Not-Quite-
SUPERMODEL

Not-Quite-
SUPERMODEL

A Novel by **KATHY TONG**

CALIFORNIA

NOT-QUITE-SUPERMODEL

Published by SWP, California
www.swppress.com

COVER DESIGN: STEPHANIE JIMENEZ SCHILLER

Publisher's Cataloging-In-Publication Data

Names: Tong, Kathy, author.
Title: Not-quite-supermodel : a novel / Kathy Tong.
Description: [Sereno], California : SWP, [2019]
Identifiers: ISBN 9781734073607 (paperback) | ISBN 9781734073614 (ePub) | ISBN 9781734073621 (mobi)
Subjects: LCSH: Models (Persons)--New York (State)--New York--Fiction. | Young women--New York (State)--New York--Fiction. | Fashion--New York (State)--New York--Fiction. | Self-esteem in women--Fiction.
Classification: LCC PS3620.O582 N68 2019 (print) | LCC PS3620.O582 (ebook) | DDC 813/.6--dc23

Library of Congress Control Number: 2019915392

PAPERBACK: ISBN-13: 978-1-7340736-0-7
EPUB: ISBN-13: 978-1-7340736-1-4
MOBI: ISBN-13: 978-1-7340736-2-1

Dedication

For my Dad, who has always been my hero.
For my Mum, who is the heart and soul of everything.
For my Sister, my best friend, my biggest champion,
and the most beautiful person I've ever known.
For Sam & Will, who are the best things that ever happened to me.
For Pete, you're my whole world.

Acknowledgements

THIS BOOK WOULD NOT HAVE BEEN POSSIBLE without the unwavering support of my friends and family who are the backbone of my world. There are no words to express the never-ending gratitude and love I have for all of you.

Richard and Ann Leav, who encouraged me and supported me every step of the way.

Mike, my brother-in-law, for enduring the long calls, texts, and emails at all hours.

Digger, the most amazing human I know who has kept a smile on my face since we were kids.

Mike, who encouraged me and never stopped believing.

Jeff, who took the time to read the very first draft of my manuscript, and silently corrected my grammar.

Jason, who read that very same draft and spent hours word-smoothing the same paragraph with me. I think we finally got it right.

Kevan Foran, your love and humour have kept me laughing out loud since the day we met.

Marianne, I fell in love with you the day we met.

Lisa, who held me up when I couldn't stand.

Simon and Ava, whose couch was like a second home.

The Schofields, the Jones, the Sacks, and the Brunns, who've been with me since the beginning.

Chloe Wing, for whom there are no words. You saved my life. Your soul is missed by everyone you touched.

Special thanks to:

Stephanie Jimenez Schiller, whose phenomenal illustrations brought Alex Emmerson and her world to life. You're quite simply amazing.

Jeff and Linda Maerov, who were the very first people to read Not-Quite-Supermodel, whose kindness, brilliant advice and encouragement kept me going.

Lucien Etori, whose unparalleled wisdom and guidance was invaluable. Without your help, shaping one of my beloved characters would not have been possible.

Alex Leav, who answered all my crazy calls and texts.

Robin Kowalski, and the team at Richard's Models who started this crazy journey with me.

Daureen Castonguay, Gina Barone who never gave up on me.

Jill Reiling and the team at CESD.

My agencies: Wilhelmina, Heffner Management, Models1, and Okay Models.

My editor, Megan McKeever and my publisher, SWP Press. We have a bright future together.

The cast and crew of Le Charlot, you know who you are.

For all those who may not have been mentioned, your names have been omitted and/or changed to protect the guilty and the innocent except perhaps Lisa Gorman who deserves honourable mention. Our outrageous escapades have been an endless source of material.

And to Leah Adams, you will be a part of Alex and me forever.

Contents

Chapter 1

I WAS ON THE VERGE OF A PANIC ATTACK and my guided relaxation app was failing. I ripped off my headphones and clung tight to my Linus, though he was doing nothing to calm my nerves. It wasn't the flight that was causing me duress, it was my recent life choices. When the fasten seat belt sign lit up somewhere over the Great Lakes, the hipster couple seated beside me started breathing heavily. I didn't know why they were stressing and I hadn't yet spoken a word to them, but maybe we could find comfort in our shared anxiety? I jerked my head to the right. "I'm totally freaking out."

They stared wide-eyed and smiling at the blank screens on the seat backs in front of them. I tried to look away as Air Canada's assigned piece of fluff fluttered on, but I had to sneak a peek. No lie, she was giving him a tug. When he finally leaned his head back and sighed, I turned to him and asked, "Well, how was it?"

"Yeah, all right, thanks."

That was it?

He smiled, balled up the blanket, and threw it on the floor. I wondered how many happy endings my blanket had seen, and discarded it immediately.

The tugger stared transfixed at my lap. "May I ask you a question?" she muttered.

I felt like I was the one who should be asking questions, but I opened my hands wide and said, "Ask away."

"Why do you keep caressing that little blue towel?"

"It's my Linus. I've had him all my life and he goes wherever I go." I ran my fingertips over his soft prickles. "He helps me relax. I guess we all have our methods of relaxation."

"Oh . . . uh-huh . . . okay." She tugged at her boyfriend's sleeve and they shifted their bodies away from me, nodding like I was insane.

Are you kidding me?

You just jerked off your boyfriend while I sat here and watched. I buried my face in my Linus. Maybe I am insane.

≶ ☺ ≷

Two months ago, I was finishing up my second year at university and working in a high- paying union job at a Safeway supermarket. My shift started at 7:30 a.m., the day after my sociology final. My essay about Durkheim and Suzanne Collins's *The Hunger Games* was, I thought, spot on. Panem had devolved into a state of anomie. My argument was sound but my professor was emphatically erudite and downright moody. Perhaps he would hate the pop culture reference. My GPA had never dipped below 3.9. Would this be its undoing?

I was fileting a halibut when this woman stepped up to the seafood counter, though it was beyond me how she could step anywhere in her thigh-high boots with six-inch spike heels. Designer clothes hugged tight to her taut body; she looked like she had just walked off the set of *Gossip Girl*. She flicked her waist-length auburn hair off her shoulders and played with the zippers on her leather jacket. I smoothed my blue and white polyester uniform, straightened my "Alex at your service" name tag, and asked, "May I help you with something?"

"How old are you?" she asked.

"I'm twenty." After fifteen seconds of wordless scrutiny, my nervous chatter kicked in. "Actually, I'm turning twenty-one in September, on the twenty-first. I'm a Virgo."

"Okay, here's the sitch." Her voice was throaty and dangerous. "My name's Robin. I'm a scout for a modeling agency in New York. You've got the right look for us. Maybe even something special."

Special, me?

"I'm guessing 5'9 ¾, and you're about 145 pounds. It's not like you're fat."

Fat?

"You'll definitely need to put down the fork and run up and down the stairs a few times. Having said that, you have a lot of potential."

"Potential for what?" I asked, dumbfounded.

"You're peddling fish, right? The modeling industry is peddling flesh. You'll be the commodity. We'll sell your image to photographers, fashion labels, and beauty products. The payout can be huge." She paused for dramatic effect. "You will be scrutinized, adored, valued, and devalued. You will be rejected. It's a runway to hell, kid, but perdition does have its perks." She threw her card on the counter. "Call me."

My best friend, Mike, gaped from the end of aisle twelve, where he was stocking shelves. He abandoned his case of salad dressing and ambled over as Robin breezed out the door. "What the fuck was that all about?"

"She works for a modeling agency in New York."

"And she spends her afternoons hanging out in the suburbs of Canada dressed like a dominatrix?" Mike asked. "What's with the boots?"

"I think she looks cool."

"She's got something," he conceded. "She's definitely worth a look."

"For your information, she thinks *I'm* worth a look. She thinks I could be a model."

Mike leaned in tight, squinting his eyes like he'd never seen me before. Finally he took a step back and said with the utmost sincerity, "I don't get it."

I didn't get it either but my hands moved to my hips and I snapped, "She happens to be an expert, and she thinks I have something special."

"Hey Al," he smirked. "You have fish guts in your hair."

≥ ☺ ≤

I called Robin the next day and we arranged to meet at her hotel in Vancouver. I finished my shift at 4:00 p.m. and shot downtown. When faced with the prospect of being late or arriving in my Safeway uniform, I had opted for the uniform. Tardiness is not part of my vocabulary. Mercifully, there was a T-shirt in the backseat of my car, but I was stuck with the blue polyester pants. I swept my hair in a bun and charged into the hotel, arriving at Robin's suite somewhat disheveled but with minutes to spare.

She was clad in the same all-black, skintight clothes, but barefoot this time. "What's with the pants?"

"They're part of my uniform."

"Is this uniform a staple in your wardrobe for interactions outside of Safeway?"

It occurred to me that in this instance, tardiness might have been the better choice.

"It's not my first choice, but it has been known to happen when I'm rushed."

"It takes a certain sense of confidence to walk around in those things," she remarked admiringly. "But please, don't bring them to New York."

She was far less intimidating in this setting, without onlookers, and without the boots.

"Do you really think I could be a model?" I asked.

"Absolutely! You're a diamond in the rough. Really rough." Her eyes were fixed on my pants. "But we can buff out the edges."

I always wanted to be talented. I'd dreamed of being on Broadway. I'd love to be special, but I'd resigned myself to reality. If you're 5'2", you're not going to play in the NBA, and if you're Alex Emmerson, you're not going to sing or dance for a living. Maybe not even in public. Studying was something I excelled at, so I was striving for success in at least one area. That's why my GPA was so freaking important. But maybe this was *my* chance to be in the spotlight. If only my high-school frenemy, Lydia Baker, could see me now. Not just her. Her whole posse of mean girls. It's pathetic how much I still care about what they think, but I do.

She grabbed a proper camera, not an iPhone, opened the curtains wide, and maneuvered me up against a wall.

"Take your hair down and let me take some pictures of you and a quick video to send to Metropolis."

"Metropolis?" It sounded like a city in a superhero movie.

"It's the agency I work with." She started snapping pictures.

"Here's the thing, doll: 20 pounds seems like a lot to lose, but it's not."

I beg to differ.

"Once you develop some healthy eating patterns, you'll discover a whole new you."

A whole new me might take more than dropping 20 pounds.

"You're going to love New York."

You know who would love New York? Lydia effing Baker. But me? Alone in New York? This is crazy.

Sweat was forming at the nape of my neck. "Yeah, but the people who go to New York are like you, or artists, or like the kids from *Fame*, or rich private school kids like the girls from *The Facts of Life.*"

I love eighties sitcoms. There's always a teachable moment and once the thirty minutes are up, everyone, for the most part, is healed and happy.

"The suburbs, and the life you're living now, will always be here waiting for you. No city is more alive than New York. It's where art happens, where music happens, where cultures collide. The sense that anything can happen, at any moment, is a wild ride."

I wanted to be bold and brazen and jump at the chance, but flying off to New York to take a stab at a modeling career sounded terrifying. Robin made it sound like *a wild ride* was the greatest experience of one's life. Every aspect of *my* life was controlled and part of a delicate ecosystem to keep my neuroses in check. Riddled with anxiety was not the vibe I wanted to convey. What would Robin think if she knew the truth?

"I'm not sure a girl from the suburbs like me will fit in." I shrugged, hoping to come off as nonchalant.

"There's a place for everyone in New York," she said, eyeing me thoughtfully.

Could she sense my fear?

I wanted to claw my way out of my own skin, but smiled as though this were the happiest moment of my life.

"This"—Robin's voice dropped two octaves— "is the opportunity of a lifetime."

I gazed out the window past Robin, past the city, past the Rocky Mountains. I didn't want my life to be filled with regret at the tender age of twenty. This may be my only chance to do something special. It wouldn't hurt if people thought I was cool.

"You only live once," I said with quivering vocal chords.

She motioned to me with a sweet smile. "Come and look at these pictures."

Scrutinizing my appearance was a nasty habit I developed in high school, and blissfully walked away from upon graduation. I was willing to revisit it in this moment for the sake of a potential modeling career.

Top-to-bottom scan: unkempt, and undeniably full-figured. Full facial inspection: enormous eyebrows match my unruly mass of brown, fuzzy curls. Depending on the camera angle, my nose is a little crooked. An ex-boyfriend once told me he would ski it to the left. My eyes are wide and deep blue. Sometimes they look gray-green depending on the light or mood. Deep blue could mean excited, nervous, or terrified. My expressions captured all three.

"She doesn't look like a model," I said.

"Not yet, doll." Robin leaned in close to the camera display. "But this girl's inner monologue is tantalizing."

If only Robin's compliments were my constant inner monologue.

"Her eyes are alive with a sense that anything could happen at any moment. You want to know her."

⋛ ☺ ⋚

When I shared the news with Mike, we were hanging in his perfectly manicured backyard. I was laying in the hammock while he planted some shrubs. We started working at Safeway on the same day, when I was sixteen and he was twenty-one. He took me under his wing, and we became fast friends. Mike didn't talk about it much, but he was bullied in high school, which is why, I think, he has a soft spot for "awkward" people like me, and rescue dogs. He brought Ben, a black Lab mix, home two years ago and they've been inseparable ever since.

Mike's edges needed buffing out, but he was a softie underneath his gruff exterior. In the past four years, we had never missed our weekly Scrabble and spliff sessions.

"I went to see that model scout. She took a video and a bunch of pictures of me and sent them to an agency in New York."

"Al, I'm not sure this is the right fucking thing for you." Mike didn't curse for effect. It was just part of his vernacular. "You love fucking Safeway."

That was true. The money was great and it was paying for my degree. The customers liked me, the staff liked me. I felt happy and comfortable at work. Mike, not so much, even though he had been promoted to assistant store manager and Safeway was paying for his new house. He had gutted and completely remodeled the two-bedroom rancher. He wanted to flip houses full-time one day.

"And you're halfway through school," he said.

That was also true, but I didn't feel happy or comfortable at university. I felt perpetually in the way of other students who were busy "finding their way."

"I can finish my degree later." I didn't have a clue what I wanted to do when I finished school. The goal was to blossom into some formidable woman, a sociologist, a professor, a writer with a brilliant career, but it might take more than a BA in sociology. My dad's an engineer, and he never loved the idea of me majoring in something "impractical," but he was relieved I'd given up my childhood dreams of Broadway. "Besides, it's not like an undergraduate degree is the key to a thriving future."

"Modeling is the fucking key?" The muscles in his neck were strained like his words.

I thought about it for a second. Although there isn't an *exact* key, clearly STEM, law, medicine, or learning a viable trade such as plumbing might open more doors, but I wasn't interested in any of those.

"Modeling could pay for grad school." My face brightened. "Robin did say the payout could be huge."

I hadn't even considered grad school, but it was a compelling argument.

Mike just rolled his eyes. For him, the whole concept of modeling was connected to the high school hierarchy. He was too jaded to see the financial upside involved.

"And you have your weird fucking plumbing thing."

Mike was the only other person on the planet, besides my parents, who knew about my plumbaphobia. It started when I was ten. I just couldn't use a bathroom except in my own house. Public restrooms and pools had become sources of torture. It has gotten progressively worse through the years. Avoidance is key, which is why:

(a) I didn't attend a single pool party in my youth.

(b) I couldn't live in a dormitory.

(c) I have acquired the skill of never needing to relieve my bladder for ten-hour periods at a time.

In my four years at Safeway, I had never once used the facilities. In the event of an emergency, I carry rubber gloves with me at all times.

"I get what you're saying." I'd spent days obsessing over the exact points he was making. The logical voice in my head screamed *Don't go!* but there was a whisper from my gut murmuring *Go . . . Go . . . Go.* When I woke up this morning, the depths of my gut howled *Go!* I knew if I didn't try, I would regret it.

"Al, don't take this the wrong way, but you're not very fucking modelly."

"Robin said I'm a work in progress. She said Jennifer Lopez wasn't always JLo. She transformed herself."

"Who's transforming you?" Mike asked.

Robin had assured me the agency would take charge of my image, but they wouldn't take me on unless I lost the weight.

"Starting tomorrow, I'm implementing a daily routine of running up and down the stairs," I said with a mouthful of Oreos.

Mike just shook his head.

"This is my chance to do something special."

"Fucking 'modeling'?" He used air quotes. He knew how much that annoyed me. "That's what you think is special?"

"I would say that a lot of people think it's special, and I want to give it a shot."

I was done trying to convince him. And why not modeling?

≥ ☺ ≤

The flight attendant announced our initial descent into New York City, and my adrenals kicked it up a notch. When I arrived at baggage claim, I was panting. A heaving crowd of people vied for space at the carousel.

I was grateful the modeling agency had arranged for a car service. My driver was holding a white sheet of paper. Written in bold capital letters was my name, Alex Emmerson. Metropolis Models.

"Hello, madam, my name is Mohammed." His accent was foreign and charming. "I will be your driver this evening. Did you have a nice flight?"

Even with my limited experience, I'm confident that "nice flight" is an oxymoron if there ever was one.

"It was one for the record books." It would take hours to wash away the remnants of that plane. My body shuddered. A shower, in a foreign bathroom.

Keep breathing.

When my agency sent me the details regarding my new living arrangements, I had requested photos, specifically of the bathroom. Instead, they sent me a snapshot of the girl I was staying with. She was an ex-supermodel with glowing skin; thick, luscious eyelashes; and a sexy sheen to her hair. Her 5'11" smoking hot body was all legs. Her goddesslike stature was at least somewhat reassuring. I imagined her bathroom must be exquisite, but one needs to be prepared. Supersonic wrist to elbow latex gloves and flip-flops with two-inch soles were tucked neatly into the front pocket of my suitcase.

New York rose up before me, flickering in the heat. I could feel its heartbeat. The view was impressive but the noise was suffocating. The sirens were relentless, and drivers were senselessly leaning on their horns. Experiments with rats have scientifically proven that constant exposure to noise causes many health problems including, but not limited to, headaches, anxiety, and nausea. I was suffering from all three when the car stopped outside a sixteen-story apartment building on the Upper West Side of Manhattan. The arched doorway was dimly lit. I pushed open the cast bronze doors and stood awestruck in the giant stone foyer.

A man dressed like a bellhop hurried toward me to ask whom I was visiting.

"Hi!" My voice was loud and loaded with enthusiasm. "I'm here to meet Lori Hastings."

He ushered me and my suitcase into a miniature elevator. "Ms. Hastings is in twelve 12C. I'll let her know you have arrived." As the doors crept closed I heard him mutter, "And you might try using your indoor voice."

≥ ☺ ≤

I was standing outside apartment 12C practicing what to say when Lori threw the door open. "Hi! Come on in here." She hugged me, which I thought was a bit premature, but her southern accent was warm and comforting. "I hear this is your first time to New York. How exciting!"

The casual banter I had practiced all went to hell. Her hair was pulled back and I wasn't sure if it was the headband or a deformity, but she looked like her skin had been stretched too thin to cover her forehead. Her eyebrows were lifted so high that she looked permanently surprised. There were spots of crusting blood set equidistant from each other underneath her hairline. Her lips were puffed up like giant pillows; she looked like she had been stung by a giant, angry bee.

"Don't mind my face. I just had an eyebrow lift and my lips injected. The swelling will go down in a few days but the staples will take a little time to heal. They actually dissolve."

She had willfully allowed someone to put staples in her head?

"How innovative," I said.

12

"Right? Let me show you around." She grabbed my hand. "The kitchen is a little small but it's not like I cook anyway. You can get anything delivered anytime you want." Soft yellow voile curtains were half open to reveal a large window.

"Check out the view. Those are the Hudson River and the George Washington Bridge. Amazing, right?" It was amazing, but I was obsessing about the staples. I managed to nod.

"This is the living room." An enormous brocade mirror hung over a white couch covered in cashmere pillows. Thick cream curtains hung on a brass rod from the ceiling to the hardwood floor framing two large windows, and a giant flat screen TV covered the wall between them. The coffee table looked like a slab of reclaimed wood, but upon closer inspection I could see it was a mix of wood and leather on a brass base.

"And this is the dining room." She laughed and gestured to the corner where a table and chairs were piled with papers and magazines. "Don't worry, the maid is coming in a few days."

She needed a maid? She couldn't handle this apartment by herself?

She glanced at herself in the mirror and sat on the couch. "This is your bed."

"What is?" I asked.

"The sofa, silly."

The agency is paying fifteen hundred dollars a month for me to sleep on a couch?

"Is it a convertible?"

"No, but don't worry, it's super comfortable. I fall asleep here myself sometimes watching TV," she said cheerfully. "Oh my gosh, I almost forgot Chloe."

She opened her bedroom door and a golden Lab came bounding out and jumped on the couch. Lori squeezed her nose. "She's a little spastic."

Spastic and seated comfortably on my bed.

"You can put your clothes in the closet by the front door."

"May I?" I asked and peeked inside. It was jam-packed with her jackets and shoes, ready to tumble out at some inopportune moment like a scene in a bad sitcom.

"There's just never enough closet space in a New York City apartment. Sometimes I need a flashlight to find anything in there. Oh, hey, you must be dying to have a shower."

Oh my God, the bathroom.

"I feel so dirty after a flight."

That's because those seats have never been steam cleaned, thousands of people sit on them every day and shamelessly spooge in the blankets.

I followed her into the bathroom. The bathtub had feet. I'd never seen that before. Part of the interior had peeled off, which left a giant grayish stain that could have been mistaken for mold. She marveled at the tub.

"I searched everywhere for this. It's an antique."

That much was clear.

"Some of the paint was starting to peel away. Don't worry, I've had it sealed so it won't come off when you take a bath. Sometimes I'm in here for hours. I light the candles and relax into Dr. Hauska's silky bath salts. Don't you love a good bath?"

A bath? I was practically dry heaving. I wasn't sure I could stand in the damn thing.

"I'm more of a shower person."

The shower curtain was covered in a milky film, as was the nozzle, which was half the size of the ones at home. The bath mat was covered in little mounds of fluff and had a gray tinge to it. I'm sure it had once been white. This would require a whole lot more than flip-flops and rubber gloves.

"Lori, I'm going to call my mother and let her know I'm here. Can we smoke inside?"

I had only recently started smoking. It was a repulsive, repugnant habit that filled me with shame and remorse. Lori smiled.

"Technically it's frowned upon, but I sneak one in every now and again. Just smoke out the kitchen window." She headed toward her bedroom. "I'll give you some privacy."

I didn't see how that was possible, as my bedroom was a couch.

⋛ ☺ ⋚

My screen saver is a picture of my parents taken last year, on their twenty-fifth wedding anniversary. My father bears a resemblance to Elvis (during the *Aloha from Hawaii* era). Jet-black hair and heavy-lidded, deep-set eyes. My mum's are bright and blue. Her cherubic face and rosy cheeks lit up the screen. Even my father was smiling. He wasn't an unhappy person, just permanently irritable. He wasn't coping well with my recent life choices.

"Have you heard about this nonsense, Elizabeth?!" he screamed when he heard the news.

"Yes, Edward. She's very excited about this modeling and so are 'we.'" My mum took supportive to a whole other level. In the unlikely event that I were to commit murder, she would insist that the victim had it coming.

"Why would she want to give up a proper job that's paying for her education?" He swatted the air in disgust, his signature move to indicate his utmost disapproval. Only the Catholic Church and the Royal Family warranted a two-handed swat. My prospective modeling career had joined their ranks. "Now we're letting her fly off to bloody New York City to work with a bunch of perverts and weirdos?"

I lit a cigarette and pressed call. "Mum, I'm here."

"Edward, she's there." I heard his leather recliner and a splash of scotch. "It's about bloody time."

"Ooh, how exciting," she said into the phone. "Let's Skype. Show me the apartment. Let's meet the supermodel."

"Forget Skype," I whispered ferociously. "The bathroom is like something out of the Dark Ages. I need a Hazmat suit! I'm freaking out. I am totally freaking out!"

"Well, don't panic. Go to your room, have a lie down and one or two Oreos."

"I don't have a room. I'm sharing a couch with a dog. And I can't eat Oreos anymore. Remember?" I stared at the open bag of Fig Newtons on the counter. "Anyway, she only has Fig Newtons."

Disgusting.

My mother was starting to sound concerned. "You are just having some anxiety. That's normal."

She was fond of the word "normal" when referencing my plumbaphobia. Professional counsel was never an option. My family is British, and British people tend to just get on with things and not complain. My mother insisted it was perfectly "normal" to despise public plumbing. "Oh, it's dreadful. It's a blessing you didn't grow up in Yorkshire. The British built ships that traveled the globe; even when the sun never set on the British Empire, they couldn't make a decent toilet or shower if their lives depended on it. You're perfectly normal."

The solid coping mechanisms designed to manage my "perfectly normal" phobia were beyond useless in this setting.

"Mum, this is a fiasco. I have to be at my best when I meet my agency tomorrow. I can't get in the shower."

"You're going to be absolutely fine."

I stared at the lights that dotted the George Washington Bridge. My mum seemed a million miles away.

"Your agency will love you."

I pressed my cheek against the phone.

"You can get in that shower, and you will get in that shower, because it will not defeat you."

I think my mum may have stood up, and I found myself standing at attention.

"And you love dogs."

A deep sigh swept through me. Mum was right. I was going to be fine. Of course I could do this. I stared at the ceiling and silently vowed, *I will not be defeated. I can get in the shower. I will get in that shower. Just maybe not tonight.* I smoked two more cigarettes, grabbed Linus, curled up on my new bed/sofa, and passed out.

Chapter 2

MERCIFULLY, I SLEPT THROUGH THE NIGHT. Lori emerged with a golden pashmina wrapped around her head and lower face at about 7:00 a.m.

"I'm taking Chloe out. Do you want a coffee?" She added a huge pair of black sunglasses to her ensemble.

"Yes, please. Milk, no sugar would be awesome. Do you have any Saran Wrap?"

"Kitchen drawer, far left."

I covered myself in Saran Wrap and stood in front of the shower naked save for my rubber gloves and sneakers.

Stepping over the side of the tub, careful to not let any part of my body touch anything, I pulled the shower curtain closed. It didn't reach the far wall and I couldn't understand how the water wasn't going to go all over the bathroom floor until I turned it on and a tiny sprinkle came out of the nozzle. I would have to run around in there to get wet. It was quite a project washing body parts individually. Unwrap, lather. Rinse, rewrap, repeat.

"Hey girl," Lori said through the door. "I left your coffee on the table. I'll be in my bedroom if you need me."

"Thank you!"

Please stay there while I stash this heap of sopping Saran Wrap and my soaking wet sneakers.

Once everything was secured in a garbage bag behind the sofa, I started on my hair.

Taming my mass of curls has never been easy. In my senior year of high school, I invested in one of those hair straighteners from the local drugstore. The smell of burned hair lingered for hours and my father was none too impressed. I accepted that smooth locks were never in my future, and wash-and-go became my default management program. The memory and lingering fear of the straightener led to my recent purchase of a new Conair 1875 hair dryer. Its infrared heat promised to help light frizz and bring out my natural shine. In the weeks leading up to my departure I committed serious time to practicing, with a modicum of success. It was a challenge to smooth out the back, but I loaded it up with John Frieda antifrizz and if you looked at me straight on, it wasn't half bad. It was a definite upgrade to my hair pre-Robin, which is how I had come to describe my life.

The steady whir of the dryer soothed my nervous system, and my hair was shaping up to be a solid 9. My nerves were holding at a 4, but jangling precariously close to a 3.

My rating scale isn't complicated. I apply it to every facet of my existence, and now things I had never considered required a rating: my hair, my clothes, my fitness regime. Despite valiant efforts, I was having trouble attaining 10's across the board. Things were so much simpler pre-Robin. I rated my performances at school, at work, and at home. Essays, the seafood counter display, the perfectly made bed, the undisturbed vacuum lines on the carpet, which required a certain degree of dexterity. The shine of the bathroom taps. The glow of the tiles in the shower. I was lost in the memory of my glorious Mr. Clean when Lori fell into a luxurious sprawl beside me.

"So what time are you meeting the agency?" Her silk robe slid open, revealing her ample cleavage and exquisite legs.

"I have an appointment at eleven." I tugged tightly to the seams of my fuzzy terrycloth robe.

"How'd you end up with Metropolis?"

"Do you know Robin Ramon?"

"The missile in stilettos?" Lori said with an air of reverence.

"She convinced me to quit school and my twenty-five-dollar-per-hour job." I swallowed hard. "She said it was the opportunity of a lifetime."

"Amen to that!" She threw her hands in the air. "A scout for Elite Models found me shopping at JCPenney in Texas. Fifteen years old, and I just packed up and went to Paris."

"That was brave."

I was talking to a woman who had staples in her head.

"Elite represented me all over the world, but I've been with Metropolis for the past ten years."

"Did you ever have a normal job?" I asked.

"Nope, I've been a model my whole life." She disappeared into her bedroom and returned with an enormous jar of coconut body lotion. "I've been in this game twenty-five years. Can you believe it?" She had begun slathering her gorgeous gams in cream.

She's forty and still modeling?

"That's amazing. I thought models had a shelf life." Robin had made it clear that I was a little old to be starting.

"Not all of us," she said defensively. "How old are you?"

"I'm turning twenty-one next month."

"Hmm." Her eyes scanned my face. "Don't tell anyone that."

"Oh, God, I hope I'm doing the right thing." Lori had been at this twenty-five years and this apartment was all she had to show for it?

"Obviously Robin saw something in you, right?" she said.

"Robin did say I was special."

She also told me that if the agency was willing to invest in me, I needed to be willing to invest in myself. I figured that if Metropolis was willing to take the risk and front all of my expenses, they must believe in my potential for success. That's what had cinched the deal.

"See? You totally did the right thing," Lori said.

I started gnawing the inside of my cheek.

"How are you getting to the agency?" she asked.

"I haven't even thought about it." I was so focused on my hair and the shower.

"Apple Maps is way better than Google. You'll be an expert on the subways in no time. Just remember, Manhattan is a grid system. The avenues run north and south and the streets run east and west. The closer you get to Fifth Avenue, the lower the number of the buildings."

So much information.

"Geography wasn't exactly my best subject in school."

"You want to arrive at the agency fresh-faced and relaxed. Skip the subway and take an Uber."

"I know it's 2014, but Vancouver and its suburbs don't have Uber yet." I felt so provincial.

"That's a must-have app," she said, and stared at me in disbelief. "Grab a cab."

"Do you have the number?"

"Just head south on West End. Stick out your hand and a taxi will stop for you."

"Great," I said, trying to sound confident.

At 10:15 a.m. I was packed and ready to go, with Linus and my rubber gloves secured neatly in my brand-new Kipling knapsack.

"This is it. I'm leaving."

Lori came running out of her room, arms wide open to hug me, but stopped abruptly. "Is that what you're wearing?"

Huh? My wardrobe was, hands down, a solid 10.

"I bought it at the Gap." I zipped up the hoodie of my sleeveless light-weight cream track suit, leaving a hint of my white ribbed tank showing.

"Ah, okay. Good luck."

As I left the building, the snarky lobby guy opened the door for me. "Enjoy your day."

It was like a hotel.

Chapter 3

I WAS STANDING ON WEST END AVENUE and West 86th with my arm in the air, as were ten other people. Taxis were whipping past, but none of them stopped.

"Excuse me," I said, approaching the woman nearest to me, who was wearing a dowdy pantsuit. "I'm sorry to bother you, but why aren't these taxis stopping?"

"Because they're unavailable. The sign needs to be lit up."

A taxi stopped less than a foot away and a different woman jumped in. "Hey!" Pantsuit screamed. "That was mine! Get the fuck out of my cab!" She lunged her arm through the window. The cab started driving away. "Fuck you, you crazy bitch."

Pantsuit glared at me. Clearly she felt that, somehow, my question had led to this missed opportunity.

"I get it now. If the light is on then the taxi is available. Thank you." I cowered away and two blocks down, then waited five minutes for an available taxi. It stank of sweat and stale aftershave and wasn't relaxing at all. Accelerator-brake, accelerator-brake. Did the driver use both feet? When we arrived in Union Square and the meter read $26.40, I wondered if the subway would have been the better choice.

Metropolis occupied the penthouse of a twelve-story building in Union Square. The elevator opened into a tiny alcove with a small desk and giant, frosted glass doors. The receptionist was emaciated, like those poor kids in the Unicef commercials. I had never seen anyone that thin, and wondered if it was on purpose. Her black dress was falling off her tiny white body, which had clearly never seen the sun. "Metropolis, please hold. Metropolis, please hold. Metropolis, please hold." The phones continued ringing, but she moved the mouthpiece away from her brightly painted red lips. She had drawn a lip line way outside her natural border in a futile attempt to mask her whippet-like upper lip.

"May I help you?" She looked me up and down, her eyes lingering a little too long on my taupe wedge sneakers.

"Yes, please. I'm Alex Emmerson. I have an appointment at eleven." I smiled.

"Do you know whom your appointment is with?"

"I just arrived from Vancouver. I think they're expecting me."

She replaced her mouthpiece. "Darlene, I have an Alex Emmerson here from Vancouver. Whom might she be seeing today?" She gestured to the doors like Vanna White. "You may go in."

Seventeen-foot soaring floor-to-ceiling windows offered sweeping views of the city below. The white leather sofa and chaise in the lounge area looked like they had never been used. A fragile, impeccably put together young Asian guy was adjusting the magazines spread across a marble coffee table. He then tiptoed across the freshly waxed hardwood floors and disappeared behind a door in the far right corner of the office. The soft white walls boasted fifty framed magazine covers. I had time to count them because I stood there for at least five minutes before a rigid woman furrowed her brow and trudged over.

"I'm Darlene." Her stubby fingers pushed her short brown, brittle hair away from her bulging black eyes. She had stuffed her 5'2" full figure into an ill-fitting black pencil skirt covered in fringe.

"You arrived safely? Lori's apartment is acceptable?" I leaned away from her as she barked sharp staccato rhetorical questions at me. Then she grabbed my arm and led me to the enormous table in the center of the office. "This is the booking table; the ten of us are bookers." The group directed aloof glances toward me. The only person to convey a sense of enthusiasm was the attractive, magnetic gentleman seated beside an empty chair at the head of the table. He was on the phone but raised his hand and fluttered his fingers.

"That's Adam." Darlene's demeanor softened. The longing in her loins was palpable. I hurried toward her as she sat down beside him.

"You'll be working with us."

My eyes darted toward Adam, willing him to finish his call, and then locked onto the forty five-by-seven cards on the wall behind him. "Wow." There were so many beautiful faces.

"Those are our girls," she said. "Nobody, I mean nobody, has models like Metropolis."

I stood before her erect as possible.

"I see you lost some weight," she said, like she was flicking lint off her sleeve. "You know, I'm not sure about you, but Robin said she saw something in you." She narrowed her eyes but shook her head, unconvinced.

"Isn't Robin here?"

She could pinpoint exactly what the "something" was.

"No, she's in London, *scouting.* I am the *Agent.*" She picked up her phone and snapped, "Nick!"

He shot back out from behind the door, took the length of the office in two strides, and stood at attention beside me.

"I assume you have different clothes and a bikini," she scowled and nodded to my Kipling, "in your knapsack."

No one told me to bring a bikini.

"This, umm, well," I stammered, motioning to my tracksuit, "this is all I have."

Nick took a step backward.

"You're wearing a tank under *that?*" I was stunned it was not a hit and immediately demoted it to an 8.

"Yes, but I'm not"—I hesitated—"wearing a bra."

"It's not like you need a bra. What are you, a 34A?" She rolled her eyes in Adam's direction. He was still deep on his call, but he caught it; there was a tightening of his jaw.

Does he think she's mean, or does he think I'm not worthy?

"Take Alex's measurements and shoot some digitals. Next time she's here, in appropriate attire, we'll do them again."

Nick marched us back to the inner offices. We walked the length of the twelve-foot hallway into a small fishbowl-like room with a desk, bare walls, and a glass facade that offered no privacy.

"Let's start with those hips, 36 inches," he said, tightening the measuring tape. "There we are, 35 ½ inches. Much better. It's all that fabric."

No it isn't. My hips are 36 inches.

"Definitely," I said.

"Okay, guurl. Lose that hoodie." I laid it tenderly on the desk.

"Waist, 25 ½ inches." He cinched tighter. "Sorry honey, that half inch isn't budging. And bust, 34A." He flipped up the collar of his polo. "Now step back and let's do this." He picked up a camera and started snapping away. "Smile. Big smile with teeth. Very nice. You have such a great smile and beautiful skin."

I caressed my cheek. "Really?"

"Totally. Now a closed-lip smile like you have a secret."

My parents don't know I'm smoking.

"Nice. Now be serious."

They're going to kill me when they find out.

"Let's get some profiles, and looking back at me. Look at your long skinny arms. Women would just die for those."

There was hope for me yet.

"And your 34As are perfect and perky." He winked. *He* knew Darlene was mean.

"Let's do some full-lengths." He turned his nose up at my Kipling. "You're sure there are no jeans or a skirt in there?"

I officially changed the wardrobe rating to a 6.

He smoothed out the creases of his tight, not quite ankle-length khakis. "Okay then, here we go."

I stood facing the camera with my beautiful skinny arms by my side and puffed up my perky breasts.

"Can you put some hip into this? Give it some shape."

Robin never asked for shape.

"Yeah. Sorry. Of course." I said and shifted my hips left and right.

"Stop jerking your body all over. Watch me." He cocked his hip out half an inch, and put a slight bend in his knee. "It's not rocket science, honey. It's modeling."

My body strained against my nervous system.

"Your shoulders are up to your ears. Relax your shoulders."

Freaking hell, the pressure. Those predictable beads of sweat were forming at the nape of my neck.

"I think we're good for today," he said, reviewing the images. "These head shots are great and these . . ." he trailed off. "Anyway, I will send them to Darlene." He sat behind the computer and glanced at my hoodie. "Don't forget this. You know the way out? Straight down the hall."

"You're not coming with me?" I didn't want to go back out there alone.

"I'm busy here. Good luck," he trilled.

Darlene had edited my digitals by the time I got back to the booking table. "These will have to do for now." She frowned at her computer screen.

Was she this bitchy to all her models?

"What is happening with your Instagram? How many followers do you have?"

"I don't have an Instagram."

"You don't have an Instagram? Are you, like, the only person in the world without an Instagram?"

"I'm sure there are a lot of people without an Instagram," I countered. "Take, for example, my friend Mike, and people in Third World countries don't even have—"

"Let me bring you up to speed in the Western world. You are the only person your age I have ever met without an Instagram. What does that say about you?"

I'm a total loser with a boring life.

"I do have a Twitter account."

"Twitter is so over. How many people follow you?"

"I'm more of a follower than, you know, a person who gets followed."

"Some of our clients won't even see girls if they don't have at least a hundred thousand followers on Instagram!" she spat at me. Spittle dribbled down her chin.

If I'd known about it before, I could have snapped Mohammed holding the sign with my name.

"I'm all over it," I assured her and wiped my cheek.

"Adam's going to arrange a test shoot with Fabio." He shot me a smile.

You couldn't get off that call for two minutes to greet me?

"Once we have the pictures, we'll start sending you on castings and go-sees."

"Go-sees?"

"A go-see is what we in the modeling world call an appointment." Her lip curled. "We're done here."

"Go-see. Got it." I was inches away from the exit when Darlene's voice belted across the office. "Fuck me, Adam. Are we wasting our time? Do you think she's worth it?"

I stared dejectedly at my Kipling and walked into an unconscionably beautiful blond girl coming through the doors.

"I'm so sorry," I mumbled. "I wasn't looking."

"That's obvious." Her voice carried a royal air of superiority.

Darlene squealed and ran toward us.

"Sheila baby, I'm soooo happy to see you. Flight was good? You're settled in? We missed our new cover girl."

Sycophantic staccato sentences for Sheila?

They kissed each other on both cheeks as I watched hopelessly, wishing someone would kiss me.

"Are those the new Proenza Schouler? I love, love them," Darlene said, salivating over Sheila baby's heels.

"Me too." I could barely pronounce the name.

"Sheila, this is Alex Emmerson." Her tone was beyond dismissive.

Sheila threw her silky golden hair over her bare shoulder and read-justed the strap of her enormous leather bag, which had its own fringe thing happening.

"Hi Sheila. It's nice to meet you." I should have split, but my nervous chatter kicked in. "I'm super excited to be here, can't wait to explore the city and kick-start my modeling career. Where are you from? When did you get here? We should get together for coffee—"

Sheila cut me off. "I'm from New York, and I don't drink coffee."

"Oh, me either." I actually put my hand over my mouth.

They walked away, arm in arm, laughing uproariously. It was a catastrophe.

I sat down on the steps in Union Square watching the people going into and out of Whole Foods. I can't recall the taste of real food.

I see you lost some *weight.* Are you kidding me, Darlene?

As it turned out, Robin was wrong about running up and down the stairs *a few times.* That didn't tip the scales. I'm not athletic, but my performances in the stairwell back home were nothing short of heroic. My pump-it-up playlist was full on Hardwell, Tiesto, Beyoncé; if those didn't get you moving, nothing could. After one week, I went from ten flights once a day to fifty flights twice a day. My rating scale was off the charts; some days I earned an 11. My father went ballistic. "What the bloody hell is going on around here? Running up and down the bloody stairs at six in the morning. All because of this bloody modeling. I won't have it, Elizabeth."

"It wouldn't hurt you to get up those stairs a few times a day," my mother chirped back. She made sure he had a scotch and soda in his hand during my evening sessions. My commitment to the stairs was futile and soul-crushing. After ten days with no change to my 145-pound frame, I resigned to give up my beloved Oreos, and that was no easy feat. Oreos are as addictive as cocaine, so wrote *The Huffington Post.* I posted the article above my bedroom mirror with a picture of Kate Moss to remind myself why I must never eat Oreos. I dreamed about them every night, and every morning my pillow was drenched in saliva. I started buying them in bulk and licking the outside of each cookie before dousing them in water and tossing them in the garbage. My father marched around the house screaming, "Has everyone in this house gone mad?! Soaking wet bags of biscuits in the bin! Elizabeth! Elizabeth!"

"Yes, Edward, I've seen them. We're being supportive."

It still wasn't enough.

My staple diet of English food, including, but not limited to, roast chicken, mashed potatoes, Yorkshire pudding, sticky toffee pudding, and bacon and fried eggs was a problem. But it's all I knew. Our family friends had all emigrated from the same part of England, and that's how every-one ate. In fact, eating was encouraged. There was no better way to show people how much you love them. My grandparents were born at the end of World War II, when rationing was still in effect. That's something that filters through the bloodline and stays forever.

Those special Sunday mornings when Mum made all my faves, sausages, scrambled eggs, and bread fried in bacon fat were utter perfection. Removing them from my life inflicted suffering far beyond the physical; it was emotional torment. I couldn't bear to be around real food. My mum started making low-calorie meals for me, which I ate in solitude in my bedroom.

Mike, a longtime vegetarian, had been pushing that whole vibe on me for years. Admittedly, the animal cruelty element to Big Agriculture is deplorable. I had given up pork for a month a few years ago. Wilbur from *Charlotte's Web* kept popping up in my dreams, but the smell of fried bacon sucked me back in. However, once I looked a cow in the eye I swore off beef forever. As per chicken, I read somewhere that if you could kill what you were going to eat, then it was morally acceptable. I couldn't kill an animal, but my father could and even my mum said she could knock off a chicken. I figured that while they were doing all the cooking, I could live with that ideology. In a perfect world I'd be a vegetarian, but it's not a perfect world and the whole food thing now went way beyond animals. Either way, vegetarianism may contribute to weight loss, but not entirely. There was still dairy, and anything that tasted good.

To add insult to injury, Lydia Baker perpetually posted about her new-found commitment to veganism, usually followed by selfies of her beach-ready body. I hadn't set eyes on her since she left for a semester in Europe, but Mike caught her peeling out of the Golden Arches drive-through in a convertible Porsche roadster. Not that it mattered; she was always skinny, and I never really cared back then. I'm smarter than Lydia and she knows that, which is part of the reason I was always the target of her passive aggressive bullying. Still, I longed for her approval. It wasn't the Porsche, her long blond hair, or her student of the year award. It was that *everyone* fawned all over her. It's all I wanted even for one day, to be the most exciting person in the school. Nobody cares about you if you're a straight A student.

But now I also care about being thin. I care a lot.

And not unlike every other facet of my existence, it had become an obsession. Here's the thing: if you look at it from an addiction standpoint, as painful and challenging as it may be, one can completely remove drugs or alcohol; but with food, you have to let the tiger out of the cage at least three times a day. That freaking tiger is tough to tame.

As my departure date for New York closed in, the pressure to lose the weight mounted. It led to massive midnight bingeing. My worst night ever I ravaged two bags of Oreos, six bagels drenched in peanut butter and honey, half a pizza, and a pint of ice cream. Never in my life had I received negative numbers on my rating scale.

I finally sought professional help from our family physician.

"Dr. Archer, I need help," I had pleaded with him with tears in my eyes. "I can't stop eating. I realize gastric bypass surgery is a bit premature, but isn't there anything you can do? Appetite suppressants?"

He was seated smugly behind his mahogany desk, littered with pictures of himself winning triathlons. "What you need, Alex, is some good old-fashioned willpower."

Really? I have a steadfast will of iron. It's worth noting that the plumbaphobia was not a case of willpower, it was accepting my condition like one accepts allergies to cats. I have never quit anything. Sure, things have quit me, but I never quit. There's a modeling career at stake here, goddamnit!

"Thank you for your encouragement."

"Have you considered Weight Watchers or Lean Cuisine?" He had pushed his glasses higher on the bridge of his nose with an air of self-importance. "It's economical and they offer balanced meal plans."

The memory of it makes me want to strangle him with his stethoscope. Nonetheless, introducing Lean Cuisine was helpful. In fact, it's all I eat now, but it didn't curb the cravings. That's how the smoking started. It turns out that nicotine is an appetite suppressant. It was gross at first, but the menthols weren't so bad, and it helped. After two weeks, I lost six pounds. When I got down to 130, my father started buying Oreos and leaving them open on the kitchen counter. My mother would then hide then from me. I found seven bags in the linen closet three days before I left for New York.

Mike wasn't impressed with the smoking or the weight loss. We were eating lunch in the parking lot during my last shift at Safeway. I had finally reached my goal weight of 125. "You do realize we are eating out here so you can suck on that cancer stick."

"I'm going to quit once I get to New York. Besides, it worked. Look at me."

"Your uniform is hanging off of you."

"I know. Isn't it marvelous? It's the new and improved me!"

"I don't know about new and improved." He walked toward his beat-up VW Bug, then stopped midway. "And the old you was just fine."

"I am through with fine!" I yelled back. If Kate Moss were here she'd give me a high five.

≥ ☺ ≤

Darlene had just shit all over my victory, and my swanky new tracksuit. I took out my phone and snapped a selfie #justmetmyagency#deflated#humiliated #neednewclothes #stillasmoker, and added it to my private album of selfies titled "Historically Speaking."

Of course, I have an account, *alexemmersonwhiterock*, but there isn't a single post; it exists for the sole purpose of spying on other people's lives. Freaking Instagram. It was just one more thing to worry about.

On a positive note, my Apple Maps experience was decent. I did have to change directions twice at 14th Street but arrived at the Seventh Avenue subway stop unscathed. That is, until I descended the stairs: it was hot as balls, and the crowds and stench were stifling. Public transportation was so much more civilized in Vancouver. True, it has a population of 610,000 as opposed to 8.4 million, but a mop and some disinfectant could go a long way down here. I almost ripped off my hoodie and embraced my braless-ness, but a man steeped in filth and dressed in garbage bags was leering at me. We boarded the same subway car. "Garbage guy" eyed me all the way to 18th Street. The screeching halt of the train shot straight down my spine as I bolted for the door. The next train was delayed; when it did arrive, it didn't stop. The crowd cursed a collective "Fuck." My tank was steeped in sweat. I surrendered my hoodie and in doing so looked like someone I vowed never to be, a contestant in a wet T-shirt contest. I crossed my arms over my 34As and kept them there until I arrived back at Lori's.

She and Chloe were on the couch. "Hey, girl, how'd it go?"

"The subway was a gong show, but it was a cakewalk compared to the shower."

"Huh?"

Did I say that out loud?

"You were right about Apple Maps. Very user-friendly."

"How was the agency?" Her lips were so swollen and puffy, I was amazed she spoke with such ease.

"Also a gong show. I have to say, they weren't very welcoming. It was like they had totally forgotten I was coming. Then this girl Sheila showed up—"

"Sheila Summerville? Blond, gorgeous, great style?"

"Do you know her?"

"Not personally. She's Darlene's new superstar in the making."

"I noticed that. She got the red-carpet treatment."

That I was expecting.

"Sheila was a total nobody and now she's *everywhere*. Who are you working with?"

"Darlene and Adam."

"That's great." She opened her eyes wide, I think, but it seemed like that was the goal.

"Adam never spoke a word to me. Darlene had a lot to say and none of it was nice."

"Darlene's a bitch, but she's a shark. She can make your career. I don't know much about Adam. He's pretty new. They have this *good cop–bad cop* thing happening."

"Is that their go-to routine? She's a bitch and he's the good guy?"

"He's the good guy, and the gay guy." She winked. "Darlene is major crushing on him."

"Darlene was pissed that I don't have an Instagram account."

"Seriously? Why not?"

Just admit it already.

"I mean, I'm on Instagram, but I've never posted anything. My life isn't that interesting."

"It's all so fake anyway," she said, and then added enthusiastically, "Do you want to see mine?"

It was unbelievable. There were only twenty-five posts, but she had a hundred and fifty thousand followers. Small wonder. The red carpets, parties, and photoshoots. Her fabulous life, her fabulous friends, and her fabulous self.

"What am I supposed to post?" I was mesmerized by a picture of her spectacular, custom-built for *Sports Illustrated* body sprawled sensually on golden sand. "Darlene said some clients won't even see you if you don't have at least a hundred thousand followers."

"The business has changed. It wasn't like this when I was younger. Nobody had this social media thing happening. Now, if you have enough followers, people will pay you to wear their clothes. You know you can buy followers, right?"

"That's good news."

"The thing is, if you have like five hundred followers but no one is liking your posts, it'll get suspicious. But don't worry, you can build up slowly. Once I'm all healed you can do some selfies with me."

It was a start.

"Don't forget, the maid is coming tomorrow."

Shit. The garbage bag.

"Oh, right. Just out of curiosity, where do we put the garbage?"

"Under the kitchen sink."

The direction the conversation was taking was uncomfortable but I tried to keep it light. "I'm such a Curious George, umm, after that, where would it go?"

"The maid will take it out."

"Right, of course. I'm just wondering where she might take it?"

"A garbage chute in the stairwell." An air of annoyance was settling over her. "Is this, like, a recycling issue?"

"Are we allowed to use the stairs for running?"

Nice save!

"You are too cute. You go for it, girl. Do some stairs for me." She sauntered back to her room. "Come on, Chloe."

I scooped up this morning's soaking wet Saran Wrap, shot out the apartment door, and dumped it in the chute. Longing for fresh air, I climbed past the sixteenth floor to the roof; my footsteps landed like lead . The door was locked and the iron stairwell stank of garbage. It was an opportune selfie moment! #stairwayfromhell#thisdoorisalwayslocked#trapped#footsteps ofdoom.

Chapter 4

I WAS GOING TO HAVE TO STOCKPILE MORE SARAN WRAP. Lori directed me to the nearest supermarket. Gristedes had all the characteristics of a grocery store: aisles of food, a deli, a bakery, and checkout lines, but it was apocalyptic in there. Who was responsible for merchandising? It was so random; I couldn't find the Saran Wrap.

"Excuse me," I said to someone in an apron, which may or may not have been a uniform.

"Could you please tell me where to find the Saran Wrap?"

The male clerk screamed toward the cashier, "Where's the Saran Wrap at?!"

"You've been here a year and you can't find the damn Saran Wrap?" That cashier turned to the cashier beside her. "Can you believe him?"

I picked up ten boxes and a minipack of Oreos. I'd earned them; besides, I hadn't eaten anything all day. I wolfed down the entire package before the cashier had finished ringing up my order.

"You have Oreo crumbs all up in your face," she said loudly, wagging her two-inch purple nails at my chin.

"Thank you." And not unlike Jay-Z when he notices dirt on his shoulders, I brushed them away. It's not like it mattered; that floor hadn't seen a broom or a mop in quite some time.

"What do you need all this Saran Wrap for?"

"I'm a plumbaphobe." I couldn't believe the word came out of my mouth, but the state of the supermarket had shocked me to my core.

"Right." She paused. "Right . . . well, whatever that is, it's gonna get expensive."

At $4.96 per roll, and 1½ rolls per shower, it was definitely going to get expensive.

⋛ ☺ ⋚

I hid the Saran Wrap in my suitcase and called Mum.

"Hi Mum. I have mastered the shower for now."

"Well done!" she said proudly. "How was your meeting with the agency?"

I didn't have the heart to tell her the truth so I gave her Sheila's version.

"How exciting, your first photo shoot."

"Say hi to Dad and tell him I haven't met one pervert or weirdo."

There was the plane incident and my roommate did have staples in her head.

"Gotta go. Mike is FaceTiming me."

"How's New York treating you so far?" Mike asked, inhaling sharply on a joint. Ben's ears flopped over Mike's knee.

"My agent hates me and my clothes, and I need to actually post stuff on Instagram."

A breeze caught the yellow curtains and drew my attention to the bridge. Maybe I could post that.

"What the fuck are you looking at?"

"Something to post," I said, shifting my focus back to his grimace. Mike doesn't even have a Facebook account and he thinks Snapchat is a precursor to Armageddon.

"I need people to think I have a fantastic, interesting life, which will make clients more likely to hire me." I would've loved to be sharing that joint with him.

"I told you, it's fucking fake. Just like fucking high school." A vein his neck was pulsating. The thought of high school elicits strange responses from a lot of people. I don't know the name of Mike's Lydia Baker, but he was clearly wretched.

"So far, it's worse. And get this! The supermarket is a shit hole. The place is filthy. Grocery carts were strewn all over the area around the checkouts, the shelves were haphazardly stuffed, the dairy aisle was covered in spilled milk, the cashiers were chewing gum, and the grocery guy didn't know where the Saran Wrap was."

"Saran Wrap? What the fuck are you buying Saran Wrap for?"

"The bathtub has feet, there's a film on the shower curtain thick enough to be removed with an ice scraper, and the bath mat looks like—" I started gagging.

"All right, pull yourself together." He squeezed his eyebrows together with his left hand, the joint still dangling between his lips. "You know, fucking plastic is destroying the planet."

"I'm in a crisis mode!" I said through clenched teeth.

"Fucking hell. How's the apartment otherwise?"

"Well." I could see a thin layer of dust on the sunflower painting on the far wall, which looked like some dollar store Van Gogh knockoff. "The apartment is really cool and artsy. She has an awesome dog and . . . oh, fuck it." I surrendered. "I'm sleeping on a couch."

"Sounds great, Al." He had mastered the art of sarcasm. "How's the hot supermodel roommate?"

"She's nice, but she has two staples in her head, kind of like Frankenstein."

"You know Frankenstein was the doctor, eh? The monster had no name."

≥ ☺ ≤

I slept with the dog last night. She jumped on the couch around midnight.

"Chloe, we need some boundaries. I like you. Who couldn't love your sweet face? She licked my hand but I wasn't having it. "Listen, if I had a pullout, I could work with you." I nudged her. "You have to sleep on the floor, buddy." She nestled her face into my knees and I caved. "Don't get used to this. I'm totally serious."

Lori found us squished together in the morning. "Oh, how sweet. Come on, baby, I'll take you out now. How about a coffee, Alex?"

"Thanks. Let me get these today."

"Don't be crazy. It's coffee." She grabbed her pashmina and glasses and headed out the door.

I needed to implement a system. There'd been no stairs in three days, and yesterday's Oreo intake required optimum stair output. My Conair was in overdrive trying to salvage my wet sneakers when I heard Lori's key. I threw my Asics aside and feigned drying my very dry hair.

"Did you already have a shower?"

I was dreading it. The sink was bad enough. Brushing my teeth in rubber gloves was a colossal pain in the ass.

"I was just pondering that situation."

"What situation?"

I picked up my hair dryer. "You know, how long it will take to dry my hair and stuff."

"What are your plans for today?" she asked.

"I'm hitting those stairs for sure." Albeit with soaking wet sneaks. "How do you stay so fit?"

She had slipped out of her Adidas pants and stood sipping her coffee in skimpy boy shorts and a tank. "There are no stairs in my future. I'm too lazy."

"Do you have a daily calorie maximum?" She couldn't possibly be that perfect.

"I eat whatever I want."

"Even carbs?" I asked doubtfully.

"Yep. This is my natural body type. Lucky, right?"

"Yeah, lucky." At least I didn't have staples in my head. "I'm not lucky and need to stock up for very my limited menu. Are all the grocery stores like Gristedes?"

"Pretty much. This isn't the suburbs. There's the organic market, and Fairway is down on 74th but it's always a zoo." She brushed past me. "I'm going to hunker down and do some healing." Her perky behind and cellulite-free legs were all the motivations I needed. I headed for the stairwell and ran to the ground floor and back to the twelfth floor twice: 220 stairs! That was a record, despite the stairwell stench and soppy sneaks. I gave myself a 10+.

$\gtrless$ ☺ $\lessgtr$

Riding that high, I worked up the courage to return to Gristedes and stock up on Lean Cuisine. The same striking young cashier who was working yesterday was at the checkout. Having now confessed—albeit accidentally—that I was a plumbaphobe, I felt somewhat connected to her. There was no basis in fact for this, but the feeling was there all the same. Her lustrous skin was flawless, and her piercing eyes had a mischievous glimmer. She was wearing a name tag, which I hadn't noticed the day before: Keisha.

"Wow, you must *really* love Lean Cuisine."

"Not exactly. I'm on a diet."

"You swallowed up those Oreos pretty quick yesterday. What's this diet called?"

The stench of patchouli suddenly engulfed the checkout as a petite hippie lady draped in love beads pushed past me with her cart.

"I'm sorry," I said, retreating into myself, almost knocking over the magazine stand.

"Why are you sorry?" Keisha demanded. "This woman here needs to be saying sorry because it ain't her turn."

Entirely unfazed, the woman continued loading up her items on the conveyer belt.

The adjacent cashier, a brunette with enormous breasts, whipped around to face us and her booming voice announced, "And she hella needs to change her perfume."

Keisha replied to this assessment with, "Amen, Tonya."

"I'm waiting," the hippie said in a haughty and what I knew was a fake English accent. No decent British person would ever dare jump a queue.

"You can just keep waiting until I'm done with her." Keisha nodded at me and I shrank away like a frightened turtle tightening my grip on my basket.

The woman fondled her love beads but she sounded pissed. "My yogurt is getting warm."

Yow-gert? I think you mean yoghurt, with the yog rhyming with jog. If you're going to pretend to be English, do your homework—or at least watch *Downton Abbey.*

"Take your stink ass," Tonya said rather mercilessly, "and your damn yogurt to the back of the line."

My eyes were darting back forth among the three of them.

"I shall not be treated in this way! The Better Business Bureau will hear about this." The faux-English hippie tilted her chin ceiling high and stormed out of the store.

"I'm sorry," I said to everyone. "I'm not sure what to do now."

"Damn girl," Keisha said. "It's a supermarket. Just give me your stuff."

"I'm sorry if that was my fault."

"You're a grown-ass woman," Keisha said, shaking her head in disbelief. "You can't let crazies like her push you around."

"That bitch is in here every damn day," Tonya said. "She's hella crazy."

Agreed on all fronts. Definitely bitchy and crazy, but were they allowed to say that in front of other customers?

"She comes in here every day?" I asked. I'd like to know what times to avoid.

"What's with that accent?" Keisha asked.

"I know!" I said. "Was it the yow-gert that gave it away? She's not English."

"Not her sorry fake English ass." She pointed her electric blue fingernails at me. "Your accent."

"You think I have an accent?" I suddenly felt exotic and interesting. "I'm from Canada."

"Oooh-kay Canada! I remember growing up in Detroit, my mom used to go all the way to this one store Glenn's on West Chicago, specifically to get some of that President's Choice pop you all be drinking up there. She loved that stuff."

"I actually don't drink pop."

"Uh-huh, 'cause you're on a diet." Keisha finished ringing up my Lean Cuisine and winked. "How much would this cost in loonies?"

"It costs a lot more in loonies." A smile spread across my face. "Thank you."

As I turned to leave, Tonya's customer, who was on her cell phone loudly lamenting the shit service at Gristedes, snatched up her shopping bags and pushed past me. "This is the fucking worst supermarket in the city."

"You're the one shopping here. What does that say about you, luv?" Tonya said, disinterested.

It was like a combat zone. I could start a new series, *Supermarket Scandals.*

Stay tuned and find out. Will Alex survive?

≥ ☺ ≤

Lori watched me stuff her freezer full of my entrées. "Wow. You're really into Lean Cuisine."

"There are some volatile shoppers and cashiers in your neighborhood." I'd have to psych myself up for my next grocery excursion. "Do you mind if I smoke?"

"Great idea. I'll have one with you." Her slender manicured fingers reached for my Craven A Menthols. "Are you sure? That's your last one."

"It is, in fact, my very last one." I nodded forlornly. "I promised I'd quit when I finished this pack."

"Here's to quitting." We raised our cigarettes and toasted the moment.

"I'm going to miss them. They helped me lose 20 pounds."

"Did you have a weight problem your whole life?"

A weight problem? My whole life?

"I didn't have a weight problem my whole life. I've had a problem since I met Robin."

"So you weren't fat before you met Robin, but then you got fat after?"

"I weighed 145 pounds when I met Robin."

"Got it. You were kind of fat. At what point weren't you fat?"

I guess I have always been kind of fat.

"Before university." I had to say something.

"Sooo many girls I went to high school with just ballooned freshman year. It's so sad."

Sad? People are starving all over the world.

"Anyway, here I am 125 pounds."

Feeling sad that I was kind of fat my whole life.

"Good for you, girl. People say losing weight when you're older is really hard."

"It's been hell." Thinking about it made me want to scream or cry, but mostly it made me hungry.

"It's so worth it. Just wait and see," she said, reaching for her Ben & Jerry's. "Chunky Monkey and cigarettes for lunch. It's getting crazy up in here."

She gestured to the enormous pint of ice cream. "I guess this isn't on the menu?"

She handed me a Lean Cuisine macaroni and cheese. "Only three hundred calories."

I discarded the plastic and fluffed up the noodles in one of Lori's multicolored Mediterranean bowls.

"I hope it's so worth it," I said aloud. Jealousy makes people ugly.

As serendipity would have it, Adam called and snapped me out of it.

"Hi sweetie." His tongue touched the top of his palate when he made the "s" sound and he held it there for a second.

"I arranged a test shoot for you with the fabulous Fabio. All you need to bring is your super fab self."

"Thanks, Adam." I loved the way he talked.

"You're so lucky. Fabio is taking you to the Hamptons. It takes about two hours, sweetie. You're meeting the team tomorrow at his studio in Soho at six a.m. You're going to do some fashion and beauty shots and some swimwear, okay?"

Swimwear? Shit!

Apparently, researching the actual art of modeling should've been higher on my priority list, but the dieting and mental preparation required to even get myself here used up all my reserves. My brain was running on fumes. I assumed there would be some kind of tutorial with the agency. What happened to the transformation team?

"Bon chance, sweetie!"

I tossed my uneaten Mac & Cheese. There would be no food for me until this shoot was over.

"Ah, Lori." I knocked on her door.

"Come in." A bronzed chandelier hung over her four-poster bed. The pint of Chunky Monkey sat empty on her bedside table, which was covered in pill bottles. She looked like she was coming out of anesthesia as she nestled into her rose-colored Egyptian cotton sheets.

"Are you okay?" It was probably a sugar coma.

"Totally. I just took a Xanax." She smiled at me through half-shut eyes.

The pint of ice cream didn't do it for you?

"Lori, I have this test tomorrow with Fabio."

"Oh, I loooove Fabio. He's amazing."

Let's hope so. I need all the help I can get.

"We're shooting some swimwear and I'm wondering if you might have reference shots lying around."

"Totally I do!" She grabbed an iPad, which was buried beneath a cashmere throw; her room was messy but fancy. "Check out my portfolio."

Lori's pictures were spectacular. Her long, thin, yet voluptuous bronzed body was perfectly positioned in every shot. She was more beautiful in pictures than in real life. I wondered if that was makeup or if this is how she looked pre-staples.

"What do you think?"

"You're a goddess."

"Thanks." She shrugged.

"I don't look like this in a bathing suit, Lori."

"Most girls don't look *this* good." She propped herself up on her expensive-looking accent pillows. "The clients need to see your beautiful shape and your gorgeous skin."

"You think I have a beautiful shape and gorgeous skin?"

"You totally do." I totally hugged her. She slid her luscious limbs over the side of the bed. Her feet landed soundlessly on her plush area rug, where she stood uninhibited in a lacy bra and underwear.

"Watch me." She leaned against the wall, elongated her body, and arched her back.

"Cock your hip and point your toes and lean forward with a little space between your arm and your body." Her body looked positively perfect with each nuanced move.

"Come and stand with me in this mirror." Her boudoir boasted three full-length mirrors. "This is my skinny mirror. I need it after that ice cream."

I stared transfixed at our calves.

OH, MY GOD, I HAVE CANKLES! How could I have not noticed this before?

She took me through pose after pose. "You're getting the hang of it from the neck up."

I was afraid to look down.

I stretched my neck, reached my arms backward, and arched my back.

"You look like you're on a runway."

"That's encouraging," I said, leaning deeper into my arch.

"Not that kind of runway. You look like you're ready for takeoff."

I slouched down, put one hand on my waist, and cocked my hip out.

"What about now?"

"Now it looks like you are about to start singing 'I'm a Little Teapot.'"

"I need a cigarette."

"I thought you just quit."

That was before I noticed my cankles.

"I just started . . . again."

⋛ ☺ ⋚

"You were like *just* here." Keisha didn't miss a beat.

"I know." I was unable to control the tapping of my foot. "I forgot cigarettes."

"We don't sell cigarettes."

"Who does?" I balled my hands into fists.

"Oh, my God, are you serious? That nicotine be calling you for real. 7-Eleven is up the block."

The 7-Eleven was at least more efficient than Gristedes. The five-person line moved like wildfire.

"A packet of Craven A Menthols please," I said to the clerk.

"What's that?"

"Cigarettes." I pantomimed smoking.

"We don't have them."

"Cigarettes?"

"We sell cigarettes, yes."

"What do you mean, you don't have them?"

"We don't have what you said." He smiled at me.

My breath was getting shallower. "They're menthols."

"We have menthol. Marlboro or Newport."

"But I don't know those brands." The walls were closing in on me, and the fluorescent lights weren't helping. "I need Craven Menthols." There was aggravated shuffling and grunting coming from the line forming behind me.

"Marlboro or Newport." He wasn't smiling anymore. Some guy at the back of the line yelled, "We don't got all day, lady!"

"I can't believe this is happening." I stared at the clerk.

"We can't believe this is happening." It was the same yeller. "Get your cigarettes already."

You can just wait your effing turn.

I couldn't risk another confrontation; I was running out of places to shop. "Fine. I'll take the Marlboros, please."

ʒ ☺ ʃ

"They taste disgusting." This brand was not part of my very delicate system. "I'm totally freaking out."

Cankles, cankles, cankles.

"Here," Lori tossed me a bottle of chewable vitamin C, "suck on those."

I stuffed three in my mouth. "That does help. Thanks."

"Listen, I have a great idea for your Instagram."

I lit another cigarette.

"Forget your old account. Start fresh tonight and tomorrow take a bunch of snaps and start posting cute, cool stuff. #firstshoot#modelona-mission#location#hamptons#beauty#glamsquad#lovemyjob."

"I think I need to work on the posing."

"You need an Instagram. They'll help you tomorrow."

That was reassuring, and I relaxed against the window frame. Perhaps tomorrow was the onset of the transformation.

"How about a Brazilian?"

"A Brazilian what?" A massage wouldn't hurt.

"Wax front to back." She eyed my lady parts.

"I don't even wax my legs."

"Once you wax, you never go back." She looked at the clock. "Eight p.m., it's too late. You'll have to tend your garden yourself." She giggled and sashayed out of the kitchen, where I collapsed and remained curled in a fetal position for a good half hour.

I had to shave. Shave everything. In that bathroom.

"Project Shave" required three rolls of Saran Wrap, four towels, and just over an hour to complete. My nervous system would never be the same.

"Wow, girl, you just spent an hour in the bath. Why do you look so stressed?"

Hmmm, let me see. Your bathroom is wretched, these Marlboros are wretched, and my cankles are wretched.

"I'm just nervous about tomorrow."

On a positive note, my adrenals have curbed my appetite and I've forgotten I'm starving.

"You'll do great."

"I took your advice about Instagram." Editing my profile and my new handle helped instill a sense of promise. "Meet *alexemmersonnyc.*"

"Alexemmersonnyc, you're gonna rock that shoot." She high-fived me.

Chapter 5

MY TAXI PULLED UP THE COBBLESTONE STREET beside two guys leaning against a white passenger van. "You must be our beautiful model. I'm Brian."

He called me beautiful. Yay.

"Hi, I'm Alex. I'm from Vancouver. I just got here two days ago."

He leaned and kissed both my cheeks, just like Sheila and Darlene had done.

Was this how all fashion people greeted each other?

"I'll be doing your hair and makeup." His silk-like skin was radiant, and he was definitely shopping at the same store as Nick. "This fab hipster, who needs to put out that cigarette, is Fabio's assistant, Carlos."

I stuffed my menthols back in my Kipling.

"Hey." He took a deep drag and smiled.

"Carlos, can you help me?!" a raspy voice hollered. A formidable six-foot-tall woman hurried toward us. She was pushing a rolling rack, which Carlos loaded into the van.

"Brian, you sweet angel." She towered over him. "You have to help me, my love. Look at what they've done to my hair." Her hair was black at the roots, sort of blondish through the center, and white on the tips, like someone spliced a zebra and a golden retriever.

"Astrid, this is Alex." I leaned in to do the kiss, but I started on the left, she started on the right, it all went pear-shaped, and we both gave up.

"I'm not Catholic. I don't know what side to start with," I said.

"I'm a recovering Catholic. There are no rules here." She took off her glasses and pulled her hair. "Please tell me you can fix it?"

"Darling, I can fix everything," Brian said.

"We were shooting in Rome last week and this amateur colorist butchered me. Fucking Italians." She turned to me. "What's your name again?"

"Alex. I'm from Vancouver."

"Right. I have pulled some amazing clothes for your gorgeous self today."

Gorgeous. Yay.

"Astrid is the best." Brian squeezed her hands and her eyes brightened. "She knows everyone and can get her hands on the top designers."

"It's true." She shrugged. "Carlos, baby, can I have a drag of that?"

"Angel," "love," "baby." I loved her casual use of the pet names. "Gorgeous" was great but I was hoping to effectuate something more intimate.

"I have cigarettes," I offered.

"No thanks. I don't actually smoke," she said and sucked on the filter of Carlos's Marlboro. "I hate it when Fabio makes us go to the Hamptons."

I'd never been to the Hamptons, and couldn't wait to embark on our adventure.

"The traffic is maddening." Brian managed to stretch ma-aa-ad-den-inng into five syllables. "But everyone summers there. The Kennedys, the Clintons, Beyoncé, Jay-Z, and tragically this year so did the Kardashians."

Summers. Etymologically incorrect, but I liked the word as a verb.

"Heads up, here he comes."

A seriously dilapidated version of his namesake of romance novel fame, Fabio was enormous and balding. The scraps he was clinging to hung in a lifeless ponytail to the middle of his back. His pants sagged around his belly, and his chest hair was pouring out of his stained white T-shirt.

Astrid mumbled to Brian, "He's always late, fucking Italians." Then she threw her arms around Fabio. "Fabio, my darling, so good to see you." More kissing.

Brian introduced us. "This is the beautiful Alex, our model today."

That was the second time he said "beautiful." I was beaming inside.

"Ciao, *bella.*" Fabio double-kissed me. Perhaps he had really moist lips, but I think he may have licked my face. "Let's go," he said.

We piled into the van. I cozied up to Linus in the back row as we headed east on the Long Island Expressway. Four lanes were already teeming with traffic. I didn't care. The Hamptons, two "beautifuls," one "gorgeous," and my first photo shoot. Yay!

⋛ ☺ ⋚

We pulled up to an enormous estate whose driveway could easily be mistaken for a quaint side street. The team set up shop in the pool house, whose French doors opened onto extensive views of golden sand and the Atlantic Ocean.

"This is bigger than my parents' house," I said.

"I know, it's outrageous," Astrid said. "Two full bathrooms, and the bedroom is sick."

"Why would someone sleep in the pool house?"

She continued reveling, "All the linens are imported from Italy. I love the Italians."

Was she bipolar?

"Fabio must be a really successful photographer," I said.

"Ah, NO." Brian wagged his finger at me. "The owner is some big hedge fund guy but he lets Fabio shoot here so he can invite all the models to his parties."

"That's why there's a bedroom." Astrid ran her tongue salaciously over her lip.

"If these precious cabana walls could talk," Brian whispered as he laid out his brushes. "We could sell scandals to *Page Six*."

"What's *Page Six*?" I asked.

Astrid looked at me with unconcealed incredulousness. I wasn't making a good case for a personalized pet name.

"It's the *New York Post*'s gossip column." Brian pulled out a chair for me. "Now let's get started on that gorgeous face." He pushed my hair behind my ears. "Alex, I don't even want to use foundation. Your skin is flawless."

Flawless. Yay.

"Astrid, what's our first look?"

She was caressing a long, camel-colored silk dress with spaghetti straps. "Calvin. I love him. Simple, elegant, ethereal beauty." She lowered her eyes and swayed side to side across the terra-cotta tiles. "Maybe carrying these K Jacques sandals?"

My heart rate was on the rise; there had to be more of a tutorial than this. "Astrid, I have never done this before and now that it's crunch time, I'm kind of freaking out."

"Everything is natural and fresh." She pulled out some reference shots for each look.

Was that it? Look at these pictures and do that?

"The Calvin dress is dreamy and sensual. Think Charlize Theron."

Charlize Theron? That's ambitious.

"We're going to shoot this Ralph Lauren Col-lec-tion"—she mouthed the word slowly, as though I'd never heard it before—"striped bikini with some boyfriend jeans and this super fab Ralph Lauren Col-lec-tion." This time I mouthed the word with her and nodded in acknowledgement, "off-the-shoulder cable knit sweater and a great necklace. It's sporty but sexy. Think Karlie Kloss."

This Karlie Kloss was doing it brilliantly, but mimicking Lori hadn't worked and that had been a live, you know, in-person instruction.

"Put your thumbs in the pockets and pull the jeans down a little so a hint of the suit shows." She acted out the moves.

"I might need more guidance. Think model-by-number."

"Just relax. You don't want tension in your face."

How does one just relax when one has no idea what one is doing?

"We'll help you." She sounded agitated. "The bikini will be the easy part. Have fun with it."

Keep breathing.

Brian massaged my shoulders. "We're going to tame this mass of glo-rious curls into soft waves, and when you slip into that dress and feel that soft silk against your skin, you're going to transform into a goddess."

His brushes felt like feathers on my skin and I started to relax.

"I don't think I need the eyelash curler. Look at those lashes." He snatched up a pair of tweezers. "However, I need to clean up these brows."

Having someone, even a skilled professional, holding sharp instruments near your eyes is unsettling, and my natural reflex was to pull away.

"The eyebrows make or break your entire appearance," Astrid announced. "I'm a victim of the nineties but I pencil them in, and that fullness makes me look younger."

I never would've noticed, but having now had my attention drawn to them, they looked unnatural and overly arched.

"Astrid's right," Brian chimed in.

To you, maybe. I didn't want those brows.

"I cannot overstate the importance of the brow." Brian pushed my hair behind my ears and held up a compact mirror. "We need some more space between the brows. If I take these stragglers growing toward the center of your nose, it will make a massive difference. May I?"

"Okay." It did twinge, but that simple tweezing tweaked my face. It made more space for my eyes. Still natural, but neat.

"These three strays here, just above your lid on both eyes, are distracting, and if I take this one, this, and this one, it will create a very subtle arch framing your perfectly shaped eye and lid. May I?"

It was more hair than I planned to part with, but for the sake of my perfectly shaped eye, I acquiesced.

"Perfect! Your beautiful eyes just pop now." Brian held up the compact. "It just opens your face up."

"Wow!" If a brow makeover could do this, what else did he have in his bag of tricks?

"Astrid, look at this hair. A roll brush and some antifrizz and it does this. Glorious natural wave."

"Yeah, glorious." Astrid snatched up one of the twenty sun hats she'd brought. "I shouldn't be allowed in public with this hair. Thank God for House of Lafayette, I'll be fashionably camouflaged until it recovers. Let's get you dressed." She yanked me out of the chair and led me into the bedroom.

After unzipping the dress, she stared at me.

WTF? She's going to dress me?

I wiggled out of my jeans and tank top.

"Okay, I never mentioned those jeans or that polyester tank."

Both recent purchases that now needed to be demoted on the rating scale to a 5.

"But what's with the Fruit Of The Loom bra and panties?"

"It's my underwear." I've never used the cringe-inducing word "panties" and was not about to start.

"Lose the bra. You might want to think about investing in some new . . .

Please don't say it again.

. . . panties. Something seamless. Brian, can you bring me my kit?" I ducked behind the bed. "It's okay, baby, he's not interested in vajayjays."

My vajayjay was fully covered. It was my fully exposed 34As I was concerned about.

"Thanks, Brian." She handed me a nude G-string. "Here, put this on."

Someone else's underwear?

Astrid was losing patience. "They're clean, okay? In fact, you can keep them."

I wish I had my Saran Wrap.

"That's so generous. Thank you."

"Brian, come here and look at Alex," she said, fitting me with a beautiful ring. "It's Alexis Bittar."

She turned me toward the mirror. The three of us stared at my reflection.

"She's gorgeous," they said in unison.

My skin was glowing and my hair, sans frizz, was flowing and cascading gently over my shoulders onto my long, beautiful, skinny arms. The silk dress caressed my body and just skimmed the tops of my can . . . no . . . ankles. In this dress, with this hair, and this skin, even my ankles looked great.

Maybe I could be a goddess.

My eyes were brimming with tears.

"I used waterproof mascara, baby girl, but don't you even think about letting one tear fall."

"Okay, goddess. Put on your game face. You got this," Astrid said.

Gorgeous. Goddess. Game face.

"I got this."

⋛ ☺ ⋚

Fabio was in the middle of the beach running sand through his fat fingers. He pointed to Carlos, who was holding a light reflector. "Come, bella, stand here. Let us begin."

I stared into the camera, tilting my head from side to side.

"Do something with your body," Fabio commanded.

He had a big role in capturing my transformation and he wasn't inspiring confidence.

I swayed back and forth, looking down, like Astrid had done in the pool house.

"Stop that. Keep your arms by your side. I don't want to see the front of your hand. You look like a gorilla."

Gorgeous. Goddess. Gorilla?

My teeth were clenched and I was squeezing my brain so hard my sight was blurred. Astrid crossed into my field of vision and I locked onto her.

"Fabio, just wait. I want her to carry these."

She handed me the K Jacques and whispered, "Fucking Fabio. Think tall. Think thin. Think of that gorgeous girl in the mirror."

That gorgeous girl in the mirror was *me*.

Astrid floated behind Fabio, mouthing, "Gorgeous. You're gorgeous." The more I heard that word, the more a part of me started believing it. I thought about how that gorgeous girl might walk on a beach.

I walked slowly toward the horizon, touching the seams of the dress, and a gentle breeze lifted my hair off my shoulders. The warmth of the sand and the smell of the sea, the feel of silk swept me away, and in that moment I felt like a woman in a perfume commercial, just like Charlize, my body shimmering across the sand. I felt like a goddess.

"Beautiful, bellisima." Fabio was snapping away.

Beautiful. Bellisima.

Operation transformation is in full go mode.

"Beautiful, bella. Now change."

We ran back to the pool house. "Astrid, you're amazing. Thank you," I said, stepping out of the dress with nipples blazing.

"It's all you!" The padded bikini top lifted my 34As into actual cleavage. I was pulling the pink, off-the-shoulder cable knit sweater over my head when Fabio started screaming, "We're losing light!" Astrid grabbed a necklace and we ran to the beach.

Brian, unfazed, massaged the roots of my hair and double-downed on the antifrizz.

"Humidity isn't my friend," I whispered.

"Your hair is gorgeous. Let's just freshen up these lips." Brian smiled.

"Now!" Fabio screeched, killing the moment, and started snapping.

Astrid was pantomiming the moves she wanted and I followed her lead, cranking up my inner Karlie Kloss. Pulling down the jeans, sitting cross-legged in the sand, throwing my head back, and laughing. I'd mastered the art of the fake laugh in high school. That skill was proving useful.

"Take off your clothes, bella! Let's go. Carlos, shade her!"

I whipped off the jeans and the sweater, and Astrid grabbed the necklace.

"Now, bella, come walk with me. Run, turn, spin."

I ran, I turned, I spun.

Fabio came in tight with his camera; the shutter was going super fast. "Yes, yes, that's it. You have such a beautiful face."

Beautiful face!

Fabio stopped and took a step back. "But you have an ugly body."

What?

Deep down I knew it all along. Twenty pounds didn't change anything. Nick was lying about my arms and my 34As. And my cankles! The shame of self-deception smothered me. My whole body is ugly. And now it's been captured on film for the whole world to see. I froze, grasping my hands in front of my face so tight I was cutting off the circulation.

"Do something, bella. Move."

Astrid ran toward me with a flowing skirt. "Ignore him."

Ignore him?

"Your body is just fine."

Fine?

"Just work the vibe with this sarong; it'll help." If a confidence boost was her intention, she missed the mark.

"Yes, Astrid, that's good." Sweat was gathering on his upper lip. "Give her something to cover her legs."

Cover my legs?

It was over for me.

"Bella, you're stiff. Come lie in the sand."

I lay there, limp and lifeless.

"Sit up. Do something."

I sat up, wrapped my arms around my legs, and buried my face.

"Look at me." Fabio swiped at the sweat oozing down his chin. "What's the matter with you?"

Well, Fabio, I haven't eaten in thirty-six hours, and I have an ugly body, which you kindly pointed out. I'm now paralyzed from the neck down, and from this moment forward I shall never wear a bathing suit again.

"Jet lag."

"It's okay, bella." After several failed attempts, he hoisted himself into a seated position.

"Anyway, you look nicer with clothes on."

I raced back to the pool house, with Brian and Astrid in hot pursuit.

"Alex, listen to me," Brian said through the bedroom door, "Fabio can be, well, Fabio. He likes rail-thin girls with large breasts."

"But not fake," Astrid added. "You can come in, baby, she's decent."

"His stupid bias is not a reflection on you." Brian rushed past Astrid, who was stretched out on the Italian linens. "Your body is just fine."

CHAPTER 5

Astrid scooped us up into a group hug. "You need a thick skin for this business, my love."

I guess utter humiliation merited a pet name.

We piled into the van and no one spoke another word the whole way back to the city.

Once Carlos had parked, I clambered over the seats, repeating "Thanks, everyone" at least ten times, waving nonstop, and avoiding all eye contact. I jumped into a taxi as they unloaded their gear. No kiss good-bye, no Instagram friends, no posts.

I stopped at Gristedes and bought two bags of Oreos. Got halfway through the first one when I reached the checkout.

"Look at you, Lean Cuisine," Keisha said, nodding with approval. "We've got a model in the house today."

"Trust me, I'm not a model."

"You won't be if you keep stuffing your face with those Oreos."

Chapter 6

I WAS STARING AT THE BACK OF MIKE'S HEAD ON MY IPAD.

"I'll never wear a bathing suit again," I muffled with a mouthful of Oreos. "Why are you so distracted?"

"I'm barbequing." He held up an ear of corn drenched in butter. It glistened in the sun.

"I've asked you not to talk about food."

"Fuck me, Alex, it's just corn. Corn is a vegetable." Melted butter dripped on the screen.

"Corn is a carbohydrate." I dropped both empty bags of Oreos in the trash and lit a cigarette.

"You're still fucking smoking?" He pointed the tip of those ridiculous yellow corn holders at me. "I thought you were quitting when you got to New York."

The diet, Darlene, freaking Fabio. One could hardly blame me. Except, of course, Mike. "There's a modeling career on the line here. Give me a break."

"Is it worth dying for?"

"You know what? Maybe it is!"

Chloe bounded into the kitchen when she heard me yell, but her tail stopped wagging when she saw the cigarette. She turned her nose up at the cookie crumbs and marched off. Even the dog was judging me.

Mike leaned back in his patio chair, the corn out of view, but it was there, an arm's reach away. Ben was licking his lips, hoping to get in on the action.

"Why don't you add 'quitting smoking' to your rating scale?"

I had considered that, but the negative numbers in the diet department were demoralizing enough. "I can't handle any more negative reinforcement."

"Fuck the fat Italian!" he yelled.

"It ended so badly. I didn't get anyone's Instagram handles, or do any posts."

Chloe's sweet paws had left marks on the cream-colored tiles; it looked intentional, like something you'd see on a hat, a T-shirt, or a mug. Perhaps Chloe's pawprint pattern was postable.

"Can't you be Internet friends, or whatever the fuck you call it, with the people who dressed you up?"

"They witnessed a big-shot photographer comment on my ugly body." I was delusional, prancing in the sand for that man. It made me sick.

"What if they tell their friends? I'll be known as the model with the ugly body."

"Just fucking relax and wait to see the pictures. And quit fucking smoking." It felt like Ben's puppy dog eyes were pleading with me too.

I covered the Marlboros' surgeon general's warning in masking tape and readied myself for all things Instagram.

≥ ☺ ≤

My social media existence didn't go much beyond Facebook. Instagram is Facebook's sleazy cousin, sly and substanceless. Spying on people is skeevey and sadomasochistic, but it's impossible to look away.

Moving beyond spying to creating is way beyond my skill set.

#modellife#glamsquad#location#sunset#setlife#lovemyjob#street-style#ilovefashion #flawlessskin#shineyourlight#inspired#minimal#natural#cool#visionary#retro#vintage#chic#modern#fashionforever#strikea-pose#burnbright #iloveny

It's a freaking virtual art gallery.

Art intimidates me; it's so directionless, and the absence of structure is upsetting. It isn't lost on me that so many of the greats killed themselves; their minds were on constant overload. Photography is also not my forte. No one in my family takes pictures, which is kind of cool. We are all too busy eating, talking, and having fun to bother with recording the experience.

There are certain people, such as Lydia Baker, who can make everything look beautiful. Her photos look like they're straight out of some artsy magazine: moody lighting, abstract angles and shadows, spectacular sunsets, golden beaches, and now her account was spattered with images of her fabulous semester abroad with her fabulous friends #iheartlondon #burberrylove #britboys #everythingsoundsbetterinbritish

Well, I have a British passport and I'm in New York City, so you can suck it!

Chapter 7

"HI SWEETIE. FABIO'S A STAR AND HAS ALREADY sent over the images! Come into the agency around two p.m. and we can go through them."

The receptionist had withered over the past few days, and I could practically see through her and her Vantablack dress. She nodded politely but grimaced when she saw my Tevas.

Seriously? Even Tevas?

"Hi again. I'm Alex Emmerson."

"Yes, of course. How could I forget?" She alerted Darlene to my arrival and nodded to the giant doors.

"Sweetie." Adam slid his hand out the tiny pocket of his skin-tight denim, which barely grazed his ankles, and linked arms with me.

We headed toward the back office, where Darlene was sorting through my test shots.

The giant computer screen was full of my pictures. Elegant and ethereal. Sporty and sexy. My skin was glowing, my hair was blowing, and my eyes were sparkling. "Is that really me?"

Darlene whipped her head around. "Pick up some magazines and work on your poses."

As she marched off, she said, "Wood, Adam. We're working with wood."

"Sweetie, this was your first photo shoot." Adam clasped my hands. "Your skin, your eyes, your smile are divine, but modeling"—he relished the word—"modeling is movement."

The street noise filtered through the giant walls of the agency, into the back room. A constant hum accompanying the continuous ring of the ten phones, for the ten bookers, for the mob of magnificent movers made up of Metropolis models.

What am I doing here?

"Don't be discouraged, sweetie. No one is expecting Coco Rocha—she's inimitable—but maybe try a dance class?"

My toes curled up like claws in a Pavlovian response.

"Let's get you up on Metropolis's website and make you some cards. For now, just go home and relax."

"Okay," I said, unclenching my feet.

"Alex"—he grabbed my shoulders and kissed my forehead—"you can do this."

☺

Adam may have understated the inimitableness of Coco Rocha. *The Study of Pose* is like a PhD in movement. Even Lori said, "No one can do what Coco does."

Flipping through the new issues of *Vogue* and *Harper's Bazaar*, something occurred to me. Darlene never mentioned my ugly body, or my cankles. Neither did Adam.

"You can do this! You can do this! You can do this!"

I went through the magazines cover-to-cover. Despite hours of practicing, my posing was still all wrong. My shoulders rotated inward, which caused my hands to face outward instead of hanging delicately alongside my body. This drew more attention to my abnormally long gorillaesque arms, which were completely disproportionate to my mammoth thighs and cankles. I'm a deformed endomorph and I can't dance.

I tried ballet when I was ten. I loved the black body suits and pink tights; the uniformity was comforting. But even at that age, there's always someone who shines brighter than the rest. Suzanne Simmons, with her halo of blond curls, was the star and the teacher's pet. She now attends Canada's National Ballet School.

Ms. Schultz never criticized my lack of coordination; she never said much at all. As our year-end recital approached, we all poured our sweet hearts into rehearsals. While practicing a routine tendu I tripped and fell. The other girls watched in horror. Ms. Schultz yelled, "Alex, be careful, sweetheart! You may cause yourself or someone else a serious injury."

On the day of the performance, I pretended to be sick. My mum chalked it up to nerves, but she didn't force me to go. My dad was secretly relieved; he hated small chairs and strangers. Ms. Schultz sent me some balloons and a card, which the whole class had signed. It was a sweet gesture but deep down I knew they were relieved by my absence.

I retired my sweet little body suit, pink tights, and ballet slippers to my memorabilia box.

Even now, ten years later, I was on the verge of tears thinking about it.

≥☺≤

Three hundred stairs this morning! I awarded myself a resounding 10.

The maid had made some progress in the bathroom. The sink was clean, the faucets had a sheen, and the dirt and hair on the tiles were nowhere to be found. But there was only so much that bleach could accomplish. Short of burning that bath mat and shower curtain and disposing of the antique tub, it was hopeless.

Accepting the repulsiveness and adapting to the shower situation was a 15. But I was running dangerously low on Saran. The most pressing issue of the day was wardrobe. I knew the black Gap tank was a repeat but it made me look thinner, as did my dark blue Bootlegger cigarette jeans. I was saving my brand-new black patent two-inch pumps for a possible night out in the Big Apple, but I needed to be at Wardrobe 10.

The taxis were cutting into my limited funds, but today's plan for the subway was thwarted by the sidewalk's metal grates, which shredded the heel of my right shoe.

I was trying to buff out the scratches when Metropolis's elevator doors jerked open and I stumbled into the receptionist's desk. Her black dress slid off her chicken bone shoulder and she blinked fifteen times in the span of three seconds.

Was she having a seizure?

I hopped toward her, pump in hand. "Are you okay?"

"Are you?" Her lip line was more pronounced than usual, and was such a dark red that it almost appeared black, which magnified the stark whiteness of her skin and teeth.

"Yes, thanks, but I'm a little bummed out about my shoe. It got stuck in one of those grate things."

"You should have left it there."

She hated these shoes too?

"Well, anyway, I'm here for Darlene and Adam."

She readjusted her mouthpiece. "Darlene, I have Alex Emmerson here for you."

My pump was beyond repair. Hopefully no else one would notice.

"You may go in, Alex."

≳ ☺ ≲

Sheila was seated comfortably in Adam's chair next to Darlene.

Did she plan her agency appearances around my appointments?

I sauntered toward the booking table, determined not to be intimidated. I had earned a right to be here.

"Hi Alex. How are things going with kick-starting your career?" Sheila did her best to muffle a giggle and fingered the chain that wrapped around her torso.

Was that a body necklace?

"Nice pumps, by the way." Now it was Darlene stifling laughter under the enormous brim of her hat. The ends of her fake blond hair lay frayed out on her shoulders.

Who wears beach hats to work?

Then I saw it. My model comp card on the wall.

You can suck it, girls!

"Sheila, would you mind passing me my new card?" Her icy blue eyes bore into me like shards of glass. "It's right there behind you."

The cover photo was a head shot from the Calvin dress series. The back had three full-length pictures: the dress, the Karlie Kloss number, and the bikini. Adam must have shrunk my cankles somehow; they looked goodish, though not Lori good, which was my new gold standard. Overall, I looked like a model.

I did it! We did it: Astrid, Brian, Carlos, Photoshop, and that fat bastard who need not be named.

"It's so beautiful," I said and tried not to cry.

"It's super fab, sweetie!" Adam exclaimed as he swept toward me. He was impeccable in a fitted short-sleeve button-down, another pair of ankle-grazing pants, and sneakers that looked like an expensive version of Converse. "Isn't it, Darlene?"

"Yes," she said from behind her obnoxious chapeau. It was the nicest thing Darlene had ever said to me.

"Now sweetie, come to the back office and I'll show you your web page." Adam's enthusiasm was infectious. "And let's get your portfolio uploaded onto your iPad. Sooo exciting, sweetie."

My web page looked awesome, maybe too awesome. The glaring discrepancies between my pictures and my real self were more noticeable on the big screen.

"Adam, umm, did anyone alter these pictures? My body seems longer and leaner."

"Camera angles have a lot to do with that."

Camera angles?

"And all the girls get a tiny magic dose of retouching."

Maybe that's why no one mentioned my cankles! Adam knew they could be fixed. If all the girls were doing it, I guess it was okay.

"You're gorgeous."

I caressed the smooth surface, running my fingers over the edges, savoring the smell of freshly cut paper and ink.

Alex Emmerson
Height 5'10"
Bust 34"
Waist 25"
Hips 35"
Shoe 9
Eyes Blue
Hair Brown

"Umm, Adam, I'm not 5'10", my waist isn't 25 inches, and my hips—"

"Is the shoe size correct?"

"Yes."

"Perfect. For a second I thought we needed to make a whole new card."

We do need to make a whole new card.

"What happens when clients meet me? Won't they know these measurements aren't right?"

"If clients fall in love with you, one inch won't matter."

My card felt heavy.

"And do NOT tell them your real age. You look so much younger than twenty-one." Adam's voice was full of tenderness now.

Could he sense my discomfort?

"You can count on me."

"How's your walking?"

"Is this because of my shoe?" It was way past exasperating.

He glanced at my feet and his lip twitched as he crossed his arms.

"Let's just focus on walking right now. Take a stroll for me to the end of the hallway and back, sweetie."

I walked the length of the twelve-foot hallway.

"Nick!" Adam shrieked, then turned back to me. "He teaches all our girls runway."

Runway? I couldn't manage a photo shoot without serious on-set coaching.

"I don't think I'm ready for runway."

I'd never even watched a Victoria's Secret fashion show. Everything was happening so fast.

"Sweetie, the shows are where designers, editors, and photographers find the new 'It' girl. We need to make you runway material."

Adam watched in dismay as I resumed walking.

"You need to put some hip into it. Don't plod around when you turn. You need to do it with deliberation."

Was it possible to turn without deliberation?

"Your strides are too long. Just a little hip, sweetie, not like you're pushing someone out of the way. Shoulders back. Long neck."

I stretched my neck, pushed my chin out, and brought my knee to waist height before putting my foot down.

"You look like a drunk ostrich!" Darlene bellowed from behind me. "Adam, where's Nick with my latte?"

"I don't know, sweetie. Starbucks can be a mare." Adam sighed.

Mare?

"Sheila, baby," Darlene simpered, "could you come here a minute?"

Sheila paraded the hallway, her hips swaying in sync with her forceful footsteps. Midway, she spun on her heel, put her hand on her hip, and struck a pose, finally coming to a stop centimeters away from my face. Her breath reeked of cinnamon.

"Oh, snap, guurl." Nick came barreling through the door. He clicked his tongue. "You just got served."

What did that even mean?

Darlene snatched her venti latte from Nick's quivering hand. "Teach her how to walk."

"This week has been such a mare." Nick sighed, watching as Darlene stormed away.

"What exactly is a mare?"

"A nightmare." He looked exasperated. "It's British slang, but everyone is using it now."

After hours with Nick in that hallway, he finally let me go. "Better, but you need to practice all weekend. And wear heels."

I am wearing heels.

I stopped at Gristedes to pick up more Saran. The deserted aisles were ideal makeshift runways. I spent twenty minutes practicing.

"What are you doing, Lean Cuisine?" Keisha caught me midsashay.

"Umm, I'm model . . . um . . . walking?"

"I thought you weren't a model."

"I'm trying to be a model."

"You could try, but you're not gonna be if you keep walking like that." She cocked her hip and sauntered past me. My jaw dropped. She was fantastic, much better than Nick or Sheila.

"I gave you Iman okay, and then I gave you Tyra okay, and then and only then did I hit you with Naomi okay. That's runway. Okay?"

Chapter 8

"MUM, YOU HAVE TO GO ONLINE RIGHT NOW to Metropolis's website," I said, iPad in hand.

"Ooh," she gasped, "aren't these lovely? What a beautiful dress. Look at your hair."

"Can you believe it? I'm on the agency wall and everything. I can't do the runway walk very well, but I'm a work in progress," I said triumphantly.

"You look very modely in these pictures . . . hmmm." Mum hesitated.

"What is it?"

"You know how your father feels about those Victoria's Secret commercials, and *Sports Illustrated*. All those girls are someone's daughter or sister. Your father wouldn't like it if men were salivating over pictures like that of you."

"Mum, it's not lingerie, and it's not *Sports Illustrated*. It's the new skinny me on a beach. They are just to show to clients. Don't worry."

"Well, we won't show them to your father just yet. Now how about Skype? I'd like to see you and your lovely roommate."

Chloe and Lori came breezing through the front door. She had switched out the gold pashmina for rose. Her lips were less puffy but she was still sporting the headband.

"Mum, it's my agency calling. I have to hang up."

Lori bypassed hello when she saw my portfolio. "Hand them over, girlfriend."

I presented it to her like Moses with the Ten Commandments.

"These are, like, totally amazing. Even Darlene must have loved them."

I should have been infused with a vibrating sense of confidence, but the glaring discrepancy between my pictures and reality, coupled with the walking, were weighing on me.

"She did, but the whole walking business isn't happening quite yet."

"All those stairs are getting your adrenaline flowing. Maybe you need to slow it down."

Chloe attacked her chewy toy. Nothing was slowing her down.

"Have you ever tried yoga?"

Yes, and I have NOTHING good to say about it.

"No."

"This is my teacher, Erin." She texted me her info. "She's way more than yoga. She'll change your life."

There's zero chance that a yoga teacher could change anything about my life, least of all my runway skills.

"I'm not sure my life can sustain anymore change."

"You're doing great. Do you have a full day on Monday?" Lori hovered over my shoulder as my email refreshed.

"Wow! I have eight appointments. I mean go-sees, or castings."

"Exciting." Lori clapped and Chloe started barking.

"They just chuck you in the deep end, don't they?"

"Girl," she put both hands on my shoulders, "it's sink or swim."

"It's the sharks I'm worried about." Darlene was vicious, and she was on my side. Who else was out there lurking and ready to bite?

"OMG! Let's do your first post!"

Lori positioned me and my new comp card in the ideal light. My smile was major.

@metropolis@lorihastingsofficial#newcomp#modellife#modelona-mission#castings#nyc

≥ ☺ ≤

"You're fucking kidding?" Mike said, sucking on a freshly rolled joint.

"Absolutely not."

"You're not going to go out all fucking weekend?"

"No."

"That's fucked up, Alex. More fucked up than our using every fucking device we own!" We were playing Words With Friends, which was super annoying because we had to have both our phones and iPad open and Mike loathed using "devices" unless absolutely necessary.

"No, it isn't. I cannot introduce any new factors into the equation. I'm maxed out."

The crisp white linens were still tucked into the corners of the sofa, and a giant faux-fur throw lay crumpled around me; an unmade bed at 2:00 p.m. was unconscionable.

"The subway, the shower, the diet, the runway walking, and freaking Instagram!"

An entire wall of Mike's kitchen was devoted to empty tequila bottles.

He had installed a recessed shelving system to accommodate them. An abstract white flower adorned the Patron bottle above his tousled chestnut hair. Could I post that? Would it cast an ugly image of drunken suburbanites?

"It's demanding acute mental and physical focus." Beads of sweat formed at my temples.

"You'd rather play Scrabble with me on your first Saturday in New York?"

"It's part of the system. Saturday, Scrabble, and spliff. Admittedly, it isn't the same without the spliff."

"Your Scrabble skills have improved but you're pretty fucking high strung, even for you."

S-T-R-U-N-G

The joint he was smoking had been burning slowly and was almost out. The last few drags are always a little raunchy. I could almost taste the resin.

R-E-S-I-N

"I would love a puff of that."

"Can't your roommate sort that out?"

"You can get arrested for a nickel bag of weed in parts of this country. I don't need to be deported right now."

"Fuck, you can't even drink there, eh?"

"Legally, not until next month. I'm hopeful I'll be in a groove by then. Working, and making friends."

"Don't set the fucking bar too high."

"What do you mean by that?"

I knew exactly what he meant. Last year my birthday celebration consisted of cake and coffee in the Safeway lunchroom, and dinner with my parents.

"You didn't exactly have a real happening social life here."

"Now I'm a model living in New York. People might find me more interesting."

"You probably fucking need to leave the apartment to meet those 'people.'"

He had a point, but this week I would be doing go-sees and castings that were bound to lead to some social interaction.

"How's Safeway?" Linus's prickles pressed the ends of my fingertips.

"It's not the same without you."

My heart swelled and I was hit by a wave of homesickness.

"How's the roommate?"

Lori had been holed up in her room all day and night watching reruns of *America's Next Top Model.* She took a break to fill me in on an episode involving a former Texan beauty pageant winner, Cassandra Jean. Tyra had insisted she cut her hair short and dye it blond, à la Mia Farrow circa 1970. "Of course Tyra's hair is long and fabulous. She's such a bitch," Lori said.

"She's seriously into reality TV."

"Alex, do us both a favor." He shot me a smile. "Try and have some fucking fun."

I was saving myself and my New York City playlist for Monday.

Chapter 9

WHAT AN ASTOUNDING START TO MY DAY!

Stairs 10

Hair 10

Lori suggested I borrow her three-hundred-dollar hair dryer to manage my frizz. "This is what the professionals use. Be careful, it gets major hot."

The Supersalono 3600 made a huge difference managing my curls. The frizzies were tamer and more subdued. I think it was clear from my pictures and my limited styling skills that my hair had a lot of potential. I revisited the Bootlegger-faded denim boot-cut jeans but rolled up the pant legs to give them that boyfriend jeans feel. They were a smidge too high and fitted on my hips to capture "slouchiness," and were a little wide at the bottom, but that made my cankles look smaller. It was almost working. The pumps weren't ideal, but the ragged heel was making the whole grunge thing happen. The Gap black tank was a three-peat but it was the most fitted thing I had. Finally, the pièce de résistance—my new Timex gold bracelet watch. It wasn't real gold but it dressed up the whole look. Just a little tweaking and this outfit had been promoted.

Wardrobe 8

Nerves 5

"What's your first stop?" Lori asked.

"Carson Curteis's studio," I said, zipping Linus, gloves, and my portfolio safely into my Kipling.

"I love Carson. He's shot everyone that's anyone. I worked with him twenty years ago."

"Do you think he'll like me?"

"You're going to do great," Lori said, hurrying out the door with Chloe.

How about "you look great"?

I took one last look at myself and cued up Katy Perry. You know what? Alex Emmerson, you do look great. Go show 'em what you're worth.

Baby, you're a firework.

The crosstown shuttle at Times Square is in the bottomless pit of the station. Heels and stairs don't mesh. The pumps were all about fashion, not function, and my feet were killing me when I arrived at Carson Curteis's penthouse studio in SoHo.

A sign on the door in large block black letters read: DON'T RING THE BUZZER. COME IN!

This was it. My first peek beyond the velvet rope.

I opened the door just a crack and peered inside. Sunlight flooded the studio. Magnificent black-and-white portraits of Christy Turlington, Giselle Bundchen, and Naomi Campbell hung on the twenty-foot walls.

A petite woman with stained teeth and long gray hair was leaning against a stone pillar in the middle of the studio and screaming into her cell phone. "Tell your Russian girls not to come here drenched in perfume. They're giving me a headache." She turned to find me stalling in the doorway.

"I'm Alex, from Metropolis. I don't even use scented soap," I spluttered and stepped inside. "Is Mr. Curteis here?"

"No. The almighty himself can't be here. I'm his wife." She zipped through my portfolio and grabbed a comp card. "Very nice, thank you for coming."

"Very nice," however brief, was positive. I walked across town to my next appointment, in TriBeCa. New Yorkers walk fast and in sync, like a well-oiled machine. It was choreographed chaos, but even moving at this pace, I didn't see how it was possible to do eight go-sees in one day.

When I arrived at the casting agency, thirty models were already waiting in the reception area.

Were we all here to see the same person?

They all looked like they just stepped off the pages of *Vanity Fair.* Clearly none of them was shopping at Bootlegger or The Gap. Skintight jeans, short skirts, and scandalously high heels accentuated their gazelle-like legs. Lots of tank tops and snug shirts hugged tight to their impossibly flat stomachs, exposing their protruding collarbones. All of them were carrying large leather bags. I took note of the labels: Balenciaga, Givenchy, and Chanel.

Chanel? I thought that was perfume?

They were huddled together in cliques watching the flashing images on the four giant screens in the lobby.

"I totally saw that photoshoot on Kelly's Instagram." A ravishing black girl took out her phone. "Check it out. They were in the Maldives."

Shit. Instagram. I should've had Lori take my picture.

#firstdayofcastings#modelonamission#modelamongstmanymodelson-thesamemission#missionimpossible#DIYboyfriendjeans #neednewbag

"Look, there's Sheila's new hair campaign," said the bombshell brunette standing closest to me. "She looks amazing."

"She totally does." I leaned into their group. They all glanced at me with raised eyebrows and nodded before turning away. I immersed myself in Words With Friends until I was called in to meet "Marcy." She was sitting cross-legged on her desk, and had one of those giant earrings that hollowed out her earlobe, and a shaved head. The walls of her office were covered in model comp cards and enormous posters of advertising campaigns. I recognized the dewy fresh faces of Haute. "I know Haute skin cream. Did you take all these awesome pictures?"

"No," she dismissed me. "This is a casting agency." I could see her tongue piercing when she talked. "I'm the filter."

I sensed I hadn't gotten past her filter when she suggested, "You might want kick up the antifrizz. It's humid out there today."

WTF, my hair was operating at a 10 when I left. Had something happened?

I checked myself out in the window of the downtown A/C train. Frizzy had indeed monopolized smooth, and to add insult to injury the subway car was devoid of air-conditioning. As the minutes ticked away, my hair morphed into a giant Afro. Pulling it into a tight ponytail didn't help; runaway curls were fuzzing up like an enormous sunflower.

I barreled through the entrance at Hudson Studios, licking my fingers and trying to mat down my hair. Fifteen girls sat perfectly posed, as though someone were ready to paint them. They turned their glorious heads of hair in unison to find me grooming myself like a rabid cat, exchanged blank glances, and returned to their iPhones. I checked my phone twenty times during the painful silence that elapsed before the photographer summoned me.

"I'm Alex from Metropolis." I handed him my portfolio. He nodded and held my gaze for a minute until I looked at the floor like a dog at obedience training. He examined each photo, exhaling loudly as he went through my portfolio. He passed it back to me and said, "You need to do something with your hair." He was bald.

I officially demoted my hair to a 4, snapped a selfie, and added it to my "Historically Speaking" collection, #badhairday#humiditysucks#rejectionsucks#demoralized. This was not the "alexemmersonnyc" I wanted the world to see.

I was running forty-five minutes behind when I arrived at Modal NYC, in the Meatpacking District. One hundred unearthly beautiful girls were sprawled across leather couches, lounging cross-legged on the floor, or leaning against the studio walls. I felt like a chuck cut amid the grade A sirloin. I stayed close to the entrance, still trying to mat down my frizz, when a statuesque blonde sauntered past me.

"Have you signed in?" she asked in a thick Eastern European accent. I abandoned my grooming and followed her toward "the list." Once she had written her name, she handed me a pen. She positioned herself in the center of a vacant sofa and I perched myself beside her. My olfactory was in overdrive.

"It looks like we're going to be here a while," I said. I'm number 103. My name's Alex."

"I'm Natalia."

"Your accent is so awesome. Where are you from?"

"Russia."

The Russian girls really do love to spritz.

"Your perfume is lovely." I was dying to know if she had been at Carson's.

She took out her iPhone, and that was the end our conversation. Two girls joined us.

"Caroline." Kiss-kiss. "Sylvia." Kiss-kiss.

Caroline crossed her golden brown legs and leaned into Natalia. "It's awful today. There are no taxis or Ubers anywhere."

An endless stream of models kept coming through the doors. There was lots of kissing and friendly chatter.

- "You look sooo good."
- "I gave up gluten."
- "Fashion Week is the only time I ever go above 14th Street."
- "My schedule is cray-cray this week."
- "It's a total mare. I'm so over it. Whatevs!"
- "Four callbacks and they didn't book me. Can you believe that?"
- "That's just wrong."
- "I know, right?"

Americans use the word "right" in the same fashion that Canadians use "eh."

American: It's so hot out there, right?

Canadian: It's so hot out there, eh?

I considered sharing my observation, but my attempts to interact with my fellow models made me feel like a nuisance. A good hour and a half passed before someone called, "Alex, 103."

I hadn't even noticed the casting director in the far corner of the studio. He was tall, maybe 6'4", chiseled, with boyish good looks, and seemed immersed in a lively discussion with Natalia. He used his hands a lot when he talked and he kept pushing his wild mass of curly brown hair behind his ears.

"Your book is great, Natalia. We are going to get some digitals of you. Thanks."

He turned and smiled at me. "Hi, I'm Walter."

"I'm Alex. I see we have something in common," I said, unleashing my hair.

"Oh, yeah? What's that?"

"Umm, our hair?"

"I don't see it."

Good-bye, confidence.

"Can I see your book?"

I glanced at Natalia, who was effortlessly posing for digitals a few feet away.

"Natalia's great, right?"

"She is." Walter looked up from my portfolio. "Do you know each other?"

"Kind of. We met here, at this casting. I like her perfume. She's Russian. I'm Canadian. We say 'eh' and Americans say 'right.'"

He handed me my book. "Thank you for coming."

Approval denied.

I glanced at my Timex: 1:30 p.m. Shit! I was supposed to be in Times Square an hour ago.

I did what readjustments were possible on the 1 train but my hair was beyond help. My tank was steeped in sweat, and blisters were amassing on my heels. Still, I was headed to Times Square! Billboards. Bright lights. Broadway. I'd be near Broadway. I cued up Alicia Keys.

These streets will make you feel brand new, big lights will inspire you.

As I fought my way through throngs of tourists, the streets did not make me feel brand new. The Great White Way was a huge letdown. It looked like abandoned warehouses with big, ugly signs. The Queen Elizabeth Theater was much nicer. Times Square was filthy, frenetic, and loud, like a video game. It felt like I was being jostled around by some amateur gamer with a joystick.

I stared up at the monolithic skyscraper, 4 Times Square. It was the setting for a climactic scene in the *Amazing Spider-Man*, which wasn't my favourite superhero movie, but Emma Stone was awesome. And I did get sucked into her and Andrew Garfield's off-screen romance. A love story is a love story, and I'm a hopeless romantic.

I took a deep breath and forged ahead. The clacking of my heels on the gleaming floors of the enormous lobby were like nails on a chalkboard. The line to pass security was eight feet long. I was now one hour and forty-five minutes late.

"I need to see photo identification," the stout security guard demanded.

"This is pretty intense, eh?"

What possible threat could a fashion magazine pose?

"I mean, it's like Fort Knox in here."

He stood up holding my visitor's badge hostage. "We don't joke about security on my watch. The NASDAQ is here."

Seriously? A mall cop is berating me for pointing out the obvious.

"Sorry, sir," I said, taking my badge.

My ears popped as the elevator climbed past the twentieth floor. The reception area was pristine and stark white. Everything was white. The walls, the leather sofas, the coffee tables, even the flowers, but the lilies and orchids did little to soften the aesthetics. The glass-like floor reflected the light. I don't know how the receptionist handled it without sunglasses. I approached her desk in full squint mode.

"Hi, I'm here to see Ron. I'm Alex, from Metropolis." I leaned in and whispered, "I'm late."

She pushed her black, waist-length hair over her shoulders. Her leather pants looked like snakeskin. People made clothes out of snakes? Note to self, make a donation to PETA.

She smiled and said, "Everyone's running late today. I'll call his assistant."

As she motioned for me to take a seat, her cropped black blazer lifted ever so slightly, revealing her washboard abs. "Make yourself comfortable."

I leaned against the wall nearest the elevator, feather-like and dainty as possible.

Caroline sauntered past reception on her way out.

"I love your Birkin," the receptionist said. "I totally pinned it ages ago."

"Thank you. It was a gift," Caroline said, modeling her bag.

"Hi Caroline."

"Do I know you?" She put on a pair of sunglasses that covered a third of her face.

"I'm Alex. We were at that casting an hour ago with Natalia."

"I don't remember."

"You were saying how things were awful because there were no taxis or Uber and—"

"Were you eavesdropping on our conversation?" she snapped as she stepped into the elevator.

"Aren't those Brazilian girls just so amazing?" the receptionist sighed.

Maybe not that one.

"Totally, right?" I said.

Five minutes later an intern arrived in the lobby. He, too, was sporting snug snakeskin slacks and a denim button-down shirt.

"I'm Craig. Ron's on a call." He escorted me to the inner offices and asked for my book. He didn't offer me a seat. He looked at each image and back at me. His eyes darted over my knapsack, my pumps, and settled for a split second on my watch.

"Can you take your hair down for me, please?"

"It's a total mare out there, right? I really need to kick up the antifrizz."

"It is quite humid." He returned my book and returned me to reception.

"Have a nice day," the receptionist chirped.

"At this point, one can only hope," I said, reaching for my phone.

Three missed calls from Metropolis! Shit!

"Darlene," I tumbled out of the elevator and into the lobby, "it's Alex Emmerson. I saw you—"

"Where the fuck are you?"

I was running toward the exit. The security guy yelled, "Leave your badge!" I threw it toward him and kept moving.

"You missed two of your appointments."

It might help if my go-sees were grouped together geographically and chronologically.

"I know, but the collective waiting time at my go-sees has been over two hours. That doesn't include travel time. I'm heading toward the subway now."

"They won't see you after 3:30 p.m. She hung up.

The 1 train stopped moving somewhere between 34th and 28th Street. None of the other commuters seemed disturbed. I leaned back in my seat and settled into my playlist. Three minutes passed before a garbled announcement came out of the broken intercom. Are you kidding me? What if this were a matter of life and death? Panic was setting in.

"Can anyone understand what they are saying?!" I shouted to the packed subway car.

Those who chose to acknowledge me just shrugged. The general malaise was infuriating. I tried to focus my attention on my playlist and the legendary Billy Joel.

I know what I'm needin'
And I don't want to waste more time

After nine painful minutes, the battered intercom blasted another muffled message. I stood up and tore off my headphones. Quite frankly, Mr. Joel, we have a vastly different version of a New York state of mind.

"What is going on?!" I yelled. The train lurched forward, my Timex and then I smashed into a pole.

The cracked face stared up at me: 3:10 p.m. There was no time to mourn as I jumped out at 14th Street and hauled ass to Milk Studios at 450 West 15th. I hobbled through the doors of Studio 2. "Hi, I'm Alex Emmerson, from Metropolis. I'm sorry . . ." I leaned against the casting assistant's tiny desk, panting, "I'm late . . . the subway . . . just one second—"

"It's all good." A perfect afro of tight blond curls framed her freckles. She waved my worries away with a flick of her delicate wrist. "We are going to five thirty today."

5:30 p.m.?

"Was there a recent schedule change?"

"Nope."

WTF Darlene?

"You're number fifty-six."

"Do I have time to get a coffee?" I hadn't eaten all freaking day.

"Totally," she answered cheerfully. "It's going slow."

I smiled. "Thank you."

You're the only person who has been nice to me all day.

"Listen," she whispered, "you might want to hit the bathroom too. You're a bit of a hot mess."

The bathroom's mood lighting was a blessing. I gloved up, threw cold water on my face, dabbed the sweat from my neck and chest, and pulled my hair into a tight bun. I never understood why people would willfully subject themselves to the physical torment of a triathlon, yet here I was drenched in sweat and covered in blisters and nowhere near the finish line.

My hopes of grabbing a coffee were dashed when the immaculate trio—Natalia, Caroline, and Sylvia—arrived at the café. Fainting from low blood sugar was a better alternative than another attempt to engage.

Every beautiful girl from around the globe had descended on New York City for Fashion Week. How could they even decide who was worthy? They just kept coming through the door, each one exquisite in her own way.

I emailed Adam to let him know that there would be no chance to do any more go-sees today; the casting at Milk would take hours.

Having now been privy to a day full of drama, I can say this: it doesn't matter what happens in between, the Entrances and Exits are key. They have been duly added to my rating scale.

- The shy, quiet girl, soundless as a geisha whom everyone wants to love - 9.
- The girl dripping with sexuality whom everyone wants to be -10.
- The all-natural, upbeat, probably believes in Jesus girl, bouncing through the door -8
- The I have better things to do and more interesting people to see girl, sauntering into the room -9

Several girls who were deemed "not digital worthy" stole the show with a grand exit. Their complete nonreaction to the casting person was followed by an elegant toss of their Balenciaga or Givenchy tote over their shoulder, a flick of the hair, and a hurried kiss meet and greet as they strutted out of the studio. Solid 10s across the board.

It's unclear to me what constitutes digital-worthy, but it would be nice to be considered.

I couldn't pull off the exits I saw here.

At 5:35 p.m. the casting assistant called, "Alex Emmerson, fifty-six." Once again, I was denied my digital moment.

>☺<

Mike leaned back in his kitchen chair. The espresso-stained table and chairs had belonged to his grandmother. I tried to talk him into an upgrade, some IKEA number, but his hate-on for consumerism won over.

"Your pictures are pretty fucking awesome, Alex. But you're looking beat up today."

Two bags of frozen peas lay atop my throbbing feet. My iPad was angled upward, held in place by Lori's salt and pepper grinders. Mike watched unimpressed as I lit a cigarette.

"My schedule is cray-cray. The subway was a total mare and I totally need a new bag."

"Why are you talking like that?"

"It's model talking."

"You sound like an idiot."

"Maybe right now, but I'll get the hang of it."

"You want to sound like an idiot?"

"Whatevs." I liked whatevs a lot. It felt very natural to me.

"Fucking whatever."

"Exactly! Whatevs is short for whatever."

His deliberate exhale was an attempt to reset. "Did people like your pictures?"

"It umm . . ."

The frost on the bags of peas was beginning to melt into small pools around the outside of my eggplant-like feet.

Drip-drip-drip.

"None of the clients wanted to take digitals of me."

Drip-drip-drip.

"But that also happened to other girls, who didn't seem to care."

Drip-drip-drip.

"Don't fucking worry about it then."

"But—"

Drip-drip-drip.

"It's like all the models are in some special club, and well"—my poor ugly body shuddered—"they aren't looking for new members." I dissolved into racking sobs.

"Alex, it sounds totally fucked up. But fucking relax, okay? It was your first day."

"Okay," I murmured.

I took a picture for my selfie collection—my feet, the peas, and my Timex

#firstdayofcastings#utterlywretched#thankgoditsover#casualties#tomorrowisanotherday.

New York was ripe for material for "Historically Speaking."

Lori and Chloe found me wallowing on the kitchen floor. Lori's lips were looking quite lovely. Very Angelina.

"I'll replace your peas tomorrow."

"No worries. Rough day?"

"It was a mare, but I'm working through it."

"Hang in there. It's so worth it."

"Totally, right?" Chloe licked my hand. I suspected she knew the truth. You can't lie to a dog; they know us better than we know ourselves. But I didn't want Lori or anyone in this scene to think I couldn't handle myself.

"What's up for tomorrow?"

"More showrooms, more studios, and some casting at a hotel."

"Are you seeing Andrew Weir?" Her eyes lit up. "Almost every girl who does Fashion Week sees him."

"The hotel casting is for James Canon."

"He's not Andrew, but he's a player."

"Hopefully my feet will have recovered by tomorrow." I held up my wrist. "I don't think my watch is going to make it."

"Once you start working you can buy a real watch. Audemars Piguet is my fave."

I love my Timex.

"Totally. Me too."

"Come with me. We're going to get you ready for Mr. Canon tomorrow."

I hobbled behind her into the living room, with Chloe at my heels.

"I did all the shows in my heyday," she said, pushing the coffee table tightly against the sofa. "New York, London, Paris, and Milan." She grabbed her pashmina from the table and hit play on her phone.

Lori strutted that living room with every morsel of her model soul.

I'm too sexy for my shirt

Too sexy for my shirt

So sexy it hurts

"I love this song. So nineties." She tossed me the pashmina, laying down the gauntlet. "Come on, girl."

And I'm too sexy for Milan

Too sexy for Milan

New York, and Japan

"Never did Japan," she said over her shoulder as she passed me on our imaginary catwalk.

"Lori, I hope your skills osmose the hell out of me."

"You're totally getting it." Chloe's tail was wagging madly against the sofa, all three of us jazzed up by our impromptu show.

"Really?"

"Almost." The music stopped.

The abrupt ending to the show sucked the life right out of me. I was ready to pass out.

"You need some of your Lean Cuisine, a good night's rest, and . . ." She disappeared into the bathroom.

Please don't be running a bath.

"These." She gave me a box of blister Band-Aids. "You're going to be great."

Chapter 10

MY HAIR WAS OPERATING AT A 7. Lori's anti-frizz was helping. My wardrobe was also a 7. My midthigh, rayon-cotton, navy tank dress was the last fitted item in my repertoire, but my cankles were exposed, so I had added a pair of black leggings to boost my confidence. But no one took digitals, and at the showrooms no one even wanted to see me walk. My exits were tragic, but earned 3's because no tears were involved. They were brimming when the uptown 6 train was delayed. I was officially late for the James Canon casting.

"Hey, Lean Cuisine!" a voice boomed from across the platform.

"Keisha?" She was curvy as hell in her high-waisted black jeans. A cropped white Tee showed off her tiny waist. Her sneakers must have had a serious platform because she was taller than I am. "What are you doing here?"

"I'm going to class. What do you think, I live at Gristedes?"

"Where do you go to school?"

"Hunter." She realized I had no idea what that was and added, "College."

"I used to go to school and work in a supermarket too, but I gave it up for the modeling."

I wished I were back at Safeway. It was more appealing than my castings.

"What's wrong with you?" She wagged her hot pink nails. "Looking all sad and sorry for yourself."

"I feel like a loser. I practiced all weekend but still no one wants to see me walk."

That's the second time that she drove me to total honesty.

"Let me see what you got."

"Here? On the subway platform?"

"YES, right here on the platform! Just be careful not to get too close to the yellow edge, or that weird guy sitting on the trash can."

My parade down the platform elicited no response from the straphangers.

"Look, you're never gonna walk like me, or Naomi. But you gotta work with what you got."

"Okay," I whimpered, and followed her into the packed subway car.

"Now you see? You still sound scared."

"I am scared. These people are really mean."

"I love to see a young girl go out and grab the world by the lapels. You've got to go out and kick ass. That's Maya Angelou talking, okay?"

"Okay," I said forcefully. Maya Angelou rocks, and when she's talking you listen.

"Better."

"Keisha, can I take a picture of us for my Instagram?" She grabbed my phone, found her best angle, and popped off five frames in rapid succession, made her selection, chose a filter, and handed it back to me. @keisha#runwaycoach#mayaangelourocks#modelonamission#6train #iloveNYC

My second Instagram post. Things were looking up.

"Go own it, Lean Cuisine!"

$\stackrel{\scriptscriptstyle\sim}{\scriptscriptstyle\sim}$ ☺ $\stackrel{\scriptscriptstyle\sim}{\scriptscriptstyle\sim}$

When I sauntered onto the glistening marble floor and into the gleaming light of the modern Deco lobby, I was ready to own it.

Then I saw the poor girl, who was four feet away, walking for James. Here, steps away from the lobby, in front of everybody? This is where we have to showcase our runway skills?

My inner Maya fell apart and my legs buckled. "Hi there. Is there a sign-in sheet?"

Entrance 2, and that was generous. Someone pointed to a coffee table and with a slight nod banished me to a vacant sofa. Everyone was checking each other out but pretending not to. Lingering glances asking: Do I have prettier hair? Do I have nicer skin? Do I have better legs? Some Brazilian girl had the nicest legs I had ever seen, and she knew it. Her skirt barely covered her who-ha, which I'm sure was waxed and fantastic. That's what it's come to. I'm now assessing women's genitalia.

"OMG, that's Sheila Summerville," whispered an awestruck waif to her willowy companion.

Sheila owned the lobby. She owned the whole damn hotel in her cut-off denim shorts, six-inch lace-up heels, and midriff-baring shimmering crop top.

"Hey Sheila." I waved. "The list is over here."

Do I kind of hate her? Yes. Can I get past that and use her to garner social acceptance? Absolutely.

She sashayed toward me. I stood up to kiss her but she grabbed the list and sat down.

"I see you're still carrying your knapsack. How practical."

A heavy floral scent engulfed the lobby as Natalia and Caroline descended on us.

"Where's Sylvia?" Sheila asked.

"She's still at the Maida Gregori Boina and Rami Fernandes casting," Natalia replied.

"Sheila, I love your shoes." Caroline was salivating.

"They're Manolo and serious cab to curb, but I can do anything in heels." She flicked her hair, which

(1) was getting old;

(2) almost took out my eye.

"Your Birkin is divine, Caroline," Sheila said as I slid my Kipling out of view.

The three of them spent the next hour discussing their fabulous bags and their fabulous lives, and only when my name was called did Sheila acknowledge me.

"Oh, Alex, good luck." I could feel her bad juju all over me.

I cannot walk in front of her.

James Canon was hot and he worked it. His fitted black Tee and charcoal gray suit emphasized his toned physique. He towered above me and locked eyes with mine.

"When did you arrive?"

"About an hour ago." I held his unnerving gaze. "To be honest, yesterday the waiting time was way worse."

"When did you arrive in New York?" I looked past James at his assistant, who stared at the ceiling, shaking his head. "Oh, right. Of course. About ten days ago."

"Didn't your agency tell you to wear heels?"

WTF? I am wearing heels.

I conjured a tear and looked up at him. "Yes, but my Manolo heels were serious cab to curb and someone stole them on the subway."

"Your book?" A quick scan, a quick nod, and a quick demand. "Walk for me, baby. Straight toward that handsome boy holding the camera, and bring it on back."

I stared at the adorable assistant and back at James. If I had one ounce of self-respect I had to do it. For me, for Maya, and for Keisha. My ego took over.

'Cause I'm a model, you know what I mean

And I do my little turn on the catwalk

Yeah, on the catwalk

On the catwalk, yeah

I walked the shit out of that hallway. Shoulders back and down, forceful yet graceful steps, and a spot-on turn.

"Thank you, Alex. We're going to take some quick digitals." The adorable assistant smiled and waved me over.

VICTORY!!!!!

Sheila and her posse glanced up at me as I strolled by. "Oh, Sheila," I flicked my hair over my shoulder, "good luck."

Exit 10!

En route to the subway, I passed a guy hawking leather bags. A black Birkin caught my eye. Black goes with everything.

"Very nice. Very nice bag, only fifty dollars."

I suspected that whomever gave Caroline her Birkin paid more than fifty dollars.

"Okay, buddy, on the level, why is this bag fifty dollars?"

It could've been stolen.

He insisted no one would know it was fake.

I snapped a selfie. My third Instagram post.

#brandnewbirkin#modelonamission#nyc#fashionweek

I arrived home the conquering hero. Lori was still in her robe. It may have been the Xanax, but her face looked more relaxed.

"Hey girl. How was it?"

"He took digitals!"

"Oh my God!" She ran toward me.

"I know!" I said, readying myself for a congratulatory embrace.

"You got a Birkin!" She looked at it closely, and her face changed. "Oh, it's a fake." She put my faux bag on the floor like it was diseased.

"How can you tell?" I wanted to punch the vendor guy right in the throat.

"The clasp is all wrong."

"I just posted it on Instagram!"

"Take it down immediately!" she shrieked.

"Oh no! The agency just liked the picture."

"Take it down and don't bring it up unless someone asks."

"This is hideous. I'm back to two posts. The stress is beyond."

"You really need to call my guru, Erin."

"I really need to smoke. Needs must when the devil drives."

"Ooh. Meryl Streep was so great in that movie, but I'm a bit of a Hathahater."

It's an idiom, not a movie.

Chapter 11

GRISTEDES WAS CRAMMED WITH SATURDAY SHOPPERS. Keisha wasn't working, which was unfortunate. She might like to know my casting was a success thanks to her coaching, and she might have talked me off the ledge. Instead, I walked home cradling a supersized bag of Oreos.

I played with them for a while spelling words, creating an Oreo exposé. They were the most inspiring photos I had taken yet.

An open-faced Oreo and three stacks towered above the letters NYC. #nyc#moon#oreo#skyline#nabisco

LOVE #love#nyc#christophercross#nabisco

If you get lost between the moon and New York City, the best that you can do is fall in love.

The best that I could do was eat. I surrounded the letters with a heart made from cookie crumbs.

EAT #loser#lonley#lame I added these pics to "Historically Speaking," a reminder that I cannot be trusted with Oreos.

I was weighing in at 124. There was some wiggle room, but the buffer was comforting. I revisited my practice of licking the outside of each cookie and throwing them in the garbage.

"Oh girl, do you do that too?" Lori had wandered into the kitchen. "Hey, it's better than throwing it up."

"I never thought about it that way." The notion was disturbing.

"Any plans for today?"

"I'm going to Central Park." I missed the dewy West Coast of Canada ocean air. Greenery might be calming, and help ready me for the week ahead.

"You're going to love it! You should try running around the Reservoir."

"I can't. The stairs, you know? I'm hyper attached to my system."

"You're too funny."

I split the moment her bacon and eggs with a side of butter-drenched pancakes arrived.

Central Park was a magical place, crowded and hectic, but peaceful somehow. I stumbled across a classical three-piece with a giant bass that stirred a melancholy deep in my soul. A saxophonist amassed a crowd of revelers with his steamy number, and ten feet away people swayed to the beats of a drum circle. All the while runners and cyclists whipped around the entire loop of the park.

I took pictures of everything. Bethesda Fountain, Bow Bridge, and Strawberry Fields, where a group of people were holding hands and singing. Although I appreciated the sentiment:

(1) They couldn't sing.

(2) They were blocking my view of the iconic *Imagine* mosaic.

I passed a groovy gang on Rollerblades who were rocking out to some deep house beats. People without wheels were also moving to the music.

Imagine being so carefree?

CHAPTER 11

My afternoon finale was a ride on the carousel. That was my favourite part of the day, and it earned a place on my Instagram. My third post. #centralpark#magical#carousel#ilovenyc.

In that moment, I really did. I loved NYC.

Chapter 12

MY LOVE AFFAIR WAS CUT SHORT ON MONDAY after another hopeless day of castings.

Maybe it's me. Maybe everyone else is having fun, but I didn't sign up for this madness. It's perdition, all right, which might be sufferable if there were any perks, but so far it's thankless. At what point do you just quit?

There was a disturbed gentleman who roamed around Lori's neighborhood. He would walk five steps, hit himself on his bald head five times, and on the fifth round, he shrieked. His glossy eyes looked sad, like somewhere deep down, way back when, he remembered something tangible that connected him to the world. What were his dreams?

"Hey, girl. How was your day?" Lori was sporting a blue pashmina, which matched Chloe's new collar.

"Brutal, and today every Brazilian girl in NYC was at my castings. I think I was geographically robbed of some innate sexiness. Whatever those women are drinking, for Godsakes someone bottle it and bring it here."

"It's so true, right? People say I look Brazilian."

My phone started blaring the theme from *Jaws*. "It's my new ring tone for the agency." It was meant to lighten the mood. It wasn't having the desired effect. Even Lori seemed freaked out.

"Hi Darlene, it's Alex Emmerson. How are you?"

"You have a request casting tomorrow. Don't screw it up." The line went dead.

I checked my email.

*****IMPORTANT*****REQUEST CASTING*****CONFIRM IMMEDIATELY

There were no details other than an address in the Meatpacking District.

"You know, when they don't give details it could mean it's a great gig."

Lori led us toward the kitchen, where she dug into a new tub of Chunky Monkey. Her natural metabolism was becoming increasingly nauseating. "When you're requested for a casting, it means that clients have filtered through the masses and you made the first cut."

Weeding the worthy.

"That's encouraging."

"Imagine this." She tossed the Chunky Monkey and took my very lit cigarette from my fingers. "A request for *Sports Illustrated*. The best of the best. We were all so young and so gorgeous. I'm not sure any of us realized how amazing we looked."

The city's voice drifted in through the window, and the voile curtain fluttered open, drawing Lori's gaze.

"It all happens so fast."

A heaviness fell over her. Her agonizing silence amplified the ominous ticking of her Audemars Piguet.

Tick-tick-tick.

"You're young and fabulous." She twirled the ends of her hair. "Everything you ever wanted is in the palm of your hand."

Tick-tick-tick.

"And poof. It's gone."

Tick-tick-tick.

"The request casting?"

Please snap out of this! This was the first time that Lori had exhibited any sense of ennui, and it was freaking me out.

"*Sports Illustrated?*"

"I killed it and they booked me." She flipped her hair and smiled brightly. "My career took off."

Phew.

"Any advice?"

"Save your money, girl."

I meant the casting, but it was sound advice. The taxis were wreaking havoc on my budget. "I need to make some. I have fifteen hundred dollars left until I start working."

"Girlfriend, I spend that in a week." She sounded horrified. "That's like below the poverty line."

Poverty line?

She could see my distress, and added, "But I'm a total mare with money. I don't even own this apartment."

She didn't own it?

"Let that be a lesson to you. Don't waste all that money you're going to make."

I nodded, feigning confidence. "Hopefully tomorrow will get the bankroll rolling."

"You walk in there like the job is already yours. If you believe that, the client will too." She turned to go. "Alex, I believe in you."

Maybe everything was going to work out just fine.

Chapter 13

MY BIRKIN WAS PACKED AND I WAS READY TO CONQUER.

"You're going to do great today," Lori assured me. She had stopped wearing the headband and pashmina and had introduced a Yankees baseball cap with aviator sunglasses. She glanced at my Bootlegger jeans and newly polished pumps, and her eyes swam with pity. "Is that what you are wearing for your big casting?"

"Yes."

"You know what you need?" She looked positively jubilant. "You need some kick-ass heels."

Heels?

"What size shoe do you wear?"

"A nine."

"Perfect. I have a pair of Jimmy Choos that are too small for me. I never should have bought them, but you know how it is."

Not really.

She hurried back to her bedroom and handed me a pair of obscenely high heels. I felt obligated to accept.

"They're yours. Just strap these on, girl, and kick some ass."

En route to my casting, a shit hot transvestite pointed out, "Girl, you don't deserve to own those shoes! Stop embarrassing yourself."

"I don't own them," I snapped, and pulled my heel out of the cobblestones.

I stumbled through the door of the studio, arms flailing, and grabbed the casting assistant's clipboard for support. She snatched it away from me.

"I'm Alex Emmerson. I'm here for the casting."

She checked off my name and adjusted her leather choker necklace. "Sit down before you break something." She remained standing guard at the entrance.

Entrance 0. In fact, negative 0

"Alex, over here."

Anyone but her.

Sweat was dripping down my neck and my hair went from a 10, to a 4 in all of three seconds. Shelia was sitting pretty in a distressed T-shirt which read *"I Shagged the Drummer"*. I'm sure she was shagging the lead singer, but that wasn't as catchy. Had the exit been closer, I would have bolted.

I have to go over there.

My intention was to saunter toward her nonchalantly, like a cat, but instead I embodied a hapless stray dog. I was ready to bail and put any ounce of remaining dignity into my exit when a blond British girl asked me, "All right, let's have it. Who's in your wank bank?"

Shelia's gorgeous posse stared up at me. I didn't want people to know that I wanked, let alone who was inspiring the wanking. When in doubt, do nothing. Be mysterious, be French, be aloof, be anything except honest.

"Well, there's my high-school crush Troy, and Robert Downey Jr. always does it for me. Now that I'm thinking about it I suppose there was the Elvis incident. When I was eight years old I watched *Blue Hawaii*, and at the end of the movie, Elvis spanks this girl. I reenacted the whole scene with my Raggedy Andy doll. It's interesting because Elvis just isn't in my wank bank. So, yeah I guess it's really only Troy and RDJ."

My volume control is hardwired to my nervous system, and it was redlining. The entire room heard me.

"You're just full of surprises. Elvis? I pegged you as a 'Belieber.'" She snickered, and the entire room burst into hyena-like laughter.

Getting the hell out of there was the only plausible course of action. I had been working on an emergency exit strategy and now was the time. "Does anyone have a cigarette?" I asked, and grabbed my bag. I feigned a phone call, smiled graciously, and hobbled outside while chatting famously with my imaginary caller. Talking on the phone denotes a sense of importance, it gives the whole exit a little something special. As far as exits go, it wasn't half bad, but nothing could salvage this wreckage. I never saw the client. Darlene was going to kill me. My feet started walking and just kept going. I had been barefoot for hours when, finally, somewhere between the West Side Highway and Central Park, she called.

Duunn dunn . . . duun . . . duun . . . duuuunnnn duun . . .

"Why didn't you see the client today?" Darlene's voice was teetering on hysteria. "They specifically asked to see you."

I was overwhelmed with conversational remorse and couldn't muster up one word.

"You know, Alex," she stressed the first syllable of Al and spit down the phone, "I don't have time and energy to waste. Do you know how many girls would love to be with this agency? If you can't sort your shit out, you can just get the fuck out."

I crossed Central Park's Great Lawn and continued walking all the way to the Upper East Side, where I accidentally lit the filter of my last Marlboro and began sobbing. I was considering developing a relationship with Jesus when someone snatched the wasted cigarette from my fingers.

"Well, this is no good," she purred in an intoxicating French accent, and slid a pack of Marlboros from her Hermès handbag.

Her jade opal-set eyes were ablaze with passion that compelled one to linger. The contour of her lips must have been crafted by the gods, because no plastic surgeon was capable of such precision. Her golden-brown skin shimmered in the sunlight, and her thick, lustrous brown hair fell to the middle of her back, casting its own shadow. My world was crumbling, and here before me was my savior. I stood smoking with Cleopatra.

"You know they are trying to make it illegal to smoke outside now? No smoking inside? This I can accept. Who wants their clothes to smell like smoke? But outside? That's a little rich. I resent someone telling me what I can and can't do."

What kind of superhuman resolve would it take to refuse this woman? She oozed an innate sexuality that crossed all frontiers.

"I find when things really fall apart, sometimes the only way forward is with nicotine. *Chérie,* it appears to me this situation also calls for wine. Come with me. Perhaps you should put on some shoes."

I stuffed my feet back into Lori's Jimmy Choos and followed her to a restaurant on the corner. The petite restaurant's facade was all windows. Twenty tables were covered with white tablecloths and small bouquets of flowers. There was a bar but no bar stools. Behind the bar sat an enormous floral arrangement that almost covered the rear wall. The remaining two were adorned with giant paintings, and a suspicious disco ball was hanging from the ceiling.

The waiters, for the love of God, the waiters, their wavy hair, slim-fit pants, and French accents, were unnervingly sexy.

Every person in the restaurant looked like they had just stepped off a runway.

Cleopatra greeted the staff and the patrons as I stood helplessly crossing then uncrossing my arms.

"Come, chérie, we'll sit on the banquet." She glided across the restaurant, radiating light.

What was this place? Who was this woman?

"I'm Virginie."

Veer-jhee-nie. It sounded exotic and inviting all at once. Her smile permeated everyone around us.

"Alex," I managed through sniffles. My eyes were swollen half shut.

"Enchanté. Do you know Le Brasserie?"

"No. I'm new to the city."

I certainly didn't belong here and wanted to crawl under the table.

"Alors bienvenue, how do you like it?"

I don't know what possessed me, but yet again I launched into a play-by-play of the nightmare that had become my life, rounding it up nicely with Robert Downey Jr.

"Ah yes, RDJ. No one can blame you for that."

One of the gorgeous waiters brought two glasses of wine to the table, and Virginie smiled. "I think we need a bottle."

"Virginie, are you a model?"

"That's not the life for me." She laughed. Even her laugh was sexy. "God didn't make us beautiful so that we would have to work hard and suffer. We are like flowers, *des belles fleurs.*" She gestured to the lavish bouquet behind the bar. "We deserve to be loved and cherished and in turn we share our nectar and beauty with the world. It's the natural order of things."

Had Virginie called me beautiful? I felt warm and fuzzy all over, but it might have been the wine. "I love beautiful things; look at this ring. My lover in London bought it for me. It brings me so much pleasure, and it gives him so much pleasure to give it to me. *Magnifique, non?* This bag, it's impossible to find anywhere in the world. My prince in Saudi Arabia sent it to me. I feel so special when I carry it. I feel like a princess, his princess. Every woman deserves to feel like a princess."

"Is he an actual prince?"

"Of course."

She was French and glorious.

"Virginie, why did you talk to me today?"

"Because, chérie, when one sees a wilting flower, one has to give it water and bring it back to life."

I wish my agency were watering me.

The restaurant door flew open. In strode a bronzed boy-man, svelte, and mercilessly chic. He marched up to the bar in his skin-tight black denim and twirled his fingers like he was directing a dance number. "Scotch on the rocks," he said in a broad English accent.

It was one of the best entrances of all time. Drink in hand, he sat down beside me, pushed aside the wisps of his disheveled black hair, and presented us with a tattered *Vanity Fair* about Liz Taylor and Richard Burton. "This is all I have to say about it."

"This is my darling friend Tyler." Virginie rubbed his shoulders. "His boyfriend keeps cheating on him, and he keeps letting him."

"The thing is, I love the fucker. If all I have for the rest of my life is his pimply ass and small penis"—he paused and put his hands over his heart—"I'm perfectly happy with that."

"It's the cheating he can't deal with," Virginie said, flipping through the magazine.

"Anyhoo, what have I missed?" He drained his entire glass of scotch.

"*Chéri*, this is Alex."

"I'm new here, and I have made a fool out of myself in front of everyone I've met."

Tyler took my wineglass out of my hand. "Listen, poodle, at some point in our lives we all have. You're not alone."

"How was your week, Tyler?" Virginie asked as he finished my wine.

"What a load of shit. We were shooting shoes and after three days they still hadn't got the shot. I finally put the damn things on myself. Walked onto the set, sat in a chair, crossed my legs, and the photographer screamed, 'That's it!'"

"You do have extraordinary legs." Virginie touched his thigh. "Tyler is an assistant stylist."

"I was working with that cow again. Her bloody *I Shagged the Drummer* T-shirt—"

"That's her!" I yelled.

"Sheila?" Virginie asked. "This is the girl you've been talking about?"

"She's a trust fund baby with a stick up her arse." Tyler refilled our glasses. They'd have to carry me out of the restaurant if we kept up this pace.

"She's never done a hard day of work in her bloody life."

Of that I was one hundred percent confident. One should never judge a person's life by the chapter one walked in on, but as it relates to Sheila, I was done giving her the benefit of the doubt, as was Tyler.

"Spend a week in Wythenshawe, darling. Those wankers would sort you out. No WAG life for that twat. None of the footballers would have her."

It wasn't clear to me to whom he was directing the conversation, but the table of people next to us were riveted.

"Tyler's from a rough part of Manchester," Virginie explained. "He won the green card lottery in 2006, and he's been here ever since."

"That was lucky," I said. "Lucky for us."

Tyler kissed my cheek. "Here's to us!"

We downed the rest of the wine.

"Listen, my loves, I think we've all had enough." Virginie threw some money on the table and grabbed my arm. Tyler grabbed the other. As they blew kisses to everyone, I looked over my shoulder and yelled, *"Merci!."* Our exit was a fabulous 10.

Chapter 14

LORI'S COUCH HAD NEVER FELT SO COMFORTABLE, and for the first time since this whole thing started, I woke up with a smile on face. Until my phone rang.

"Sweetie, get over there NOW!" Adam was screaming, which was so out of character that I screamed back.

"What's happening?!"

"James Canon's people just called. LumiYa lost two girls. Double booked. Flight delayed. Milk Studios now, sweetie!"

"Lori!" I was still screaming.

She came flying out of her bedroom. "What is it?"

"I booked a show! I need to be at Milk Studios now!"

"Whose show is it?"

"LumiYa!"

"Never heard of it. Don't stress. I doubt anyone important will be there."

Still, with my limited options, I tried to dress to impress. Faux-boyfriend jeans, sleeveless hoodie sans bra, taupe wedge sneakers, Astrid's thong. Wardrobe 7, Hair 2. "I haven't even showered."

"They'll fix you there." Lori threw me into the hallway and pushed the elevator button.

≳ ☺ ≲

Chairs had been arranged to form a makeshift runway. The media were everywhere. Production people were scurrying from chair to chair, assigning name tags. The lighting guys were running tests; there was no time to think.

Oscar, the show's coordinator, grabbed me. "You're the Metropolis girl, right? Hair and makeup now. You missed dress rehearsal, but LumiYa is going to brief the girls."

Brian was backstage wearing a Redken T-shirt. I beelined straight to him. "Brian, thank God. I'm freaking out. I've never done this before."

He stopped me before I sat down. "You sweet thing, I'm 'key' makeup on this but Miguel will take good care of you."

Sheila, also rocking a Redken shirt, slipped into Brian's chair. A swarm of models and media gathered to fawn over her. Her hair and makeup looked finished, but Brian was milking it for the cameras.

"Wheels up, people, LumiYa is en route." Oscar strode backstage as the hair and make-up underlings scurried from model to model. Miguel pushed me into his chair. He had cut the sleeves off his Redken shirt, exposing the tattoo that covered his entire upper arm.

"Hi, I'm Alex. This is my first—"

"I don't want to hear it, honey. I've heard it all before." His makeup brushes were impeccably arranged in his section of the six-foot-long table, which was shared by five other makeup artists and their assistants. "Just sit there and let me work my magic."

"Miguel, can I Instagram you working your magic?"

"NO social media until the show's over."

"Can I least have a Redken shirt?" I could Instagram myself wearing that later. He blasted his Solano 3600 in my ear and shouted, "You didn't wash your hair?"

Sheila rolled her eyes and then had the audacity to wave as Miguel's blow-dry job ripped my hair out by the roots.

She pointed to me and announced over the whir of the dryer, "She's what they got to replace Nadia. It's a mare."

Maybe I wasn't their first choice, but they picked me.

All the models were sporting the same look anyway. Our hair was pulled back in loose buns with a harsh center part, and the makeup was dewy and fresh. You could barely tell us apart, which was the point, according to Miguel.

"It's about the clothes, honey. Now go work it."

"Gorgeousness, everyone. Brilliant work. Thank you." Brian's approval was encouraging.

A sense of calm enveloped me. Sheila's black cloud could not permeate me. My heart even warmed as I realized that if she weren't such a raging bitch, I might never have walked for James. If only Keisha could see me now, taking life by the lapels and kicking some ass. Thank you, Maya Angelou.

A wardrobe assistant whisked me away from Miguel and led me to my rack of clothes.

A digital picture of Nadia and her stats—Height 5'10.5", Bust 34A, Waist 24", Hips 35"—were attached to the rack.

"I'm not Nadia," I said.

"Clearly." A tape measure hung around her ostrich-like neck. She had cut a deep V into her Redken shirt, and even I recognized that might have been the wrong choice.

"I'm Alex. This is my first show."

"Uh-huh." She didn't tell me her name. She didn't even look at me.

"I'm wondering if I could have a Redken shirt."

"Uh-huh."

I wasn't leaving until someone gave me a shirt.

Nadia had one outfit: a high-waisted pair of coral palazzo pants, and a floral embroidered organza crop top. On the bright side, there would be complete cankle coverage; however, the six-inch block heels were concerning. I should have done a whole lot more to prepare for these beyond cab-to-curb heels. But this was no time to start berating myself.

The wardrobe assistant turned to go, and I grabbed a fistful of her Redken shirt.

"I was just wondering if there was perhaps another selection from LumiYa's collection that I might be better suited for."

"I'll make this work. I'm the master pinner."

"Yeah, I was thinking more about footwear. Think flats."

She looked confused and dislodged my grasp. "Are you, like, on drugs?"

I was desperate to tell her that I wished I were on drugs, but I just winked. She seemed to enjoy that.

"I'll try and find you a Redken shirt," she said and started pinning the pants to accommodate the height difference between Nadia and me. I strapped on the heels and grabbed the rack for support. Keep breathing. If Britney and Beyoncé could dance in heels, if Sheila could do anything in heels, then goddammit, so could I.

Out of the corner of my eye I saw Shelia watching me. Arms

outstretched, as if on a tightrope, I stepped toward her. The shoes were a big problem.

Still, the vibe backstage was buzzing; it was infectious.

Everyone gathered around LumiYa when she arrived. I was expecting an Asian man, but she was French and exquisite, like Audrey Tautou. Her flawless pixie cut complemented her petite features. Her semisheer, muted-gray oversized boyfriend shirt was tucked into high-waisted pleated tailored pants, which were a deeper shade of gray. The minimalistic ensemble hung effortlessly on her delicate frame. It was stunning.

"Girls, you can do that model thing or you can be animated. Lady's choice." Her brown eyes were blazing. They landed on me and I nodded.

You can count on me, LumiYa.

"Have fun and be gorgeous."

I felt gorgeous. Animated, you better believe it. I knew my Disney.

Sheila, you can back off, Barbie, because I am ready to kick it up a notch.

$$\gtrless \odot \lessgtr$$

Sheila was opening the show. We were all lined up behind her.

"Cue music, lights, and action." Oscar signaled, and I choked.

I can't do this. WTF was I thinking?

"I'm having a panic attack," I wailed.

Three girls pushed past me.

"Go, go, go!" Oscar yelled.

No, no, no. Oh, F@*k it!

I launched myself onto the center of the catwalk. The lights and cameras bore down on me. Every chair was occupied, and revelers were vying for standing room only. A single bead of sweat ran down my back. Then something magical happened.

My spirit left my body, and Disney took over. I kicked off my shoes, threw my arms in the air, and skipped on down that catwalk, waving at the audience. The crowd was aloof at first but seemed to enjoy me more when I blew them kisses.

I reached the end of that runway prepared to own my moment. My Rockette-worthy high kick elicited uproarious laughter. One of the cameramen was laughing so uncontrollably he could barely hold up his camera. I laughed with them.

Thank you, Walt Disney.

No one was laughing louder than Sheila when I came backstage. Then I saw her, LumiYa. Her pixie cut had morphed into a sort of Mohawk, and her left eye was twitching uncontrollably in my direction. The crowds applauded as she stepped out to take her bows. Oscar and the other models chatted about an after party, but no one extended an invitation. An uneasy feeling crept over me. I grabbed my Kipling and slipped out unseen without a Redken shirt.

≥ ☺ ≤

When I arrived back at the apartment, Lori was wearing sunglasses and watching TV.

"How was it? Did you love it?" She patted the sofa, inviting me to join her.

Hmmm.

"Totally loved it."

The mass of papers and magazines on the dining room table had now spread to the coffee table.

"Ooh. Love the makeup."

"Yeah. Me too."

I didn't give a toss about the dewiness of my face. "There was an after party somewhere, but I didn't catch the address."

"Who cares? If you've been to one after party you've been to them all."

That was easy for her to say. She's been to them all. I'd like to see one, just one.

"No one really said good-bye. I thought there would be a group hug or something."

"Girl, this is fashion. Everyone is on to the next show."

"Short of another fatality, I think I'm done for this season." I leaned back into the cushions. "Sheila opened the show and LumiYa, who was French and a woman, told us to do that model thing or be animated. I opted for animated."

I paused to gauge her reaction, which was a challenge with the massive sunglasses.

"My walk seemed to go over really well, but LumiYa wasn't exactly happy when it was over. People were laughing but also applauding. So, you know?"

"Who was laughing?" She took off her frames. An air of concern, or maybe morbid curiosity, fell over her face.

"The audience."

"Huh." She put her sunglasses back on and grabbed my hand. "Let's have a cigarette."

"I think my high kick was a highlight." I leaned against the window frame for support. The cigarette did little to soothe the dense dread deepening in my core.

"A high kick?" Lori asked gently.

"Upon reflection"—I willed myself to say something—"I've decided that my performance was neither good nor bad, but interesting."

Before Lori could address what we both knew was a lie, I finished my smoke and announced, "That's all I have to say about that."

$\geq \odot \leq$

That was not all my agency had to say about that. Darlene, Adam, Nick, and I were sequestered in the agency's media room watching my performance on a giant sixty-inch screen.

"Why didn't you tell us she couldn't do runway?" Darlene howled at Nick, who was shuddering in the far corner of the room. She replayed the footage over and over, pointing at the screen and firing the same questions.

"What the fuck is that? Are you skipping? Have you ever seen a model skip on a runway? Are you waving? What the fuck is that supposed to be? Are you blowing kisses? What the fuck do you think this is? A Miss America pageant?"

I nodded, absorbing every word of her assault. When it came to the high kick, Nick covered his eyes.

"Clearly"—my voice quivered—"animated means something different to LumiYa."

"Animated?" She slapped the monitor. "This is an absolute shit show! You have embarrassed LumiYa, this agency, and you will not be compensated for it."

"I'm not getting paid?"

"No, and neither are you, Nick!" Darlene marched out of the media room.

"Sweetie, it's okay." Adam grabbed both my shoulders as tears streamed down my face.

"This may be the last show of your career, but Fashion Week is over tomorrow, okay?"

"Okay," I said through sniffles and he kissed me on the forehead.

"There's been a lot of interest in you. Let's start again next week."

﹗☺﹗

"We're starting fresh next week," I said, undeterred.

The kitchen counter was cluttered with take-out containers, an empty bag of Fig Newtons, and an invitation printed with embossed lettering.

"I guess you're not going to any of the end of Fashion Week parties?" Lori asked.

"Nope."

The gold letters VIP caught a glint of sun, burning the rejection deeper into my soul.

"It will take years for my nerves to recover. I'm not sure my self-esteem ever will."

"You have to call Erin. She'll help you with that."

"Lori, I hate yoga."

"She's not just a yoga teacher. Everyone calls her 'the Guru.'"

Guru? I just wanted a party invitation.

"She'll give you a mantra and everything."

I wasn't sure some magic phrase will help, but I had nothing to lose. "I'll call her."

Chapter 15

I STEPPED OVER THE HOMELESS MAN SLEEPING outside Erin's Lower East Side apartment building and climbed the six steep flights of a decrepit stairwell where Erin's door was ajar, awaiting my arrival.

"Welcome." She took my hands and ushered me into her sanctuary. Two giant windows on the far right of the studio bounced light onto the soft, warm-colored walls and natural hardwood floors.

"Please sit down." There was no sofa, or chairs, and no shoes were allowed. Erin sat cross-legged next to a giant Buddha draped in a mala and handed me a sari-covered pillow. Her billowy pants splayed out around her like a halo. She swept her mass of curly brown hair into a high bun, and loose tendrils fell delicately to her golden brown shoulders. Her ethereal presence was a cross between Oprah and Galadriel, with a dash of Beyoncé; she was beautiful. She closed her eyes and inhaled deeply.

I put Linus on my lap. "He helps me relax."

"That's great. Maybe we can find some new ways to help you cope."

I doubt it.

"Linus goes where I go."

How could anyone possibly be comfortable sitting so straight, with crossed legs on a cushion? I stuck with it in the event that it was part of the whole life-altering experience.

"How are you feeling, Alex?" She had the kind of smile that made you want to keep talking.

"I'm in a crisis situation. My modeling career is at stake."

"Are you interested in fashion?"

No one had ever asked me that before.

"I don't think so."

"What would make you want to be a model?" There was a gentleness in her mannerisms that guided me toward the unabridged, unconditional, organic truth.

"I guess I want to be important. I want to be special."

"A job doesn't make you special."

"That's true if you work at Safeway in the suburbs."

"Did you enjoy Safeway and the suburbs?"

"Yes. But slicing fish doesn't have much of a cool factor."

"What makes you feel that way?"

"Everyone feels that way."

Except Mike.

My eyes were drawn to the chimes at the base of the Buddha. I'd been to a few yoga classes during my last year of high school. Lydia Baker and her posse had jumped on the Spiritual Gangster train, and I wanted a ticket. The teacher, Sara, had those chimes, and a mala. She wore an anklet and was always sporting T-shirts with a message. She espoused a lot about spirituality and individuality, but her yoga class felt a whole lot like high school. Her 5:00 p.m. was mostly girls from my grad class, who all dressed the same, and who had all begun talking "yoga-speak"—divine beings, releasing, freeing the self, and Namaste-ing. Still, when Sara ended the class with those chimes and said "May all beings be happy and free from suffering," I held out hope.

Huge Mistake.

Lydia and her posse went right on making me suffer when they cornered me in the parking lot.

"What's with the sweatpants? Why don't you pick up some Lululemons?"

That fateful day was the last day I ever attended a yoga class. For it was the wise, enlightened Sara who remarked to Lydia that being enlightened meant she had to change her mind-set about girls like *me*. "You know, the ones who aren't cool."

It was almost as if Erin had waited for the memory to pass before she spoke. "I don't feel that way."

Erin was cool. A different kind of supercool that made everything I had to say even more ridiculous.

"Yes, but *most* people do feel that way. I know it isn't very yoga-like, but external validation is high on my priority list."

"Humans are pack animals. We're constantly seeking approval and a sense of community." Her tone wasn't patronizing, but I had the sneaking suspicion that she wasn't on board with the whole modeling scene.

"Are you suggesting I shouldn't be a model?"

"You can be anything you want to be. If you choose modeling, I'm sure it will be a success."

"That's encouraging." Erin's confidence felt like a victory.

"Do you feel like it's the right community for you?"

"If it's right is irrelevant." I felt an overwhelming urge to hit those chimes. "I have to make it the right community."

"I work with some lovely girls who model."

I noticed that for Erin, "model" wasn't a noun. It was a verb.

"Some enjoy the experience and some don't. Often the girls who struggle are not at ease with themselves."

"Oh God, is that it?" I said. "I've never been at ease with myself. Not as a child, not in high school, and not at university."

Definitely not now.

"High school is a challenging part of most people's lives."

Suddenly I was struck by the need to confess my life story. Erin seemed like one of the few people on the planet who could keep a secret.

"Erin, I tried out for every school team and didn't make any of them. I did win a medal for trying so hard. That's actually what they called it."

In all fairness, it was the only year in the history of the school that they awarded the *Trying So Hard* medal.

"That's very special. You're not afraid to keep trying. Celebrate that wonderful quality."

"Yes, failure is certainly something to celebrate." I groaned.

"You're courageous."

"My triumphant failure in the athletic department led to my foray into theater. I auditioned for Rizzo in the high school production of *Grease*. I rehearsed in the shower for weeks."

"Did you enjoy singing?"

"Yes."

I loved it. My mum and I are rabid musical theater fanatics. My dad once took us to a matinee performance of *The Phantom of the Opera*. He hated it so much that he didn't return after intermission, and waited for us at a bar near the Queen Elizabeth Theater. But Mum and I were hooked. We've seen all the major productions that came to Vancouver. *Les Misérables* is our favourite; we sobbed throughout the entire performance. Eponine's solo was the highlight for me. I suppose lots of kids dream of becoming a singer. I, too, longed for the bright lights and the chance to sing "On my Own." But it was never meant to be.

"My audition song was, 'There Are Worse Things (I Could Do).'"

I remember it like it was yesterday. The air conditioner was broken and the auditorium was sweltering. All the seats were taken; there were at least seventy-five of us at the tryouts. Lydia Baker was there to support another vapid blond member of her posse.

"I had breezed onto the stage, ready to belt it out to the bleachers. But it all went south."

Erin listened with not just her ears, but also her eyes.

"I didn't know how truly terrible my singing was until confronted with an audience.

When my song ended there was a sort of stunned silence and no one was clapping except Mr. Singh, the music teacher."

The words were tumbling out of my mouth at record speed.

"He took me aside and said, 'Alex, I applaud your efforts, but my dear, this is not your path.' He assigned me to the last row of the chorus." My lip started to quiver. "And asked me to lip-sync."

The tears started flowing. "Now I'm failing at modeling. I can't move, I can't walk, and the other girls are mean. Meaner than Lydia Baker!"

"Was Lydia Baker part of your high-school experience?"

"Oh, my God." I gasped and grabbed the Buddha for support.

"Alex, are you okay?"

"*You know, Alex,*" I said, trying to emulate Lydia's condescending tone.

"By the way, that's me being Lydia."

"Thank you for clarifying," Erin said.

"It's interesting how your arms are so thin but you try to hide them. You'd look great in a sleeveless shirt. You should start wearing them."

I'll never forget flying home from school that day and tearing apart Mum's sewing basket. I wanted the sharpest pair of scissors in the house. There was no room for error. I had cut all the sleeves off my T-shirts. Weeks passed before Lydia pointed out she had been wrong, and that, in fact, the no-sleeve look only emphasized what was wrong with my body.

"You're bottom-heavy, but don't worry, it's not like you have cankles."

"I'm not sure where you're going with this," Erin said.

"I do have cankles! Lydia knew it, and was being passive-aggressive. And you just know she told EVERYONE!"

The image of Lydia and her posse giggling to themselves, parading the halls arm in arm, made me gag.

"I lost all this weight and I still have cankles, which I didn't even realize until a few weeks ago. And now I know that everyone always knew that I had cankles."

I rolled up my sweatpants, revealing my grotesque knotted elephant ankles. "They're hideous. My roommate's are perfect."

"How do you measure the perfection of an ankle?"

"Let's start with girth."

"In twenty years, you never noticed your alleged cankles, and now you're convinced they exist?"

"Correct."

Let's not forget that people were probably talking about them all through high school.

"Do you think it might be possible that nothing has changed except your perception of things?"

"It's not a perception. Cankles are real. I just never noticed mine before."

"When I'm centered and connected, I'm able to see things more clearly. Why don't we try to breathe a little bit?"

Breathe?

"I thought we were supposed to do yoga."

"We practice a lot of things in this studio." A cool breeze filtered through the windows. "Self-compassion is high on the priority list."

"What about the life-altering mantra?"

Unfazed, Erin wrote on a textured piece of paper and gently placed it in the center of my palm.

"Try working with this mantra."

I am worthy of love and success.

"The life-altering experience is the breathwork."

We spent the duration of our session noticing our breath, and what was going on internally.

Whatever was happening inside my baby toe wasn't interesting or relaxing, and I started spluttering like a broken lawn mower.

"You see? I can't even breathe right."

Erin erupted into laughter. "You must be breathing right or you'd be dead. Try to stick with it."

After a valiant effort, I bagged it. "I hate this, Erin."

"A lot of people feel that way when they start."

At least I fit in somewhere.

"You know what would be awesome?"

"What would be more awesome than taking time to just breathe?" she asked.

"If you took a picture of me in a kick-ass yoga pose," I said and scrambled to find my phone. "Or we could do a selfie together. You're so beautiful. Everyone will be impressed. You know, something like: Thanks to my beautiful teacher, Erin. #yogis#warriors#powerful#innerbeauty#soulsisters #fit#modelonamission. Stuff like that."

"Alex, do those hashtags resonate with you?"

"It's just Instagram lingo."

None of it resonated with me.

"I have to write vapid, generic model things so people think I'm cool and successful."

"In my heart, yoga is about love, compassion, and kindness. It keeps me centered, reminds me to breathe and stay in the moment so that I can fully experience life."

That's not going to sound too catchy in a post.

"My real hashtags, for my real life, are honest, but they're just for me."

And nothing like what you just said.

"Why don't you spend time exploring those hashtags? Those moments?"

I was pretty clear about all things "Historically Speaking", but just starting to get a grip on the fake ones.

"Okay. But for now, as it pertains to this post, how about I throw in #joy #love? What's your handle?"

"I don't have a handle."

"How's that even possible? You could be huge!"

"My students come to me via word-of-mouth referrals. I'm very lucky."

"But big brands would pay you to wear their clothes."

"But I love teaching," she said softly.

You are a Guru.

"Try to take five minutes every day and focus on breathing. It will help you, I promise."

"I'll try, but you're now privy to my past success record."

She laughed again. A deep belly laugh, the contagious sort, and it followed me all the way home.

≶ ☺ ≷

Erin was worth way more than eighty-five dollars, and I was determined to fit her into the budget. The breathing practice was introduced into my routine after morning stairs. Five minutes felt like an eternity; I preferred repeating my mantra twenty times per day.

I am worthy of love and success.

By midday on Thursday, when I still hadn't heard from the agency, nothing was helping.

"Lori, I'm freaking out. I'm totally freaking out." I was halfway through my pack of Marlboros. "Pretty soon I won't be able to pay for this nasty habit, which, as you know, all started with Metropolis."

"The agency hasn't called, huh?"

"No."

"I agree it hasn't been a good start, but there has been a lot of interest in you," she said cheerfully. "That's encouraging, right?"

I hadn't considered that. I'd been so busy failing; it never occurred to me that I had been afforded the opportunity to fail.

The kitchen faucet had been leaking since the maid's last visit. The dripping was doing my head in.

Drip-drip-drip.

"Adam said we were regrouping. Why hasn't he called?"

Drip-drip-drip.

"If they were going to drop you, Darlene would have done it by now."

Drip-drip-drip.

"Do you think?"

Drip-drip-drip.

"Totally."

"If this all blows up, I want you to know how much I appreciate—"

"Listen, girl, we both need this to work out. How else am I going to pay the rent?"

Not only did she not own the apartment, she couldn't pay the rent?

"Hey, by the way, the maid said she found a garbage bag full of wet Saran Wrap behind the sofa."

F@CK*

There was no possible way to explain myself out of this.

"Umm. That, that, that's mine."

"Obvs. But what are you doing with it?"

"Recycling."

"Is that like a Canadian thing? Does everyone recycle Saran Wrap?"

"I'm pretty sure it's my own thing."

The great thing about Lori was she didn't press for details. She wandered off, back to her own wacky world.

Meanwhile, in my woebegone world, my Saran stash needed to be restocked. I'd been avoiding Gristedes, but there was no way to postpone it any longer. I grabbed a cigarette and headed out the door.

Keisha wasn't working the till. Worse still, she was buying her lunch and ended up behind me in line at Tonya's register.

"Hey, Lean Cuisine. You stink like an ashtray."

"I know. It's hideous."

"Then quit," Tonya said.

"I'm working on it."

"Work harder."

My ten boxes of Saran Wrap were crawling down the checkout's conveyer belt, which was in dire need of a scrubdown.

"Girl, what's with you and the Saran Wrap?" Keisha asked. She grabbed her sandwich, hoisted her bag onto her shoulder, and we walked out together.

"What are you carrying in that bag?" Her shoulders were lopsided from the weight of its contents.

"Books."

"What are you reading?" My mind was myopically focused on diverting the conversation away from anything having to do with me.

"*Pioneers of Psychology.*"

"Sounds like some light stuff." I was still working my way through *War and Peace*, which I had been hell-bent on finishing this year, but that was pre-Robin.

"Girl, please, it's seriously dry." She waved me away with her three-inch silver nails. "It's for school."

"You're studying psychology?"

"I'd like to understand what makes seemingly sane people do messed-up shit."

Me too.

"Is that book offering any insights?"

She laughed like she was genuinely amused. "All right now, what's your name again?"

"Alex."

"All, right cool. Can I still call you Lean Cuisine?" She flashed a mischievous smile.

"That's cool," I said and I felt cool just walking up the block with Keisha. It's true what people say, everything about New York does make you feel like you're in a movie. We covered a lot of ground in just a few blocks. Keisha lived with her mom, and her dad was back in Detroit. She hated Gristedes but it was close to home and school, and she didn't have time for much else now that she had applied to grad school at Hunter.

"If people wanna spend their whole damn lives, and racks on racks on racks psycho-analyzing the shit out of their selves, they can pay me."

"Do you think we'd all be happier if we lowered our expectations?"

"Girl, are you not valuing yourself?" she asked and we both burst out laughing.

We walked up Broadway, crossing at 89th Street, where there was a grassy island in the center of the frenetic traffic.

"Seriously, you gotta break this down for me." Keisha sat on a bench. "What's up with damn Saran Wrap?"

I'd already confessed the first day we met. She may as well know the details.

"Okay, Keisha. You mentioned sane people doing messed-up shit?" I didn't bother to sit, just launched into the story of my plumbaphobia, and the coping mechanism I devised to deal with Lori's bathroom.

She leaned into the bench and glanced up at me. "You're wrapping yourself in Saran Wrap? Girl, do you know how this sounds to actual noncrazy people?"

As my father would say, 'What cannot be cured must be endured.'

"Yes." I sat down beside her and sighed. "But I can't explain it."

"All right. I mean, I don't know why I'm still listening to R. Kelly, but I am."

"Thanks." There was a certain sense of relief of involved, but it was not in having relayed the details. It was the manner in which she received the news. Accepting my reality and likening it to something simple, like someone's taste in music. It was that simple to me. Plumbaphobia was just a part of my makeup.

"Hey, what happened with your runway thing?"

"I got the job," I said, avoiding direct eye contact.

"Damn girl, you did good." She beamed with pride. "I knew you would."

"It was all you and Maya." That was all I wanted to say about the show. The LumiYa debacle was the more embarrassing subject for me, which in and of itself needed psychoanalyzing. "But Walt Disney also played a role," I added.

"Way to own it, Lean Cuisine," she said as she pulled a giant textbook from her bag. She grabbed her Beats headphones, and that was my cue to leave.

I looked back at her from across the street. Headphones or not, how could anyone read, never mind study in the midst of that chaos?

$$\gtrless \odot \lessgtr$$

I arrived home and googled the Coles Notes for *War and Peace*. It turns out that Americans call them CliffsNotes. I know this because I spent two minutes reading about it on Wikipedia. It was tough to accept, but I had fallen for click bait. My ability to concentrate was becoming more challenging. My brain welcomed any quick distraction from my current situation. A situation that definitely called for wine. That idea is what inspired me to call Virginie.

Could I call her? She did give me her number. I practiced some possible openers:

"Hi Virginie. Last week was so fun. How about an encore?"

"Hi, it's Alex. Wanna grab some wine?"

"Hi Virginie. It's Alex. Remember me, the wilting flower you watered?"

I lit a cigarette and summoned up the courage. "Hi Virginie. It's Alex."

"How wonderful to hear from you." Her voice was luscious and warm and put me at ease.

"Umm, so, not unlike the last time we saw each other, things have hit a bit of a snafu. I may've even outdone myself this time."

I laid out the fiasco that was the show. She laughed and I could feel her smile all over me.

"Why don't you come to my apartment and we'll try to put things back together?"

My jaw dropped when she opened the door to her penthouse. The place looked like a page out of *Architectural Digest.* Vaulted ceilings, hardwood floors, and an entire wall of windows overlooking Central Park.

"Chérie," she said, kissing me, "welcome. It's wonderful to have you here."

"Your apartment is incredible."

"It is prime Upper West Side real estate," she said. "I used to have a loft in SoHo, but I love having a private roof deck and three bedrooms. And you really need the two and half baths when you have company."

I marveled at the open living space. A beautiful vase of sunflowers adorned a grand kitchen island, and orchids lined the mantel of the fireplace. She touched the tips of the white flowers and leaned in to smell them. A childlike grin spread across her exquisite face.

"Do you do a lot of entertaining?"

"I had a chef who handled my dinner parties, but Michael refuses to pay anymore, and it's just not worth the fight. I refused to give up the maid. You have to pick your battles."

"Who is Michael?"

"He's just a man in my life."

She couldn't be more clear about his insignificance. She wasn't unkind, merely bored by the whole idea of him.

"Does Michael live here too?"

"*Mais non!* Thank goodness." She gestured to a giant white couch that was nestled between lush plants and an Indian vase full of peacock feathers. I burrowed into the cushions.

"I never want to leave." I put Linus in my lap. "I love it here."

"Stay as long as you like." She poured two glasses of wine.

"Virginie, how old are you?" I assumed she was young, but her disposition was that of an older woman who'd seen thing or two.

"Do I look old to your young eyes?" She laughed, her irresistible sexy laugh, "I'm twenty-eight."

"You look perfect."

I'd never felt at ease with another member of my own sex. I was always working so hard to impress them, but Virginie didn't want to be impressed. Her main objective in life was to enjoy it, and that meant everyone she surrounded herself with needed to be enjoying it too. She was akin to the most intriguing, lovable character of any a novel I'd ever read. This was a woman who would inspire poets, composers, and authors. No one had yet created a *Virginie*, but someone needed to; Natasha Rostova paled in comparison.

"How long have you been in New York?" I asked her.

"All my life, at least the part that counts." She had an air of mystery that kept luring you in, and it intensified my developing girl crush.

"Chérie, is that your *doudou?*" She led me away from my questions and I followed her like an excited child.

I looked down. "This is Linus. He goes wherever I go."

"He goes everywhere with you?" I appreciated that she referred to Linus as "he" without hesitation.

"Since I was four years old."

"You sweet girl." She kissed me and set up a bottle of champagne and three glasses.

"A toast to my new beautiful friend, and Linus."

We drank several toasts.

"Virginie, could we take a picture together?"

"Of course."

"I'm trying to build an Instagram."

Virginie styled a mini photo shoot with the Veuve Clicquot champagne bottle, candles, and orchids. I posted everything.

#newfriends#celebrate#veuveclicquot#champagneisalwaysagood-thing#love#nyc.

A few comments popped up almost immediately. It looked like the lovely Lydia Baker had discovered alexemmersonnyc.

"Latching onto the cool kids. So Alex" (with a nauseating wink emoji).

The most empowering reply was #noreplyatall. I relished in the thought of her pulling out her blond hair while waiting for me to answer.

Virginie was midway through her second wardrobe change, a cropped flowing tulle blouse with gold sequins, ripped jeans, and sky-high strappy gold sandals.

I scrolled through her feed. "How do you come up with all these beautiful pictures?"

"I just post things that inspire me." She sat down on the bed and elevated her leg ever so slightly. She touched the shoe like it was a breathing entity with a soul. "Like these Louboutins. Christian just does it perfectly."

She did everything perfectly.

"I'm not going to lie to you, Virginie, I don't get the shoe thing."

She slipped into a bright red pair of pumps with spiked heels. They looked cheap and completely out of character.

"That looks like a stripper shoe."

"Aha, you see, this is a bedroom shoe. It's purely sexual. It is mildly painful to stand in, and it's more painful to walk in. It's almost masochistic while you become accustomed to the pain, but you develop a relationship to the sexuality of the shoe. There's magic in that."

She was magic.

"Chérie, your shoe is an extension of you. When a woman puts on pair of heels, everything changes—her posture, her walk, even her personality. Any man will love this shoe. The sex will be extraordinary."

"I've never had ordinary sex."

I couldn't bring myself to tell her the story of Chad Baker, who was my first and, to date, my last. We met in English Lit., and two weeks into our relationship, we sealed the deal in Stanley Park. After five minutes of thrusting and moaning, he cried out, "Alex, can you feel me deep in your beautiful flower?" My flower? I'm permanently scarred. RDJ and I have been responsible for my own climaxing ever since.

"A beautiful woman like you? A man would take such joy in pleasuring you," she said and caressed my hand.

"The guy gave it his all, but nothing was happening. So I faked it."

She pulled her hand away. "No, no, no, you must never fake it. *Jamais, jamais, jamais.*"

"I can take care of it myself. It all happens in about three minutes and—"

She let go a horrified gasp. "Then you haven't truly experienced a real orgasm. This is the right of every woman. Here, come, I will teach you."

I backed away when she took my hand.

"No, no, I got this. No demonstrations needed. How about we break it down orally, not orally, but with words."

She lit a cigarette. "I actually squirt when I have an orgasm."

"I had no idea women could do that."

"It takes practice, but together with your lover, it is a wonderful experience. This is a piece of yourself you need to unlock and explore."

"I don't think I'm ready for that."

"You'll get there." She cued up a deep sensual house track and started to dance with herself. "Close your eyes, my love, and let the music move you."

That seemed unlikely, and once having tripped over the coffee table, I was afraid to move anywhere. I stood in one spot and swayed back and forth with my arms pinned at my side, like a pendulum in a grandfather clock.

Chapter 16

"HAPPY BIRTHDAY!" MY MUM WAS SMILING back at me, and my dad was grimacing.

"I hate it that you're all alone in New York on your special day. Twenty-one—it's a milestone. I hope you're not having Lean Cuisine today."

Mum usually makes a roast chicken dinner with Yorkshire pudding, and a Duncan Hines chocolate cake with Smarties. Proper English Smarties. The orange ones actually taste like an orange.

"As long as she bloody eats something. Look at her. I've seen more fat on a cold French fry," my dad said.

"We've sent your card and some money but"—Mum started to cry and Dad looked traumatized—"we've got you a brass key and we're keeping that for you until you come home." The key is an English thing. It symbolizes that you've grown up and earned your own key to the house. I didn't feel grown up, and wanted to be curled up at home with parents.

"We love you." Mum couldn't pull it together, and that got me started.

"Right then, you go get something to eat. Happy birthday and all the best." Dad was trying to hang up but he didn't know how to disconnect

Skype. "How do I hang this bloody thing up?"

Lori found me blubbering in the kitchen. "What's going on in here? What are all these tears about?"

"It's my twenty-first birthday."

"Don't tell people that." She gave me a tight squeeze. "We need to celebrate. How about when I'm all healed and ready to make my debut, I take you somewhere fabulous like Le Brasserie."

"I was there on Friday."

"Watch out for those waiters, girlfriend. Trouble!"

"They're all gorgeous, it's insane."

"We have a date to celebrate, but right now it sounds like someone's FaceTiming the birthday girl." She gave me another big squeeze and left me alone with my iPad.

"Happy fucking birthday!" Mike held up Ben's paws, waving them at me and then presented some weed paraphernalia wrapped with a red bow.

"Thanks." I couldn't mask my lack of enthusiasm.

"Do you even know what this is?" He looked ready to jump out of his hammock.

"A bong?"

"This is a fucking vaporizer," he said, mightily impressed with his gift.

"I'm really okay with a joint."

"We can always pass around a fucking joint, but this is special."

I offered another uninspired, "Thanks."

"What the fuck is wrong with you?"

"I don't know how to begin answering that." My eyes teared up again and I slumped on the kitchen floor, rattling off the details of the casting and the show.

"Robert Downey Jr., eh?" He laughed.

"That's what you took away from all of that?" My tear ducts dried up.

"Alex"—he set the vaporizer aside and stared straight at me—"your first few weeks at Safeway weren't the fucking brightest."

Hmmm.

There was the time I spilled mop water all over the produce department and a few customers' shoes. And the day I hit someone's new car while collecting shopping carts, and of course the time I knocked over six cases of glass pickle jars. The stockroom stank for a week.

"But you fucking got through it!"

Yeah! Everyone makes mistakes, maybe not on the same scale as Van Gogh and his ear or me and LumiYa, but still.

"You got fucking promoted, and all was well until the dominatrix showed up."

"The dominatrix is MIA, but I did meet the most amazing woman imaginable."

I couldn't conjure up the words to describe Virginie. "And some other awesome people."

"There you go! Call these people and go fucking celebrate your birthday!"

≳ ☺ ≲

"Happy birthday, chérie!" Virginie's esprit sparkled over the phone. "Let's meet at Le Brasserie and we will celebrate you!"

A severely gorgeous waiter brought us two glasses of champagne, and then the manager approached our table. His walk was deliberate, but he carried himself like he didn't have a care in the world.

"Dante, let me introduce you to Alex, my beautiful friend from Canada. It's her birthday!"

"Happy birthday, Alex." His jet-black hair fell across his olive-toned, chiseled cheekbones as he kissed me à la fashion, fabulous, and French people style. I was lost for words and feeling rather warm in my nether regions. "It's lovely to meet you."

"Thanks." It was a simple word and yet and I sounded confused.

"Please excuse me, ladies." He wore his confidence on his sleeve and carried his charisma with ease.

He settled on the opposite side of the restaurant with none other than Sheila, who flashed her famously fake smile and waved.

"Oh, God. She really is everywhere."

Sheila's skin was glowing and she was wearing sunglasses.

Inside the restaurant?

"WTF? How is she all bronzed and gorgeous like the Brazilians?"

"That's a spray tan, and a very good one," Virginie said with a measure of appreciation.

"My agent, Darlene, worships her."

"Alex," Virginie eyed me thoughtfully, "when was the last time you were in the agency?"

"I haven't seen them since the show fiasco."

"You must always make yourself beautiful for the agency, not just for the castings."

"I do. I try. The last time I was there I did my hair kind of like now, smooth in the front and a little curly in the back."

"Aha, it looks like this on purpose?" She sighed. "What were you were wearing?"

"Actually, I was wearing this."

"I love your sporty look, but this is not an agency outfit."

I looked dejectedly at my champagne glass. "I know."

"Alex, it's time you show your agency you mean business."

I do mean business.

"You need to work it, like Sheila. Come shopping with me tomorrow and I will book an appointment with my stylist, Eduardo. He'll know what to do with your hair."

"Ciao, Virginie." Sheila strode by in her infamous Manolo Blahniks. "Bye, Alex."

She didn't even look at me. But Dante did, just in time to see me watching him watching her. A slow smile worked its way across his lips, and I let my eyes linger on them.

"Virginie, I don't have any money."

"You must have a credit card."

"For use in the event of an emergency." I had oodles of credit. Virgos are prepared for anything. It's not just a star sign, it's a sickness.

"This constitutes an emergency." She motioned for Dante to join us. "Besides, there may be a way for you to make some extra money until your career takes off."

Dante sat down with a glass of red wine in his hand. "May I join you?"

"Of course, Dante," Virginie cooed.

"Alex, what is a beautiful Canadian doing here in NYC?"

Beautiful?

The warmth of his come-hither accent swirled around me. I took a sip of champagne and managed a single word. "Modeling."

"Are you enjoying it?" A sincere curiosity shone from his dark chestnut eyes.

"Enjoying" might not be the appropriate word.

"It's been interesting."

"That's a tough business."

"She is already doing amazing things. All the top people ask to see her." Virginie nudged me under the table.

"Yep!" I gulped back the last of my champagne. "Although I'm sleeping on a couch with a dog and I'm broke."

There was an unsettling lull in the restaurant.

"Maybe I can help?" There was that smile again.

He reminded me of my high-school crush and resident bad boy, Troy Sephton. All the girls were besotted with him. Even Lydia. No one got into more trouble than Troy. I was mad about him.

"Help me how?"

"Would you like a job here?"

Virginie flashed a triumphant smile. This was her plan all along.

"Umm, I can fillet a mean fish, but don't you have chefs for that?"

"My darling, I want you to bartend."

My darling? Was that a French thing or was it me?

"I don't know how to bartend."

"That's not a problem." He laughed and touched my arm.

Now the touching?

"You just pour wine and champagne and act friendly. The guys and I will help you with the rest."

Virginie grabbed my hands. "Alex, it's a brilliant idea. You'll be amazing."

"Let me think about it."

"Why don't you beautiful ladies join us for brunch on Saturday? You'll be my guests."

The scent of something sweet and spicy lingered as he walked away.

Guys like him don't go for girls like you.

Chapter 17

VIRGINIE, ME, AND MY VISA stepped onto the curb at 61ˢᵗ and Madison, ready to engage in some hugely irresponsible behavior.

"This is Barneys," Virginie said an unwavering reverence. She smiled at the doorman as he welcomed us inside.

The store had a doorman?

"Do you recognize the area, chérie? Le Brasserie is a few blocks up."

Dante was a few blocks away.

"Mmm, can you smell that? It smells like money laced with leather." It was wall-to-wall designer bags and accessories. "We're going to skip this department today."

"Isn't the bag a necessity?" Replacing my "Birkin" with the real deal was at the top of my list.

"Alex, the authentic version of your Birkin is worth more than ten thousand dollars."

It's inconceivable to me that ANYONE would pay that astronomical sum for a piece of leather.

"But you're going to look so fabulous no one will even notice it's fake."

If Virginie was convinced, maybe it was possible. We headed straight to the seventh floor. "The denim bar is the best in the city."

Virginie, with sales associates hot on her heels, danced among the racks of clothes, pausing to drape herself in the fabrics and colors that pleased her. She loaded up a dressing room and stuffed me inside. It was so *Pretty Woman*, but Richard Gere wasn't picking up the tab.

"Nothing too outlandish. We're just shedding off those suburbs," she said.

Thank you J Brand, and thank you Frame; my butt had never looked so good. The Alexander Wang Tees hung effortlessly while maintaining a nice silhouette.

"You need a pair of super amazing boots for running all over town on your castings."

The Classic Newbury 3½-inch stacked heel was totally manageable. My kick-ass model must-have boots seemed like the ideal way to finish our retail foray, but Virginie had other plans.

"Now it's time." She stepped off the escalator.

"For what?"

She intertwined our fingers. "You need a pair of exquisite heels."

She led me toward the to-die-for shoe floor. The walls were white marble. The tables made of glass and wood were wrought through with shards of sunlight and everything looked like it had been sprinkled with fairy dust.

"It's time to for you to discover your shoe. Remember, the shoe chooses you."

Then they saw me. The thrusting heel of the Pigalle pump and its naughty red sole screamed sex.

I screamed, "That's it!"

"Good girl," purred Virginie as we sauntered toward Christian Louboutin. The manager placed it on my foot. I felt hot and flushed.

"Let's take them for a walk." Virginie held my arm. It wasn't walking so much as being walked. "You were meant for these, chérie."

I was breathing heavily when I took them off. "Virginie, I think I get it. The shoe thing." My $675.00 120mm Pigalles might take some practice, but they were worth every penny.

We loaded the bags into a taxi and shot down Fifth Avenue. We popped into TopShop, All Saints, and Zadig-et-Voltaire.

I was on the verge of collapse, as was my Visa, when we arrived at Eduardo's SoHo salon.

It was small and sleek in contrast to his taut muscular body, which looked like it might explode out of his black leather pants and black Tee.

"I love it here, Eduardo." Virginie caressed one of the three white leather chairs. "What you've done with this space is beyond. The floating mirrors are perfection."

"It's spectacular, right?" he said admiringly. "It cost a fortune but the architects outdid themselves."

"Do you rent out a chair?" Virginie asked.

"Sometimes, but I'm done with salon drama." Eduardo was massaging my scalp.

"You have beautiful hair, darling. Let's just get rid of these split ends, give you a deep conditioning treatment, and add some minimal highlights."

"How's your love life, chéri?"

"The woman I'm obsessed with is married."

Woman?

"Are you bisexual?" I asked.

"I'm a very straight man. Not all male stylists are gay."

Virginie laughed. "Alex, I adore you."

"Her husband is oblivious. We're insatiable. We had sex in the back closet last week and the salon was packed."

Among the shopping, the shoes, and the scandals, I felt like a movie star.

"Eduardo, you're a genius," Virginie said when he finished my blowout. My hair was silken with sheen, and the sun picked up hints of caramel.

"It's glorious," I gasped. Eduardo's six-hundred-dollar fee suddenly seemed like a paltry sum.

"Alex, put on the Zadig-et-Voltaire camisole." She caressed my hair and the hem of my shirt. "Beautiful clothes, beautiful hair, beautiful salon."

Virginie wrapped up her impromptu photo shoot, snapping a selfie in the floating mirror. "I love this city."

#glamsquad#style#magicmoment#saloneduardo#hairguru#gorgeoushair#highlights#beauty#shopping#barneys#louboutingirlforever#girlsjustwanttohavefun#fashion

#inspired #ilovenyc

It's worth noting, Lydia had nothing to say, and her selfies were a bit of a bore now that she was back from Britain.

"Virginie, we could publish these," Eduardo said. "Fucking superb."

My posts had a hundred likes in ten minutes, but Metropolis wasn't one of them.

"Ladies, would you care to smoke a joint?" Eduardo asked, presenting a crisp rolled spliff.

"What a perfect way to end the day." Virginie leaned back into her chair.

"Today was perfect," I said. "Totally perfect."

Our final selfie, glassy-eyed and smiling, was for my private collection.

"You know what's missing?" Virginie reached into her quilted Chanel bag and handed me a pair of aviator Ray•Bans. "They're yours, timeless and classic, just like you."

I slid into the sleek shades, and Virginie turned me to face the mirror. "Alex, now you're ready."

Chapter 18

"THE AGENCY STILL HASN'T CALLED, so I'm showing up there unannounced to debut the new me!"

"Love, love, love the highlights," Lori said, stroking my hair.

"Are those Frame?" She stepped back, admiring me like a piece in a museum.

"Yep!" I was loving my skinny black jeans, with just the right amount of distress.

"This Tee, with this piece"—Lori fingered my braided bronzed-gold feather necklace— "it's rock-chic perfection."

We double high-fived.

"I can hardly tell your bag is fake anymore."

It's working. Yay!

"I can't wait to show the agency the new me."

"You look fab. Go work it, girl!"

Wardrobe 10++

Hair 10++

I cued up Katy Perry.

I got the eye of the tiger, a fighter
Dancing through the fire
Metropolis was going to hear me roar.

≳ ☺ ≲

I considered waking into the office wearing my aviators but decided I didn't have the cool factor to pull it off. The receptionist removed her headset when I stepped out of the elevator. Her eyes locked onto my hair and landed on my boots.

"You look A-Ma-Zing."

Your predictable funeral attire is fetching today.

"Thanks."

She replaced her headset. "I'll let them know you're here."

I paused before making my grand entrance. "What's your name?"

"Mitsy."

I couldn't have scripted a better name for her. "Thank you, Mitsy."

I strolled casually toward the booking table.

"Hi Darlene. Hi Adam. I just popped in to pick up some new cards."

"Sweetie, you look gorgeous! Look at your hair!" Adam gasped. "I'm so happy I don't have to tell you to buy new clothes."

"Nick was showing me your Instagram this morning." Darlene leaned back in her chair, her raised eyes boring into me, and she smiled.

YAY!

"Who's that girl you're with?"

"She's my new friend, Virginie."

"Who's her agent?"

"Virginie's not a model."

"Let her know I'm interested." Darlene handed me her business card. "She could be huge."

So . . . my makeover isn't doing it for you?

"She doesn't want to work this hard." It was all I could do to not stuff her card down her throat.

"I'm the person who works hard here. Do you have your bikini with you today?"

"I didn't even think about that." My shoulders drooped and my words withered.

"That's why it's so frustrating when a girl makes my job more difficult."

"Sweetie"—Adam winked at me and handed me some of my cards—"I just emailed your castings for Monday."

YES!

Nick flew past me with his tray of coffees. "Can't talk. You. Makeover. Super gorge. Posts. Love."

I paraded out of the office, stopping to nod at Mitsy, who watched me slide on my aviators before the elevator doors closed.

≷ ☺ ≶

It didn't play out exactly as I had envisioned, but I had casting for Monday, the agency liked all my posts, and Mitsy was now following me on Instagram. I strolled confidently down 14th Street toward Seventh Avenue and the dreaded 1 subway line. I stopped to grab a Starbucks and saw Virginie nestled in the corner with some guy. He was young, handsome, and surprisingly sporty. There was nothing European about him; he was straight-up America and wearing classic Adidas sweats.

She leaned into him, digging her fingers into his blond tousled hair, but I could sense her eyes darting around behind her Prada sunglasses, which seemed more like camouflage than fashion. I couldn't hear what they were saying but she hung on his every word. When she spoke, he kissed her fingertips.

Watching them felt like spying, but approaching them felt awkward. I slinked out of the Starbucks unseen and sent her a text.

"Didn't want to interrupt your lovely coffee break." (heart emoji/wink).

She never responded. He must be someone special; Virginie's an instantaneous text responder. There would be a story to look forward to later, but I do wish she'd seen my outfit.

I rocked my aviators all the way home. On the streets, in the subway, down Gristedes's frozen food aisle, and into Keisha's checkout line.

"You're looking good, Lean Cuisine. Tell me that runway gig paid for these bougie clothes?"

"It inspired the shopping."

That much was true.

"I'm liking this hair on you. This whole thing you got going on here," she stepped back and sprinkled her fingers at me, "it's working for you. You own that, okay?"

"I owned it today, Keisha."

My ego was sheening with pride when I FaceTimed Mike. Ben was sprawled out on the La-Z-Boy recliner, a wretched burgundy thing that Mike picked up at a garage sale. Mike was on the floor. That dog owned him.

"Why the fuck are you wearing those sunglasses inside?"

"They were a gift from Virginie and I'm owning it."

"You look like an idiot."

"You will not believe what's kicking off here! Virginie took me shopping. I spent about eight thousand dollars, but it's already working! The agency was super impressed!"

He wasn't, and wore his contempt openly.

"I'm in the club now!"

"What club?" he said, like he'd never heard it before.

"The model club. I can wear sunglasses inside now. I'm one of them!"

"Let me just break this down. You had one job that you didn't fucking get paid for and you fucking spent eight thousand dollars on clothes?"

"And my hair." I ran my fingers from the roots to the silky tips to remind myself that I had done the right thing.

"Your hair looks fucking great."

At last! Some positive reinforcement.

"But how long will it stay like that?"

I had taken that under consideration myself. There was still a level of reason governing my actions. The running and the sweating would make my hair situation more challenging, but it was manageable.

"A semiweekly blowout will keep it in check."

"What's a fucking blow job worth?"

"Blowout." His disdain did little to burst my bubble. "It's nothing, like forty dollars."

"And the fucking eight-thousand-dollar membership fee? Does that guarantee you any work?"

"Not exactly. I might give bartending a go in the interim." I had to do something keep my credit card's exorbitant interest fees at bay.

"What the fuck? Now you're a bartender?"

Of all the people in the world I thought would be excited for me, it was Mike. Me, Alex, neurotic kid from the suburbs, taking the reins and control of my circumstances in New York City.

"I'm just a girl who decided to go for it." I jumped around like a rabid bunny, hoping he could get the "it" factor of this moment. "FYI, that's a super fab idea for my next Instagram post."

"Alex, are going fucking crazy?"

"No! But my Insta-life is making Lydia Baker crazy!"

"Your Insta-life? What the fuck?"

"I have a casting next week, and I think it's time my Louboutins make their first appearance."

Mike stared in disbelief as I held out my shoe and pressed it to my heart.

"And I finally get the shoe thing!"

"There's just no fucking telling where this could lead. The yellow brick road?"

Clearly, the feminine side of him wasn't open enough to understand my experience.

"Listen to me. A bedroom shoe can change your sex life. I've never had a real orgasm and Virginie is a squirter—"

"A squirter? I thought that was urban legend." The masculine side of him was all over that part.

"What's important here is that I'm having life-changing epiphanies."

"Alex, is it just you, or does modeling make everyone fucking crazy?"

If my best friend couldn't celebrate this moment with me, it was his problem, not mine.

I hung up and whispered to the wicked red sole, "Tomorrow you'll make your debut."

Chapter 19

MY LOUBOUTIN STEPPED ONTO THE CURB, followed by my All Saints ultraskinny black metallic jeans. My Zadig-et-Voltaire crêpe de chine camisole left just enough to the imagination.

Wardrobe 10++

Hair 10++

I scanned the crowd clustered outside the restaurant. Dante wasn't there.

Tyler took my hand and whispered, "You're fucking gorgeous, poodle."

I tried not to look when a hooded Emma Stone and her companion strolled out of the restaurant.

"Did you see that?" My grip on Tyler's arm left a mark.

"Baby lamb, pull yourself together. We're just as interesting as those people."

"We need to do a photo-op for Instagram." This was the ideal setting to boost my image.

"Sorry, poodle. What happens at Le Brasserie stays at Le Brasserie."

Virginie arrived, carrying two huge bags from Roberto Cavalli and acknowledging the revelers with a gracious wave and smile.

"Alex, you look beautiful." She and Tyler, with me sandwiched between them, glided through the crowd. Dante was waiting at the door.

Please knees, don't give out on me.

"Dante, you're an angel," Virginie said, and her effervescence filtered through the air. "Thanks for keeping my favourite table."

"It's my pleasure." He put his hand on my shoulder, and my entire body shuddered. He hesitated, but his hand remained firm as he led us to the prime location on the banquet. "Champagne for the ladies? Tyler, scotch?"

There was a lingering tension; my impression was he could sense my internal gasp, but it was tough to read him.

"Wonderful, Dante." As he walked away, Virginie turned to me. "Chérie, he couldn't keep his eyes off of you."

"It's true, poodle. FYI, I'm not interested in food today." Tyler's eyes were glued to his phone. "My twat of a boyfriend hasn't been seen or heard from since last night."

Virginie ordered for both of us. "Le Brasserie is famous for their Cajun chicken and frites."

Although I was too nervous to eat my Lean Cuisine for breakfast, it didn't justify French fries. The alcohol intake was already a huge concession.

"Virginie"—I chugged my champagne—"there's something you need to know before the food arrives."

"Please tell me this isn't a bloody gluten issue. What a load of shite."

I wasn't sure if Tyler was talking to us or his phone.

"I eat the same thing every day and French fries aren't on the menu."

"Alex, I really do adore you," she said with her sexy laugh. "But it would be a sin not to taste it."

It's the scene. Make an exception.

"Okay. But it can't be a regular thing."

But oh, how I wished it could be. The chicken melted in your mouth and I'm not sure if it was the three-month absence of potatoes from my regime or the fries themselves, but the dining experience was euphoric.

"Right, that's it!" Tyler slammed his hand on the table. "I've just texted the fucker. It's over." He marched behind the bar, where Dante poured him a very stiff drink.

"Don't listen to him, Alex. It's been like this forever," Virginie sighed. "Raoul isn't worth it."

"Is the Starbucks guy worth it?"

She froze. It caught her off guard, but with an air of nonchalance and a flick of her

French-manicured nails, she dismissed the question. I didn't press her.

"Raoul will show up when things get going."

"How much more going could it get?"

The restaurant was already slammed. The waiters were like contortionists navigating the clusters of tables.

"It hasn't even begun, chérie."

Dante returned to our table with two more glasses of champagne. "Did you enjoy your lunch?"

Liquid courage was kicking in and I looked him the eye. "I loved it." One of the waiters waved him over.

"You must go to bed with him, Alex. I hear he is a very good lover," Virginie said.

"What?" It was like someone had just punched me in the stomach, hard. "Who told you that?"

"Many girls."

This was dismal news.

"I can't sleep with someone who's had sex with half the city."

"Tyler is sleeping with Raoul and he had sex with half the city."

Tyler, swinging a glass of champagne and totally sloshed, traipsed back to our table. "Go on now, poodle," he slurred. "Let him shag you stupid."

"Uh-oh," Virginie said. "Sheila has just arrived with some friends."

Sheila, flanked by Sylvia, Caroline and her posse, took up residence across the restaurant.

We locked eyes. She did her best to mask her surprise at my revamped look. She hadn't even seen my shoes yet. It was revolting watching her fawn over Dante. Four glasses of champagne arrived at her table as he sat down to join her. She nestled into him.

"Please tell me he's not sleeping with her."

"He's not." Virginie laughed. "He likes you. It's written all over him."

It's Sheila who was all over him.

Tyler passed me my glass and I downed the whole thing. The music had been getting incrementally louder. The disco ball lit up and everyone started dancing, including the waiters, who weaved into and out of the chaos. Dante came back over to our table with more champagne. I was three sheets to the wind already.

"Alex, what do you think of Le Brasserie?" he asked.

I'd never seen anything thing like it. "Bewildered" was a good word. How would I explain this to Mike? It was a must-see situation.

"Brunch at The Keg back home is nothing like this."

"Can we persuade you to work here with us?" I imagine he could persuade a great many women to do a great many things. It required serious effort not to succumb to his charm.

"Umm, maybe."

"Let me know." His touch on my wrist made me shiver.

Again with the touching?

As he walked away to greet new guests, he said, "You look beautiful today, Alex."

"Tyler, did you hear that? Do you think he means it? Do you think he's telling everyone the same thing?"

"I heard it. He definitely meant it. And he's definitely telling everyone the same thing." He nodded toward Sheila, who was pawing at Dante, damn near dry humping his leg.

"I think it's time for a cig." Tyler made for the door.

"Virginie, look at her grinding up against him."

"We can dance too. Come on, Alex."

All eyes were on Virginie as she swayed like a samba dancer, all hips and sex. My body would never move like that, not even after a lifetime of classes with Erin.

"I think I'll go have a cigarette with Tyler."

I weeded my way toward the door, narrowly avoiding contact with Shelia, and found Tyler holding court outside.

"Do you all know the lovely Alex from Canada?"

My curtsy was ridiculous, and I leaned into Tyler's shoulder to hide my face. "Sheila is in there dancing up a storm with Dante and I can't dance under the best of circumstances. Never mind in these heels."

"My bastard of a boyfriend is sulking over there," he said, and unlaced his Chuck Taylors. Raoul was leaning against the brick facade of a three-story brownstone, six feet away. He was bald, a tad pudgy, and pouting like a petulant child.

"Should I say hello?"

"No! Shun the cheating pig!" he yelled loud enough for Raoul to hear, and handed me his sneakers.

"What am I supposed to do with these?"

"You are going to put them on, get in there, stand on a table, and start shaking your ass!" he ordered. "Now give me your shoes."

"My Louboutins? Why?"

"Because I am going to shake my ass out here."

Tyler stuffed me into his Chuck Taylors and slipped his dainty lady-size foot into my shoes.

"My darlings, Naomi Campbell ain't got nothing on me."

His full-on strut commanded applause and cheers from the crowd. He was spectacular.

I skipped back into the restaurant, beelined to Virginie, stood on the table, and started clapping. It was hardly dancing but it was the best I could do. A bunch of brunchers joined me atop tables and chairs, whooping and hollering. The disco ball was spinning, the bass was thumping, and then I had a near brush with death when I fell off the table. Virginie came to my rescue.

"It's time to go."

"But the party is still crazy."

"A woman is sexy when she is glowing from the champagne, but it's not pretty when she gets sloppy."

She took my hand and led me outside. Tyler was still in my Louboutins, presiding over the sidewalk. He kissed me good-bye and announced, "Can we have a round of applause for Alex, who has survived her first brunch?"

I blew kisses to the clapping masses as my taxi drove away. Exit 10+

Chapter 20

"LORI, I'M NOT EVEN HUNGOVER." I SLID OFF THE SOFA.

"It must've been something, girl. You slept in your shoes."

I lay back down, crossed my feet, and snapped a pic. My Instagram was looking good. #themorningafter #brunch #chucktaylors #soworthit #wheresmylouboutins#cinderella

Boom. Lydia Baker, within seconds, commented, "Life's not a #fairy tale, lost shoe=drunk."

"It was amazing. These aren't even mine. Long story."

"Le Brasserie, it happens to all of us."

Lori was looking quite lovely in her Lululemon attire. Her hair was pulled back in a low ponytail, and her lips were touched with a hint of gloss. She, however, was unimpressed.

"Look at this." She had mustered up a millimeter of skin and pinched it together. "This is back fat."

Please let me not care about this shit when I'm forty.

"I don't see fat on any part of your body."

"I'm heading to LA in the next couple of weeks and I need to be in tip-top shape." She winked at me. "I have a major request, but it's top secret. Shh."

This was the first mention of her career in the present and she was vibrating, flitting from mirror to mirror. Her bed was buried in wardrobe possibilities for her top-secret casting.

I hoped for both our sakes that she would, in her words, "kill it," as per the rent situation. But she wanted it so much, and that made me want it so much for her. Lori had given her whole life to this business. Maybe Erin had given her a mantra.

"Casting aside, I'm ready to get my social life back on track."

No one ever came to the apartment, but she had been healing.

"Do you have a massive Tay-Swift kind of posse?"

"God, no." She sounded relieved. "I have two besties, and we get in tons of trouble, but they don't live in the city. What I have is a cool crowd and they're crazy connected." Her brown eyes were ablaze with excitement. "Art galleries, restaurant openings." She shrugged off the notion of night-clubs: "I'm done with that scene."

How had we never have discussed her social life? Maybe I had become too wrapped up in myself.

"When my pseudoboyfriend was around, I went out six nights a week." There was a twitch at the corner of her mouth.

"How long hasn't he been around?"

"Six months." More twitching.

Lori's Instagram was chock-full of fabulousness but her last post was six months ago, and there weren't any photos that captured a #ManCrushMonday vibe.

"Out of sight, out of mind."

Maybe she had scrubbed her account of any images of him.

"He's never in LA, which is a plus." She twirled the tips of her hair, her default habit when she was deep in thought. "Resurging on the scene is bound to cause a stir. Killing at that casting will change everything."

"Lori, I believe in you."

⋛ ☺ ⋚

Tyler answered his door wearing a bathrobe and a towel fashioned into a turban, cradling a lone Pigalle. He looked like he had been dragged a few blocks by a bus.

"What happened to you?"

"Le Brasserie, poodle. It happens to all of us."

"Can I do something for you?"

"Talk quieter." He winced.

The scent of sandalwood wafted through the sheer Egyptian fabric draped across every corner of the room. The burgundy and orange intertwined and wrapped around the chain of a cast iron chandelier.

"Wow."

"It's only a five hundred and fifty square foot studio. One does what one can." He nodded at my shoe and motioned to his bed.

"Poodle, I have bad news." He inhaled. "Something unfortunate has happened to your other shoe."

"Can I see it?"

"No."

"Where is it?"

"I threw it at Raoul somewhere near Bagatelle at four a.m."

A sense of panic rose in me. I read somewhere that sandalwood can induce a meditative state, but it was suffocating. Aromatherapy wasn't in my future.

"We were at Gold Bar, another great place we need to take you. Anyway, this beautiful godlike Grecian sculpture of a man was standing at the bar." His dramatic prayer-like gesture to the heavens wafted more sandalwood my way, but he was oblivious to my mounting distress. "Then out of nowhere there was Raoul, mounting his leg."

"Aren't you broken up?"

"Yes," he said adamantly. "I stormed over to the Adonis and said he's not worth it, honey, I've seen his cock. Raoul dragged me outside screaming in Spanglish."

Tyler paused, silently seething as he lit a cigarette, his face running with wrath.

"And then what?" I asked.

"I took off your shoe and aimed the heel right at his head."

I snatched my Louboutin from him. "Is it possible Raoul kept the shoe?"

"No." He reached under the bed and pulled out a pair of briefs ripped almost in half.

"We ended up half naked in a taxi and came back here, where he shagged me sideways."

Tyler pried the sole Louboutin from my hand and placed it on the shelf atop his bed.

"I'll replace them, darling." He stared at me, despondent. I stared at my shoe, equally despondent. "I am deeply sorry."

I removed his Chuck Taylors from my knapsack, laid them at the foot of his bed, and walked wordlessly down the six stories of his West Village apartment building.

It was disappointing that my Louboutins would not be a part of the week ahead, but it was awesome that *my* shoes were part of all the drama. My kick-ass boots would have to suffice until my beloveds were replaced. If there was a huge need for huge heels, I had Lori's Jimmy Choos.

Chapter 21

I HADN'T MENTIONED THE LUMIYA SHOW TO MY MUM, and was thrilled to be sharing some good news.

"Your hair is lovely. You look like a proper model."

The transformation only cost eight thousand dollars.

"The agency loves it too."

"Look at you, tackling a modeling career, and that bathroom." Her cherub cheeks were glowing with pride.

You should probably buy shares of Saran Wrap.

"You just needed a cup of confidence." All our Skype calls happened in the small third bedroom of my parents' house that was now "the computer room," unless they had guests. I tried to convince them to go with a user-friendly Mac, but they opted for some dinosaur Dell number, which was a nightmare. My dad still hadn't managed to print something without help.

"How's Dad coping with things?"

"He's seen your pictures and he thought they were lovely."

"Even the bikini?"

It's doubtful that he's slept through the night since I left. The world could use a pair of my mum's rose-colored glasses.

"He's very impressed."

"Mum," I said.

"He's coming around, in his own way."

I'm sure the scotch is helping. My poor dad.

"Tell him I made some new friends."

"We're both very proud of you."

Chloe came bounding into the kitchen, licking my face. "Mum, this is the little rascal who tries to sneak into my bed every night." Lori popped her around the corner and waved.

"I still haven't met your lovely roommate."

Lori mouthed, "One second."

My mum rattled on about dusting and vacuuming and needing to Swiffer twice a day, while I relocated to the living room, which hadn't seen a Swiffer since the maid's last visit. Lori didn't own a Swiffer, or a vacuum, for that matter. The moment she sauntered out of her room, none of that mattered.

She was in full makeup, smoky black eyes, glossy lips, and her JBF Victoria's Secret hair cascaded around her shoulders. Her IRO leggings, which looked spray-painted-on, and her Giuseppe Zanotti six-inch stiletto ankle booties were dressed down with a distressed vintage Rolling Stones Tee. She put herself together in all of four minutes. She looked phenomenal.

"Mum, I'd like to introduce you to Lori."

I reversed the camera and watched my mum's eyes widen as Lori Hastings, supermodel, walked casually toward my iPad, waving and smiling.

"Hi there, Mrs. Emmerson. It's so nice to meet you."

I presented my iPad to Lori, so she wouldn't have to sit or move or do anything but stand there in all her model glory.

"It's lovely to meet you. My goodness, aren't you tall? You're just as beautiful as Alex told us. Thank you for being so kind to our daughter."

"It's been fun having her here, she's like the little sister I never had. Y'all enjoy your Skype, I'm heading out to check the mail." That was the first time she had turned up the Texas drawl.

"Now doesn't she just look like a supermodel?"

My eyes followed Lori's soaring silhouette as she swaggered out the door.

"And what a lovely accent. Is she always that well put together?"

Hmmm.

"Oh, yeah, she's the real deal." Why not keep the fantasy alive? "Anyway, say hi to Dad. Love you."

Lori came back with a stack of mail, tossed it on the dining room table, and shrugged. "More bills."

"Lori, you look unbelievable. My mother was speechless."

"Thanks." She grabbed her phone and took thirty pictures from every angle, in every possible light, until she settled on our selfie. #glamsquad#roomies#sisters#nofilter#modellife, which I posted immediately. And Lydia Baker commented immediately, "Your roommate is so super gorge (star emoji). Maybe she's got some pointers (winking emoji)."

Gorge? Really? Now you're doing fashion lingo?

Chapter 22

I WAS AT HAIR AND WARDROBE 10 FOR MY CASTING, in a simple yet exquisite cami and my Paige Skyline ankle jeans. It was unthinkable that the quaint cobblestones of the Meatpacking District had once caused me so much grief. I guided Lori's Jimmy Choos across the pavement and floated through the doors of Milk Studios with an air of nonchalance and a cupful of confidence. Entrance 10.

Thanks, Mum.

The regular cast and crew were sequestered in the corner, trolling through Instagram and planning their weekends, when the blond British girl from THE casting strolled in.

"Oy, look who we have here. The lovely lady who is wanking with RDJ."

Somebody just shoot me already.

"He's a bit too scruffy for me, darling. Now that Chris Hemsworth, he keeps me up at night."

Everything does sound more interesting with an English accent.

"Lisa, he keeps all of us up at night." A breathtaking young black girl was smiling at me. "I'm Ashley. She's a troublemaker, this one."

"Alex, babes, there's a party on Saturday. It's going to be massive," Lisa said.

Is it my hair? Is it my fab outfit?

"We'll be havin' it. You in?"

"Totally in."

Whatever, wherever, I was IN!

"Right. I'll give you a ring——"

The group squealed a collective cheer, and the focal point of the moment shifted from me to a petite porcelain blonde who looked like a life-size Tinker Bell.

"You look so gorgeous! We were totally just looking at your Instagram." The girls were talking over each other. "When did you get here?"

"I just got back from Paris yesterday." If Disney's Tinker Bell did speak, I imagine that's how she would sound, high-pitched, and erratic with a sweetness to her tone.

"Have we met before?" she asked me. "You look so familiar."

"I don't think so." There was no way I could forget that face; her skin was flawless and she had the thickest eyelashes I had ever seen.

"I know what it is! You're in this video at Metropolis."

Video?

"You were in the LumiYa show."

I toyed with ripped seams of my Paige jeans. "Lisa, what were you saying about this weekend?"

"They make new girls watch it to show them"——Tinker Bell couldn't suppress her giggling——"what NEVER to do on a runway."

OMFG!!!

"If I can't be a good example, at least let me be a horrible warning." I laughed while my model membership slipped through my fingers. I implemented my emergency exit and threw in a wink as I strutted out the door.

≥ ☺ ≤

At what point do you just quit? Ideally with your dignity still intact, and I was way past that. I stormed out of Metropolis's elevator, swept past Mitsy, who dared not stop me, and threw open the doors. Nick ceased his futile rearranging of magazines; the 856-page September issue of *Vogue* fell to the floor with a thud. An ember of shame flickered in his eye, and he dropped to his knees to rescue Joan Smalls, Cara Delavigne, and Karlie Kloss.

I know that you were part of this.

I marched steadfastly toward Darlene.

"You made a video of me? Showing girls what never to do?"

Every hue of color drained from Adam's face. There was a tightening of his jaw, like the day we first met. He failed to summon words.

I know that you didn't know.

"Like Sheila said, let us all learn from your mistakes." Darlene's saccharine-soaked speech made me sick. "At least it wasn't all for nothing."

"Darlene"—I tore my Metropolis comp card to shreds—"we are done."

"I knew the minute we met that you didn't have what it takes to make it in this city," she said with a shit-eating grin. "You'll never be a model."

"Frankly, Darlene, I don't give a damn." I marched out with my head held high.

≥ ☺ ≤

"Of course I give a damn. This is hideous, and so NOT worth it."

"Look at the positive side," Lori said, "no other girl will follow in your footsteps."

"There's a slim to no chance that ever would've happened."

Lori nodded and sighed. "Are you going home?"

"I don't know what I'm going to do." Although Oreos, alcohol, and another pack of cigarettes would be involved.

"Why don't you sleep on it? That sofa is paid up through the end of next week." She gave me a squeeze. "But you can have it until the end of the month."

I FaceTimed Mike who, mercifully, picked up.

"Darlene put together a video of me to show models what NEVER to do on a runway."

"What a fucking bitch!" he yelled and Ben shot out from underneath the hammock.

"The clothes, the hair are a total sham. Everyone can see me for what I am. I'm just a big fake, worse than my Birkin." I tore off my necklace. "Of course, my model membership has been revoked." Salty tears were burning my eyes.

"Have you noticed that almost every time you call me you end up fucking crying?"

"You were right about all of it!" I lit a cigarette, which helped stifle the tears. "I'm now shoeless, broke, and agentless. I quit."

"You're fucking quitting now?" He appeared incredulous, which was bizarre since he'd been against the #modellife since the beginning.

"I'm going to ask for my job back at Safeway, but they won't pay my union wage as I'll be a new hire. I can sort out something with university."

The more I thought about going home, the harder I stared at that freaking sunflower painting. No one wonder poor Vincent offed himself. It's a cruel world. To put everything you have into your dream and have it all fall apart? I was done with big dreams. Fame does cost, a whole lot more than sweat.

"The fucking stairs? The fucking Lean Cuisine? The fucking Saran Wrap?"

"It's hideous. Quite frankly, I blame you for letting it go on this long."

I don't, but it's a relief to have somewhere else to direct the self-loathing.

"It's so worth it? Fucking remember that, Miss L'Oréal?"

Mike knew the L'Oréal slogan?

"I don't get it, but you fucking want it. You've come this far. You're telling me that fucking Metropolis is the only agency in all of fucking New York City?"

"No." He had a valid point. But they were developing me and paying my rent, which was due next week.

"Stop feeling fucking sorry for yourself. Find a new agency, and in the interim, take the fucking bartending job." He flashed his infamous crooked smile and hit every one of his words hard, hammering his point home. "You Can Fucking Do This."

≥ ☺ ≤

Virginie, Tyler, and I stared at my lone Louboutin. Tyler had surrounded it with white candles, and the flames burned like a shrine.

"You've been to Barneys?" The sequins on her gold Alice + Olivia Sequin slip tank shimmered in the glean of the Pigalle. "The shoe is no longer available?"

He shook his head and they sat on the bed simultaneously.

"This is a terrible loss." Virginie was transfixed with my shoe.

"This isn't why I wanted to see you both." I blew out the candles. "I need a new agent."

Virginie and Tyler nestled into his silky gray sheets, swaddled in the scent of sandalwood, which did nothing to soothe their nerves when they heard about Darlene's video.

"Fuck Darlene and Metropolis Models. You need to summon up a little GFY spirit."

"GFY?"

"Go Fuck Yourself!" Tyler yelled. "Darlene can go fuck herself. Sheila can go fuck herself, and God knows Raoul can go fuck himself!"

He grabbed some pom-poms from the under his bed, which was odd, but his cheerleading number was awesome.

"We've got spirit, yes we do, we've got the GFY spirit, how about you?"

I immediately wanted to run out and make a shirt emblazoned with "GFY Spirit."

"You know what? They all can go fuck themselves." I grabbed a pom-pom. "I'm taking that job as a bartender, I'm finding a new agency, and I'm going to make this work!"

Chapter 23

"LORI, I TRIPLED MY STAIR OUTPUT, and smoked ten cigarettes already. My hands are still shaking."

How could I pour wine like this? I had to be there in an hour.

"Relax, you'll do great. You look super sexy. The exposed back of that shirt is beyond."

This morning's salon blowout was the icing on a very decadent cake. Wardrobe/Hair 10+

"It's me who should be worried," Lori said, while digging through shopping bags strewn across her bedroom floor. "My daddy is going to kill me. He put money in my account to pay the rent but I was walking past Bergdorfs." She grabbed my hands like we were about to break into a verse of "Kumbaya." "I can't wait for them to break out the window trimmings at Christmas. Anyway, I bought these new Jimmy Choos and they carried me all the way up Madison, where I stopped into Michael Kors and of course that led to Cavalli and here we both are with no money for rent."

"How much is your rent?"

"Six thousand dollars a month."

"Good Lord." I choked. "How much did your shopping spree set you back?"

"Much, much more than that. I didn't pay last month's rent either. Maybe I need a job at Le Brasserie." She laughed at herself. "Daddy knows I'm a compulsive shopper, but he doesn't know about the plastic surgery." She was looking resplendent and refreshed, in a plastic-fantastic kind of way. "That's on the QT. Your rent is part of the plastic surgery payment plan."

"Let's hope tonight is a success then." I took one last look in the mirror and stuffed Linus in my bag.

"Go get 'em, girl!"

The restaurant was empty save for a gorgeous specimen who was behind the bar opening wine.

"Hi, I'm Alex. I'm your new bartender."

"I'm Patrick." When he smiled his brilliant sea-blue eyes crinkled. His gelled black hair and chiseled jaw emphasized his movie-star good looks. Taking my hand, he led me behind the bar, which was the size of a pantry closet. "Shall I help you get started?" He didn't have a hint of a French accent.

Laurent, on the other hand, I could barely understand. He came barreling through the doors with headphones on, singing something in French. He pushed his mop of curly brown hair out of his eyes. "You're that Canadian girl? I remember you standing on the tables."

"Falling off the tables," Patrick corrected him.

"You guys saw that, eh?"

"That was hard to miss." They both laughed, but it felt like they were laughing with me, not at me.

I hope.

"You guys were amazing. I don't know how you do it." They had impeccable style. "And you're all so good-looking."

"We know," Laurent said with a schoolboy grin.

"Is that a prerequisite?" I asked.

"We lowered our standards for you." He was the kind of guy who could get away with that cheeky banter. "What's your story? Model? Actress? Trying to find a rich guy?"

"I guess you could say I'm a model."

"I guess you can say Patrick's an actor."

"I am an actor," Patrick said. "I'm in the process of finding a new agent."

"Me too. It's stressful, eh?"

"Just find yourself a rich guy. Plenty of them eat here," Laurent said.

"I pay my own bills. Why else would I be working with you?"

"You're going to fit in just fine here." Patrick grinned at me.

It was the complete opposite of my first day of high school, when cramming myself into my locker seemed a preferable option to facing Lydia and her posse. In this place, in these clothes, and with these guys, it is going to be a whole lot different.

"Let me familiarize you with the bar. This is the house champagne. These are the cabernets, the merlots, the chardonnays, and the pinots."

But I'm not going to be an overnight sommelier.

"Can we go over all that one more time? Maybe two more times? Maybe we could start with the wine opener?"

I'd drunk more wine in the past month than I had in my entire life. Shockingly, however, I hadn't opened any of those bottles. "I can't pronounce the names of the wines you just showed me, much less remember which is which."

"Good thing they have labels on them," Laurent said.

"Aha, so you have never bartended before," Patrick said. "I'll take the lead tonight. You can start by cleaning the area underneath the bar."

I scrubbed away, humming to myself. Once satisfied with my exemplary efforts, I came face-to-face with Dante's crotch.

"Hello." I tried to arrest the rush of blood to my cheeks.

Laurent leaned over the bar. "Enjoying the view?"

"Are you going to be this annoying all night?" I asked from my squatted position.

"I see everyone is getting along," Dante said, and then did the kiss-hello thing, which brought on tiny heart palpitations.

"Alex, you look stunning. Everyone's going to love you."

I just wanted him to love me. Or at least like me a lot.

"Patrick was getting some love in the bathroom last week." Laurent spun around and whistled. "Oh, yeah."

"In the bathroom? While you were working?" The thought of being half naked in there made me cringe.

Patrick smiled at me. "You see, Alex, we're all very sophisticated here."

I busied myself with a mountain of dirty wineglasses. The sense of satisfaction derived from cleaning is directly proportional to the immediate result, and perfecting wineglasses brought swift satisfaction. A night of this would be a breeze.

Dante and Laurent were going through the reservation book when a couple walked in and asked for a table.

"I'm sorry, madame, but we are full for this evening." Dante escorted them out of the restaurant.

"You guys are booked solid tonight?" That was some serious pressure for my first night.

"No, but those aren't the right people for our restaurant," Dante said.

"Did you see her sweatpants?" Laurent asked.

They weren't allowing them to eat here because of their clothes?

"I've worn sweatpants here."

"Yeah, but you came with Virginie, so we let that shit slide," Laurent said.

This presented a dilemma. I was living the hellish life of a rejectee daily. How could I allow myself to be a rejecter?

"You guys, I'm not telling people they can't come in because they don't look right."

"It's not your problem, sweatpants. Dante handles the door."

"That's outrageous."

"Speaking of." Laurent picked up my bag. "Is this a fake Birkin?"

"Listen, jackass, it's weird that you are well versed in woman's handbags." I snatched it out his hands. "There are valuable things in here, okay?"

"Like what?" He grabbed Linus and pulled him out. "This rag?" He wiped his forehead.

I staggered backwards, gasping for air. Linus now required a bath before bed; the laundry room was grim at midday, much less at midnight.

"Alex, you look pale. Maybe you should sit down," Dante said.

I stared straight at Laurent, lowering the pitch of my voice. "Give that to me."

"Why are you talking like Darth Vader?" he asked, eyeing me like I needed institutionalizing.

"This is Linus. He goes wherever I go," I explained without a hint of shame.

"I don't know what's worse, the fake bag or that rag." Laurent shrugged.

I don't know what possessed me, but I ran behind the bar, grabbed some ice, and stuffed it down his shirt.

"Yes, it's all very sophisticated," Patrick said.

The dinner crowd started rolling in at about 6:00 p.m. They were older than the brunch crowd and drenched in wealth. No one spoke to me except the guys who were giving me their drink orders. When I wasn't pouring wine, I just stood behind the bar smiling, trying to appear busy. It was awkward, but no worse than my castings. In fact, it was great practice.

Virginie sauntered through the door at about nine, and within minutes the volume of the restaurant increased. She covered me in kisses and joined a table with two older gentlemen. I wondered if one of them might be Michael.

And where was the guy from Starbucks?

"One of our patrons asked for your number." Dante cozied up to me behind the bar.

He nodded toward a man sitting at one of the front tables. Even his fancy clothes couldn't hide his belly, and his dye job only enhanced his bald spots.

"I'm surprised he got past the door." That barb hit him hard, and I smirked.

"Alex, I'm not an asshole. Le Brasserie has a reputation. We are known for our elite clientele."

I was surprised to see him so vulnerable.

"If we let everyone eat here we would lose that exclusivity and we wouldn't be a hot spot anymore. None of us would make any money."

The strained silence between us spoke volumes.

"If it makes you feel better, I was fired from my last job because I refused to serve a guy wearing jeans and a T-shirt."

A guy like Dante was fired?

"Wasn't that the right move?"

"Turns out he's one of the richest guys in town. The manager fired me on the spot, right in front of him."

He told me this story without an inkling of shame or remorse. I'd feel humiliated.

"That's terrible."

"We all have to learn the ropes." He shrugged and nodded toward the table Laurent was serving. "He's actually a cool guy and he's sitting right over there."

The guy was dining alone and decked out in some expensive-looking digs. Laurent was admiring his watch.

"I don't get it. He has to dress up when he comes here?"

"That guy has so much money that he can do whatever he wants. My job is to know who's who, and make them happy."

There was something impressive about the way he handled his role in the scheme of things. None of it seemed to affect him.

"The customer asking about you also has a lot of money. Are you sure you don't want me to give him your number?"

If I said yes, would he be jealous?

"I pay my own bills, but thanks."

His face radiated a sense of satisfaction, and a hint of a smile formed at the right corner of his upper lip.

"Besides, I think I'm going to like working here."

"It would be unfortunate to lose you so soon."

"Tragic even," I said.

Well done.

He cleared his throat. "Things are going to get a little crazy soon. Have some champagne."

At about ten, people started dancing. The music was thumping, and customers began ordering drinks directly from me. It was madness. No one seemed disappointed with my first attempts at mixing highballs. The tip jar was overflowing.

"Alex, you're amazing!" Virginie yelled above the chaos. The crowd parted like the Red Sea as she made her way to the exit. People were still ordering drinks when Dante hit the lights at 11:45 p.m., but he had everyone out by midnight.

"Good job tonight, sweatpants," Laurent said, and handed me my cut.

"Oh, my God! Four hundred dollars?"

"We'll see you tomorrow night then?" Patrick asked.

"That's a promise." I was completely enamored. Dante escorted me outside and hailed me a cab.

"I look forward to seeing you tomorrow." He kissed me on the cheek, letting the warmth of his lips linger. I was ready to offer him my other cheek but he walked away.

That wasn't the standard French and fabulous kiss good-bye. Was there some secret meaning in that?

Chapter 24

"HOW WAS IT?" Mike was sprawled out on the grass, taking in some rays back home.

"I'm not very good, but no one seemed to mind, and I walked out with four hundred dollars."

"Maybe you should give up the fucking modeling entirely and become a professional bartender."

At least I was on my way to being able to pay my rent now; the Visa bill would take some time.

"I love the guys who work there."

I wasn't ready to tell him about Dante. My feelings about him were too fresh and fragile.

"There was a team vibe, like Safeway, except it's a restaurant and we drink at work, and everybody's rich and good-looking."

"Easy now, are you saying I'm not fucking good-looking?"

Mike, of all people, had no need for external validation. He'd blossomed since his geeky high-school days, and was confident in his lumberjack-es-que appearance.

"What's going on with you?"

He held up the vaporizer, which had been getting stellar reviews across the board. I was looking forward to breaking it in myself.

"I may have found the perfect house to flip, but it's not going to work out with the blonde I was dating. She's allergic to dogs and she wants kids."

Mike was part of the Voluntary Human Extinction Movement. He gave me a bumper sticker for Christmas last year: *May we live long and die out.* It sounded doom and gloom, but the movement is an upbeat, positive bunch of tree huggers. It's their notion that the planet would be better off without humans. Although my feeling was there was some truth in that, I never put the sticker on my car.

My cell phone's new ring tone, Destiny's Child's "Survivior," kicked off. "I have to get this, it's Virginie."

"Ah, yes, the squirter."

"Seriously?" 'End call' didn't carry the same weight as slamming down the receiver on an old-school phone. Note to self: never get rid of parents' rotary phone.

"Hi Virginie." My voice never failed to convey the intensity of my girl crush.

"You were wonderful last night. How was it with Dante?" she said over the street sounds in the background.

"I think he was flirting with me. It could just be a French thing, but when he kissed me good-bye, he kissed only one cheek."

"There's definitely something special about that."

"Virginie, do you believe in love?" It sounded childlike, but she was so passionate about me and Dante, which couldn't make me happier. But it felt like she was living the experience of falling hard for someone through me.

She never used the word "love" when she talked about the men in her life.

The phone went dead.

"Hello?"

"I, yes, it's . . ." she stammered, her voice heavy with sorrow.

"Are you okay?"

"I believe in love." Her whisper hung on the line.

The Starbucks guy.

The moment was stolen by the ceaseless yapping of someone's dog. She dropped right back into her fabulous self.

"Wardrobe for tonight?"

"Sorted. All Saints top, and Frame skinny jeans." The whole look embodied effortless class. Wardrobe 10.

"Have fun. Enjoy every moment with Dante."

"That's a promise."

≳ ☺ ≲

I loved the restaurant at this hour. Calm, serene, and beautiful. The wall art, the bouquets of flowers, and the bar looked different in daylight. It was like a French painting that we were bringing to life.

Patrick looked up from his script. "How's our bartender today?"

"Patrick, why don't you have a strong French accent like these two?"

"I grew up in Switzerland, studied theater for years, and took vocal training."

"Everyone here has a backstory, eh?"

What was Dante's story?

"Dante told me you live with Lori. She's an incredible woman—"

"Yeah, you would know," Laurent interrupted. "Carnal knowledge on the premises, my man."

Good Lord!

"Lori? How many women have you had sex with here?"

"Patrick? Or the staff collectively?"

"Collectively," I said emphatically and glanced at Dante.

"Twenty-five. Give or take."

"Alex," Dante grabbed me by the shoulders, "what happens at Le Brasserie stays at Le Brasserie, okay?"

What is this, Vegas?

"Your secrets are safe with me, gentlemen," I promised.

"New York City, baby." Laurent tried to engage in a salsa but I stood there motionless as he danced around me. "You need to loosen up, sweatpants. Where's your rag thing?"

"Linus doesn't dance, and neither do I."

"Why don't you dance?" Dante touched the tips of his hair when he asked questions. It was a provocative tendency that made it hard to concentrate.

"Umm, it's, umm, dancing and me aren't a winning combination."

"Do you eat?" An amused smile spread to his eyes. "It's going to be a long night."

"No thanks."

The savory smell of French fries permeated my pores; every ounce of me was salivating.

"Do you starve yourself like all the models?" Laurent asked.

"I can assure you Lori doesn't starve herself, and I have an ongoing love affair with Oreos."

"You know guys don't like skinny chicks."

"Really, Laurent? Lori is pretty damn skinny."

"But she has boobs. And they're real."

The night started winding down at about midnight, and I was stuffing $467 into my wallet when Dante threw the keys to Laurent. "Lock up for me and put this one in a cab."

"Where is our fearless leader off to tonight?" I asked Laurent once Dante was gone.

"Our apartment. Some girl is waiting for him there. Do you want to come out with me and Patrick? The night's just beginning."

For Dante and some girl.

"Maybe next time."

"Cool. Rest up for tomorrow's brunch, sweatpants."

I spent most the night obsessing about Dante and the girl waiting for him. What did she look like? Did she come to Le Brasserie? Did he kiss her on one cheek? Virginie must have read too much into that. Read? I remember reading books in bed back home. Those days seemed like a lifetime ago.

⋛ ☺ ⋚

My first brunch shift seemed like the ideal time to debut my Kate Moss TopShop cami, which I paired with my Frame black skinny jeans and Rag & Bone jacket. Wardrobe 10. My hair was also a 10. I was feeling almost sure of myself when I arrived at the restaurant.

"Sweatpants, are you ready for today?" Laurent sambaed past me. "It's going to get wild."

Dante walked through the door with a box of croissants and greeted us all with the kiss hello. Why didn't everybody kiss hello? How did that get lost on us non-Europeans?

"Hello, beautiful." Even with black circles under his eyes, he was gorgeous. "By three p.m. I want to see everyone in this restaurant with a shot glass in their hand, including you."

"Is that on me?" I asked.

Dante smiled, and Laurent added, "You're the bartender, sweatpants."

"Laurent, you have to lose the 'sweatpants.' I'm over it," I said.

"I'm also over it." Patrick put his script away. "Come here, beautiful. I'll teach you how to make shots."

It isn't just Dante. All the Frenchies call girls "beautiful".

Dante and Laurent were engaged in a covert conversation in French. "What's with the whispering?" I asked. "By the way, I studied French in high school."

I didn't understand a word.

"Let's speak English for Alex," Patrick said. "And please continue. It sounds like Dante had a delightful evening."

"Yeah, Dante. I found her G-string on the dining room table," Laurent said.

Did I just throw up in my mouth?

Dante glared at Laurent and he tried to walk it back. "But they could've been old, like from a different night."

I wasn't sure if Dante rubbing his temples was out of frustration or a hangover, but when he caught my eye, a sheepish look came over his face and he looked away.

"It's settled then." Patrick clapped his hands together. "At some point, Dante was having sex on his dining table. Very sophisticated."

The thought of it affected me way more than it should have. He was the manager of the restaurant where I worked. A giant flirt and a man whore. Nothing more.

"Never a dull moment with you guys." My fake high-school laugh was lighthearted as ever.

"There definitely won't be today," Laurent said with a wicked smile.

Chapter 25

I WOKE UP ON THE BATHROOM FLOOR haphazardly covered in Saran Wrap and wearing one of my rubber gloves. I wrapped myself in a towel and crawled to the living room. Pieces of yesterday's wardrobe made a trail from the couch to the bathroom door. Lori came out of her bedroom, picked them up one by one, balled them up in my jacket, and put them under my head. "Le Brasserie. It happens to all of us."

Of two things I was certain:

(1) I had spent a good part of the night throwing up. Furthermore, I was so drunk that Lori's bath mat seemed like a good place to pass out.

(2) I would not be running the stairs today. Stairs 0.

"Relax, recover, and when you're ready, relay all the details."

"To be honest, I'm struggling to piece it together." My voice was hoarse and gravelly.

"You were home by six p.m., singing and laughing. I couldn't understand a word you were saying, then you passed out around seven."

"And the onset of the projectile vomiting commenced when?" I rasped.

"I'd say ten. I guess that's why you're wearing rubber gloves."

A single rubber glove.

"I was going to get up and check on you, but I figured you'd want privacy."

Where was the other glove?

"That was considerate of you."

"Then my Xanax kicked in and I passed out."

Maybe she has some painkillers floating around her bedside table.

"I distinctly remember making the first round of shots for the entire restaurant at about two p.m."

"Ooh, that was early, even by Le Brasserie's standards."

"It was complete pandemonium. The guys were screaming drink orders at me, the disco ball was going, and the customers were spraying people with the soda gun."

"I love it when they do that."

"At some point, Patrick stood on the bar and announced that it was my first time working brunch."

I was staring at Lori's ceiling, willing myself to remember, and then it hit me. Where it all went wrong. Le Brasserie had bought shots for everyone to celebrate, which I had to personally deliver to every table.

"Everyone made me drink a shot with them. I physically couldn't do my job after that."

I slid off the sofa, which had begun rocking like a floating dock, and lay flat on the floor. "You think they would've sent me home."

"The guys can't lose their shit, but everyone loves when the bartender gets drunk."

"I begged Dante to let me leave, but he flatly refused."

Lori nodded as if to say that was his only course of action.

"I stumbled around from table to table kissing people, talking absolute nonsense. I told a table of Swedish people I'd been to Sweden and how much I loved it there. I've never been to Sweden."

"I know lots of Swedish models." Lori patted my arm. "I'll introduce you."

That'll make me more credible.

"Lori, although we have never discussed it"—I closed my eyes—"you may as well know, Fabio told me I had an ugly body."

"You do not have an ugly body! I've heard he can be an asshole."

That information might have been useful going into that shoot.

"Worse still, I shared that unfortunate nugget with an entire group of people who were outside, smoking."

"Noooo." She fell backward like she had just been slapped across the face.

"I spent the remainder of my shift having an in-depth discussion about how women are sexualized in the mainstream media, yet when they express themselves sexually they are labeled a whore. Something I assured everyone that I abhorred wholeheartedly."

Unlike the Sweden story, there is some truth to that. I have nothing but respect and admiration for brazen women. History has not been kind to women of ill repute; it hasn't been kind to women, period. Short of the pagans, not too many orthodoxies support women getting down with whomever they want, whenever they want.

Women, the giver of life, shouldn't be shagging unless someone tells us so?

Intelligent people believe in this hypocrisy. I do not, but am nonetheless a victim of those sitcoms and afterschool specials, and their "just say no" motto. To say that I, personally, am sexually liberated would be a lie.

The irony of all the nonsense I was spouting is that it ties back to

Sweden. Those Scandinavians are notoriously liberal and freewheeling.

"And then I pointed out that I wasn't even wearing a bra."

"You didn't need a bra with the shirt you were wearing."

"Mercifully, Dante put me in a taxi before I had the chance to prove it."

"Phew, girl. Let me get you more water and some Advil."

I lay staring at the ceiling. The ultimate humiliation had been omitted in the retelling of events. The last thing Dante whispered to me as I fell into the taxi was, "You don't have an ugly body."

My cell phone shrilled from somewhere in the apartment.

"Alex," Lori yelled from her bedroom, "your phone is in the kitchen!"

Please bring me the Advil!

My phone, and the contents of my entire bag, were on the kitchen floor.

"Hello," I managed to say while sifting through the wreckage.

"Chérie, are you okay?"

My missing rubber glove and the seven hundred dollars in my wallet jeered at me.

"No."

"You've seen the video," she said with a heavy sigh.

"Someone took a video of brunch?"

What happens at Le Brasserie stays at Le Brasserie? I'd kept up my end of the agreement.

"Oh, dear." The gravity of her words seemed somewhat misplaced. "Someone posted the Metropolis video "What Never to Do on a Runway" on YouTube. It has a hundred thousand hits already."

Lori came flying into the kitchen. "Girl, have you seen it?"

The two sides of my brain just fell apart, and catatonia set in.

Chapter 26

"AT SOME POINT YOU'LL HAVE TO LEAVE THE APARTMENT." Lori offered me an enormous pair of Burberry sunglasses. "Camouflage."

"Thanks."

"Maybe just start with a shower," she suggested.

I'd spent two days prostrate on the sofa, swathed in a bathrobe.

"I'm headed to LA in a couple of days."

I'd forgotten all about her top-secret casting, having now willed myself to disassociate from anything to do with reality.

"Any new developments?" I said, trying to sound enthusiastic.

"There's serious interest. You gotta cross your fingers for me because this could . . ." She hesitated, taking in the close-up view of my woeful state. She patted my grotesque thighs. The three pints of Chunky Monkey, three bags of Oreos, and the three—that's right, three—pizzas in two days had taken a toll.

"Probably not the best time to talk shop."

"It's not your fault my career is over."

The video was truly wretched. Darlene had doctored the high-kick, so it happened three times in a row. I couldn't bear to look at it again.

Runway? What was I thinking?

"Don't talk like that. Think huge comeback."

Comeback from what?

"Thanks."

She wrenched a suitcase from the closet. I'm ashamed to admit there was a small piece of me that wanted that sitcom moment where, at last, everything would tumble out in shambles.

Wallowing in misery was one thing, but wishing it on someone else was bad karma and obviously there were some shady moments in a past life that were haunting my current existence. I couldn't afford any more bad juju.

The soothing energy of Erin's studio was downright celestial. Her mass of glorious tight corkscrew curls fell unfettered past her golden shoulders. Her staple billowy yoga pants and loose-fitting Tee draped on her figure like they were a second skin. But even if she were bald and naked, it wouldn't alter her magnificence.

"Alex, hair and clothes don't change a person. Those things changed the way you see yourself."

"I can see clearly now. Reality has set in. My modeling career is over."

"I'm sorry this happened." Erin clasped my hands. "You have a bright light burning inside. Shine your beautiful light."

"You're mistaken. I'm now a black hole." There wasn't even a flicker at the end of my tunnel.

"I believe that the Universe supports us and that circumstances and people come into our lives for a reason."

"Darlene and Shelia? I'm having trouble with the reasoning behind any of the aforementioned events."

"The Universe is going to keep sending you Lydia, Darlene, and Sheila—"

"Thank you, Universe, for the gifts that keep on giving."

Erin laughed, but continued in a more serious tone. "I know it's a cliché, but other people's acceptance isn't important. You need to accept yourself."

"Oh, is that it?"

She clasped my hands and asked, "Do you think it's possible that we were supposed to meet?"

That was an encouraging proposition, like Frodo was meant to have the Ring.

"Maybe you're like my Gandalf, guiding me through this mess."

"I don't see a mess. I see a journey."

Let's hope my journey doesn't entail the despair and horror of dear Frodo's.

"Try to focus on your breathing, and turn your gaze inward." I watched as a fleck of dust fell on the Buddha. "We all have a place in the Universe."

A warm glow started in the depths of my heart and saturated my soul.

"Erin, you're my Gandalf."

≷ ☺ ≶

"Hey, Lean Cuisine, you have some nasty old food on your face," Keisha said and shook her head in disbelief.

Remnants from yesterday. Mirrors were currently banned, as I was focusing on my inward gaze.

"I kind of fell off the wagon the past few days." I emptied my cartful of Lean Cuisine, Saran Wrap, and an *O* magazine.

"Uh-huh. You're feeling sorry for yourself because of that video?"

My runway coach, my inspiration, my motivator knew my dirty secret. "You saw it, eh?"

"I saw it too. It was sad," Tonya said. "Like Miley Cyrus twerking sad!"

I removed the Lori's Burberrys and sniffled. "Do you want me to take down our Instagram post?"

"Now you see, there you go again." She hit me in the chest with a box of Saran Wrap. "You gotta own that!"

The stench of patchouli swallowed the checkout. There she stood, the faux-English hippie, stroking her swag of love beads.

Time for another exciting episode of Supermarket Scandals.

She placed an iceberg lettuce, an assortment of Campbell's soups, and Doritos on the conveyer belt and stood tapping her foot. "I'm waiting and my items are perishable."

There were enough chemicals in her perishables to withstand a nuclear attack and I glanced at her with a baffled expression.

She shot daggers at me and shrieked, "Do I need to get the manager involved?!"

"You need to get a voice coach very involved so you can lose that fake-ass accent, and I'm with a customer." Keisha's fifteen-second eye roll landed squarely on me. "I keep on telling you whatever it is, no matter how messed up, own your shit."

"Yeah, but I shouldn't have to own this. Someone else made this shit."

"Is that you"—she wagged her purple-sparkled nails from my head to my toes—"doing whatever that was, in that video?"

"Yeah, but—"

"You own the damn Saran Wrap, but you got a problem with this?"

Plumbaphobia is a condition I can accept and that Keisha was also willing to accept.

I could understand how this might look from her perspective, but the problem with *this*, the LumiYa video, is that I screwed up and *everyone* knows.

"Fine," I surrendered. "I made an artistic choice on the runway and it was obviously a bad choice."

"Now, that is owning it." She nodded with approval.

"But Keisha, everyone is laughing at me. I look like an idiot and I feel like a loser."

"Oh, hell no! You need to start believing in your inner Beyoncé."

The line of shoppers rustling behind the hippie moved over to Tonya's checkout, but she wouldn't budge. She was practically frothing at the mouth.

"This is outrageous!" the hippie said, stuffing her face with Doritos. "If you two don't shut up and—"

Keisha and Tonya were ready to pounce but I piped up, "You may not speak to me that way, nor may you speak to the staff that way. The only person who needs to shut up is you."

Keisha and Tonya directed a satisfied, and I daresay impressed, glance my way.

"Keep owning it, Lean Cuisine." She smiled. "Proud of you, girl."

I marched out of the supermarket like a victorious gladiator. Not only did I survive, I also conquered.

Chapter 27

EMBRACING MY INNER BEYONCÉ MAY BE HELPING me own the show fiasco, but there was still the rest of my life to figure out. If anyone could help you find your way in the Universe, it was Erin. But a dose of Oprah couldn't hurt, and I settled into my *O* magazine.

What to wear. Save your hair. Love your skin. Recipes, yoga routines, book suggestions, and even a little Suze Orman on bringing down your debt. I'm now feeling guilt-ridden about the lack of fresh vegetables in my diet, the absence of any skin care regime, and my massive Visa bill. The advertisements were endless and left me longing for an Oreo.

OREO. GRAB 'em, POP 'em, LOVE 'em.

I sure do. Thanks, Nabisco.

CALGON. Take me away.

Right this instant, I beg you.

ALWAYS. Keep that just-showered feeling all day long.

Maybe not this shower.

Then it hit me. Who were these girls?

Kohl's? JCPenney? Kmart? Who's wearing their clothes?

It isn't Kate Moss, Giselle, or Karlie Kloss.

Lori came out of her room and found me savagely ripping up her magazines.

"Alex, are you okay?"

"I'm not a runway model, I'm not a supermodel, but why can't this be me?" I showed her the torn pages.

"That's 'lifestyle modeling.'" She used air quotes, and her face tightened. "It's like supermodels being put out to pasture."

We really are like cattle.

"I mean, if you're Karlie and you have your own brand named after you, that's one thing. But it's like has-been celebrities doing *The Apprentice* or *Dancing with the Stars*."

It felt like the apartment walls were pressing in on us.

"It's demoralizing." Her tone switched to steadfast determination. "Lori Hastings is not going out like that. I'm going out on top."

Condensation formed on her bottle of kombucha. For a brief moment I dared not breathe or speak.

"Listen." Her prolonged exhale brought her focus back on me and my future. "There's a HUGE market for catalogs, and lifestyle, and those girls make bank."

"I could do lifestyle. I could make bank." My career wasn't exactly playing out in the Hollywood fashion I had envisioned, but the Lifetime made-for-TV version was still promising. Darlene could just suck it because I am going to be a model!

"I could be a not-quite-supermodel."

"Not quite supermodel. That's cute." With a nod of approval and a double high five, she said, "You go, girl!"

Not-Quite-Supermodel! NQS!

Mike wasn't down with the whole concept. "You went to New York to be a supermodel and now you might model tampons?" He suggested I might not want to give up the bartending just yet. He was right about that. There would not be modeling of any kind until I found a new agent.

꒰ ☺ ꒱

"Listen, I have HUGE news!" The importance of this moment could not be understated, and I presided over Tyler's bedroom like Éponine, ready to belt out my solo.

"I'm NQS!"

"Jesus wept, is that like a disease?" Tyler recoiled in horror.

"How do you know?" Virginie clutched at Tyler's hand.

"Oprah Winfrey, goddammit!"

"Oprah Winfrey, the bloody guru of daytime TV, gave you NSS?!" Tyler yelled. "I told you she was a sham. Lord knows how many lives she has ruined."

"I don't *have* NQS. I *am* NQS."

The tension in Virginie's brow was out of character, and Tyler was positively rigid with confusion.

"I lost my place in the Universe. But I found it a mere day ago, via an *O* magazine."

A bottle of wine and half a joint later, Virginie wrote NQS on the flap of an empty pack of Zig-Zags and lay it against the heel of my lone Louboutin, which had taken up permanent residence on the mantel. It just may be my favourite Instagram post to date. #NQS #thanksOprah #findyourniche #thefutureisyours

Lydia's comment was her most impressive yet, although she might have wanted to get me arrested. She got the acronym wrong but it was a solid effort, "#notquitesure is that #legal #zigzags."

"You see, baby lamb"—Tyler kissed me on the forehead—"trust the Universe. Our angels are guiding us."

Virginie threw her arms around me and directed a throaty growl at Tyler. "They had better guide you to that shoe."

Chapter 28

LORI'S NERVES ABOUT LA, COUPLED WITH MY ANXIETY about my first night back at Le Brasserie, filled the apartment with palpable tension.

"I'm sure the guys have seen the video," I said through clenched teeth.

"Something way more interesting is bound to happen, and everyone will forget about you."

Could it happen right now?

"Chloe is with the dogsitter, by the way."

I could've used the company.

"My car is going to be here, like any minute." She started pacing, circling her three suitcases for a three-day jaunt, and repeating the same sentences over and over. "Not my first rodeo. Gonna kill it. Back by Monday."

The doorman arrived to collect Lori and her Louis Vuitton luggage. She faltered, falling back against the door, and stared at me like a frightened child.

"I believe in you, Lori Hastings."

She snapped right out of it, slid on her Burberry shades, and pronounced, with the fierceness of a drag queen, "I'm gonna kill it! This is the start of something HUGE!"

It didn't have the same effect when I announced to myself, *I believe in you, Alex Emmerson.* I would just have to put my best foot forward, and Lori's Jimmy Choos were the ideal way to raise my game tonight. Lori had restuffed the closet in the most illogical fashion, and as karma would have it, everything tumbled out on me. The last thing to fall was an unused suitcase, which hit the shoe at the precise angle to snap the heel in half.

⋛ ☺ ⋚

"Hey, hey, sweatpants." Laurent had been waiting all week for this moment. He cued up the clip. "That's you, right?"

"Yes, it is," I said, matter-of-factly.

"Was it like publicity for something?"

"No." My intention was to act cool, but the sweat forming at my hairline hijacked my mojo.

"You did that for real?"

"Yes." Laurent was so stunned that he couldn't muster up a single barb.

"Hi Alex," Patrick emerged from the wine cellar, "how goes the agent search?"

"Well, I—"

"Not good, my man," Laurent interjected. "Look at this."

"Is this a joke?" Patrick looked concerned.

Own it.

"That was my first foray into runway, okay?"

"And hopefully your last," Laurent said, and hysterical laughter mushroomed between us. "We're all very s-s-so . . ." Patrick doubled over, struggling to get his words out. "Sophisticated," he finally managed.

Dante strode into the restaurant, and my laughter shriveled up like burned bacon. Laurent, however, couldn't compose himself and put the video on a loop.

"Look at her, my man."

"More than two hundred thousand views?" Dante gave an impressed nod. "Not bad for your first show."

I could've kissed him.

"Can we just move on?" I was done owning it.

Virginie strolled in alone at about nine to say hello, but it was more a show of support. I love that woman. When she left, Laurent remarked that of all the women who come to the restaurant, Virginie is the one he'd like to have sex with the most. He doesn't even know about the squirting.

"Hey guys, have a great night." I stuffed my three-hundred-dollar take into my bag.

"Alex, wait." Dante followed me outside. "I'll get a taxi for you."

"I've got the hang of it now."

"You know the guys are just having fun with that video." Three taxis slowed at the corner of Madison, but neither of us stopped them. "I don't ever want you to feel uncomfortable here."

"This is one of the few places in the world where I do feel comfortable."

The lights were dim inside the restaurant, creating soft shadows of our silhouettes on the sidewalk.

"That's good to hear. And you know what?"

You're offering me a full-time job here?

"If you can't find an agent, you can audition for the Rockettes."

The French ladies' man has a sense of humour.

"*A Chorus Line* is really more my thing."

He leaned into me. The cool evening air breezed against us. "I have something for you." He handed me a packet of Oreos.

"Thanks for remembering," I whispered.

"You're hard to forget."

I could feel his breath on the nape of my neck, but then he pulled away and whistled for a taxi. I stared at him in the rearview mirror.

I called Mike from the taxi. Now was the time to talk about Dante.

"Here's the deal. The manager, Dante, is gorgeous, and he kind of flirts with everyone, which is part of his job, I think. But he acts like he is super into me, and Virginie thinks he's into me. He's super touchy-feely, tons of compliments, and tonight he gave me a packet of Oreos."

"I'm guessing that this really fucking good-looking guy, who manages this really fucking exclusive restaurant, has a lot of options." Mike's keys were jangling in the background and he whistled for Ben. "Alex, I don't want be the fucking bad guy, but remember how all the good-looking guys in high school would do whatever it took to fuck who they wanted?"

"You really don't think the Oreos mean anything?"

"Alex." He sighed. He sensed how much this mattered, and I sensed he was trying to find the right words to say, which I didn't want to hear.

"Don't shit where you eat. It sounds like nothing but fucking drama."

"Did I mention the Oreos were double-stuffed?" I said haughtily and hung up. I knew I would never open this package and considered having it bronzed.

Maybe his gift was just a ploy to bed me, but the Disney deep inside my soul was clinging to the fairy tale. After all, they were double stuffed.

Chapter 29

HOPE AND SELF-DOUBT RICOCHETED inside me all night. Self-loathing got mixed up in there this morning when my mum called to wish me luck with my castings. Metropolis and NQS were still on the QT, never mind the bartending.

Dante looked up when I arrived for my shift, and I caught him staring at my metallic jeans. What I wouldn't give for a whisper of his internal dialogue.

Instead I was the target of Laurent's annoying outspokenness. "Are you ready for brunch tomorrow, sweatpants?"

I flat-out refused to have an encore performance at brunch, but Laurent wasn't having it.

"Hey, don't wear a bra again, everyone loved that."

"That was very sophisticated, Alex," Patrick said. "Thank you for staying in theme."

"I'm not doing shots with you guys all afternoon." With feet rooted to the floor, I said, "That's final."

"Is it?" A throaty voice monopolized the restaurant.

There she was, thigh highs and all. Laurent and Patrick watched mesmerized as her hips swayed toward us.

"Robin, you're looking ageless as always," Dante said. "Have you met our new bartender?"

"Indeed I have." She leaned up against the bar and addressed us like she had just stepped up to a podium. "Gentlemen, I discovered Ms. Safeway here behind a fish counter in Canada, and here she is behind the bar of one New York City's notorious hot spots."

"We're the Dream Team," I said. "Look who I get to work with every day. Best job ever."

"Might I steal your bartender away for a moment?"

I followed her outside with fingernails digging into clenched fists.

"You look gorgeous, doll. This revamped version of yourself is fab. I saw the possibilities the moment I set eyes on you."

"Darlene had a tougher time seeing those possibilities." My nails were close to drawing blood.

"Darlene's a bitch. She's always hated me."

That explains a lot.

"May I ask, where have *you* been?" My accusatory stance was begging for a much-deserved apology.

"All over the place. Doing my job. Scouting."

The casualness in her demeanor, the way she leaned into her hip, and the ease with which she delivered her words; the whole shtick that had been intriguing was now infuriating.

"Just FYI. Meanwhile, here in New York, the purgatory has been unparalleled."

"Life isn't a sitcom, doll." Her face softened, but her eyes lit up like the first time we talked about New York. "It's raw and gritty. With real highs and real lows."

"I'm in violent agreement with you."

Robin fought back an amused smile and lit a cigarette.

"I'd love a cigarette."

"When did that start?"

"Around the same time all my troubles started." It was my turn to pause for dramatic effect. "When I met you."

"I thought you knew what you signed up for."

"Are you aware that I'm an unwitting star on YouTube now?"

"Indeed I am."

"Well"—I stubbed out my cigarette at the foot of her Sergio Rossi boots—"I'm also a not-quite-supermodel now."

"I'd like to cock an eyebrow, but I got Botox last week."

"Lifestyle modeling is my future."

"Have you found yourself an agent?"

Seriously?

"We've been here before." My entire self was shaking with rage. "It didn't end well."

She reached into her Phillip Lim tote and produced a business card. "Just look at it."

RADIANT MODELS, Robin Ramon, President.

"I opened my own agency last week." She led me away from the dinner crowd arrivals. "I'm not allowed to poach any of Metropolis's girls, but quite a few followed me. When I heard your relationship with them had come to an end, I started snooping around to verify the rumors."

We were getting close to Park Avenue and the steady hum of traffic when Robin stopped. "I want to represent you. Come with me to RADIANT."

I threw my arms around her, and Robin Ramon, the missile in stilettos, gave me a giant squeeze hug.

"Darlene doesn't want me, or my girls, to do well. She posted the video to YouTube."

"That freaking bitch is Satan incarnate."

"She did you a huge favor. You know how many hits that thing has? Post it to your Instagram #firstshowofmycareer#lastshowofmycareer#no-runwayinmyfuture.

Thankyou@LumiYa#gifted#brilliant#designer #understanding#accepting#nobodysperfect

#grateful."

She rattled it off so fast I had trouble keeping up.

"You think you're the first model to mess up at a show?" It was a rhetorical question. "I've never seen anything quite like *that* before," she shrugged, "but own your image. Don't be a victim."

Keisha would love that.

"I'm in!"

"Welcome aboard, Ms. Not-Quite-Supermodel." And with those words, she sauntered away like a high-heeled gazelle.

Chapter 30

MADISON AVENUE'S SERENADE OF STREET SONG started later on the weekend, and the restaurant was bizarrely quiet on Saturday mornings—the calm before the storm. Today more so than usual. The guys were late, and Dante and I were alone.

He was making cappuccino. The fluidity of his movements hypnotized me. I felt safe to stare when his back was to me.

"Are you excited about working with Robin?" he asked, turning to face me.

"Totally! I'm meeting her on Monday."

"I'm surprised she didn't go out on her own before now. Robin has a great reputation."

Virginie and Tyler felt the same way. Tyler's exact words were "She's bloody GFY incarnate."

"She believed in me." Robin's faith spurred a newfound confidence in myself and my career.

"She still believes in me."

"So do I." He smiled and disappeared into his own thoughts.

I swallowed hard. I almost said "I believe in you too" but there was something unbearably intimate about that statement, and the moment left me breathless.

"I believe in her," I whispered.

He leaned back in his chair, his eyes searching mine, and offered me a chocolate croissant. "You won't even taste it?"

"No, thank you." I was relieved the conversation was moving in a manageable direction. "I've had breakfast."

"Do you really eat the same things every day?"

"Yes." My Lean Cuisine Canadian bacon English muffin was, in fact, superb.

"If you go to a restaurant, what do you do?"

"My system doesn't involve restaurants."

"You've been in New York for months and have never been to a restaurant?"

I've eaten here once.

"No." I felt ridiculous. It was impossible to explain.

"I hope we can introduce a little fun and new dining experiences into your system."

We?

"Laurent knows everyone. He can get a table anywhere."

So the royal "we," not "you and me."

An intense sense of irritation was building inside me. Disappointment masquerading as irritation. Maybe Mike's right—this is nothing but drama.

"Perfect," I said, hoping my smile could mask my true feelings. "By the way, I'm not getting drunk today."

"You don't need to get drunk. Just have fun."

I didn't speak to him unless necessary for the duration of my shift.

⋛ ☺ ⋚

"Alex, can you come to my place right away?" The urgency in Virginie's voice was alarming.

"Is everything okay?"

"Just get here as fast as you can."

I flew uptown and was standing outside Virginie's apartment fifteen minutes later.

She threw the door open, grabbed my hand, and pushed me onto the sofa. "Close your eyes."

"What's going on?" This frenetic behavior was so out of character.

"Just do it and no peeking."

"Okay, okay." I covered my eyes to prove my commitment to her request.

"And now . . . open them."

Tyler was standing in front of me holding a brand-new pair of Louboutins. "See, poodle, our angels are guiding us."

"How can this be? I thought we couldn't find them anywhere."

"Virginie works miracles," Tyler said, genuflecting.

Shoe boxes, garment bags, and mountains of designer clothes were laid out on the dining room, and a trail of enormous shopping bags led to the living room.

"I found them in London when Michael took me shopping."

"You went shopping in London?"

"I wanted to go to Harrods." She spoke of it as though it was the most natural thing in the world. When one wants to go to Harrods, one goes. I wanted to be just like her, a French Holly Golightly.

"You were only gone three days."

"We flew on his private jet. Anyway, they're yours."

"I can't accept these, Virginie." Tears swelled up in my heart.

"It's my gift to celebrate all the wonderful things that are happening." She smiled at me, and everything felt right with the world.

I hugged my shoes tightly to my chest and my tears were poised to fall when Tyler asked, "Can I keep the spare? My bastard boyfriend has done it again!"

Freddie Mercury was the first gay man I fell in love with. Then there was Christian, the Jungian from Psychology class, but I'm partial to the stereotype of the fashionistas, and their larger-than-life personas. Tyler was the most magical of anyone I'd ever met. "Please explain why you put up with this guy."

"We lost a shoe because of this asshole." I'd never heard Virginie swear.

"Where's your GFY spirit?" I asked.

"You're right. GFY!" Tyler declared, throwing in an eye-high leg kick. "I'm leaving him for good."

The high kick was stupendous, but the words behind them were weak. I wouldn't put money on that bet.

"You deserve an incredible man in your life," Virginie said, stroking Tyler's arm. "And Alex, so do you."

Chapter 31

ROBIN HAD TRANSFORMED HER twenty-four-hundred-square-foot TriBeCa studio into RADIANT's offices.

The sharp, sleek lines of the sparsely furnished space were modern and edgy, with just the right element of soft.

"You look great, doll," Robin said. "The whole thing you have going on is working."

This morning's salon special was an exceptional 10+ My Paige jeans had been out of the rotation for a while, and it was a happy moment when they slid easily over my hips.

My All Saints leather jacket made its first appearance today, and my boots were beginning to take on that perfect amount of lived-in look. Wardrobe 10+.

"Thanks." My smile was bursting with a sense of pride.

"Don't lose any more weight, and don't change your hair."

The diet and stairs were back on track, but I couldn't say the same for the breathing practice.

"You're cool, right? Mastered the subway, living with Lori still okay?"

Plumbaphobia notwithstanding.

"Yes." I was studying RADIANT's wall of model comp cards like it was a sacred monument. "Is that Lisa?" The blond British girl that was wanking with Chris Hemsworth.

"She was the first to come with me." Robin glanced up at her girls. "This is the wall of fame, or shame, depending on the hour. You'll fit right in."

"How many Metropolis girls came with you?"

"Ten. For now."

Please don't let her be up there.

Sheila may well be Darlene's baby, but loyalty didn't strike me as her redeeming quality.

"Umm." I hesitated. "Did Sheila join RADIANT?"

"Sheila Summerville?" She acted like she had never heard the name. "Hey Stefanie," Robin yelled toward the booking table in the rear of the office, "what do you think about Sheila Summerville?"

Stefanie ambled toward me. Her waist-length strawberry blond hair probably weighed more than she did. All 5 feet, and 2 inches of her couldn't weigh more than a hundred pounds soaking wet, but she had a commanding presence. "Too much drama."

"No drams here, doll." Robin pulled up my page on RADIANT'S website. "Digitals fab, and your page is fab."

"Fab," Stefanie reiterated, devoid of any enthusiasm. "I took out the bikini shot, but it was also fab."

"You don't have cankles," Robin said, clearly flustered. "Don't let this business mess with your head."

It was a bit late for that.

"It's not the business. I've always had cankles."

"No swim. It's your career, and you make the decisions. I'll get you the work." She handed me a RADIANT portfolio.

"Let's shoot that," Stefanie said. "Instagram. What's your handle?" @ alexemmersonnyc#newrecruit#readyset#RADIANT

"You're all set. I'll email your appointments for tomorrow—Macy's, Soft Surroundings, Blair, some Ecommerce—it's not sexy, but it pays."

"Are you sure about posting the YouTube clip to my Instagram?"

"Trust me," Robin said. "Trust Stefanie, she's the social media expert."

"Post it," Stefanie said.

"Done." I shrugged, but my tone revealed the magnitude of my reservations.

"Listen, doll," Robin's face softened, "it's gonna be great."

"Thanks, Robin." The words carried more sentiment than they could convey.

⋛ ☺ ⋚

"Hey, girl." Lori threw open the apartment door, and then slammed it once the doorman had deposited her suitcases. Her boundless glow lit up the room.

"You look positively perfect. How—"

She flew toward me and dragged me to the bedroom. Once sequestered in her sanctum, she whispered, "I'm not allowed to say anything."

Then why are we hiding in here?

"It's still not for sure, but I killed it."

"Of course you did. You're Lori Hastings."

"Right?" She buried her face in her silken sheets and let go an ecstatic squeal. "I'm in their top three."

Robin was right about those highs and lows, but there was something about this business that took those emotions to intense extremes. Every part of me was rooting for Lori. I don't think either of us could bear the pain of her not getting this job.

"Oh my God, I totally forgot. Robin called me when I was in LA." Lori was rooting for me too. "Soooo?" She practically sang it. "What's happening?"

"I just left RADIANT's office," I said, trying to smile.

"You don't sound too excited."

"We decided to post that clip to my Instagram."

I'd been back at the apartment for more than an hour and everything was ready to go, but I couldn't bring myself to hit "share."

"Just do it. Like a Band-Aid, rip it off!" she yelled. It was my turn to scream into the sheets, but it was more a terrified howl.

"Come with me."

I followed her into the kitchen, phone in hand, and fought against my fumbling fingers until Lori snatched it away and posted it for me.

We smoked three cigarettes in silence. I counted the sunflowers in that stupid painting: six, I'd never noticed that before. Lori counted the minutes on her watch.

Tick.

Tick.

Tick.

The incessant ticking of her freaking Audemars Piguet was insufferable, even for Lori. "Okay, that's enough time for something to be happening. I'm going to like your post, and say something cute. Love this! Love this girl! The little sister I always wanted #sisters#modellife#love."

"Thanks, Lori."

"Don't thank me. Thank your ten thousand followers!"

"What?" It was surreal. The momentum was insane. Robin and Stefanie were right. *Darlene, you can just suck it!*

"The power of social media, right?" Lori said, and then I passed out.

"Alex." Lori was blowing on my face, which was an odd revival technique. "Are you okay?"

"I have to delete that post immediately!"

Until a moment ago, showcasing my glossy new life had yielded a positive response. Was there a sense of validation involved? Maybe. Was I happy that strangers liked my posts? Kind of. Was I prepared for the vile, venomous vitriol the video had spawned? Hell No!

Lydia's comment, "OOPs. You can take the girl out of the suburbs, but you can't take the suburbs out of the girl #notmadeforfashion," didn't even rate in the top worst one hundred.

- what career? #delusional
- epic fail, like your dad's condom #modelfail
- ur too fat for runway #wannabe#weightwatchers#modelfail
- runway—it'saprivilegenotaright#massivemodelfail#careersuicide
- bitch be like monday, everybody hate you #bitch
- i hate you #justbecause
- everyone hates you #justsaying
- you crucified LumiYa's collection #sabotage#megabitch
- kill yourself already #careersuicide

"Kill myself?"

Thank God my mother isn't on Instagram.

"It's great that you have more followers and you can delete the mean comments. Don't let it get in your head."

How could it not get in your head?

The massive hate-on was crippling. Robin and Stefanie had to talk me off the ledge.

"Have you seen what people are saying?" My vocal chords were trembling.

"People say mean shit all the time." Stefanie's voice was devoid of emotion. "Don't trip." Our discussion was happening via conference call. Had we been up close and personal, they might have agreed to delete the freaking thing. The neighborhood crazy guy had nothing on me. I was literally knocking my head against the wall.

"I'm looking, doll, it's eighty percent positive stuff here," Robin said.

"Focus on your castings," Stefanie said. "Don't look at your Instagram."

I scanned it quickly one last time before retiring for the night.

@danteDelavalette nothing is more beautiful than a woman who can laugh at herself. #beautyinsidendout

Dante, I'm a little bit in love with you right now.

@keisha way to own it girl! #ownit#noshade

Keisha, I'm a little bit in love with you too.

Chapter 32

"HOW ARE YOU THIS MORNING?" Lori wheeled what I assumed was her emptied luggage into the living room.

Recovering from my vulnerability hangover.

"Okay, I think. Prepping for my first day of castings with RADIANT."

"I may have just the perfect thing for today." She buried her face in her Vuitton valise. "Voilà." She handed me a Burberry trench. "It's yours!"

"Lori, I can't accept this."

"You have to," she said, delighted with herself. "I went shopping in LA and I bought a new one."

I slipped my arms into my almost-brand-new Burberry. "I love it."

"We have to shoot that. You look fab!"

@burberry#trenchcoat#fallfashion#britsdoitbetter

What, Lydia, no comment? Look who's wearing Burberry now? #Suck it.

"I have more awesome stuff for you."

"Th-th-hank you," I stammered as she showered me with her almost-never-worn designer digs.

"You need to share your good fortune. Pay it forward. You know what

I'm saying?"

Her eyes were bulging and she was moving her hands like we were in the midst of a game of charades. I'm well versed in charades; it's a family Christmas tradition. I'm not one to brag, but my talents are unmatched.

"The casting?"

"I'm *still* not allowed to say anything," she trilled. "Not yet anyway."

I killed it on the stairs 10, and masterfully touched up yesterday's blow-out, hair 10.

The sassy IRO sweater Lori had gifted me jazzed up my Frame jeans, and the Burberry was to die for. Wardrobe 10.

Breathing practice 0. That part of the program needed work, but it wasn't my top priority. It was also time to add quitting smoking to my rating scale, but I'd wait until my first week of castings were over.

The venues hadn't changed much. Sandbox, Splashlight, Jack Studios, and I recognized a lot of the girls.

"Hey, Alex." Lisa waved me over. "The sign-in sheet is over here, babes."

"Hey, Lisa."

Please don't let this moment be awkward.

"You're with RADIANT now? Fucking brilliant."

"Robin is the reason I came to New York. She scouted me in Canada."

"Respect. Fucking selfie here for Robin right now."

#RADIANT#robinramone#radiantgirls#castings#respect#modellife

"Hopefully she'll help me turn things around." This was the first intentional, honest moment I'd shared with another model other than Lori.

"More than half of these show ponies aren't working consistently."

"Show ponies" was priceless, and I laughed out loud. It sounded nicer than "cattle."

"I was a coat check girl at Capitale for six months."

She had a casual way about her, but I felt like she could conquer the world if she were so inclined.

"Do you work consistently?"

"Yeah, but I have no ego about it, babes. Catalog, lifestyle, whatever. Let's make some fucking dollar."

"Fucking dollar" was another gold nugget and needed to take up a permanent place in my repertoire, but it wouldn't sound the same without that accent. This was the most fun I'd ever had at a casting.

"Bartending at Le Brasserie is currently my main source of income."

"What happens at Le Brasserie stays at Le Brasserie." Her wicked laugh was incendiary and infectious. "Brunch is brilliant."

"The money's great, but I'm not sure my liver can withstand too many more."

"I've fallen off a few tables there myself."

The casting people called her name, and as she stood up to leave she said, "Oy, that video is fucking priceless, babes."

I gave her a thumbs up. I was done talking about that video.

I was digital-worthy at all of my castings. By midafternoon a sense of euphoria set in. I had time to kill before my next appointment and moseyed around the Meatpacking District, stopped for a coffee, and took a stroll on the High Line's supersweet stretch of park. It brought me back to my first trip to Central Park, and the first time I felt connected to the city. People say you have to spend ten years here before you can call yourself a "real" New Yorker, but I suddenly felt like one. Mastered the bathroom from hell, survived extreme humiliation, vanquished an evil agent. That was serious bad-assery. As I was staring at the skyscrapers and the madness below, a feeling of blissful calm wrapped itself around me. I caressed the sleeves of my Burberry and fell into the sensation. A sitcom writer couldn't script a happier ending to this episode.

However, everything can change in a New York minute, and that dreamy sensation was vaporized by the streets of Chinatown. The stenches of garbage, urine, and sweat permeated my pores. Times Square was a jaunt in an English garden compared to this. My playlist was at full volume. Even Pharrell Williams couldn't drown out the noise.

Bring me down

Can't nothing

Bring me down

The halting traffic, rabid pedestrians, and screeching vendors were kind of bringing me down. Happy? Hardly.

The casting for Macy's was one block north of Canal. The whole neighborhood changed—the cobblestone streets appeared clean, the noise dissipated, and the buildings were in good repair. I was mentally clapping along with Pharrell when Lisa and the breathtaking Ashley joined me in the elevator.

"You remember Alex, from that video?" Lisa said, laughing.

"I told you she was trouble." Ashley smiled.

We had barely signed in when the casting director ushered us into a windowless room with bright lights and a video camera.

This is new.

"Okay, girls." She addressed us like we were being invited to a party. "First we are going to slate, name, agency, and profiles. I'm going to put on some music. Forgive me, it's a terrible song," she said with a dismissive wave. "Dance, have fun, and do some huge smiles to camera."

WTF now I needed to dance?

Madonna's "Holiday" was an odd number, but Lisa and Ashley worked it. I managed to sandwich myself between them, and smiled bug-eyed at the camera.

"Great. Thank you, ladies. You're outta here."

"Alex, babes," Lisa said, "we're headed to Le Brasserie. You in?"

"Thanks, but I have one more casting," I lied, and then called Erin. If dancing at castings was the new norm, something needed to be done. Mike always says everyone can dance if vodka is involved, but that wasn't an option, and he'd never seen me dance.

≥ ☺ ≤

"Hi." Erin hugged me and ushered me into her studio. The freshness of the air filtered through my pores.

"I know we weren't supposed to see each other until tomorrow, but I have a situation."

"Come sit down and tell me how you're feeling."

It took a good fifteen minutes to bring Erin up to speed.

"Ultimately it was you and a little bit of Oprah that led to this moment."

"It's you who changed your life." She made a namaste gesture. "You should feel proud of yourself."

"I guess, kind of I am, but—"

"No 'but.' Celebrate your victories in life. Don't let them pass unnoticed. Honor them."

Conversation ceased for a moment because Erin wanted her words to resonate. My mind was fixated on the bigger picture.

"Moving on, today I had to dance at a casting."

"That makes you uncomfortable?"

"I can't dance. I've known since I was ten."

Erin erupted into her joyous laughter. "Everyone can dance. It's a delightful part of being human."

If Erin said everyone could dance, then maybe there was hope.

"Would you like to try something fun?"

"Oh, God, yes." I wasn't sure what she had in mind, but "fun" sounded very promising.

"We need to get into your sacroiliac joint and loosen it up. It will help you with dancing."

We spent thirty minutes on a series of yin poses that involved a lot of breathing. It was not fun in any way.

"Now, how about we turn on some music and dance?" My face must have conveyed my trepidation because she added, "We're just playing."

Erin cued up Lana Del Rey and sang along. "I get my red dress on tonight." Her voice was deeper and two octaves lower when she sang.

I stood before her, rocking back and forth. She put her hands on my hips. "Can you feel how the movement is coming from your knees?"

I had no idea what was happening, but it felt ridiculous.

"Put the weight on the balls of your feet. Feel that?"

"I think I do feel something." Something was loosening.

"Now move your hips." She guided me to the rhythm of the music. "Close your eyes. Don't think, just feel."

The music moved from my knees to my hips, which began swaying from side to side.

"That's it," Erin said. "Beautiful."

It was hardly classical ballet, but a huge part of me felt like my ten-year-old self. Tears poured down my cheeks as I pranced around the studio, savoring every moment, and I promised to do a lot more dancing in the future, but preferably not in public.

Chapter 33

MIKE HAD LAUGHED OUT LOUD when I told him we had to dance at castings, but it was his view that "Videogate" had worked out great and that I seemed less stressed out since the dominatrix resurfaced. He was right. The whole model scene felt different. The castings seemed less showy and weren't teeming with schadenfreude. Maybe I was acclimating. My first casting of the day was at *O*prah magazine. Perhaps Oprah was actually in the offices of the forty-six-floor high-rise; I needed security clearance just to get to the elevators at Hearst Magazines. I wore my visitor's pass like a badge of honor.

Two soon-to-be supermodels boarded the elevator with me. Their Etro and Lanvin patchwork boots were clearly the season's "IT" footwear, but I oozed confidence in my Newburys. The elevator stopped at the twenty-fifth floor, home of *Harper's Bazaar.* The delightful duo exited and kindly pointed out that one didn't actually have to wear the pass. "You look like an idiot."

They could just suck it. Oprah may not be high fashion, but her headquarters were on the thirty-sixth floor, and I would be keeping my badge as a souvenir.

O mag's offices were a total letdown. The glass doors opened into a room full of those stupid cubicles. Even the carpet looked dingy. However, the beauty editor was a vision in a mango-colored silk EQUIPMENT button-down.

"Where are you from?" she asked in a soft dulcet tone as she flipped through my book.

"Canada."

"Ah, I thought I heard a hint of an accent. Canadian, eh?" She laughed.

"You have an awesome accent. Where are you from?"

"Barbados."

Whatever the Barbadian women are drinking, please also bottle that and bring it here. Rhianna's "Diamonds" started playing in the recess of my mind. It's such a great song and one of my Rhi Rhi faves.

If only I had said that. Instead these words steamrolled of my tongue:

"Now, how does that work? If you're from Barbados, you're not African American. Of course, if you're black and Canadian you wouldn't say that either. I think you'd say black. What do you call yourself?"

"Rashana." She smiled.

Several members of the staff looked up from their cubicles to get a closer look at the white jackass discussing how to "label" people of color at *O*prah magazine. The woman nearest to us shoved her chair away from her desk and headed my way when Rashana handed me my portfolio.

"Your book is beautiful. Thanks for coming in."

Thank you, Rashana.

I hightailed it out of there. It was a total shit show, and I was midway through my third cigarette when Robin called to tell me that Jane Taylor asked to see me.

"Get over to Jack Studios right away."

There was no way to reset; self-condemnation would be accompanying me for the rest of the day. Doubtless for the rest of my life. I jumped into a cab and headed straight down the West Side Highway to 601 West 26th Street.

Jack Studios' enormous space housed seven studios. The aquarium and Ping-Pong table seemed oddly out of place, but the studio café was a nice touch. It was my favourite venue.

I passed Studio 1: *L'Oréal*, Studio 2: *Lingerie CLOSED SET*, and arrived at Studio 3: *Jane Taylor*.

When the art director waved me over, my eyes locked on his bulging crotch. His jeans were so tight his business was pulsating.

Was it real? Did he stuff socks down there?

"I'm Marcel, and I'm up here, girlfriend." He clapped his hands twice, which must have been a challenge because his wrists were buried under masses of chains.

"I'm so sorry. I just, you know, I bet you get that all the time."

"Uh-huh." He flipped through my book and directed a speculative glance at my footwear. "Nice boots. Nice book."

What if he didn't like my boots? Were they a factor?

"Please try some things on for us." His chains rattled as he directed me to wardrobe.

I tripped over thirty pairs of shoes, almost taking out the steamer and four racks of clothes, and collapsed onto the wardrobe stylist.

"This is madness!" the stylist lisped, and brushed me off.

"I'm so sorry."

"It's okay, honey. I'm Davide."

Davide, pronounced Da-vi-day, was clad in Prada from head to toe.

He handed me a pair of black stretch dress pants and a black-and-white sweater set. The standard style for ladies like my mum. "Today's been a mare."

I squished myself into a corner and squirmed out of my jeans, rushing to get into the outfit as Davide stamped his foot. When I presented myself to him, the cami of the sweater set was stuck in my underwear.

"You might want to consider revamping your lingerie drawer," he said.

I didn't know there would be a fitting.

I presented myself to Marcel for inspection. He looked me up and down and nodded.

"Listen, honey, he loved you."

You know that from the nod?

"We'll see you soon," Davide said through a tight-lipped smile.

"Great!" I said a little too forcefully.

"But honey, don't come back here in those granny panties."

Underwear aside, the casting felt like a victory, and I stopped by the studio café to celebrate with a latte. Standing at the bar was an arresting young Asian girl, and Sheila, whose blond locks full of body and curl looked like she had just stepped off the set of a Pantene commercial.

"Not working at Le Brasserie today?" she asked.

"Ooh, I love Le Brasserie." The Asian girl's hair fell perfectly to her waist, unlike her white fluffy jacket and leather tank, which hung just below her rib cage, revealing her concave stomach. Her six-foot frame was all legs, and she towered over me.

"What casting could *you* be here for?" Sheila asked.

All my GFY abandoned me, and the saliva in mouth dried up. I knew Sheila had seen it before, but my emergency exit strategy was my only option.

"I have to take this."

"Take what? I don't hear anything." Sheila looked around the café.

"My phone is on vibrate. Anyway, nice seeing you."

"Oh, Alex. Kiss Dante for me."

Mike is definitely right.

Two fire trucks whizzed by me on Tenth Avenue. A police entourage, alarms blaring, weaved into and out of traffic on Ninth Avenue, and an ambulance screeched past me on Broadway. This made the unusual calm of Gristedes all the more unsettling. I stopped in, hoping, and dreading, to see Keisha.

She was the lone cashier and stood filing her nails, which were now crimson red, like her lipstick.

"Hey, Lean Cuisine. Only one roll today?"

"Hey, Keisha." I wasn't there for the Saran Wrap; it was a ruse, but it felt like the most organic way to get to the heart of the issue. "Umm, so remember when you asked me about my accent?"

"Uh-huh."

"And remember how I said the angry hippie had a fake English accent?"

"Uh-huh." She was waiting for me to pay and seemed flummoxed by my awkward fumbling while I reached for my wallet.

An angry shopper, who looked like a homeless person, pushed his cart toward me with the intent to maim.

"Are you gonna let him get away with that?"

I wanted to tell him that he wasn't allowed to treat me that way. But all I could think of was Rashana and what Keisha would think about my performance at Oprah. I couldn't muster up my GFY spirit, and stood there helplessly while he pushed his cart into my thigh.

Keisha put her nail file on the belt, sashayed out from behind the register, pushed past me, and placed the "Checkout Closed" sign on top of his cart.

"Girl, what's up with you today?"

The words shot out of me like a machine gun. "I asked a black woman if I should call her black."

"Tonya"—she tossed her name tag on the checkout and yelled toward the rear of the store—"I'm on break."

My eyes fell to the floor and followed her Air Jordans out the door. We walked one block before she stopped.

"I'm guessing you don't have too many black folks in your life back in Canada?"

"Umm, no."

"When you meet a black woman, you might not want to open with, 'Should I call you black?'"

"I'm so sorry," I whimpered. "We were talking about our accents."

"You gotta taste your words before spitting them out, okay?"

"Okay." They were like acid burning my throat.

She massaged her temples in exasperation. "I can't deal with you without my latte."

The sea of pedestrians parted as we made our way to 90th and Broadway, where we stopped at Dunkin' Donuts. It prompted a pang of homesickness in the pit of my stomach, and the feeling rose to my face.

"What? You wanted Starbucks?"

All I wanted was a donut, but I ordered a nonfat latte.

"No. It's just that donuts make me think of home. Canadians are serious about their donuts."

Keisha was serious about her coffee. A French vanilla latte, four shots, and three caramel swirls. We sat at the counter, facing the tiny store's four occupied tables.

"I like that you're real with people," she said.

"The thing is when I'm really real, it's unintentional."

"You got your shit. The Saran Wrap, the Oreos, and your damn videos. But we all got shit."

The girl who was working behind the counter was nodding in agreement, and every patron's eyes were on me and Keisha.

"I went to a casting at *O* magazine and the woman I met was black, but from Barbados, and I asked her in front of other black people if she wanted me to call her black because African American didn't apply."

Keisha kept on swirling her caramel, but the girl behind the counter, who was black/ African American, was now shaking her head. I directed all conversation to her.

"I'm so sorry, but I'm Canadian and it really was all about accents but then the thought occurred to me, and it was totally out of curiosity because, you know, I'm not black or American."

Condensation was forming on the inside of the windows, and all activity ceased. Even the background music was inaudible.

"I'm sorry. I'm just trying to be a model, who might even model tampons, and I have no idea what I'm doing." I was now addressing everyone in the entire Dunkin' Donuts and there was no way to stop the words tumbling out of me.

"I'm so sorry. The thing is sometimes my brain is going really fast and the more nervous I get the more I talk and everything goes south."

"Okay, see now this here . . . this is why I like you, Lean Cuisine."

I wasn't sure the girl behind the counter liked me too much, and I was ready to apologize some more, but Keisha stood and walked out. I waved good-bye and chased her outside.

"I don't think she likes me."

"No, she doesn't. You've got to keep it real even if someone doesn't like you and what you have to say." She leaned up against the brick facade, feet crossed, sipping her French vanilla latte. "But you need to understand there's a time and a place for some things."

"I'm such an idiot." I buried my face in my sweater. Thinking about it now, Rashana didn't seem angry, but everyone heard me. "Should I go back to Oprah and apologize?"

"Hell no," she said emphatically.

"Because my inane babbling would likely make things worse?"

"Yes." She took a slow sip. "It's okay to make mistakes, but you need to learn from this, girl. Black or African American, whichever they chose to identify as, a woman is a woman, and we don't need labels."

"That's not how it sounded in my head." A wave of nausea hit me, and I willed myself not to throw up. "I'm so embarrassed."

"Stick with your model thing, and tackle race relations when you get control of your mouth."

"I'm sorry, it's all so stressful. I feel like such a loser."

"I keep telling you, girl, you gotta kick up your Sasha Fierce!"

She tilted her head, cocked her hip like no one else could, and swayed southbound down Broadway.

Chapter 34

THERE WAS A CHILL IN THE AIR that called for cashmere. I had even introduced nonfat, no- whip pumpkin lattes into the menu, but only on Sundays and Wednesdays.

Videogate had subsided, my Instagram was looking #awesome, although far from #real, and I no longer read the comments. Robin and RADIANT had made the #modellife a whole lot easier, which is why my sessions with Erin had become so infrequent. The breathing portion of my program had somewhat petered out, but my steadfast commitment to the rest of my system was keeping me centered and my generalized anxiety had subsided. It took some coaxing but today was the day to revamp my underwear drawer, and I turned up the heat on the stairwell.

"Look at you. You're drenched," Lori said with admiration and a hint of disgust as I wiped away sweat. "I know it's Monday but don't you think you've earned a pumpkin spice today?"

"No, just coffee, but thanks."

"I just gave Chloe a bath," she said on her way out the door. "It's a bit of a mess."

When Lori returned with the coffee, I was standing on the street smoking, shivering in my bathrobe and rubber gloves.

"Why are you out here smoking?"

Well, Lori, your bathroom has surpassed grotesque. Dog hair is everywhere, caked onto the shower curtain, and in puddles of filth scattered across the tiled floor. I'm permanently traumatized and may never be able to return to your apartment.

"Just getting some fresh air. Thanks for the coffee."

"You do know the maid is coming tomorrow, right?" She pointed to my gloves.

Could she come now, before I have to go back in?

After fifteen minutes the doorman insisted I put some clothes on or he would have to escort me upstairs.

If you thought my indoor voice was loud, you are in for a rude awakening.

I marched past him and the elevator and slammed the door to the stairwell. I would have preferred the elevator but the slamming made for more GFY drama.

The uncontrollable retching started the minute I stepped into the apartment. There was no way around it; I couldn't go back in that bathroom. The kitchen sink, Method dish soap, and paper towels served as my shower.

I threw on my J Brands and an impossibly soft V-neck cashmere sweater and headed straight to the salon. Hair therapy may be chair therapy, but a spectacular blowout did little to soothe my nerves. Nonetheless, my commitment to my lingerie drawer was unwavering.

Bloomingdale's intimate apparel department took up half of the second floor. There were more brands of underwear than there are chewing gum. I needed a professional.

"Virginie, I have a situation," I whispered into my cell. "I need new underwear."

"Ooh, is something special in the cards for you and Dante?"

"What? Oh, God, no."

All my fantasies about Dante never involved my underwear, or my nakedness, for that matter.

"I'm at Bloomingdale's."

"Not my first choice," she said with an edge of excitement in her voice. Just the notion of shopping sent her adrenals soaring. "Panties, bras, what are you looking for?"

Panties? The word should be deleted from the global lexicon.

"Whatever models wear."

"When you're shooting a job, you should wear nude bras and thongs. Calvin Klein has a great line."

I beelined it straight to the Calvin section.

"Done. What would someone wear if they weren't working, and just going on castings?"

"I love lingerie, but it depends on my mood. Aubade and La Perla are deliciously sensuous."

"I don't even know what those are. Can we keep it simple?" How did underwear become so overwhelming?

"What are you wearing, chérie?"

"Fruit Of The Loom."

"Oh, dear." I could hear the despair in her voice. "Just pick up some Hanky Panky. Everyone loves the low-rise thongs."

Hanky Panky. I passed that section at the entrance.

"I don't know," I said, fingering the lace bralette. "It looks a little burlesque."

"Alex, BUY IT NOW! And I will require proof of purchase."

I scooped up five sets, all in black, and headed straight to Virginie's.

"It's a good start," she said, sifting through my little brown bag. "But here's some inspiration for you." She tucked the torn pages of her *Vanity Fair* into my Birkin. "It's Cara Delevingne in La Perla."

"Virginie, we have another situation." Tension crawled from the depths of my being, contorting my face. I looked like a cast member from the *Real Housewives* of somewhere.

"Chérie, whatever it is, I believe this situation calls for wine."

"Only four other people on the planet are privy to this information."

"I'll take it to my grave," she said solemnly.

An entire minute passed before she was able to speak. "Plumbaphobia?" She even managed to make my neuroses sound exotic.

"You've had this your whole life?"

"Pretty much."

"You poor thing. You want me to find a doctor for you?"

"I'm really okay with it, but I can't stay at Lori's."

"I wish you could stay here, but Michael refuses to let me have long-term guests. He says the apartment isn't my hotel." She dismissed the notion with an air of annoyance. Virginie was accustomed to having things her way, and this concession was an obvious source of contention.

"It is his apartment," I said.

"In his point of view. I breathe life and beauty into these walls. I should be able to do whatever I like."

Why shouldn't she have full control of someone else's apartment? She almost had me convinced. But how could her untamable spirit be happy with this? She made it sound like she made the rules, but when I played her words back in my head it was Virginie who played by his rules. Someone else was in control. Either she genuinely didn't see it that way or she was lying to herself. And where did the mysterious Starbucks guy fit into all this?

"If you won't let me find you a rich man, we just have to find you a new apartment."

"Do you think we can find it soon?"

"Absolutely!" Her optimism was infectious.

"I also don't want to hurt Lori's feelings. She has been so great to me, and my fifteen-hundred-dollar monthly rent is part of her plastic surgery payment plan."

"Fifteen hundred dollars? Per month?"

"I know it's outrageous."

"Alex, this is Manhattan. It's hard to find studio apartments for less than three thousand dollars per month."

"Three thousand dollars? How do people survive?" Le Brasserie would cover rent but not much more.

"I guess we all just do what we have to." Her eyes seemed suddenly hollow and forlorn. They wandered toward the vaulted ceilings and lingered on a vase of flowers, but it was the stupendous view of the park that held her gaze. "Real estate is a hobby of mine. Let's not give up hope."

The exorbitant rent rates weren't the biggest problem. If the bathroom in Lori's apartment is what you get for six thousand dollars, I was screwed.

Virginie saw my face drop.

"Alex, why don't you spend the night here with me?"

It was a tempting offer, but in the morning's mad rush I had left my gloves at home.

"Come on, let me show you my bathroom."

Subtle hints of lemon verbena enveloped my senses as I stepped into her custom-built spa.

"It's out of this world."

"I know."

"It looks like it's been styled for a travel magazine." The room exclusively for the toilet was twice the size of Lori's entire bathroom. Soft white candles surrounded her stone sunken bathtub.

"Virginie, I've never seen such a magnificent bathtub, but despite my British heritage, I don't take baths."

"You're missing out on one of life's simple pleasures."

Toiling around in water tainted with one's own filth is repulsive.

"I'm a big fan of showers."

"Then this will make you very happy." The shower's immaculate glass doors opened inward into the marble-tiled masterpiece. I had never been in a shower with two shower heads.

"Maybe this infinity shower can break you in gently. Perhaps you won't need Saran Wrap and gloves." She took my hand, tracing the marble with my fingertips. A shudder shot up my spine, but I surrendered to the soothing scent of verbena.

"Step inside."

There was no way to will myself into the shower. The drain was sneering at me.

"We've made huge progress here, Virginie, but I can't go in here without flip-flops."

She wrapped me in the luxury of a sixty-five-gram double-rolled Egyptian cotton bath sheet and snuggled into it. "I have some spa sandals from my trip to Fiji."

Standing nestled together caressing the marble of Virginie's infinity shower may well have been one of the happiest, most peaceful moments of my entire young life.

"I love you, Virginie."

"I love you too."

My overnight care package included an electric toothbrush, organic toothpaste, Crème de la Mer face cream, and an unopened box of rubber gloves. I didn't use the gloves, only the spa sandals. The shower was divine decadence.

"You do all these wonderful things for me and I don't do anything for you."

"You do everything just by being in my life."

We curled up together in our pajamas with Linus and a joint. Virginie restarted the movie she was watching during my hour-long shower.

"Have you seen this movie, *Swept Away?*" she asked. "This is the final scene of the film."

The haunting face of a woman stared through an airplane window as it lifted off the runway.

"This is the Italian version. It's so beautiful." She dissolved into gut-wrenching sobs.

"I'm a crier too," I said, cuddling her. "My dad won't watch movies with me for fear of my ghastly emotional scenes."

"It's not the movie." She buried her face in my lap, and her tears became so violent, she was heaving. I was staring to panic.

"Virginie, what's wrong?"

"I'm in love, hopelessly in love."

"The Starbucks guy?"

"His name is Caleb. He's an artist. A brilliant one. His paintings will be in a gallery one day. We met last summer in the Hamptons. The moment I saw him, I fell in love, and he said the same about me. Our souls connected." The peacock feathers fluttered in the rush of air behind her words.

"I could see that connection from a distance at Starbucks."

"We made love every night under the stars." She had a glow about her, the kind of glow you only have when you're in love.

"What's the problem?"

"He's poor. I grew up poor. I don't want to be poor ever again."

Her body couldn't hold her sorrow, and it spilled out into every corner of the apartment.

She unraveled the mystery of her youth with quivering breaths and withering tears. Virginie was from a fishing village in the North of France, a place she despised so much she wouldn't tell me the name. Her mother was once a beautiful woman, but she married the wrong man, and the bitterness of an unhappy life had taken its toll. She died when Virginie was young. She hadn't seen or spoken to her father in more than ten years.

"I met a group of businessmen on the train to Paris, which led me here. Nothing beautiful existed before New York. My life started in this city."

She had reinvented herself, and no one knew really anything about her. She was so whimsical and magical and completely entrancing that I, myself, never gave any thought to her backstory.

"I want people to take care of me and buy me beautiful things. But Alex, the sex, the passion; he's with me body and soul. I don't know how to live without him."

"Why have you never spoken about him?"

"I don't talk about Caleb with anyone. It would be bad if anyone knew."

She turned away from me. "It's complicated."

It wasn't complicated. The gravy train would come to an abrupt halt if there was a man in her life.

"Does Caleb know about your life?"

"Yes," she whispered. "He's the only other person who knows everything."

I'd never felt so connected to anyone, ever, except maybe Mike, but he was a guy. This was different.

"Does he know about all your paramours?"

"Yes, but now he is giving me an ultimatum. He wants me to give them all up and move in with him or he'll leave me."

It was unfathomable that a woman such as Virginie would deny herself the possibility of an extraordinary life, a real life, full of real love, because of money. It was tragic.

"*Swept Away* is the story of a woman married to a very rich man. She has everything she ever wanted. But then she falls in love with the sexiest, most incredible human being. A true, real, all-consuming love." She was using every part of her body to convey her inner torment. "But she flew away from him because she didn't want to give up her glamorous life." Her voice was raw and ravaged. "That's me."

"Virginie, you can rewrite the ending of that movie for yourself. Choose love, choose Caleb."

"Where we will live? You said yourself, how do people survive?"

"You can make your own money." She recoiled from the idea. "You said real estate was a hobby? You could sell sand to the Arabs."

"Hmmm, it's funny you should say that." She sniffed. "My prince is in town next week. He said he's bringing me something out of this world."

"Tell him you're in love with Caleb."

"That won't matter to him."

What is wrong with these people? How could it not matter?

"I'm sure it'll matter to Caleb!"

"Of course it would." I could sense the wheels or her mind whirling, searching for a way to spin this part of the story. "Can't I just see him and get my out-of-this-world present?"

"Absolutely not."

"It's not like I have to have sex with him. It's just dinner, and maybe a blow job."

"Oh, well, if that's all it is."

"Exactly," she said definitively. Sarcasm wasn't lost on her. It was nicer to believe that I understood and was in agreement.

"No more blow jobs, no more presents, no more of this." My arms spread wide open to the lush surroundings, which had lost all their appeal. "You have to walk away or you'll regret it forever."

She acquiesced. "Like all the people who watched Madonna's version of *Swept Away.*"

Chapter 35

"**HI LORI. I'M HOME.**" I headed straight to the bathroom and peered inside. Kudos to the maid, who had made some improvement, but there was a photo in my mind's eye that would haunt me forever.

#plumbaphobia#youtakethegoodyoutakethebad#bathroomfrom-hell#haunted

"Hey girl." Lori leaned against her bedroom door, naked save for her lacy underwear. Her glorious black silly mane cascaded over her shoulders "Can I trust you?"

"Of course." I was hardly a vault, but Mike was my biggest confidant, and whatever she had to say would doubtless have no bearing on our life back home.

"The casting." I thought she might explode then and there. My fingers and toes were crossed. "It's to be a judge on a new reality TV show," she squealed. "It's between me and one other girl, who is a total has-been, but the producer is way into me. I know reality TV."

"You're an expert." All the time she spent glued to those shows was paying off. "You're going to be amazing on that show!"

"I know, right? I'm so over Tyra. I'm bringing drama back to reality."

I wanted to hug her but the overt nakedness was still awkward for me. "When will you know?"

"I'll know when they know. I can't wait to be bicoastal."

How could she be so casual about the not knowing? How could she sleep?

"Lori, this is huge!"

"Girl, I killed at that casting," she said, flicking her hair and exposing her nipples. "You believed in me."

Every time the phone rang, my body froze. Could this be it? Did she get it? Chloe must have sensed my anxiety, because when my phone rang, she jumped on the couch and put her head in my lap.

"You booked Jane Taylor. Way to go, doll." Robin delivered the news with a measure of casualness. Business as usual, but I suspected she was more excited for me than she let on. "I'll shoot you an email with the details."

"I did it!" I yelled, and Lori flew out of her bedroom. But no one was more excited than Chloe, who continued barking for five straight minutes.

"A real job! My first booking with RADIANT is this Friday! Fifteen hundred dollars for a ten-hour day!"

Lori displayed the same enthusiasm for my victory.

"Things are heating up in this apartment!" She bypassed the high five and went straight in for a naked hug.

My mum was over the moon when she heard the news, and my dad muttered something supportive but unintelligible in the background. Mike emoted a subdued degree of enthusiasm; he didn't want me to get overly excited until the job was over. Virginie and Tyler wanted to meet for a glass of wine, but I wanted to stay low key all week to mentally prep for Friday.

There was no way I would be able to sleep tonight. I'd never been this excited about anything, except maybe when I still believed in Santa Claus.

I texted Dante to tell him I couldn't work Thursday. He didn't ask any questions, and answered "No problem," with an emoji blowing me a kiss.

Hmmm.

⋛☺⋚

I stopped into Gristedes to pick up some Saran Wrap, but mostly I wanted to tell Keisha about Jane Taylor. At least something positive came from my day at *O* magazine.

She was leaning against her register, flipping through a *Soap Opera Digest.* Her hair was longer, and she was wearing makeup. Her fake eyelashes were fab.

"Keisha, you look amazing."

"Girl, I always look amazing, but I turned up the heat today."

"Why'd you turn up the heat?"

"Me and my girls are celebrating tonight," she said with a shoulder shimmy, "because I got accepted into grad school at Hunter."

"Keisha is smart as fuck," Tonya said.

"Yay!" I got my shimmy on too.

"Girl, I don't know what that is," Keisha said while assessing my moves.

I leaned over the conveyer belt to give her a hug.

"Damn girl," Keisha said, leaning away from me. "It's all good but no hugging."

"You're extra," Tonya said, returning to her phone. I assumed *extra* wasn't a compliment.

"Well, congratulations! That's awesome." My news seemed somewhat minor now, but it was still worth sharing. "I know it's not grad school awesome, but I wanted to tell you I got a job modeling for Jane Taylor."

"Jane Taylor?" Tonya looked at me and scrunched up her face. "Those are some ugly ass clothes."

At least she was honest.

"You can shut your mouth, Tonya," Keisha said, and Tonya just shrugged.

Keisha smiled at me like my catalog job was just as much cause to celebrate as getting into Hunter's graduate program. "Proud of you, girl."

Chapter 36

ALTHOUGH THERE WOULD BE A HAIR AND MAKEUP team beautifying me, I was bringing my A game, which included a blowout, a manicure, and a pedicure. Thank you "Ballet Slippers" by ESSI, my hands and feet had never looked so marvelous. Despite the shower conundrum, my entire self was operating at a 10. A Joie cardigan draped over a simple gray Tee, my Burberry open and relaxed, captured a classic urban vibe. My rag & bone boyfriend jeans made their first public appearance, and hidden beneath them were my new nude Calvins. I couldn't wait to show Davide. I strode into the studio wearing my aviators.

"Hello." Marcel greeted me with a double kiss. He was sporting the same jeans and remarkable bulge. "Grab some breakfast and head straight to hair and makeup. It's going to be a long one today."

Nothing should have made me happier than finding Lisa, with a head full of rollers, munching on a breakfast burrito, but Miguel—LumiYa's Miguel—was doing her hair.

Heat prickled in my jaw and rose up my neck, but I stood my ground with confidence. "Hello."

"Hi baby," Miguel said. "You look super gorge."

All is forgiven.

"Hey babes," Lisa said, "we have thirty shots. Let's bang this shit out."

"Brian is going to be here any minute," Miguel said.

Could it be my Brian?

He whisked into makeup with his homemade tofu scramble. "How's my beautiful Canadian girl? I saw your name on the call sheet."

"Yay, it's you." My connection to everyone on the team fed my confidence. My epic failures were behind me. Jane Taylor entrusted us with her brand, and we were going to bang out thirty shots for her ecommerce.

Davide strode in, whipped off his Prada sunglasses, and tossed his Salvatore Ferragamo tote over his shoulder. "Marcel has got to stop stuffing those socks in his jeans."

I knew it.

"He thinks he's, like, an ad for H&M. Going all David Beckham on us."

"Let's get started on you, Miss Canada," Brian said. I sat down and put Linus on my lap. "I have a towel, my lovely. You don't need that."

"This isn't a towel. It's Linus. He goes wherever I go."

There was a collective adoring gasp, and we made an awesome Instagram collage starring Linus. Everyone loved him. Did I love everyone touching him, and wearing him like a scarf? No. It was horrifying. But our posts got tons of likes, and I picked up some new followers.

#Linus#hegoeswhereverIgo#securityblanket #janetaylor#modellife#studiolife #glamsquad #lovemyjob

"Nice Calvins, honey," Davide whispered as he finished pinning my outfit.

I marched out onto the set ready to rock that white backdrop.

"I'm Tony," the photographer said, and picked up his camera. "You know what to do."

There were considerably more people in the studio since my arrival at 7:45 a.m. and they were all gathered around a boardroom table watching me, which was somewhat unnerving. But when Marcel said, "You look gorgeous, Alex," I went for it.

My hand went straight to my slightly cocked hip.

"No. We don't do hands on hips here."

No problem. I dropped that hand and flashed my red-carpet-ready smile.

"No. Softer smiles. Can you do something with your arms?"

No problem. I crossed my arms, and stared down that lens with a hint of a smile.

"No. We don't like crossed arms. Do some looks away from the camera."

No problem. I turned profile and looked up.

"No. Now we can't see the clothes. Try using the pocket of the pants."

Hmmm.

"No. Just a thumb in the pocket."

The shift in the studio's energy was stifling. Brian, that sweet man, came to me and pretended to touch up my lips.

"You're doing great," he whispered. "Put a little space between your arm and your body."

"Try a small step to camera," Tony said. He looked unimpressed with my attempts and added, "Watch your mark, Alice."

Alice?

"Alice, you see that black tape. Stop there or you're out of focus, okay?"

Tony's assistants were trying not to look at me as the train wreck unfolded. The frustrated murmurs throughout the studio were gaining momentum and volume.

"Hey Davide." Tony stopped shooting. "Is Lisa ready?"

She stepped effortlessly onto the set and lit up the studio. Stepping, jumping, and prancing gracefully toward the camera, always hitting her mark.

"Alice, are you watching?" Tony asked as he snapped away. "Just do it like her."

Highly unlikely.

Despite valiant efforts on my behalf, and a full fifteen minutes, no one was satisfied with my first outfit. Lisa ended up wearing it, and had finished ten shots before noon. I was still struggling with my second.

Lisa, Brian, and I sat together at lunch. Davide was sandwiched between Marcel and Miguel at the opposite end of the table, dining with the rest of the crew who had abandoned me. I could hear Marcel murmuring over the munching of their quinoa and kale salad. "Fuck. So much for wrapping early. She's a mare."

"The first day is always the hardest, babes," Lisa reassured me. "Marcel's a wanker. Ignore him."

"Look, girls, we started something this morning," Brian said.

Instagram was lit up with peeps and their versions of Linus and childhood stuffies.

#nevergonnagiveitup#kidsforever#goeswhereverIgo#memories#bffs4ever#love.

Of course, there was Lydia. "I remember your towel." #memories#highschool #sheneededhersecurityblanket

Her passive-aggressive Insta-bullying was more than I could bear today, and Brian spent the duration of the lunch rubbing my shoulders as I fought back tears.

There was some minimal progress on the sweater-set portion of the afternoon. There wasn't a lot of movement, but there was much less stiffness.

"Remember talking hands, Alice," Tony said, trying to mask his irritation. "Pretend you're talking to someone."

This was a helpful hint. Feigning conversation was a skill set in my repertoire, and my hands no longer looked like they belonged in a morgue. However, when the dresses appeared, the afternoon spiraled on a downward trajectory. Lisa shot twenty-two outfits, ten of which were the dresses. I didn't know what to do with my legs and was convinced everyone was discussing my cankles.

"Davide, we're going to be here all night." Marcel's ceaseless foot tapping grew louder in response to any move I made.

A cock of the hip to the left.

Tap.

Tap.

Tap.

A twirl to the right.

Tap.

Tap.

Tap.

"Give the damn dresses to Lisa. Put her in a sweater set."

Marcel didn't even use my name?

It was over for me, just like that day in the Hamptons. My whole body was overcome with lockjaw. When at last my shot was finished, Marcel announced, "We're going to have to reshoot that, Davide, but I'm way over it today."

I can't even catalog model.

The shame and the guilt were insufferable. I didn't bang out anything. It was my fault we wrapped late. I was bucking under the emotional baggage and shrank farther into myself. "I'm so sorry to all of you," I said, clenching every muscle to contain my tears, and ran out of the studio.

There was no time to mourn. My shift at Le Brasserie started in half an hour, and there were no taxis anywhere. I hightailed it to the subway. The train was approaching as I shot down the stairs, shamelessly pushing people out of the way. I flew across the platform and launched myself through the sliding doors, which closed on my Birkin.

Really?

I wrenched it out, ripping the faux leather, and fell backward, almost taking out some German tourists. The train lurched forward and then I saw him. Linus was trapped between the doors.

"Linus!" My piercing shrill shot through subway car. I grabbed him and pulled with every ounce of strength that my sad, skinny gorilla arms could muster. As the train sped up Linus started slipping through my fingers.

"Help! Help! Please anyone, help me!" I was laying on the ground with my feet braced against the doors, engaged in an epic life-or-death tug-of-war. The other passengers distanced themselves from me and watched emotionless as Linus was ripped from my raw, throbbing hands. I lay curled in a fetal position, sobbing inconsolably.

When we reached the next stop people just stepped over me. The German tourists were laughing, and an obnoxious obese Texan quipped, "Only in New York, kids, only in New York." Once having manipulated myself to an upright position, I glimpsed at my reflection in the window. Miguel's magnificent hair had morphed into a wild rat's nest, and my tear-stained cheeks were streaked with wretched subway filth. Mercifully, Brian had used waterproof mascara. Every passenger was staring at me. As we approached the Fifth Avenue station, I smoothed out my classic Burberry, which was now a disturbing shade of dirt, and said, "My Linus is dead and every one of you let it happen."

$\overset{>}{\sim} \odot \overset{<}{\sim}$

"Alex, what happened to you?" Dante put his arm around me. "Sit down, beautiful. Laurent, get her some water."

"Linus is dead."

"I'm so sorry." Laurent rubbed my shoulders. "Is he your grandfather?"

"No," I said despondently.

"Your grandmother?"

"No."

"It's her blue towel," Dante said.

He remembered.

"Patrick, could you pour us all a glass of wine?"

"All this because of that rag?" Laurent asked as he pulled out a chair. The four of us sat together and drank a toast to Linus.

"Thank you, guys." Tears flowed down my cheeks, past my chin, and onto my lap, where Linus should have been. "I know how this must look, but we've been together my whole life."

"Is it just me, or does everyone else think this is crazy?" Laurent murmured to Patrick, but when he saw my tear-stained face, he smiled and handed me a napkin.

"Alex, do you want to go home?" Dante asked gently.

I didn't have a home, not without Linus. "I think it's better to be as busy as possible."

Laurent scrunched up his face. "You might want to freshen up."

Oh, God. Another bathroom.

I grabbed my torn Birkin and gloved up. After wiping away layers of dirt with Le Brasserie's sandpaper-like toilet paper, I emerged looking no less haggard, with my hair up in a very sad bun.

The restaurant was busy, which kept me physically occupied, but everything was on rote. Psychologically, I had shut down. Nothing eased my suffering, not even two bottles of house champagne. The dark cloud hanging over me seemed to engulf the guys too; there was a heaviness in all our movements. Laurent and Patrick both screwed up an order. We mentally willed the last of the dinner crowd out of the restaurant before midnight.

"Please, let us put you in a taxi," Patrick offered.

"I'm going to have a cigarette. I got this."

Laurent looked ready to crawl out of his skin as he shuffled toward the door. "Sweatpants, are you okay?"

I'm drunk, in mourning, and headed back to Lori's apartment to sleep on a couch.

"Really, I'm fine."

Dante waved them both away. "I've got this."

He let me smoke inside the restaurant while he finished cashing out. Words escaped me, and he was kind enough not to force conversation. Midway through my fourth cigarette, he said, "Alex, why don't you come home with me?"

This was an interesting turn of events.

"What the hell? Why not? Let's go home together."

Chapter 37

"SPRING STREET BETWEEN BROADWAY AND WOOSTER," Dante said. I plastered myself to the far side of the taxi. "Are you going to try and stay this far away from me all night?" "Probably."

We pulled up to an Italian restaurant, where a clique of girls was outside, smoking. They were indiscernible from each other; all of them were short, with fabulous long brown hair, and seventy-five percent of their über-thin bodies was exposed to the elements. At what point would hypothermia set in?

"Hi Dante," they cooed, crooning to see who was getting out of the taxi with him.

He smiled and quickly ushered me into the building and up three steep flights of stairs. "Come in and relax."

The loft's hardwood floors and brick walls amplified the sound of my choppy breathing.

"I thought you were used to stairs." Dante glanced in the enormous mirror hanging over a distressed wood dining table, which certainly was large enough for an intimate encounter. He settled into the enormous leather couches that had been custom made to fit the room. "What do you think?"

"Hmm," I said, staring at the stripper pole in the center of the room. "Do you get a lot of use out of this?"

"It's fun. You should try it."

"You've tried it then, have you?"

"No, but that's what the girls tell me."

"What girls might that be?" I peered out of the eight-foot windows, which overlooked Spring Street. "The lovely ladies downstairs, perhaps?"

"I think they may have had a go." A Cheshire catlike grin took over his face.

"Are you familiar with Lewis Carroll?"

"Alex in Wonderland?" He was smooth. "No, it's Alice. *Alice in Wonderland.*"

"The photographer called me Alice all day. The whole shoot was a fiasco."

"Why don't you sit down and chill? Would you like some wine?"

"I drank two bottles of house champagne already. I might have to drink myself into a stupor every night for the rest of my life." I collapsed on the couch and buried my face in a pillow. "I can't sleep without Linus."

"It was hard for me to give up my doudou when I was four years old. At twenty-one, it must be devastating." He worked hard to suppress a smile.

"I know it's hard to understand, but he's a part of me."

"I think most children feel that way."

"I'm not a child. I'm not Alice."

"Alex, I'm kidding. I see it's painful, and I'm sorry."

I was mesmerized by his hands as he wrapped his long, slim fingers around the shaft of the wine opener, gently piercing the cork and easing it out of the bottle.

"That's impressive." My voice was breathy and heavy.

"Years of practice. I studied food service, restaurant management, and culinary arts in Paris."

"How long have you been in New York?"

"Eight years. I was turning twenty-one and my English was terrible." He smiled, fingering the cork. "Luckily, I met Laurent. He got me a job at Le Brasserie and offered me a place to stay."

"What about the place you got fired from?"

"When they fired me, Le Brasserie took me back. After a few years, they made me the manager."

"Now what?"

"I'd like to open my own restaurant. Are you almost through with your interrogation?"

I was just getting warmed up, and unwrapped a new pack of Marlboros.

"Did you always want to go to New York?" I asked.

"It's the greatest city in the world. How about you?"

"I don't know where I wanted to go." My eyes followed the wisps of smoke from my cigarette.

"If you don't know where you're going, any road will get you there." He shrugged. "The Cheshire Cat."

The sapiosexual in me wanted to devour him. "Every adventure requires a first step," I said, staying in theme.

"Are you enjoying your adventure here in the city?"

"I like my friends, and Le Brasserie, but the modeling thing is freaking hard."

"What made you want to do it?"

I ran through some plausible answers. Easy money. Traveling would be fun. What came out of my mouth was a surprise to both of us.

"I wanted people to think I was cool."

Seriously, Alex? Is it the wine?

"That's interesting," Dante said.

The word you're looking for is "pathetic."

"Have you satisfied your need to feel cool?"

I'm more insecure now than ever.

"No."

"For what it's worth, I think you're cool, even in your sweatpants."

"You know what? I love those sweatpants." I was sick of defending them.

"That doesn't make you less cool. It just means you have bad taste."

I threw a pillow at him, which he successfully dodged without spilling his wine.

"You prefer Sheila's taste in clothes?" She had been festering in my subconscious; her name left a sour residue on my tongue.

"You said that with poison in your voice."

"I kind of hate her. She's part of what has made things so hard."

Her, Darlene, and my ugly body's inability to model.

"Sheila's not so bad."

"You're not a girl."

"That's true." He laughed out loud. "Alex, you're beautiful, and people like you."

I liked the way he said "beautiful." He used the word a lot, but his inflection was different, and it carried more meaning. "Girls can be weird with each other." I liked the way he shook his head in a perplexed fashion. He didn't understand mean girls either. "She was born gorgeous and rich. That's not her fault."

It's her fault that she's a bitch.

"Her father is one of the investors of Le Brasserie."

WTF?

"We work for Sheila's father?" My blood had passed boiling point and my skin was pulsating.

"Not exactly." Dante approached his explanation with kid gloves. "Stuart is a silent investor. He's never even been to Le Brasserie."

Dante knows Sheila's father?

"I have to quit."

"Alex, relax." My jaw was clenched so tightly, my teeth were starting to hurt.

Sheila Summerville's father and Le Brasserie?

"I have to quit." Today may have been the worst day of my life so far, and this recent development spawned the behavior of a feral animal.

"The Summervilles have a lot of money invested in restaurants and real estate all around New York."

"Is that why everyone fawns all over her?"

"People really like her. She's a New York City socialite, she's fun, and she's sexy."

"I have to quit." There were other bartending jobs. There had to be another way.

"You have to quit because of Sheila? That's crazy. Alex, everyone loves you."

I was pacing like the poor guy who hits himself. I felt dizzy and powerless.

"What's the deal with you and her? Were you a thing? Are you a thing?"

"There is no deal. We're weren't a thing. We aren't a thing."

That revelation definitely improved my vibe, and under different circumstances it might have given me more satisfaction than a bag of Oreos, but there was no way to un-know what I now knew.

"What about you? Do you have a thing? Someone back in Canada?"

"No."

"No lovers?"

There was no way to suppress the blood rushing to my cheeks. "Is this a French thing? First Virginie, and now you. Why is my sex life a point of interest?"

"I believe you started the conversation."

"How many women have you slept with?"

And down the rabbit hole we go.

"I don't know the exact number."

Why did it matter? I had no claim to him. And even if we were involved, was there a number that would be unacceptable? Doubtful. I might even find solace in his colorful past. Nobody wants a fumbler.

He picked up the empty bottle of wine. "Do you think you are drunk enough to fall asleep, or shall I open another?"

I should have been facedown on the floor by now but rage, adrenaline, and pheromones were coursing through my veins.

"We should probably call it a night."

"You're welcome to stay here. The couch is really comfortable."

The couch? I had a couch at Lori's.

"Thanks, but I'm going home."

Dante followed me to the door and offered me my jacket.

That's it?

"Dante, thanks for tonight."

"It's my pleasure. If there's anything I can do—"

Laurent barreled through the doorway, knocking the two of us ass over tip. We lay sprawled on top of each other.

"You couldn't wait to get upstairs?"

"Alex was just leaving," Dante said.

"So you just finished upstairs."

"Laurent, enough." Dante stood and brushed himself off. "Alex, I'm sorry."

"All good." My bladder was about to explode. It'd been approaching a crisis situation an hour ago. "See you guys tomorrow."

There was no way to sleep without Linus, and although I'd sworn it off, I even ventured onto Instagram. Anything to get my mind off everything that had happened in the past twenty-four hours. The first post to pop up was all the reason I needed to stop venturing. Lydia Baker, with her legs wrapped around Troy Sephton, my high-school crush, on a beach in Hawaii. #lookwhoifound#there-arenoaccidents#loveconnection#surf#sand#him&me#forever.

I'm sure it wasn't an accident because we all knew that Troy was a surf instructor somewhere in Hawaii. He didn't have an Instagram account, one more reason to love him, but it couldn't have been that hard to find him. Nonetheless, they looked great together, #bronzed #beachready and radiating #JBF.

Barf.

Why would Troy hook up with her? He avoided that love connection all through high school. You and her forever? For the love of God, why Troy? Why did Dante offer me the couch? Why didn't he try to have sex with me? He couldn't be that selective. What was wrong with me? How can I keep working at Le Brasserie? My brain was in meltdown mode, like my own personal Chernobyl.

Chapter 38

MY LINENS WERE FOLDED AND I WAS SEATED rigidly upright, staring at a blank TV screen when Lori sauntered into the living room at 7:30 a.m.

"Morning. You got home late." Her Ambien-heavy eyes brightened when she asked, "Did you do anything fun?"

"I was hanging out with the guys at their apartment. I didn't get much sleep."

I didn't get any freaking sleep.

"You look good considering, minus those bags under your eyes. There's some cucumber in the fridge."

"I'm not hungry." At least something was positive.

"Not to eat, silly. Cut two slices, lay them over your eyelids, and cover them with a warm facecloth for ten minutes. You'll be fresh as a daisy. I'll grab some coffees."

Two flights of stairs were all I could muster but that merited an 8, when taking recent events into account. The cucumbers were refreshing but my mood was sallow and pasty.

"Oooh, your eyes look so much better, but you seem a little forlorn. Is everything okay?"

CHAPTER 38

I don't know how to begin answering that question.

"I drank way too much last night, and I have to work brunch today."

Did I mention Sheila's father's investment in Le Brasserie?

"I'm just not up for it."

"I totally get it. Sometimes when I'm really low energy I take a Ritalin."

"Is that like Adderall?"

Adderall is one compound away from methamphetamine, and I refused to get involved with that even to study.

"Lord no! It's like strong coffee that gives you a little kick to jump-start your day. Do you want one?"

"What the hell? Why not? I would love a Ritalin."

"I'll have one too."

She brought out a shoe box full of pill bottles. "Now where is that dang Ritalin?"

"Are you sure you should be taking all that stuff?" I was reconsidering my decision.

"They're all prescription. It's not like it's oxycodone." She handed me a little pink pill and a coffee. "Bottoms up."

My skills with a blow-dryer were becoming worthy of Lori's hair-dryer. It wasn't a salon blowout, but after thirty-five minutes of effort, my hair was shaping up to be a solid 8. My wardrobe was in recycle mode, but today was still special because peeking out of my Paige jeans was a hint of my black lace Hanky Panky thong. Wardrobe 10. My spirits were on the rise.

"Lori, I'm leaving. Thanks again. I feel better already."

She popped her head out of the bathroom. "Great! And the Ritalin hasn't even kicked in yet."

It hasn't kicked in yet?

"By the way, you might have trouble sleeping tonight. It can cause insomnia."

Insomnia?

"But it's such a low dose, I wouldn't worry." She tossed the bothersome side effect away with a flick of her hand. "Have fun today."

⫸ ☺ ⫷

My heart hurt when I stepped onto the sidewalk, looking up at the awning and its gold seraphim letters "Le Brasserie." The tarnish would never fade; I could never feel comfortable here now.

"Hey sweatpants," Laurent said. "Today is going to be crazee." The hip gyrating hadn't lost any of its charm. "You two probably need a triple espresso this morning. Patrick, our bartender, was leaving our place at four a.m."

Dante winked at me but I didn't acknowledge it. He was an angel last night, but among the Oreos, the Cheshire Cat, the ladies, the stripper pole, and the couch offer, his flirting was giving me whiplash. It came to me in the cab ride. Arianna and Iggy had popped up on my playlist.

One less problem without ya!

"I'm not interested," Patrick said. "But would you like a coffee, Alex?"

I most certainly didn't need a coffee and probably wouldn't need a coffee for the rest of my life.

"Alex, are you okay?" Dante asked.

Thoughts were coming into my mind so fast I didn't have time to process them, much less answer any questions. I grabbed the bar to steady myself. It felt like a freight train was running through my body. My two-finger salute, followed by a harried walk to the bathroom, did little to convey a sense of okay.

I fell against the door and collapsed on the terra-cotta tiles. I couldn't work like this. I couldn't do anything like this. For the love of God, I was sitting on the floor of a public bathroom.

Alex! You have to get your shit together! You have to get out there and do your job!

In a blink, the intensity of the kick in began to subside. My body and my brain were vibrating with a sense of control I'd never known. If this was what invincible felt like, then let me show up as a superhero in the next life.

I paraded into the middle of the restaurant. "Let's do this."

"Yeah baby," Laurent said.

"Patrick, how's the acting?" I asked, whipping through my bar setup. "New agent? New auditions? It's a tough gig, eh?"

"Alex, you're talking really fast."

"I'm not good on no sleep."

"What's going on with you?" Dante asked as the lunch crowd rolled in. "You can't stand still and your eyes are like saucers."

"It's all good. Brunch, let's do it."

Sheila and her glam squad sauntered in at about 2:00 p.m. Natalia, Caroline, Sylvia, and the Asian girl from Jack Studios, who was wearing the exact same outlandish outfit, took over the entire banquet on the left side of the restaurant. I downed a glass of champagne and waved at them.

"Hi ladies! You all look amazing. Big kiss."

Sheila threw her arms around Dante and flashed her plastic-fantastic smile.

Were those her real teeth? Socialite skank.

All the attention Sheila worked so hard for landed square on a true showstopper when Virginie arrived moments later. She made her rounds, graciously greeting everyone, including Sheila, then beelined straight toward me.

"Alex, you're glorious. How are you, chérie?"

"The shoot was a nightmare. Linus is dead. Sheila's father owns part of Le Brasserie. I went home with Dante, but nothing happened."

"Mais non!" I'm not sure which she found the most disturbing, but I was about to up the ante.

"And I'm on Ritalin."

"Do you have ADD?"

Huh?

"Do I look like I have it?"

"In this moment, yes."

Tyler swaggered through the doors, acknowledging the crowd's whistling, and strutted straight to the bar, where I was huddled with Virginie.

"Ladies, why so secretive?"

"Alex is on Ritalin," Virginie said.

"That could be fun. Do you have any more?" Tyler looked at my eyes and grimaced. "How much did you take?"

"Not much, but I feel really good." Laurent was waving a check at me. "I have to go."

They both grabbed me and said in unison, "Don't drink too much."

Dante was watching me from Sheila's table, where she had been groping him for the past half hour. They certainly looked like "a thing," but his exploits were no longer of interest to me under accordance with my new purely platonic plan.

Ooh, I like that. PPP. It sounded like the name of some hip eighties band. *PPP, yeah, PPP . . .*

Patrick's sudden grasp on my arm scared the crap out me. "Get a lighter ready."

"What? Where? When?"

"Alex, keep it together. We need you." He stood on the bar. "Ladies and gentlemen, may I have your attention? Let's wish the lovely Keiko a very happy birthday."

Sheila's friend Keiko threw off her fluffy white jacket, exposing her gaunt midsection.

She had been wolfing down frites since she arrived. Maybe she only ate on Saturdays.

The clapping and cheering commenced when Patrick cued up Stevie Wonder's "Happy Birthday." Laurent danced his way to Sheila's table with a magnum of Veuve Clicquot alit with sparklers.

"Shots for everyone!" I yelled, and personally delivered them to every table, even Sheila's, where Keiko actually hugged me.

"I know you got kicked out of Metropolis and Sheila doesn't like you, but you're the best bartender ever." She stood on the banquet and yelled, "Let's hear it for the bartender!" She then fell ass backward on top of me. It's hard to believe I buckled under all 110 pounds of her. Alas, there we were splayed across the dirt, wine, and general filth of Le Brasserie's floor. I offered Keiko my hand. "Le Brasserie, it happens to all of us."

Sheila and Dante brought her outside, where she vomited all over the sidewalk.

"Her digestive tract probably hasn't seen food in weeks. Silly bitch," Tyler said.

Dante was hailing a taxi for Sheila and Keiko, but there was no way Sheila was leaving before I set the record straight.

Tyler was hot on my heels. "Hold up, baby lamb, where are you going?"

"Sheila, oh, Sheila," I sang the words. The eighties were happening for me today.

"What do you want?" she snapped.

"Just to be clear, I left Metropolis. They didn't kick me out."

"Just to be clear, I could care less."

"You *couldn't* care less," I corrected her. "If you could care less, there's room for some more caring. Thank you for caring, Sheila."

We stood nose-to-nose. "Do you want me to tell all these people about RDJ? What would Dante think about that?"

"We never got into that last night. I guess we just ran out of time."

"Details, baby lamb," Tyler said.

I turned my back on Sheila, which was a small lapse in judgment on my part because my brain didn't register that she would be privy to what I was saying.

"I left at four a.m. but nothing happened. He didn't even try. Bizarre, right?"

"You're just not his type." Sheila strolled toward Dante, kissed him on the lips, and whispered something before her voluptuous silhouette dissolved into the taxi.

"Let's get inside before you do any further damage," Tyler said.

We were but moments from the door when someone hollered, "Is the bartender wearing a bra today?!"

Ooh how exciting. Suddenly it was all about me.

"Yes, friends and lovers, I'm in Hanky Panky from top to bottom." I fingered the lace of my thong. "They make everyone's ass look great, don't they, girls?"

I then turned and kissed Tyler, deep, wet, tongue, and all.

After several rounds of shots, I gave up my post behind the bar and was gutted when Dante killed the music at 5:00 p.m.

"Alex, why don't you pick up your cut next week. I think it's time for you to go."

He was telling me to go? Whatevs.

Virginie and Tyler put us in a taxi. "What are going to do now? I'm ready for anything."

"I noticed," Tyler said.

"OMG I kissed you! Have you ever kissed a woman before? Did you like it?"

"It was too much tongue, baby lamb. Is it really up to a gay man to teach a woman how to kiss?"

"Chérie, you're a hot mess. Let's go to my apartment and smoke a joint."

Three joints later, I was still flying, but it wasn't fun. The candles burned like spotlights, dust bunnies were drifting everywhere and settling on my skin. "When will the Ritalin stop?"

"You just have to let it run its course." Tyler opened one eye. "The bloody FDA puts an approved label on everything, but pharmaceuticals are drugs."

"This is hideous."

Virginie brought me a pale blue facecloth. "I know it's not Linus, but it is Frette."

It was soft and pretty, but it didn't have prickles and wasn't soothing at all.

꒰ ☺ ꒱

The full moon lit up Manhattan's skyline, and glints of light speckled the terrace. The Ritalin was finally wearing off. Shattered and shivering in the dark, there were no tears left to cry.

"Look at yourself!" I said aloud.

"Look at you indeed." Virginie closed the sliding glass door and joined me on the terrace, wrapping us in a cashmere throw. We stayed there and watched the sunrise.

"Virginie, Sheila's father is an investor in Le Brasserie."

"Don't let things that don't matter upset you." She waved it away. "Nothing's changed. It's still the same Brasserie." She snuggled into me. "Dante is still the same."

"Dante and I went home together and he didn't even try to kiss me."

"Maybe that's because you're special. Be open to the possibility of love."

I wanted to be open. I wanted her words to hypnotize me as they always had.

"Lydia Baker is in Hawaii and she's bewitched my high-school crush. They're in love."

"Your heart is here. Follow where it's leading you."

It wasn't leading me anywhere fun, that much was becoming clear.

She marveled at the sky. "The colors are so beautiful, the blues, the fuchsia, and the luminescence of the clouds. The feminine moon and the masculine sun shining simultaneously, reflecting each other's magnificence. The world is wonderful."

It didn't feel wonderful. My teeth were chattering.

"Alex, you're freezing. Come inside."

Tyler was awake and spellbound by his cell phone. He fondled the Queu Queu—black marble case. "Poodle, this may not be the best time, but it's better to hear it from me."

"Freaking hell, what now?"

The three of us huddled around Virginie's laptop, watching a video of Linus's death.

"Bloody Germans. They should be ashamed of themselves."

"It's true, chérie. Someone should have helped you."

After having watched the clip ten times, I'm wasn't so sure. I looked like an escapee from a mental asylum.

"You should start your own YouTube channel, baby lamb. Five hundred and seventy thousand views—you're an Internet sensation."

Drugs, alcohol, cigarettes. I'm a bad sitcom episode, but there was no teachable moment in this mess. I was stone cold sober in that video.

"I'm out," I said.

"Out of what?" Virginie asked.

"The whole scene."

"It's crazy for everyone when they first get to the city. My time here has been a wild ride but I don't regret one minute of it." She grabbed a remote and the surround system belted out, "*Non, rien de rien. Non, je ne regrette rien.*" Virginie sang along.

"She is saying that she has no regrets. All the memories, the good and the bad, made her part of who she is."

You don't want anyone to know the parts of you that made you who you are.

"You're comparing me to Edith Piaf?"

The iconic Edith Piaf, who, incidentally, died of liver failure?

"She is sweeping away the memories and starting fresh and so can you! Live your life anyway that you choose."

Didn't I recently give you the exact same advice?

"Forget the bloody video." Tyler shut the laptop.

Yeah, like that's going to make it go away. Was I this delusional about my modeling career?

"GFY, baby lamb. GFY."

"GFY? Seriously? How's that working with Raoul? Did you break up with him?" Tyler couldn't look at me, but I couldn't quit. "Is it just him, or do you let every man in your life treat you like shit? Are you waiting on an STD?"

"Chérie, take it easy."

"What about Caleb?" Tyler looked at Virginie.

"Tyler is one of your best friends and he doesn't even know his name." Blood rushed to my cheeks, and sweat was breaking out at the base of my scalp. "You know, all this time I've looked up to you, idolized you like you were some reincarnated Cleopatra overseeing an empire, or Natasha Rostova, or Holly Golightly, but you're a French Scarlett O'Hara who'd lie, and cheat"—she recoiled from my words—"and fuck anyone to get what she wants. So she'll never be poor again."

"Don't you dare judge me." She growled at me with all the ferocity of a caged animal.

"You've never been poor!"

"You twist the truth and make this false world you live in so intoxicating that stupid people like me want to live in it with you!"

"You have some serious issues, Alex. It's not your towel or your rubber gloves."

She called Linus a towel? An uncontrollable combustible anger was steadily building in my core. I was shaking.

"Your blue-collar background has jaded your views of the world. You have serious issues with people who have money because you're so insecure about yourself!"

I never realized until she said it but there is a piece of me that does resent rich people.

"Just because I want to make my own money doesn't mean I have issues. It's called self-respect. But what would you know about that?" I balled up her cashmere throw and chucked it across the room. "What's cashmere worth? A blow job? How about the apartment? How often does Michael need to be serviced?"

She put her hand over her heart like she'd been stabbed, her breath shallow.

"I created my life. I make the rules. I take the risks."

"You don't take real risks. You don't make the rules. You play by the rules. You play a part in the fantasy." My voice was trembling, and then my core exploded. "This is not real life!"

She looked at me like she'd never seen me before. "You're so insecure and too terrified of your own shadow to have a real life. Fear created your life."

I folded her blue Frette and laid it on the dining table. "I'm out."

I walked out and all the way back to Lori's.

Chapter 39

"HI DAD." Today, of all days, he picked up the phone. "Is Mum home?"

"No, she's at her exercises."

Shit. Sunday. Aquacize.

"How are you?" A blanket of cracked Himalayan sea salt coated the kitchen sink, each grain a symbol of all my experiences here in New York. Lori's salt grinder was indefatigable, and I kept making more.

"Watching some nonsense about Kate Middleton's pregnancy," he said.

I could hear the two-handed swat and readied myself for him to speak ad nauseam on the subject of the Royal Family, which would lead into the Catholic Church. He had the utmost respect for the Queen but resented the fact that she wasn't elected by "the people."

"Intelligent people behaving like sycophants, and they didn't even get to vote."

I wasn't sure in what direction he was going. The Pope, the Queen; either way, it was time to get off the phone.

"I'll leave you to it, Dad."

"Hold on then. How's New York?"

"Terrible. I lost Linus to the subway." The black pepper almost covered the salt-coated sink; there weren't enough peppercorns to crack for Linus.

"It's about bloody time. I've told your mother a grown woman shouldn't be carrying around a security blanket."

Now I'm a grown woman?

"A grown woman should be able to fly off to New York whenever she chooses, shouldn't she?" The pepper grinder was empty now, and the sink's interior was as black as my insides.

"Right then." There it was, the splash of scotch. Things were about to get serious.

"Your mother showed me some lovely pictures. She said the modeling was going quite well."

I was grateful he didn't know how to use Skype because if he saw me now, all his worst fears would be realized.

"It's not."

"You've had some jobs?"

"I've had two." I traced the number two in the sink and then turned on the Kohler taps to wash away the memories.

"Dad, they've been massive failures. I don't know what I'm doing."

"You've got to acquire the skills."

I guess it was time they knew. I threw cold water on my face and announced, "And I'm bartending on the side because I don't have any money."

"There you are then." I could hear the ice cubes rattling in his glass.

Huh?

"You're self-sufficient! It takes courage and ingenuity to make these artsy things work." This wasn't the response I was expecting from my stoical father. It bordered on supportive of my current life choices.

"I think"—the words got stuck in my throat—"I'm ready to come home." A lone tear fell down my cheek. The last of the pepper-salt water seeped down the drain.

"Look here, do you like what you're doing?"

Do I like what I'm doing?

I let the question churn inside me. The first thing that came to my mind was "Historically Speaking"—all the selfies chronicling every hopeless moment of my life. It's a constant reminder of my ever-mounting failures. That's why I need systems and rating scales; it's to prevent future failure. To gauge my progress, thwart unforeseen mishaps, and minimize the damage. I need to feel some semblance of control.

Maintaining control is a whole lot easier in the safety of controlled environments such as Safeway, university, and Mike's backyard. Now all the variables had changed.

I am afraid—all the time—of doing the wrong thing, saying the wrong thing, and wearing the wrong thing. Virginie is right: fear has created my life. Fear does control my decisions.

But here in New York, I face those fears every day. I keep getting it wrong, but I keep on going. I didn't know where it would take me but I'd never felt so alive. I don't need to be a model to be special. I can be anything I want! Maybe not a dancer or a singer, but maybe I could write lyrics, maybe I could write a book. My time here had given me loads of material. Little ol' messed-up me was finding her way in this crazy city, taking life by the lapels, and kicking some ass.

"Hello?!" my Dad yelled. "What's going on over there?"

"Dad, I love what I'm doing."

"You know what Winston Churchill said, 'Never, never, never give up.'"

"I love you, Dad."

Chapter 40

LOVING WHAT I WAS DOING WAS ALL WELL and good, but to move forward, three things needed to happen, and in this order: Erin, Robin, and Dante.

Rain pelted the windows as my taxi flew down the FDR. Dread was setting in. Today wasn't going to be great for me, or my hair. How is it possible that the classic Burberry trench, born in Great Britain, where it rains two hundred days a year, doesn't have a hood? I ran up the stairs to Erin's building cowering under the *New York Post*.

"Hi Erin. Thanks for seeing me last minute."

"How are you?" She instinctively radiated vulnerability and an openness that created space for me to fall apart. Tears gushed out of me, unleashing years of emotional trauma. Admittedly, a considerable amount was self-inflicted.

"Tired." Striving for acceptance and perfection throughout one's entire existence was exhausting. "I am not a cardboard cutout from a Target, Victoria's Secret, or freaking Jane Taylor catalog! I am not a carbon copy of a L'Oréal, Pantene, or Clinique campaign! I'm stepping out of that box and into myself, whomever that may be."

"*Namaste,*" Erin said.

"But to live that truth, I need to get real and honest with myself."

"That's a big challenge, but it will set you free."

"The rating scales, the systems, and the crippling insecurity might be hindering the process of self-discovery."

"Maybe we can work on letting go of the things that no longer serve you."

"I don't know how to let go of Linus." I didn't want to let go of him, ever.

"How about 'letting go' of your rating scale? It might ease some anxiety. Keeping a journal could be fun."

Journaling about disturbing events and unpleasant emotions didn't sound like stress relief.

"The Universe doesn't give you things that you're unable to deal with. Try to let go, breathe, and surrender."

Freaking hell, the Universe has been raining buckets of piss all over me for months. I surrender.

"Is that all you have in your bag of tricks?"

"It's the only way."

The half hour we spent mindfully breathing was mildly soothing, but it was über challenging without Erin guiding me through the process.

"Be gentle with yourself. These are big changes."

Living a less rigid life would be challenging, but my commitment to my real, honest self was unwavering.

"By the way, if I could be any of those women, I'd opt for the Victoria Secret models."

"Is it because of their ankles?" Erin asked, which sent us into paroxysms of laughter.

≥ ☺ ≤

There was nothing to be done about my hair, and it was operating at a 3 when I arrived at RADIANT's offices.

"Whatever is happening with you today isn't working," Robin said, eyeing my fro, my taupe wedge sneakers, and my subway-stained Burberry, which now looked polka-dotted from the enormous drops of rain. Wardrobe 3. In my defense, my boots hadn't been weatherproofed.

"Robin, they hated me at Jane Taylor. I ruined the whole shoot."

"You think you're the first girl who had a bad experience onset? You're a bit of a drama queen, doll."

Stefanie, who had mastered the art of multitasking, was on the phone, setting up a web page for one of Robin's new recruits. She held up a sign from the booking table: NO DRAMA.

"I don't know how to catalog-model." I felt ridiculous.

"No one does until they try. I gather Marcel and company weren't too helpful." She shrugged like she'd heard all this before.

"Catalog modeling is all technique. We can teach you those poses."

Stefanie, with the phone still cradled to her ear, moseyed over and performed a stunning series of catalog poses.

"It's not hard once you know what to do."

Stefanie positioned my hips, hands, and feet and guided me through some poses. My robotic modeling lacked all the fluidity of her movements.

"You're a little stiff, but you're getting there. Keep practicing, doll."

It occurred to me that Marcel and company didn't have to be such assholes. They could have shown me a few poses. If everyone had been as supportive as Brian and Lisa, the day would have gone much smoother, but they preferred to torture me. They enjoyed making make me feel like a loser. What's worse is I let them.

"This is why you asked to have a meeting?" Robin leaned back and propped her Sergio Rossi stilettos on her desk.

"That was Part A. Part B involves YouTube."

"I'm going to have to call you back," Stefanie said.

I watched them watching the clip. I couldn't look at the screen; the heartbreak was still too near.

"What is this?" Stefanie asked. "Drugs?"

"Linus's death caught on someone's phone. It's tragic on so many levels. He made his Instagram debut earlier that day at that freaking Jane Taylor job."

"Instagram?" Stefanie's cool demeanor was beginning to crack and she pulled up my feed. "This is good stuff. Your #setlife looks great." She executed a deliberate calm exhale.

"He was a sensation," I said as they examined the images and comments he had inspired.

"We'd been together since I was four. He wasn't just a security blanket. To speak of him as an inanimate object does a disservice to his memory." My finger wrapped around the lonesome curl that had fallen on my face. "I hate Instagram but I'm grateful that people got to see what he was and the joy he brought into the world. The horrific circumstances surrounding his demise will haunt me for the rest of my life."

"Fuck me," Stefanie said. "She needs some drugs."

"You're a public relations nightmare, doll."

"Are you going to drop me?"

"No."

I flew across the office and threw my arms around both of them.

"Enough with the hugging," Stefanie said.

"Is there anything else I need to know before going forward?" Robin asked.

"I'm addicted to Oreos, and I'm a plumbaphobe." I took my Playtex rubber gloves from my haggard Birkin. "I don't go anywhere without these."

"This one has more issues than *Vogue*," Stefanie said.

"Hmmm. She's real," Robin said, mulling over the words. "She lives her truth."

"That's not true," I said. "But that's the goal."

"True. Free. Real," Stefanie said.

"Are you guys asking me? Because it's become a running theme."

Stefanie turned her back to me and slammed the desk. "She's honest!"

"Are you thinking what I'm thinking?" Robin asked.

"Let's do it," Stefanie said.

"Do what?" I asked.

"Post the video to your Instagram," they said simultaneously.

"Are you crazy?" Their look to me spoke volumes. Clearly I wasn't the right person to be asking that question.

"Listen, doll, you're a mess. Owning that makes you likable."

"Keisha, the cashier, said that. Not a Safeway cashier; she works at Gristedes, she gave me some runway coaching."

"She could be a reality show, Robin," Stefanie said.

"She could be," I said. "She's amazing!"

"Not her. You."

Me? Reality TV? Lori would love that.

"I'm too sensitive. Instagram gives me a vulnerability hangover."

"Get ready for the biggest hangover of your life, doll."

Chapter 41

IT WASN'T THE IDEAL TIME TO QUIT SMOKING, but it had to go. Lori had pointed out that nicotine was more addictive than heroin and that quitting would be so much easier with Chantix, but my foray into pharmaceuticals was over. It was cold turkey all the way.

I had also given up my rating system and would therefore be robbed of the joy of seeing 10's in every column. I was up all night writing in my new journal about my anxiety. Journaling would have been a far more pleasant experience if at the end of the journaling session I could rate my performance.

Mike had promised me a Scrabble match to help cope with the loss of Linus, but canceled at the last minute. His 9:00 a.m. FaceTime call was a slap in the face.

"Enjoyed your evening, did you?"

"Whatever. Fuck. I'm sorry." I'd never seen him look worse. It was worse than the morning after our infamous "Jenga & Jell-O Shot Tournament."

"I was fucking looking at houses, and the broker was fucking smoking, and—"

"Fine." I wasn't in the mood for details. "I'm sorry about my email." It was five pages, three taken almost verbatim from my journal entry, and the rest was about friendship, complete with quote cards essentially shaming him for letting me down when I needed him most.

"Alex, you can't post that fucking video. You look psychotic."

"Robin has a plan. It's called marketing." This wasn't what I wanted to focus on. Dante, and quitting Le Brasserie sans notice, were the priorities.

"Are you modeling fucking straitjackets?"

"I'm living my truth. Free, real, honest, stuff like that."

"Alex, that business is so fucked. Nothing is free, real, or fucking honest."

"True, but in real life I'm trying to be all of the above."

"Why the fuck not?" He surrendered. "I doubt your situation can't get any more fucking fucked."

"I'm taking control," I said with a surety that paralleled Maggie Smith's Dowager Countess. "And I'm quitting smoking." He might already know; it was in page two of the email.

"Thank fuck for that."

"I'm quitting Le Brasserie today." Pages two and three.

"Thank fuck for that."

ᗒ ☺ ᗕ

Hitting the reset button and trying to be true to myself brought me back to the beginning, which is why I wore my Gap sweatpants, with the matching hoodie and taupe wedge sneakers, to Le Brasserie. To be fair, my All Saints leather jacket and killer blowout added an element of cool to the non-fashion ensemble. The urge to rate my hair and wardrobe was killing me. It was worse than the need to smoke.

Dante was standing outside alone, taking a long drag of his Marlboro, when my taxi pulled up. My beloved sweats tripped me up and sent me flailing onto the sidewalk.

"Are you okay?" he asked as he helped get me back on my feet.

"Do you have a minute to talk?"

"Of course."

It suddenly occurred to me that he might want to talk to me. Quitting was my goal, but maybe firing me was his, which took the awkwardness of the whole situation to another level. The restaurant was empty except for Patrick, who had his nose in a script.

We settled into a secluded corner table as Dante asked, "Would you like some champagne?"

It wouldn't hurt, but the daily drinking was part of the "things that no longer served me." "Just water."

"My darling, what would you like to talk to me about?"

The pet names were still unnerving even though he used them for every woman in the city.

"About Saturday, the details aren't important. I'm really sorry."

"Le Brasserie, it happens to everyone. Even our beautiful bartender."

He wasn't firing me but it might have been easier if he were. I had rehearsed it several different ways but there was no way to make it sound better.

"About the bartending." I swallowed hard. "I know it's last minute but I have to quit, effective today, and it's got nothing to do with Sheila."

"Are you quitting me too?"

Huh?

"It's not about you."

"Have dinner with me tonight."

I spit out my water and as he wiped it off his shirt, he asked, "Is that a no?"

"No. Not 'no' about dinner. No about no. You know?"

"Will you make an exception with your menu plan?"

Letting go of things that no longer served me was finally serving me.

"Okay." I made it sound like a sacrifice.

"Torrisi in Nolita, say eight p.m.?"

Who eats dinner at eight p.m.?

"Is there a dress code?"

"You can wear your sweatpants." His disarming smile took over his face.

Chapter 42

DANTE'S INVITATION SENT ME FLYING, and I had been walking aimlessly around the Upper East Side, trying to process it, ever since. The one person in the world I wanted to talk to was Virginie, but how could I face her? A lying, cheating slut? How often does Michael need to be serviced?

Keisha's words whirled in my world: "*You gotta taste your words before spitting them out.*"

The rancid, rotten, repulsive aftertaste of my words had been with me ever since. My plan had been to just show up at her apartment with flowers, pour my heart into an in-person apology, but I was terrified the damage couldn't be undone. I texted her instead, to test the waters. "Can we talk?"

My phone rang in the split second that my text read, "Delivered."

"You will not believe what is happening!" Virginie said. She was speaking so loudly I had to hold the phone twenty centimeters from my ear. "Can you come to my apartment?"

When she threw open the door, my stare locked onto her opal-set jade eyes. Before I could speak, she said, "I find when things really fall apart, sometimes the only way to put it back together is with nicotine. Chérie, this situation also calls for wine."

Our friendship had come full circle, and we collapsed into each other's arms.

"I'm so sorry for judging you, and you're better than any heroine in any book I've ever read."

"It's hard to hear the truth, especially from your friends." She wiped away a tear. "I'm sorry for what I said too."

"Virginie, you were right about all of it. I love you for telling me the truth."

Our tears washed away the lingering residues of anger, hurt, and guilt.

"I love your Linus, and your plumbaphobia."

She pulled me toward the dining room, which was littered with real estate magazines.

Two blue wineglasses and an open bottle of champagne sat in the center of the fray.

"I know how terrifying it is to have a crush, especially on a guy like Dante."

My Dante story may be huge, but whatever she wanted to tell me was bubbling inside her, and I gave her the floor.

"These glasses are Daum Crystal Louis XV," she said as she poured the champagne. "For very special occasions."

However huge her news may be, I wasn't breaking my commitment to abandon the weekday drinking.

"I told Michael it's over," she said solemnly.

"Oh my God!" This required a minimum of one sip.

"It's all because of you, and Oprah." She ran to her bedroom and returned with a tattered copy of *The Secret* held tightly to her chest. "She introduced me to this glorious book."

I was familiar with the book, but how it had intervened in the past three days was beyond me.

"What happened?"

"I spent the past few days putting out to the Universe that I choose love."

I noticed that the cashmere throw I had chucked across the room was still balled up in the corner.

"What did Michael say about Caleb?"

"I didn't tell him about that." She laughed like I was insane. "You can't just change the rules." Her elegant display of certainty promised she had a plan to make the playbook to work in her favor. She moved throughout the apartment taking in every corner, the walls, the window, the view. "He wants to sell the apartment."

"Wow."

"I also put it to the Universe"—she smiled as she sauntered toward me—"that I don't want to be poor."

"Did the Universe have any solutions?"

"Real estate! Look out, Barbara Corcoran."

It was actually me who had first suggested real estate.

"That's perfect for you!"

"Once I'd convinced him, Michael loved the idea of me being an independent woman." The fire in her eyes burned straight through me. "And he wants to help me in any way that he can."

How she convinced him was in and of itself fascinating, but to have twisted the scenario to one in which he wanted to help was surreal. But if she wanted to reveal the details, she would have. Questions would only tarnish the air of mystery she so loved.

"And he's putting this apartment on the market tomorrow for fifteen million dollars, and I get the six percent commission."

"Holy shit!"

She manifested this in all of three days. Maybe I needed to reread *The Secret.*

"Wait a second." I have no working knowledge of the real estate industry, but there had to be some legalese involved. You can't just sell other people's apartments. "Don't you need a license of some kind?"

"I'll get my broker's license. Eventually. This is just a start-up fund."

"Basically, Michael is just giving you nine hundred thousand dollars."

"Basically, yes." She thought about what she had said and added, "But not until I find the buyer. I'm going to miss this apartment." She collapsed beside me. "But Caleb is worth it."

"Does Caleb know about the start-up fund?"

"He's okay with it as long as we move in together as soon as possible."

"Where will you go?"

"Alex, everything just happened. I haven't gotten that far."

This wasn't the time for logistics, and my question was selfishly motivated. I wanted to know she was staying in the city.

"It's your turn. Tell me everything!" Virginie's eyes welled up again as I took her through my epiphanies. "We're both living our truth. It's so amazing."

Living her truth didn't involve the same degree of humiliation and commitment. Lying by omission is hardly a lie in Virginie's world. It was part of her doctrine, "The Natural Order of Things," which always has a happy ending. But to be fair, she was playing by new rules.

"We'll see what happens, but quitting Le Brasserie worked out well. Dante just asked me to dinner!"

Virginie insisted we have one more sip of champagne. "Finally!"

We FaceTimed Tyler, who was brandishing a spanking brand-new copy of *The Secret.* He'd already heard all about Virginie. "Poodle, tell me everything."

"I'm really sorry about what I said. About STDs and everything." I wanted to reach through the screen and squeeze him tightly.

"Under the bridge, darling, under the bloody London Bridge where my twat of a boyfriend belongs."

He'd made no progress in that arena? I'd said horrible things for nothing? He must have read my mind.

"Listen, baby lamb, our angels are guiding us. They may not have led me away from the bastard"—he lit a cigarette and lay back on his cozy gray sheets—"but they are currently guiding a Greek Adonis to my flat."

"The Adonis from Gold Bar?" The story of Raoul mounting a stranger's leg was not one I would ever forget.

"The very same." He blew us kisses and signed off with, "Love and light, ladies."

"Let's get you ready for tonight!" Virginie ran into her bedroom. "We'll shoot a bunch of wardrobe options and post everything." #firstdate#torissi #crushing#whattowear

"No way! Tonight is precious, personal, and private." My Instagram had already become way too detailed for me as a public persona. There was no chance I would ever post something this intimate about my real life.

"But it's so exciting," she said, topping off her Mother-flared jeans and suede fringed shirt with a House of Lafayette burgundy hat. "Look at this Coachella throwback." The touch of the fabric and the movement of the clothes were almost as thrilling to her as my date night. "We have to shoot this."

#happyhumpday#welovefashion#justbecause#bohochic#houseofla-fayette#motherdenim

#coachella#throwback

"You could totally wear this boho-chic at Torrisi. Love it."

"No."

A fashionista I would never be, but it was always fun to play dress-up with Virginie. From the far reaches of her walk-in closet, she yelled, "Ooh, how about a minidress with Freda Salvador ankle boots?!"

"Never."

"Still, Alex? You won't wear a dress?"

"It's not just Fabio—or Jane Taylor, for that matter." Although that did play a role. "I'm not comfortable in dresses. I never know what to do with my legs."

She shimmied out of her jeans, slipped on the ankle boots, and perched against the windowsill with her legs delicately crossed as she bent over to adjust the booties' ankle straps. "Just watch me."

"Virginie, I need to be me," I said, admiring her Imelda Marcos–like shoe selection.

Then *they* saw me, sparkling from the far reaches of the closet. It looked as though they had been sprinkled with flecks of gold. The white-and-gold-tone leather was emblazoned with a star and a stripe patch. An ideal side zip fastening ensured the exquisite crisscross pattern of the golden laces. The magnificence of the über cool high-top sneakers was amped up by the distressed detailing. I cradled them close to my heart.

"You just go where your high-top sneakers sneak, and don't forget to use your head." *The Cheshire Cat*

"Golden Goose Deluxe Brand." Virginie nodded and smiled encourage-ment. "Italian. Even their sneakers are perfect."

We paired them with Mother ankle-frayed faded jeans and Zadig & Voltaire's simple but stunning satin tunic. Virginie draped her AYR Atelier coat over my shoulders. A modern take on classic and effortlessly chic; it was perfect.

"You look beautiful, but something is missing." She grabbed a perfume bottle shaped like a star. "Angel by Thierry Mugler," she said, reveling in its mist. "This is Alex sprinkled with special. Dante won't be able to resist you. You must go to bed with him."

"I'm not going to bed with him." Not tonight. There wasn't anyone, any-where, whom I would rather explore my sexuality with, but I didn't want to be just another notch in his headboard.

"Living True? Real? Honest? You're trying everything. Why not a real orgasm?" she said.

"I don't have my rubber gloves with me." Which was unprecedented, but my brain was fogged in prior to my meeting with Dante. "That's the Universe saying 'Not tonight.'"

⊰ ☺ ⊱

Torrisi was nothing short of perfect. The exposed brick setting and open kitchen entertained only six tables; it felt like I had been invited into the owner's personal dining room and he was having one hell of a dinner party.

Dante's corner table was the best seat in the house. He was leaning back in his chair, watching me take it all in. There was a certain mischief in his eyes when he stood to greet me.

"You look beautiful, Alex. Is that Angel I smell?"

How could he possibly know that?

"It's my first foray into perfume."

"Angel's my favourite."

Did Virginie have inside information? Note to self: pick up a bottle of Angel ASAP.

"You Europeans sure do love perfumes." In my experience, North Americans aren't as attached to the spritzing.

"Don't you like it?" He smelled delicious. I wanted to bury myself in his Salvatore Ferragamo cashmere sweater.

"Sometimes it can be a bit suffocating." Natalia wafted into my mind.

"Am I suffocating?"

"Yes." I managed to stop myself before giving him my response in its entirety, which was, "It's not your cologne, it's pretty much you as a whole."

"In the future," he laughed, "I'll be sure to keep my cologne to a minimum."

Hmmm. The future.

"Shall I order some wine?"

"Not for me. I'm giving up alcohol during the week."

"Can we make an exception tonight?"

"I've already had two sips of champagne. Virginie and I were celebrating." That was all he needed to know about that.

"I'll order a glass of cabernet, and maybe you can have one more sip to make it a lucky three." His charismatic approach to things was both unnerving and captivating at the same time. "But you agreed to make an exception with your diet."

I looked up at the chalkboard menu. The ricotta and salmon withstanding,

I couldn't pronounce the names of any of the dishes. An awkwardness registered on my face, and he graciously remedied the situation.

"Please allow me to order for our table."

Dante greeted our waiter and asked him take our picture. "It's your Brasserie retirement dinner. We need to capture the moment."

At some point between the sublime tuna southern mulberry and the equally divine salmon cannelloni, my phone started blasting its new ring tone, "Don't Stop Believing."

Steve Perry wouldn't quit and everyone in the restaurant was staring at me.

"I'm so sorry," I addressed the entire room. "I can't find my phone."

I stood up and leaned over my Birkin, almost emptying its contents, hoping to illustrate that it wasn't for lack of effort. I finally wrapped my sweating fingers around the freaking thing and ripped it out of my bag for everyone to see. "Found it," I sang, and threw in some jazz hands before sitting back down. All that for a freaking robocall.

"I'm so sorry."

"That was entertaining." He smiled, leaving my limited poise intact. "But something fell out of your bag." He slid a condom, which was taped to a pair of shiny new rubber gloves, across the table. Attached was a note, scrawled in Virginie's handwriting, "The Universe has ways of making everything possible. Just in case you change your mind."

I'm going to kill her.

My frantic effort to conceal Virginie's "surprise" care package resulted in Dante's wine- glass shattering to the floor. I held my head in silent prayer.

"Normally, in a situation like this, I would implement my emergency exit strategy."

"You have an exit strategy?" I couldn't bear to look at him and just nodded in response.

"Alex, why don't we perform your emergency exit strategy as a duet?'

This was an exciting proposition, but mine was a solo act; we'd have to improvise. We *could* act as though whomever called me was so distraught that they were now phoning Dante.

"Okay," I whispered. "Pretend your phone is ringing, and hand it to me."

I gasped when Dante passed me his phone, then leaned in and whispered, "Now we have to leave immediately."

He signaled the waiter and nodded solemnly as I grabbed my bag and slipped out with harried steps that carried a sense of urgency.

Feigning an imaginary caller in distress took the performance to new heights. I paced the sidewalk, waiting for him to join me. His forehead creased, and with a cigarette already dangling from his lips, Dante's determined stride outside polished off the exit with great finesse. He took my hand and headed north on Mulberry Street.

Was the hand part of the exit?

"You were fantastic." I returned his phone. "FYI, I'm never going there again. I'm so sorry."

"Torrisi is shuttering its doors soon. I'm happy you got to experience one of my favourite restaurants."

I'm happy you're still holding my hand.

"Although it was the first time I've ever finished dinner by nine-twenty."

"I'm sorry, but just think of all the people who are now enjoying their dinner in peace."

"You say 'sorry' a lot."

"It's cultural. Anyway, I really am sorry about dinner."

"Would you like to go back to the restaurant and say 'sorry' to everyone again? Perhaps we can break into St. Patrick's Old Cathedral and you can say penance instead."

Glimmers of moonlight flickered in the stained-glass window above the church's arched red doorway.

"That's a beautiful building."

"Of course. The architect was French."

"You know why Canadians always say sorry? We're a humble nation."

"Everyone likes Canadians."

"Conversely, French people are always saying how *fantastique* they are. One might say you're arrogant."

He shrugged his shoulders. "It's okay to be arrogant when you're fantastique."

They are fantastique.

"Canada is partly French, and a multinational country. We're a proud, kick-ass, nature- loving, peaceful people."

"Do all Canadians carry condoms attached to rubber gloves?"

Part of me had hoped we could spend the rest of our lives pretending that never happened.

"Virginie had a clear vision of how this night would end. The condom speaks for itself."

"And the rubber gloves are like a sexual fetish?" he asked, wholeheartedly unperturbed, which was disconcerting.

I braced myself, hoping the reality would be as well received, and blurted out, "I'm a plumbaphobe."

"I don't know this word."

"It's not a real word, but I can assure you it's a real thing."

It was beginning to drizzle. The water droplets were gradually increasing in size and soaking the pavement. The night had started so promising, and now here we were in the rain discussing my deepest secret.

"Can you spell it for me?"

"P-l-u-m-b-a-p-h-o-b-i-a." Each letter emphasized my glaring defect, and to add insult to injury, feckless frizzies were forming at my hair follicles.

"Aha. This is a fear of some kind?"

"I have a crippling aversion to public plumbing scenarios. I carry rubber gloves with me at all times in the event that I need to use a public restroom."

I would have preferred to end the confession there, on the steps of St. Patrick's, but Dante wanted details.

"What about swimming pools, showers?"

"Off-limits."

"What about Lori's apartment?"

"I wear sneakers and cover my body in Saran Wrap."

"How are you getting clean if your body is wrapped in Saran?"

He was the first person to ask me that. I appreciated the analytical approach to his questioning.

"I remove a layer, wash said body part, replace the Saran, and continue said process through to its natural conclusion."

"It must take you hours to get ready."

"You have no idea."

"And this fuzzy mess," he said, ruffling my hair, "how long does it take fix this?"

I just revealed my deepest secret and he was making fun of my hair?

"I like it curly." He started to laugh. "You're like sheep. Bah."

"You don't think I'm crazy?"

"We're all mad here; it's the Cheshire Cat." He put his arm around me and ushered me down Prince Street. "All the crazy people come to New York. That's why I love it."

"Where are we going?"

"For a walk in the rain."

We crossed the chaos at Sixth Avenue and Waverly Place and wandered down a quaint crooked street, where we stopped in front of a black shiny door.

"This was my first apartment in the city, 7 Gay Street, apartment 3S. A small studio with a working fireplace; it was perfect." His gaze wandered to the third-floor window. "I never wanted to leave."

Why was he so emotional? Was it a girl?

"Do you follow football? Real football? European football?"

"I don't follow any sports, but my family watches the World Cup."

England, God love her, hadn't won the tournament since 1966, but we've never given up hope.

"In 2006 France was set to win the World Cup. We were a much better team than Italy." His upper lip curled, graduating to a full-on teeth-baring snarl. "I was living with the guys from Le Brasserie. We watched every game together. The day after France beat Portugal, July sixth, 2006, I moved here."

His words were laden with guilt, and his shoulders stooped under their weight.

Did someone die?

"Everyone begged me not to move until after the final game because it was bad luck, but I was excited to be in my new apartment."

The rain came down heavier and quiet thunder rumbled in the distance.

"France lost to Italy on July ninth, 2006. Les Bleus." He crossed himself.

"I'll always blame myself. I broke my lease and left my rent-controlled piece of paradise the next day. I left everything except my phone and the clothes on my back."

Everything?

"You're quite the devoted fan."

"I was also drinking way too much, and I made a crazy bet on that game."

Gambling?

"How crazy?"

"Five thousand dollars crazy."

I didn't want to interrogate him; I wanted to let the details unfold naturally, but my facial expression gave me away.

"It was a one-off." He pulled me toward him and gave me a tight squeeze, and I relished those brief seconds.

"But it took a while to pay back. Laurent helped me get back on track."

The joker, the goofball, the samba dancer?

"Laurent?"

"He's a great friend; I'm lucky to have him." Dante smiled to himself. "I'm also lucky that he comes from a wealthy family. He loaned me the money."

"Okay, here's a question. Why is Laurent a waiter if his family is wealthy?"

"Laurent is an interesting character. He wants to find his own footing and who he is outside of his family's money."

Everyone really does have a backstory. There's a teachable moment here for me. Not everyone who was born into a wealthy family is a spoiled rich kid. Laurent was in the trenches with us at Le Brasserie and no one knew about his family.

It was raining hard now, and puddles were forming on the sidewalk.

"Well, Alex . . . now we know each other's secrets."

A stream of water ran down my neck. We were both soaking wet. "What happens now?" I whispered.

He grabbed the back of my hair and tilted my chin up to face him. "Now, Alex Emmerson, I'm going to kiss you good night."

My body crumpled into a taxi. I traced the contours of my lips, knowing his kiss would be with me forever. RDJ and Troy had been usurped. We'd had a good run, but now there was only room for Dante.

Chapter 43

AFTER ANOTHER SLEEPLESS NIGHT, I arrived for my meeting RADIANT fresh as a daisy.

"Hey doll," Robin said, "you're glowing."

"She had a date last night." Stefanie joined Robin behind her desk.

"How did you know?" I asked.

"Because your Brasserie guy posted it on his Instagram."

#torrisi#celebrate#retirementdinner#missheralready#brasserie#neednewbartender

His post depicted a version of our night that kept something precious and personal for us. I hoped like hell Sheila saw that post.

"Aw sweet," Robin said.

It was sweet. We looked adorable. We looked like a thing.

Dante had also posted a picture of the Cheshire Cat with the caption "We're all mad here."

#secrets#allthecrazypeoplecometonyc

"What's with the Cheshire Cat?" Stefanie asked. "Did you talk to him about posting that video?"

"No." I was hoping he'd never find out about it. People had stopped looking at the freaking thing. Half the comments were in German. Interest had peaked. "I don't want to post it."

"I get that," Robin said. "It's your decision, but we have a plan."

"Hear me out," Stefanie said. "Haute is working on a new line of products."

"Haute. As in skin care?"

"Correct. My girlfriend works for the advertising firm handling the new launch."

Stefanie is a lesbian?

"What's wrong with you?" Stefanie asked. "Why are you smiling?"

"I've never met a lesbian in person. It's exciting."

She turned to Robin. "Please, I beg you, let's pitch a fucking show. They wouldn't even have to script it. Just get a camera and a mic and let her talk."

"No show," Robin said. "Moving on. Haute always goes for the superstar, the supermodel type. But they're getting on board the honest skin care train—organic, pure, natural. Models everywhere—doing yoga, meditating, drinking kombucha—are living pure, organic, honest lives."

"What isn't everywhere is a model who shares raw, real, honest moments. None of this #nofilter#nomakeup#lovemyjob#wokeuplikethis to increase your likability crap," Stefanie said.

"The LumiYa debacle was funny. New model learning the ropes." Robin cued up the Linus video. "But this is raw."

"This is fucking honest," Stefanie said. "And your Brasserie guy has gifted us the Cheshire Cat."

"I think I'm in love with him."

"You and countless other men and women. The guy's a wank-bank star for sure."

The thought of Dante appearing in other people's wank banks disturbed me almost as much as the notion of posting the video.

"Post pictures of you and that towel, childhood stuff. Some heartbreaking quote about loss. Drum up some sympathy." I had to admire Stefanie's commitment to her idea. She had put a lot of energy into this pitch. "More issues than *Vogue* is perfection; I'm sure it's a quote card."

"Maybe 'Historically Speaking' could play a role in all this. I do have a cache of disastrous selfies that no one's ever seen. Think #loner#loser#lame."

"Now's the time to #tbt the worst of the worst." She was intent on hijacking my Instagram.

Nothing is worse than the video.

"Get creative. Your comp, a bottle of water, and the rubber gloves peeking out of your bag." #modelonamission#castings#can'tleavehomewithoutthese.

"My rubber gloves?"

"You think you're the only person who has a weird plumbing thing?" Robin said. "When I was a model working on location, my bowels would be backed up for days."

"What's weirder is the person who does take a shit in the RV," Stefanie said. "The point is, everyone has something."

"I've been wrapping myself in Saran to brave Lori's shower. The bathtub has feet."

"Robin, come on?" Stefanie pleaded with her. "That's the teaser for the show right there."

You know what? Everyone does have something. Stefanie wants to make my thing into a TV show. The people I love know about my things, and they don't care. I'm done caring about what other people think!

"I'll do it."

"Yes! Any wiggle room on the show?"

"No!" Robin and I said in unison.

"You're sure you want to do this, doll?" Robin asked, inspecting the groove marks on the pen she'd been gnawing. "People are going to say some ugly shit."

"It couldn't get uglier than 'kill yourself already,'" I said. "Besides, what I'm going to post is real, so what if people know the truth?"

"The truth shall set you free."

"It kind of already has."

⌇ ☺ ⌇

An exquisite vase filled with two dozen scarlet roses was waiting for me at Lori's.

"When the doorman sent these up, I thought for sure they were for me," she said. "But the envelope is addressed to you."

The card was blue and the words were written in a simple white font.

"Some people walk in the rain, others just get wet."

Inside it read,

"Thank you for a perfect evening.

Bisous,

Dante."

Five petals fell to the floor; I placed the card beside them.

#luckygirl#grateful#warmautumnrain

That would be my only post for the day, and it saved something precious and personal for us.

"Damn girl. Someone's in love," Lori said.

I hope so.

My hands were trembling as I dialed his number. "Thank you for my flowers."

"You're welcome." His voice wrapped around me. Love, lust, the whole thing. He has my heart, and he can have the rest of me.

"Now, about the Cheshire Cat." I gathered up the will to not unravel, and texted him the link. "There's something you need to see."

It's not like he didn't see the end result of the experience, but the video captured a crazy far beyond even Wonderland.

"My darling, this is terrible," he said, struggling to stifle his laughter. "Who filmed this?"

"Some sadistic tourist."

"They did a nice job. The fat Texas guy is hilarious. 'Only in New York, kids,'" Dante said in a southern accent, and then lost all control.

You're going to need that sense of humour.

"Please let me show Laurent?"

"It's funny you should ask." I laid out RADIANT's plan with a frenzied enthusiasm that rivaled Stefanie. "What do you think?"

"It sounds like a crazy idea, but you seem convinced."

Definitely crazy. Hopefully liberating.

"It's going up today."

"You'll make Laurent's day." In his kissable, come-hither way, he added, "You'll make mine if you agree to meet me tomorrow after brunch."

I buried my smile in my hands. "See you tomorrow."

⤜ ☺ ⤛

My mum managed to scan six pictures of Linus and me through the years, which was an impressive feat in light of her limited working knowledge of any and all things technological.

"Sweetheart, are you sure you're okay?"

"Sleeping is tricky, but I have a teacher who's helping, and my new agency is one hundred percent behind me."

"I'm very sorry about your Linus, but your father is pleased that you've given him up."

How "I lost Linus to the subway" became "I've given up Linus" was beyond comprehension, and my entire body vibrated with a violent contempt for both my parents. There was a piece of me that longed to show them the video of Linus being wrenched from my poor, miserable hands, but they didn't deserve the anguish that might cause. Besides, it might raise some concerns about my sanity. Fortunately, neither of them had ever looked at YouTube.

"I'm just so proud of you," she said, gearing up for a sensational crying session. "Bartending, modeling, and now Linus." Maybe the loss of Linus symbolized something to Mum about my growing up and out of childish things. But Linus was never childish, and I had planned to spend the rest of our lives together.

"I love you, Mum."

⤜ ☺ ⤛

Project Honesty started at 1:00 p.m. EST. As per Stefanie's instructions, my first posts were pictures of Linus and me, and the quote about loss, which resulted in two hours of sobbing to Radiohead's "How to Disappear Completely."

I'm not here,

This isn't happening.

When I finally posted the video, my eyes were swollen half shut. #linus#love#brokenheart#treasure#traumatized#worstsubwayexperienceever

As there were to be no cigarettes or alcohol, Oreos would have to suffice. I headed to Gristedes and picked up two family-size boxes, one of which I promptly opened and started eating.

"Hey Lean Cuisine. Are you planning to eat that whole box at my checkout?"

"Keisha," I mumbled with a mouthful of Oreos, "I'm in mourning and doing some serious owning."

"I saw your Instagram." She stopped scanning my Saran Wrap. "Girl, you took it to a whole other level."

"That shit was real?" Tonya chimed in.

"That was some crazy shit. But you keep it real. That's why I like you."

"Whateva, Keisha. That guy won't want her now."

Tonya had seen Dante on my Instagram.

"And a touch of crazy is a turn-on." Keisha directed these words to me. "A real man loves an honest woman."

"Keisha, you're so awesome. Owning it changed my life. Thank you."

I literally skipped the six blocks back to Lori's.

"Hey girl." Lori was naked save for her Hanky Panky. "You're getting some traffic."

The momentum was kicking off. No one loved the video more than Laurent, who commented every half hour, but amid all the crazy-faced emojis he offered a sincere, "I'm sorry, sweatpants. I know you loved that rag."

The virtual venom was predictable.

- "This is staged."
- "Attention whore."
- "Cunt on the tube."
- "People will do anything to get on TV."
- "Kill yourself already."

Lydia Baker's comment was the most sickening of them all: "My heart is breaking for you my sweet childhood friend. You're too fragile for New York. #timetocomehome

Whatevs, Lydia. FYI, I can't stand you.

Was the cyber hate-on still wretched? Beyond! But the #modelife "live" experience was far worse, and I had managed to survive that with some remnants of dignity still intact. Unto all the Insta-hater trolls I offer a colossal GFY.

Besides, there were overwhelming outpourings of love and support from complete strangers. Sharing my painful experience and having people acknowledge it made it easier to hold. Maybe there is something to be said for virtual connectedness.

For the first time in my life, I felt free, and next week #tbt would begin, and my gloves were going up. I'd still probably die a plumbaphobe, but whatevs. I'd come to this city with a suitcase and a dream. I had unpacked my neuroses and was ready to stuff my "Samsonite" full with lots of new, neato things, including another bag of Oreos.

Chapter 44

ALTHOUGH YESTERDAY'S OREO BINGE had been justified, permissible, and forgiven, rectifying the behavior was the next step. Based on past experience, I had calculated the amount of stairs required to repair the damage. It was impossible to ascertain what might be involved with the Reservoir, but I was committed to letting go of the system.

"Lori, I'm going to run around the Reservoir this morning." My voice was full of enthusiasm, but my journal was full of all the reasons why it seemed like a bad idea.

Shaking? Shortness of breath? Hyperventilating? The anxiety and jaw clenching commenced the moment the words took shape on the page. Any alteration to my systems requires mountains of planning. I need to prepare for whatever physical response my body chooses. Why upset the very delicate balance of my diet and exercise regime? It will only make me want to eat more to soothe my nervous system, and that will defeat the whole point of running in the first place.

"You're gonna love it," she said.

I doubt that.

It was brisk and fresh, and three laps seemed sufficient. I did run up the stairs upon returning to the apartment, and those ten flights felt a whole lot better than the Reservoir but smelled a whole lot worse. Lori wrenched the door open the second she heard my key.

"I got the show!" she squealed. A mega-high-pitched squeal, like those girls in sorority movies.

I squealed with her. "Yay!"

"They just called! Filming starts in three weeks."

"I'm so freaking happy for you!"

My jazz hands were in position, and I was going to launch into "There's No Business Like Show Business."

But Lori spoke first. "I was thinking if things don't work out for you here, you could be on the show and we could, like, totally try and fix you."

Only Lori could make that offer without sounding offensive.

"Thank you," I said with the uttermost sincerity. "But Dante isn't in LA."

"Girl, love looks so good on you."

"Success looks good on you, and I think you've lost weight?" She looked exactly the same, but I knew that would make her happy. "Should we go out and celebrate?"

"Girl, three weeks isn't enough time to pack. I needed to start, like, yesterday. You go have a drink for me."

The abandoning of my daily system continued at Chelsea's Le Grainne, which was the ideal place to for a girl's brunch. The petite restaurant boasted the charming atmosphere and décor of a true Parisian café. I felt fabulous and French sipping my rum with milk and honey. It was, after all, a Saturday.

Virginie swept into the restaurant, her Hermès twill scarf flowing behind her. She had mastered the art of an entrance. It truly was a pity my rating scale was being phased out.

"Chérie"—she squeezed my hands and leaned in tightly toward me—"his post. Your post. The flowers." She was near to tears. "Tell me everything."

"It was the most amazing night of my life, but your jacket and sneakers got soaking wet. I'm so sorry."

"A jacket and sneakers are a small price to pay for the most amazing night of your life."

Her devotion to materialism was inconsequential when her friend's happiness was at stake.

"Please tell me you went to bed with him."

Or their sex life.

"No, but he did find your care package."

"*Mais non*," she gasped.

"*Mais oui.* Now he knows all my secrets."

"Has he seen your Fruit Of The Loom panties?" She looked horrified.

My underwear was more disturbing to her?

"Not yet," I said in my most menacing tone.

"Promise me you'll throw them away."

They had been disposed of weeks ago.

"I promise, but only if you stop using the word 'panties.'"

The Nutella banana crepes and oeufs maison were sensational. But it was impossible to calculate the stair output or the laps required to account for this melt-in-your-mouth, out- of-this-world-delicious cuisine.

"Did anything sexy happen?" She slid her tongue over a spoonful of banana, begging me for some erotic details.

"He kissed me good night in the pouring rain."

She wasn't at all disappointed with my reply.

"I put it out to the Universe that you and Dante would fall in love."

Ah, the magic of Virginie. I could feel her spell all over me, but at this point all that was certain was that I was in love.

"What's happening in your and Caleb's universe?"

She dissolved into a lovestruck schoolgirl. "I'm going to meet him in the Hamptons tonight."

"Does he know what's happening?"

"Not everything." There was softness about her when she talked about him, but her scintillating sensuality was sparkling just below the surface. She was giving off heat. "I want to wait until I see him in person."

"When do I get to see him in person?"

"He's coming into the city next week so we can look at apartments."

"It's time to celebrate!" For the first time in my life, I ordered a bottle of champagne. It felt rock star-esque. "This is BIG. I'm so freaking happy for you."

"Everything I've been putting out to the Universe is happening." She was uncharacteristically giddy. "Your career is bound to take off now that you have a hundred and fifty thousand followers. It's the law of attraction, Alex."

"A hundred and fifty thousand? Really?"

"And most of the comments are nice." Her flare for embellishment may have overstepped believability there. "I've manifested something else."

How much more could there be? We saw each other three days ago.

"I found a buyer for Michael."

The cork popped, and for a second the world stopped and I reveled in her magnificence.

"Already? How's that even possible?"

"*The Secret*!"

This was beyond *The Secret*, but tonight I'm downloading that book.

"The buyer is my prince." She drifted away into a fleeting moment of melancholy, holding tightly to a piece in her life she'd never know again. "He's buying it for his mistress."

That guy really gets around.

"My prince was so thrilled with the apartment"—she reached into her Proenza Schouler tote and handed me a Tiffany blue box—"he gave me these most precious platinum and diamond earrings."

It made me think of Holly Golightly's remark "You can always tell the kind of person a man really thinks you are by the earrings he gives you." The prince was a pig, but he clearly thought highly of Virginie, who couldn't take her eyes off the box.

Jewelry never interested me. What is with the diamond fetish?

"They're beautiful." My lack of enthusiasm was upsetting her.

"This was my out-of-this-world present. Don't you see?"

She filled her glass, and her eyes filled with tears. "I didn't have to give him a blow job."

Finally I understood. She got everything she wanted and she never cheated on Caleb.

"Thank you, Universe," we said.

≷ ☺ ≷

The contents of Le Brasserie had poured out onto the street. Watching the scene play out from one block away wasn't nearly as entertaining as being in the middle of the action. Despite indulging with Virginie, I didn't have enough liquid courage to face the brunch crowd. Lord knows who may have seen the video. Laurent I could handle, but the masses would cause vulnerability paralysis. Dante could meet me around the corner.

I was set to send him a text when I spotted Sheila following him out of the restaurant. The whispering in his ear was revolting; the sensual pawing at him made my blood boil. Hadn't she seen our Instagram posts? Marching over there was the only plausible course of action. My Newburys were going to walk all over her.

But then she took out her phone and passed it around to her posse. The unbridled hysteria could mean only one thing: the video.

What was I thinking posting that?

I watched it myself while I waited, trying to will myself to walk over there. But I couldn't do it. This is Sheila's stomping ground, and her daddy's an investor. Not caring what people think of me is entirely different than not caring what people thought of us—Dante and me. Everybody loves Sheila. Even though she is a raging snatch, she's a superstar socialite, with superstar friends, with superstar lives. People will think Dante is crazy for hooking up with the nut-job bartender, wannabe model.

The longer I stood there watching them, the more I began to doubt myself and Dante's feelings for me. He probably does just want to have sex with me, and he knows the right things to say. He's a playboy, and an amazing lover, according to numerous reports from Virginie.

Come on, Alex! GFY spirit!

You're independent, you're funny—even if it's not on purpose—and you're pretty. He even likes your sheep-like hair. Bah.

Dante was looking at Sheila's phone now and laughing with her.

I'm the laughingstock of Le Brasserie. Our date felt like a lifetime ago, and a total sham. The Disney deep inside me had colossally failed me once already. It was time to stop believing in fairy tales. Guys like him don't go for girls like me. Mike's right, and Keisha is way off base on this one.

I cowered away and sent him a text saying that brunch with Virginie hadn't ended well and it might be food poisoning, offered up massive apologies, and canceled our plans.

≳ ☺ ≲

I texted Mike 911. We made a pact two years ago that no matter what was going on, if either of us texted 911, we had to drop everything and answer the phone. It all came about because of some horror movie he made me watch wherein the main character's death could have been prevented if only her friend had picked up the phone. I had nightmares for months. Anyway, I'd never used that signal until today. It wasn't an actual 911, but he answered my FaceTime. Mike was the one person whose honesty I could count on in this situation.

"It's not really 911," I blurted out. My teetering glass of wine and the half- empty bottle beside me painted the wrong picture.

"No fucking kidding." He was leaning back in the La-Z-Boy, drinking tequila.

"You were right about the video, and Dante." I brought him up to speed on everything.

"Did he fucking ask you why you canceled five minutes before your date?"

"I told him it might be food poisoning."

Dante even offered to come take care of me. I'd felt a pang of guilt about lying but it was better than his knowing the truth.

"What's the fucking problem here, Alex?"

"Sheila's a quasi-supermodel. They look perfect together. And her daddy is an investor at the place where he works." It made me sick every time I thought about that.

"Alex, who gives a fuck about her dad? If Lydia fucking Baker's parents were somehow invested in Safeway, would you really fucking care? Would you have quit?"

It was a valid point; I wouldn't care, and I wouldn't have quit, but this was different. Safeway is an enormous company, and there's only one Brasserie, and only one Dante.

"I didn't quit because of Sheila. But it's like she has some claim to him."

"You fucking had dinner?" Ben put his head on Mike's lap, and his features softened. "He knows about all your shit? Sent fucking flowers?"

"You said he did all that because he wanted to have sex."

"When people fucking like each other, it usually leads to sex."

I shriveled at the mental image of Sheila's flawless figure wrapped around Dante. "Sheila's perfect, like retouched perfect, even naked." I'd never seen her naked but some things you just know.

"Alex, she's a fucking trust fund bitch who hasn't grown out of the high-school mean-girl phase." He paused and smiled. "Meanwhile, look at you." He seemed overwhelmed by his sense of pride. "You're in New York, with your fucking plumbing thing. Your fucking Linus is gone, and you've publicly fucking humiliated yourself daily."

I appreciated what he was saying, but this wasn't just about me. My heart was out there. Way out there.

"You're special."

There are certain people in your life who know exactly the right words to say, at exactly the right time. Today, in this moment, it was my BFF.

"Sounds like the philandering Frenchman has fucking figured that out."

My vocal chords were paralyzed with emotion. A full thirty seconds passed before Mike said, "Sometimes you just have to fucking go for it."

$$\geqq \odot \lessgtr$$

Sometimes you do have to fucking go for it, but sometimes rabid snatches like Sheila make that impossible. Once Dante was convinced my full and speedy recovery was on its way, he spent the night out on the town. I spent the night trolling through Sheila's Instagram. She had begun posting collages of her #yoga #pure#organic #love#honest life. As if that wasn't nauseating enough, tonight she was wearing the infamous *I Shagged the Drummer* Tee. She and her posse had a big night out. #Metropolis #glamsquad #girlsnigh-tou t#girlswanttohavefun #topofthestandard#domperignon #invitationonly. Even Darlene had even joined in the fun, flapping her bat wings all over the city. I'm sure Badgley Mischka offered a cocktail dress with sleeves. They #endedupat10ak, and coincidentally, so did Dante. Sheila couldn't get enough of her #frenchie #lovehim #frenchforever #boyswanttohavefuntoo #thenightsstillyoung.

Really? Sheila posted that at 4:00 a.m.

The moral of the story, according to my journaling, was had I not lied, and lived my truth, and told Dante I didn't think I was good enough to be his girlfriend, then I too might have #endedupat10ak. I could have told Darlene in person that her outfit was way in the negative numbers.

There was an entire novella devoted to how I missed my rating scale. A few pages were committed to rationalizing why staying home and getting drunk alone was a better alternative to freaking #endedupat1Oak with that lot. Who needed the drama? The last two pages of my journal entry looked like something out of *The Shining.* GFY! GFY! GFY! GFY! GFY! GFY! GFY! GFY! GFY! GFY! GFY! GFY! GFY! GFY!

I looked like something out of *The Shining,* with my fixed psychotic stare, sheen of boozy sweat, and rabid lip curl.

"Hey girl." Lori found me hunched over my journal somewhere around 8:00 a.m. "Did you fill that whole notebook?"

"Yes."

"Did you drink that whole bottle of wine?"

"Yes."

"Did you get any sleep?"

"No."

Lori's glossy Ambien eyes searched the room for something to take this conversation in a positive direction. I gave her one.

"But I didn't smoke."

Celebrate your victories.

"That's great," she said, trying to convey a sense of enthusiasm.

"And I have an appointment with Erin in an hour."

"Amen!"

Now, that was enthusiasm.

She slipped into to a Deep South, church-loving, Sunday morning mode that I'd never seen before. We didn't need Joel Osteen in this apartment, we had Erin.

"I never would have booked that show without her." She waved her hands at the remnants of my evening and tattered soul. "She can help you with all this."

Chapter 45

I had spent hours lying on the floor of Erin's studio and never noticed the painting on the ceiling. "That's beautiful," I said.

"It's the Sanskrit symbol for namaste. Two of my students painted it ten years ago."

"How's it possible that I missed that?"

"Sometimes when we are wrapped up in our own thoughts we miss things that are right in front of us."

Had I become that self-absorbed? That was a big thing to miss. It covered a large portion of the ceiling.

"That's why breathing is so important. It helps to keep us in the moment and see things more clearly."

The ceiling aside, I was pretty clear on everything. Venturing into unchartered territory with Dante and abandoning my systems were colossal mistakes. Things were falling apart.

"Changing my life isn't working out too well."

"Change takes time and gentleness." A tenderness lit up her eyes.

"I'm being gentle."

She exploded with laughter. "Alex, less than a week ago, you made a decision to let go a little bit and begin exploring yourself."

"I ate new food, ran around the Reservoir, and started journaling." Those elements of the program were triumphs from my perspective.

"You opened your heart to someone, and you shared intimate experiences on a social platform. Now you expect your fragile self to get on board."

"No, no. I've given up fragile."

Erin couldn't suppress a smile.

"Not caring what other people think is far more complicated now because Dante is part of the equation."

"Equation?" she asked. "I wasn't aware we'd be doing math today."

I made a mental note to keep that line in my repertoire, but stayed myopically focused on Dante.

"What if people think I'm not good enough to be his girlfriend?"

"You are enough," she said firmly. "That's your new mantra. I am enough."

I had to wonder how one convinces oneself of something they don't truly believe. Something stupendous had to happen to instill that feeling.

"A mantra might not be enough to inspire, you know, enoughness."

"Stop looking outside yourself to satisfy that need." She paused for a deep inhale, and on the exhale said, "The goal is to feel satisfied when you're with yourself."

"I'm not that interesting."

"Alex Emmerson, you're very special. I suspect that this young man feels the same way."

"I'm terrified." Looking back now, this was most terrified I'd ever felt in my life.

Not letting fear create your life required a level of commitment that far surpassed even orthodontic headgear. My mouth started twitching.

"Why don't we try and breathe a little bit?"

Erin talked me through a meditation that ended with a vibrating bell chime. The bell was a first.

"Erin, that really worked. I feel much better," I said before noticing that I was lying on the floor wrapped in her pashmina with a pillow under my head.

"You did really well for three minutes and then you fell into a deep sleep for two hours."

"I haven't been sleeping much."

"Keep working on the breathing practice. It will help you relax."

The breathing practice was a challenge when it was in the system and on the rating scale.

"I'll try."

"Remember, be gentle. You're doing great."

⋛ ☺ ⋚

"Chérie, are you okay? I've been calling you for hours." The sound of the ocean was faint in the background. Virginie and Caleb were still in the Hamptons, but she must have seen Sheila's Instagram.

She's interrupting their getaway for me. That's real friendship right there.

"You're amazing. Thanks for calling."

"I'm sorry. The Universe has really let you down."

"The Universe played no part in it. This one is on me."

Once she had recovered from the shock of my play-by-play, she started quoting *The Secret.* "You are the one who calls the law of attraction into action."

"I know."

"We attract what is happening in our lives." The treble in her voice went up a notch.

"I got it."

"Decide what you want. Believe you can have it. Believe you deserve it. Believe it's possible for *you!*" The treble peaked on *you.*

There was no longer an imminent need to download the book. It was unlikely, bordering on impossible, that Virginie had ever felt "not enough." Nor would she ever feel "not enough." It wasn't in her makeup, but she had tons of empathy.

"Right now I'm working on getting comfortable with myself."

"You will be life altering—comfortable with yourself if you meet me on the Upper East Side at five tonight. I'll text you the address."

En route to this mysterious life-altering rendezvous, Dante called.

"Hi beautiful. How are you feeling?"

Sickened by your and Sheila's PDA at 10ak, while I suffered through a sleepless night of crippling insecurity.

"Much better. How was your night?"

"It would've been better if you were with me."

That might have interfered with your time with Sheila.

"What did you do?"

"Hit a few hot spots, and everyone ended up at 10ak."

"Everyone?" There was an edge to my voice but he didn't acknowledge it. I resolved to try harder to convey my passive-aggressive behavior.

"The usual cast of characters."

My taxi went zipping by Le Brasserie. I hadn't even noticed that we had crossed the park. The breathing practice needed to become top priority. What else had I been missing my whole life?

"We need to take you out dancing, Alex."

My commitment to dancing more often was a solo adventure. Furthermore, life was passing me by and Dante had just omitted Sheila from his retelling of the evening's events.

"I'm all booked up tonight. Virginie has something outrageous planned."

"That sounds dangerous."

"That's the new me, remember? Out of the system? Living dangerously."

"Did you pack your gloves?"

Of course I packed my gloves.

"Not today!" I lied. The whole conversation had been a lie, but at least it had been consistent.

"I can't wait to hear the details," he said with an air of mystery.

If anyone was waiting to hear details, it was me!

"I'll post them to my Instagram." I hung up. There wasn't a shred of honesty in my words. I was hardly the poster child for Haute.

Virginie was waving famously from the steps of a shabby six-story walk-up. She grabbed my hand, flew up the six flights, and threw open the door of apartment 6E.

Tyler was nestled into a dreamy cream-colored sofa, surrounded by the soft glow of tea lights. Virginie whipped off her Phillip Lim motorcycle jacket and snuggled up beside him. They were proudly sporting custom-designed matching T-shirts, a baby doll for her, a simple white Tee for him, which were emblazoned with bold jet-black letters: GFY Spirit.

"This is for you," Virginie said. Tyler handed me my own custom baby doll Tee.

The day may come when floods of tears aren't my only response to a sudden influx of emotion, but today was not that day. Virginie, who was always prepared, handed me a box of organic tissues.

"Do you like it?" Tyler asked.

"I love it," I said between sobs. "I'm never going to take it off."

"Not the shirt, chérie."

"The apartment." Tyler presented the five-hundred-square-foot studio like a charismatic talk show host. "Hardwood floors, a tad scratched but they sure are shiny, sweetheart. Cream stucco walls, not my first choice, but love the shabby-chic vibe." I wanted him to spend the whole night talking like Caesar Flickerman. Gay men make the world a better place. "How about the view, kids?" Two tiny windows overlooked a dreary cement courtyard.

"And check out this spanking brand-new fully equipped kitchenette." He scrapped the showy American accent when he said, "All you need is the bloody microwave and the Bialetti."

"Is this your new place?" I asked.

"It's yours," they said in unison. Virginie handed me the tissues again. "It's rent stabilized, fifteen hundred dollars per month including utilities."

"What? It's perfect. But when?" I was tripping over words, trying to convey my sense

of gratitude and excitement. "How's this possible?"

"The Universe and my real estate career."

"Did you get your license?" I asked.

"Not important." That would be a resounding no. "I have connections."

"What if things don't work out? I can't sign a lease."

"Everything is going to work out, baby lamb." Tyler opened a bottle of champagne and laid a freshly rolled spliff on the IKEA coffee table.

"You don't have to sign a lease. It's month to month, but there's a catch."

I was learning that some of Virginie's fairy tale moments tended to have a "catch" clause.

"I'm not giving anyone a blow job."

"Not if your skills in that arena are as lacking as your kissing, poodle."

"Just so you know, I'm dying inside." Kissing Tyler was hardly the most humiliating part of that brunch, but it was up there.

"If anyone asks you have to pretend you're sleeping with my friend," Virginie said.

"Rent-stabilized apartments have rules. Just put up a picture of the two of you, pretend you're a thing, and no one will ask questions."

In her world it seemed morally acceptable—normal, in fact—to pretend you were intimately involved with someone you'd never met. Tyler could read my body language and sensed my reservation.

"You don't even have to meet the guy," he said.

"His family has three apartments in this complex, and they're very connected to the management company. It's a no-brainer," Virginie said.

"What about you and Caleb?" Didn't they need to find something right away?

"My friend with these apartments knows Michael, and it's way too small for us."

"What about Tyler? Don't you want it?" It only seemed fair that he got first dibs.

"The Upper East Side?" He rolled his eyes, affecting an exaggerated look of disdain. "I don't think so."

"Ummm." I glanced at the bathroom door and froze. Virginie squeezed my hand and guided me toward it.

"It's a prewar building but I've done what I can."

It may have smelled like the sweet lemon verbena of Virginie's bathroom, but in comparison it was Third World standard at best. The magnificent white bath mat was working hard to mask the vinyl flooring's tinge of gray, and although the shower tiles were freshly grouted, they still looked like they'd been pulled from the wreckage of a dilapidated housing demolition, as did the tub. At least it didn't have feet. Massive efforts had been made to ensure that both the shower and sink faucets sparkled, but there was no hope for the sink's exposed pipes. Virginie closed the lustrous white shower curtain.

"How do you feel, chérie?"

The verbena was helping. I fixed my stare on the darling wicker basket filled with a set of dazzling white Frette towels, a roll of Saran Wrap, and a pair of rubber gloves that sat atop the very new, very shiny toilet. But my heart rate had skyrocketed, hyperventilation was creeping up on me, and my right eye was twitching.

"It's fucking brilliant, isn't it?" Tyler joined us in the bathroom.

"You can do it, Alex."

Breathe. Notice your breath. Breathe.

I could feel my rapid pulse beginning to subside. Of course I could do this. I stared at the ceiling and silently vowed, *I can get in the shower. I will get in that shower. Just maybe not tonight.*

"Do what, poodle? What's going on?"

Midway through the joint and his second glass of champagne, Tyler said, "You've never sought professional help?"

"No."

"And you've shared that bloody video with the world? And the marigolds?"

British people call rubber gloves "marigolds," which has a much nicer ring to it but not without the fab accent, you'd sound like a poser.

"Video, yes. Gloves, not yet."

"I'm gone for a few days and everyone's gone bloody barmy."

"Someone else shared that video. I just took control of my image." Stefanie was the true mastermind.

"What is it that you're going for?" Tyler asked.

"Honesty."

"You've got the effing gold, baby lamb."

"If you can't get rid of the skeletons in your closet, make them dance," Virginie said.

"I'm rocking a graveyard," I said proudly.

It took a little more convincing but we got Tyler on board and we shot some fab GFY spirit selfies. #gfyspirit#bffs#iloveny#uppereastside#grateful#newpad

"Alex, post the skeleton quote someone famous said, and the graveyard part, and #honesty."

"Stefanie said no honesty hashtags. Too obvious, but the rest is great."

Tyler was miffed there would be no smoking in my new apartment and headed outside. "Christ, we can't even smoke in our own bloody apartments. We're social pariahs."

We're not. I was one-week nicotine-free.

"Chérie, your Instagram looks so good. You have two hundred thousand followers from all over the world."

"It stresses me out. I just post and get off the freaking thing, lest I get sucked into Sheila's Instagram."

"It's interesting that Dante didn't even like her posts from last night."

"That is interesting."

He wasn't that into Instagram; he'd only posted maybe thirty times, but he has tons of followers. Still, protocol would dictate that he like the picture of them together. Unless he didn't want me to see that he liked it. He didn't even tell me she was there.

"What are you thinking?" Virginie asked.

"Honestly? Honesty."

Tyler strolled in reeking of cigarettes. It was a repulsive habit; nonetheless, I was dying to smoke.

"Speaking of honesty, what's happening with Raoul?"

"I love the fucker, I really do, but now the Adonis is involved. These things take time."

I wasn't clear on exactly how the Adonis may be involved. Were they involved collectively? We spent an hour putting it out to the Universe that Tyler would summon up his GFY spirit to sort out his love life. The thing is, what he truly loves, for now anyway, is the drama.

Chapter 46

"**IS THAT A TIFFANY BLUE BOX?**" Lori gasped.

"I might just be the luckiest girl in the world." My eyes were welling up again. There was no shortage of moisture in my tear ducts.

"Dante?"

"No." Virginie and Tyler had engraved GFY on a Tiffany key chain. "It's the keys to my new apartment."

"Oh, thank God."

That was not the reaction I expected. Was this about Dante? What would give her any plausible reason not to be happy if the blue box had been a gift from him?

"I'm being evicted. We have to be out by the end of the week."

WTF?

"Are you freaking out?" I was on the verge myself. Hopefully we could bump up my move-in date.

"I knew it was coming," she said with a shrug. "I haven't paid the rent in eight months."

Thank you for keeping our pending homelessness to yourself.

"And now you've found a place." She snuggled up to Chloe. "My baby and I are headed to la-la land."

She was already there.

How was she going to pack up this apartment in six days? There was shit everywhere!

"The only meh part of this"—she traced the corners of her mouth—"I wanted a little collagen touch-up before we started filming."

"Isn't LA the capital of enhancements?"

"Totally, but that's not the issue."

The issue was the production company, which was handling her relocation. When Lori demanded they reschedule her moving day, with almost no notice, they insisted on immediately shooting a promo piece.

"The diva card doesn't get you what it used to." She shrugged. "We're shooting the promo on Friday."

"This Friday?" I had an overwhelming desire to hit pause. "When are you leaving?"

"In two days."

"Lori, I—"

"I'm going to miss you too." She dabbed at her Miss America tears, the ones poised to fall but never do.

Shocked, blindsided, bushwacked were more representative of my emotional state, but I got on board with her farewell train drama.

"You've been so good to me, and I can't thank you enough for helping me."

"Alex, you've been such an important and special person in my life."

Important and special? Really?

"You've made a lasting impression," I said.

"This isn't the end for us." She shook out her mane, stared past me at an imaginary camera, and performed a well-rehearsed speech. "When people ask me how I knew I could mentor young models, I'm going to tell them about Alex. This fragile, youngish Canadian girl, who didn't even have an Instagram account, that I helped blossom into a badass, not-quite-supermodel."

First point of contention, that isn't even proper English. Second, you turned your nose up at lifestyle modeling. Third, above all else, Not-Quite-Supermodel, is my baby.

"You've been quite the role model."

"Thank you." She blinked back her faux tears and blew kisses at the pretend paparazzi.

I really was going to miss her.

⋛ ☺ ⋚

The early morning air was crisp and the sky was an azure blue, which matched the tone of my Vince cashmere sweater. My wardrobe, my hair, and the rest of me were having a lovely morning. There was no need to put a number on things. Lots of things don't require a unit of measurement, but my loins yearned for some numbers.

Castings 1 and 2 were uneventful, and no one had mentioned the video. En route, to Jack Studios and casting 3, I stopped at a bodega to pick up the *Post.* That's when I happened upon Sheila's fake smile, which was plastered across the cover of some Spanish fashion rag. Smiling right at me like she knew I was looking at her. Like she knew when my phone rang that it was Dante.

"Hi beautiful," he said.

"Hi." I softened a little, but just a little.

"What are you doing?"

I'm in line to buy a magazine that, once outside, will be ripped into tiny pieces.

"Just heading to a casting."

"You don't sound too excited for someone who has a new apartment."

I should have called him to share the amazing news, but the truth is I wasn't ready to let go of what was, in my opinion, his lying by omission. Besides, it was clear from my true, pure, and honest Instagram what had happened.

"I wanted to tell you in person."

"Where's your casting?" Construction work on his end overpowered his voice.

"Near the West Side Highway." A siren overpowered mine.

"Meet me at the Underline Café in an hour?" he yelled over the pounding of a jackhammer.

"Okay." I stuffed Sheila in my bag. I didn't want to rush the joy of destroying her cover. I headed west on 26th Street, plotting out my conversation with Dante.

True, honest, real.

Just ask him about freaking Sheila and 10ak? Tell him Sheila's a better fit?

Sheila wasn't meeting him for coffee. I was, goddammit! I'm good enough to be with him!

I am enough. I am enough I am enough.

My obsess mode was in full swing when I ran into Lisa at the casting. She commended me on being the most insane person she'd ever met.

"My first thought was Stefanie had dreamed up some reality show for you and staged the whole thing. Fucking brilliant!"

In an industry and a city full of crazies, I had earned top billing in Lisa's mind. All those years of trying to be the best at everything; here, at last, I had succeeded in being the craziest.

Well done!

Quite frankly, someone as crazy as myself who is also a semi-functioning citizen is hard to come by. Dante is lucky to have me. A mantra I repeated forty times after casting 3. I was midway through the forty-first repetition when Dante wrapped his arms around me.

"Are you talking to yourself?"

He brushed his lips against mine. My insides fell apart outside the Underline. We sat at one of the two top tables, nestled into our extra-foamy cappuccinos and sweet Nutella toast.

"It's nice to see you try something new. Coffee and toast is at least a start."

"The Nutella is not new. Virginie and I had crepes at La Grainne."

"I hope you don't have the same experience with this toast." The way he licked the Nutella from the corner of his lip stirred a sensation in me I'd never felt before.

"I'm pretty sure I didn't get food poisoning from the Nutella." My eyes were glued to the floor.

"Hey, I'm up here." He raised his cappuccino cup like a flute of champagne. "Shall we toast your new apartment?"

"Ah, yeah, definitely," I stammered, straining to contain my desire. "Keep that cup raised for Virginie, who made it all happen."

"Is she also planning a housewarming party?"

"I'm not sure about a party."

With Lori permanently relocating to LA, that would bring the guest list to maybe five people.

"I have to be low-key."

"How about sleepovers?" He dipped his finger in the foam of my cappuccino and offered it to me. Licking his finger was beyond question the most erotic moment of my life thus far, but fear gripped me, crawled up my spine, and landed hard in my jaw. The inescapable response was to clamp down on his knuckle.

"This is very BDSM of you, Alex." I immediately unclenched.

"I'm not sure what the D stands for." My breath was growing heavy and fast. It certainly sounded like I was aroused.

"Discipline," he said.

"I'm super disciplined, but it's more of a challenge without my systems." My grasp on the conversation was slipping away.

"Alex, are you okay?"

The sleepover wasn't the issue. It just occurred to me that I would be falling asleep and waking up alone every day and every night in my new apartment. In the excitement of Tyler and Virginie and GFY, the realities of my new living arrangement didn't register, but now they swirled around me. My mind was caught in an out of control eddy, thoughts whipping up into a category 4 typhoon.

"I've never lived alone. I've never had a guy sleep over, never mind the disciplined S and M kind. And I have to post pictures of my gloves."

"Let's get out of here." He ushered me outside and headed for the Highline. We sat on a bench overlooking the Hudson. "You don't need to be afraid. You can call me or your friends every night and every morning. You won't be alone."

That brought me some relief. My friends were a phone call away and I could sleep with the lights on. But he didn't need to know that.

"I'll only sleep over if you want me to. No pressure." He pushed my hair behind my ear. The moment was starting to feel like a chapter in a young adult novel.

"I'm not a virgin. The sleepover part is great."

"Then I can bring the handcuffs?" He leaned in, his lips touching the nape of my neck.

That whole scene wasn't for me. What if that was his thing? I didn't even have a bedroom shoe. Every muscle in my body clenched.

"Relax, Alex, I'm kidding."

"If I said yes, would you have brought them?"

"Yes."

Did this make him more or less desirable? There was a moistening beneath my Paige skinny jeans.

"You're into all that stuff?" I asked.

"Some of the girls I've been with were into it."

I stood so I could look down at him, and even threw in a finger wag. "Let me just be clear, I'm not into it."

"Got it. But will you wear your gloves for me?"

"I'll wear them for you right now." I ripped open the box of my brand-new purple Playtex gloves and flashed a winning smile. A moment Dante captured beautifully with his iPhone.

"There's your Instagram post. Now we've solved all your problems."

#Alexfindsthegloves#wonderland#prettyinpurple#highline#hudson #cantleavehomeithoutthem#modellife#plumbaphobe#highline#RADI-ANT

"Tyler has already liked this," Dante said. "What's a marigold?"

"It's what they call rubber gloves in England."

"That's much nicer than Playtex," he said.

Playtex is a giant umbrella for a plethora of products, but it's the image of tampons that sticks with you.

"Let's do a selfie in your marigolds," Dante said in a hopeless Anglo accent. I wrapped my arms around him and buried myself in his sweater.

#fitslikeaglove#justlikeus

Dante, stylist extraordinaire, directed my preoccupied stare to the Hudson and perched my Birkin beside me with gloves draped over the ripped faux leather. A bottle of Fiji and my comp card peeked over the edge the bag.

#modelonamission#Hudson#iloveny#whatsinmybag#RADIANT#modellife

"Why do you have Sheila's latest cover in your bag?"

F*@K!

"Why didn't you tell me Sheila was at 10ak?"

"I told you it was the usual crowd."

I wasn't aware she was a part of the usual crowd.

"She was there with a bunch of Metropolis girls." He picked the magazine out of my bag. "Maybe they were celebrating this. It's a great picture of her."

If only Lori had a shredder.

"She plastered pictures of you all over her Instagram."

"I thought you stopped looking at Instagram," he said.

Your complete indifference to my questioning will lead to my stalking Sheila's account.

"I did. Virginie showed me."

Again with the lying?

Karmically, it didn't bode well for Haute, or Dante.

"Virginie certainly is a woman in the know, but there's a covert operation under way that even she isn't privy to."

He had effortlessly guided the conversation away from Sheila. The detour did not go unnoticed, but now I was curious.

"What?"

"I could tell you but I'd have to kill you," he said, then stood up and strolled away.

"Hey!" I yelled from the bench, but he kept walking. I broke a sweat running to catch up with him, which wasn't a bad thing; I needed to burn off the toast.

"Come on," I begged.

"Laurent and I want to open our own restaurant. We've been checking out locations for a while, and we've found the perfect venue in the Meatpacking District."

The planets must be aligning for everyone I love. This was huge for Laurent and Dante. I had to let the Sheila thing slide.

For now.

"This is so exciting!" Grabbing him, wrapping my legs around him, and covering his face in a quick succession of kisses was the only course of action.

Their plan was to have a Brasserie-type vibe, but a more intimate setting, like Torrisi.

Torrisi, our first date, our special place.

"We have investors, and we're ready to sign."

He had to catch me before I fell face-first on the boardwalk. They have investors? Did that mean Sheila's father would be involved? I didn't need to ask; the question was written all over my forlorn face.

"I'm sure Stuart Summerville would invest in our venture, but I guess you and I are both lucky that Laurent comes from a wealthy family."

YES!

Dante explained that Laurent's parents were the only investors. They had *that* kind of money. Old money and they hadn't wanted their son working in restaurants.

"They struggled with his decision, but they came around."

"My dad didn't want me to model, but he came around."

He traced the contours of my face with my fingertips. "One day I'll have to thank him."

"I would've come around if Sheila's dad was an investor, but I'm not going to lie to you, it would've been a struggle."

There was something about the way he laughed that made me think how ridiculous it is that it would matter to me. God only knows how many silent investors are involved in business ventures all over the freaking world. It's not like her dad was some drug lord.

"It's not about him, by the way, it's about her. She acts like she has some claim to you."

"I have to tell you something," he said.

A sailboat appeared in the distance, heading out for a sunset sail on the Hudson. When I was a kid, my dad used to make paper boats for my mum and me. We'd write a wish on the paper; we called them Little Wish Boats. My dad would take them down to Crescent Beach and pretend to release them. On our birthdays or sometimes on a random weekday, he'd come home bearing something we had written on our wish boats. I stared at the approaching schooner, wishing like hell that whatever Dante was going to say wasn't about her.

"Sheila and I hooked up a few years ago."

It didn't just take the wind out of my sails, it was a whirlwind that whipped me backward so fast that I fell flat on my ass.

"You lied to me." I swatted his hand away and clamored to my feet.

"I didn't lie. We were never a thing. We spent one night together."

My mind was bombarded with images of them naked with whips and handcuffs and blindfolds. It was torture.

"Lying by omission is lying."

"Alex, I'm sorry."

Everyone's nice to Sheila because she's a socialite?

"Did you sleep with Sheila to get promoted?"

It's interesting that the idea of it made me sick, but had it been Virginie using sex for advancement, I would have been more forgiving.

"You have it all wrong." Savagely rubbing his temples wasn't going to help me get it right, but I enjoyed watching him suffer. "I didn't know about her father."

So . . . it's not ridiculous that it matters to me.

"I don't know if her father would care but—"

"But what?"

"When I found out, I talked to Sheila and I told her it's better if we didn't get involved."

So . . . she does have a claim to you.

"Nobody knows."

Sheila and Dante share a secret.

"Except Laurent. Maybe she told her friends, but no one has ever said anything to me."

Sheila was playing that hand close to her chest. The schooner was far

351

off in the distance now, gliding across the river, chasing the dazzling hues of orange and scarlet on the horizon. Sheila Summerville can even ruin a beautiful sunset.

"Now that her father isn't involved, does that change things?" I asked.

"Come on, Alex, obviously not for me."

The indignant disbelief that registered in his entire demeanor was comforting.

"I can't speak for Sheila."

It does change things for Sheila. You've shared this secret for years, and now you're going out on your own.

"She's clearly still into you. Why didn't you tell me this before?"

"When you asked me about her before, things weren't like they are between us now."

"What are things like between us now?"

He entwined our fingers and announced with all of his innate charisma, "Things are like you're my girlfriend."

The giddy feeling that can happen only when your crush has a crush on you morphed into pure ecstasy at the notion of our newfound boyfriend-girl-friend status. And looking up at him, I knew we could handle anything together, even Sheila, and I decided in that moment not to put him on the cross for a past that I wasn't a part of.

Chapter 47

MOVING DAY WAS IN FULL SWING. Lori was shouting out hysterical commands to the team of packers accumulating in the apartment. Robin's phone call came amid the morning's chaos.

"Haute wants to see you, doll." Her voice had none of its usual inflection.

My muffled screech brought the action to a halt.

"It's just a casting. They're seeing lots of girls. Be cool."

I was trying to be cool, but Dante and I fit like a glove, I was moving into my new apartment, and the people behind Haute's new Honest line had just requested to see me. Containing my excitement was impossible. Fortunately, Robin couldn't see me bounding among the movers like a victorious Olympian.

"What should I wear?"

"I'll send you the details. Stefanie wants to talk to you."

What if this request casting wasn't about me? My victory dance came to an abrupt end.

"Do you think they want to see me because of Stefanie's girlfriend?"

"No." Robin laughed. "But Stefanie's lady will be at the casting."

Lady? It sounded so Hollywood. Would Dante refer to me as his lady?

"This is not about my girlfriend." Stefanie sounded exasperated.

Had she been on the call the whole time?

"It's about you. They want to see your personality. Show them the real you." A smile swallowed my face.

The action in the apartment was at a standstill. The Xtreme Movers crew weren't interested in me, but Lori still had her hand in the air to indicate the need for total silence. It wasn't her commanding presence, but rather her skimpy boy shorts and sports bra that held their attention.

"Well?" Lori asked.

"Haute wants to see me."

Lori unleashed a high-pitched squeal, waved her hand to recommence the packing, and swept toward me. "Do you know how good this will make me look? You have to get that job!"

When the last of the movers had carried the last of the boxes out of apartment 12C, all that remained were their dirty footprints and the couch.

"I'm leaving it for you," Lori said with a solemnness reserved for a sacrament.

I didn't want the damn thing.

She pushed her Maybach Monarchs into her magnificent mane. Somehow, amid the mayhem, she had switched to supermodel mode and her Giuseppe Zanottis were ready to strut out the door. She stopped to snap a selfie.

#ihategoodbyes#helloLA#nextchapter#realitytv#star

"Lori, thank you for everything."

She pressed a finger to my lips and shook her head. Then continued her performance in the hallway, where she paused to bite her lip and place a hand over her heart. Her new flare for drama would be great for the show.

"Let us not say good-bye, but au revoir. And remember, I believe in you." She stopped the elevator door as it slid closed and added, devoid of any soupy sentiment, "Book that job."

I snapped a pic of the couch and then bade it farewell.

#modellife#couch#couchsurfing#goodriddancetobadbeds#newbeginnings

The bitchy doorman was quite touched when I offered it to him, and graciously carried my bags to the black town car, which Virginie had arranged, waiting to take to my new apartment.

I watched the sun slip behind the trees as we crossed Central Park at 86th Street, and the streets fall away in the last of its light.

The driver brought my suitcases to the sixth floor and wouldn't accept a tip. I imagine Virginie had taken care of that too.

My hands tightened their grip on my GFY Tiffany key chain. "Okay, this is it," I said aloud, and unlocked the door to my very own apartment.

$$\geqslant \odot \lessgtr$$

A spliff, a bottle of Veuve Clicquot, and Virginie's baby-blue Frette washcloth were waiting for me. She and Tyler had stocked my freezer with a week's worth of Lean Cuisine and framed a picture of us in our GFY shirts. Their note read,

"HAPPY HOUSEWARMING! We love you," and included the Wi-Fi password GFY2014.

A complete sense of calm and contentment washed over me.

Wash, hmmm.

The time had come. Virginie had selected my shower accessories, as she called them. The lavender gloves matched the purple mosaic of my two-inch-thick TEVA Mush flip-flops.

My floral-esque ensemble did not inspire the freshness of spring, and I shuddered with every step toward the bathroom.

The lustrous white shower curtain was half open.

Inhale the sweet, smoothing scent of verbena.

Exhale the bright, balmy bouquet of bleach.

I glanced at the roll of Saran Wrap peeking out of the Restoration Hardware wicker basket.

Inhale the sweet, smoothing scent of verbena.

Exhale the bright, balmy bouquet of bleach.

I was going to give it a go command, the gloves and the flops notwithstanding,

Inhale the sweet, smoothing scent of verbena.

Exhale the bright, balmy bouquet of bleach.

At Erin's behest, I had assigned new words to describe the setting of my very own, quaint Old World bathroom. I gingerly stepped over the vintage-tinged bathtub.

Inhale the sweet, smoothing scent of verbena.

Exhale the bright, balmy bouquet of bleach.

The freshly grouted shower tiles, fighting against the tides of time, told tales of glory days gone by. The fearless Irish immigrants who'd made New York their home, the singers, the dancers, the out-of-work actors hoping to make a Broadway debut; maybe, just maybe, their spirit lived on in these tiles. They had all come here with a dream. We had all come here with a dream. I lathered up my L'Occitane shea butter bar and traced my name with purple fingertips; the soapy letters sparkled upon the dinge. I closed my eyes and let the warmth of the water wash away my waning anxiety.

Inhale the sweet, smoothing scent of verbena.

Exhale the bright, balmy bouquet of bleach.

This bathroom and I were part of history, and someday I hope to make total peace with that. But today would not be that day, and it was unlikely that I would ever be able to shower here without my "accessories." Still, this moment was a monumental victory. I collapsed into a stark white bath towel and dissolved into tears, dabbing at them with the baby-blue Frette.

No one was happier than my mum that I had conquered my very own shower, but Dante was a close second, and we made a date to celebrate on the weekend. He and Laurent were on double duty; they had given Le Brasserie a month's notice, and construction had begun on their new place.

Things were full-on for my boyfriend, and as for me, my kick-ass casting was tomorrow, and tonight was my first night in my very own apartment. I was feeling like a super bad-ass woman whom anything could happen to, but I would be sleeping with the lights on.

Chapter 48

SHEILA SUMMERVILLE WALKED OUT of the studio at Godlove Casting, fawning all over the casting director.

"So good to see you," she said in her sickly sweet falsetto fashion, followed by her predictable phony smile and, of course, the hair flick. Then her eyes met mine. I returned her poisonous stare, the corners of my mouth turned up with a casual confidence.

"Alex Emmerson?" the casting director said, searching the waiting area. I nodded.

"You're on deck."

There you have it. I was on deck, sporting a black tank and jeans, just like Sheila and all the other girls who were waiting and none of whom was speaking. Sheila broke the silence with none of her contrived charm.

"How's Dante?" she hissed. "Excited about his new venue?"

I know all about you guys, Sheila, and I don't care.

"We both are," I said with eyes sparkling. My mojo was back on track.

She slivered to the elevator, seething but still smiling, and I sauntered into Studio 2.

The five women seated behind a TV monitor inspecting me were unnerving, but knowing that one of those women was Stefanie's lady made me feel safe, like someone working undercover was on my side. Trying to determine which one of 'the five' she might be was so intriguing that for a brief moment I forgot my nerves entirely.

Only one of 'the five' wasn't wearing a wedding ring. She was striking, with dark, exotic features—Stefanie's polar opposite. Tyler had pointed out that Stefanie was what one called a lipstick lesbian. The term now made total sense to me. I imagine that watching the two of them kiss would be quite erotic.

"Hi Alex. I'm Dana." The casting director's introduction interrupted my mental detour. "We're going to slate, have you tell us something about yourself and do some face appreciation."

Face appreciation?

"Great," I said.

"Alex, where are you from?"

"Canada."

"How are you liking the city?"

"Honestly, it was a rough entry but I'm starting to love it. I just moved into my own apartment." Low murmurs and whispering hummed beyond the monitor.

"Can you tell us about any special moments?"

"I'm falling hopelessly in love for the first time in my life." Nods of approvals and 'the fives' soothing collective "Aw" begged for more.

"And I braved my friend's shower without wearing rubber gloves," I said with a jubilance that was met with a stunned silence. Dana didn't know where to take the interview.

The dark, exotic (possible lipstick lesbian) woman asked, "Why do you wear rubber gloves in the shower?"

"I'm a plumbaphobe." My declaration laden with pride, I continued, "I carry a pair of rubber gloves wherever I go. There's some in my faux Birkin right now."

There's some honesty right there.

Her dark eyes flickered. She gave me a satisfied smirk and nodded at Dana, who proceeded to the face appreciation component of the casting.

"Use the lens of the camera like a mirror," Dana said.

And then something happened. A surreal out-of-body experience. I was transported back in time. Staring at Alex Emmerson pre-new and improved, pre-makeover. She wasn't thin but she wasn't fat, she was cool in her weird sort of way, and she didn't have cankles!

"Alex, the lens is a more of a bathroom mirror. Your face is your focus," Dana said.

"Oh, right. Sorry. I just realized that I don't have cankles."

The studio erupted into laughter, which rippled inside me as I thoughtfully stroked my face, appreciating my youthful, lustrous skin.

"Thank you. Great job."

I could feel 'the fives' silent applause as it followed me out of the studio.

☉

My personal victories aside, the entire week had been a raging success. Patrick had landed a recurring role on a daytime soap, and Virginie had found a swanky two-bedroom loft in TriBeCa. My first Friday night stop was Leonard Street to meet the elusive Caleb Baker. His tousled blond hair framed his chiseled features; his green eyes were spotlights that followed Virginie's every move. His 6'6" frame towered over us, but he moved with artful agility. Physically, he was all varsity sports, but he had a quiet magnetism about him. He was soft-spoken and gentle with his words.

"It's a sincere pleasure to finally meet you, Alex. Please excuse the mess." Moving boxes and clothes were scattered across the bamboo floors.

"I've heard so much about you," I said.

Blood rushed to his cheeks and he steered the conversation away from himself.

Aw, he's shy.

"Gigi is still getting ready."

"That's what he calls me, chérie" Virginie sang from somewhere amid the chaos. "Isn't it wonderful?"

Gigi? There couldn't be a more perfect name. "The Night They Invented Champagne"

would be stuck in my head all evening.

"How many wardrobe changes have there been so far?"

"Four." He laughed and guided me to the kitchen, where three Daum Crystal Louis XV glasses were waiting.

Virginie flitted toward us with all the carefree fabulousness of Audrey Hepburn's Gigi.

"Let's drink to true friends and true love."

Caleb smiled with tears in his eyes and I almost fell apart, but the night was young and the celebrating had barely begun. The festivities commenced at Indochine with Dante, Virginie, Caleb, and me.

Between stolen kisses on all sides, Dante whispered that Virginie was a completely different person with Caleb. Her sexuality was pervasive as ever, but only she and Caleb were lassoed inside. He'd never spent time with Virginie outside Le Brasserie and didn't know her sweet, funny side.

"Dante, I can't believe you . . ." She laughed until her sides hurt, unable to get out her words. "F-f-f found the condom and the rubber gloves."

Caleb hadn't heard the entire story and asked me to clarify the plumba-phobia element. Tears were streaming down his face when I reached the Saran Wrap portion of the program.

We #endedupat10ak with Tyler, who was sloshed and solo. Raoul had a little problem with the INS and had been shipped back to Spain. The Universe, it would seem, had intervened. "It's not like I turned him in," Tyler said with a mysterious twinkle in his eyes.

"And the Adonis?" I asked.

"Done, baby lamb. He's dull and dizzy as dishwater. But you see that man in the corner?"

He looked like a Roman statue that had been chiseled out of granite.

"Let's ask the Universe to send him home with me tonight."

I'm sure Tyler would be shagging him sideways until dawn. Laurent and Patrick met us when they finished their shift.

I'm not sure who was picking up the check for our bottle service, but the champagne and the vodka didn't stop flowing. The dance floor was hopping and dead center was Virginie, and Lisa, who was grinding up against a Chris Hemsworth doppelgänger. Leonardo DiCaprio was sequestered somewhere in the back of the club and there were rumors that Rhi Rhi might make an appearance. The entire evening was the ultimate in beyond the velvet rope. My Louboutins glittered in the darkness as I relished the madness.

"Come on, sweatpants," Laurent said. "Let's have a dance."

Without a moment's hesitation, I grabbed his hand. We weaved our way through the masses, entranced by the melodic house beats. The track peaked and crescendoed; I kicked up my heels, balled my hands into fists, and exploded into motion. Arms flailing, my elbow almost took out Lisa's eye and my sidestep sent Virginie sprawling. She even fell with finesse. No one seemed to mind, and I kept dancing until 3:00 a.m.

"Wow, sweatpants," Laurent said. "Your skills on the dance floor are worse than your runway skills."

"You can just suck it, Laurent."

I had danced on the tables, whirled around the floor, drank champagne, and twirled out the door.

"It may behoove you to know that I kicked ass at a big-time casting."

"And I'm going to kick your ass big time if you don't shut up." Dante lunged at him, but Laurent was whisked away by a generic bottle blonde whom I recognized from Sheila's Instagram.

"Usual cast of characters?" I asked.

"Your place or mine?" Dante answered.

≷ ☺ ≶

I leaned into the stripper pole and asked, "Why did you choose your apartment?"

His hair fell over his eyes as he glanced toward the slow-burning ash of his cigarette.

"Your apartment is nonsmoking, and this is where we fell down the rabbit hole."

"The pole here played no part in your decision making." He seemed uncomfortable with it standing between us.

"This isn't where I want our night to end."

His bedroom was immaculate, white all over, even the hardwood flooring. His low bed, buried in deep charcoal-gray bedding, was the room's centerpiece. With each kiss on my fingertips, he led me closer to it. There was a calm on his face as he lit two candles on the bedside table. My attempt at a seductive smile failed.

"Are you nervous?" He looked deep into my eyes.

"Are there any handcuffs hiding in here?"

He laughed. "You might find some hidden in the top drawer of that dresser."

It was pressed against the far wall. I clamored over him, shot across the room, and wrenched open the drawer. The handcuffs didn't bother me, but there was something balled up lurking beneath them. The room started spinning.

It can't be.

Rage coursed through my veins and burned my tears as I unraveled the *I Shagged the Drummer* T-shirt. I met his chestnut eyes, daring him to say something. "Is it hers?"

"Yes."

"Why is it in your dresser?"

"I don't know."

I grabbed the rancid thing and ran down the stairs with Dante, who was shirtless, in hot pursuit. I'd almost made it out of the door when Laurent stumbled in and knocked all three of us down.

"Again with you two? Learn some control." Sound advice from a man whose neck looked battle-scarred from his leechy pick of the night.

"I was just leaving," I said from my precarious position sandwiched between them.

"It's always crazy when you leave this place, sweatpants."

"Not to worry," I said, shoving him off of me. "I'm never coming back."

Dante heaved himself up, and we stood face-to-face with Laurent still sprawled between us.

"Alex, it's not what you think."

"What is it then?"

Laurent watched with bated breath, trying his best to remain invisible.

"A bunch of people kept stopping by this week to congratulate us. Everyone was just celebrating our new place."

He celebrated their new place with her.

"And Sheila stopped by and celebrated by taking her clothes off?" I asked.

Laurent felt this was a good time to weigh in. "Oh, yeah, she worked that pole better than anyone." We both glared at him and he pantomimed zipping his lip and maintained his position on the floor.

"I was going to tell you, but—"

"You wanted to sleep with me first?"

"I wanted to see you first." Dante ran his fingers forcefully through his hair. "You just moved into your apartment, the shower, your castings. I didn't want to upset you."

"How considerate of you." The stink of her sickly perfume and his after-shave made it difficult to breathe. I flung myself through the door.

Laurent's eyes were wide as saucers when he caught sight of Sheila's T-shirt.

"Fuck! Wait, sweatpants, Alex!" Laurent yelled after me. "I put it in the dresser!"

I took the three flights of stairs, three at a time, and threw myself into the nearest taxi. It wasn't until I collapsed onto the floor of my apartment that I allowed the tears to flow.

Chapter 49

I SPENT SATURDAY MORNING ALONE, cocooned in my apartment with a box of Oreos. I refused the flowers that arrived around noon, and shredded Dante's handwritten note in front of the poor delivery guy.

He wouldn't give up, and left messages in thirty-minute intervals all day, all of which I deleted without even listening. His persistence didn't end there; he enlisted the services of my friends, which was bang out of order. Virginie, Tyler, and even Caleb begged me to take his calls, but Sheila's T-shirt, doused in her foul perfume, sneered at me from atop my TV. I had yet to devise the diabolical plot for its demise.

Laurent gave up on calling and instead texted me a dozen times, but I refused to answer, and stopped looking after his sixth attempt at contact.

"Sweatpants, I put Sheila's T-shirt in Dante's dresser."

I'm not sure I believe you.

"Sweatpants, Alex, it was a joke."

A joke?

"Alex, it was me. I'm sorry."

I don't care.

"Alex, I did it. It was supposed to be funny."

Why would that be funny? Why would Dante think it was funny?

"Alex, it was a bad joke. I'm sorry."

Really bad.

"ALEX!!!! IT WAS ME!"

I DON'T CARE!

"A Great Big World & Christina Aguilera" was set to repeat on my playlist. I journaled the hell out of the whole experience. Two notebooks-full, front to back. Why didn't he tell me Sheila was at their apartment? If he didn't sleep with her, what did he do with her? What did she do on that pole? What happened with the handcuffs? What BDSM antics played out in his industrial-chic bedroom? Did Laurent really put the T-shirt in his dresser? Did Sheila?

The unendurable wretchedness of it all led to the lifting of my no smoking ban, which prompted a late night visit to 7-Eleven that resulted in two packs of Marlboro menthols and another box of Oreos. I was halfway through the second pack of cigarettes when Lori's promo popped up. *So You Think You Can Model?* There she was in all her glory, nailing her speech about how she "blossomed some young-ish Canadian girl into a bad-ass not-quite-supermodel." I gave her a well-deserved standing ovation and uncorked the champagne. "Thank you for believing in me, Lori Hastings. New York isn't the same without you."

Alcohol and cigarettes truly do encourage the whole "feeling satisfied with oneself," though stimulants weren't part of Erin's program. Nonetheless, I felt pretty darn satisfied with myself, all alone, in my new apartment on Saturday night. I could pee without gloves, sleep without Linus, and take care of business without Dante. As of this moment, he was officially booted from the wank bank. Welcome back, RDJ. I fell asleep watching *Iron Man*.

ᗢ ☺ ᗜ

Mike FaceTimed me Sunday morning at 7:00 a.m. EST. I crawled to my iPad with one eye open.

"Is that a bowl of cigarette butts on the windowsill?" he asked.

"No one is more disgusted by myself than myself." Which was a sharp turn from five hours ago.

"You have Oreos in your fucking hair." His voice carried a degree of concern.

"I don't care."

"I'm sorry for being off the fucking radar." He barely responded to my texts about my apartment, my shower, or the Haute casting.

"Might I inquire as to the timing of your resurgence?" It was 4:00 a.m. at home.

"Well, the broker fucking just left." He looked triumphal, laid back in his recycled-wood rocking chair. "I got the mortgage on that house, and I'm quitting Safeway."

His reno-and-flip plan meant as much to him as modeling had meant to me. Floods of tears poured out of me, soaking the baby-blue Frette. "I'm so happy for you."

"Enough with the fucking crying." Mike wiped his eyes. "Let's see this fucking apartment."

My body was still shaking from that brief intense cry, but I reversed the direction of the camera.

"What's with the shirt on the TV?" That was it for the tour. I re-reversed the camera.

"Oh, that's just Sheila's T-shirt," I said nonchalantly, "that I just happened to find in Dante's drawer, moments before we almost had sex."

"Fuck." Mike knew it was bad, really bad, because I was past the point of tears on this subject. Rage permeated my every word. Verbalizing each minute detail of the week's events was far more soothing than the journaling, but an ugly hangover was settling in.

"I need to lie down."

"Let's fucking address your situation one issue at a time. One, quit fucking smoking. Two, nice fucking work on the shower. Three, nice work on the skin casting. Finally, call the fucking Frenchman."

"Are you kidding me?"

Had he missed something in the retelling of events?

"It's not like he fucked her. She just took her fucking clothes off. So what?"

"He never told me she was at his apartment! She stripped for him! That's what!"

"Sounds like she fucking stripped for everyone. Give him a chance to explain."

"Fuck that."

Expletives were a rare thing for me, but *fuck* that. The only thing I was going to give him was the packet of double-stuff Oreos that he gave me. I had considered a number of ways to destroy them, but returning the packet unopened and unspoiled felt the most empowering.

"His roommate said he put the T-shirt there." The steady rocking of his chair was making me nauseous.

"Laurent's his best friend. He'd lie for him. I'd lie for you."

A fact that might not be in theme with #honest, but it was #true #real. That touched his heart in some way, and he looked like he might cry again.

"I'd lie for you too, but I'd never lie to you. I believe the fucking roommate. Give Dante a chance." That's the first time he had ever said Dante's name.

"You know what? He's no longer my concern." I hung up.

The Oreos, the cigarettes, and the entire bottle of champagne, however, were at the top of my list. Once the remnants of all my vices had been discarded, I settled into self-pity Sunday. Why wasn't anyone telling me Dante's an asshole? It felt like my entire inner circle were somehow siding with him. Wallowing in a vast pit of misery, and journaling about all the people and all the ways I had been wronged, droned on for hours. It was Keisha's voice that snapped me out of the funk.

"There you go feeling sorry for yourself. You gotta own your shit!"

My neighborhood Gristedes was one block away, but I called an Uber and headed to the Upper West Side.

Please let Keisha be there. Please let Keisha be there. Please let Keisha be there.

꒰ ☺ ꒱

Gristedes was markedly quiet for an overcast Sunday afternoon. Tonya was at the checkout, on her phone, and didn't look up when she said, "Where've you been?"

"I moved to the Upper East Side, my freezer's full of food, and I stopped buying Saran Wrap."

For now.

"Damn girl, you gotta quit smoking." Keisha sidled up to her register. "Do you want yellow teeth?"

The stench of day-old cigarettes was repulsive. "Everything's gone to shit."

"That hot guy left you 'cause of that video, huh?" Tonya was immersed in a video game, and the noises, coupled with the wretched fluorescent lighting, were bringing my hangover full frontal.

"Not exactly."

I wasn't sure if Keisha was shaking her head in exasperation about me, or the state of the shoppers who had started streaming into the store. The faux-English hippie in her swag of beads; a rather robust man whose crisp linen shirt was trying hard to cover his girth; an upscale, uptight brunette who was screaming at her phone; and the poor guy who walks around hitting himself in the head were among the crew.

"You didn't come here to talk about your new apartment," Keisha said. "But I liked that GFY."

"I came to talk about the guy."

"Told you," Tonya shot back.

"You better start talking. You see all the people who just came in here, okay?"

I started talking, and kept on talking while Keisha kept on checking out customers.

Tonya and the hippie shared some contentious words, but in true New York fashion, I let the chaos roll right off my back. If not for my circumstance, I might have celebrated that small victory.

Keisha interjected my monologue with a lot of uh-huhs and okays. She didn't speak to any of her customers, except the guy who hits himself. His eyes were glossed over with a confused stare. He was holding M&M's and two dollar bills but didn't seem to know the next step.

"You like the peanut ones, huh? I like the originals." Keisha touched his hand. "You get home safe." He nodded like he understood and shuffled out the door.

She directed her hip my way. A signal for me to continue.

"So, the day after our first date, we were supposed to meet up. But I was watching him with the cool crowd, and Sheila in the middle fawning all over him. I felt like I'll never be good enough—"

"You gotta stop with this shit!" She stopped scanning the upscale, uptight brunette's items, and her eyes bore right into the heart of me.

The brunette ceased talking on her phone. I could see her hands trembling.

"You need to start valuing yourself!" Keisha said. "You alone are enough. Okay?"

The brunette dissolved into hysterical crying. "Thank you. That's just what I needed to hear." She hugged me on her way out.

Maya Angelou really speaks to people. It's wasn't lost on me that Erin had said almost the same thing.

"Okay. But then I found out he slept with her."

"Told you," Tonya said.

"He cheated on you?" All activity ceased. I was afraid, not for myself, but for anyone who dared try to cross this woman.

"No, no, no. He slept with her two years ago, before me."

It felt like Gristedes itself unleashed a sigh of relief.

"Don't go messing up the present because you're looking at the past."

"But—"

"I don't got all day. Just tell me why you have those damn Oreos all up in your hair."

"On Friday night, I found her T-shirt rolled up in the top drawer of his dresser, moments before we were about to have sex."

Keisha threw her apron on the checkout stand. "Tonya, I'm on break."

I hurried after her, and rapid fired all the details of the entire week, the apartment, the shower, the casting, and building up to the crescendo of Sheila, the stripping, and the T-shirt. I was ready for her to go apoplectic when we arrived at Dunkin' Donuts, but she was reserved and pensive. It felt like a lifetime had passed before she spoke.

"You gotta go in there and get my latte." She handed me five dollars, but this wasn't about her coffee; the girl who didn't like me was working and looked none too happy to see me outside.

"Look at me." My sweatpants and the stale smell of smoke weren't my biggest hang-ups, but the Oreos in my hair? I'd been through enough. "Please don't make me go in there, not right now."

"You've nothing to prove to anyone."

I willed my taupe wedge sneakers right up to the counter, refusing to cower to the stink-eye aimed right at me.

"I'd like a French vanilla latte, four shots, and three caramel swirls, and a nonfat latte, please."

She didn't answer me. She took the money and glared at me the entire time I stood there waiting. It took the last remnants of resolve in the recesses of my very being not to launch into nervous chatter. I stood my ground and stared her down.

I did, however, say "Thank you."

It was an empowering moment. I feel like shit, I look like shit, but I will not be intimidated by someone else's shit.

Another life lesson from Keisha. I insisted on paying for the coffee, and we sat on that same bench in the center of bustling Broadway.

"You better be proud of yourself. That girl in there is as mean as they come."

"Actually, I do feel proud. It was kind of liberating."

"You're on the right track, girl."

"Not with him." I summarized the Sheila-Dante drama, the denials, the flowers, his handwritten note, his phone calls, my friend's phone calls, and Laurent's insistence that it was him. "What do you think?"

"It doesn't matter what I think. It doesn't matter what your friends think. It only matters what you think."

"I know." My concession was a feeble attempt to hide my longing for her words of wisdom. Keisha's uplifting speeches had been beacons of hope throughout this journey.

We sat there sipping our coffee, tuning out the traffic and the pedestrians passing by.

"You know, you could have your own TV show. Owning it with Keisha. People could call in and ask for advice."

The corners of her lips turned up in a half laugh-smile.

"I told my agent about you."

"I don't want nothing to do with that messed-up world. I'm sticking with psychology."

There couldn't be a more perfect profession for her.

"I could take up permanent residence on your couch."

"You've been great practice for me." She shot me a sideways glance and grinned. "You love this guy?"

"I think so."

"Does this guy love you?"

"I think so."

"Have enough courage to trust love one more time—"

"And always one more time," I said with a knowing smile.

In one fluid movement, fueled with finesse, she stood and tossed her empty latte in the trash.

"Don't be a stranger, Lean Cuisine."

She sauntered off under the rainbow taking shape within the clouds.

I arrived home feeling inspired, liberated, and empowered, but totally unable to make peace with the whole situation. I gave the breathing a shot, but shifting my focus inward took serious effort, and it didn't feel good. My baby toe was burning hot, like the rest of me. Probably a side effect of rage. Clarity still lingering in the beyond, I laced up my Asics, cued up Rachel Platten, and headed to Central Park.

This is my fight song

Take back my life song

I breezed past the Reservoir, ready to tackle the entire 6.1-mile loop around the park. My feet pushed through the pavement, my thoughts racing with the rhythm of my legs, fueling the flames in my heart. I'd found my place in all this madness, a place that I love. Shelia needed to become background noise, like the traffic and the sirens that I'd learned to drown out. The fire burning in me exhausted near the 65th Street Transverse, Sheila smoldering in the ashes.

Chapter 50

I KICKED MONDAY OFF WITH SOME BADASS girl power anthems—thank you, Queen Bey.

We flawless, ladies tell 'em

I woke up like this

I didn't exactly wake up like this. My killer blowout was straight from the salon, and I was rocking it with my distressed Paige jeans and my ba&sh faux fur coat. My whole vibe screamed urban chic.

Say I, look so good tonight

Goddamn, Goddamn

It was actually noon, but still Goddamn, Goddamn. I was headed downtown to meet Robin, who had asked me to stop by RADIANT. My arrival was met with resounding applause and whistles from the entire agency, which was bizarre. My entrance was entirely pedestrian, sans panache.

"Here she is," Robin said.

"The new face of Haute Honest!" Stefanie said, her voice gushing with emotion that I didn't know was possible.

"You're shitting me," I said.

"We're still talking numbers," Robin said with a predatory smile, "but I'm thinking eighty, maybe a hundred grand."

"You're shitting me."

Once convinced it was real, I launched myself across the office and wrapped my arms around Stefanie. She squirmed herself out of my bear hug and handed me off to Robin.

"You nailed the casting, doll."

"The cankle thing was a stroke of genius," Stefanie said.

"The cankle thing wasn't a thing. It was an out-of-body experience. I saw myself seeing myself, and I realized I don't have cankles."

"Amen!" Robin said.

"My girlfriend said that sealed the deal," Stefanie said.

"She's dark and exotic-looking?" I asked, and Stefanie nodded. "I knew it! I recently learned that you're a lipstick lesbian. And she was the one I would enjoy watching you kiss the most."

"You couldn't script this stuff." Stefanie smiled to herself.

I was whirling in a wave of emotions. "Thank you for believing in me," I said and wiped my nose on my sleeve.

"You did this, doll," Robin said proudly. "Go celebrate."

≥ ☺ ≤

"We're so pleased for you," Mum said and dabbed her eyes. She held the seams of her apron in a death grip and kept adjusting her hair. Dad stood rigidly by her side. We both knew she was on the verge of a ghastly emotional scene, and were set to end the call before her British poise fell apart.

"Right then." I think there was the beginning of a smile on my dad's face. "We knew you could do it. Churchill has never led us astray."

I hung up and hugged my phone tightly to my chest as my taxi screeched to a halt on Broome Street. My tattered, torn, and tired Birkin was perched beside me. We had been on the front lines together, abused, laughed at, and outcast; this triumph belonged to both of us, but my faux Birkin's part in this journey was over. It was time to make a monumental purchase.

> ⊰ ☺ ⊱

"Fucking nice!" Mike's face disappeared in his smile. "Take your agent's advice and fucking celebrate."

"The festivities have already begun," I said and presented my Madewell ruggedly cool, leather carryall.

"You're fucking celebrating with a bag?" Mike yelled.

"Not quite," I said. "It's what's inside the bag."

Here's the thing. "Bags" would never have made my rating scale. They didn't matter to me. It was my brand-new (fresh off the shelf from their Broome Street boutique), kick-ass, beyond spectacular, Golden Goose Deluxe Brand-Slide hi-top sneakers that were rocking my world.

"More fucking shoes?" He was on the verge of a violent diatribe.

"I have two bottles of champagne on ice." That stuffed a cork in him. "I'm going to invite my friends to help me celebrate," I said with all the fabulousness of a soap opera grande dame.

"I have some fucking news that might ice the fucking cake for the celebrations."

The proverbial cake he was hiding was well and truly frosted, and I couldn't wait to take a bite.

"Fucking Lydia's back from Hawaii. Troy broke up with her."

The news of her just desserts brought me a certain sense of satisfaction.

"He's a heartbreaker, that one." If anyone deserved some heartache, it was the lovely Lydia Baker, but maybe this would be the catalyst to her becoming a nicer person.

"Alex, I'm proud of you. Go celebrate for real!"

I snapped my iPad shut and dialed Virginie. "I booked Haute!" I screamed.

"Alex booked the skin-care campaign!" she screamed, and then whispered, "I'm at Le Brasserie with Caleb and Tyler. Sheila is sitting directly across from us."

"The daft bitch got sent home from our shoot yesterday for behaving like a twat." Tyler made no attempt at discretion, nor to mask his outright loathing. There was no doubt Sheila heard what he said. I could have kissed him, not like that Ritalin kiss, but nonetheless a kiss.

"Good job, sweatpants." It sounded like Laurent was leaning into Virginie's phone. "I'd text you but your phone sucks."

"Is Dante there?" I asked.

"No." Her ominous tone was telling. Telling me that we were thinking the same thing. There could be no sweeter way to celebrate. It was time to scatter Sheila's ashes. I stuffed Miss Summerville's T-shirt in my Madewell tote, grabbed my All Saints leather jacket, and slipped into my GGDB Slide hi-tops. Give a girl the right shoe and she can take over the world. My kicks and I were poised to make the entrance of a lifetime.

Chapter 51

SHEILA WAS PERCHED ON THE LEFT BANQUET with her posse, which today gloriously happened to include Darlene. Her catcher's mitt sneered up at me as I stepped brazenly through the doors of Le Brasserie.

My massive moment was upended when Dante smiled at me from behind the bar. I glared at Virginie. Clearly, this was part of her plan. His eyes locked with mine and he glided across the restaurant. I had no idea in what direction to take the entrance now. Dante swept me up into his arms, spun me around, and kissed me hard on the mouth.

"I'm sorry. I should have told you sooner. She won't be coming back."

How could I not give him a chance? He was a key component to my most cinematic entrance of all time.

"I love you, Alex." Professing his love for me sealed the deal, but he had me at "I'm sorry."

"Same," I said.

Darlene had barely picked her gaping jaw up off the floor when I passed by their table and deposited Sheila's T-shirt in her lap. "I guess you're not his type."

Sheila, with her ego in ashes and bereft of her bravado, executed my emergency exit strategy. Darlene and company followed suit.

Patrick opened a bottle of Dom Perignon. "Let's raise our glasses to our retired bartender's new campaign and to The Dream Team's new beginnings. *Santé.*"

"Here's to the next chapter," I said leaning into Dante, savoring this perfect moment.

We stayed glued to each other as we walked back to my apartment. The door had barely closed when in one sweeping motion Dante's jacket hit the floor and I was in his arms. "Virginie told me you've never had a real orgasm. Let's just see what we can do about that."

Photo by Lisa Houlgrave Photography

About the Author

MEET KATHY TONG, AUTHOR AND (NOT-QUITE-SUPER-) MODEL.

Kathy was discovered at the ripe old age of 20 behind the seafood counter at Canada Safeway.

That's right, she was slicing fish. And, studying at Simon Fraser University—but she walked away from all that to take a stab at a modeling career.

By all shapes and standards she was way too old to start modeling, and, at 5'8, kind of short. However, one Marie Claire cover and 28 years later (much older and no taller), she is still doing it. Of her career, she says this: "It isn't exactly playing out in the Hollywood fashion I had envisioned but the Lifetime made-for-TV version is still promising."

Not-Quite-Supermodel is Kathy's juicy first novel. How semi-autobiographical is it? She'll never tell.

She has no plans to go back to slicing fish…yet.

The villages are arranged by geographical region

• Forêt d'Écouves, forest; Château de Carrouges (12–19 miles/19–31 km).
• Parc naturel régional Normandie-Maine, nature park; Carrouges (19 miles/31 km).
• Bagnoles-de-l'Orne (25 miles/40 km).
• Haras National du Pin, national stud (34 miles/55 km).

Did you know?
In the 15th-century chapel built on the site of the Saint Céneri hermitage, there is a statue of the hermit and a granite stela, said to have been used by him as a bed, and believed to heal incontinence. Legend has it that, if young girls pushed a needle into the feet of the saint's statue, they would be able to find a husband.

A map introduces each geographical region

Northwest: pp. 12–53

Northeast: pp. 54–81

Southeast, pp. 82–151

Southwest, pp. 152–267

La Réunion, pp. 268–69

All of the villages are listed alphabetically in the index
pp. 270–71

🧺 Local Specialties
Artisanal produce and local delicacies; crafts and artistic activities in the village.

🗓 Events
Markets and key events in the village calendar (fetes, festivals, exhibitions, etc.).

🦋 Outdoor Activities
Excursions and activities in the open air (walking, watersports, mountain-biking, etc.).

🌿 Further Afield
Tourist attractions, towns, and other Most Beautiful Villages of France (marked with an asterisk before their name) within a thirty-mile (fifty-km) radius, or a one-hour drive.

Did you know?
An anecdote, historical detail, or cultural particularity of the village.

THE MOST BEAUTIFUL
VILLAGES
OF FRANCE

English Edition
Editorial Director: Kate Mascaro
Editors: Helen Adedotun and Samuel Wythe
Editorial Assistance: David Ewing and Isabella Grive
Translated from the French by Kate Ferry-Swainson and Anne McDowall
Design: Audrey Sednaoui
Copyediting: Penelope Isaac
Typesetting: Gravemaker+Scott
Proofreading: Samuel Wythe and Nicole Foster
Production: Titouan Roland
Color Separation: IGS-CP, L'Isle d'Espagnac (16)
Printed by GPS in Bosnia and Herzegovina

Simultaneously published in French as *Les Plus Beaux Villages de France:*
Guide officiel de l'Association Les Plus Beaux Villages de France
© Flammarion, S.A., Paris, 2019

First English-language edition
© Flammarion, S.A., Paris, 2016
This second English-language edition
© Flammarion, S.A., Paris, 2019

editions.flammarion.com

19 20 21   3 2 1

ISBN: 978-2-08-020390-8

Legal Deposit: 02/2019

THE MOST BEAUTIFUL
VILLAGES
OF FRANCE
THE OFFICIAL GUIDE

Les Plus Beaux Villages de France® association

Flammarion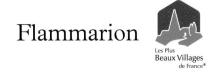

Les Plus
Beaux Villages
de France®

Preface

Come and discover, explore, wonder at, and stroll through The Most Beautiful Villages of France. Listen to the stones tell their story, linger on a café terrace, feel the cool water of a fountain run between your fingers, marvel at the skills of artists and craftspeople, fall asleep in a fairy-tale castle or dovecote, follow delightful walking trails, share in local celebrations and festivals, sample all the regional delicacies, and bring home choice items from the village market.

The Official Guide to the Most Beautiful Villages of France invites you to experience both simple and extraordinary pleasures, in exceptional locations that will awaken all your senses. Nearly 160 distinctive destinations—boasting a wealth of outstanding heritage and architecture, and buzzing with the vibrant energy and enthusiasm of their inhabitants—celebrate the French way of life, in all the diversity of their regions: from Alsace to the Basque Country, from Brittany to Provence, from Picardy to Languedoc, via Corsica and even the overseas department of La Réunion.

Whether you are seeking a short break or an extended vacation, whatever the season or occasion, this guide is the perfect traveling companion to help you enjoy these magical places to their fullest and to organize your stay with ease. If you are longing for a memorable rural getaway, The Most Beautiful Villages of France are ready to welcome you.

Maurice Chabert
President of Les Plus Beaux Villages de France association,
Mayor Emeritus of Gordes, in the Vaucluse

The Most Beautiful Villages of France

Inside story

The association of Les Plus Beaux Villages de France® was founded in the early summer of 1981 when one man encountered a certain book. That man was Charles Ceyrac, mayor of the village of Collonges-la-Rouge in Corrèze, and the book was *Les Plus Beaux Villages de France*, published by Sélection du Reader's Digest. This book gave Ceyrac the idea of harnessing people's energy and passion to protect and promote the exceptional heritage of France's most beautiful villages. Sixty-six mayors signed up to Charles Ceyrac's initiative, which was made official on March 6, 1982 at Salers in Cantal, France.

Today, this national network of almost 160 villages works to protect and enhance the heritage of these exceptional locations in order to increase their renown and promote their economic development.

Three steps to becoming one of The Most Beautiful Villages of France

Three preliminary criteria

In the first instance, the village looking to join the association must submit an application showing that it meets the following criteria:
- a total population (whether village or hamlet) of no more than 2,000 inhabitants
- at least two protected sites or monuments (historic landmarks, etc.)
- proof of mass support for the application for membership via public debate

Twenty-seven evaluation criteria

If these three conditions are met, the application is accepted. The village then receives a site visit. After an interview with the local council and a photographic report have been completed, a table of twenty-seven criteria is used to evaluate the village's heritage, architectural, urban, and environmental attributes, as well as its own municipal initiatives to promote the village.

The verdict of the Quality Commission

The finished evaluation report is put before the Quality Commission, which alone has the power to make decisions on whether a village should be accepted (an outcome requiring a two-thirds majority in the vote). About ten candidates apply each year, and about 20% of applications are successful. The approved villages are also subject to regular re-evaluation in order to guarantee each visitor an outstanding experience.

A concept that has traveled the globe

Interest in preserving and enhancing rural heritage transcends national boundaries, and several initiatives throughout Europe and the rest of the world have given rise to other associations on the French model: Les Plus Beaux Villages de Wallonie (Belgium) in 1994; Les Plus Beaux Villages du Québec (Canada) in 1998; I Borghi Più Belli d'Italia in 2001; The Most Beautiful Villages of Japan in 2005; and Los Pueblos Mas Bonitos de España in 2011. Collaborating with the Federation of the Most Beautiful Villages of the World, these associations are now taking their particular expertise to emerging networks.

Join us on www.facebook.com/LPBVT

To read more about the association, visit www.lesplusbeauxvillagesdefrance.org

BECOME A FRIEND OF THE ASSOCIATION

Join us and play your part in protecting the heritage of French villages by becoming a **Friend of The Most Beautiful Villages of France**. In return for your membership fee you will receive special privileges, gifts, and discounts to help you get the most out of your stay. Participating establishments are marked with a ♥ in this guide.

Membership details are available at the back of this book.

Preface

Come and discover, explore, wonder at, and stroll through The Most Beautiful Villages of France. Listen to the stones tell their story, linger on a café terrace, feel the cool water of a fountain run between your fingers, marvel at the skills of artists and craftspeople, fall asleep in a fairy-tale castle or dovecote, follow delightful walking trails, share in local celebrations and festivals, sample all the regional delicacies, and bring home choice items from the village market.

The Official Guide to the Most Beautiful Villages of France invites you to experience both simple and extraordinary pleasures, in exceptional locations that will awaken all your senses. Nearly 160 distinctive destinations—boasting a wealth of outstanding heritage and architecture, and buzzing with the vibrant energy and enthusiasm of their inhabitants—celebrate the French way of life, in all the diversity of their regions: from Alsace to the Basque Country, from Brittany to Provence, from Picardy to Languedoc, via Corsica and even the overseas department of La Réunion.

Whether you are seeking a short break or an extended vacation, whatever the season or occasion, this guide is the perfect traveling companion to help you enjoy these magical places to their fullest and to organize your stay with ease. If you are longing for a memorable rural getaway, The Most Beautiful Villages of France are ready to welcome you.

Maurice Chabert
President of Les Plus Beaux Villages de France association,
Mayor Emeritus of Gordes, in the Vaucluse

The Most Beautiful Villages of France

Inside story

The association of Les Plus Beaux Villages de France® was founded in the early summer of 1981 when one man encountered a certain book. That man was Charles Ceyrac, mayor of the village of Collonges-la-Rouge in Corrèze, and the book was *Les Plus Beaux Villages de France*, published by Sélection du Reader's Digest. This book gave Ceyrac the idea of harnessing people's energy and passion to protect and promote the exceptional heritage of France's most beautiful villages. Sixty-six mayors signed up to Charles Ceyrac's initiative, which was made official on March 6, 1982 at Salers in Cantal, France.

Today, this national network of almost 160 villages works to protect and enhance the heritage of these exceptional locations in order to increase their renown and promote their economic development.

Three steps to becoming one of The Most Beautiful Villages of France

Three preliminary criteria

In the first instance, the village looking to join the association must submit an application showing that it meets the following criteria:
- a total population (whether village or hamlet) of no more than 2,000 inhabitants
- at least two protected sites or monuments (historic landmarks, etc.)
- proof of mass support for the application for membership via public debate

Twenty-seven evaluation criteria

If these three conditions are met, the application is accepted. The village then receives a site visit. After an interview with the local council and a photographic report have been completed, a table of twenty-seven criteria is used to evaluate the village's heritage, architectural, urban, and environmental attributes, as well as its own municipal initiatives to promote the village.

The verdict of the Quality Commission

The finished evaluation report is put before the Quality Commission, which alone has the power to make decisions on whether a village should be accepted (an outcome requiring a two-thirds majority in the vote). About ten candidates apply each year, and about 20% of applications are successful. The approved villages are also subject to regular re-evaluation in order to guarantee each visitor an outstanding experience.

A concept that has traveled the globe

Interest in preserving and enhancing rural heritage transcends national boundaries, and several initiatives throughout Europe and the rest of the world have given rise to other associations on the French model: Les Plus Beaux Villages de Wallonie (Belgium) in 1994; Les Plus Beaux Villages du Québec (Canada) in 1998; I Borghi Più Belli d'Italia in 2001; The Most Beautiful Villages of Japan in 2005; and Los Pueblos Mas Bonitos de España in 2011. Collaborating with the Federation of the Most Beautiful Villages of the World, these associations are now taking their particular expertise to emerging networks.

Join us on **www.facebook.com/LPBVT**

To read more about the association, visit **www.lesplusbeauxvillagesdefrance.org**

BECOME A FRIEND OF THE ASSOCIATION

Join us and play your part in protecting the heritage of French villages by becoming a **Friend of The Most Beautiful Villages of France**. In return for your membership fee you will receive special privileges, gifts, and discounts to help you get the most out of your stay. Participating establishments are marked with a ♥ in this guide.

Membership details are available at the back of this book.

Create your own adventure!

Whether you're looking for a made-to-measure or an off-the-shelf vacation, you'll receive a warm welcome in nearly 160 outstanding villages just waiting to give you a wonderful experience.

Book online

The website of Les Plus Beaux Villages de France® has a dedicated online booking system that is compatible with tablets and smartphones. You can make reservations direct with our partner establishments without paying a booking fee. Choose your destination, click on the dates you want, and choose from the options available.

Visit www.lesplusbeauxvillagesdefrance.org

Take "La Route des Plus Beaux Villages de France"

With the company 4 roues sous 1 parapluie ("Four Wheels under an Umbrella"), you can set off in a 2CV on two amazing car rallies: "Villages Tour Paris–Cannes" (seven days) in May, and "Villages Tour Paris–Deauville" (four days) in September. From behind the wheel of the iconic French convertible, you'll take part in an original treasure hunt through a series of beautiful villages before

making a star's entrance right in the middle of a cinema festival.

4 roues sous 1 parapluie:
+33 (0)800 80 06 31
www.4roues-sous-1parapluie.com

Bespoke trips around the villages

If you prefer to travel under your own steam, you can organize an independent vacation with "My Trip Tailor," which offers bespoke tours that you can select and reserve online. Select your departure date, and reserve accommodation and activities along your chosen route.

Book tours at
www.lesplusbeauxvillagesdefrance.org

Book accommodation and activities at
www.mytriptailor.com

Save the date

Get to know The Most Beautiful Villages of France from every angle—heritage, cuisine, craftsmanship—and in every season, by taking part in events aimed at those who enjoy the finer things in life.

Journées Européennes des Métiers d'Art® (European Festival of Arts and Crafts), 1st weekend in April

Every year, in collaboration with the Institut National des Métiers d'Art, the association harnesses the villages' creative skills to host its European Festival of Arts and Crafts. Events include open studios, demonstrations, workshops, exhibitions, and art and craft fairs.

Visit www.lesplusbeauxvillagesdefrance.org
www.journéesdesmetiersdart.fr
(in French only)

Marché aux Vins des Plus Beaux Villages de France® (The Most Beautiful Villages of France Wine Festival), 2nd weekend in April

Since 1998, the village of Rodemack in Moselle—which borders Luxembourg, Belgium, and Germany—has hosted The Most Beautiful Villages of France Wine Festival. During this event, local wine producers welcome you to their vineyards and their villages.

Tourist information—Communautaire de Rodemack: +33 (0)3 82 56 00 22
www.tourisme-ccce.fr

Journées Européennes du Patrimoine® (European Heritage Festival), 3rd weekend in September

This event has become unmissable for anyone who is passionate about heritage and history, and is undoubtedly one of the best times to discover The Most Beautiful Villages of France.

Visit www.lesplusbeauxvillagesdefrance.org

Nuit Romantique des Plus Beaux Villages de France® (The Most Beautiful Villages of France Romantic Evening), June

On the Saturday following the summer solstice, The Most Beautiful Villages of France (and also its sister associations in Italy, Belgium, and Spain) organizes magical evening events around the country to celebrate the launch of the summer season, including guided walks, plays, concerts, tours, and themed dinners.

www.lesplusbeauxvillagesdefrance.org

JOIN US ONLINE

Go online at **www.lesplusbeauxvillagesdefrance.org** to keep up with the latest news, enjoy virtual sightseeing, share photos and itineraries, and choose your next destination, or follow us on social media.

Scan the QR code below to access the mobile website directly (available in French only).

f www.facebook.com/LPBVT
◎ www.instagram.com/lesplusbeauxvillagesdefrance
𝕏 www.twitter.com/LPBVF

Lille

Arras

Charleville-
Mézières

Amiens

Laon

Rouen

Beauvais

Châlons-
en-Champagne

Pontoise

St-Lô   Caen

Évreux

PARIS

St-Brieuc

Alençon   Chartres

Troyes

Melun

Rennes   Laval

Quimper

Le Mans

Auxerre

Vannes

Orléans

Nantes   Angers

Tours   Blois

Bourges

La Roche-s.-Yon

Nevers

Châteauroux

Poitiers

Moulins

Niort

Guéret

La Rochelle

Clermont-
Ferrand

Angoulême

Limoges

St-Étienne

Tulle

Le Puy-
en-Velay

Périgueux

Privas

Aurillac

Mende

Bordeaux

Cahors

Agen

Rodez

Mont-de-Marsan

Montauban

Albi

Nîmes

Auch

Pau

Toulouse

Montpellier

Tarbes

Carcassonne

Foix

Perpignan

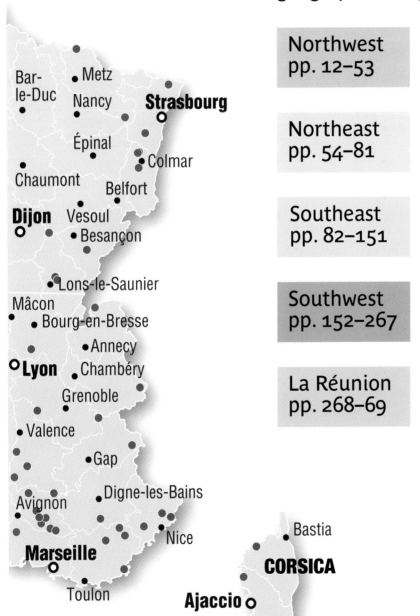

The 158 Most Beautiful
Villages of France by
geographical region

Northwest
pp. 12–53

Northeast
pp. 54–81

Southeast
pp. 82–151

Southwest
pp. 152–267

La Réunion
pp. 268–69

©éditerra

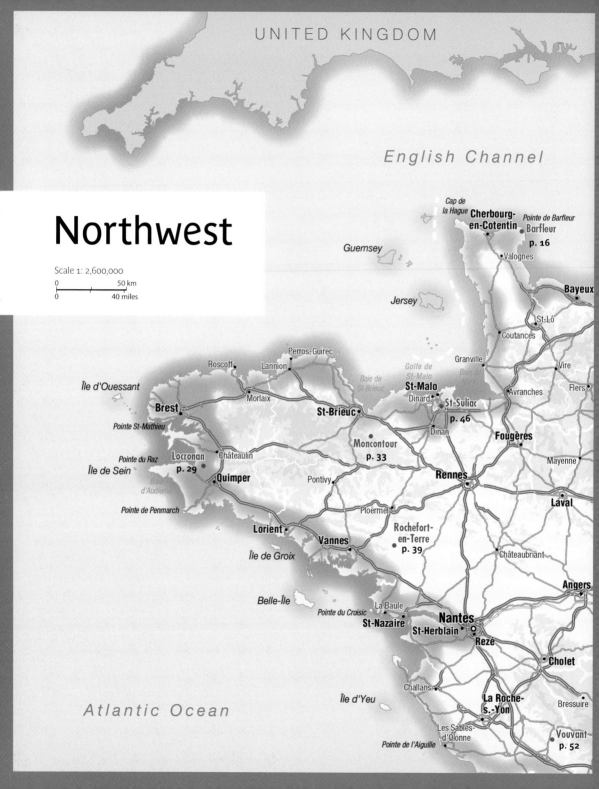

Northwest

Scale 1: 2,600,000

UNITED KINGDOM

English Channel

Atlantic Ocean

Cap de
la Hague · Cherbourg-
en-Cotentin · Pointe de Barfleur
Barfleur
p. 16
· Valognes

Guernsey

Jersey

Bayeux
· St-Lô
Coutances
Granville
Vire
Flers
Golfe de
St-Malo
Baie de
St-Brieuc
St-Malo
Dinard · St-Suliac
p. 46
Avranches
Fougères
Mayenne
Laval

Île d'Ouessant
Roscoff
Perros-Guirec
Lannion
Morlaix
St-Brieuc
Dinan
Moncontour
p. 33
Rennes

Brest
Pointe St-Mathieu
Pointe du Raz
Locronan
p. 29 · Châteaulin
Quimper
Pontivy
Ploërmel
Île de Sein
Baie
d'Audierne
Pointe de Penmarch
Lorient
Vannes
Rochefort-
en-Terre
p. 39
Châteaubriant

Île de Groix
Belle-Île
Pointe du Croisic
La Baule
Angers
La Roche-
s.-Yon
Nantes
St-Herblain
Rezé
Cholet
St-Nazaire

Île d'Yeu
Challans
Bressuire
Les Sables-
d'Olonne
Vouvant
p. 52
Pointe de l'Aiguille

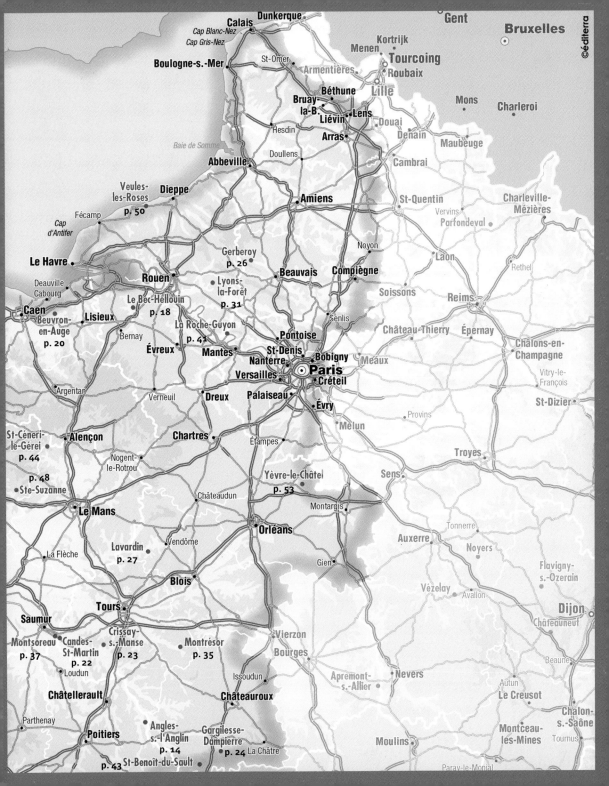

Angles-sur-l'Anglin
Traditional skills and ancient wall carvings

Vienne (86) • Population: 395 • Altitude: 331 ft. (101 m)

The *jours* (openwork embroidery) of Angles is a traditional skill that is still practiced in this village on the banks of the Anglin.

From the top of the cliff, the ruins of the fortress, built by the counts of Lusignan between the 11th and 15th centuries, overlook the river. At the top of the village, the Église Saint-Martin, with its Poitiers-style Romanesque bell tower, stands next to the 12th-century Chapelle Saint-Pierre. The "Huche Corne" offers a magnificent view of the lower part of the village, where the Chapelle Saint-Croix, an old abbey church with a 13th-century doorway, faces the river, which is bordered with weeping willows. With its old bridge and its mill wheel, this romantic environment is the perfect spot for providing artists with inspiration. Several lanes—les Chemins de la Cueille, le Truchon, l'Arceau, and la Tranchée des Anglais—run from top to bottom of the village and are lined with pretty pale stone houses. Nearby, the site of the Roc aux Sorciers (Sorcerers' Rock) houses a unique Paleolithic frieze carved into rock 15,000 years ago, which is now protected.

Angles has been famous for its *jours* for 150 years. Threads are drawn from fabric (such as linen or cotton) using very fine and sharp scissors, and the openings are then embellished with embroidery. Angles has for many years provided Parisian department stores with luxury lingerie.

By road: Expressway A10, exit 26–Châtellerault Centre (22 miles/35 km).
By train: Châtellerault station (21 miles/34 km); Poitiers TGV station (31 miles/50 km). **By air:** Poitiers-Biart airport (37 miles/60 km).

ⓘ Tourist information:
+33 (0)5 49 21 05 47
www.tourisme-chatellerault.fr

👁 Highlights
• **Forteresse d'Angles** (July and August): Remains of the fortress built in the 11th–15th centuries.
• **Maison des Jours d'Angles et du Tourisme:** Demonstration of the *jours* technique and sale of embroidered linen. Further information: +33 (0)6 82 00 78 95.
• **Village:** Guided tour Fridays at 3 p.m. for individuals; groups by appointment only: +33 (0)5 49 48 13 82.

♂ Accommodation
Hotels
♥ Le Relais du Lyon d'Or***:
+33 (0)5 49 48 32 53.
Guesthouses
Artemisia***: +33 (0)5 49 84 01 83.
Le Grenier des Robins:
+33 (0)5 49 48 60 86.
La Ligne: +33 (0)6 18 34 17 96.
Lorna and Tony Wilkes:
+33 (0)5 49 48 29 85.
Gîtes and vacation rentals
www.tourisme-chatellerault.fr

🍴 Eating Out
Le 15, tea room: +33 (0)5 49 91 01 25.
Crêperie d'Angles: +33 (0)5 49 48 95 53.
L'Amaretto, pizzeria: +33 (0)5 49 48 57 89.
Le Goût des Mets, gourmet restaurant:
+33 (0)5 49 84 36 02.
La Grange des Dames:
+33 (0)5 49 84 54 78.
Le Patio: +33 (0)5 49 84 18 37.
Le Relais du Lyon d'Or, brasserie:
+33 (0)5 49 48 32 53.

🧺 Local Specialties
Food and Drink
Broyé du Poitou (butter cookies).
Art and Crafts
Antiques • Secondhand bookstore • *Jours* (openwork embroidery) • Artists • Cross-stitch, lace, gifts • Custom clothing, hats, and accessories • Wood carving.

② Events

April: Spring flea market (Easter weekend)
May–October: Exhibitions.
June: Journée du Petit Patrimoine
de Pays, local heritage day.
July: Crafts days (weekend of 14th).
August: firework display with music
(1st Sunday); "Des Livres et Vous,"
book festival (week of 15th).
September: Journées du Patrimoine,
local heritage days; flea market.
November: Rouge et Or (arts and crafts
fair), street performances.

✺ Outdoor Activities

Canoeing • Rock climbing • Fishing •
Walking • Mountain-biking • *Pétanque*.

✿ Further Afield

• Parc de la Brelle (3½ miles/6 km).
• Abbaye de Fontgombault
(5½ miles/9 km).
• La Roche-Posay (7½ miles/12 km).

• Musée Mado Rodin, Yseures-sur-Creuse
(7½ miles/12 km).
• Abbaye de Saint-Savin (10 miles/16 km).
• Le Blanc (11 miles/18 km).
• Archigny: Ferme Musée Acadienne
(15 miles/24 km).
• Chauvigny (16 miles/26 km).
• Le Grand-Pressigny (20 miles/32 km).
• Parc de la Haute-Touche
(21 miles/34 km).
• Futuroscope, theme park
(30 miles/48 km).
• Poitiers (31 miles/50 km).

⚑ Did you know?

The village takes its name from the
unruly Germanic tribe of the Angles.
Charlemagne led descendants of this
people to the banks of a river—a tributary
of the Gartempe called the Angle, and
later the Anglin—where they settled,
hence the name Angles-sur-l'Anglin.

15

Barfleur

A port facing England

Manche (50) • Population: 600 • Altitude: 10 ft. (3 m)

In the Middle Ages, Barfleur was the principal port on the Cotentin Peninsula, and the village's history is tied to that of the dukes of Normandy and England.

It was a man from Barfleur named Étienne who, in 1066, carried William on the longship *Mora* to conquer England. In 1120 William Adelin (heir to King Henry I of England) and Henry's illegitimate son Richard perished when the *White Ship* ran aground at Barfleur Point. In 1346, at the beginning of the Hundred Years War, the English returned to the port, which they looted and burned. The 11th-century Romanesque church, which occupied the present-day site of the lifeboat station, was replaced by the Église Saint-Nicolas, built between the 17th and 19th centuries. Surrounded by its maritime cemetery, the building contains—by way of an ex-voto—a three-masted whaleboat, offered at the birth of the artist Paul Blanvillain (1891–1965). The Chapelle de la Bretonne, built in 1893 by the people of Barfleur in honor of the beatification of Marie-Madeleine Postel, features some remarkable stained-glass windows tracing the life of the saint, as well as numerous statues adorning its walls. Alongside humble fishermen's cottages surrounded by pretty little gardens, the opulent-looking houses of the Cour Sainte-Catherine (15th century), facing the fishing port and marina, are built—like those of the Bourg, La Bretonne, and the old Augustinian Priory (18th century)—from the gray granite that is part of Barfleur's austere charm.

By road: N13, exit Valognes (16 miles/26 km); expressway A84, exit 40–Cherbourg (66 miles/106 km). **By train:** Valognes station (16 miles/26 km); Cherbourg station (17 miles/ 27 km). **By air:** Cherbourg-Maupertus airport (11 miles/ 18 km).

ⓘ **Tourist information:**
+33 (0)2 33 54 02 48
www.barfleur.fr

👁 **Highlights**
• Église Saint-Nicolas: Built in the 17th–19th centuries on a rocky promontory at the center of a maritime cemetery, it is in the classical style and contains a superb Visitation by the Flemish school of the 16th century, which is listed as a historic monument.
• Old Augustinian Priory (18th century) and its garden.
• Chapelle de la Bretonne: Listed stained-glass windows tracing the life of Marie-Madeleine Postel.
• Cour Sainte-Catherine: The remains of a former mansion (late 15th–early 16th century).
• Lifeboat station: The first lifeboat station to be built in France, in 1865, modeled on English ones.
• Village: Guided tour in summer. Further information: +33 (0)2 33 54 02 48.

🗝 **Accommodation**
Hotels
Le Conquérant**: +33 (0)2 33 54 00 82.
Guesthouses, gîtes, walkers' lodges, vacation rentals, and campsites
Further information: +33 (0)2 33 54 02 48
www.barfleur.fr

🍽 **Eating Out**
Café de France: +33 (0)2 33 54 00 38.

Chez Buck, crêperie:
+33 (0)2 33 54 02 16.
Le Comptoir de la Presqu'île:
+33 (0)2 33 20 37 51.
La Marée: +33 (0)2 33 20 81 88.
Le Phare: +33 (0)2 33 54 10 33.

🧺 Local Specialties
Food and Drink
Shellfish and fish.
Art and Crafts
Antique dealer • Decoration • Art gallery •
Ceramic artist.

📅 Events
Market: Tuesday and Saturday in summer
(Saturday off-season), 8 a.m.–1 p.m.,
Quai Henri-Chardon.
June–August: Painting and sculpture
exhibitions.
Late July to early August: Été Musical
de Barfleur, classical music festival.
August: Village des Antiquaires, antiques
fair (3rd or 4th weekend).

🦋 Outdoor Activities
Walking: Route GR 223; hiking and
mountain-biking trails.
Watersports: Sailing, kayaking, diving.

🥬 Further Afield
• Barfleur Point (2 miles/3 km).

• Gatteville lighthouse (2 miles/3 km).
• Montfarville: church and its paintings
(2 miles/3 km).
• La Pernelle: viewpoint (4½ miles/7 km).
• Saint-Vaast-la-Hougue: Vauban towers
(9½ miles/15.5 km).
• Valognes, "the Versailles of Normandy"
(16 miles/26 km).
• Cherbourg; Cité de la Mer, science park
(18 miles/29 km).
• Château de Bricquebec (24 miles/39 km).

ℹ Did you know?
Some come here just for the Barfleur
"Blonde." This wild mussel, from
natural beds near the port, is fished
by professional fishing boats equipped
with a mussel dragnet, and is best
eaten between June and September.

Le Bec-Hellouin

Spiritual resting place in the Normandy countryside

Eure (27) • Population: 419 • Altitude: 164 ft. (50 m)

Between Rouen and Lisieux, this typical Normandy village takes its name from both the stream that flows alongside it and the founder of its famous abbey. The abbey at Bec was founded in 1034, at the time of William the Conqueror, duke of Normandy and England's first Norman king. Its first abbot was Herluin (Hellouin), knight to the count of Brionne. Both Lanfranc and Anselm followed Herluin into the abbey and were trained by him; both left their mark on Western Christianity. Lanfranc was a scholar and teacher who developed the abbey school; he served as archbishop of Canterbury in England from 1070 to 1089. Saint Anselm, philosopher and theologian, succeeded Lanfranc as prior of Bec Abbey and became abbot on the death of Herluin in 1078. He also became archbishop of Canterbury (1093–1109). Destroyed and rebuilt several times, Bec Abbey fell into ruin during the French Revolution and Napoleon's Empire. The only remaining part of the medieval abbey complex is the tower of Saint-Nicolas (15th century), which still dominates the site. In 1948 new life was breathed into the abbey by the arrival of a community of Benedictine monks. While Le Bec-Hellouin certainly owes its reputation to the religious prestige of this remarkable building, the village itself is also well worth visiting, with its half-timbered houses and flower-decked balconies nestling in the heart of a verdant landscape of woodland and fields.

By road: Expressway A28, exit 13– Le Neubourg-Brionne (3½ miles/5.5 km).
By train: Brionne station (4½ miles/7 km); Bernay station (16 miles/26 km).
By air: Deauville-Saint-Gatien airport (5 miles/8 km).

ⓘ Tourist information—Pays Brionnais:
+33 (0)2 32 45 70 51
www.tourismecantondebrionne.com
www.lebechellouin.fr

👁 Highlights

• **Abbaye de Notre-Dame-du-Bec:** Maurist (Congregation of Saint Maur) architecture of 17th and 18th centuries; abbey church, cloisters. Further information: +33 (0)2 32 43 72 60.
• **Église de Saint-André** (14th century): Important 13th–18th-century statuary.
• **Organic farm:** production and research site, permaculture school, resource center for permaculture, agroecology, and horticulture. Further information: +33 (0)2 32 44 50 57.
• **Village:** Guided tours Tuesday 2.30 p.m. in summer, by tourist information center.

🔑 Accommodation

Hotels
Auberge de l'Abbaye***: +33 (0)2 32 44 86 02.
Gîtes and vacation rentals
Le Petit Moulin***: +33 (0)2 32 35 40 22.
Au Chant des Oiseaux: +44 (0)1386 765972.
La Maison du Bec: +33 (0)6 14 20 12 22.
La Parenthèse: +33 (0)2 32 45 97 51.
Campsites
Camping Saint-Nicolas*** (March 15–October 15): +33 (0)2 32 44 83 55.

🍴 Eating Out

L'Antre de Cloches, tea room:
+33 (0)6 16 51 63 07.
L'Archange, crêperie: +33 (0)2 32 43 67 64.
Auberge de l'Abbaye: +33 (0)2 32 44 86 02.
La Crêpe dans le Bec, crêperie:
+33 (0)2 32 47 24 46.
L'EDEN: +33 (0)2 32 44 86 15.

🧺 Local Specialties

Food and Drink
Organic produce • Chocolates and cookies.
Art and Crafts
Art and antiques • Monastic crafts •
Art gallery.

📅 Events

April: Plant market; book and printed
ephemera fair (last Sunday).
July: General sale (closest Sunday to 14th)
and "Gourmand'Art," outdoor produce
market (Sunday after the 14th).
July–August: Exhibitions of painting
and sculpture.
August: Les Estivales du Bec, festival of
local produce and crafts (1st weekend).

🦋 Outdoor Activities

Horse-riding • Fishing (Bec stream) •
Walking (3 marked trails) and green route
(27 miles/43 km) of multi-trail paths along
the former railway line (walking, cycling,
roller-skating).

🌿 Further Afield

• Brionne: keep, former law court,
watersports on the lake (3½ miles/5.5 km).
• Harcourt: castle, arboretum
(8 miles/13 km).
• Sainte-Opportune-du-Bosc: Château
de Champ-de-Bataille (8½ miles/13.5 km).
• Le Neubourg: Musée de l'Ecorché
d'Anatomie, museum of anatomy
(11 miles/18 km).
• Pont-Audemer, "the Venice of
Normandy": Musée A.-Canel, museum
(12 miles/19 km).
• Bernay: museum, abbey church
(14 miles/23 km).
• Beaumesnil: museum, castle
(24 miles/39 km).
• Évreux: cathedral, Gisacum religious
sanctuary (27 miles/43 km).
• Rouen (27 miles/43 km).

Beuvron-en-Auge

The flavors of Normandy

Calvados (14) • Population: 246 • Altitude: 33 ft. (10 m)

Nestled between valleys dotted with apple trees and half-timbered farmhouses, Beuvron, centered around its covered market, is a showcase for the Pays d'Auge.

In the 12th century, Beuvron consisted of only a small medieval castle and a church. By the end of the 14th century, however, reflecting the fame of the resident Harcourt family, the town was in its heyday. This Norman family with royal connections helped establish the town's commercial activities right up until the French Revolution, and built the present church and chapel of Saint-Michel de Clermont overlooking the Auge valley. Bedecked with geraniums and decorated in rendered plaster or pink brick, the façades of the wooden-frame houses recall the village's four centuries of glory, while the steep roofs are covered with slates or tiles. The houses and businesses huddle around the magnificently restored covered market. On the edge of the village, farms, manors, and stud farms stretch out into the woods and farmland, keeping alive the region's local traditions and specialties.

By road: Expressway A13, exit 29–Cabourg (4½ miles/7 km). **By train:** Lisieux station (18 miles/29 km); Caen station (19 miles/31 km). **By air:** Caen-Carpiquet airport (26 miles/42 km).

ⓘ Tourist information:
+33 (0)2 31 39 59 14
www.beuvroncambremer.fr
www.beuvron-en-auge.fr

👁 Highlights
• **Church** (17th century): 18th-century main altar, stained-glass windows by Louis Barillet, pulpit in Louis XVI style.
• **Chapelle de Saint-Michel-de-Clermont** (12th–17th century): Statues of Saints Michael and John the Baptist.
• **Stud farm Haras de Sens:** Visit a stud farm that breeds, raises, and trains horses; groups by appointment only: +33 (0)2 31 79 23 05.
• **Espace des Métiers d'Art:** In the former school are five art and craft studios, and a multipurpose exhibition space. Further information: +33 (0)2 31 39 59 14.
• **Village:** Guided visits for individuals in summer, and for groups by reservation. Further information: +33 (0)2 31 39 59 14.

⚷ Accommodation
Guesthouses
♥ Le Clos Fleuri ***: +33 (0)2 31 39 00 62.
Aux Trois Damoiselles: +33 (0)2 31 39 61 38.
M. and Mme Pierre de La Brière: +33 (0)2 31 79 10 20.
Domaine d'Hatalaya: +33 (0)2 31 85 46 41.
Manoir de Sens: +33 (0)2 31 79 23 05.
Le Pavé d'Hôtes: +33 (0)2 31 39 39 10.
Le Pressoir: +33 (0)6 83 29 42 52.
Gîtes
M. Patrick De Labbey***: +33 (0)2 31 79 12 05.
La Maison du Haras: +33 (0)6 98 25 51 84.
RV parks
Further information: +33 (0)2 31 39 59 14.

🍴 Eating Out
Le Café du Coiffeur: +33 (0)2 31 79 25 62.
Le Café Forges: +33 (0)2 31 74 01 78.
La Colomb'Auge, crêperie: +33 (0)2 31 39 02 65.
L'Orée du Village: +33 (0)2 31 79 49 91.
Le Pavé d'Auge: +33 (0)2 31 79 26 71.

🧺 Local Specialties
Food and Drink
Cider AOC, Beuvron cider • Calvados.
Art and Crafts
Antique dealers • Artists' studios • Fashion designer • Painter • Sculptor, *Santon* (crib figure) maker, animal painter • Ceramic artist • Cabinetmaker

📅 Events
April: Boogie blues at Sens stud farm.
May: Geranium fair.
July: Antiques fair.
July–August: Art and craft exhibitions.
August: Grand flea market.
October: Large market and traditional cider festival, boogie-woogie at Sens stud farm.
December: Christmas market.

🦋 Outdoor Activities
Fishing • Walking (one marked trail).

🌿 Further Afield
• Manor houses and castles in the Beuvron region (½–6 miles/1–9.5 km).
• Cambremer (6 miles/9.5 km).
• Côte Fleurie, coast in bloom, Cabourg (9½ miles/15 km).
• Caen (19 miles/31 km).

❗ Did you know?
The covered market in Beuvron's main square is not as old as it looks. It was actually built in 1975 on the site of the previous market building, using materials recycled from farms and barns set to be demolished when the Normandy expressway was being built.

Candes-Saint-Martin

Bright reflections where rivers meet

Indre-et-Loire (37) • Population: 229 • Altitude: 131 ft. (40 m)

Built on a hillside, Candes gazes at its own reflection in the waters of the Vienne and Loire. Springing up where two rivers merge, Candes was for centuries a village of barge people, who contributed to the busy traffic on the Loire and the Vienne by selling local wines, plum brandies, and tufa stone from their *toues* (traditional fishing boats) and barges on the Loire. Indeed, the striking whiteness of tufa stone beneath the dark slate and tiled roofs still brightens the houses and the imposing collegiate church in the village. Built between 1175 and 1225 and fortified in the 15th century, the church is dedicated to Saint Martin, the bishop of Tours, who brought Christianity to Gaul. One of its stained-glass windows recreates the nocturnal removal of his body by monks from Tours. More than sixteen centuries after his death, Saint Martin is still revered through legends of his many miracles. Undoubtedly the best tells the story of how, when his remains were taken by boat to Tours on November 11, 397, the banks of the Loire burst into unseasonal summer blooms. This was the first ever *été de la Saint-Martin*—also known as an Indian summer.

By road: Expressway A85, exit 5–Bourgueil (6 miles/9.5 km). **By train:** Saumur station (8½ miles/13.5 km); Saint-Pierre-des-Corps TGV station (42 miles/68 km). **By air:** Tours-Saint-Symphorien airport (43 miles/69 km).

ⓘ Tourist information—Azay–Chinon Val de Loire: + 33 (0)2 47 93 17 85 www.azay-chinon-valdeloire.com

👁 Highlights
• **Collégiale Saint-Martin**, collegiate church (12th and 13th centuries): Plantagenet Gothic style, fortified in the 15th century.
• **Centre Permanent d'Initiative à l'Environnement du Patrimoine Fluvial:** Find out about the area's river heritage; boat trips in July and August: +33 (0)2 47 95 93 57.
• **Village:** Guided tours given by the Association des Amis de Candes: +33 (0)2 47 95 90 71.

⚷ Accommodation
Guesthouses
La Basinière: +33 (0)2 47 95 98 45.
Gîtes and vacation rentals
Le Château de Môh**** and ***:
+33 (0)2 47 58 88 88.
Le Gîte de la Confluence****:
+33 (0)2 45 95 87 12.
Les Lavandières: +33 (0)2 47 95 86 62.
Le Logis de la Renaissance***:
+33 (0)2 41 62 25 21.
Le Moulin Saint-Michel: +33 (0)2 41 51 18 23.
Campsites
Camping Belle Rive: +33 (0)2 47 97 46 03.

🍴 Eating Out
La Brocante Gourmande, bookshop and tea room: +33 (0)2 47 95 96 39.
L'Onde Viennoise, brasserie:
+33 (0)2 47 95 90 66.
La Route d'Or: +33 (0)2 47 95 81 10.

🧺 Local Specialties
Food and Drink
AOC wines from Tours, Chinon-Tours, and Saumur-Tours.
Art and Crafts
Ceramic artist • Silver- and goldsmith • Perfumer • Photographer • Painter.

② Events
Country market: Saturday mornings, 9 a.m.–1 p.m., east car park.
Throughout the year: Concerts: +33 (0)2 47 95 90 61.
July and August: "Flâneries Piétonnes" (village closed to traffic, various activities): Sundays 2–6 p.m.; village festival.
November: Fête de la Saint-Martin.

🦋 Outdoor Activities
Bathing: Confluence beach (no lifeguard) • Fishing • Boat trips • Walking: path along the Loire, via Sancti Martini • Cycling: "Loire à Vélo" trail.

🌿 Further Afield
• *Montsoreau (½ mile/1 km), see pp. 37–38.
• Abbaye de Fontevraud (4½ miles/6.5 km).
• Seuilly: La Devinière, Rabelais's house (9½ miles/15.5 km).
• Chinon (11 miles/18 km).
• Châteaux of the Loire and Indre (12–23 miles/19–37 km).
• *Crissay-sur-Manse (24 miles/39 km), see p. 23.

Crissay-sur-Manse

Renaissance charm in the Touraine

Indre-et-Loire (37) • Population: 116 • Altitude: 197 ft. (60 m)

A former *crisseium* (Latin for "where a fortress stands") in the 9th century, Crissay has retained its castle, its houses, its gardens, and two washhouses bordering the river Manse, which meanders beneath the poplars.

Originally a castellany belonging partly to Île-Bouchard, a large town at this time, and partly to the archbishopric of Tours, Crissay became the stronghold of Guillaume de Turpin and his descendants for nearly five centuries. The Château de Crissay was built on the foundations of the fortress in the 15th century. Of this seigneurial residence, which was never completed nor lived in, there remains only the main building, the keep from the 11th and 12th centuries, and underground shelters. Built in 1527 at the instigation of the Turpins, the church contains two 16th-century wooden statues representing Saint John and the Virgin, a piscina with floral *rinceaux* in the chancel, and the tomb of Catherine du Bellay, a cousin of the poet Joachin du Bellay (c. 1522–1560). On the upper square, the 15th-century houses recall Crissay's golden age with their mullioned windows and ridged dormers.

By road: Expressway A10, exit 25–Saint-Maure-de-Touraine (7½ miles/12 km).
By train: Noyant-de-Touraine station (6 miles/9.5 km); Tours station (29 miles/47 km); Saint-Pierre-des-Corps TGV station (30 miles/48 km).
By air: Tours-Saint-Symphorien airport (31 miles/50 km).

ⓘ **Town hall:** +33 (0)2 47 58 54 05
www.crissaysurmanse.fr

👁 Highlights
• Castle (15th century): By appointment only: +33 (0)2 47 58 54 03.
• Église Saint-Maurice (16th century): 16th-century statues.
• Village: Guided tour by appointment: +33 (0)2 47 58 54 05.

🗝 Accommodation
Hotels
L'Auberge de Crissay: +33 (0)2 47 58 58 11.
Guesthouses
♥ Les Vallées: +33 (0)2 47 97 07 81.

Gîtes
Le Puy Renault: +33 (0) 6 35 29 45 49.
Rochebourdeau: +33 (0)2 47 95 23 84.
La Vieille Chaume: +33 (0)2 47 97 07 33.

🍽 Eating Out
L'Auberge de Crissay, wine bar/restaurant: +33 (0)2 47 58 58 11.

🏪 Local Specialties
Food and Drink
Goat cheeses • Honey • Chardonnay, *vin de pays*, and AOC Chinon wine.

Art and Crafts
Art galleries • Historic bookshop.

📅 Events
February: Children's carnival.
April: Walk (3rd Sunday).
Pentecost Sunday: Foire aux "Vieilleries," rummage sale.
June: Feast of St. Jean.
July and August: Classic and modern theater in the castle courtyard (2nd fortnight of each month).

🦋 Outdoor Activities
Walking: 2 marked trails • *Boules* playing field • Communal garden • Park • Fishing.

🌿 Further Afield
• Roches-Tranchelion: collegiate church (1 mile/1.5 km).
• Vienne valley: from Île-Bouchard to Chinon (4½–14 miles/7–23 km).
• Panzoult: Cave des Vignerons, sculpted wine cellars (4½ miles/ 7 km).
• Tavant: church frescoes (7 miles/11 km).
• Azay-le-Rideau: castle (12 miles/19 km).
• *Candes-Saint-Martin (24 miles/39 km), see p. 22.
• *Montsoreau (24 miles/39 km), see pp. 37–38.

Gargilesse-Dampierre

Inspiration for a novelist

Indre (36) • Population: 325 • Altitude: 476 ft. (145 m)

This romantic village, with its harmonious houses overlooked by the château and church, stretches out over a sloping headland rich in vegetation. In 1844, novelist George Sand discovered this village, whose "houses are grouped around the church, planted on a central rock, and slope down along narrow streets toward the bed of a delightful stream, which, a little further on and lower down, loses itself in the Creuse." Only a postern and two round towers survive of the medieval castle, the rest of which was destroyed in 1650 during the Fronde (civil wars, 1648–53) and the extant château was built on its ruins in the 18th century. The 11th–12th-century Romanesque church, with its fine white limestone stonework, adjoins it. Its nave houses a set of capitals decorated with narrative scenes, including the Twenty-Four Elders (Revelation 4:4) at the crossing and scenes from the Old and New Testaments in the apses. The crypt is decorated with 12th–16th-century frescoes of rare beauty, representing the instruments of the Passion and various scenes from the lives of Christ and Mary. Following in the footsteps of Claude Monet, many artists—such as Paul Madeline (1863–1920) and Anders Österlind (1887–1960)—have been inspired by the charm of the village.

By road: Expressway A20, exit 17–Argenton-sur-Creuse (11 miles/18 km).
By train: Argenton-sur-Creuse station (8 miles/13 km); Châteauroux station (25 miles/40 km). **By air:** Limoges-Bellegarde airport (62 miles/100 km).

ⓘ Tourist information:
+33 (0)2 54 47 85 06
www.gargilesse.fr

👁 Highlights
• **Château** (18th century): Art gallery: +33 (0)6 81 19 65 53.
• **Romanesque church** (12th century): Capitals decorated with narrative scenes, including the Twenty-Four Elders from Revelation and scenes from the Old and New Testaments; crypt, 12th–16th-century frescoes representing the instruments of the Passion and various scenes from the lives of Christ and Mary; painted wood Virgin (12th century); guided tour daily in summer: +33 (0)2 54 47 85 06.
• **"Villa Algira," Maison de George Sand:** Collection of the author's personal effects in her former vacation home: +33 (0)2 54 47 70 16.
• **Musée Serge Delaveau:** Collection of works by the painter who lived at Gargilesse. Further information: +33 (0)2 54 47 85 06.

⚹ Accommodation
Hotels
Les Artistes: +33 (0)2 54 47 84 05.
Guesthouses
Le Georges Sand: +33 (0)2 54 47 83 06.
Le Haut Verger: +33 (0)9 53 54 17 78.
Gîtes
Further information: +33 (0)2 54 47 85 06
www.gargilesse.fr

Municipal campsite and chalets
La Chaumerette**: +33 (0)2 54 47 84 22.

🍴 Eating Out
Les Artistes: +33 (0)2 54 47 84 05.
Auberge La Chaumerette:
+33 (0)2 54 60 16 54.
Café de Dampierre: +33 (0)2 54 47 84 16.
Le George Sand, in summer:
+33 (0)2 54 47 83 06.

🛍 Local Specialties
Food and Drink
Goat cheese (*Gargilesse*).
Art and Crafts
Picture framer • Metalworker • Art
galleries • Pottery • Jewelry • Sculptor.

📅 Events
May: Flower and farm produce market
(2nd Sunday).
June–September: Concerts and
exhibitions.
August: Free art exhibition in the street
(Sunday before the 15th); harp and
chamber music festival (3rd week).
September: Journées du Livre book fair
(last weekend).

🦋 Outdoor Activities
Swimming • Fishing • Walking: Routes
GR Pays Val de Creuse and 654, Chemin
de Compostelle (Saint James's Way),
and marked trails.

🌿 Further Afield
• Gorges of the Creuse (1 mile/1.5 km).
• Lac d'Éguzon, lake (7 miles/11.5 km).
• Argenton-sur-Creuse (8½ miles/13.5 km).
• Crozant (11 miles/18 km).
• *Saint-Benoît-du-Sault (15 miles/24 km),
see p. 43.
• Nohant-Vic (24 miles/39 km).

❕ Did you know?
George Sand wrote of Gargilesse, where
her dry-stone house, Villa Algira, provided
a contrast to her grander mansion at
Nohant: "While waiting for fashion to
extend her scepter on this rustic solitude,
I am careful not to name the village
in question: I simply call it my village,
as one might speak of one's discovery
or one's dream."

Gerberoy
The roses of Picardy

Oise (60) • Population: 97 • Altitude: 617 ft. (188 m)

On the border between two villages that were once rivals, the houses in Gerberoy combine Normandy and Picardy traditions, featuring wattle-and-daub half-timbering and brick slabs.

The village, on the edge of the Pays de Bray, acquired a castle in 922 at the instigation of the viscount of Gerberoy. His son and successor completed the structure with the addition of a keep, a hospital, and a collegiate church in 1015. Given its strategic position at the crossroads of two kingdoms, the village of Gerberoy was soon coveted and contested. The fortified town belonged to the lords of Beauvais, then was successively besieged by John the Fearless, the Burgundians, and the Catholic League. The square tower that controlled the curtain wall is the only remnant of the castle that once adjoined the collegiate church of Saint-Pierre. Rebuilt in the 15th century after having been burned by the English, the latter still contains treasure in its chapter house. From the tower gate can be seen, down below, the paved courtyard and house that hosted Henri IV in 1592 after he was wounded at the Battle of Aumale. Captivated by "the silent Gerberoy," the postimpressionist painter Henri Le Sidaner (1862–1939) created beautiful Italian-style gardens here that are visible from the ramparts, and helped to make Gerberoy a village of roses, which have been celebrated every year since 1928.

By road: Expressway A16, exit 15–Beauvais-Nord (12 miles/19 km); expressway A29, exit 16–Hardivillers (20 miles/32 km). **By train:** Marseille-en-Beauvaisis station (6 miles/9.5 km); Milly-sur-Thérain station (7 miles/11.5 km); Beauvais station (14 miles/23 km). **By air:** Beauvais-Tillé airport (16 miles/26 km); Paris-Roissy-Charles de Gaulle airport (63 miles/101 km).

ⓘ Tourist information—Picardie Verte et Ses Vallées: +33 (0)3 44 46 32 20 or +33 (0)3 44 82 54 86
ot.picardieverte.free.fr / www.gerberoy.fr

👁 Highlights
• Collégiale Saint-Pierre (11th and 15th centuries): 15th-century stalls.
• ♥ Jardins Henri Le Sidaner: Designated a "remarkable garden" by the Ministry of Culture; terraces of the old fortress transformed into 1-acre (4,000 sq.-m) gardens by the artist Le Sidaner; artist's studio/museum: +33 (0)6 59 09 36 77.
• Jardin des Ifs: Award-winning garden unique in France for the age and size of its yew trees: +33 (0) 6 11 85 57 04.
• Musée Municipal: Archeology, crafts, and paintings and drawings by Le Sidaner.
• Village: Guided tour for groups all year round by appointment only: +33 (0)3 44 82 54 86 or +33 (0)3 44 46 32 20.

⚷ Accommodation
Guesthouses
Le Logis de Gerberoy****:
+33 (0)3 44 82 36 80.

🍴 Eating Out
Les Remparts****, restaurant and tea room: +33 (0)3 44 82 16 50.
IF**, local bistro: +33 (0)6 11 85 57 04.
Le Vieux Logis**, restaurant and tea room: +33 (0)3 44 82 71 66.

Les Jardins du Vidamé, bistro: +33 (0)3 44 82 45 32.
Tea rooms
L'Atelier Gourmand de Sarah***: +33 (0)6 73 19 02 06.
La Terrasse: +33 (0)3 44 82 68 65.

🏛 Local Specialties
Art and Crafts
Rose products (soaps, preserves, candles).

2 Events
April–September: Art and crafts exhibitions.
June: Moments Musicaux de Gerberoy music festival; Fête des Roses (3rd Sunday).
November: Country market (last Sunday)

🦋 Outdoor Activities
Walking: Route GR 125 and 3 marked trails.

🍂 Further Afield
• Picardy valleys: Songeons; Hétomesnil; Saint-Arnoult (6–25 miles/9.5–40 km).
• Pays de Bray, region: Gournay-en-Bray; Saint-Germer-de-Fly (8 miles/13 km).
• *Lyons-la-Forêt (22 miles/35 km), see pp. 31–32.

Lavardin

Grottoes and Gothic architecture

Loir-et-Cher (41) • Population: 220 • Altitude: 262 ft. (80 m)

This village, near where the poet Ronsard was born in 1524 (the Promenade du Poète that runs along the Loir river is named after him), bears the marks of centuries of occupation, from prehistoric cave complexes to the Renaissance and beyond. Lavardin became famous when it withstood Richard the Lionheart's attack in 1118, thanks to its castle's tiered defenses. However, the lords of the region were not in a position to fight back when they faced Henry IV—the king of Navarre—and his troops. Furious when his subjects refused to convert to Protestantism, the young king and the duke of Vendôme destroyed the fortresses of Montoire, Vendôme, and Lavardin. Today, the castle ruins command the village from the top of a limestone cliff. A tufa-stone Gothic bridge with eight arches spans the Loir. Standing tall at the heart of the village is the Romanesque church of Saint-Genest, whose nave and choir are decorated with murals from the 12th and 16th centuries. Almost every period of history has left its mark on Lavardin, which blends troglodyte, Gothic, and Renaissance houses. White façades rub shoulders with half-timbered houses topped with flat tiles. Larvardin also boasts the only grottoes in France in which, according to a widely held legend, a powerful druidic sect indulged in bloody sacrificial rites.

By road: N10 (7 miles/11 km); expressway A10, exit 18–Château-Renault (21 miles/34 km). **By train:** Vendôme station (16 miles/26 km); Vendôme TGV station (19 miles/31 km). **By air:** Tours-Saint-Symphorien airport (32 miles/51 km).

ⓘ Tourist information—Vendôme – Vallée du Loir: +33 (0)2 54 77 05 07
www.vendome-tourisme.fr
Town hall: +33 (0)2 54 85 07 74
www.lavardin.net

👁 Highlights

• **Castle** (11th and 14th centuries): Lodge, outbuildings, drawbridge, grand staircase, guardroom, keep. Open May–September: +33 (0)6 81 86 12 80.
• **Église Saint-Genest** (11th century): Wall paintings from 12th and 16th centuries, representing Christ's Baptism and Passion: +33 (0)2 54 85 07 74.
• **Musée de Lavardin**: Village history and castle heritage. Open May–September.

🔑 Accommodation

Guesthouses
À la Folie: +33 (0)2 54 72 60 12.
Gîte de l'Arche: +33 (0)6 21 21 78 36.
Gîtes
À la Folie: +33 (0)2 54 72 60 12.
Gîte de l'Arche: +33 (0)6 21 21 18 36.
Les Roches Neuves, cave-dwellers' gîte: +33 (0)2 54 72 26 56.

🍴 Eating Out

Le Relais d'Antan: +33 (0)2 54 86 61 33.

🧺 Local Specialties

AOC Coteaux du Vendômois wines • Regional produce (honey, goat cheese, charcuterie, mushrooms, cider, ice cream).

② Events

January: Fête de Saint-Vincent.
March: World Chouine (traditional card game) Championships, (1st Sunday).
Ascension: "Peintres au Village" painting contest.
June: "Feu de la Saint-Jean," bonfire.
July: "Embrasement du Château," celebration with fireworks.
December: Christmas market (1st weekend).

🦋 Outdoor Activities

Walking: Routes GR 35 and GR 335, and 3 marked trails.

🦋 Further Afield

• Troo: collegiate church, cave-dwellers' settlement; Couture-sur-Loir: Ronsard's manor (5–9½ miles/8–15.5 km).
• Thoré-la-Rochette: tourist train; Vendôme (6–12 miles/9.5–19 km).

♟ Did you know?

Each year Lavardin hosts the world championships in *chouine*, a card game that has been played since the 16th century.

Locronan

Thread and stone

Finistère (29) • Population: 810 • Altitude: 476 ft. (145 m)

A historic weaving village dominated by granite, Locronan owes its name to Saint Ronan, the hermit who founded it.

In the 6th or 7th century, while still haunted with memories of druidic cults, the forest of Névet became home to the hermit Saint Ronan. In the 15th century, thanks to the dukes of Brittany, Locronan became one of the jewels of Breton Gothic art. The priory church was built between 1420 and 1480, while the Chapelle du Pénity (15th–16th centuries), next to the church, houses Saint Ronan's recumbent statue. During the Renaissance, the village became famous for its weaving industry, providing canvas sails for the East India Company and the ships of the French Navy. The East India Company's offices still stand on the village square, as well as 17th-century merchants' dwellings and residences of the king's notaries. Locronan's Renaissance granite buildings regularly provide movie backdrops, for productions such as *A Very Long Engagement* (with Audrey Tautou and Jodie Foster) and *Tess* (directed by Roman Polanski). In the old weaving quarter, the 16th-century Chapelle Notre-Dame-de-Bonne-Nouvelle contains stained-glass windows by the abstract painter Manessier.

By road: N165, exit Audierne-Douarnenez (3 miles/5 km). **By train:** Quimper station (11 miles/18 km). **By air:** Quimper-Cornouaille airport (11 miles/18 km); Brest-Guipavas airport (39 miles/63 km).

ⓘ Tourist information:
+33 (0)2 98 91 70 14
www.locronan-tourisme.bzh

👁 Highlights

• **Église Saint-Ronan** (15th century): 15th-century stained glass, statues, treasure.
• **Chapelle du Pénity** (15th–16th centuries): Recumbent statue of Saint Ronan in Kersanton stone (15th century).
• **Chapelle Notre-Dame-de-Bonne-Nouvelle** (16th century): Modern stained-glass windows by Alfred Manessier; cross and communal washing place.
• **Musée d'Art et d'Histoire:** "L'Industrie de la toile" (the work of an 18th-century weaver, traditional costume collection) and "Locronan, Étape de la Route des Peintres en Cornouaille" (collection of paintings by 50 early 20th-century painters), Breton headdresses and costumes, reconstructed Breton interior; temporary exhibitions.
• **Village:** Guided visits for groups or individuals. Further information: +33 (0)2 98 91 70 14.

🗝 Accommodation

Hotels
Latitude Ouest***: +33 (0)2 98 91 70 67.
Le Manoir de Moëllien***: +33 (0)2 98 92 50 40.
Le Prieuré**: +33 (0)2 98 91 70 89.
Guesthouses
Mme Camus***: +33 (0)2 98 91 85 34.
Mme Douy: +33 (0)2 98 91 74 85.
Mme Le Doaré: +33 (0)2 98 91 83 97.
Vacation rentals
Further information: +33 (0)2 98 91 70 14
www.locronan-tourisme.org
Campsites
Camping Locronan***: +33 (0)2 98 91 87 76 or +33 (0)6 28 80 44 74.

🍽 Eating Out

Au Coin du Feu: +33 (0)2 98 51 82 44.
Le Comptoir des Voyageurs: +33 (0)2 98 91 70 74.
Le Grimaldi: +33 (0)2 56 10 18 37.
Le Prieuré: +33 (0)2 98 91 70 89.
Crêperies
Ar Billig: +33 (0)2 98 95 22 75.
Breiz Izel: +33 (0)2 98 91 82 23.
Chez Annie: +33 (0)2 98 91 87 92.
Le Temps Passé: +33 (0)2 98 91 87 29.
Les Trois Fées: +33 (0)2 98 91 70 23.
Ty Coz: +33 (0)2 98 91 70 79.

🏺 Local Specialties

Food and Drink
Galettes • Breton cake • *Kouign amann* (buttery cake).
Art and Crafts
Watercolorist • Antiques • Ceramic artists • Leather and tin worker • Bronze worker • Leatherworker • Painters • Art photographer • Glass-blowers • Weavers • Wood sculptors • Marriage-spoon sculptor.

🗓 Events

Market: Every Tuesday morning, Place de la Mairie.
May: Flower market.
July: Pardon de la Petite Troménie, procession (2nd Sunday).
July–August: "Les Marchés aux Étoiles," evening craft and local produce market (Thursdays, mid-July–mid-August); concerts (Tuesdays); flea markets and antiques fairs.
December: Illuminations and Christmas market.

🦋 Outdoor Activities

Walking: Route GR 38 and marked trails (Névet forest, circular walk; wheelchair accessible) • Mountain-biking (Névet forest).

🦋 Further Afield

• Douarnenez (6 miles/9.5 km).
• Châteaulin; Nantes–Brest canal (10 miles/16 km).
• Quimper (11 miles/18 km).
• Audierne (19 miles/31 km).
• Crozon peninsula (19 miles/31 km).
• Pays Bigouden, region; Pont-l'Abbé (24 miles/39 km).

ⓘ Did you know?

Locronan is one of the few Celtic settlements still to have a *nemeton* in the landscape. This large rectangle of land (making a circuit of 7½ miles/12 km) contains 12 markers corresponding to the 12 months of the Celtic year. It had a sacred purpose: to represent on earth the passage of the stars in the sky. Every six years, the Grande Troménie religious procession takes place in honor of Saint Ronan, and the inhabitants of Locronan walk this sacred path.

Lyons-la-Forêt
Village in a clearing

Eure (27) • Population: 759 • Altitude: 312 ft. (95 m)

Standing in the middle of one of the most beautiful beech groves in Europe, in Normandy's largest forest, Lyons's attractive half-timbered buildings are typical of the Normandy style of the 17th and 18th centuries.

Gallo-Roman in origin, Lyons-la-Forêt stretches along the Lieure river. The church of Saint-Denis (12th–16th centuries) and the historic Benedictine and Cordelier convents look down over the river. Right at the heart of Lyons-la-Forêt, the village center encircles the remains of the castle, where Henry I of England, son of William the Conqueror, died—supposedly from a surfeit of lampreys—in 1135. The village also clusters around its 18th-century market hall, in a triangle bustling with all the shops and businesses you'd expect from the region's county town. Built of colored cob, bricks, or half-timbers, the houses are bedecked with flowers. The Vieux Logis (coaching inn), the Sergenterie (sergeants' residence), the house of Benserade (a poet at Louis XIV's court), the Fresne (where Maurice Ravel composed), and the former bailiwick court (now the town hall) are the main attractions.

By road: Expressway A16, exit 15–Beauvais centre (37 miles/60 km); expressway A13, exit 20–Criquebeuf (21 miles/34 km).
By train: Rouen station (21 miles/34 km).
By air: Rouen-Vallée de la Seine airport (17 miles/27 km); Beauvais-Tillé airport (34 miles/55 km); Paris-Roissy-Charles de Gaulle airport (71 miles/114 km).

ⓘ Tourist information—Lyons Andelle: +33 (0)2 32 49 31 65
www.lyons-andelle-tourisme.com

👁 Highlights
• **Hôtel de Ville:** Prison cell and 18th-century law court: +33 (0)2 32 49 31 65.
• **Village:** Guided visits for groups by appointment only: +33 (0)2 32 49 31 65.

🗝 Accommodation
Hotels
La Licorne****: +33 (0)2 32 49 62 02.
Le Grand Cerf ***: +33 (0)2 32 49 60 44.
Les Lions de Beauclerc:
+33 (0)2 32 49 18 90.
Guesthouses
L'Escapade de Marijac: +33 (0)6 31 44 04 19.
Le Vieux Logis: +33 (0)6 80 40 00 40.
Gîtes
Les Hirondelles: +33 (0)6 31 44 04 19.
Further information: +33 (0)2 32 49 31 65
www.lyons-andelle-tourisme.com
Campsites
Saint-Paul***: +33 (0)2 32 49 42 02.
Le Bois Mareuil, naturist club:
+33 (0)6 63 98 00 45.

🍴 Eating Out
Le Commerce: +33 (0)2 32 49 49 92.
Le Grand Cerf: +33 (0)2 32 49 60 44.
La Halle: +33 (0)2 32 49 49 92.
La Licorne Royale, gourmet restaurant:
+33 (0)2 32 49 62 02.
Les Lions de Beauclerc:
+33 (0)2 32 49 18 90.
Le Petit Lyons: +33 (0)2 32 49 61 71.

🛍 Local Specialties
Food and Drink
Local Normandy produce.
Art and Crafts
Antiques • Gifts • Fashion accessory and homeware designers • Weaver • Artists.

📅 Events
Market: Thursday, Saturday, and Sunday 8.30 a.m.–1.00 p.m.
1st May: "Foire à Tout," general sale.
Pentecost: Craft fair.
July: Fête de la Fleur, flower festival (1st weekend).
October: Fête de Saint-Denis (mid-October).
December: Christmas market.

🦋 Outdoor Activities
Arboretum • Horse-riding • Walking • Cycling.

🌿 Further Afield
• Abbaye de Mortemer; castles at Fleury-la-Forêt, Heudicourt, Vascoeuil, and Martainville; Abbaye de Fontaine-Guérard; Musée de la Ferme de Rome (3–12 miles/5–19 km).
• Château-Gaillard; Château de Gisors; Rouen (12–22 miles/19–35 km).
• *Gerberoy (23 miles/37 km), see p. 26.

🔖 Did you know?
Lyons-la-Forêt has twice been the location for film versions of *Madame Bovary* by Gustave Flaubert. The first was filmed in 1933 by Jean Renoir. The second was made in 1991; directed by Claude Chabrol, it starred Isabelle Huppert.

Moncontour

A product of revolution

Côtes-d'Armor (22) • Population: 957 • Altitude: 394 ft. (120 m)

In a spot where two green valleys meet, Moncontour is girdled by its imposing medieval ramparts.

The village was founded in the 11th century as part of the defenses for nearby Lamballe, capital of Penthièvre. Despite being damaged in numerous clashes during the Middle Ages and partly dismantled during the French Revolution by order of Richelieu, the walls still boast eleven of its original fifteen towers, together with the Porte d'en-Haut and Saint Jean's postern. From the 18th century until the Industrial Revolution (and echoing its Finistère neighbor Locronan), Moncontour developed around the production of *berlingue* (canvas and linen cloth), which was exported to South America and the Indies. In this granite-and-slate world, the grand mansions, the town hall, and the Église Saint-Mathurin are reminders of this prosperous era. The Maison de la Chouannerie et de la Révolution reveals how the republican General Hoche established his headquarters in a mansion on the Place de Penthièvre during the French Revolution.

By road: N12, exit Moncontour (8½ miles/ 13 km). **By train:** Lamballe station (10 miles/16 km); Saint-Brieuc station (16 miles/26 km). **By air:** Saint-Brieuc airport (22 miles/35 km); Rennes-Saint-Jacques airport (60 miles/97 km).

ⓘ Tourist information:
+33 (0)2 96 73 49 57
www.tourisme-moncontour.com

👁 **Highlights**
- **Église Saint-Mathurin** (16th and 18th centuries): Listed 16th-century stained-glass windows: +33 (0)2 96 73 49 57.
- **Maison de la Chouannerie et de la Révolution:** Permanent exhibition about the Chouan guerrilla movement of the 19th and early 20th centuries: +33 (0)2 96 73 49 57.
- **Théâtre du Costume:** Permanent exhibition on knights in the Middle Ages, and costume from Louis XII (1498–1515) to 1900. Further information: Carolyne Morel, +33 (0)6 81 87 33 40.
- **Village:** Heritage walk, "The medieval fortress" (90 mins). Guided tours available for individuals in summer (Thursdays), and throughout the year for groups by appointment; themed guided tours in summer; carriage rides Mondays in summer: +33 (0)2 96 73 49 57.

🗝 **Accommodation**
Hotels
Hostellerie de la Poterne**:
+33 (0)2 96 73 40 01.
Guesthouses
À la Garde Ducale***: +33 (0)2 96 73 52 18.
La Vallée**: +33 (0)2 96 73 55 12.
Gîtes and vacation rentals
Mme Georgelin** +33 (0)2 96 73 44 24 or +33 (0)6 71 20 13 72.
Mme Leroux** : +33 (0)2 99 64 52 28 or +33 (0)6 87 48 30 21.

M. Ruffet**: +33 (0)2 56 26 91 05 or
+33 (0)6 33 38 37 18.
Moncontour Cité Médiévale :
+33 (0)2 96 61 46 85.
Mme Picard: +33 (0)2 96 61 46 85 or
+33 (0)6 61 94 38 45.
Campsites
La Tourelle**: +33 (0)2 96 73 50 65 or
+33 (0)6 76 74 85 04.

🍽 Eating Out
Adana Kebab: +33 (0)2 96 76 02 72.
Au Coin du Feu, crêperie/pizzeria:
+33 (0)2 96 73 49 10.
Le Chaudron Magique: +33 (0)2 96 73 40 34.
La Mulette: +33 (0)2 96 73 50 37.
La Poterne: +33 (0)2 96 73 40 01.
Les Remparts: +33 (0)2 96 73 54 83.

🏛 Local Specialties
Art and Crafts
Ceramic artist • Dressmaker and hatter •
Beadmaker • Stylist • Costume designer •
Painter • Stained-glass artist • Résidence
des Arts (exhibitions and residencies by
artists and craftspeople).

📅 Events
Market: Local produce, Monday evenings.
Pentecost: Pardon de Saint-Mathurin
procession, Pentecost festivities.
July–August: Sporting and cultural
activities (daily).

August (odd years): Fête Médiévale,
medieval festival (1st Sunday).
September: "Journée des Peintres"
painting contest; Festival Dell Arte,
street art (1st weekend).
December: Ménestrail, cross-country trail.

🦅 Outdoor Activities
Walking, horse-riding, and mountain-
biking • Nordic walking • Fishing.

🦋 Further Afield
• Plémy (3 miles/5 km).
• Hénon, Quessoy, and Trébry: parks
and residences of Ancien Régime
notables (3½–5 miles/5.5–8 km).
• Saint-Glen: Village des Automates,
clockwork and robotic toys (July and
August) (6 miles/ 9.5 km).
• Lamballe (10 miles/16 km).
• Saint-Brieuc (16 miles/26 km).
• Loudéac (17 miles/27 km).
• Quintin: castle and Musée Atelier
du Tisserand et des Toiles, working
weaving museum (18 miles/29 km).
• Le Foeil (20 miles/32 km).

Montrésor

In the heart of the Loire valley, on the banks of the Indrois

Indre-et-Loire (37) • Population: 350 • Altitude: 328 ft. (100 m)

Montrésor get its name from the Treasurer (*Trésorier*) of the chapter house at Tours Cathedral, which owned this area in the 10th century.

In the early 11th century, the powerful count of Anjou, Foulques III, nicknamed "Foulque Nerra" (Fulk III, the Black), began to build a fortress at Montrésor in order to defend the approaches to the Touraine. Remains of the double ring of defenses are still visible. Inside its wall, at the end of the 15th century, Imbert de Bastarnay (advisor to the French kings Louis XI, Charles VIII, Louis XII, and François I) built the present castle in the Renaissance style. He is also responsible for the collegiate church of Saint-Jean-Baptiste, which houses an Annunciation painted by Philippe de Champaigne (1602–1674), as well as tombs of members of his family. In 1849, the castle became the property of Xavier Branicki, a Polish count and friend of Napoléon III. He restored it and filled it with many works of art: sculptures by Pierre Vanneau, and Italian Renaissance and Dutch paintings. Count Branicki also gave his name to one of the streets cut into the rock, where half-troglodytic and half-timbered houses rub shoulders. Cardeux Market, once the wool market, has been restored as a cultural center and exhibition space, and recalls village life in bygone days. The 16th-century Chancelier's Lodge, which has a watchtower, houses the present town hall. The riverside walk, "Balcons de l'Indrois," provides wonderful views of the village from the footbridge to Jardinier Bridge, which was built by Eiffel's workshop.

By road: Expressway A85, exit 11–Bléré (17 miles/27 km); N76 (17 miles/27 km). **By train:** Tours station (34 miles/55 km); Saint-Pierre-des-Corps TGV station (34 miles/55 km). **By air:** Tours-Saint-Symphorien airport (42 miles/68 km).

ⓘ Tourist information:
+33 (0)2 47 92 70 71
www.loches-valdeloire.com

👁 Highlights

• **Castle** (11th–15th centuries): "Musée d'Art Polonais": +33 (0)2 47 92 60 04.
• **Collegiate church of Saint-Jean-Baptiste** (16th century): Alabaster tomb with three recumbent statues, Annunciation by Philippe de Champaigne, stained-glass windows, 16th-century stalls and paintings, reliquary with the skullcap of Pope John Paul II.
• **Cardeux wool market** (18th century): Permanent exhibition of *gemmail* stained glass and the history of Montrésor.
• **Banks of the Indrois:** Walking paths and information points along the river.
• **Village:** Guided tours for groups only and by appointment: +33 (0)2 47 92 70 71.

⚷ Accommodation

Guesthouses
Le Moulin de Montrésor★★★:
+33 (0)2 47 92 68 20.
La Grenache: +33 (0)2 47 92 71 39.
Gîtes and vacation rentals
Maisons de Charme: +33 (0)6 86 44 63 72.
Further information: +33 (0)2 47 27 70 71.

🍴 Eating Out

Café de la Ville: +33 (0)2 47 92 75 31.
Crêperie Barapom: +33 (0)2 47 19 27 48.
La Légende: +33 (0)2 47 92 61 90.

🧺 Local Specialties

Food and Drink
Montrésor macarons • Montrésor rillettes.
Art and Crafts
Local crafts (Maison de Pays shop) • Painter.

📅 Events

July–August: "Nuits Solaires" evening festival, illuminated trail accompanied by music and events on the banks of the Indrois; painters' and sculptors' fair (August 15).
December: Christmas market.

🦋 Outdoor Activities

Boules playing field • Fishing • Walking: 2 marked trails • Cycling • Horse-riding trails.

🌿 Further Afield

• Lac de Chemillé, lake (1½ miles/2 km).
• Chartreuse du Liget (2½ miles/4 km).
• Loches, Indre valley (11 miles/18 km).
• Beauval Zoo (12½ miles/20 km).
• Chedigny (12½ miles/20 km).
• Château de Montpoupon; Cher valley: Chenonceaux; Loire valley: Amboise (18½–28 miles/30–45 km).
• Château de Valençay (19 miles/31 km).

ℹ Did you know?

According to legend, the young Gontran, who became king of Burgundy from 561 to 592, fell asleep in his equerry's lap on a riverbank and dreamed of treasure hidden in a cave. The equerry saw a small lizard run over Gontran's face; it dashed toward a nearby hill and returned covered in gold. When the king was told this vision, he quickly had the hill excavated and discovered enormous wealth there. But the chronicles of the Middle Ages reveal that this estate belonged to the Treasurer of Tour Cathedral's chapter house. This explains why during the 10th century it was called Mons Thesauri (mount of the Treasurer), which later became Montrésor.

Montsoreau

The lady's castle

Maine-et-Loire (49) • Population: 447 • Altitude: 108 ft. (33 m)

Montsoreau sits between Anjou and the Touraine, in a land of history, sweetness, and harmony.

Lying between the Loire and a hill, and very close to the royal abbey of Fontevraud, Montsoreau grew up around its 15th-century castle. The village draws a rich heritage from the Loire river and Montsoreau's lady, Françoise de Maridor: Alexandre Dumas wrote tales about her passionate and fatal love affair with Bussy d'Amboise. There is something for everyone here: wander the village's flower-lined paths that climb toward the vineyards, and admire its white tufa-stone residences and immaculately tended gardens. Stroll the courtyards and alleyways, beyond which the Loire stretches into the distance; roam the Saut aux Loups hillside, where historic cave dwellings nestle. Taste some famous Saumur-Champigny and Crémant de Loire wines at a local vineyard.

By road: Expressway A85, exit 5–Bourgueil (7½ miles/11.5 km). **By train:** Saumur station (8 miles/13 km). **By air:** Angers-Marcé airport (39 miles/63 km); Tours-Saint-Symphorien airport (45 miles/72 km); Nantes-Atlantique airport (110 miles/177 km).

ⓘ Tourist information:
+33 (0)2 41 51 70 22
www.ot-saumur.fr
www.ville-montsoreau.fr

👁 Highlights

• **Castle** (15th century): Further information: +33 (0)2 41 67 12 60.
• **Église Saint-Pierre-de-Rest** (13th–18th centuries): +33 (0)2 41 51 70 15.
• **Le Saut aux Loups mushroom farm:** Within a group of 15th-century cave dwellings, now used as a mushroom farm, a reconstruction of an early 20th-century mushroom farm: sculptures, exhibition, geological collection: +33 (0)2 41 51 70 30.
• **Maison du Parc Naturel Régional Loire-Anjou-Touraine:** Permanent fauna and flora experience, exhibitions, shop. Further information: +33 (0)2 41 38 38 88.
• **Vins de Loire market:** In a cave dwelling, experience the wines of the Loire valley in 10 stages from Nantes to Sancerre: +33 (0)2 41 38 15 05.
• **Village:** Guided tours. Further information: +33 (0)2 41 51 70 22.

🔑 Accommodation

Hotels
La Marine de Loire****: +33 (0)2 41 50 18 21.
Le Bussy***: +33 (0)2 41 38 11 11.

Guesthouses
La Fauvette: +33 (0)6 08 93 85 61.
La Forge: +33 (0)2 41 52 35 47.
Juliette: +33 (0)2 41 51 75 70.
Gîtes and vacation rentals
Further information: +33 (0)2 41 51 70 22
www.ville-montsoreau.fr
Campsites
L'Isle Verte****: +33 (0)2 41 51 76 60.

🍴 Eating Out

Le 2, art gallery and tea room: +33 (0)6 51 51 23 36.
Aigue-Marine, floating restaurant: +33 (0)2 41 38 12 52.
La Cave du Saut aux Loups: +33 (0)2 41 51 70 30.
La Dentellière, crêperie/salad bar: +33 (0)2 41 52 41 68.
Diane-de-Méridor, gourmet restaurant: +33 (0)2 41 51 71 76.
Fleur de Sel, crêperie: +33 (0)2 41 40 82 99).
Le Lion d'Or, crêperie: +33 (0)2 41 51 70 12.
Le Mail, brasserie: +33 (0)2 41 51 73 29.
Le Montsorelli: +33 (0)2 41 51 70 18.

Le P'tit Bar, brasserie/grill: +33 (0)2 41 51 72 45.

🛒 Local Specialties

Food and Drink
Mushrooms • Organic apples and pears • AOC Saumur, Saumur-Champigny, Crémant de Loire wines.
Art and Crafts
Antiques dealers and art galleries.

2⃣ Events

Market: Sundays, 8 a.m.–1 p.m., Place du Mail.
July–August: Les Musicales de Montsoreau music season at the castle and church.
Throughout the year: Montsoreau flea market (2nd Sunday of each month).

🦋 Outdoor Activities

Pony trekking • Mountain-biking • Loire river cruises • Fishing • Watersports on the Loire • Walking: Route GR 3, 1 marked trail (11 miles/18 km), and "Au Temps des Mariniers de Loire" heritage trail from Montsoreau to Candes-Saint-Martin • Cycling: "Loire à Vélo" trail.

🕊 Further Afield

• *Candes-Saint-Martin (½ mile/1 km), see p. 22.
• Abbaye de Fontevraud (2½ miles/4 km).
• Saumur (7½ miles/12 km).
• Chinon (12 miles/19 km).
• *Crissay-sur-Manse (24 miles/39 km), see p. 23.

❗ Did you know?

A unique location at the heart of the village plays host to the ancestral game of *boule de fort*. At the Société l'Union, in Montsoreau's old market, is a circular pitch on which players, who must wear slippers, roll *boules* of 6-in. (13-cm) diameter with flattened sides; the balls must get as close as possible to the *maître*, the smallest *boule* at the center of the pitch.

Rochefort-en-Terre

Brittany in flower

Morbihan (56) • Population: 710 • Altitude: 164 ft. (50 m)

Halfway between the Gulf of Morbihan and "Merlin's Forest" (Brocéliande Forest), this village was once a *roche fort* (stronghold), which controlled the trading routes between land and sea.

A medieval village that dates back to the 11th century, Rochefort-en-Terre is one of the oldest fiefdoms in Brittany. Its location, on a rocky outcrop surrounded by deep valleys, gave it a strategic position and a leading role. Traces of this rich history can be seen in the upper village—a legacy of a prosperous past linked to the exploitation of slate quarries—with its old covered market, 12th-century collegiate church, ruins of the medieval castle of the counts of Rochefort, and the 19th-century château, as well as the 16th- and 17th-century mansions with their richly embellished granite and shale façades. Rochefort-en-Terre became an artists' town in the early 20th century, thanks to the American portraitist Alfred Klots, and has retained its pictorial as well as its floral tradition.

By road: N166, exit Bohal (9½ miles/ 15.5 km); N165, exit 17–Marzan (14 miles/ 23 km). **By train:** Questembert (6 miles/ 9.5 km), Redon (16 miles/26 km), Vannes (20 miles/32 km) stations; Rennes TGV station (62 miles/100 km). **By air:** Rennes-Saint-Jacques (60 miles/97 km), Nantes-Atlantique (62 miles/100 km), Lorient-Lann Bihoué (64 miles/103 km) airports.

ⓘ Tourist information:
+33 (0)2 97 26 56 00
www.rochefort-en-terre.bzh

👁 Highlights

• **Parc du Château:** View of the ruins of the medieval castle and of the 19th-century château built on the site of 17th-century stables.
• **Collegiate church of Notre-Dame de la Tronchaye** (12th–14th centuries).
• **Village:** Sightseeing tour of the Petite Cité; guided tours all year round for groups, booking essential; every Tuesday and Thursday morning in July and August, and Fridays and Saturdays in December when the Christmas lights are on, for individuals: +33 (0)2 97 26 56 00.
• **Naïa Museum:** Contemporary, fantastic, digital, and kinetic art museum; Parc du Château: +33 (0)2 97 40 12 35/ www.naiamuseum.com

🗝 Accommodation

Hotels
Le Pélican**: +33 (0)2 97 43 38 48.
Aparthotel
Domaine Ar Peoc'h: +33 (0)2 97 43 37 88.
Domaine du Moulin Neuf:
+33 (0)5 55 84 34 48.
Guesthouses
François Pinat: +33 (0)2 97 43 30 43.
La Tour du Lion: +33 (0)2 97 43 36 94 or
+33 (0)6 63 34 77 27.

Gîtes and vacation rentals
Further information: +33 (0)2 97 26 56 00
www.rochefort-en-terre.bzh
Campsites
Camping Au Gré des Vents:
+33 (0)2 97 43 37 52 or
+33 (0)6 23 32 51 53.

🍴 Eating Out
À l'Heure de l'Apéro: +33 (0)2 97 68 49 66.
L'Ancolie: +33 (0)2 97 43 33 09.
Les Ardoisières: +33 (0)2 97 43 47 55.
Freine le Temps: +33 (0)2 97 43 31 63.
Les Grées, pizzeria: +33 (0)2 97 44 73 89.
Le Pélican: +33 (0)2 97 43 38 48.
Le Rouge, tapas bar: +33 (0)6 85 67 65 03.
La Terrasse: +33 (0)2 97 43 35 56.
Voyage Gaufré: +33 (0)9 50 44 96 58.
Crêperies
Le Café Breton: +33 (0)2 97 43 32 60.
La Crêperie du Puits: +33 (0)2 97 43 30 43.
La Petite Bretonne: +33 (0)2 97 43 37 68.
La Tour du Lion, crêperie/brasserie:
+33 (0)6 63 34 77 27.

🧺 Local Specialties
Food and Drink
Breton shortbread, *kouign amann* (buttery
cake) • *Pain d'épice* (spice cake) • *Galettes
bretonnes* (butter cookies) • Honey •

Chouchen (type of mead) • Cider •
Apple juice.
Art and Crafts
Wooden handicrafts • Metal handicrafts •
Slate handicrafts • Handmade candles •
Embroidery • Jewelry and sculpture •
Leather craftsman • Artists • Soap-maker.

📅 Events
June: "À travers chants" choir festival.
June–September: Temporary exhibitions
of work by artists, painters, and sculptors;
events at the château.
July: Potters' market.
August: Medieval fair (around 15th);
Pardon de Notre-Dame de la Tronchaye
procession (Sunday after 15th); music
festival.
July and August: Concerts at the Café de
la Pente (every Thursday) and at the Salle
de Spectacle at the Étang Moderne.
December: Christmas lights.

🦋 Outdoor Activities
Walking: Route GR 38 and marked trails
around Rochefort.

🌿 Further Afield
• Malansac: Parc de Préhistoire
de Bretagne (2½ miles/4 km).

• Caden: Musée des Maquettes de Machines
Agricoles, museum of models of farming
machinery; arts center (6 miles/9.5 km).
• Questembert: 16th-century covered
market (6 miles/9.5 km).
• Malestroit (10 miles/16 km).
• La Gacilly: handicrafts, Végétarium
Yves-Rocher, photography festival
(11 miles/18 km).
• La Vraie-Croix: 13th-century chapel
(11 miles/18 km).
• Le Guerno: Branféré animal painter
(12 miles/19 km).
• La Roche-Bernard (12 miles/19 km).
• Forêt de Brocéliande, forest (22 miles/
35 km).
• Vannes (22 miles/35 km).
• Gulf of Morbihan: Île d'Arz, Île aux Moines
(25 miles/40 km).

ℹ️ Did you know?
In 1911, four years after buying the castle,
the American painter Alfred Klots created
a floral window display competition to
brighten up the village's old houses,
offering each inhabitant some geranium
cuttings to bedeck their windows. The
floral-decoration tradition has continued,
earning Rochefort high honors in this area.

By road: Expressway A13, exit 14–Vernon (7 miles/11.5 km) or exit 11–Mantes-la-Jolie-Est (11 miles/18 km). **By train:** Vernon station (8½ miles/13.5 km); Mantes-la-Jolie station (10 miles/16 km); Paris TGV station (47 miles/76 km). **By air:** Paris-Roissy-Charles de Gaulle airport (55 miles/89 km); Paris-Orly airport (56 miles/90 km).

ⓘ **Town hall:** +33 (0)1 34 79 70 55
www.larocheguyon.fr

La Roche-Guyon

A castle by the Seine

Val-d'Oise (95) • Population: 520 • Altitude: 394 ft. (120 m)

In a bend of the Seine carved into cliffs of chalk and flint, La Roche-Guyon mixes Île-de-France architecture with Normandy half-timbering.

The village, which was originally troglodytic, consisted of *boves*: dwellings cohabited by animals and men that are now used as out-houses. The 12th-century keep is surrounded by a curtain wall and linked to the castle by an impressive secret passage more than 330 ft. (100 m) long. Built in the 13th century and rebuilt in the 18th, the castle has retained its corner pepperpot turrets from its feudal past. The main building was completed with corner pavilions and ter-races during the reign of Louis XV. Located on the main road between the castle and the Seine, the castle's kitchen garden, cre-ated in 1741, was restored in 2004 following the original 18th-century plans, and provides a setting for artistic creations by sculptors and landscape designers. The village's old streets invite one to stroll around and to follow the Charrière des Bois or de Gasny to the banks of the Seine. The village forms part of the regional nature park of French Vexin and of the Coteaux de la Seine nature reserve.

👁 Highlights
• **Castle** (13th–18th centuries): Themed tours (medieval route, salons route, keep and chapels route, bunker and *boves* route), kitchen garden; activities for children; cultural events:
+33 (0)1 34 79 74 42.
• **Église Saint-Samson** (15th century): Marble statue by François de Silly, who owned the castle in the 17th century:
+33 (0)1 34 79 70 55.

🗝 Accommodation
Hotels
Les Bords de Seine**: +33 (0)1 30 98 32 52.
Guesthouses
M. Buffet: +33 (0)1 75 74 41 85.
Vacation rentals
La Cachette: +33 (0)1 34 75 45 98.
Le Logis du Château: +33 (0)6 98 70 58 77.
Walkers' lodge
Further information: +33 (0)1 34 79 72 67.

🍽 Eating Out
Les Bords de Seine: +33 (0)1 30 98 32 52.
La Cancalaise, crêperie:
+33 (0)1 34 79 74 48.
Casa Mia, pizzeria: +33 (0)1 34 79 70 73.
Cuisine en Seine: +33 (0)1 34 79 67 05.
Le Relais du Château: +33 (0)1 34 79 70 52.

🏛 Local Specialties

Art and Crafts
Metalworker • Mosaic artist • Jeweler • Potter • Weaver.

2 Events

May: "Plantes, Plaisir, Passions" plant festival (1st weekend).
Ascension: Big flea market.
June: Country market (2nd Sunday).
July 14: Citizens' banquet.
November: Wine fair (1st weekend) and Advent market (last weekend).

🦋 Outdoor Activities

Walking: Marked walks in the forest and village (topographic guide from the town hall) • Mountain-biking.

🌿 Further Afield

• Route des Crêtes, scenic drive; Route GR 2, hiking trail (1 mile/1.5 km).
• Haute-Isle: underground church (2 miles/3 km).
• Vétheuil (3½ miles/5.5 km).
• Giverny: Claude Monet's house and gardens (5½ miles/9 km).
• Chaussy: Château de Villarceaux; golf course and manor house (6 miles/9.5 km).
• Vernon (8 miles/13 km).

• Mantes-la-Jolie (10 miles/16 km).
• Les Andelys: Château-Gaillard (19 miles/31 km).

❗ Did you know?

In February 1944, Field Marshal Rommel set up his headquarters at the castle. Opposed to Nazi theories and eager to end the war, he made contact with the German Resistance. The castle became the setting for secret meetings to negotiate peace with the Allies, while he tried to persuade Hitler of the futility of his fight. Rommel did not have time to execute his plans: the Allies landed on the Normandy beaches on June 6, 1944.

Saint-Benoît-du-Sault

A priory on the edge of Limousin

Indre (36) • Population: 615 • Altitude: 722 ft. (220 m)

Built on a granite spur, the village of Saint-Benoît-du-Sault overlooks a broad bend of the Portefeuille river.

Enclosed by partially intact double ramparts, Saint-Benoît has preserved its medieval past in the form of a fortified gateway, a 14th-century belfry, and an old wall-walk. At the tip of the rocky promontory, a Benedictine priory offers a view over the valley. The church, majestic and sober, from the first Romanesque period, contains carved capitals and an 11th-century baptismal font. At the heart of the village, 15th- and 16th-century houses line the narrow, often steep streets: the Portail and Maison de l'Argentier, with its carved lintel, are the most remarkable. Walking trails invite visitors to explore the village, built in the shape of an amphitheater, and the priory, which is reflected in the water below. The priory is due to be restored soon and will house a cultural and tourist center.

By road: Expressway A20, exit 20–Saint-Benoît-du-Sault (5 miles/8 km). **By train:** Argenton-sur-Creuse station (13 miles/21 km). **By air:** Limoges-Bellegarde airport (50 miles/80 km).

ⓘ Tourist information:
+33 (0)2 54 47 67 95
www.saint-benoit-du-sault.fr

👁 Highlights
• **Church** (11th, 13th, and 14th centuries): Stained-glass windows by contemporary master stained-glass maker Jean Mauret.
• **Priory:** Open to the public for exhibitions.
• **Village:** Guided tour on Wednesday and Saturday: +33 (0)2 54 47 67 95.

🗝 Accommodation
Hotels
Le Centre: +33 (0)2 54 47 51 51.
Guesthouses
La Châtille***: +33 (0)2 54 47 50 12.
Le Portail***: +33 (0)2 54 47 57 20.
Outre-l'Étang: +33 (0)2 54 24 83 97.
La Treille: +33 (0)9 60 02 10 50.
Gîtes
Loisir Accueil Indre +33 (0)2 54 27 58 61.
Walkers' lodge
La Maison des Voyageurs:
+33 (0)2 54 47 51 44.

🍴 Eating Out
L'Auberge du Champ de Foire:
+33 (0)2 54 27 43 77.
L'Entrecôte, pizzeria/steak house:
+33 (0)2 54 47 66 82.
Hôtel du Centre: +33 (0)2 54 47 51 51.

🧺 Local Specialties
Art and Crafts
Publisher of artists' and poetry books •
Engraver and painter • Angora wool dyer and designer.

🈁 Events
March: Festival de Ciné-concert (movies with live music, late March).
April: Pays de la Loire wine fair.
June: Contemporary art exhibition.
July: Flea market (13th).
July and August: Theater, concerts.
August: Inter-regional ram show (4th), local saint's day (15th), cattle show (last week).
December: "Foire Grasse d'Oies et Canards de la Région de Brive," goose and duck produce fair.

🦋 Outdoor Activities
Fishing • Tennis • Walking trails.

🌿 Further Afield
• Dolmens of Les Gorces and of Passebonneau (1–2 miles/1.5–3 km).
• Roussines: church (2½ miles/4 km).
• Parc Naturel Régional de la Brenne, nature park (3–31 miles/5–50 km).
• Château de Brosse, ruins (6 miles/9.5 km).
• Creuse valley; Musée Archéologique d'Argentomagus; Lac de Chambon, lake; Crozant: ruins (11–17 miles/18–27 km).
• *Gargilesse-Dampierre (15 miles/24 km), see pp. 24–25.

Saint-Céneri-le-Gérei

A painter's paradise

Orne (61) • Population: 140 • Altitude: 417 ft. (127 m)

At the heart of the Mancelles Alps, Saint-Céneri-le-Gérei combines water, stone, and wood.

The village, which nestles in a bend in the Sarthe river, was founded by Saint Céneri, an Italian-born monk who created a monastery that was later burned by the Normans. A church was built on the site in the 11th century. Today, topped with a saddleback roof and a tower adorned with columns and belfry openings, it emerges above the trees. Inside, it houses recently restored 12th-century murals and a ceiling that is unique in France. The village's old houses surrounding the church have been preserved. Below is a charming 15th-century chapel. On the opposite bank is the miraculous spring created by Saint Céneri in 660, which, according to popular belief, has the power to cure eye problems. Over the years, the village has charmed many famous painters, including Camille Corot (1796–1875) and Eugène Boudin (1824–1898), and at the Auberge des Sœurs Moisy, which they frequented, you can still see charcoal portraits of artists and villagers sketched by candlelight.

By road: Expressway A28, exit 18– Alençon centre (12 miles/19 km), N12 (7½ miles/12 km). **By train:** Alençon station (12 miles/19 km). **By air:** Caen-Carpiquet airport (83 miles/134 km).

ⓘ Tourist information— **Alpes Mancelles:** +33 (0)2 43 33 28 04 or +33 (0)2 33 27 84 47 www.saintceneri.org

◉ Highlights
• **Église Saint-Céneri** (11th century): Murals, Stations of the Cross.
• **Chapel** (15th century): Statue of Saint Céneri.
• **Auberge des Soeurs Moisy:** Museum of 19th- and 20th-century painters.
• **Village:** Audioguide tour (www.saintceneri.org).

⚷ Accommodation
Gîtes and vacation rentals
La Cassine: +33 (0)2 33 26 93 66.
Chez Martine: +33 (0)2 33 32 23 93.
La Giroise: +33 (0)2 43 33 79 22.

⦿ Eating Out
Auberge des Peintres: +33 (0)2 33 26 49 18.
Auberge de la Vallée: +33 (0)2 33 28 94 70.
L' Échoppe Gourmande: +33 (0)2 33 81 91 21.
La Taverne Giroise: +33 (0)2 33 32 24 51.

🍽 Local Specialties
Art and Crafts
Marquetry • Restoration of paintings • Artists • Painter-sculptor.

② Events
Pentecost: Artists' event.
July: "Saint Scène" (music).
August: Open-air rummage sale (1st Sunday).

🦋 Outdoor Activities
Canoeing • Fishing • Walking: Route GR 36, several marked trails via the Normandie-Maine regional nature park and the Chemin des Arts toward the Mont des Avaloirs • Mountain-biking • "Monts et Marche" (signposted walk).

🦋 Further Afield
• Saint-Léonard-des-Bois (3 miles/5 km).
• Alençon: Musée de la Dentelle, lace museum (9½ miles/15.5 km).
• Mont des Avaloirs (9½ miles/15.5 km).

• Forêt d'Écouves, forest; Château de Carrouges (12–19 miles/19–31 km).
• Parc naturel régional Normandie-Maine, nature park; Carrouges (19 miles/31 km).
• Bagnoles-de-l'Orne (25 miles/40 km).
• Haras National du Pin, national stud (34 miles/55 km).

⚕ Did you know?

In the 15th-century chapel built on the site of the Saint Céneri hermitage, there is a statue of the hermit and a granite stela, said to have been used by him as a bed, and believed to heal incontinence. Legend has it that, if young girls pushed a needle into the feet of the saint's statue, they would be able to find a husband.

Saint-Suliac
Between land and sea

Ille-et-Vilaine (35) • Population: 930 • Altitude: 69 ft. (21 m)

With a stunning view over the Rance estuary, Saint-Suliac sits in a beautifully unspoilt landscape.

The impressive steeple of the Église de Saint-Suliac rises loftily above an old cemetery that represents a unique kind of churchyard in Haute Bretagne. The church is set in the center of a maze of narrow alleyways lined with fishermen's houses and low granite garden walls. Paths from the village lead to a variety of delightful attractions: the tide mill; the old salt marshes at Guettes, created in 1736; the standing stone of Chablé, dubbed the "Dent de Gargantua" (Gargantua's Tooth), and the intriguing remains of a Viking camp. The port, busy with both fishing and pleasure boats, evokes Saint-Suliac's rich maritime history. This was a population of sailors, and the Vierge de Grainfollet (patron saint of Newfoundland), sitting above the village, reveals the heavy price that these coastal folk paid the sea in order to support their families.

By road: Expressway A84, exit 34–Saint-Malo (32 miles/51 km); N175 then N176, exit Châteauneuf-d'Ille-et-Vilaine (2½ miles/4 km). By train: Saint-Malo station (8 miles/13 km); Dinan station (16 miles/26 km). By air: Dinard-Pleurtuit airport (16 miles/26 km); Rennes-Saint-Jacques airport (43 miles/69 km).

(i) Tourist information:
+33 (0)2 99 58 39 15
www.saint-suliac.fr

◉ Highlights
• Church (13th century): Stained-glass windows, wood carving, sailors' shrine.
• Village: Guided tour by appointment only; Guillemette Tremaudan:
+33 (0)2 23 15 03 85.

⚶ Accommodation
Guesthouses
L'Acadie****: +33 (0)2 23 15 04 94.
La Chabossière: +33 (0)2 99 58 32 87.
Entre Terre et Mer: +33 (0)2 23 15 00 92.
Les Mouettes: +33 (0)2 99 58 30 41.
Les Salines de la Rance:
+33 (0)2 99 58 21 37.
La Vie en Rose: +33 (0)2 23 15 07 97.
Gîtes
L'Escale****: +33 (0)2 99 82 38 61.
Brigitte Lefrançois***: +33 (0)5 62 95 08 61.
La Métairie du Clos de Broons***:
+33 (0)2 99 89 12 30.
Aventures Isolées: +33 (0)6 22 65 36 35 or
+33 (0)1 30 52 67 90.
Gîte de Jayne et Ian Perry:
+33 (0)6 08 12 24 71 or
+33 (0)2 99 58 30 48.
Gîte du Mont Garot: +33 (0)2 23 15 07 80.
Maison de Pêcheurs: +33 (0)2 99 98 86 22
or +33 (0)6 35 96 93 11.
La Villa Marine: +33 (0)6 08 09 20 86 or
+33 (0)6 11 75 88 92.
Campsites
Les Cours**: +33 (0)6 07 80 48 51.
Mobile homes
Le Bigorneau: +33 (0)6 59 87 71 72.

⊕ Eating Out
Le Bistrot de la Grève: +33 (0)2 99 58 95 84.
La Ferme du Boucanier:
+33 (0)2 23 15 06 35.
Le Galichon: +33 (0)2 99 58 49 49.
La Guinguette: +33 (0)2 99 58 32 21.

⌂ Local Specialties
Food and Drink
Cider • Buckwheat *galettes* (pancakes) •
Fish and shellfish.
Art and Crafts
Flowercraft • Painter.

▣ Events
Market: Summer market, Tuesday evenings, July and August.
June: "Feu de la Saint-Jean," Saint John's Eve bonfire (2nd fortnight); triathlon (last weekend).
August: "Saint-Suliac Autrefois," historical event (1st weekend); Pardon de la Mer ceremony at Notre-Dame-de-Grainfollet (15th).

September: "Copeaux d'Abord," sea festival (last weekend).
December: Christmas market and living Nativity (1st and 2nd weekends).

⚑ Outdoor Activities
Swimming • Fishing • Sailing • Horse-riding • Walking: 3 marked trails, Route GR34 and GR route in the Pays Malouin • Mountain-biking.

⚶ Further Afield
• Saint-Malo (6 miles/9.5 km).
• Cancale (11 miles/18 km).
• Mont-Dol (12 miles/19 km).
• Dinan (14 miles/23 km).
• Mont-Saint-Michel (19 miles/31 km).

Sainte-Suzanne

Beauty and rebellion

Mayenne (53) • Population: 1,008 • Altitude: 525 ft. (160 m)

This medieval village, the "pearl of Maine," perched on top of a rocky peak dominating the Erve valley, resisted attacks from William the Conqueror.

When relics of Saint Suzanne (patron saint of fiancés) were brought back to Saint-Jean-de-Hautefeuille from the Crusades, the village was renamed in her honor. The medieval village was fortified in the 11th century; both beautiful and rebellious, it proudly resisted William the Conqueror, but had to surrender to the English during the Hundred Years War. Atop a mound opposite the village, the site of Tertre Ganne, occupied by the earl of Salisbury's troops during the 1425 siege, offers a fabulous view of Sainte-Suzanne's striking profile. The keep partly survived this tumultuous period, but the double wall of 12th-century ramparts owes its present appearance to Guillaume Fouquet de La Varenne, comptroller general of posts, who also built the Renaissance lodge and took over ownership of the citadel from Henri IV. The hamlet of La Rivière, where the "Promenade des Moulins" path winds, offers the loveliest vistas toward the medieval village.

By road: Expressway A81, exit 2–Sablé (12 miles/19 km). **By train:** Évron station (4½ miles/7 km); Laval station (21 miles/34 km). **By air:** Angers-Marcé airport (45 miles/72 km).

ⓘ Tourist information—
Sainte-Suzanne – Les Coëvrons:
+33 (0)2 43 01 43 60
www.coevrons-tourisme.com
www.ste-suzanne.fr

👁 Highlights
• **Castle** (17th century): Centre d'Interprétation de l'Architecture et du Patrimoine de la Mayenne, visitor center; exhibitions and activities: +33 (0)2 43 58 13 00.
• **Romanesque keep** (11th century): Self-guided visit (interior staircases and gangways).
• ♥ **Musée de l'Auditoire** (16th century): 3,000 years of the village's history: +33 (0)2 43 01 42 65.
• **Grand Moulin** (15th–19th centuries): Former communal mill belonging to the village's lords, the only one in France to produce flour, paper, and electricity using the same wheel. Guided visits, manufacture and sale of artisanal paper: +33 (0)2 43 90 57 17.
• **Camp des Anglais:** Fortified camp, William the Conqueror's base during the siege of 1083–86, military fortifications, self-guided visit: +33 (0)2 43 01 43 60.
• **Dolmen des Erves** (2 miles/3km): 6,500-year-old megalith.
• **Medieval town:** Guided tours by appointment: +33 (0)2 43 01 43 60.
• **Chapelle Saint-Europe** (18th century): altarpiece dating to 1706.
• **Tertre-Ganne:** panorama over the town (1½ miles:2 km).

🗝 Accommodation
Hotels
Hôtel Beauséjour** : +33 (0)2 43 01 40 31.
Guesthouses
Côté Jardin**** : +33 (0)2 43 98 93 66.
Gîtes
Les Fiancés de Sainte-Suzanne**** : +33 (0)2 43 53 52 43 or +33 (0)6 09 11 40 70.
♥ Les Gîtes des Remparts**** : +33 (0)6 42 78 11 71.
Le Passe-Muraille**** : +33 (0)6 42 78 11 71.
Le Grand Moulin*** : +33 (0)820 153 053.
L'Écrin de Verdure: +33 (0)6 46 20 51 26.
La Maison Formidable: +33 (0)2 43 98 13 31.
Le Nid des Mésanges: +33 (0)2 43 01 44 16 or +33 (0)6 03 83 25 07.
Farmhouse accommodation
La Sorie, equestrian farm: +33 (0)2 43 01 40 63.
Vacation villages and campsites
VVF-villages "La Croix Couverte"*** : +33 (0)2 43 01 40 76.
Sainte-Suzanne Camping-Caravaning et Glamping** : +33 (0)6 33 76 87 70.
RV parks
La Madeleine RV park: +33 (0)8 05 69 48 69.

🍴 Eating Out
La Cabane, light meals (in summer): +33 (0)6 11 32 58 01.
Café des Tours, light meals: +33 (0)2 43 66 81 10.
Hôtel-restaurant Beauséjour: +33 (0)2 43 01 40 31.
Péché de Gourmandise, Le Bistrot: +33 (0)6 83 75 10 76.

🧺 Local Specialties
Food and Drink
"La Suzannaise" beers and local lemonade • Honey.
Art and Crafts
Antiques • Medieval crafts • Candles • Painting, sculpture, and jewelry • Local soaps.

🗓 Events
Market: Saturday mornings, Place Ambroise-de-Loré.
May: "Les 6 Heures de Sainte-Suzanne," race and sports festival.
May–September: Local flea market (1st Sunday of the month).
June: Soirée Bodega, street party.
July: "Journée des Peintres dans la rue," art festival and photography competition (3rd Sunday), medieval activities.
July–August: "Nuits de la Mayenne," theater festival.
August: Medieval activities (Wednesdays); Tournoi du Maine, jousting tournament.
September: Fête des Vieux Papiers et des Métiers de Tradition, rummage sale and fair celebrating traditional skills and antique paper products (1st Sunday); le Roc Suzannais, mountain-biking.
December: Christmas market.

🦋 Outdoor Activities
Recreation area (La Croix Couverte) • Horse-riding trails • Walking and mountain-biking (maps from tourist information center).

🌿 Further Afield
• La Promenade des Moulins, history trail; La Rivière, hamlet (½ mile/1 km).
• Tertre Ganne: view across to the village (1 mile/1.5 km).
• Pays d'Art et d'Histoire Coëvrons-Mayenne, regional cultural heritage: Évron, Saulges, Jublains, Mayenne (3–22 miles/5–35 km).
• Gué de Selle, lake (7½ miles/12 km).
• Laval (22 miles/35 km).
• Le Mans (34 miles/55 km).

Veules-les-Roses

Beach resort in the Pays de Caux

Seine-Maritime (76) * Population: 586 * Altitude: 260 ft. (79m)

Nestled between land and sea, in the hollow of a valley located on the Caux plateau and ending in a cliff overlooking the Côte d'Albâtre, Veules-les-Roses is bursting with charm. Inhabited since the 4th century, it takes its name from the ancient Saxon word *well*, meaning "water source." Water is everywhere in the local landscape and has shaped the village's history since its foundation. The sea brought prosperity in the Middle Ages, and in the 19th century prompted the development of one of the first beach resorts to be frequented by famous artists and writers. Other tales speak of the Veules, the "shortest river in France," which powered weaving mills and flour mills, and irrigated the still-active watercress beds before flowing into the English Channel. And there are also accounts of the village's rebirth, since history has left its mark even in this little corner of Normandy, in the form of barbarian invasions, the Wars of Religion, and World War II. From its sea front and bathing huts to the heart of the village where fishermen's houses rub shoulders with thatched cottages and villas with flowering gardens, Veules-les-Roses still presents visitors with a variety of architecture and landscape that makes it an unmissable stopping point on the road to Fécamp and Dieppe.

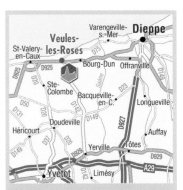

By road: Expressway A150, exit 4–Saint-Valery-en-Caux (20 miles/32 km); expressway A29, exit 8–Yvetot (25 miles/40 km); expressway A28, exit 10–Les Hayons (32 miles/52 km). **By train:** Dieppe station (16 miles/26 km); Yvetot station (21 miles/34 km). **By air:** Rouen-Vallée-de-Seine airport (47 miles/75 km); Deauville-Normandie airport (61 miles/98 km). **By bus:** 61 Dieppe—Saint-Valéry-en-Caux (4½ miles/7 km).

ⓘ Tourist information—Plateau de Caux Maritime: +33 (0)2 35 97 63 05
www.plateaudecauxmaritime.com
www.veules-les-roses.fr

👁 Highlights

• **Église Saint-Martin** (13th–16th centuries): Painted murals recently uncovered in the choir vault; polychrome statuary from 15th–17th centuries.

• **Route along the "shortest river in France"**: Follow the Veules to see the local nature and architecture of the village and the beach resort (cliff, mills, religious buildings, cress beds, drinking troughs, thatched cottages, villas). Self-guided tours; guided tours for groups all year round by appointment, and in July–August for individuals: +33 (0)2 35 97 63 05.

⚲ Accommodation

Aparthotel
Relais Hôtelier Douce France: +33 (0)2 35 57 85 30.
Guesthouses
La Petite Maison***: +33 (0)2 35 57 36 10.
Le Moulin des Cressonnières***: +33 (0)2 35 97 60 27 or +33 (0)6 13 17 34 67.
La Maison de la Rose**: +33 (0)2 35 97 60 16 or +33 (0)6 82 32 28 81.
♥ Le Jardin Saint-Nicolas: 33 (0)6 48 74 47 13.
Gîtes and vacation rentals
Mme Bourdin***: +33 (0)1 39 31 49 35 or +33 (0)6 04 16 54 58.
Champs Elysées***: +33 (0)2 35 97 63 08 or +33 (0)6 22 51 39 77.
La Dame d'à Côté***: +33 (0)6 81 49 42 23.
Les Embruns***: +33 (0)2 35 91 31 51 or +33 (0)6 31 89 57 25.

Les Hortensias***: +33 (0)2 35 60 73 34 or +33 (0)2 35 97 47 13.
La Maison Bleue***: +33 (0)6 78 99 97 00.
A l'Abri des Roses**: +33 (0)6 79 13 84 05.
Les Bains**: +33 (0)3 44 47 80 39 or +33 (0)6 83 49 42 05.
M. Claire**: +33 (0)9 82 37 35 97 or +33 (0)6 59 60 52 00.
M. Defosse**: +33 (0)2 35 97 19 77 or +33 (0)7 85 85 34 25.
Les Lobelias**: +33 (0)2 32 53 82 79 or +33 (0)6 25 63 24 45.
Les Logis de la Plage**: +33 (0)2 35 40 32 48 or +33 (0)6 70 29 83 38.
M. Lambion*: +33 (0)6 61 87 89 76.
Résidence Le France—M. Beurel**: +33 (0)6 95 68 15 32.
Résidence Le France—Mme Paumelle*: +33 (0)6 74 43 09 68.
Vacation village
VVF Village***: +33 (0)2 35 97 68 04 or +33 (0)4 73 43 00 43.
Campsite
Les Mouettes***: +33 (0)2 35 97 61 98.

🍴 Eating Out

4 d'Alice: +33 (0)2 35 97 76 41.
L'Abreuvoir: +33 (0)9 51 39 92 81.
Les Galets, gourmet restaurant: +33 (0)2 35 97 61 33.
Le Pinocchio, pizzeria: +33 (0)2 35 97 38 10.
Relais Hôtelier Douce France: +33 (0)2 35 57 85 30.
Le Tropical, brasserie: +33 (0)2 35 57 17 36.
Le Victor Hugo, brasserie: +33 (0)2 35 97 98 98.
Light meals
Bar des Voyageurs, fast food: +33 (0)2 35 57 32 53.
Comme à la Maison, fast food: +33 (0)9 81 05 63 11 or +33 (0)6 64 96 16 12.
La Cressonnière, crêperie: +33 (0)2 35 57 25 32 or +33 (0)6 43 34 35 29.
Le P'tit Veulais, crêperie: +33 (0)2 35 57 32 53.
Tea rooms
Atelier 2—L'art du thé: +33 (0)2 35 97 07 95.
Un Jour d'Été: +33 (0)2 35 97 23 17.

🏛 Local Specialties

Food and Drink
Cress • Veules oysters.
Art and Crafts
Artists' galleries • Upholsterer • Interior designer.

📅 Events

Market: Wednesday mornings.
April: Cress festival.
May: "Salon des Arts," art show.
May and June: "Rose en Fête," rose and garden festival (weekend of Father's Day).
June and August: Exhibitions.
July: Book show; linen festival (2nd weekend).
July and August: Exhibitions; "Read on the Beach," evening market for artisans and designers.
October: "Festival de l'Image," photography and film festival.
September: SITU Festival (theater, circus, cinema).
All year round: "Ciné-Objectifs" film screenings; "Les Vendredis du Patrimoine" (last Friday of month).

🦋 Outdoor Activities

Bathing (beach) • Watersports • Fishing: sea and shore • Walks (4 circuits).

🌿 Further Afield

• Saint-Valery-en-Caux: Maison Henri IV (4½ miles/7 km).
• Sainte-Marguerite-sur-Mer: Vasterival gardens: (9 miles/15 km).
• Tourville-sur-Arques: Miromesnil castle (10 miles/16 km).
• Varengeville-sur-Mer: church and sailors' cemetery; Bois des Moutiers ornamental gardens (12 miles/20 km).
• Dieppe (16 miles/26 km).
• Fécamp: Benedictine palace, museums, abbey church (25 miles/40 km).
• Etretat: cliffs and Notre-Dame-de-la-Garde chapel (35 miles/56 km).

ℹ Did you know?

In the 19th century, many writers and artists flocked to Veules-les-Roses on vacation, among them the Goncourt brothers and Victor Hugo. The latter liked to gaze out to sea and chat with locals while sitting in a cave on the cliff road.

Vouvant

Village of painters and legends

Vendée (85) • Population: 919 • Altitude: 361 ft. (110 m)

Deep in the forest of Vouvant-Mervent, the Mère river winds through a landscape that has inspired both art and mystery.

William V, duke of Aquitaine (969–1030), discovered the site of Vouvant while hunting. Struck by its strategic position, he built a castle, a church, and a monastery here in the 11th century. In the church, the 12th-century portal, the 12th-century apse, and the 11th-century crypt are all well worth seeing. The castle has retained only its keep, the Mélusine Tower, sections of the ramparts, and a 13th-century postern gate, which was used by Saint Louis (King Louis IX). A Romanesque bridge straddles the river Mère, linking the two riverbanks. Everyday life in the village is enhanced by numerous artists who form the "Vouvant, Village de Peintres" art association, which organizes a wide range of cultural events.

By road: Expressway A83, exit 8–Fontenay-Ouest (11 miles/18 km).
By train: Fontenay-le-Comte station (10 miles/16 km); Niort TGV station (35 miles/56 km). **By air:** La Rochelle-Laleu airport (40 miles/64 km).

ⓘ Tourist information:
+33 (0)2 51 00 86 80
www.tourisme-sudvendee.com
www.vouvant.fr

👁 Highlights

• **Église Notre-Dame** (11th and 13th century).
• **Nef Théodelin** (11th century): Exhibition center.
• **Mélusine Tower** (13th century): 115 ft. (35 m) high; views over the village and the Vendée landscape.
• **Village:** Guided visits of 1½ hours by appointment: +33 (0)2 51 69 44 99.

🗝 Accommodation

Guesthouses
La Grange aux Peintres****:
+33 (0)6 98 24 12 00.
La Porte aux Moines***:
+33 (0)2 53 72 01 37.
Auberge de Maître Pannetier**:
+33 (0)2 51 00 80 12.
M. and Mme Berland: +33 (0)2 51 00 83 56
+33 (0)6 17 27 87 35.
Les Pousses Vieilles, Pierre Blanche:
+33 (0)2 51 00 36 48.
M. and Mme Roy: +33 (0)2 51 52 65 67.
Gîtes
Bruno and Isabelle de la Pintière***:
+33 (0)2 51 69 66 94.
Louis and Anne-Marie Robin***:
+33 (0)2 51 69 64 38.
Family vacation centers
Relais Mélusine: +33 (0)2 51 00 80 14.
Vacation villages
La Girouette: +33 (0)2 51 50 10 50.

🍴 Eating Out

Auberge de Maître Pannetier:
+33 (0)2 51 00 80 12.
Café Cour du Miracle: +33 (0)2 51 00 54 93.

Café Mélusine: +33 (0)2 51 00 81 34.
La Serre Gourmande:
+33 (0)9 66 96 43 97.

🧺 Local Specialties

Food and Drink
Brioches and cakes • Pâtés, foie gras, and duck confit • Honey.
Art and Crafts
Artists' studios • Art galleries • Icon painter.

📅 Events

Market: Summer local produce and crafts market, Monday mornings, June–mid-September.
July–August: "Vouvant, Village de Peintres," exhibitions and activities.
August: "Festival des Nuits Musicales en Vendée Romane," music festival.

🦋 Outdoor Activities

Horse-riding • Fishing • Tennis • Walking and mountain-biking: 3 marked trails.

🌿 Further Afield

• Forêt de Vouvant-Mervent, forest; Mervent (4½ miles/7 km).
• Fontenay-le-Comte (10 miles/16 km).
• Marais Poitevin, region (19 miles/31 km).
• Puy-du-Fou, theme park (28 miles/45 km).

❗ Did you know?

Mélusine—half-woman, half-serpent or fish—often appears in legends told in the north and west of France, the Low Countries, and Cyprus. She is said to have built the castle in Vouvant in one night, "with three aprons-full of stones and one mouthful of water."

Yèvre-le-Châtel
(commune of Yèvre-la-Ville)
A medieval inspiration for modern artists

Loiret (45) • Population: 231 • Altitude: 361 ft. (110 m)

On the boundary between the regions of Beauce and Gâtinais, Yèvre-le-Châtel is a happy blend of medieval heritage and contemporary art.

Yèvre Castle, built in the 13th century under King Philip Augustus and recently restored, commands the Rimade valley and a wide horizon. Its high ramparts and four round towers dominate the Romanesque church of Saint-Gault and the unfinished nave of Saint-Lubin. There is a circular walk around the curtain wall and, from the top of the towers, there are stunning views over the surrounding landscape, as far as the forest of Orléans. All along the flower-bedecked streets from the Place du Bourg, near the old well, to the Pont de Souville straddling the Rimarde, old houses and gardens hide behind limestone walls. The village seduced many 20th-century painters, including Maria Vieira da Silva (1908–1992), Árpád Szenes (1897–1985), and Eduardo Luiz (1932–1988), and continues to attract artists and galleries.

By road: Expressway A6, exit 14–Malesherbes (27 miles/43 km), N152 (5½ miles/9 km); N20 (21 miles/34 km); expressway A19, exit 7–Pithiviers (8½ miles/13.5 km). **By air:** Paris-Orly airport (59 miles/95 km).

(i) Tourist information:
+33 (0)2 38 34 25 91
www.yevre-la-ville.fr

👁 Highlights
• Castle (13th century): +33 (0)2 38 34 25 91.
• Église Saint-Gault (12th century).
• Église Saint-Lubin (13th century).
• Village: Guided tour by appointment: +33 (0)2 38 34 25 91.

⚔ Accommodation
Gîtes
M. and Mme Liger****: +33 (0)2 38 62 04 88.
M. and Mme Blanvillain***: +33 (0)2 38 34 25 22.

🍴 Eating Out
Le Courtil, tea room: +33 (0)2 18 13 21 52.
La Rolancière: +33 (0)2 38 34 28 47.

🧺 Local Specialties
Food and Drink
Farm produce: e.g. oil, honey, saffron, cider, wine, jam.
Art and Crafts
Art galleries.

📅 Events
Market: Sunday mornings, Place du Bourg.
May–September: Art and sculpture exhibitions indoors and outside.
July–August: Concerts in Église Saint-Gault.
August: Medieval games and activities.

🦋 Outdoor Activities
Walking: Route GR 655 and Rimarde valley.

🌿 Further Afield
• Boynes: Musée du Safran, saffron museum (3½ miles/5.5 km).
• Pithiviers (3½ miles/5.5 km).
• Pithiviers-le-Vieil: Gallo-Roman site (5 miles/8 km).
• Vrigny: Maison du Père Mousset, rural history museum (7½ miles/12 km).
• Château de Chamerolles (12 miles/19 km).
• Malesherbes (16 miles/26 km).
• Montargis (26 miles/42 km).
• Orléans (28 miles/45 km).

🎗 Did you know?
Yèvre and its castle charmed Victor Hugo, who, in a letter to his wife dated August 22, 1834, said, "I had an admirable journey to Pithiviers and its surrounding area. Yèvre-le-Châtel, which is two leagues away and where I went on foot with holes in my shoes, keeps all to itself a convent and a castle, ruined but complete. It is magnificent. I am drawing everything I see." Indeed, two of these drawings are kept at the Maison de Victor Hugo, Paris.

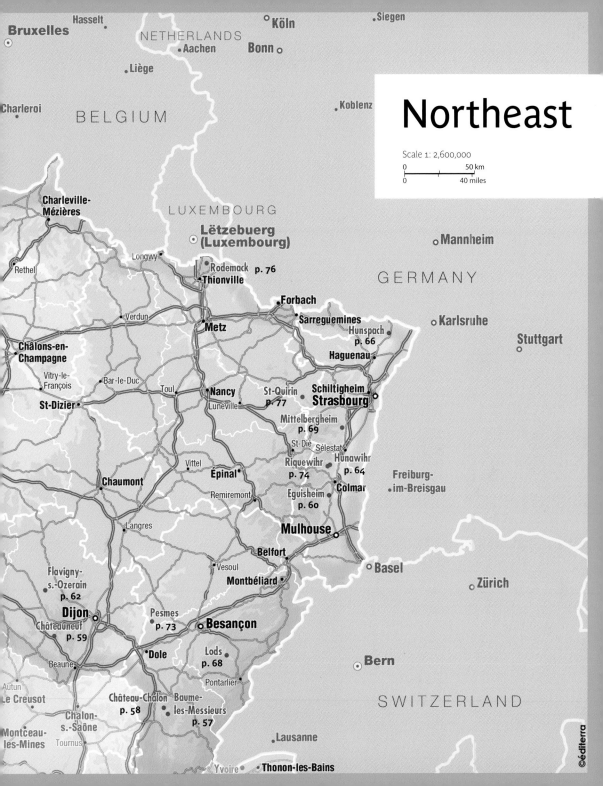

Northeast

Scale 1: 2,600,000

0   50 km
0   40 miles

Bruxelles

Hasselt

NETHERLANDS

Köln

Siegen

Liège

Aachen

Bonn

Charleroi

BELGIUM

Koblenz

Charleville-
Mézières

LUXEMBOURG

Lëtzebuerg
(Luxembourg)

Mannheim

GERMANY

Rethel

Longwy

Rodemack
p. 76

Thionville

Verdun

Forbach

Sarreguemines

Hunspach
p. 66

Karlsruhe

Stuttgart

Metz

Châlons-en-
Champagne

Vitry-le-
François

Bar-le-Duc

Toul

Nancy

St-Quirin
p. 77

Haguenau

Schiltigheim

Strasbourg

St-Dizier

Lunéville

Mittelbergheim
p. 69

Vittel

St-Dié

Sélestat

Épinal

Riquewihr
p. 74

Hunawihr
p. 64

Freiburg-
im-Breisgau

Chaumont

Remiremont

Eguisheim
p. 60

Colmar

Langres

Vesoul

Mulhouse

Belfort

Flavigny-
s.-Ozerain
p. 62

Dijon

Pesmes
p. 73

Montbéliard

Basel

Zürich

Châteauneuf
p. 59

Beaune

Dole

Lods
p. 68

Besançon

Bern

Autun

Le Creusot

Château-Chalon
p. 58

Pontarlier

SWITZERLAND

Montceau-
les-Mines

Chalon-
s.-Saône

Tournus

Baume-
les-Messieurs
p. 57

Lausanne

Yvoire

Thonon-les-Bains

©éditerra

Apremont-sur-Allier
The garden village

Cher (18) • Population: 77 • Altitude: 581 ft. (177 m)

Overlooked by a castle surrounded by landscaped gardens, the village—which was entirely restored in the last century—is reflected in the Allier river.

To the east of the Cher river, Apremont is part of the Berry region, which is evident not only from the wooded countryside around and the high, leafy hedges within, but also from the very ground on which it is built: for a long time, this peaceful village of quarrymen and bargemen dispatched, via the Allier and then the Loire, cut stones that still dress Orleans Cathedral and the Abbaye de Saint-Benoît-sur-Loire. The Maison des Mariniers, at the end of the village, preserves this aspect of the village's history. However, it was in Burgundy that its fate was twice decided. In the Middle Ages, the Château d'Apremont, the westernmost possession of the duchy of Burgundy, was a powerful fortress. Four centuries later, in 1894, Eugène II Schneider, third in the dynasty of powerful industrialists based around Le Creusot, married Antoinette de Saint-Sauveur, a direct descendant on the female line of the family that had owned the castle since 1722. Until his death in 1942, Schneider worked tirelessly, with the aid of his architect and decorator, M. de Galéa, to restore this château and every house in Apremont in the Berry style. His grandson Gilles de Brissac continued his work, and in 1970 created a floral garden at the foot of the castle, inspired by Vita Sackville-West's garden at Sissinghurst in England. Among ponds, waterfalls, and the scents and colors of more than a thousand tree and flower species, a Chinese covered bridge, a Turkish pavilion, and a gazebo decorated with Nevers faience, designed in the style of the 18th-century "manufactories," add a nice, exotic touch.

By road: Expressway A77, exit 37–Bourges (8½ miles/13.5 km); N7, exit 76–Bourges (20 miles/32 km).
By train: Nevers station (10 miles/16 km).
By air: Clermont-Ferrand-Auvergne airport (98 miles/158 km).

ⓘ Tourist information—
Val d'Aubois: +33 (0)2 48 74 25 60
www.mairie-apremontsurallier.info

👁 Highlights
• **Floral gardens** (classed as "remarkable" by the Ministry of Culture): Musée des Calèches, permanent and temporary exhibitions, and a walk around the castle ramparts: +33 (0)2 48 77 55 06.
• **Village:** Guided tour by appointment only: +33 (0)2 48 74 25 60.

🍴 Eating Out
La Brasserie du Lavoir:
+33 (0)2 48 80 25 76.
La Carpe Frite: +33 (0)2 48 77 64 72.

📅 Events
May: Fête des Plantes de Printemps (3rd weekend); classical music festival.
June: Brocante de Charme, flea market (4th weekend).
October: Fête du Vin et de la Gastronomie, wine and food festival (3rd weekend).

🦋 Outdoor Activities
Fishing • Walking on the Chemin de Compostelle (Saint James's Way) via Route GR 654; strolling along the banks of the Allier • Cycling: "Loire à Vélo" trail.

🦋 Further Afield
• Bec d'Allier and Pont-canal (aqueduct) du Guétin (3 miles/5 km).
• Espace Métal/Halle de Grossouvre—museum of industry (6 miles/9.5 km).
• Nevers (9½ miles/15.5 km).
• Abbaye de Fontmorigny (12 miles/19 km).
• Château de Sagonne (16 miles/26 km).

Baume-les-Messieurs

An imperial abbey in the Jura

Jura (39) • Population: 196 • Altitude: 1,083 ft. (330 m)

Baume-les-Messieurs combines the simplicity of a village with the spirituality of the abbey that inspired the founding of the Order of Cluny, which spread throughout the West during the Middle Ages.

Nestled in a remote valley typical of the Jura landscape formed by the Seille river, Baume Abbey experienced remarkable growth throughout the Middle Ages. Developed from the 9th century at the instigation of Abbot Berno, later the founder of Cluny, it enjoyed such widespread influence that Frederick Barbarossa made it an imperial abbey. Of great architectural wealth (Romanesque with alterations in the 16th century), the abbey contains several convent buildings, a 16th-century Flemish altarpiece, a tomb-chapel, and Burgundian statuary. During the French Revolution, the abbey was divided up into private dwellings. Lulled by the gentle sound of the cloister fountain or by the louder noise of the Seille, which cascades in waterfalls not far off, the pale-fronted, brown-roofed houses live in harmony with this green, wild valley, whose rich soil produces some fine wines.

By road: Expressway A39, exit 8–Lons-le-Saunier (17 miles/27 km).
By train: Lons-le-Saunier station (8½ miles/13.5 km). **By air:** Dijon-Bourgogne airport (61 miles/98 km); Geneva airport (68 miles/109 km).

ⓘ Tourist information—Coteaux du Jura: +33 (0)3 84 44 62 47
www.tourisme-coteaux-jura.com

Maître Denise: +33 (0)3 84 44 61 48.
Further information: +33 (0)3 84 44 99 28
www.tourisme-coteaux-jura.com

👁 Highlights
• **Imperial abbey:** Abbey church, 16th-century Flemish altarpiece, 15th-century Burgundian statuary, tomb-chapel, permanent exhibition on the abbey's history. Option of guided tour. Further information and bookings: +33 (0)3 84 44 99 28; audioguides in French, English, and German.
• **Baume caves:** Considered to be among the most spectacular in Europe, with ½ mile (1 km) of accessible galleries and new lighting effects. Further information and bookings: +33 (0)3 84 48 23 02.
• **Cascade des Tufs:** waterfalls.

🗝 Accommodation
Guesthouses
Ghislain Broulard**: +33 (0)3 84 44 64 47.
Rex Andrews*: +33 (0)3 84 44 65 72.
Bernard Lechat: +33 (0)3 84 85 26 49.
Chez Josette: +33 (0)6 42 69 34 47.
Daniel Coudorc: +33 (0)3 84 44 61 84.
Didier Favre: +33 (0)3 84 44 68 37.
Le Dortoir des Moines: +33 (0)3 84 44 97 31.
Félicette Debonis: +33 (0)3 84 85 29 28.
La Grange à Nicolas: +33 (0)3 84 85 20 39.
Gîtes, vacation rentals, and campsites
Laroche Nathalie: +33 (0)6 76 54 31 37.

🍴 Eating Out
L'Abbaye: +33 (0)3 84 44 63 44.
Des Grottes et Des Roches: +33 (0)3 84 48 23 15.
Le Grand Jardin: +33 (0)3 84 44 68 37.

🧺 Local Specialties
Food and Drink
AOC Jura and Côtes du Jura wines • Honey • Abbey produce.
Art and Crafts
Puppets and figurines made from plants • Potter.

📅 Events
December: Christmas market (1st weekend); Les Fayes, celebration of the winter solstice (25th).

🦋 Outdoor Activities
Walking, riding, and mountain-biking: Route GR 59 and 5 themed trails.

🌿 Further Afield
• Voiteur (3 miles/5 km).
• *Château-Chalon (7½ miles/12 km), see p. 58.
• Châteaux of Le Pin and Arlay (10 miles/16 km).
• Lons-le-Saunier (11 miles/18 km).
• Lac de Chalain (16 miles/26 km).
• Cascades du Hérisson, waterfalls (19 miles/31 km).

Château-Chalon

Flagship of the Jura vineyards

Jura (39) • Population: 162 • Altitude: 1,529 ft. (466 m)

Overlooking the valley of the Seille and the Bresse plain, Château-Chalon watches over its vineyards, the birthplace of *vin jaune*, the white wine that resembles a dry sherry.

Between the grasslands and forests of the Jura plateau and the vineyards huddled beneath the cliff, the village emerged around a Benedictine abbey, as is evidenced by the Romanesque Église Saint-Pierre, covered with limestone *laves* (flagstones), and a castle, now reduced to a ruined keep. Lined with sturdy winemakers' houses, which are often flanked by a flight of steps and pierced with large arched openings, nearly every street in Château-Chalon leads to one of the four viewpoints overlooking the vineyards, where Savagnin reigns supreme. In the secrecy of their cellars, winemakers use this distinctive grape variety to make *vin jaune*, ageing the nectar in oak casks for at least six years and three months. At the heart of the village, the old cheese factory has been revived to reveal the secrets of the manufacture and ageing of Comté. The former school, which has been reconstructed as it was in 1928, relives yesteryear, while the Maison de la Haute-Seille houses the tourist information center, as well as an interactive museum on wine and terroir.

By road: Expressway A39, exit 7–Poligny (7½ miles/11.5 km).
By train: Lons-le-Saunier station (9½ miles/15.5 km). **By air:** Dole-Jura airport (30 miles/48 km).

ⓘ Tourist information—Coteaux du Jura: +33 (0)3 84 24 65 01
www.tourisme-coteaux-jura.com

👁 Highlights
• **Maison de la Haute-Seille:** Interactive museum and an introduction to the Jura vineyards. +33 (0)3 84 24 76 05.
• **Église Saint-Pierre:** Romanesque and Gothic art; murals, rich furniture, treasure belonging to the abbey (reliquaries, goldware, statues).
• **École d'Autrefois:** School furniture and teaching materials from 1880 to 1930; activities from April to October: +33 (0)3 84 44 62 47.
• **Old cheese factory:** Guided tours: +33 (0)3 84 44 92 25.
• **Vigne conservatoire:** A plot of 53 old Jura grape varieties from the 19th century: +33 (0)3 84 44 62 47.
• **Landscape:** Listed as "outstanding."

🗝 Accommodation
Guesthouses
La Tour Charlemagne****: +33 (0)3 84 47 21 98.
La Maison d'Eusébia: +33 (0)6 86 60 03 23.
Le Relais des Abbesses: +33 (0)3 84 44 98 56.
T'Nature: +33 (0)3 84 85 29 83.
Gîtes
La Maison d'Anna: +33 (0)3 84 52 50 87.
Les Marnes Bleues: +33 (0)3 84 44 62 86.

🍴 Eating Out
Le P'tit Castel: +33 (0)3 84 44 20 50.
Les Seize Quartiers: +33 (0)3 84 44 68 23.
La Taverne du Roc: +33 (0)3 84 85 24 17.

🧺 Local Specialties
Food and Drink
Cheeses • AOC Château-Chalon, Côtes du Jura, Crémant, Macvin, and Vin de Paille wines • Bresse chicken cooked in the local *vin jaune*.

2️⃣ Events
April: Fête de la Saint-Vernier festival (3rd Sunday).
June: "L'art se dévoile," major art fair (Pentecost).
June–September: Entertainment, tasting evenings, gourmet walks: +33 (0)3 84 44 62 47.
July: Sound and light show.
December: Les Fayes, winter solstice festival (25th).

🥾 Outdoor Activities
Walking: Route GR 59 and 5 marked trails for discovering the vineyards • Mountain-biking: 5 certified circuits • Exploring the area by electric bike.

🌿 Further Afield
• Château de Frontenay (3½ miles/5.5 km).
• *Baume-les-Messieurs (7½ miles/12 km), see p. 57.
• Château d'Arlay (7½ miles/12 km).
• Poligny; Arbois (7½–9 miles/12–14.5 km).
• Lons-le-Saunier (9½ miles/15.5 km).

Châteauneuf
A castle in Auxois

Côte-d'Or (21) • Population: 87 • Altitude: 1,558 ft. (475 m)

The castle is situated to the fore of this village, the waters of the Burgundy Canal reflecting its medieval military architecture.

The fortress was built in the late 12th century by Jean de Chaudenay to control the old road from Dijon to Autun. It owes its austere bearing to its polygonal curtain wall flanked by massive towers and wide moats, which are crossed via one of the old drawbridges transformed into a fixed bridge. In the inner courtyard, the original keep is surrounded by two 15th-century *corps de logis* (central buildings). Below the castle, the church contains a Renaissance-style pulpit and a 14th-century Virgin and Child. Opposite the building is the Maison Blondeau, one of many old merchant houses of the 14th, 15th, and 16th centuries. Distinguished by their turrets, ornamented cartouches, mullioned windows, and ogee lintels, these houses are a recurrent feature of the fortified village, which stretches from the north gate to the spectacular mission cross viewpoint on the hilltop. From there, the view takes in the wooded hillsides of Auxois, with, in the background, the mountains of Morvan and Autun.

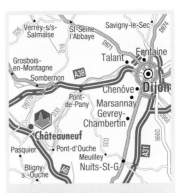

By road: Expressway A6, exit Pouilly-en-Auxois (5½ miles/9 km); expressway A38, exit 24–Autun (5½ miles/9 km).
By train: Dijon station (27 miles/43 km).
By air: Dijon-Bourgogne airport (35 miles/56 km).

ⓘ Tourist information—Pouilly-en-Auxois: +33 (0)3 80 90 74 24
www.pouilly-auxois.com
www.chateauneuf-cotedor.fr

👁 Highlights
• **Castle:** 12th-century keep, 15th-century grand *logis* (Flemish tapestries, medieval furniture), residence of Philippe Pot (15th century), chapel (15th-century "distemper" paintings, copy of the recumbent statue of Philippe Pot retained at the Louvre), 14th-century south tower; multimedia visitor interpretive center; medieval garden; medieval-themed activities for children: +33 (0)3 80 49 21 89.
• **Église Saint-Jacques-et-Saint-Philippe** (16th century): Statues, 14th-century Virgin and Child: +33 (0)3 80 49 21 59.
• **Village:** Guided tour by appointment only: +33 (0)3 80 49 21 59.

🗝 Accommodation
Hotels
Hostellerie du Château**:
+33 (0)3 80 49 22 00.
Guesthouses
Au Bois Dormant***: +33 (0)6 79 49 25 62.
Mme Bagatelle***: +33 (0)3 80 49 21 00.
Mme Vigneron: +33 (0)3 80 27 91 54.
Gîtes and vacation rentals
Notre Maison d'Antan: +33 (0)3 80 49 21 92.
Further information: 03 80 90 74 24/
www.pouilly-auxois.com

🍽 Eating Out
Au Marronnier: +33 (0)3 80 49 21 91.
Hostellerie du Château:
+33 (0)3 80 49 22 00.

L'Orée du Bois: +33 (0)3 80 49 25 32.
La Pizz' du Castel: +33 (0)3 80 49 26 82.

🛍 Local Specialties
Art and Crafts
Antique dealers • Ceramicists • Sculptors • Artists • Wood-carvers.

🗓 Events
July (in even years): Medieval market (last weekend).
October: Mass of Saint Hubert and gourmet and local produce market (1st Sunday).
December: Christmas Mass with living Nativity scene (24th).
All year round: Art and crafts exhibitions, concerts, theater.

🐾 Outdoor Activities
Riding • Fishing • Mountain-biking • Cycle route • Walking around the Auxois lakes, Romanesque chapels trail.

🌿 Further Afield
• Castles in Auxois: Chailly-sur-Armançon, Commarin, Mont-Saint-Jean (5–19 miles/8–31 km).
• Burgundy Canal: boat trip; Pouilly-en-Auxois (6 miles/9.5 km).
• Abbaye de la Bussière; Ouche valley (7½ miles/12 km).
• Beaune; Burgundy vineyards (22 miles/35 km).
• Dijon (27 miles/43 km).

Eguisheim

Enter the round

Haut-Rhin (68) • Population: 1,802 • Altitude: 689 ft. (210 m)

Just a short distance from Colmar, Eguisheim—the birthplace of wine-growing in Alsace—winds in concentric circles around its castle.

Whether around the castle at the center of the village, which witnessed the birth of the future Pope Leo IX (1002–1054), or along the ramparts that encircle it, Eguisheim encourages visitors to go round in circles. With every step, from courtyard to fountain, lane to square, the ever-present curve changes one's perspective of the colorful houses arrayed with flowers, half-timbering, and oriel windows. Rebuilt in the Gothic style, the Église Saint-Pierre-et-Saint-Paul is distinguished by its high square tower of yellow sandstone, and a magnificent tympanum depicting Christ in Majesty flanked by two saints, as well as the Parable of the Wise and Foolish Virgins.

The winegrowers' and coopers' houses, with their large courtyards, are a reminder that—as well as being a feast for the eyes—Eguisheim also delights the palate with its *grand cru* wines, which are celebrated with festivals throughout the year.

By road: Expressway A35, exit 27–Sainte-Croix-en-Plaine (4½ miles/7 km). **By train:** Colmar station (4½ miles/7 km). **By air:** Bâle-Mulhouse station (35 miles/56 km); Strasbourg-Inter airport (45 miles/72 km).

ⓘ **Tourist information:**
+33 (0)3 89 23 40 33
www.ot-eguisheim.fr

👁 Highlights

• Chapel of the Château Saint-Léon (19th century, neo-Romanesque style): Relics of Pope Leo IX.
• Église Saint-Pierre-et-Saint-Paul (11th–14th centuries): Polychromed wooden statue known as "the Opening Virgin" (13th century), porch of the old church.
• Parc des Cigognes (stork garden): Free entry to the enclosure, information board on the life of Alsace's legendary bird.
• Vineyards: Guided tour of the wine route followed by a guided tasting session of the wines of Alsace. By arrangement with the winegrowers, and on Saturdays from mid-June to mid-September and on Saturdays and Tuesdays in August: +33 (0)3 89 23 40 33.
• Village: Guided tours all year for groups and by arrangement, and Thursdays from mid-June to mid-September: +33 (0)3 89 23 40 23; guided tour on a tourist train and tour of the area on the Train Gourmand du Vignoble Tuesdays and Thursdays: +33 (0)3 89 73 74 24, discovery tour of the old village (information boards with QR codes).

🔑 Accommodation

Hotels
Auberge Alsacienne***: +33 (0)3 89 41 50 20.
Ferme du Pape***: +33 (0)3 89 41 41 21.
♥ Hostellerie du Château***: +33 (0)3 89 23 72 00.
Hôtel Saint-Hubert***: +33 (0)3 89 41 40 50.
À la Ville de Nancy**: +33 (0)3 89 41 78 75.
Auberge des Trois Châteaux**: +33 (0)3 89 23 70 61.
Hostellerie des Comtes**: +33 (0)3 89 41 16 99.
Auberge du Rempart: +33 (0)3 89 41 16 87.
Aparthotel
Résidence*** Pierre et Vacances: +33 (0)3 89 30 41 20.
Guesthouses
M. et Mme Bombenger +33 (0)3 89 23 71 19.
Other guesthouses, gîtes, and vacation rentals
Further information: 03 89 23 40 33
www.ot-eguisheim.fr
Campsites
Les Trois Châteaux***: +33 (0)3 89 23 19 39.

🍴 Eating Out

À la Ville de Nancy: +33 (0)3 89 41 78 75.
Auberge Alsacienne: +33 (0)3 89 41 50 20.
Auberge du Rempart: +33 (0)3 89 41 16 87.

Auberge des Trois Châteaux:
+33 (0)3 89 23 70 61.
Au Vieux Porche: +33 (0)3 89 24 01 90.
Caveau des Douceurs: +33 (0)3 89 23 10 01.
Caveau Heuhaus: +33 (0)3 89 41 85 72.
Le Dagsbourg: +33 (0)3 89 41 51 90.
Ferme du Pape: +33 (0)3 89 41 41 21.
La Grangelière: +33 (0)3 89 23 00 30.
Hostellerie des Comtes:
+33 (0)3 89 41 16 99.
Le Pavillon Gourmand:
+33 (0)3 89 24 36 88.
Wistub-Bierstub Kas Fratz:
+33 (0)3 89 41 87 66.

🏛 Local Specialties
Food and Drink
Pretzels • *Pain d'épice* (spice cake) •
Mushrooms • Alsatian charcuterie •
AOC Alsace wines and Eichberg and
Pfersigberg *grands crus.*
Art and Crafts
Artists' studios • Art gallery • Painting •
Upholstery and decoration.

2 Events
July: Eguisheim wines week and
"Nuit des Grands Crus" wine festival
(2nd fortnight).
August: Discovery Day, Parc à Cigognes
(1st Sunday), guided wine tasting
(1st week), Fête des Vignerons,
winegrowers' festival (last weekend).
September: Fête du Vin Nouveau,
new wine festival (last weekend).
October: Fête du Vin Nouveau
(1st weekend), Fête du Champignon,
mushroom festival (last weekend).
November and December: Christmas
market (daily for the four weeks of Advent).

🦋 Outdoor Activities
Discovery of the village by microlight •
Standard and electric bike rental •
Walking: 12 marked trails • Segway rides.

🌿 Further Afield
• Hautes Vosges, region: Munster
valley; Col de la Schlucht (3–19 miles/
5–31 km).
• Colmar (3½ miles/5.5 km).
• Alsace wine route: Turckheim (5 miles/
8 km); Rouffach (7 miles/11.5 km);
Kaysersberg (8 miles/13 km);
*Riquewihr (11 miles/18 km), see
pp. 74–75; *Hunawihr (12 miles/19 km),
see pp. 64–65; Guebwiller (13 miles/
21 km).
• Château du Hohlandsbourg and
Five Castles route (5 miles/8 km).
• Neuf-Brisach (13 miles/21 km).

🛈 Did you know?
Here, if stones could speak, they would tell
the story of the illustrious family of the
counts of Eguisheim, into which was born
a certain Bruno, son of Hugh IV. A high-
ranking nobleman, he was called to papal
office. Bruno went to Rome on foot, stick
in hand, cape on his shoulders, just as he
is depicted in his statue on the Place du
Château. On his arrival, he was acclaimed
by the people of Rome and enthroned as
Pope Leo IX.

Flavigny-sur-Ozerain
A sweet-smelling spot

Côte-d'Or (21) • Population: 338 • Altitude: 1,398 ft. (426 m)

The site of an abbey, Flavigny also produces an aniseed candy that is enjoyed throughout the world; its sweet fragrance perfumes the air here.

The Romans chose this location during the siege of Alesia in 52 BCE; the town grew with the founding of the Benedictine abbey of Saint-Pierre, which is where the famous candies are now produced. The parish church of Saint-Genest, whose nave and aisles are partially surmounted by a 13th-century gallery, contains stalls made by the brotherhood in the 14th century and fine Burgundian statuary from the 14th and 15th centuries. At Flavigny's heart, the village's artisanal and commercial prosperity is visible today in the bay windows of single-storey houses such as the Maison au Donataire, which contains the "Point I" visitor center. The medieval fortifications of the Portes du Val and du Bourg still stand, as do Flavigny's ramparts, from where the view stretches out over the green hills of Auxois.

By road: Expressway A6, exit 23–Bierre-lès-Semur (14 miles/23 km). **By train:** Venareyles-Laumes station (5 miles/8 km); Montbard TGV station (15 miles/24 km). **By air:** Dijon-Bourgogne airport (45 miles/72 km).

ⓘ **Tourist information—"Point I" visitor center:** +33 (0)3 80 96 25 34
www.flavigny-sur-ozerain.fr
Tourist information—Pays d'Alésia et de la Seine: +33 (0)3 80 96 89 13

👁 Highlights
• Crypt of the Abbaye Saint-Pierre (8th century).
• Église Saint-Genest (13th–16th centuries): Gothic style with 15th-century stalls and relics of Saint Reine: +33 (0)3 80 96 25 34 or +33 (0)3 80 96 21 73.
• Aniseed factory: In the former Abbaye Saint-Pierre; free entry and tasting: +33 (0)3 80 96 20 88.
• Maison des Arts Textiles et du Design: Algranate museum—collection, exhibitions, traditional Auxois weaving workshop: +33 (0)3 80 96 20 40.
• Village: Guided tour for groups by appointment only: +33 (0)3 80 96 25 34.
• Flavigny-Alésia vineyards: Self-guided visit of the winery and free tasting: +33 (0)3 80 96 25 63.

🗝 Accommodation
Guesthouses
L'Ange Souriant***: +33 (0)3 80 96 24 93.
Les Adages: +33 (0)6 64 52 18 60.
Chez Elle: +33 (0)3 80 96 28 23.

Couvent des Castafours: +33 (0)3 80 96 24 92.
Le Logis Abbatial: +33 (0)6 87 25 60 08.
Le Logis de l'Ozerain: +33 (0)6 84 83 18 99.
La Maison du Tisserand: +33 (0)3 80 96 20 40.
Mme Troubat: +33 (0)3 80 96 24 00.
Gîtes, bunkhouses
Further information: +33 (0)3 80 96 25 34/ www.flavigny-sur-ozerain.fr

🍽 Eating Out
Le Garum: +33 (0)3 80 89 07 78.
La Grange des Quatre Heures Soupatoires, farmhouse inn: +33 (0)3 80 96 20 62.
Le Relais de Flavigny: +33 (0)3 80 96 27 77.

🏛 Local Specialties
Food and Drink
Abbaye de Flavigny aniseed, specialty confectionery • Charcuterie • Cheese (Époisses) • Burgundy wines; vins de pays des Coteaux de l'Auxois.
Art and Crafts
Wrought ironworker • Art galleries • Lithographer • Organic wool and vegetable dyes.

📅 Events
Ascension weekend: Walks open to all.
June: Pimpinella music festival.
July: Village meal (14th).
August: PontiCelli cello workshops (early August).
October: Marché de la Saint-Simon, market (penultimate Sunday).
December and January: Nativity scenes exhibited in the streets, and at the old *lavoir* (washhouse) on January 1.
Winter: "Hors Saison Musicale" concerts.

🦋 Outdoor Activities
Hunting • Fishing • Mountain-biking • Walking and riding from Bibracte to Alésia and 5 marked trails.

🌿 Further Afield
• Alésia: archeological site; Château de Bussy-Rabutin (3–6 miles/5–9.5 km).
• Venarey-les-Laumes: Burgundy Canal (5 miles/8 km).
• Semur-en-Auxois (11 miles/18 km).
• Montbard; Buffon: foundry; Abbaye de Fontenay (12–16 miles/19–26 km).

❗ Did you know?
According to the writer Saint-Simon, Louis XIV loved aniseed candies, which he liked to keep with him in special box in his pocket. Madame de Sévigné, Madame de Pompadour, and the comtesse de Ségur also enjoyed the aniseed treats, which they used to offer to their friends.

Hunawihr

The colors of the vines

Haut-Rhin (68) • Population: 603 • Altitude: 525 ft. (160 m)

Situated on the Alsace wine route amid the vineyards, Hunawihr is a typical Alsatian village, bedecked with flowers.

Hunawihr owes its name to a laundrywoman, Saint Huna: according to legend, she lived here in the 7th century with her husband, the Frankish lord, Hunon. The 15th–16th-century church contains 15th-century frescoes that recount the life of Saint Nicholas. Surrounded by a cemetery fortified by six bastions, it is built on the hill overlooking the village, whose attractions include the Saint June Fountain with its washhouse, the town hall (formerly the corn exchange), the Renaissance-style Maison Schickhart, half-timbered houses, and bourgeois residences from the 16th and 19th centuries. Nature-lovers can visit the center for reintroducing storks and otters, and the butterfly garden—both magical places.

By road: Expressway A35, exit 23–Ribeauvillé then N83 (5½ miles/9 km).
By rail: Colmar station (11 miles/18 km).
By air: Bâle-Mulhouse airport (47 miles/76 km).

ⓘ **Tourist information:**
+33 (0)3 89 73 23 23
www.hunawihr.fr

👁 **Highlights**
• **Church** (15th and 16th centuries) **and its fortified cemetery:** Saint Nicholas frescoes (15th century).
• **Centre de Réintroduction des Cigognes et des Loutres:** NaturOparC, 12-acre (5-ha.) wildlife park dedicated to reintroducing and preserving storks, otters, and other local species: +33 (0)3 89 73 72 62.
• **Jardin des Papillons:** Several hundred exotic butterflies from Africa, Asia, and the Americas, living in a lush garden: +33 (0)3 89 73 33 33.
• **Village:** Guided tour of the church and village every Wednesday and Friday in July and August, meet at 6.15 p.m. at the church: +33 (0)3 89 73 23 23; Randoland, recreational discovery trail around the village.
• *Grands crus* wine trail: Permanent discovery trail; guided tour by a winemaker and free tasting sessions in summer. Further information: +33 (0)3 89 73 23 23.

• **Vineyards:** Guided tour followed by a guided tasting session every Thursday at 3.30 p.m. in July and August. Further information: +33 (0)3 89 73 61 67.

🗝 **Accommodation**
Guesthouses
Further information: +33 (0)3 89 73 23 23
www.ribeauville-riquewihr.com
www.hunawihr.fr
Gîtes and vacation rentals
Further information: +33 (0)3 89 73 23 23
www.ribeauville-riquewihr.com
www.hunawihr.fr

🍴 Eating Out

Caveau du Vigneron: +33 (0)3 89 73 70 15.
O'Goutchi: +33 (0)3 89 58 88 23.
Wistub Suzel: +33 (0)3 89 73 30 85.

🧺 Local Specialties

Food and Drink

Distilled spirits • AOC Alsace wines,
Crémant d'Alsace, and *grand cru* Rosacker
(Gewürztraminer, Riesling, Pinot Gris).

📅 Events

August: Hunafascht, Alsatian open-air
evenings under paper lanterns (1st Friday
and Saturday).

🦋 Outdoor Activities

Cycle touring • Walking • Mountain-biking,
1 marked trail • Chemin de Compostelle
(Saint James's Way) trail.

🌿 Further Afield

• Alsace wine route: *Riquewihr
(1 mile/1.5 km), see pp. 74–75; Ribeauvillé;
Bergheim; Kintzheim; *Eguisheim
(12 miles/19 km), see pp. 60–61.
• Haut-Koenigsbourg (8½ miles/13.5 km).
• Colmar; Sélestat (9½ miles/15.5 km).
• *Mittelbergheim (23 miles/37 km),
see pp. 69–70.

ℹ️ Did you know?

The village joined the Reformation in
1537, but after Alsace was annexed
to France in 1648 Catholicism was
reintroduced. "Simultaneum"—whereby
Protestants and Catholics share a church
but worship at different times—was
instigated in 1687 and is ongoing.

Hunspach

Alsace "beyond the forest"

Bas-Rhin (67) • Population: 700 • Altitude: 525 ft. (160 m)

Situated in the heart of the Parc Naturel Régional des Vosges du Nord (nature park), Hunspach features houses with white cob walls and half-timbering that are typical of the Wissembourg region, showing that, in this village, the carpenter is king.

At the end of the Thirty Years War, Hunspach was almost on its knees; it owes its salvation to French refugees and, in particular, to the Swiss immigrants who were granted farmland here. With wood and clay to hand, they built black-and-white half-timbered houses, just like those back home; the village owes its charm and attractiveness to these buildings. With their hipped gables and tiled canopies, they make a lovely sight lined up along the main road and around the pink sandstone bell tower of the Protestant church. Everywhere geraniums bloom at windows or on walls but, in this village where everything is neat and tidy, there still remains some mystery. The balloon-shaped windowpanes of Hunspach work like distorting mirrors, giving passers by a false reflection and preventing them peering inside. Behind their windows, the residents can see out without being seen.

By road: Expressway A35, exit 57–Seltz (12 miles/19 km); expressway A4, exit 47–Haguenau (24 miles/39 km). **By train:** Hunspach station (1 mile/1.5 km); Wissembourg station (6 miles/9.5 km). **By air:** Strasbourg-Inter airport (48 miles/77 km).

ⓘ Tourist information:
+33 (0)3 88 80 59 39 / www.hunspach.com

🗓 Events
June: Fête du Folklore (last weekend in spring).
July–August: Folklore activities and evenings: +33 (0)3 88 80 59 39.
December: Christmas country market (2nd Sunday of Advent).

🦋 Outdoor Activities
Pedestrian trail around village.

🕊 Further Afield
• Route around picturesque villages: Hoffen, Seebach, Steinselz, Cleebourg (2–6 miles/3–9.5 km).
• Alsace wine route: Steinselz, Oberhoffen, Rott-Cleebourg (4½ miles/7 km).
• Pottery-making villages: Betschdorf, Soufflenheim (5–11 miles/8–18 km).
• Wissembourg (6 miles/9.5 km).
• Germany: Palatinate region, vineyards, the Black Forest (6–25 miles/9.5–40 km).
• Haguenau (14 miles/23 km).
• Niederbronn-les-Bains (17 miles/27 km).
• Strasbourg (34 miles/55 km).

🛈 Did you know?
Fort Schoenenbourg, designed to accommodate 600 men and be self-sufficient for three months, was heavily bombarded as German forces streamed over the Belgian border into France in June 1940; the fortress crews nevertheless held firm. But the French General Staff ordered its surrender to German troops on July 1, 1940.

👁 Highlights
• **Fort Schoenenbourg** (Maginot Line): World War II fortress built 1930–40; the most important Maginot Line construction in Alsace open to visitors. Visit the military blocks, command post, gallery, infantry casemates, kitchen. Accessible for wheelchair users: +33 (0)3 88 80 96 19.
• **Village:** Guided visit for groups of 15+ by reservation: +33 (0)3 88 80 59 39; self-guided trail around the historic site (map available from tourist information center).

⚷ Accommodation
Guesthouses
Mme Billmann***: +33 (0)3 88 54 76 93.
Maison Ungerer***: +33 (0)3 88 80 59 39.

Gîtes
Mme Billmann***: +33 (0)3 88 54 76 93.
Maison Ungerer*** and **:
+33 (0)3 88 80 59 39.
Mme Lehmann**: +33 (0)3 88 80 42 25.
Vacation rentals
Mme Derrendinger: +33 (0)3 88 80 43 95.

🍴 Eating Out
Au Cerf : +33 (0)3 88 80 41 59.
Chez Massimo: +33 (0)3 88 80 42 32.

🧺 Local Specialties
Food and Drink
Wine • *Dickuechen* (brioche loaf) • *Fleischnacka* (meat and pasta roulade).
Art and Crafts
Painter • Alsace artifacts • *kelsch* household linen.

Lods

Born from the river

Doubs (25) • Population: 231 • Altitude: 1,214 ft. (370 m)

Exploiting the energy of the Loue river as it tumbled through the valley, the inhabitants of this little village built thriving iron forges and produced wine in the relatively mild climate.

The smithies may be idle now, and Lods may no longer produce grapes, but the village still has its 16th- and 17th-century wine-growers' houses with their spacious vaulted cellars, clustered higgledy-piggledy around the 18th-century church and its tufa-stone bell tower. The Musée de la Vigne et du Vin (vine and wine museum), which is housed in a beautiful 16th-century building, the old smithy on the other side of the river, and a historical trail through the village all tell the stories of the blacksmiths and winegrowers who used to live here.

By road: Expressway A36, exit 3–Pontarlier (41 miles/66 km); N57 (7 miles/11.5 km).
By rail: Pontarlier station (15 miles/24 km); Besançon-Viotte station (23 miles/37 km).
By air: Geneva airport (87 miles/140 km); Dijon-Bourgogne airport (92 miles/148 km).

ⓘ **Tourist information—Ornans-Vallées de la Loue et du Lison:**
+33 (0)3 81 62 21 50
www.destinationlouelison.com
www.lods-village.fr

Trout • Mountain ham • Comté cheese • Cancoillotte cheese.
Art and Crafts
Painters.

🐾 Outdoor Activities

Canoeing • Fishing • Walking • Mountain-biking.

🦅 Further Afield

• Source of the Loue river; Pontarlier; Joux Fort; Lac de Saint-Point, lake (6–31 miles/9.5–50 km).
• Loue valley; Ornans; Besançon (7½–23 miles/12–37 km).
• Ornans: Musée Courbet and Musée du Costume (7½ miles/12 km).
• Dino-zoo (12 miles/19 km).

👁 Highlights

• Église Saint-Théodule.
• Musée de la Vigne et du Vin:
+33 (0)3 81 60 90 11.

🗝 Accommodation

Hotels
Hôtel de France: +33 (0)3 81 60 95 29.
Guesthouses
Au Fil de Lods***, licensed fishing lodges:
+33 (0)3 81 60 97 51.
La Truite d'Or*: +33 (0)6 76 87 58 50.

Gîtes and vacation rentals
Further information:
+33 (0)3 81 62 21 50.
Campsites
Le Champaloux**: +33 (0)3 81 60 90 11.

🍴 Eating Out

Hôtel de France: +33 (0)3 81 60 95 29.

🧺 Local Specialties

Food and Drink
"Jésus de Morteau" smoked sausage •

❗ Did you know?

The heyday of Lods' wine production was in the 17th and 18th centuries, when wine from Lods was exported to Switzerland and Alsace. The development of railway routes brought cheaper wines from Algeria and the South, drastically reducing local production; by the end of the 19th century, phylloxera had also wreaked havoc in the vineyards, marking the end of a hitherto thriving local industry.

Mittelbergheim

Rainbow colors and fine wines

Bas-Rhin (67) • Population: 682 • Altitude: 722 ft. (220 m)

On the wine route in Alsace, at the foot of Mont Sainte-Odile, Mittelbergheim sings with color and produces excellent wines.

Mittelbergheim was founded by the Franks near Mont Sainte-Odile, and was dedicated to Alsace's patron saint; for many years it belonged to nearby Andlau Abbey, erected in the 9th century by the wife of Emperor Charles le Gros. The village is devoted to wine production. Glowing with vibrant colors in fall and wild tulips in springtime, it is surrounded by vineyards from its base (where the Rhine Plain begins) to the Zotzenberg vineyard on the hilltop. Here the Sylvaner grape is grown, among other varieties, making some of the very best *grand cru* wines. Vines are ubiquitous in the landscape—and also in Mittelbergheim's architecture. The façades of the houses lining the streets have a remarkable unity of style. Dating from the 16th and 17th centuries, they are superbly preserved, adorning the streets with their eye-catching pink sandstone frontages. Their massive wooden gates open wide in the morning to reveal huge interior courtyards at the center of buildings dedicated to wine production. Once closed, they guard the secret of the cellars, where Zotzenberg Sylvaner—the only Sylvaner in Alsace classified as *grand cru*—is aged, alongside Rieslings, Pinot Gris, and Gewürztraminers.

By road: Expressway A35, exit 13–Mittelbergheim (2 miles/3 km). **By train:** Barr station (1 mile/1.5 km); Strasbourg TGV station (23 miles/37 km). **By air:** Strasbourg Inter airport (19 miles/31 km); Bâle-Mulhouse airport (63 miles/101 km).

ⓘ Tourist information—
Pays de Barr et du Bernstein:
+33 (0)3 88 08 66 65
www.pays-de-barr.fr
www.mittelbergheim.fr

👁 Highlights
• **Former oil mill** (18th century).
• **Museum "Mémoire de Vignerons":** Conserving wine-producing heritage with a large collection of relevant artifacts; open every Sunday July–October, and by appointment: +33 (0)3 88 08 00 96.
• **Wine path:** Open all year.
• **Village:** Guided tour by appointment only; self-guided visit with a dozen information boards; map available: +33 (0)3 88 08 92 29.

🔑 Accommodation
Hotels
Winstub Gilg**: +33 (0)3 88 08 91 37.
Guesthouses
Henri Dietrich: +33 (0)3 88 08 93 54.
Christian Dolder: +33 (0)3 88 08 96 08.
Jacqueline Dolder: +33 (0)3 88 08 15 23.
Marie-Paule Dolder: +33 (0)3 88 08 17 49.
Daniel Haegi: +33 (0)3 88 08 95 80.
Paul Hirtz: +33 (0)3 88 08 54 86.
Le Petit Nid: +33 (0)6 87 36 11 17.
Charles Schmitz: +33 (0)3 88 08 09 39.
Nicolas Wittmann: +33 (0)3 88 08 95 79.
Gîtes and vacation rentals
Further information: 03 88 08 66 65
www.pays-de-barr.fr

 Eating Out
Am Lindeplatzel: +33 (0)3 88 08 10 69.
Au Raisin d'Or: +33 (0)3 88 08 93 54.
Winstub Gilg: +33 (0)3 88 08 91 37.

Local Specialties
Food and Drink
Preserves • Honey • AOC Alsace and
grand cru Zotzenberg wines.
Art and Crafts
Artist.

Events
January–June: Exhibitions.
March–April: "Henterem Kallerladel,"
open house at wine cellars (end March–
beginning April).
July: Fête du Vin, wine festival
(last weekend).
July–August: "Sommermarik," country
market (Wednesday evenings).
October: Fête du Vin Nouveau, new
wine festival (2nd weekend).
December: "Bredelmarik," market for
Alsatian Christmas cakes (1st Sunday).

Outdoor Activities
Walking: Routes GR 5 and GR 10;
marked trails, including wine path and
"Randocroquis" (walk and draw trail) •
Horse-riding • "Sentier des Espiègles"
(family fun trail) • Mountain-biking.

Further Afield
• Barr (1 mile/1.5 km).
• Andlau; Le Hohwald; Champ-du-Feu
(1–12 miles/1.5–19 km).
• Obernai (6 miles/9.5 km).
• Mont Saint-Odile (9½ miles/15.5 km).
• Sélestat (12 miles/19 km).
• Haut-Koenigsbourg (17 miles/27 km).
• Strasbourg (22 miles/35 km).
• *Hunawihr (23 miles/37 km),
see pp. 64–65.
• *Riquewihr (24 miles/39 km),
see pp. 74–75.
• Colmar (26 miles/42 km).

Did you know?
At "Mittel," as the locals call it, there is a
long history of wine-growing. Behind its
elegant Renaissance façade on the main
street, the town hall holds the *Weinschlag*,
a precious document that contains many
records of vineyards and wines, dating
from 1510.

Noyers
Medieval Burgundy

Yonne (89) • Population: 644 • Altitude: 620 ft. (189 m)

Curved around a meander on the Serein river, Noyers is a typical medieval fortified town.

The village is still protected by ramparts studded with sixteen towers and three fortified gateways: the Tonnerre, topped with lava tiles; the Venoise, on the old castle site; and the painted gateway, with culverin points on the machicolated gatehouse. Renaissance houses rub shoulders with half-timbered and corbeled ones on the Place de la Petite-Étape-aux-Vins, the Place du Marché-au-Blé, and the Place du Grenier-à-Sel. At the base of the village, stone steps outside winegrowers' houses fall smartly into line. In the center of the village, the church of Notre-Dame is in the Flamboyant Gothic style. While decidedly medieval within its ramparts, Noyers moves with the times: it organizes vibrant cultural activities that combine music and craftsmanship with a stunning collection of naive art.

By road: Expressway A6, exit 21–Nitry (7 miles/11.5 km). **By train:** Tonnerre station (14 miles/23 km); Montbard TGV station (20 miles/32 km). **By air:** Dijon-Bourgogne airport (84 miles/135 km).

ⓘ Tourist information—Noyers-Montréal: +33 (0)3 86 82 66 06
www.noyers-et-tourisme.com

👁 Highlights
• **Musée des Arts Naïfs et Populaires de Noyers** (in the 17th-century college): Extensive naive art collection; collection of folk art: +33 (0)3 86 82 89 09.
• **Site of the former castle:** Self-guided visit: +33 (0)3 86 82 66 06.
• **Tour of the ramparts:** +33 (0)3 86 82 61 75.
• **Village:** Guided tours at 3 p.m. Thursdays and Fridays in July–August, for individuals (contact tourist information center first), and throughout the year for groups by appointment only: +33 (0)3 86 82 66 06.

⚒ Accommodation
Guesthouses
Le Tabellion***: +33 (0)3 86 82 62 26.
Le Clos Malo: +33 (0)3 86 75 04 52.
La Porte Peinte: +33 (0)3 86 75 05 11.
La Vieille Tour: +33 (0)3 86 82 87 69.
Gîtes and vacation rentals
Further information: +33 (0)3 86 82 66 06
www.noyers-et-tourisme.com
Nature zone
Further information: +33 (0)3 86 82 83 72
www.noyers-et-tourisme.com

🍽 Eating Out
Le Faubourg: +33 (0)6 01 07 38 89.
Les Granges: +33 (0)3 86 55 45 91.
Le Marquis Perché: +33 (0)3 86 75 16 70.
Les Millésimes: +33 (0)3 86 82 82 16.
La Petite Étape aux Vins: +33 (0)7 68 75 40 61.

Tom et Mozza, pizzeria: +33 (0)6 20 14 86 34.
La Vieille Tour: +33 (0)3 86 82 87 36.

🧺 Local Specialties
Food and Drink
AOC Chablis wines.
Art and Crafts
Antiques • Contemporary art • Ceramic artist • Medieval illuminator • Maker of feathered masks • Wrought ironwork • Gallery • Jewelers • Tapestry artist • Leather craftsman • Potters • Weaver.

📅 Events
Market: Wednesday mornings.
July: Musical events, part of the Festival des Grands Crus de Bourgogne; "Gargouillosium," sculpting gargoyles.
July–August: Flea markets (Saturday mornings).

August: Festival Vallée et Veillée (1st weekend).
September: Illuminations as part of the Heritage Weekend (3rd weekend).
October–November: Truffle market.

🦋 Outdoor Activities
Swimming (no lifeguard) • *Boules* area • Fishing • Walking: 3 marked trails.

🦋 Further Afield
• Vausse Priory; Buffon: foundry; Fontenay Abbey (9½–25 miles/15.5–40 km).
• Castles at Ancy-le-Franc, Tanlay, Fosse Dionne, and Tonnerre Hôtel Dieu (12–19 miles/19–31 km).
• *Vézelay (25 miles/40 km), see pp. 79–81.

Parfondeval

In the vanguard of the Reformation

Aisne (02) • Population: 500 • Altitude: 725 ft. (221 m)

A compact village of red bricks and silver-gray slate roofs, Parfondeval is typical of this region and remains characterized by farming life.

During the reigns of Louis XIII and Louis XIV, to defend themselves against hordes of brigands, the villagers of Parfondeval constructed a fortified church dedicated to Saint Médard, around which they built squat houses that served as ramparts. To get to the church, you have to go through a porch that is set into a house, then pass between two round towers. The road leads to a square that is partially occupied by a pond. In the early 19th century, the village had six others, which provided drinking water for animals. Walking through the village, the visitor sees houses decorated with glazed bricks in diamond shapes, half-timbered façades, and, surprisingly, at the end of the Rue du Chêne, a Protestant church. The latter reflects the peculiarity of Parfondeval's religious history. During the 16th century, villagers and others from the Thiérache region, returning from the annual harvest in the Pays de Meaux, brought back to Parfondeval copies of the Bible translated into French and communicated the new ideas of the Reformation. The present church bears witness to the continuing presence of this community. Apple orchards, pastures, and cornfields separated by copses make up the landscape of Parfondeval, which is almost entirely devoted to farming.

By road: Expressway A34, exit 26–Cormontreuil then N51 (22 miles/35 km); expressway A26, exit 13–Laon then N2 (24 miles/39 km).
By train: Vervins station (21 miles/34 km); Laon station (30 miles/48 km).
By air: Reims-Champagne airport (39 miles/63 km).

(i) Tourist information—Thiérache:
+33 (0)3 23 91 30 10
www.tourisme-thierache.fr

👁 Highlights
• **Village:** Self-guided tour with audioguides on the signposted walk. Further information: +33 (0)3 23 91 30 10.
• **Église Saint-Médard** (16th century): Daily 9 a.m.–6 p.m.
• **Protestant church** (1858).
• **La Maison des Outils d'Antan:** Collection of 2,000 farming tools and everyday items from the 1900s: +33 (0)3 23 97 61 59.

🗝 Accommodation
Guesthouses
Françoise and Lucien Chrétien**: +33 (0)3 23 97 61 59.

Gîtes
Le Village***: +33 (0)3 23 97 62 54 or +33 (0)6 48 73 29 77.

🍴 Eating Out
Françoise and Lucien Chrétien, farmhouse, afternoon tea: +33 (0)3 23 97 61 59.
Le Relais de la Chouette (Tuesday–Sunday): +33 (0)3 23 91 34 97.

🍽 Local Specialties
Food and Drink
Cider and apple juice.

2 Events
June: Village fête.
August: Flea market (Sunday after the 15th).
October: "Potironnade," squash tastings and guided walk (4th Saturday).

🦋 Outdoor Activities
Walking, horse-riding, and mountain-biking ("Par le Fond du Val" trail).

🌿 Further Afield
• Aubenton (8 miles/13 km).
• Saint-Michel: abbey (17 miles/27 km).
• Liesse-Notre-Dame: basilica (21 miles/34 km).
• Marle: Musée des Temps Barbares, museum of the Middle Ages (21 miles/34 km).
• Rocroi, star-shaped fortified town (31 miles/50 km).

❗ Did you know?
Parfondeval is the only village in Thiérache to have both a Catholic and a Protestant church as well as a Catholic and a Protestant cemetery. In the past, Catholics used to live at the top of the village, where the Catholic church is located, while Protestants lived further down, near their place of worship.

Pesmes

A village with a prosperous past

Haute-Saône (70) • Population: 1,128 • Altitude: 689 ft. (210 m)

On the banks of the Ognon river, Pesmes bears witness to the work of winemakers, the glory days of the old lords of the town, and the heyday of Franche-Comté's metalworking industry. Pesmes is approached through the valley. At the end of the avenue of hundred-year-old plane trees, the sight of the gap-toothed castle, with houses nestling at its feet, and of the impressive ramparts reflected in the calm waters of the river takes one's breath away. Founded in the Middle Ages on the route leading from Gray to Dole, and coveted for its strategic position, the town was by turns Frankish, Germanic, Burgundian, and Spanish, before becoming French during the reign of Louis XIV (1643–1715). At that time, it was a major trading post that brought together merchants and burghers. The village bears witness to this rich past: along the streets and the alleyways, where private residences and winemakers' houses rub shoulders, visitors can discover the Église Saint-Hilaire, built and rebuilt between the 13th and 17th centuries, with its imperial bell tower; the castle ruins; and the Loigerot and Saint-Hilaire gateways. The old forge, founded in 1660 by Charles de La Baume, marquis of Pesmes, and built on the site of an old mill, was operational until 1993 and has now been converted into a museum.

By road: Expressway A39, exit 5–Saint-Jean-de-Losne (16 miles/26 km); expressway A36, exit 2–Dole (12 miles/19 km). **By train:** Dole station (15 miles/24 km); Besançon-Viotte station (32 miles/52 km); Dijon TGV station (32 miles/51 km). **By air:** Dole-Jura airport (21 miles/34 km).

ⓘ **Tourist information:**
+33 (0)9 50 17 09 00 or +33 (0)6 87 73 13 05
www.ot-pesmes.fr

👁 Highlights
• Château de Pesmes (17th–18th centuries).
• Église Saint-Hilaire (13th–17th centuries): Interior decoration, altarpiece, 16th-century statues, pipe organ.
• Hôtel Châteaurouillaud (14th century).
• Musée des Forges: Collection of machines and tools in the former workshops, forge-owner's house:
+33 (0)6 87 73 13 05 or
+33 (0)3 84 31 23 37.
• Village: Guided tour: +33 (0)6 87 73 13 05.

🗝 Accommodation
Hotels
Hôtel de France**: +33 (0)3 84 31 20 05.
Guesthouses
La Maison Royale: +33 (0)3 84 31 23 23.
Gîtes
Further information: +33 (0)3 84 31 22 77 or +33 (0)3 84 31 20 15.
Campsites
La Colombière**: +33 (0)3 84 31 20 15.

🍴 Eating Out
Hôtel de France: +33 (0)3 84 31 20 05.
Les Jardins Gourmands:
+33 (0)3 84 31 20 20.
O'Ma Pizza, pizzeria: +33 (0)3 84 31 29 68.

🍲 Local Specialties
Food and Drink
Oil • Poulet d'horloger (local recipe with potatoes and Cancoillotte cheese) • Pesmes pie and tart • Wine.
Art and Crafts
Cutler • Leatherworker • Wrought ironworker • Artist • Potter • Sculptor.

② Events
Market: Wednesday morning, Place des Promenades.
May: Handicrafts fair (Saturday and Sunday).
July: Fête de l'Île festival (2nd fortnight).
July and August: Art exhibition at the Voûtes.
August: Flea market, open-air rummage sale (1st Saturday); Fête de la Saint-Hilaire (festival).
All year round: Cinema, theater, and entertainment at the Forges de Pesmes.

🦋 Outdoor Activities
Watersports • Canoeing • L'Île des Forges • Fishing • Hiking and Nordic walking; 4 marked trails • Rock climbing • Mountain-biking.

🌿 Further Afield
• Ognon valley: Malans ("Île Art" sculpture park), Acey (Cistercian abbey), Marnay (fortified town) (3–12 miles/5–19 km).
• Moissey; Forêt de la Serre, forest; Dole (6–12 miles/9.5–19 km).
• Gray; Musée Baron Martin (16 miles/26 km).
• Grotte d'Osselle, cave (19 miles/31 km).
• Arc-et-Senans: Saline Royale, royal salt-works (28 miles/45 km).

Riquewihr
The pearl of Alsatian vineyards

Haut-Rhin (68) • Population: 1,308 • Altitude: 728 ft. (222 m)

Producing wines that, for centuries, have matched the quality of its architecture, Riquewihr remains a center of Alsatian heritage and lifestyle.

Behind its ramparts, today besieged only by the vines, the village was for a long time linked to the duchy of Wurtemberg. Now it is associated with excellence: that of the architecture of its houses, with their splendid inner courtyards, and of its powerfully aromatic wines, produced on the Sporen and Schoenenbourg hillsides. Walking along the narrow streets, one never tires of admiring the large houses, which—from the richer bourgeois residences of the 16th century to more modest dwellings—are masterpieces of colorful half-timbered façades, carved wooden window-frames, flower-decked balconies, decorated windowpanes, and "beaver-tail"-tiled roofs, which often hide magnificent painted ceilings. Some of the old store signages are the work of Jean-Jacques Waltz (1873–1951), known as "Hansi," an Alsatian illustrator and caricaturist to whom the village has dedicated a museum. From the Dolder, the tall half-timbered bell tower, there is a stunning view over the village and neighboring vineyards.

By road: Expressway A35-N83, exit–Riquewihr (5 miles/8 km); N415, exit–Colmar (19 miles/31 km). **By train:** Colmar TGV station (9½ miles/15.5 km); Strasbourg TGV station (43 miles/69 km). **By air:** Strasbourg-Inter airport (40 miles/64 km); Bâle-Mulhouse airport (45 miles/72 km).

ⓘ Tourist information—
Pays de Ribeauvillé et Riquewihr:
+33 (0)3 89 73 23 23
www.ribeauville-riquewihr.com
www.riquewihr.fr

Le Manala, *winstub* (traditional Alsatian brasserie): +33 (0)3 89 49 01 51.
Le Médiéval: +33 (0)3 89 49 05 31.
L'Originel: +33 (0)3 89 73 28 90.
Le Sarment d'Or: +33 (0)3 89 86 02 86.

🍽 Local Specialties
Food and Drink
AOC Alsace and *grands crus* Schoenenbourg and Sporen wines • Beer and distilled spirits • Alsatian cookies • Honey.
Art and Crafts
Handicrafts • Gifts • Art galleries.

📅 Events
Market: Friday morning, Place Fernand Zeyer.
June: International male choir festival; Fête de la Quenelle Alsacienne, local dumpling festival.
December: Christmas market and activities, daily 10 a.m.–7 p.m.

🦋 Outdoor Activities
Fishing • Walking: Route GR 5 and marked trails (including the Saint James's Way and the *Grands crus* wine trail) • Mountain-biking.

🌿 Further Afield
• Alsace wine route: *Hunawihr (2 miles/ 3 km), see pp. 64–65. Ribeauvillé (4½ miles/7 km), *Eguisheim (10 miles/16 km), see pp. 60–61.
• Kaysersberg (6 miles/9.5 km).
• Colmar (7½ miles/12 km).
• Haut-Koenigsbourg (16 miles/26 km).
• *Mittelbergheim (24 miles/39 km), see pp. 69–70.
• Écomusée de Haute-Alsace, local heritage museum (28 miles/45 km).

👁 Highlights
• **Musée de l'Oncle Hansi:** Watercolors, lithographs, etchings, decorative tableware, posters, video projections, play area, and store: +33 (0)3 89 47 97 00.
• **Musée du Dolder** (local history): The history of Riquewihr from the 12th to the 17th centuries: +33 (0)3 89 73 23 23.
• **Tour des Voleurs et Maison de Vigneron:** A former Riquewihr prison and its instruments of torture; the interior of a winegrower's house from the 16th century: +33 (0)3 89 73 23 23.
• *Grands crus* **wine trail:** Self-guided visits all year round; guided tour led by a winemaker followed by a visit to the wine cellar, with tastings in summer: +33 (0)3 89 73 23 23.
• **Village:** Guided tour led by tourist information center guides: +33 (0)3 89 73 23 23); tour of the village and vineyard by tourist train: +33 (0)3 89 73 74 24.
• **Signposted nature trail in Riquewihr Forest:** +33 (0)3 89 73 23 23.

🔑 Accommodation
Hotels
À l'Oriel***: +33 (0)3 89 49 03 13.
Le Riquewihr***: +33 (0)3 89 86 03 00.
Le Schoenenbourg***: +33 (0)3 89 49 01 11.
La Couronne**: +33 (0)3 89 49 03 03.
♥ Saint-Nicolas**: +33 (0)3 89 46 01 51.
Le Sarment d'Or**: +33 (0)3 89 86 02 86.
Guesthouses
Bernard Bronner**: +33 (0)3 89 47 83 50.
Mireille Schwach: +33 (0)3 89 47 92 34.
Gîtes and vacation rentals
♥ Les Remparts de Riquewihr*** to *****: +33 (0)6 08 03 37 52.
Further information: +33 (0)3 89 73 23 23 www.ribeauville-riquewihr.com
Campsites
Camping de Riquewihr: +33 (0)3 89 47 90 08.

🍴 Eating Out
À la Couronne: +33 (0)3 89 49 02 12.
Le Cep de Vigne: +33 (0)3 89 47 92 34.
La Charbonnade: +33 (0)3 89 71 63 31.

ℹ Did you know?
When, in the 18th century, one of the lords of Riquewihr found himself saddled with debt, he borrowed 500 livres from the writer Voltaire by mortgaging the vineyards of his estate. The sum was eventually repaid, so Voltaire never became owner of Riquewihr.

Rodemack
The little Carcassonne of Lorraine

Moselle (57) • Population: 1,110 • Altitude: 722 ft. (220 m)

Rodemack, near Luxembourg, owes its nickname—"the little Carcassonne of Lorraine"—to its impressive medieval heritage.

In 907, Rodemack was exchanged by the monks of Fulda, passing into the hands of the abbots of Saint-Willibrord and thus influenced by Germano-Luxemburgian culture. A fief of the house of Luxembourg, Rodemack lived in relative peace and experienced five centuries of prosperity. The fortress, built in the 12th century, then gave way to a castle, which was later extended and rebuilt. The village grew up around the church, built in the 10th century, and the ramparts were erected in the 13th and 15th centuries. Fought over by France and Germany, Rodemack was attacked, occupied, and retaken many times. In 1815, during Napoléon's Hundred Days, it was defended by General Hugo, father of the poet Victor Hugo. Walk along the Ruelle de la Forge, Rue du Four, and the Place de Gargants to discover its defensive walls and towers: the Boucour, Barbacane, and twin towers. The village itself is surrounded by a second wall with demi-lune (half-moon) towers and gateways flanked by round towers. The 14th-century Sierck Gate was built by the villagers themselves. Inside the city wall, narrow streets lead to the old post office, the *lavoir* (washhouse), and the former Officers' Pavilion.

By road: Expressway A13, exit 10–Frisange (3½ miles/5.5 km); expressway A31, exit 38–Thionville centre (11 miles/18 km). **By train:** Thionville TGV station (10 miles/16 km). **By air:** Luxembourg-Findel airport (20 miles/32 km); Metz-Nancy Lorraine airport (43 miles/69 km).

ⓘ Tourist information—Communauté de Communes de Cattenom et Environs: +33 (0)3 82 56 00 02 / www.tourisme-ccce.fr www.mairie-rodemack.fr

👁 Highlights
• **Village:** Guided tour for groups all year round, booking essential. Further information: +33 (0)3 82 56 00 02.
• **Citadelle de Rodemack:** Park opening mid-June 2016.
• **Jardin Médiéval** (medieval garden): All year round.

⚔ Accommodation
Gîtes
Mme Bertrand: +33 (0)6 29 33 31 09.
Gîte Morisseau: +33 (0)3 54 54 15 89.
Mme Herfeld: +33 (0)3 82 50 01 49.
M. and Mme Kremer: +33 (0)3 82 51 23 07.
Mme Schuster: +33 (0)6 23 40 18 98.
M. Werner: +33 (0)3 82 51 24 07.
Communal gîtes +33 (0)3 82 83 05 50.

🍽 Eating Out
La Grange à Georges (Café Terroir de Moselle), concerts: +33 (0)3 83 50 35 24.
La Petite Carcassonne: +33 (0)3 82 82 08 78.

🧺 Local Specialties
Food and Drink
Artisan beers.
Art and Crafts
Designers • Artists • Photographers • Jewelry • Ceramics • Leatherwork.

📅 Events
Market: "Le Noyer," large organic vegetable market, Saturday mornings, 9 a.m.-12.30 p.m., Route de Faulbach.
April: Most Beautiful Villages of France wine festival (mid-April).
May: Flower market (1st weekend).
June: Rodemack Solex (bike) Tour (mid-June); "Rodemack, Cité Médiévale en Fête," festival (late June).
July and August: Summer activities.
August: Fête de la Grillade barbecue (mid-August).
September: Antiques and collectors' fair.

🏑 Outdoor Activities
Walking • Mountain-biking.

🌿 Further Afield
• Mondorf-les-Bains (3½ miles/5.5 km).
• Sierck-les-Bains; Manderen: Château de Malbrouk (7½–12 miles/12–19 km).
• Schengen: Musée de l'Europe (10 miles/16 km).
• Thionville (10 miles/16 km).
• Luxembourg (16 miles/26 km).
• Veckring: Ouvrage Hackenberg, Maginot Line fortification (19 miles/31 km).
• Neufchef: Ecomusée des Mines de Fer de Lorraine, local iron mining museum (22 miles/35 km).
• Metz: (31 miles/50 km)

Saint-Quirin

A place of pilgrimage

Moselle (57) • Population: 821 • Altitude: 1,050 ft. (320 m)

At the foot of an amphitheater of hills, the village is surrounded by the vast and game-filled Vosges forest, where beech and oak grow alongside spruce and larch.

Higher up, the archeological site of La Croix-Guillaume contains important Gallo-Roman remains of the 1st, 2nd, and 3rd centuries, which bear witness to the ancient culture of the peaks. Saint-Quirin is named after Quirinus, the military tribune of Rome who was martyred in 132 CE under the Emperor Hadrian, and whose relics lie in the priory church. Many buildings testify to the village's glorious past: the priory and the Baroque priory church (1722), with its Jean-André Silbermann organ (1746), which is a listed historic monument; the Église des Verriers, a beautiful Rococo-style edifice built in 1756 at Lettenbach; and the Romanesque-style high chapel dating from the 1180s. Below the church, the water from the miraculous spring is said to have healed skin diseases through the intercession of Saint Quirinus. The village thus became a place of pilgrimage and of devotion to its healing saint.

By road: Expressway A4, exit 44–Lunéville (20 miles/32 km), then N4 (16 miles/26 km). **By train:** Sarrebourg station (11 miles/18 km). **By air:** Strasbourg airport (65 miles/105 km); Metz-Nancy Lorraine airport (78 miles/126 km).

ⓘ Tourist information:
+33 (0)3 87 08 08 56
www.saintquirin.fr

👁 Highlights

• **Priory church** (18th century): Silbermann organ, relics of Saint Quirinus, large crystal chandelier.
• **High chapel** (12th century): Stained-glass windows by V. Honer de Nancy.
• **Chapelle Notre-Dame-de-l'Hor** at Métairies-Saint-Quirin (15th and 18th centuries): Statue of the Immaculate Conception, paintings.
• **Gallo-Roman archeological site** of La Croix-Guillaume: +33 (0)3 87 08 08 56.

⚔ Accommodation

Hotels
Le Prieuré**: +33 (0)3 87 08 65 20.
Guesthouses
Le Temps des Cerises: +33 (0)6 78 15 76 02.
Gîtes
Further information: +33 (0)3 87 08 08 56
www.saintquirin.fr
Campsites
Camping municipal**. Further information: +33 (0)3 87 08 60 34.

🍴 Eating Out

Auberge de la Forêt: +33 (0)3 87 03 71 78.
Hostellerie du Prieuré: +33 (0)3 87 08 66 52.

🧺 Local Specialties

Food and Drink
Honey • Salted meats and fish.
Art and Crafts
Painting and sculpture workshop • Furniture and paintings gallery • Artist • Sculpture in stone and wood • Glassblower.

📅 Events

March: "La Ronde des Chevandiers" car rally.
May: Saint-Quirin-Marmoutier evening market (2nd Saturday).
Ascension: Procession and fair.
June: Organ recitals.
July: International hiking festival.
August: "Barakozart" music festival.
September: Plant sale (4th Sunday).
November: Mass of Saint Hubert.
December: Christmas market, giant Advent calender (1st weekend).

🦋 Outdoor Activities

Fishing • Walking: Route GR 5 and 5 "Moselle Pleine Nature" marked trails.

🌿 Further Afield

• Abreschviller (3 miles/5 km).
• Sarrebourg, Chagall trail (11 miles/18 km).
• Rhodes; Parc Animalier de Sainte-Croix: wildlife park (12 miles/19 km).
• Massif du Donon, mountain; Col du Donon (14 miles/23 km).
• Saint-Louis-Arzviller, inclined plane (16 miles/26 km).
• Phalsbourg (19 miles/31 km).
• Baccarat, crystal glass-making (25 miles/40 km).
• Saverne, Palais des Rohan (25 miles/40 km).
• Lunéville, Château des Lumières (31 miles/50 km).

🕯 Did you know?

In 1049, Geppa, sister of Alsace-born Pope Leo IX, returned the relics of the tribune Quirinus, who had been tortured in 132 CE under Emperor Hadrian, to Rome. The convoy passed the night on a hill overlooking the village of Godelsadis. The following day, it proved impossible to move the reliquary containing the precious relics. Godelsadis thus became Saint-Quirin, and a chapel was built on the hill to house Quirinus's remains.

Vézelay
The hill where the spirit soars

Yonne (89) • Population: 450 • Altitude: 991 ft. (302 m)

Gazing at the Monts du Morvan, Vézelay sits on a steep hill surmounted by the basilica of Sainte-Madeleine.

Built in the 12th century in honor of Mary Magdalen, whose relics are believed to lie there, the abbey was both a pilgrimage destination and a departure point for Compostela. The arrival in 1146 of the abbot and reformer Bernard de Clairvaux subsequently made it an important Christian center. Beautiful Romanesque and Renaissance residences survive from this thriving era, rubbing shoulders with charming winegrowers' houses in a symphony of stone façades and rooftops, all covered with the flat, brown tiles typical of Burgundy. The basilica was restored in the 19th century by the architect Viollet-le-Duc, and both it and Vézelay hill were listed as UNESCO World Heritage Sites in 1979. The basilica is renowned for its Romanesque art and continues to attract visitors from all over the globe, while the house of writer Jules Roy and the Musée Zervos demonstrate the village's appeal to artists of all kinds.

By road: Expressway A6, exit 22–Avallon (14 miles/23 km); expressway A6, exit 21–Nitry (18 miles/29 km). **By train:** Sermizelles station (6 miles/9.5 km). **By air:** Dijon-Bourgogne airport (81 miles/130 km).

ⓘ **Tourist information:**
+33 (0)3 86 33 23 69
www.vezelaytourisme.com

👁 Highlights

• **Basilique Sainte-Madeleine** (12th–19th centuries): Carved tympana, Romanesque-style arches, Gothic choir, relics of Mary Magdalen, numerous 12th-century carved capitals. Guided visits for individuals or groups by the Fraternités de Jérusalem: +33 (0)3 86 33 39 50.
• **Maison du Visiteur:** Multimedia exhibition on the world of the 12th-century builder, as preparation for a visit to the basilica and to help interpret it. Slide-show, models, architecture, light show at solstices: +33 (0)3 86 32 35 65.
• **Musée de l'Œuvre-Viollet-le-Duc:** Romanesque capitals and fragments deposited by Viollet-le-Duc during his restoration work at the basilica: +33 (0)3 86 33 24 62.

• **Maison Jules-Roy** (house and gardens): House of the writer, reconstructed study; literary exhibitions and receptions: +33 (0)3 86 33 35 01.
• **Musée Zervos** (modern art 1925–65), in Maison Romain-Rolland: Collection bequeathed to the village by art critic and publisher Christian Zervos. Founder of *Cahiers d'art*, a journal published 1926–60, which courted the major artists of the time: Picasso, Chagall, Laurens, Léger, Calder, Kandinsky, Giacometti, Hélion, Miró, Poliakoff. Works by them are exhibited in the museum. Temporary exhibition each year: +33 (0)3 86 32 39 26.
• **Village:** Guided tour for individuals in summer: +33 (0)3 86 33 23 69; for groups all year round by appointment with Guides de Pays des Collines: +33 (0)3 86 33 23 69, or Guides de l'Yonne: +33 (0)3 86 41 50 30.
• **Village and basilica:** Guided tour (art, history, symbolism, tradition) by Lorant Hecquet, professional tour guide, by appointment: +33 (0)3 86 33 30 06; or with Guides de l'Yonne: +33 (0)3 86 41 50 30.

🔑 Accommodation

Hotels
La Poste et Lion d'Or***: +33 (0)3 73 53 03 20.
Le Compostelle**: +33 (0)3 86 33 28 63.
Le Cheval Blanc: +33 (0)3 86 33 22 12.
Les Glycines: +33 (0)3 86 47 29 81.
Le Relais du Morvan: +33 (0)3 86 33 25 33.
SY La Terrasse: +33 (0)3 86 33 25 50.

Guesthouses
Au Poirier de la Perdrix***: +33 (0)3 86 33 20 17.
À l'Atelier**: +33 (0)3 86 32 38 59.
Cabalus: +33 (0)3 86 33 20 66.
Charlou: +33 (0)3 86 41 01 50.

Gîtes and vacation rentals
Further information: +33 (0)3 86 33 23 69
vezelaytourisme.com

Group accommodation
Auberge de Jeunesse: +33 (0)3 86 33 24 18.
Centre Sainte-Madeleine, Maisons Saint-Bernard et Béthanie: +33 (0)3 86 33 22 14.

Campsites
L'Ermitage*: +33 (0)3 86 33 24 18.

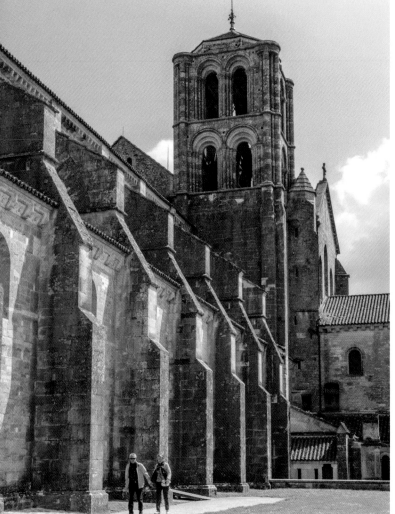

🍽 Eating Out

Auberge de la Coquille: +33 (0)3 86 33 35 57.
Le Bougainville: +33 (0)3 86 33 27 57.
Le Cheval Blanc: +33 (0)3 86 33 22 12.
La Dent Creuse: +33 (0)3 86 33 36 33.
La Poste et le Lion d'Or:
+33 (0)3 73 53 03 20.
Le Relais du Morvan: +33 (0)3 86 33 25 33.
SY La Terrasse: +33 (0)3 86 33 25 50.
Le Vézelien, brasserie: +33 (0)3 86 33 25 09.
Tea rooms
Au Tastevin: +33 (0)7 86 63 22 96.
Les Macarons de Charlou:
+33 (0)3 86 41 01 50.
Vézelay: +33 (0)3 86 33 23 01.

🛒 Local Specialties

Food and Drink
Honey • Heritage bread • AOC Vézelay
wine • Chablis wine.
Art and Crafts
Antiques • Illuminator • Earthenware
potter • Icons • Books • Metal, stone, and
fabric crafts • Painter-sculptors, galleries •
Monastic crafts • Sculptor • Weaver.

📅 Events

Market: Wednesday mornings,
May–October.
April–October: Exhibitions
(Salle Gothique).
May–October: Concerts in the basilica.
July: Pilgrimage Sainte-Madeleine (22nd).
August: Festival d'Art Vocal
(2nd fortnight), organic produce market.
November: Truffle market.
December: Christmas celebrations.
All year round: discussion groups,
pilgrimages, workshops, and conferences.

🦋 Outdoor Activities

Canoeing, rafting • Horse-riding •
Fishing • Walking: Routes GR 13 and 654,
Chemin de Compostelle (Saint James's
Way), 4 circular trails • Mountain-biking:
5 circular trails.

🦋 Further Afield

• Église d'Asquins (1 mile/2 km).
• Fontaines-Salées: archeological site;
Saint-Pèresous-Vézelay: church
(1 mile/2 km).
• Chamoux: Cardo Land, fantasy
prehistoric park (4½ miles/7 km).
• Château de Bazoches-du-Morvan
(6 miles/9.5 km).
• Avallon (9½ miles/15.5 km).
• Château de Chastellux (11 miles/18 km).
• Grottes d'Arcy-sur-Cure, caves
(12 miles/19 km).
• *Noyers (25 miles/40 km), see p. 71.

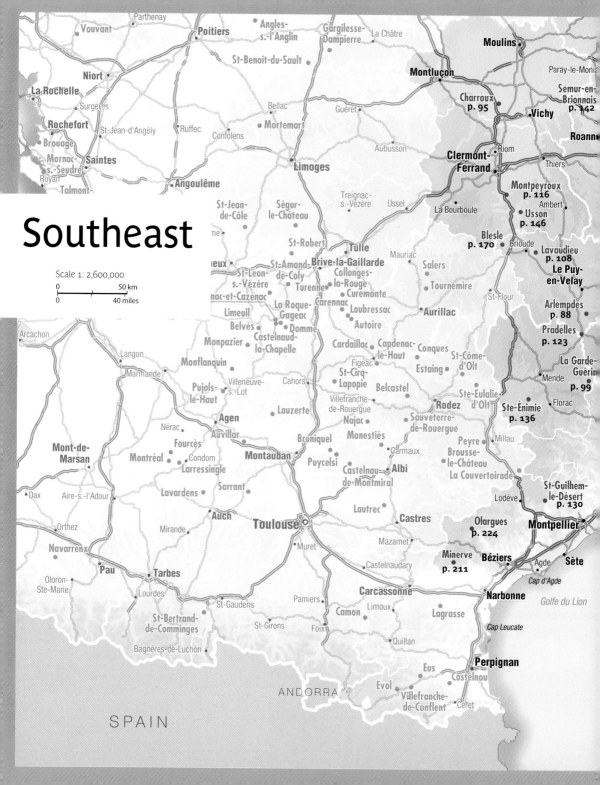

Southeast

Scale 1 : 2,600,000

0 — 50 km
0 — 40 miles

Vouvant · Parthenay · Poitiers · Angles-s.-l'Anglin · Gargilesse-Dampierre · La Châtre

Moulins · Paray-le-Monial

Niort · St-Benoît-du-Sault

Montluçon · Charroux p. 95 · Semur-en-Brionnais p. 142

La Rochelle · Bellac · Guéret · Vichy

Rochefort · St-Jean-d'Angély · Ruffec · Confolens · Aubusson · Clermont-Ferrand · Riom · Roanne · Thiers

Brouage · Mortemart · Limoges · Treignac-s.-Vézère · Ussel · La Bourboule · Montpeyroux p. 116 · Ambert

Mornac-s.-Seudre · Saintes · Angoulême · St-Jean-de-Côle · Ségur-le-Château · Usson p. 146

Royan · Talmont- · Blesle p. 170 · Brioude · Lavaudieu p. 108

St-Robert · Tulle · Mauriac · Salers · Le Puy-en-Velay

St-Amand-de-Coly · Brive-la-Gaillarde · Collonges-la-Rouge · Tournémire · St-Flour · Arlempdes p. 88

St-Léon-s.-Vézère · Turenne · Curemonte · Aurillac · Pradelles p. 123

nac-et-Cazenac · Carennac · Loubressac · St-Côme-d'Olt · La Garde-Guérin p. 99

Limeuil · La Roque-Gageac · Autoire · Mende · Florac

Belvès · Domme · Cardaillac · Capdenac-le-Haut · Conques · Estaing · Ste-Eulalie-d'Olt · Ste-Énimie p. 136

Arcachon · Castelnaud-la-Chapelle · Figeac · St-Cirq-Lapopie · Belcastel · Rodez · Peyre

Langon · Monpazier · Cahors · Villefranche-de-Rouergue · Sauveterre-de-Rouergue · Brousse-le-Château · St-Guilhem-le-Désert p. 130

Marmande · Monflanquin · Villeneuve-s.-Lot · Najac · Monestiés · Millau · La Couvertoirade

Pujols-le-Haut · Lauzerte · Bruniquel · Carmaux · Lodève · Montpellier

Agen · Auvillar · Montauban · Puycelsi · Castelnau-de-Montmiral · Albi · Olargues p. 224

Mont-de-Marsan · Nérac · Fourcès · Condom · Lautrec · Castres · Minerve p. 211 · Béziers · Sète

Dax · Montréal · Larressingle · Sarrant · Mazamet · Agde · Cap d'Agde

Aire-s.-l'Adour · Lavardens · Auch · Toulouse · Castelnaudary · Narbonne · Golfe du Lion

Orthez · Mirande · Muret · Carcassonne · Limoux · Lagrasse · Cap Leucate

Navarrenx · Pau · Tarbes · Pamiers · Camon · Quillan

Oloron-Ste-Marie · Lourdes · St-Gaudens · St-Girons · Foix · Eus · Perpignan

St-Bertrand-de-Comminges · Castelnou

Bagnères-de-Luchon · ANDORRA · Evol · Villefranche-de-Conflent · Céret

SPAIN

Aiguèze
A phoenix from the ashes

Gard (30) • Population: 220 • Altitude: 292 ft. (89 m)

A fortress perched on a cliff overlooking the Gorges of the Ardèche, Aiguèze protects its medieval heritage, cultivates vines, and ensures its inhabitants are always friendly and welcoming.

Like any strategic defense site, Aiguèze has had a turbulent past. From 725 to 737 CE, the region was occupied by the Saracens, who gave their name to one of the village's towers. The fortification of the site dates back to the 11th century: it was the work of the count of Toulouse, who wanted to make Aiguèze the outpost for his operations against the region of Vivarais. In 1360, uprisings caused Aiguèze its last great period of turmoil: local peasants, oppressed by hefty taxes, became restless, and the village endured more destruction and looting. Often attacked but always liberated afterwards, Aiguèze survived, and managed to preserve traces of its history. The village owes much of its present-day appeal to Frédéric Fuzet, archbishop of Rouen and a local man, who, in the early 20th century, devoted his time and means to its conservation and modernization, notably the main square shaded by plane trees and the 11th-century church. In the narrow cobbled and vaulted streets arch-covered balconies, mullioned windows, and arched doorways are on display. They lead to the *castelas*, the old ramparts of the castle, from where there is a splendid view of the Ardèche, *garrigue* (scrubland), and Côtes du Rhône vineyards.

By road: Expressway A7, exit 19– Bollène (14 miles/22 km), N86 (8½ miles/ 13.5 km). **By train:** Montélimar TGV station (27 miles/43 km). **By air:** Avignon-Caumont airport (42 miles/ 68 km).

ⓘ **Tourist information—Gard Rhodanien:** +33 (0)4 66 39 26 89 or +33 (0)4 66 82 30 02
www.tourisme-gard-rhodanien.com

👁 Highlights
• **Church** (11th century): Open daily.
• **Village:** Guided tours in summer, and by appointment off-season: +33 (0)04 66 39 26 89.

🗝 Accommodation
Hotels and Aparthotels
Le Castelas**: +33 (0)4 66 82 18 76.
Le Rustic Hôtel*: +33 (0)4 66 82 11 26.
Guesthouses
Les Jardins du Barry***: +33 (0)4 66 82 15 75.
Le Clos des Vignes: +33 (0)9 74 56 24 75.
Les Mazets d'Aiguèze: +33 (0)4 66 82 34 28.
La Sarrazine: +33 (0)352 661 511 023.
Gîtes, vacation rentals, and campsites
Further information: +33 (0)4 66 82 14 77 or +33 (0)4 66 39 26 89.

🍽 Eating Out
Le Belvédère, pizzeria: +33 (0)4 66 50 66 69.
Bistrot La Charriotte: +33 (0)4 66 82 11 26.
Le Bouchon, café and wine bar: +33 (0)4 66 39 47 70.
Café Chabot: +33 (0)4 66 33 80 51.
Le Drillo: +33 (0)9 86 12 84 80.

🧺 Local Specialties
Food and Drink
AOC Côtes du Rhône wines • Honey • Goat cheese (*pélardons*).
Art and Crafts
Art gallery • Pottery • Craft studios.

📅 Events
Market: Thursday mornings, mid-June to mid-September.
April: Flower market (2nd weekend).
Pentecost: Flea market (weekend).
Mid-July and mid-August: Welcome days for vacationers, activities.
December: Christmas market (2nd Sunday).

🦋 Outdoor Activities
Swimming in the Ardèche river • Canoeing and boating trips down the Ardèche river • Walking: Trail from Castelvieil *oppidum* (main settlement), walk through the vineyards.

🦋 Further Afield
• Chartreuse de Valbonne, monastery (4½ miles/7 km).
• Gorges of the Ardèche; Vallon-Pont-d'Arc; Grotte Chauvet, cave; Aven d'Orgnac, sinkhole; Grotte de la Madeleine, cave; Grotte de Saint-Marcel-d'Ardèche, cave; Aven-Grotte de la Forestière, cave (4½–22 miles/7–35 km).
• Pont-Saint-Esprit (6 miles/9.5 km).
• *Montclus (9 miles/14.5 km), see p. 115.
• *La Roque-sur-Cèze (11 miles/18 km), see pp. 124–25.
• Cornillon; Goudargues (12 miles/19 km).
• Castles at Suze-la-Rousse (17 miles/27 km) and Grignan (27 miles/43 km).
• Orange: Roman theater (21 miles/34 km).
• *Lussan (22½ miles/36 km), see p. 111.

ℹ Did you know?
The Aiguézois (as the villagers are known), who enjoy a joke, have concealed a few hoaxes around the village's narrow streets. Was it really Honoré Agrefoul who invented absinthe? Is Andris Nali really a professor of *"expansiologie"*? Find out for yourself during your tour of the village.

Ansouis

A fan-shaped refuge in southeast France

Vaucluse (84) • Population: 1,140 • Altitude: 968 ft. (295 m)

Standing at the heart of the Pays d'Aigues, with the Grand Luberon mountain range and the Durance river on the horizon, the hilltop village of Ansouis is crowned by an old château.

Spread out in a fan shape, open to the sun, the village is crisscrossed by a maze of streets and alleys that remain shady and cool. From the Place Saint-Elzéar, the Rue du Petit-Portail climbs up to a peaceful little square: bordered by the 12th-century perimeter wall, which serves as the façade of the Église Saint-Martin, and by the elegant 13th-century presbytery, it offers a vast panorama of a landscape of vines overlooked by the Grand Luberon. At the top of the village, the castle, owned for generations by the Sabran family, condenses a thousand years of castle architecture. The austerity of the medieval fortress on the north side contrasts with the classical southern façade of the 17th-century residence, which overlooks the terraced gardens with their box topiary.

By road: Expressway A7, exit 26–Sénas (22 miles/35 km); expressway A51, exit 15–Pertuis (7½ miles/12 km). **By train:** Aix-en-Provence TGV station (30 miles/48 km). **By air:** Marseille-Provence airport (37 miles/60 km).

ⓘ Tourist information:
+33 (0)4 90 09 86 98
www.luberoncotesud.com

ℹ Did you know?

Elzéar, count of Sabran, was born in 1285 at the Château d'Ansouis and was married very young to Delphine de Signe. The two took a vow of chastity and lived a life of prayer, penance, and devotion to the poor. Elzéar was canonized by Pope Urban V and the cult of Delphine was approved by Pope Innocent VII. This popular cult has survived the centuries and, every year in September, the villagers of Ansouis gather in the village church for a Mass in honor of their saints.

👁 Highlights

• **Castle:** Erected in the 12th and 13th centuries and rebuilt in the 17th century, this imposing fortress has been completely restored and is open to the public from April to October: +33 (0)4 90 77 23 36.
• **Église Saint-Martin:** Fortified 12th-century church, formerly the castle's law court; 18th-century statues and altarpieces.
• **Musée Extraordinaire:** This Provençal building presents artistic creations as well as a collection of fossils, shells, and furniture belonging to its owner, a painter and diver: +33 (0)4 90 09 82 64.
• **Musée des Arts et des Métiers du Vin:** More than three thousand objects used by the winemakers and grape-pickers of the Château Turcan: +33 (0)4 90 09 83 33.

🗝 Accommodation

Guesthouses
Bastide Saint-Maurin*****:
+33 (0)6 25 04 44 20.
Le Jardin d'Antan***: +33 (0)4 90 09 89 41.
Le Mas du Grand Luberon***:
+33 (0)4 90 09 97 92.
Un Patio en Luberon***:
+33 (0)4 90 09 94 25.
La Maison de Clémentine**:
+33 (0)4 90 09 97 68.
L'Atrium: +33 (0)6 62 70 17 27.
La Bastidette: +33 (0)6 34 60 09 59.
Le Mas de la Farigoule:
+33 (0)6 51 04 07 45.

Le Mas de la Huppe: +33 (0)4 90 09 08 41.
Le Petit Pibareau: +33 (0)6 09 85 24 10.
Gîtes and vacation rentals
Further information: +33 (0)4 90 09 86 98
www.luberoncotesud.com

🍴 Eating Out

Bar des Sports: +33 (0)4 90 08 44 33.
La Closerie: +33 (0)4 90 09 90 54.
Le Grain de Sel, restaurant and wine bar:
+33 (0)4 90 09 85 90.
Pâtisserie d'Antan, tea room:
+33 (0)6 28 41 45 73.

🛍 Local Specialties

Food and Drink
Homemade ice cream • AOC Luberon wines.
Art and Crafts
Santon (crib figure) maker • Bronze sculptures and jewelry • Artist.

📅 Events

Market: Sunday morning, Place de la Vieille-Fontaine.
May: Les Botanilles, festival and flower market (last two weeks).
June: Ansouis en Musique (music festival).
July and August: Various activities.
September: Fête de la Saint-Elzéar (mid-month).

🦋 Outdoor Activities

Walking: 3 marked trails.

🕊 Further Afield

• La Tour-d'Aigues (5 miles/8 km).
• Villages on the Durance river: Cadenet, Pertuis, Mirabeau (6–12 miles/9.5–19 km).
• *Lourmarin (7 miles/11.5 km), see pp. 109–10.
• Aix-en-Provence (19 miles/31 km).
• *Ménerbes (21 miles/34 km), see pp. 112.
• *Roussillon (21 miles/34 km), see pp. 126–27.
• *Gordes (24 miles/39 km), see pp. 102–3.

Arlempdes
The first château of the Loire

Haute-Loire (43) • Population: 131 • Altitude: 2,756 ft. (840 m)

Arlempdes (pronounced "ar-lond") sits at the top of a volcanic peak in the Velay, close to the source of the Loire river. The remains of the castle built by the Montlaur family in the 12th–14th centuries are at the top of a basalt dike, into which the Loire has cut deep, wild gorges. Crenellated ramparts and curtain walls enclose the ancient courtyard, dominated by the round tower of the keep and the Chapelle Saint-Jacques-le-Majeur, probably built in the 11th–12th centuries on the site of a Celtic sanctuary, standing some 330 ft. (100 m) above the river. At the foot of this imposing castle, behind a 13th-century gateway, the village spreads out around a peaceful square. This serves as the forecourt of the Romanesque Église Saint-Pierre, noteworthy for its polylobed door and its four-arched bell gable. From this square, a path leads to the castle, whose entrance is via a Renaissance porch. On the plateau through which the Loire has carved its course, agricultural production has been given a new lease of life by the Puy green lentil, which, benefiting from the area's volcanic soil and microclimate, was the first dried legume to be awarded an AOC, in 1996, and it obtained an AOP in 2008.

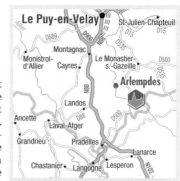

By road: Expressway A75, exit 20–Le Puy-en-Velay (56 miles/90 km), N102-N88 (5½ miles/9 km). By train: Puy-en-Velay station (17 miles/28 km). By air: Clermont-Ferrand-Auvergne airport (91 miles/146 km).

ⓘ Tourist information—
Pays de Pradelles: +33 (0)4 71 00 82 65
www.gorges-allier.com
www.village-arlempdes.com

👁 Highlights
• **Castle:** Remains; visits possible: +33 (0)4 71 00 82 65 or +33 (0)4 71 57 17 14); guided tours every afternoon in July and August.
• **Écomusée de la Ruralité** (museum of rural life): Tools and ways of life of a bygone age.
• **Église Saint-Pierre.**

🗝 Accommodation
Hotels
Le Manoir: +33 (0)4 71 57 17 14.
Guesthouses
La Freycenette***: +33 (0)4 71 49 43 43.
Gîtes and vacation rentals
Le Clos des Fontaines***: +33 (0)4 66 48 47 51.
L'Estaou***: +33 (0)4 71 49 43 43.
Gîte N° 0001223***: +33 (0)4 71 49 43 43.
La Grotte***: +33 (0)6 09 97 31 72.
Les Sources***: +33 (0)4 71 49 43 43.
Gîte N° 0001165**: +33 (0)4 71 49 43 43.
Meublé**: +33 (0)4 71 03 04 16.
Le Presbytère** and *: +33 (0)4 71 49 43 43.
La Vicairie*: +33 (0)4 71 49 43 43.
Further information on other gîtes and vacation rentals: +33 (0)4 71 00 82 65
www.gorges-allier.com

🍴 Eating Out
• Le Manoir: +33 (0)4 71 57 17 14.

🧺 Local Specialties
Food and Drink
Cheeses • AOP Puy green lentils.

🗓 Events
July: Open-air rummage sale (around the 15th).
August: Fête du Pain, bread festival (1st fortnight).
November: Hot-air balloon flights (1st fortnight).

🦋 Outdoor Activities
Swimming (no lifeguard) • Fishing • Walking: Route GR 3 and several marked trails • Mountain-biking.

🌿 Further Afield
• *Pradelles (11 miles/18 km), see p. 123.
• Lac du Bouchet, lake (11 miles/18 km).
• Le Monastier-sur-Gazeille (14 miles/ 23 km).
• Lac d'Issarlès, lake (16 miles/26 km).
• Le Puy-en-Velay (17 miles/27 km).
• Mont Gerbier-de-Jonc (28 miles/45 km).

ⓘ Did you know?
The marquis d'Arlandes, whose family was from Arlempdes, made the first manned hot-air-balloon flight on November 21, 1783, accompanied by the science teacher and aviation pioneer Jean-François Pilâtre de Rozier.

Balazuc

The sentry of the Ardèche

Ardèche (07) • Population: 352 • Altitude: 600 ft. (183 m)

Facing the sunset, Balazuc clings to a steep limestone cliff overlooking the Ardèche river. From the early Middle Ages until the Wars of Religion, the lords of Balazuc—simple knights, crusaders, and troubadours—made this village into an important stronghold. Its historic stature is evident in the 13th-century castle, rebuilt in the 17th and 18th centuries (now privately owned); the 13th-century square tower, whose façade still retains an iron rod on which the public scale for weighing silkworm cocoons used to hang; the fortified Romanesque church, crowned with a Provençal bell gable; and its gates, the Portail d'Été and the Porte de la Sablière. Balazuc has also kept its distinctive layout from the medieval period: a veritable maze of narrow, winding streets, vaulted passageways, and steps carved into the rock. Outside the village, the Chemin Royal leads slowly toward the Ardèche river and, beyond the bridge, to the reemerging hamlet of Le Viel Audon.

By road: Expressway A7, exit 17–Montélimar-Nord (32 miles/51 km), N102 (7½ miles/12 km). **By train:** Montélimar TGV station (25 miles/40 km). **By air:** Avignon-Caumont airport (80 miles/129 km).

ⓘ Tourist information—Pont-d'Arc Ardèche: +33 (0)4 28 91 24 10 or +33 (0)4 75 37 75 60 (in summer). www.pontdarc-ardeche.fr

👁 Highlights
• **Romanesque church** (11th century): Restored in 2007 and decorated with stained-glass windows by Jacques Yankel. Exhibitions March–September. Further information: +33 (0)4 75 37 75 60 or +33 (0)4 75 37 75 08.
• **Museum de l'Ardèche:** Exceptional collection of fossils representing 350 million years of natural history: +33 (0)4 28 40 00 35.
• **Le Viel Audon:** This hamlet includes an environment and sustainable development training center.
• **Village:** Guided tour, Wednesday mornings in July and August. Further information: +33 (0)4 75 37 75 60 or +33 (0)4 75 37 75 08.

🗝 Accommodation
Guesthouses
Château de Balazuc: +33 (0)4 75 88 23 27.
La Cloche Qui Rit: +33 (0)6 07 48 94 71.
Les Dolines: +33 (0)4 75 89 17 70.
Gîtes, walkers' lodges, and vacation rentals
Further information: +33 (0)4 75 37 75 08 www.ot-pays-ruomsois.com
Campsites
La Falaise***: +33 (0)4 75 37 74 27.
Beaume-Giraud**: +33 (0)4 75 89 09 36.
Le Retourtier**: +33 (0)4 75 37 77 67.
Barbine, farm campsite: +33 (0)4 75 37 70 16.
La Croix du Bois, natural area: +33 (0)4 75 37 70 20.

🍴 Eating Out
Le Buron (summer only): +33 (0)4 75 37 70 21.
Le Celtis (summer only): +33 (0)4 75 87 13 61.
Chez Paulette: +33 (0)4 75 87 17 40.
Le Cigalou (summer only): +33 (0)4 75 37 02 15.
Le Fazao, snack bar (summer only): +33 (0)4 75 37 04 44.
La Fenière, crêperie/pizzeria: +33 (0)4 75 37 01 08.
La Granja Delh Gourmandás (summer only): +33 (0)6 30 11 67 08.
Le Viel Audon, local dishes (summer only): +33 (0)4 75 37 73 80.

🧺 Local Specialties
Food and Drink
Goat cheeses • Herbal produce (syrups, etc.) • AOC Côtes du Vivarais wines and Coteaux de l'Ardèche *vins de pays.*
Art and Crafts
Pottery • Jeweler • Sculptor.

📅 Events
Market: Tuesdays, 6.30 p.m., Place de la Croisette (July and August).
July: Village festival.
July and August: Concerts and art exhibitions in the Romanesque church.
August: Folk dance.

🦋 Outdoor Activities
Swimming in the Ardèche river (no lifeguard) • Canoeing (rental) • Rock climbing • Fishing (Ardèche river) • Walking: marked trails • Mountain-biking.

🌿 Further Afield
• *Vogüé (4½ miles/7 km), see p. 149.
• Ruoms; Largentière (6 miles/9.5 km).
• Labeaume: village and gorges (9½ miles/15.5 km).
• Vallon-Pont-d'Arc; Caverne du Pont d'Arc, cave (11 miles/18 km).
• Aubenas (12 miles/19 km).
• Gorges of the Ardèche (12–35 miles/19–56 km).
• Aven d'Orgnac, sinkhole (24 miles/39 km).

Bargème
A mountain in Provence

Var (83) • Population: 217 • Altitude: 3,599 ft. (1,097 m)

Facing the Canjuers and Var mountains, Bargème is, at 3,599 ft. (1,097 m), the highest village in the Var—still Provençal, yet almost alpine. Sheltered by the ruins of the Château Sabran-de-Pontevès, the silhouette of the feudal village stands out on the steep slopes of the Brouis mountain. In 1393, the lordship of the village passed to Foulques d'Agoult de Pontevès, and it remained in the hands of the Pontevès family for the following two centuries. The region was by then suffering great religious upheaval; the people of Bargème avenged the neighboring village of Callas, which had been betrayed by Jean-Baptiste de Pontevès, by bringing the line of châtelains to an end. After murdering his grandfather, father, and uncles, inhabitants of Bargème slit Antoine de Pontevès's throat in the middle of Mass in 1595. The parliament of Aix-en-Provence issued a judgment requiring the inhabitants to build an expiatory chapel, Notre-Dames-des-Sept-Douleurs, which is located at the end of the esplanade leading to the castle. The village retains its defensive perimeter wall—the two fortified gates, the Levant and the Garde, were added in the 14th century—as well as the white-stone Romanesque church. Under the patronage of Saint Nicholas, this 12th-century church has an apse that ends in a semidomed vault. It has three altarpieces, one of which, dedicated to Saint Sebastian, is a triptych carved in half relief.

By road: Expressway A8, exit 36–Draguignan (33 miles/53 km); N85, exit Nice (50 miles/80 km). **By train:** Draguignan station (25 miles/40 km). **By air:** Nice-Côte-d'Azur airport (57 miles/92 km).

(i) Town hall: +33 (0)4 94 50 21 94
www.mairie-bargeme.fr

👁 Highlights
• **Château Sabran-de-Pontevès** (July and August): First mentioned in 1225, it was partially destroyed during the Wars of Religion but has retained its outer defensive elements: +33 (0)4 94 50 21 94.
• **Église Saint-Nicolas** (July and August): This 12th-century Romanesque church was restored, along with its altarpieces, from 1990 to 2000.
• **Village:** Further information: +33 (0)4 94 50 21 91.

🔑 Accommodation
Guesthouses
La Fontaine: +33 (0)6 15 84 09 04.
Vacation rentals
Pierre Chassigneux***: +33 (0)6 72 95 39 21.
Thiébaut Renger**: +33 (0)6 50 77 66 26.
Gîtes, teepees, wooden trailer
La Ferme Saint-Pierre: +33 (0)4 94 84 21 55.

🍴 Eating Out
L'Amandier Rose, crêperie: +33 (0)9 81 28 00 83.
Le Goustadou, local specialties: +33 (0)6 22 75 79 22.
Les Jardins de Bargème: +33 (0)06 86 85 26 69.

🛒 Local Specialties
Food and Drink
Cheeses • Beef and lamb • Vegetables • Sheep yoghurts • Tastings of local specialties.
Art and Crafts
Art gallery • Painter-sculptor • Sculptor • Flea markets.

📅 Events
June: Transhumance festival.
August: Saint-Laurent festival (2nd weekend).

🦋 Outdoor Activities
Walking and riding: Route GR 49 and 2 marked trails • Hang gliding • Mountain-biking.

ⓘ Did you know?
Just over a mile (2 km) south of the village, on the roadside, stands a chapel dedicated to Saint Petronilla. Shepherds used to visit this chapel for their sheep to be blessed before they led them up to their summer pastures. Every year, on May 31, a Mass is still celebrated to bless bread and salt, which once formed the shepherds' main diet.

🌿 Further Afield
• Route Napoléon (6 miles/9.5 km) and views on the way to Castellane (18 miles/29 km) or Grasse (27 miles/43 km).
• La Bastide: summit of Montagne de Lachens (7½ miles/12 km).
• Le Grand Canyon du Verdon (16 miles/26 km).
• *Seillans (21 miles/34 km), see pp. 140–41.
• *Tourtour (29 miles/47 km), see pp. 144–45.

Les Baux-de-Provence

Geological grandeur

Bouches-du-Rhône (13) • Population: 465 • Altitude: 715 ft. (218 m)

Perched on a rocky outcrop of the Alpilles hills in Provence, the village of Baux stands high above the Crau and the Camargue like a beacon.

Rock reigns supreme in the strange landscape of the Val d'Enfer. Outlined against the sky, the *baux* (from the Provençal word *baù*, meaning rocky escarpment) is a majestic outcrop 3,000 ft. (900 m) by 700 ft. (200 m) that dominates the Baux valley, in a landscape that opens into the Camargue and Mont Sainte-Victoire. Since the dawn of time, humans have sought refuge in this rocky mass; but the story of Baux really begins in the 10th century, when its lords built a fortress right at the top of this eagle's nest. They reigned here for five centuries, during which time they waged countless battles against the other lords of the region. The ruins of the medieval citadel still bear witness to the lords' power: they dominate both the Entreconque valley's olive groves and vineyards, and the La Fontaine valley, where the Mistral wind rushes into the gaping mouths of ancient quarries. The Renaissance, too, has left its mark on the center of the village—in the form of the Maison du Roy (the tourist information center), which bears the Calvinist inscription "Post Tenebras Lux" (Light After Darkness) on its window; and in many town houses, such as the Hôtel de Manville (the present town hall), Hôtel de Porcelet (Musée Yves Brayer), Hôtel Jean de Brion (Fondation Louis Jou), and even the former guardroom (Musée des *Santons*). Given a new lease of life by its hoteliers, restaurateurs, oil and wine producers, and artists, this beautiful village today recalls a lost way of life.

By road: Expressway A7, exit 24–Avignon Sud (18 miles/29 km); expressway A9-A54, exit 7–Arles (12 miles/19 km); expressway A54-N113, exit 7–Avignon (12 miles/19 km).
By train: Arles station (11 miles/18 km); Avignon TGV station (22 miles/35 km).
By air: Nîmes-Arles-Camargue (22 miles/ 35 km), Avignon-Caumont (25 miles/ 40 km), and Marseille-Provence (37 miles/ 60 km) airports.

(i) Tourist information:
+33 (0)4 90 54 34 39
www.lesbauxdeprovence.com

👁 Highlights

• **Carrières de Lumières:** Multimedia show projected onto giant natural backdrops throughout the year: +33 (0)4 90 54 47 37.
• **Château des Baux:** Medieval castle with keep, Sarrasine and Paravelle towers, lords' dovecote, castle chapel, Chapelle de Saint-Blaise (showing the movie "A bird's-eye view of Provence"), former Quiqueran hostel, exhibition of medieval siege engines, guided tours; treasure hunt (children age 7–12), medieval activities April–September and during fall school holidays:
+33 (0)4 90 54 55 56.
• **Fondation Louis Jou:** Exhibition of the works of Louis Jou (master typographer, engraver, printer, publisher) discovered in his workshop, and of his personal collection of incunabula, antiquarian

books, engravings by Dürer and Goya, paintings, sculptures, and ceramics; by appointment only: +33 (0)4 90 54 34 17.
• **Musée Yves Brayer:** Oil paintings, watercolors, sketches, engravings, and lithographs. Temporary exhibitions April–September: +33 (0)4 90 54 36 99.
• **Musée des *Santons*:** Varied collections of china figurines, including 17th-century Neapolitan figurines, 19th-century church figurines, works by local *santon* (crib figures) makers Carbonnel, Fouque, Jouve, Peyron Campagna, Toussaint, Thérèse Neveu, Louise Berger, Simone Jouglas; Christmas Nativity scenes:
+33 (0)4 90 54 34 39.
• **Village:** Take the unique "history and architecture" walking trail for individuals, and for groups on request; visit the Trémaïe and take the perfumed trail; enjoy

the natural and man-made heritage at the foot of the village; guided visit on request for groups only; accessible visit for the visually impaired: audioguide and touch tours, large print and Braille guides; free E-visit app: town visit accessible for all (general public, visual and hearing impaired): +33 (0)4 90 54 34 39.

🗝 Accommodation
Hotels
Baumanière Les Baux de Provence*****: +33 (0)4 90 54 33 07.
Domaine de Manville*****: +33 (0)4 90 54 40 20.
La Benvengudo****: +33 (0)4 90 54 32 54.
♥ Le Mas de l'Oulivié****: +33 (0)4 90 54 35 78.
Le Fabian des Baux***: +33 (0)4 90 54 37 87.
Le Mas d'Aigret *** : +33 (0)4 90 54 20 00.
Hostellerie de la Reine Jeanne**: +33 (0)4 90 54 32 06.
Guesthouses
♥ Mas Derrière Château: +33 (0)4 90 54 50 62.
Le Prince Noir : +33 (0)4 90 54 39 57.
Vacation rentals
Further information: +33 (0)4 90 54 34 39
www.lesbauxdeprovence.com

🍴 Eating Out
Auberge du Château: +33 (0)4 90 54 50 48.
Au Porte Mages, restaurant and crêperie: +33 (0)4 90 54 40 48.
Le Bautezar: +33 (0)4 90 54 32 09.

Les Baux Jus, organic salad and juice bar, vegan-friendly: +33 (0)9 83 24 29 19.
La Benvengudo: +33 (0)4 90 54 32 54.
Le Bouchon Rouge: +33 (0)4 90 18 26 07.
La Cabro d'Or: +33 (0)4 90 54 33 21.
Le Café du Musée: +33 (0)4 90 54 21 47.
Hostellerie de la Reine Jeanne: +33 (0)4 90 54 32 06.
Le Mas d'Aigret: +33 (0)4 90 54 20 00.
Oustau de Baumanière: +33 (0)4 90 54 33 07.
La Suite, tapas and tea room: +33 (0)4 90 54 32 06.
La Table and Bistro at Domaine de Manville +33 (0)4 90 54 40 20.
Les Variétés: +33 (0)4 90 54 55 88.

🧺 Local Specialties
Food and Drink
AOP Vallée des Baux-de-Provence olive oil • Pierced black olives and AOP marinated olives • AOC Baux-de-Provence wines • Local wines of the Alpilles.
Art and Crafts
Studios and art galleries • Silver/goldsmith and jewelry studio • Household linen, Provençal specialties • Natural and organic aromatic products • *Santon* (crib figure) workshop • Soaps and beauty products • Weaver • Hatter.

📅 Events
April–October: Exhibitions in cultural spaces (self-guided visits).
June: Fête de la Saint-Jean, Saint John's feast day.

July and August: Festival "A-part" (contemporary art).
September: Festival of Ceramics and Glass.
October: Exhibition of designers and *santon* (crib figure) makers.
December: "Noël aux Baux-de-Provence" exhibition and Christmas activities, dawn ceremony, Midnight Mass, and living Nativity.
All year round: Monuments and rocks in the village, family activities (themed walks, olive oil workshops, costumed tours, smartphone photography workshops).

🦋 Outdoor Activities
Golf: 18 holes (Domaine de Manville) • Walking: Route GR 6, 1 marked trail and 1 wine-lovers' trail at Saint Berthe, the Trémaïe Path (restricted access to forested massifs June–September).
Further information: +33 (0)8 11 20 13 13.

🌿 Further Afield
• Landscape and villages of the Alpille hills: Eygalières, Fontvieille, Maussane, Saint-Rémy-de-Provence (3–22 miles/5–35 km).
• Arles (11 miles/18 km).
• Avignon (19 miles/31 km).
• Les Saintes-Maries-de-la-Mer (36 miles/ 58 km).

Bonneval-sur-Arc

A village of open spaces

Savoie (73) • Population: 244 • Altitude: 5,906 ft. (1,800 m)

Lying between the Vanoise national park and the Grand Paradis national park in Italy, Bonneval's backdrop is nature writ large.

Ringed by dark mountains at the end of the Haute-Marienne valley, for centuries Bonneval was cut off from the rest of the world. But now each winter, when the road to the Col de l'Iseran closes, the inhabitants of Bonneval turn their isolation to their advantage by developing their own breed of tourism that respects both this remarkable environment and the ancient traditions of shepherds and artisans. Just down the road from Tralenta, whose buildings lining the Arc river lead straight to ski slopes, the huge stone houses topped with *lauzes* (schist tiles) and bristling with chimneys still nestle around the cheese dairy, the manor house, and the old village church. A few miles from the village, the hamlet of Écot, which built up around a listed 12th-century chapel, is a perfect example of Bonneval's traditional architecture. Above the rooftops, the Albaron, Levanna, and Ciamarella mountains, rising to nearly 13,000 ft. (4,000 m), tower over an exquisite amphitheater of glaciers: 42 square miles (11,000 hectares) twinkle in the winter silence, or gurgle to the music of summer streams and waterfalls. Bonneval really gets up close and personal with the mountains.

By road: Expressway A43, exit 30–Modane (17 miles/27 km). **By train:** Modane station (27 miles/43 km). **By air:** Chambéry-Aix airport (96 miles/154 km); Lyon-Saint-Exupéry airport (144 miles/232 km).

ⓘ Tourist information:
+33 (0)4 79 05 99 06
www.haute-maurienne-vanoise.com

👁 Highlights
• Musée "Espace Neige et Montagne" (snow and mountain museum): Daily life and local crafts, winter sports and historic mountaineering at Bonneval: +33 (0)4 79 05 99 06.
• Village: Guided tours for groups and individuals: +33 (0)4 79 05 99 06.

🔑 Accommodation
Hotels
Le Glacier des Évettes**: +33 (0)4 79 05 94 06.
Guesthouses
La Rosa***: +33 (0)4 79 05 95 66.
L'Auberge d'Oul: +33 (0)4 79 05 87 99.
La Greppa: +33 (0)4 79 05 32 79.
Gîtes, walkers' lodges, and vacation rentals
Further information: +33 (0)4 79 05 99 10
www.haute-maurienne-vanoise.com
Mountain refuges
Bonneval Village, alt. 5,938 ft. (1,810 m): +33 (0)6 86 66 90 12.
Le Carro, alt. 9,055 ft. (2,760 m): +33 (0)4 79 05 95 79.
Les Évettes, alt. 8,497 ft. (2,590 m): +33 (0)4 79 05 96 64.

🍽 Eating Out
L'Atelier du Tralenta (winter only): +33 (0)4 79 05 47 99.
Auberge d'Oul: +33 (0)4 79 05 87 99.
La Benna, pizzeria: +33 (0)4 79 05 83 78.
La Cabane: +33 (0)4 79 05 34 60.
Chez Mumu, at l'Écot: +33 (0)6 87 83 90 52.
Le Criou, mountain-top restaurant (winter only): +33 (0)4 79 05 97 11.
Les Évettes: +33 (0)4 79 05 94 06.
La Greppa, tea room: +33 (0)4 79 05 32 79.
La Pierre à Cupules: +33 (0)6 81 31 88 23.
Le Vieux Pont: +33 (0)4 79 05 94 07.

🏛 Local Specialties
Food and Drink
Charcuterie, salted meats, and fish • Cheeses (Beaufort and Bleu de Bonneval).
Art and Crafts
Local crafts.

📅 Events
Market: Every Sunday in winter and summer seasons.
January: La Grande Odyssée (international dog-sled race); ice-climbing rally.
April: "Chants du Monde" music and world singing festival.

July: L'Iserane bicycle touring rally; Fête du Rocher.

December: Christmas festivals (Christmas Eve and Saint Sylvester's Eve).

✹ Outdoor Activities

Summer
Mountain sports (mountaineering, canyoning, climbing, glacier walks, Via Ferrata) • Paragliding • Fishing in the lake and mountain streams • Lake (bathing and fishing) at Bessans (3½ miles/5.5 km) • Mountain hiking • Summer skiing on the Pisaillas glacier at the Col de l'Iseran.

Winter
Winter sports (Alpine skiing from Christmas through end of April, 5,900–10,000 ft. /1,800–3,050 m, 8 ski lifts, 3 chair lifts; ski touring and walking; snowshoe treks; ice-climbing) • Natural ice-skating.

✹ Further Afield
• Vanoise national park.
• L'Écot (2½ miles/4 km).
• Haute-Marienne valley: Bessans and surrounding hamlets, Lanslevillard, Termignon (4–19 miles/6.1–31 km).
• Col de l'Iseran (8½ miles/13.5 km).
• Haute-Tarentaise valley and resorts: Val-d'Isère, Tignes (19–27 miles/31–43 km).
• Col du Mont Cenis: lake (22 miles/35 km).

⚑ Did you know?
In 1957, after the Arc river burst its banks and a torrential flood destroyed half the village, the inhabitants decided to rebuild and to diversify their activities while still protecting their environment. The shepherds and farmers became businessmen, creating a cooperative and building a modern cheese dairy in a traditional chalet-style; their milk production increased tenfold in 15 years. They even took out loans to build dressed-stone chalets as vacation *gîtes* for tourists. In 1968, the village itself borrowed money to develop a proper ski resort, with all the necessary infrastructure, around the hamlet of Tralenta.

Charroux

A trading town in Bourbonnais

Allier (03) • Population: 387 • Altitude: 1,355 ft. (413 m)

At the crossroads of Roman roads, Charroux became a tax-free stronghold at the time of the dukes of Bourbon.

The rise of Charroux was linked to the charter of franchise that it obtained in 1245. The fortified city flourished in the Renaissance owing to its tannery and winemaking, as well as the fairs and markets that it held regularly, and thus attracted merchants, notaries, doctors, and clergymen. Evidence of this intense economic activity can be seen throughout the streets, some of which are named after the professions or trades that were carried out there at that time. The Halle (covered market), built in the early 19th century, has retained its old wooden pillars, which are protected from horse-and-cart collisions by large stone blocks. Despite the church being burned twice during the Wars of Religion, Charroux has retained its Église Saint-Jean-Baptiste, whose truncated bell tower remains a mystery. Adopting the arrangement of a *bastide*, the village is organized around its square. From the Cour des Dames, a magical place in the village center, the narrow streets pass by the house of the Prince of Condé and finish at the gates of the ramparts, one of which, the Porte d'Occident, received the village clock in the 16th century. During recent years, Charroux has reclaimed its identity as a place of trade, and now attracts many local producers and craftsmen.

By road: Expressway A71, exit 12–Vichy, then exit 14–Gannat (7½ miles/12 km).
By train: Vichy station (21 miles/34 km).
By air: Clermont-Ferrand-Auvergne airport (37 miles/60 km).

ⓘ Tourist information— Pays Saint-Pourcinois:
+33 (0)4 70 56 87 71
www.charroux03.fr

Rose-Thé: +33 (0)4 70 56 83 26.
La Table d'Océane: +33 (0)6 80 12 46 75.

🏛 Local Specialties

Food and Drink
Charroux jams • Charroux mustard •
Walnut and hazelnut oil • Charroux
saffron • Handmade candies and organic
sugar • Cheeses and salted meats and
fish • AOC St-Pourçain-sur-Sioule
wines • Teas and coffees • Fruit juices •
Chocolates • Cookies.

Art and Crafts
Mother-of-pearl objects • Jewelry •
Candles • Stone objects • Decorative
objects • Earthenware potter, sculptor •
Bead and wirework artist • Potter •
Soap-makers • Stained-glass artist • Silk
crafts • Textile accessories • Alpaca wool •
Upholsterer/decorator • Art galleries •
Flea market.

🗓 Events
April: Antiques fair (last Sunday).
May: Printemps des Saveurs, wine
and local produce fair (1st weekend).
August: Fête des Artistes et Artisans,
art and craft fair (1st Sunday).
November: Fête de la Soupe (1st Saturday,
unless November 1).
December: Christmas market
(3rd weekend).

🦋 Outdoor Activities
Walking: 3 marked trails.

🌿 Further Afield
• Bellenaves: Musée de l'Automobile,
car museum; Chantelle: abbey; Jenzat
(Maison du Luthier) (3–4½ miles/5–7 km).
• Gannat: Paléopolis, theme park
(8 miles/13 km).
• Gorges of the Sioule (8 miles/13 km).
• Saint-Pourçain-sur-Sioule: Musée du Vin,
wine museum; vineyards (12 miles/19 km).
• Vichy (19 miles/31 km).

👁 Highlights
• **Musée de Charroux** (popular arts
and traditions): Discover the town of
Charroux, which became a village in
the 20th century: +33 (0)4 70 56 87 71.
• **Maison des Horloges:** Antique clock
mechanisms: +33 (0)4 70 56 87 39.
• **Les Pots de Marie:** Exhibition of more
than 500 spice pots: +33 (0)4 70 56 88 80.
• **Église Saint-Jean-Baptiste** (12th century).
• **Village:** Guided tour, by appointment
only, all year round for groups; for
individuals, Wednesday at 11 a.m. in July
and August. +33 (0)4 70 56 87 71.

🗝 Accommodation
Guesthouses
♥ La Maison du Prince de Condé****:
+33 (0)4 70 56 81 36.
Le Relais de l'Orient: +33 (0)4 70 56 89 93.

Gîtes
Gîte du Vieux Four****:
+33 (0)4 70 56 88 37.
Gîte du Peyrou**: +33 (0)9 88 99 67 78.

🍽 Eating Out
L'Auberge du Beffroi:
+33 (0)4 70 56 86 82.
La Ferme Saint-Sébastien:
+33 (0)4 70 56 88 83.
La Palette Vintage; +33 (0)9 73 01 69 76.
Le Petit Café Bleu: +33 (0)4 70 56 88 16.

ⓘ Did you know?
Mustard is a specialty of Charroux. Since
the early 19th century, Messieurs Favier,
Portier, and Poulain have distinguished
themselves here as master mustard-
makers, with two oil presses nearby.
Traditionally prepared with Saint-Pourçain
wine, Charroux mustard becomes purple
when made from grape must instead of
white wine.

Coaraze

The sunshine village

Alpes-Maritimes (06) • Population: 783 • Altitude: 2,083 ft. (635 m)

A short distance from the Parc National du Mercantour, Coaraze is a medieval village bathed in sunlight.

In the middle of olive trees, the cobblestone lanes of Coaraze lead to the 14th-century church, the multicolored interior of which was embellished in the Baroque style of Nice in the 18th century with 118 cherubs. The Blue Chapel—decorated with frescoes in different shades of blue by Angel Ponce de Léon in 1962—is an oratory dedicated to the Virgin Mary. The Chapelle Saint-Sébastien, which is decorated with 16th-century frescoes, stands alongside the old mule track that linked the village to Nice. With its steep, narrow streets, its houses with pink-tiled roofs, roughcast walls, and pastel shutters, and its fountains and squares, Coaraze is evocative of nearby Italy. Many artists have contributed their designs to Coaraze's sundials, including Jean Cocteau, Henri Goetz, and Mona Christie.

By road: Expressway A8, exit 55–Nice-Est (13 miles/21 km). **By bus:** 300 and 303 from Nice bus station (16 miles/26 km). **By train:** Nice-Ville TGV station (16 miles/26 km). **By air:** Nice-Côte-d'Azur airport (23 miles/37 km).

ⓘ Tourist information:
+33 (0)4 93 79 37 47
www.coaraze.eu

👁 Highlights
• Chapelle Saint-Sébastien: 16th-century frescoes.
• Église Saint-Jean-Baptiste: Built in the 14th century, Baroque interior.
• Chapelle Bleue: Old oratory dedicated to the Virgin Mary; frescoes by Angel Ponce de Léon.
• Musée Figas (in L'Engarvin): Museum dedicated to the fantastical futurist paintings of artist Marcel Figas from Nice, by appointment only: +33 (0)6 67 15 66 85.
• Village: Guided tour by arrangement: +33 (0)4 93 79 37 47.
• Tour of the olive groves: Organized by the Comité Régional de Tourisme de Nice (tourist board).

🔑 Accommodation
Guesthouses
La Feuilleraie: +33 (0)6 38 83 02 16.
Oliveraie de la Leuzière:
+33 (0)6 22 75 19 91.
La Pitcholine: +33 (0)6 46 64 70 58.
Communal gîtes
Gîtes du domaine de l'Euzière***:
+33 (0)6 40 81 58 28.
Walkers' lodges
Gîtes du Prestbytère
Further information: +33 (0)4 93 79 34 79.

🍽 Eating Out
Au Fil des Saisons: +33 (0)4 93 79 00 62.
Bar Les Arts "Chez Yanis":
+33 (0)4 93 79 34 90.
Lo Castel, May–September:
+33 (0)6 75 24 43 24.

🧺 Local Specialties
Food and Drink
Organic olive oil • Honey, jams.
Art and Crafts
Local crafts on sale at the tourist information center (pottery, turned wood).

📅 Events
March: Le Printemps des Poètes (poetry).
May: Journée du Vide-Grenier (open-air rummage sale, May 1), Voix du Basilic (literary events).
June: La Jòia de la Saint-Jean (cart racing).
July and August: Pilo (traditional sport from Nice) world championship; summer concerts; De l'Olivier (choral events); olive tree festival; Coartjazz (music), Côte d'Azur Mercantour trail.
October: Nuit de l'Écrit (writing night).
December: Marché de Noël d'Ici et d'Ailleurs (Christmas market).

🏃 Outdoor Activities
Walking: 30 marked trails.

🌿 Further Afield
• Old village of Rocca Sparviera (3½ miles/5.5 km).
• Hilltop villages of Lucéram, Contes, Berre-les-Alpes, Peillon (5½–12 miles/9–19 km).
• Châteauneuf-Villevieille: ruins (11 miles/18 km).
• Nice; Côte d'Azur (16 miles/26 km).
• Peira-Cava; Forêt de Turini, forest; Col de Turini (17 miles/27 km).
• *Sainte-Agnès (24 miles/39 km), see p. 134.

La Garde-Adhémar
The white nymph of the Tricastin

Drôme (26) • Population: 1,177 • Altitude: 558 ft. (170 m)

Set on a limestone spur, La Garde-Adhémar looks out over the Rhône valley and the Tricastin plain.

La Garde-Adhémar has retained its medieval structure—fortifications with gates and curtain wall, elements of the castle and fortified town, narrow streets, and old houses—and is today mostly restored. At the end of the village are the remains of the Renaissance castle built by Antoine Escalin. The Romanesque Église Saint-Michel, a testimony to Provençal architecture of the 12th century, has three naves and a western apse. Nearby, the old Chapelle des Pénitents-Blancs houses an exhibition devoted to the heritage of the Tricastin region. About a mile (1.5 km) away, the Val des Nymphes was a Gallo-Roman, and later a Christian, worship site. Only the 12th-century Chapelle Notre-Dame now remains. During that century, the inhabitants deserted this fertile valley to seek refuge in the fortified town of Adhémar.

By road: Expressway A7, exit 18– Montélimar Sud (8 miles/13 km), then N7 (3½ miles/5.5 km). **By train:** Pierrelatte station (3½ miles/5.5 km); Avignon TGV station (42 miles/68 km). **By air:** Avignon-Caumont airport (43 miles/69 km).

(i) Tourist information:
+33 (0)4 75 04 40 10
www.la-garde-adhemar-ot.org

👁 Highlights
• Église Saint-Michel (12th century).
• **Jardin des Herbes:** A remarkable medicinal garden with 200 species, plus a ¾-acre (3,000-sq. m) botanical garden.
• **Val des Nymphes and its chapel.**
• **Village:** Guided tour by arrangement: +33 (0)4 75 04 40 10.

🗝 Accommodation
Guesthouses
Mas Bella Cortis**** +33 (0)6 22 00 20 36.
Gîte du Val des Nymphes***:
+33 (0)4 75 04 44 54.
Les Esplanes: +33 (0)4 75 49 04 16.
La Ferme des Rosières:
+33 (0)4 75 04 72 81.
La Part des Anges: +33 (0)4 75 52 14 38.

Gîtes
La Cour des Calades: +33 (0)6 85 36 69 16.
Further information: +33 (0)4 75 04 40 10
www.la-garde-adhemar-ot.org

🍴 Eating Out
L'Absinthe, local bistro: +33 (0)4 75 04 44 38.
L'Auberge Fricot: +33 (0)4 69 26 67 36.
Côté Pizza: +33 (0)4 75 46 40 89.
Le Prédaïou: +33 (0)4 75 04 40 08.
Le Tisonnier: +33 (0)4 75 04 44 03.

🏪 Local Specialties
Food and Drink
Goat cheeses • Fruits • Olive oil • Truffles • Wines.
Art and Crafts
Designer • Ceramicist and enameler • Gifts.

🦋 Outdoor Activities
Walking: 2 marked trails and Sentier des Arts • Mountain-biking (marked trails) • Horse-riding trail.

🌿 Further Afield
• Pierrelatte: crocodile farm (4½ miles/7 km).
• Tricastin villages: Clansayes, Saint-Paul-Trois-Châteaux, Saint-Restitut (4½–9½ miles/ 7–15.5 km).
• Châteaux de Grignan and de Suze-la-Rousse, Valréas (11–17 miles/18–27 km).
• *Séguret (25 miles/40 km), see p. 139.

La Garde-Guérin
(commune of Prévenchères)
In the knights' shadow

Lozère (48) • Population: 281 • Altitude: 2,953 ft. (900 m)

The archetype of the fortified village, La Garde-Guérin has retained its 12th-century structure.

The fortified village can be seen from afar, built as it is at nearly 3,000 ft. (900 m), and remarkably situated 1,300 ft. (400 m) above the nearby Chassezac Gorge. The site is crossed by the Régordane Way, a natural communication route linking the Mediterranean to the Auvergne through Nîmes and Le Puy. In the Middle Ages, a community of knights, known as the *chevaliers pariers* (knights with equal rights), settled in the village to provide protection to travelers using this route and safeguard their animals and goods. Inside the ramparts stand the tall watchtower and the Chapelle Saint-Michel, which date from the 12th century, and the walls of the castle that the Molette de Morangiès family built in the 16th century. Today, the site's history and its rugged natural landscape lend a wild and mysterious beauty to La Garde-Guérin.

By road: N88 (22 miles/35 km). **By train:** Villefort station (5 miles/8 km); La Bastide-Puylaurent station (11 miles/18 km). **By air:** Nîmes airport (72 miles/116 km); Montpellier-Méditerranée airport (97 miles/156 km).

ⓘ Tourist information:
+33 (0)4 66 46 87 12
Tourist information—Villefort en Cévennes: +33 (0)4 66 46 87 30
www.lagardeguerin.fr

👁 Highlights
• **Village:** Guided tour for groups:
+33 (0)4 66 46 87 12 or +33 (0)6 74 97 22 32.
• **Église Saint-Michel** (12th century):
Romanesque former chapel of the village; gilded wooden statue of Saint Michael (18th century), painting of the Crucifixion.

🗝 Accommodation
Hotel
Auberge Régordane**: +33 (0)4 66 46 82 88.
Guesthouses
La Butinerie, Albespeyres:
+33 (0)4 66 46 06 47 or +33 (0)6 81 98 90 56.
Chez Chiff's, Prévenchères:
+33 (0)4 66 46 01 53.
Le Vieux Tilleul, Prévenchères:
+33 (0)4 66 46 85 86.
Vacation rental
Solène Marzio, Prévenchères:
+33 (0)6 78 00 46 48 or +33 (0)6 74 10 38 69.
Municipal campsite
La Cascade des Cévennes**:
+33 (0)6 81 51 80 10.

🍴 Eating Out
Auberge Régordane: +33 (0)4 66 46 82 88.
Auberge Le Vieux Tilleul, Prévenchères:
+33 (0)4 66 46 85 86.
Comptoir de la Regordane:
+33 (0)4 66 46 83 38.

🧺 Local Specialties
Food and Drink
Farm produce.
Art and Crafts
Craftspeople's collective.

2️⃣ Events
June: Transhumance, movement of livestock to fresh pasture (1st Sunday after the 15th).
August: Prévenchères festival (1st weekend).

🦋 Outdoor Activities
Canyoning • Rock climbing and Via Corda • Walking and mountain-biking: Routes GR 700 (Chemin de Régordane) and GR 70 (Chemin de Stevenson); numerous marked trails • Caving • Golf: 9 holes • Trout fishing (Chassezac).

🌿 Further Afield
• Lac de Villefort and Lac de Rachas, lakes (3 miles/5 km).
• Prévenchères: Château de Castanet, 12th-century church and its *tilleul de Sully*, a historic lime tree (3½ miles/5.5 km).
• Mas de La Barque and Mont Lozère (16 miles/26 km).
• Langogne (23 miles/37 km).

By road: Expressway A57, exit 13–Le Luc
(23 miles/37 km); expressway A8, exit 36–
Draguignan (22 miles/35 km), N98
(3½ miles/5.5 km). **By train:** Fréjus-Saint-
Raphaël TGV station (22 miles/35 km);
Les Arcs and Draguignan stations
(23 miles/37 km).
By air: Golfe de Saint-Tropez airport
(6 miles/10 km); Toulon-Hyères airport
(30 miles/48 km); Nice Côte-d'Azur airport
(58 miles/93 km).

ⓘ **Tourist information:**
+33 (0)4 98 11 56 51 / www.gassin.eu

👁 **Highlights**
• **Village:** Free guided tour Wednesday at
4 p.m. from Easter to end October, 6 p.m.
in July and August, departing from the
viewpoint indicator: +33 (0)4 94 55 22 00.
• **Church** (16th century): Listed font,
18th-century bust of Saint Lawrence.

🗝 **Accommodation**
Hotels
Le Kube*****: +33 (0)4 94 97 20 00.
Le Mas de Chastelas*****:
+33 (0)4 94 56 71 71.
Villa Belrose*****: +33 (0)4 94 55 97 97.
La Bastide d'Antoine****:
+33 (0)4 94 97 70 08.
Le Domaine de l'Astragale****:
+33 (0)4 94 97 48 98.
Le Brin d'Azur***: +33 (0)4 94 97 46 06.
Les Capucines***: +33 (0)4 94 97 70 05.
Dune***: +33 (0)4 94 97 00 83.
Bello Visto**: +33 (0)4 94 56 17 30.
Aparthotels
Caesar Domus: +33 (0)4 94 55 86 55.
Odalys: Le Clos Bonaventure et Les Jardins
d'Artémis: +33 (0)4 94 97 73 34.
Guesthouses, gîtes, and vacation rentals
Further information: +33 (0)4 98 11 56 51
www.gassin.eu

Gassin
A haven on the Côte d'Azur

Var (83) • Population: 2,887 (500 in the village itself) • Altitude: 656 ft. (200 m)

From its ridge surrounded by vineyards and forests, Gassin has a
unique view of the peninsula and Gulf of Saint-Tropez.
 Alongside the protection of the surrounding landscape, the development of the new village next door has also been sensitively handled,
a feat recognized by several international awards. In addition to the
delight of exploring the new village is the pleasure to be had from
strolling, accompanied by the fragrance of oleanders and bougainvil-
lea, along the maze of winding lanes in the old village, with its façades
weathered by time. From the Deï Barri terrace, the view stretches
from the Îles d'Hyères to the Massif des Maures and, when the Mistral
has blown the clouds away, to the snow-capped summits of the Alps.

Campsites
Domaine de la Verdagne:
+33 (0)4 94 79 78 21.
Jauffret farm campsite:
+33 (0)4 94 56 27 78.
Parc Saint-James Montana:
+33 (0)4 94 55 20 20.
Roche Club: +33 (0)4 94 56 12 29.

🍴 Eating Out
Le 1999: +33 (0)4 94 55 22 14.
Au Marius: +33 (0)4 94 97 20 00.
Au Vieux Gassin: +33 (0)4 94 56 14 26.
Bello Visto: +33 (0)4 94 56 17 30.
Le Carpaccio: +33 (0)4 94 97 48 98.
La Ciboulette: +33 (0)4 94 56 25 52.
Golf Country Club restaurant:
+33 (0)4 94 17 42 41.
Le Micocoulier: +33 (0)4 94 56 14 01.
Le Pescadou: +33 (0)4 94 56 12 43.
Le Pitchoun: +33 (0)4 89 99 45 11.
Le P'tit Chef: +33 (0)4 94 43 06 71.
Les Sarments: +33 (0)4 94 56 38 20.
La Table du 1K: +33 (0)4 94 97 20 00.
La Table du Mas: +33 (0)4 94 56 71 71.
La Torpille: +33 (0)4 94 56 52 80.

La Verdoyante: +33 (0)4 94 56 16 23.
Villa Belrose: +33 (0)4 94 55 97 97.

🧺 Local Specialties
Food and Drink
Jams • Organic olive oil • AOC Côtes
de Provence wines.
Art and Crafts
Gifts • Pottery.

📅 Events
April: Internationale Granfondo cycle
race; opening of the art-exhibition
season.
May: La Gassinoise cross-country run.
June: "Fête de la Saint-Jean," Saint John's
feast day; Brazilian festival.
July: Polo Masters at the Haras de Gassin
(international tournament).
August: Fête Patronale de la Saint-
Laurent; August 15th Ball.
December: Noël des Enfants (children's
Christmas).

All year round: Exhibitions, concerts,
activities for children, mountain-biking
competitions, polo tournaments.

🦋 Outdoor Activities
Swimming (no lifeguard) • Walking •
Mountain-biking • Golf • Sailing.

🌿 Further Afield
• La Croix-Valmer; Ramatuelle
(2½–3 miles/4–5 km).
• Saint-Tropez (3½–6 miles/5.5–9.5 km).
• Calvaire, Grimaud, Sainte-Maxime
(6 miles/10 km).
• Massif des Maures, uplands; La Garde-
Freinet (8½ miles/14 km).
• Collobrières: Chartreuse de la Verne
(21 miles/34 km).
• Fréjus; Saint-Raphaël (25 miles/40 km).
• Le Lavandou (25 miles/40 km).

🏆 Did you know?
Gassin lays claim to the smallest street
in the world, called the "Andnuno."
Its name comes from the words *andros*
(man) and *uno* (one)—meaning that only
one person can pass at a time.

Gordes
Jewel of the Luberon

Vaucluse (84) • Population: 2,100 • Altitude: 1,171 ft. (357 m)

Like an eagle's nest perched on the foothills of the Monts de Vaucluse, facing the famous Luberon mountain, Gordes is the archetypal Provençal village.

Surrounded by a mosaic of holm oaks, wheat fields, and vines, the village's dry-stone houses—solidly attached to the rock—seem to tumble down in cascades. Its history, its rich architecture and heritage, its marvelous views, its cobbled winding lanes, and its fountain shaded by a plane tree on the Place du Château have appealed to numerous artists, from André Lhote (1885–1962) and Pol Mara (1920–1998) to Victor Vasarely (1906–1997). A short distance from the village, at the end of a lavender field, which in springtime enhances the pale stone of its façade, the Abbaye de Sénanque is a perfect example of Cistercian architecture and is still inhabited by monks.

By road: Expressway A7, exit 24–Avignon Sud (17 miles/27 km).
By train: Cavaillon station (11 miles/18 km); Avignon TGV station (25 miles/40 km).
By air: Avignon-Caumont airport (19 miles/31 km); Marseille-Provence airport (48 miles/77 km).

(i) Tourist information—Luberon Monts de Vaucluse: +33 (0)4 90 72 02 75
www.luberoncoeurdeprovence.com

👁 Highlights

• **Abbaye de Sénanque** (12th century): The church, dormitory, cloister, and chapter house can be visited on guided tours. Further information: +33 (0)4 90 72 02 75.
• **Cellars of the Palais Saint-Firmin:** Situated beneath a large house, the cellars feature caves, cisterns, and an old seigneurial oil press; documentary, museum, MP3 audioguide. Further information: +33 (0)4 90 72 02 75.
• **Moulin des Bouillons and Musée du Vitrail:** One of the oldest preserved oil mills with all its workings, presses from the 1st to the 14th centuries, collections of oil lamps, amphorae; at the same site, the Musée du Vitrail recounts the history of glass and stained-glass windows via a large collection: +33 (0)4 90 72 22 11.
• **Castle** (16th century): Of medieval origin, rebuilt during the Renaissance. Exhibitions by artists who have lived in Gordes or that relate to the history of the village; also temporary exhibtions: +33 (0)4 90 72 02 75.
• **Village des Bories:** Museum of rural dry-stone dwellings (*bories*) that served as housing until the middle of the 19th century: +33 (0)4 90 72 03 48.
• **Village:** Guided tour by arrangement: +33 (0)4 90 72 02 75.

🗝 Accommodation

Hotels
La Bastide*****: +33 (0)4 90 72 12 12.
Les Bories*****: +33 (0)4 90 72 00 51.
♥ La Ferme de la Huppe****: +33 (0)4 90 72 12 25.

Auberge de Carcarille***:
33 (0)4 90 72 02 63.
♥ Le Jas de Gordes***: +33 (0)4 90 72 00 75.
♥ Le Mas des Romarins***:
+33 (0)4 90 72 12 13.
Le Mas de la Sénancole***:
+33 (0)4 90 76 76 55.
Le Petit Palais d'Aglaé****:
+33 (0)4 32 50 21 02.

Guesthouses, gîtes, and vacation rentals
Further information: +33 (0)4 90 72 02 75
www.luberoncoeurdeprovence.com

Aparthotels
La Bastide des Chênes +33 (0)4 90 72 73 74.

Campsites
Les Sources***: +33 (0)4 90 72 12 48.

🍽 Eating Out
Restaurants
L'Artégal: +33 (0)4 90 72 02 54.
♥ Auberge de Carcarille:
+33 (0)4 90 72 02 63.
La Bastide: +33 (0)4 90 72 12 12.
Le Bistro de la Huppe: +33 (0)4 90 72 12 25.
Les Bories: +33 (0)4 90 72 00 51.
Casa Rosario: +33 (0)4 90 72 06 98.
Les Cuisines du Château:
+33 (0)4 90 72 01 31.
♥ L'Esprit des Romarins: +33 (0)4 90 72 12 13.
L'Estaminet: +33 (0)4 90 72 14 45.
L'Estellan: +33 (0)4 90 72 04 90.
La Farigoule: +33 (0)4 90 76 92 76.
Le Jardin: +33 (0)4 90 72 12 34.
Le Loup Blanc: +33 (0)4 90 72 12 43.
Le Mas Tourteron: +33 (0)4 90 72 00 16.
Le Renaissance: +33 (0)4 90 72 02 02.
Les Sources: +33 (0)4 90 72 12 48.
Le Table d'Euphrosyne: +33 (0)4 32 50 21 02.
Le Teston: +33 (0)4 32 50 21 74.

Light meals
La Crêperie de Fanny: +33 (0)4 32 50 13 01.
L'Encas: +33 (0)4 90 72 29 82.
Le Goût de la Vie: +33 (0)4 90 72 57 44.

🧺 Local Specialties
Food and Drink
Honey • AOC Côtes du Ventoux wine •
Olive oil.

Art and Crafts
Jewelry • Art galleries • Potters • Sculptor.

📅 Events
Market: Tuesday mornings, Place
du Château.
January: Fête de la Saint-Vincent
(2nd fortnight).
April–October: Painting and sculpture
exhibitions in the municipal halls.
July and August: Numerous concerts
at the Théâtre des Terrasses.
August: "Les Soirées d'Été," festival
(1st fortnight); Fête du Vin des Côtes
du Ventoux, wine festival (1st Sunday).
December: "Veillée Calendale," Christmas
songs and tasting of the thirteen desserts,
representative of Jesus and his apostles
(1st fortnight); Christmas market.

🦋 Outdoor Activities
Walking: Route GR 6 and 2 marked trails •
Mountain-biking/Electric mountain-bike
rentals.

🐦 Further Afield
• Véroncles: water mills (1 mile/1.5 km).
• Murs (5½ miles/9 km).
• *Roussillon (5½ miles/9 km),
see pp. 126–27.
• *Ménerbes (7 miles/11.5 km), see p. 112.
• Fontaine-de-Vaucluse (7½ miles/12 km).
• *Venasque (9½ miles/15.5 km),
see pp. 147–48.
• *Lourmarin (18 miles/29 km),
see pp. 109–10.
• Avignon (24 miles/39 km).
• *Ansouis (24 miles/39 km), see pp. 86–87.

Gourdon

Between sea and sky

Alpes-Maritimes (06) • Population: 396 • Altitude: 2,493 ft. (760 m)

Built on an isolated rock above the Loup valley, Gourdon looks out over the Gorges of the Loup toward the blue waters of the Mediterranean. Designed to repel Saracen invasions in the 8th–10th centuries, Gourdon has often served as a stronghold. Protected by the gorges to the south, the village built fortifications on the side facing the mountain. A first fortress was constructed in the 9th century. In the 12th century, the castle was built, overlooking the whole valley. Sheltered by the imposing fortress, and crisscrossed by infinitely narrow streets, the village showcases its restored houses, the Romanesque Église Saint-Vincent, and numerous artists' stalls; at the end stands its showpiece, the Place Victoria. Immortalized by Queen Victoria's visit in 1891, this panoramic viewpoint offers a breathtaking vista, from Nice and Cap Ferrat in the east as far as the cape of Saint-Tropez and the Massif des Maures in the west, via Antibes, Cannes, the Îles de Lérins, and the Massif de l'Esterel. In the late 19th century, the village spread to the hamlet of Pont-du-Loup, at the foot of the rock, in the Loup valley, where the climate was more conducive to growing herbs.

By road: Expressway A8, exit 47–Villeneuve-Loubet (16 miles/26 km).
By rail: Grasse station (9½ miles/15.5 km); Nice TGV station (24 miles/38 km).
By air: Nice-Côte d'Azur airport (20 miles/32 km).

ⓘ Tourist information:
+33 (0)4 93 09 68 25
www.gourdon06.fr

👁 Highlights
• **Place Victoria:** Panoramic viewpoint of the Côte d'Azur.
• **Église Saint-Vincent** (12th century).
• **Galerie de La Mairie:** Exhibitions: +33 (0)4 93 09 68 25.
• **Castle gardens designed by André Le Nôtre** (1613–1700). Further information: +33 (0)4 93 09 68 02.
• **Saut du Loup waterfalls** (Gorges du Loup): Guided tours of the waterfalls and viewpoint over the valley, from May to October: +33 (0)4 93 09 68 88.
• **Lavanderaies de la Source Parfumée:** Fields of flowers and herbs; guided tours for groups by a master gardener: +33 (0)4 93 09 68 23.

🛏 Accommodation
Gîtes and vacation rentals
Further information: www.gourdon06.fr

🍴 Eating Out
Auberge de Gourdon: +33 (0)4 93 09 69 69.
Les Grands Hommes: +33 (0)4 93 77 66 21.
La Taverne Provençale: +33 (0)4 93 09 68 22.
Au Vieux Four: +33 (0)4 93 09 68 60.

🛍 Local Specialties
Food and Drink
Nougat and *calissons* (candy) • *Pain d'épice* (spice cake).
Art and Crafts
Perfumery • Soap factory • Glassworks.

📅 Events
August: Open-air theater festival.
November–March: Theater festival (last Fridays), Pont-du-Loup.

🦋 Outdoor Activities
Paragliding • Walking: Chemin du Paradis and numerous marked trails.

🌿 Further Afield
- Gorges of the Loup (5 miles/8 km).
- Grasse (8½ miles/13.5 km).
- Valbonne; Biot; Tourrettes-sur-Loup; Saint-Paul-de-Vence (9½–19 miles/ 15.5–31 km).
- Côte d'Azur: Cannes, Antibes, Nice (17–22 miles/27–35 km).
- Corniche de l'Esterel, coastal drive (22–43 miles/35–69 km).

♟ Did you know?
In the early 20th century, there was no road to link Gourdon to Pont-du-Loup. Locals traveled from one village to the other by mule, on the Chemin du Paradis. Until 1900, caravans of mules could still be seen passing each other on this rocky Provençal road.

La Grave
On top of the world

Hautes-Alpes (05) • Population: 500 • Altitude: 4,757 ft. (1,450 m)

With its larch trees, rich pastures, and abundant snow, La Grave invites visitors to explore a spectacular mountain.

Teetering on a rocky outcrop, La Grave packs its robust stone houses tightly along narrow streets called *trabucs*, which climb to the top of the village. The Romanesque–Lombard-style Église Notre-Dame-de-l'Assomption, which adjoins the Chapelle des Péni-tents-Blancs, offers a breathtaking view of the Massif des Écrins, and in particular La Meije mountain. This legendary summit, which reaches 13,070 ft. (3,983 m), has made La Grave a mecca for mountaineers; laid to rest in the cemetery next to the church, beneath simple wooden crosses, are climbers that the mountain has claimed. Since the 1970s, La Grave has also gained an international reputation for its unique off-piste ski area. In summer, the Meije glaciers' cable cars enable visitors to reach the Col des Ruil-lans and the Glacier de la Girose. La Grave and Les Traverses—the hamlets scattered on its southern slope—provide ideal starting points for numerous walks.

By road: Expressway A480, exit 8–Vizille (43 miles/69 km). **By rail:** Briançon station (24 miles/39 km). **By air:** Grenoble-Isère airport (73 miles/117 km); Chambéry-Aix airport (90 miles/145 km); Lyon-Saint-Exupéry airport (103 miles/166 km).

ⓘ Tourist information:
+33 (0)4 76 79 90 05
www.lagrave-lameije.com

👁 Highlights

- **Église Notre-Dame** (11th century): 18th- and 19th-century furnishings; cemetery. Further information: +33 (0)4 76 79 90 05.
- **Hamlet of Le Chazelet:** Traditional houses, church, communal oven.
- **Meije glaciers** (alt. 10,500 ft./3,200 m) by cable car: Daily mid-June–mid-September. Further information: +33 (0)4 76 79 94 65.
- **Le Chazelet oratory:** Splendid view of La Meije.

🛌 Accommodation

Hotels
L'Edelweiss***: +33 (0)4 76 79 90 93.
Le Castillan**: +33 (0)4 76 79 90 04.
La Meijette**: +33 (0)4 76 79 90 34.
Le Sérac**: +33 (0)4 76 79 91 53.
Panoramic Village, appart'Hôtel: +33 (0)4 76 79 97 97.
Hôtel des Alpes (in winter): +33 (0)4 76 11 03 18.
Gîtes, walkers' lodges, vacation rentals, family vacation centers, and campsites
Further information: +33 (0)4 76 79 90 05
www.lagrave-lameije.com
Mountain huts
Évariste Chancel, alt. 8,200 ft. (2,500 m): +33 (0)4 76 79 92 32 or +33 (0)4 76 79 97 05.
Refuge Goléon, alt. 8,000 ft. (2,440 m): +33 (0)6 87 26 46 54.

🍴 Eating Out

Alp'Bar, crêperie: +33 (0)4 76 79 96 67.
Auberge Chez Baptiste: +33 (0)4 76 79 92 09.
Au Vieux Guide: +33 (0)4 76 79 90 75.
Le Castillan: +33 (0)4 76 79 90 04.
Le Chalet des Plagnes, crêperie/pizzeria: +33 (0)4 76 79 95 23.
L'Edelweiss: +33 (0)4 76 79 90 93.
Les Glaciers: +33 (0)4 76 79 90 07.
La Meijette: +33 (0)4 76 79 90 34.
La Pierre Farabo: +33 (0)4 76 79 95 25.
Pizza et Pasta: +33 (0)6 86 12 43 00.
Lou Ratel: +33 (0)4 76 79 92 10.
Le Sérac: +33 (0)4 76 79 91 53.

🧺 Local Specialties

Food and Drink
Goat cheeses • Honey.
Art and Crafts
Fabric designers • Creator of decorative objects (mobiles, pictures) and jewelry.

📅 Events

Markets: Thursday morning, Place du Téléphérique (off-season) or Place de la Salle-des-Fêtes (summer); local farmers' market every Sunday morning (July–August).
January: Rendez-Vous Nordique au Pays de la Meije (end January), "Reines de la Meije," girls' weekend (3rd weekend).
February: Ultimate Test Tour, freeride and security equipment fair (mid-February).
April: Derby de la Meije, ski race (1st weekend).
June: La Grave'y Cîmes mountaineering (2nd weekend), Rencontres de la Haute Romanche arts festival, country trails.
July: Messiaen au Pays de la Meije, music festival (last ten days).
August: Fête du Pain du Chazelet, bread festival (2nd weekend); Fête des Guides de La Grave, celebration of mountain guides (August 15); Tour du Plateau d'Emparis, foot and mountain-bike race (3rd Sunday).
September: Ultra Raid de la Meije, mountain-bike race (3rd weekend).

🦋 Outdoor Activities

In summer
Guided walk on the glacier, Via Ferrata, Via Cordata • Mountaineering • Rock climbing, climbing wall • Paragliding • Walking, walking with donkeys with packsaddles • Mountain-biking • Cycle touring • Astronomy • Fishing • Rafting.
In winter
Ski area (alt. 4,920–11,650 ft./1,500–3,550 m) of the Meije glaciers (off piste) and Le Chazelet (3 ski lifts, 1 chairlift): Downhill skiing, ski touring, off-piste and hiking trails, monoski, kiteboarding, snowboarding, surfing, telemarking, snowshoeing, mountaineering, ice-climbing, and dry tooling, snow and ice school • Sled dogs.

🌿 Further Afield

- **Villar-d'Arène:** Historic bread oven and water mill (2 miles/3 km).
- **Jardin Botanique Alpin du Lautaret,** botanic garden (open during summer) (6 miles/9.5 km).
- **Col du Lautaret:** Maison du Parc National des Écrins, national park visitor center (6 miles/9.5 km).
- **Col du Galibier** (11 miles/18 km).
- **Bourg-d'Oisans:** Musée de la Faune et des Minéraux, museum of geology and wildlife (17 miles/27 km).
- **Saint-Christophe-en-Oisans:** Musée de l'Alpinisme, mountaineering museum (25 miles/40 km).

❗ Did you know?

In La Grave, locals continue to make black (rye) bread, as they did in the past. This custom is celebrated every year on All Saints' Day.

Lavaudieu

In God's valley

Haute-Loire (43) • Population: 228 • Altitude: 1,411 ft. (430 m)

In the Middle Ages, Benedictine monks built a monastery in the Senoire valley, turning it into *la vallée de Dieu* (God's valley), which gave the village its name. Robert de Turlande, first abbot of La Chaise-Dieu abbey and later Saint Robert, founded the abbey at Lavaudieu in 1057. Nuns lived here until the French Revolution. It is the only monastery in the Auvergne with a Romanesque cloister. Running along the wall of the refectory, with its line of columns featuring carved capitals, is a 12th-century Byzantine-inspired mural. The abbey sheltered Cardinal de Rohan, when he fled La Chaise-Dieu after the Affair of the Diamond Necklace (an intrigue involving Marie Antoinette, Rohan, and the costly necklace). The 11th–12th-century church adjoining the monastery lost its steeple during the French Revolution. Inside, a 15th-century Pietà in polychrome stone sits alongside 14th-century Italian-influenced murals of an allegory of the Black Death. In the center of the village, the Musée des Arts et Traditions Populaires de Haute-Loire displays a typical Auvergne interior.

By road: Expressway A75, exit 20–Brioude (13 miles/21 km); N102 (5 miles/8 km).
By train: Brioude station (6 miles/9.5 km).
By air: Clermont-Ferrand-Auvergne airport (48 miles/77 km).

ⓘ Tourist information—Brioude et sa Région: +33 (0)4 71 74 97 49 or +33 (0)4 71 76 46 00 / www.ot-brioude.fr www.abbayedelavaudieu.fr

👁 Highlights

• **Abbey:** Cloisters, refectory (12th-century mural); Église Saint-André (Pietà, murals); further information: +33 (0)4 71 76 08 90 or +33 (0)4 71 76 46 00.
• **Musée des Arts et Traditions Populaires:** Reconstruction of a traditional Auvergne interior (joint tickets with abbey).
• **L'Atelier Nature:** Bookshop specializing in engravings and old books; collection of rare insects (July–August): +33 (0)7 61 22 39 52 or +33 (0)4 71 74 39 25.

✒ Accommodation

Guesthouses
La Buissonnière***: +33 (0)4 71 76 49 02.
Le Colombier***: +33 (0)4 71 76 09 86 or +33 (0)6 86 17 96 81.
La Maison d'à Côté***: +33 (0)4 71 76 45 04 or +33 (0)4 71 50 24 85.
Gîtes
M. and Mme Perrey***: +33 (0)4 71 76 82 39.
M. and Mme Watel***: +33 (0)4 71 76 45 79.

🍴 Eating Out

Auberge de l'Abbaye: +33 (0)4 71 76 44 44.
Auberge de la Fontaine: +33 (0)4 71 76 08 03 or +33 (0)7 71 72 53 26.
Court la Vigne: +33 (0)4 71 76 45 79.

🍽 Local Specialties

Food and Drink
Honey.
Art and Crafts
Essential-oil distillery.

② Events

June: Festi'Car (Pentecost).
July: Fête de la Barrique, barrel festival, and outdoor rummage sale (weekend after 14th).
July and August: Choir festivals; music concerts at the abbey; further information: +33 (0)4 71 76 46 00; exhibitions.
December: Christmas market (1st Saturday).

🦋 Outdoor Activities

Climbing • Swimming pool (at Brioude) • Walking: 3 marked trails.

🌾 Further Afield

• Brioude (5 miles/8 km).
• *Blesle (19 miles/31 km), see pp. 170–71.
• La Chaise-Dieu (24 miles/39 km).
• Allier valley: gorges (31 miles/50 km).

ⓘ Did you know?

The Fête de la Barrique, held each year on the Sunday after July 14, has its origins in the French Revolution, when Lavaudieu's inhabitants surrounded the abbey in order to seize the clergy's possessions—in particular the wine destined for the monks of La Chaise-Dieu. During the festival, this historic village traditionally places a barrel of wine in the square for everyone to share.

Lourmarin

The Provence of Camus and Bosco

Vaucluse (84) • Population: 1,188 • Altitude: 722 ft. (220 m)

Standing at the mouth of a gorge in the Luberon clawed out by a dragon, Loumarin attracted the writers Albert Camus and Henri Bosco, who slumber in the shade of the cemetery's cypress trees.

The rough gash created by the Aiguebrun river is the only route—and an ancient one—through the Luberon mountains, and the water tumbles under an old shell bridge. It is the reason why Lourmarin sprang up around a modest Benedictine monastery and a simple castle, the Castellas, belonging to the lords of Baux-de-Provence. Surrounded by a plain dotted with fortified Provençal *mas* houses, where fruit and olive orchards mingle with vines, the village today winds along streets lined with fountains, and sun-kissed rooftops that cascade around the Castellas (now a belfry and clock tower) and the Romanesque church of Saint-Trophime-et-Saint-André. A stone's throw away is the Protestant church, which recalls the tragic massacre of the Vaud people in the 16th century, survivors of which converted to Protestantism. Just beyond it, the castle of La Colette, built in the 15th and 16th centuries, looks down over fields and terraced gardens. The castle was rescued in the early 20th century by the benefactor Laurent Vibert; he created a stunning collection of furniture and objets d'art, and each year welcomes painters, sculptors, musicians, and writers to the castle.

By road: Expressway A7, exit 26–Sénas (17 miles/27 km); expressway A51, exit 15–Pertuis (13 miles/21 km).
By train: Pertuis station (12 miles/19 km); Cavaillon station (25 miles/40 km); Avignon TGV station (40 miles/64 km).
By air: Avignon-Caumont airport (34 miles/55 km); Marseille-Provence airport (41 miles/66 km).

ⓘ Tourist information—
Luberon Coeur de Provence:
+33 (0)4 90 68 10 77
www.luberoncoeurdeprovence.com

👁 Highlights

• **Castle** (15th and 16th centuries): First Renaissance castle in Provence, furnished throughout; collection of engravings and objets d'art: +33 (0)4 90 68 15 23.
• **Village tours:** All year round for groups, and from mid-June to mid-September for individuals, by appointment only: +33 (0)4 90 68 10 77.
• **Protestant church** (19th century), included in village tour: Huge organ attributed to the Lyon manufacturer Augustin Zieger.
• **Romanesque church** (11th century), included in village tour.
• **La Ferme de Gerbaud:** Plants and herb farm. Tastings available Thursdays, booking essential: +33 (0)4 90 68 11 83.

⚷ Accommodation

Hotels
Hôtel Bastide de Lourmarin****:
+33 (0)4 90 07 00 70.
Le Mas de Guilles***: +33 (0)4 90 68 30 55.
Auberge des Hautes Prairies:
+33 (0)4 90 68 02 89.
Le Moulin: +33 (0)4 90 68 06 69.
Le Paradou: +33 (0)4 90 68 04 05.

Guesthouses
La Cordière***: +33 (0)4 90 68 03 32.
La Luberonne**: +33 (0)4 90 08 58 63.
1784 Domaine de Lourmarin:
+33 (0)6 88 37 39 66.
Ancienne Maison des Gardes:
+33 (0)4 90 07 53 16.
La Bastide aux Oiseaux:
+ 33 (0)4 90 08 51 67.
La Bohème: +33 (0)6 49 86 00 95.
La Chambre d'Hôte: +33 (0)6 07 18 97 92.
Côté Lourmarin: +33 (0)6 09 16 91 80.
Le Galinier de Lourmarin:
+ 33 (0)4 90 08 92 46.
Maison Collongue: +33 (0)4 90 77 44 69.
La Maison de la Place: +33 (0)6 79 72 12 26.
Les Oliviers: +33 (0)4 90 68 37 30.
La Villa Saint-Louis: +33 (0)4 90 68 39 18.

Gîtes, walkers' lodges, and vacation rentals
Further information: +33 (0)4 90 68 10 77
www.luberoncoeurdeprovence.com

Campsites
Les Hautes Prairies***: +33 (0)4 90 68 02 89.

🍴 Eating Out

Restaurants
L'Auberge du Père Panse:
+33 (0)4 90 68 27 97.
Le Bamboo Thaï : +33 (0)4 90 68 04 05.
Le Bouchon : +33 (0)4 90 68 17 29.
Le Café de la Fontaine:
+33 (0)4 90 68 36 96.

Le Café Gaby: +33 (0)4 90 68 38 42.
Le Café de l'Ormeau: +33 (0)4 90 68 02 11.
Le Club: +33 (0)4 90 77 89 98.
Le Comptoir, wine bistro:
+33 (0)4 90 08 49 13.
L'Entre 2, pizzeria: +33 (0)4 90 07 30 20.
L'Insolite, brasserie: +33 (0)4 90 68 02 03.
La Louche à Beurre, crêperie:
+33 (0)4 90 68 00 33.
Maison Reynaud: +33 (0)4 90 09 77 18.
Le Mas de Guilles: +33 (0)4 90 68 30 55.
Le Moulin: +33 (0)4 90 68 06 69.
Le Numéro Neuf: +33 (0)4 90 79 00 46.
L'Oustalet: +33 (0)4 90 68 07 33.
Le Pan Garni, pizzeria:
+33 (0)4 90 68 84 43.
Pizzeria Nonni: +33 (0)4 90 68 23 33.
La Récréation: +33 (0)4 90 68 23 73.
La Réserve: +33 (0)4 90 77 83 53.

Tea rooms
La Calade: +33 (0)4 90 68 84 43.
Helene Lunch and Cakes:
+33 (0)6 79 42 32 18.
La Luce d'Angeuse: +33 (0)4 90 68 89 45.
La Maison Café: +33 (0)4 86 78 48 16.

🍽 Local Specialties

Food and Drink
Herbs • Olive oil and regional produce • AOC Côtes du Luberon wines.

Art and Crafts
Jewelry maker • Fashion designers • Smith • Art galleries • Household linen • Potters • Sculpture • Tools in Damask steel.

2️⃣ Events

Markets: Fridays 8 a.m.–1 p.m., Place Henri-Barthélemy and Avenue Philippe-de-Girard; farmers' market with street food, 5–7 p.m., March–April and November–December, and 5–8.30 p.m., May–October.
April: Renaissance festival at the castle.
May–September: music festival at the castle, lectures, shows.
June: Festival Yeah (pop/rock/electro).
July–August: "Rencontres Méditerranéennes Albert Camus," literary festival; craft fairs; artists' markets.
August: "Salon du Livre Ancien," antiquarian book fair.

🦋 Outdoor Activities

Mini-golf • Walks around Lourmarin: PR and GR routes • "Le Luberon à vélo" cycle route.

🌿 Further Afield

• *Ansouis (6 miles/9.5 km), see pp. 86–87.
• Fort de Buoux (6 miles/9.5 km).
• Durance valley; Cavaillon (6–21 miles/9.5–34 km).
• Lourmarin valley; Forêt de Cèdres, forest; Apt (7–11 miles/11.5–18 km).
• *Ménerbes (14 miles/23 km), see p. 112.
• *Roussillon (14 miles/23 km), see pp. 126–27.
• *Gordes (18 miles/29 km), see pp. 102–3.
• Aix-en-Provence (21 miles/34 km).
• *Venasque (28 miles/45 km), see pp. 147–48.

Lussan

A medieval epic in the backlands of Uzès

Gard (30) • Population: 502 • Altitude: 978 ft. (298 m)

Set on a rocky plateau high above the *garrigue* scrubland, the walls of Lussan bear traces of a rich medieval history.

With its near-circular silhouette surrounded by ramparts, a panoramic view over the Cévennes and Mont Ventoux, and stone façades bleached by the Midi sunshine, Lussan is the archetypal medieval village of the Languedoc region. Only a few remains are left of the earlier castle, founded in the 12th century by the lords of the village, but its 15th-century counterpart stands almost completely intact in the heart of the village. Proudly showcasing its four round towers, including one belfry tower, the castle boasts a magnificent painted ceiling and is today home to the town hall. Façades topped with distinctive *génoise* tiles line the narrow streets that tell the tale of the once-turbulent relations between Catholics and Protestants. Two mills bear witness to the village's role in the more recent regional history of silk production. It is also worth setting out from the village to discover the impressive Conclures—a set of immense gorges carved out by the Aiguillon river, a tributary of the Cèze, that make for a novel walk in the summer when the water has run dry. Along the way, the menhir known as the "Planted Stone" provides evidence of human presence dating back to prehistoric times.

By road: Expressway A7, exit 19–Bollène (27 miles/43 km), N86 (7½ miles/12 km); expressway A9, exit 25–Alès (36 miles/58 km), N106 (22 miles/35 km). **By train:** Alès station (18 miles/29 km); Avignon TGV station (37 miles/60 km). **By air:** Avignon-Caumont airport (42 miles/67 km); Montpellier-Méditerranée airport (68 miles/110 km).

ⓘ **Tourist information:**
+33 (0)4 66 74 55 27 / www.mairie-lussan.fr

👁 Highlights
• **Castle (town hall):** 17th-century listed painted ceiling. Visits during town hall opening hours: www.mairie-lussan.fr.
• **Jardin des Buis:** Garden dedicated to well-being; a Mediterranean interpretation of *niwaki*, the Japanese art of tree-sculpting: +33 (0)4 66 72 88 93 / buisdelussan.free.fr
• **Forge:** Restored former forge. Artists' studio and exhibition space, dedicated to the arts. Open all year round. Further information: +33 (0)4 66 74 55 27.
• **Village:** Free guided visit from June to September. Further information: www.mairie-lussan.fr.
• **The Conclures:** Gorges cut by the Aiguillon river, walks in summer; site and discovery trail.
• **L'Aiguillon d'Art:** Walking trail that climbs through the village, via a series of artworks. Further information: +33 (0)4 66 74 55 27.

🔑 Accommodation
Hotels
♥ Auberge des Marronniers:
+33 (0)4 30 67 29 46.
Guesthouses
♥ Les Buis de Lussan***:
+33 (0)4 66 72 88 93.
Le Bistrot de Lussan: +33 (0)4 34 04 86 85.

Domaine d'Aubadiac: +33 (0)4 66 72 70 70.
Les Elzears: +33 (0)4 66 57 62 51.
La Filature: +33 (0)4 66 72 97 55.
L'Occitane: +33 (0)4 66 72 94 39.
Gîtes and vacation rentals
Further information: +33 (0)4 66 74 55 27 www.mairie-lussan.fr

🍴 Eating Out
♥ L'Auberge des Marronniers:
+33 (0)4 30 67 29 46.
Le Bistrot de Lussan: +33 (0)4 34 04 86 85.
Les Buis de Lussan, tea room:
+33 (0)4 66 72 88 93.
Station du Mas Neuf, weekday lunch only:
+33 (0)9 60 07 77 06.
La Table d'Azor, farmhouse inn:
+33 (0)9 66 84 27 95.

🏛 Local Specialties
Food and Drink
Goat cheese • Sheep cheese • Truffles.
Art and Crafts
Gallery • Pottery • Wrought ironworker.

📅 Events
April: Art & Garden Festival (last Sunday).
July–August: Artists' exhibitions at the castle.
August: Farmers' market; Festival de Lussan (1st fortnight); "Lussan se Livre" literary festival (last Sunday).

🦋 Outdoor Activities
Walking: 155 miles (250 km) of marked trails, see map-guide "Garrigues et Conclures autour de Lussan" • Horse-riding.

🌿 Further Afield
• Grotte de la Salamandre, cave (7½ miles/12 km).
• Uzès (12 miles/19 km).
• Tour of the châteaux around Uzès (11–18 miles/18–29 km).
• *La Roque-sur-Cèze (12½ miles/20 km), see pp. 124–25.
• *Montclus (16 miles/25 km), see p. 115.
• Alès (19 miles/30 km).
• *Aiguèze (22 miles/36 km), see pp. 84–85.
• Vallon (23 miles/37 km).
• Grotte Chauvet, cave (25 miles/40 km).

Ménerbes

Tranquility and beauty in the Luberon

Vaucluse (84) • Population: 1,144 • Altitude: 735 ft. (224 m)

Perched on a ridge clinging to the side of the Luberon mountains, Ménerbes looks down over fields of vines and cherry trees. It has been inhabited since prehistoric times, as shown by La Pichoune dolmen (funerary monument), unique in Vaucluse. But it was during the Middle Ages and the Renaissance that the village acquired its heritage buildings, for example the abbey of Saint-Hilaire, the priory where Saint Louis (1214–1270) stopped on his return from the Crusades. Once the Protestant capital during the Wars of Religion, Ménerbes retains some very fine 16th- and 17th-century residences that survived this turbulent period. In a symphony of luminous, golden stone, these houses are dotted along the fortified rocky spine, facing the Vaucluse mountains. The citadel, reinforced after a siege to protect the town's inhabitants, strikes an imposing silhouette at one end of the village. Also noteworthy are Le Castellet, home of painter Nicolas de Staël (1914–1955); an 18th-century townhouse, owned by Picasso and bequeathed to his sometime partner, the artist and poet Dora Maar (1907–1997); and the Hôtel d'Astier de Montfaucon, a historic hospice that today houses the Maison de la Truffe et du Vin du Luberon.

By road: Expressway A7, exit 24–Avignon Sud (17 miles/27 km). **By train:** Cavaillon station (9½ miles/15.5 km); Avignon TGV station (25 miles/40 km). **By air:** Avignon-Caumont airport (19 miles/31 km); Marseille-Provence airport (43 miles/69 km).

ⓘ Tourist information—Luberon Pays d'Apt: +33 (0)4 90 72 21 80
www.luberon-apt.fr
www.menerbes.fr

👁 Highlights
• **Abbaye Saint-Hilaire** (13th century): Former Carmelite convent; chapel, cloisters, chapter house, refectory (April–November).
• **Maison de la Truffe et du Vin** (mansion of Astier de Montfaucon, 17th–18th centuries): Showcase for truffles and wines of the Luberon; wine collection, exhibitions, shop: +33 (0)4 90 72 38 37.
• **Maison Jane Eakin:** House/museum of the American painter (1919–2002), open in summer: +33 (0)4 90 72 21 80.
• **Musée du Tire-bouchon at La Citadelle:** Collection of more than 1,200 historic and modern corkscrews: +33 (0)4 90 72 41 58.
• **Chapelle Saint-Blaise** (18th century).
• **Église Saint-Luc** (16th century, recently restored).
• **La Pitchoune dolmen** (funerary site).

🗝 Accommodation
Hotel
La Bastide de Marie: +33 (0)4 90 72 30 20.
Guesthouses
La Bastide de Soubeyras: +33 (0)4 90 72 94 14.
La Bastide du Tinal: +33 (0)4 90 72 18 07.
Le Jardin des Cigales: +33 (0)4 90 04 87 18.
Mas du Magnolia: +33 (0)4 90 72 48 00.
Nulle Part Ailleurs: +33 (0)6 72 22 81 03.
Les Peirelles: +33 (0)4 90 72 23 42.
Le Rayon de Soleil: +33 (0)4 90 72 25 61.

Gîtes and holiday rentals
Further information: +33 (0)4 90 72 21 80/
www.tourisme-en-luberon.com

🍽 Eating Out
Le 5 [cinq]: +33 (0)4 90 72 31 84.
La Bastide de Marie: +33 (0)4 90 72 30 20.
Le Café du Progrès, country fare: +33 (0)4 90 72 22 09.
Café Véranda: +33 (0)4 90 72 33 33.
Du Côté de Chez Charles: +33 (0)4 86 69 63 51.
Le Galoubet: +33 (0)4 90 72 36 08.
Maison de la Truffe et du Vin, wine bar and truffle restaurant: +33 (0)4 90 72 38 37.
Les Saveurs Gourmandes: +33 (0)4 32 50 20 53.
La Table de Régis, communal dining: +33 (0)4 90 72 43 20.

🏛 Local Specialties
Food and Drink
Fruit and vegetables • Luberon truffles • AOC Côtes du Luberon wines.
Art and Crafts
Gifts • Fashion • Painters • Potter • Art photographer • Ironworker.

🗓 Events
Market: April–October, village market.
July: Fête des Vignerons (winegrowers' festival), and "OEno-vidéo" (movies and wine).

July–August: Les Musicales du Luberon; La Strada (open-air cinema).
August: Fête de Saint-Louis (3rd weekend).
October: Outdoor rummage sale (1st Sunday).
December: Christmas market; truffle market (last weekend).

🦋 Outdoor Activities
Walking: 10 marked trails • Cycling: "Autour du Luberon à Vélo," Luberon by bike (regional nature park) • Mountain-biking.

🦋 Further Afield
• *Gordes (7 miles/11.5 km), see pp. 102–3.
• Cavaillon; Apt; Avignon (10–25 miles/16–40 km).
• Fontaine-de-Vaucluse (10 miles/16 km).
• *Roussillon (10 miles/16 km), see pp. 126–27.
• *Lourmarin (15 miles/24 km), see pp. 109–110.
• *Venasque (15 miles/24 km), see pp. 147–48.
• *Ansouis (21 miles/34 km), see pp. 86–87.

Mirmande

Hilltop orchard in the Rhône valley

Drôme (26) • Population: 504 • Altitude: 640 ft. (195 m)

Mirmande clambers up the hill to the Église Sainte-Foy, from where there are far-reaching views of the Rhône valley and the Vivarais mountains. The high façades of Mirmande scale the north face of the Marsanne massif, emerging from the ancient ramparts and overlapping each other to seek protection from the Mistral. Dominating the Tessonne valley, where thousands of fruit trees bloom in spring, this jewel in the Drôme valley is a maze of lanes, cobblestones, and steps, all ablaze with flowers. At the top is the delightful 13th-century Église Sainte-Foy. Mirmande stopped breeding silkworms at the end of the 19th century, but several silkworm nurseries keep the memory of this industry alive. The town was given a new lease of life by growing fruit, and thanks to the input of two individuals: the cubist painter and writer André Lhote (1885–1962), who created his summer school here, and the geologist Haroun Tazieff (mayor 1979–89). The old houses have been beautifully restored; many have been brought back to life by the talent and imaginative spark of local artists and craftsmen.

By road: Expressway A7, exit 16–Loriol (5 miles/8 km). **By train:** Loriol-sur-Drôme station (5½ miles/9 km); Livron-sur-Drôme station (8 miles/13 km); Montélimar TGV station (12 miles/19 km); Valence TGV station (32 miles/51 km). **By air:** Lyon-Saint-Exupéry airport (96 miles/154 km).

ⓘ Tourist information—Val de Drôme: +33 (0)4 75 63 10 88
Town hall: +33 (0)4 75 63 03 90
https://valleedeladrome-tourisme.com

👁 Highlights
• **Église Sainte-Foy** (12th century): Exhibitions and concerts.
• **Chareyron orchard:** Open all year, self-guided visit.
• **Village:** Guided tours throughout the year for groups, booking essential. Further information: +33 (0)4 75 63 10 88.

⚒ Accommodation
Hotels
La Capitelle***: +33 (0)4 75 63 02 72.
L'Hôtel de Mirmande: +33 (0)4 75 63 13 18.
Guesthouses
Le Bruchet***: +33 (0)4 75 63 22 52.
Domaine Les Fougères***: +33 (0)4 75 63 01 66.
Le Petit Logis***: +33 (0)4 75 63 02 92.
Les Vergers de la Bouliguaire***: +33 (0)4 75 63 22 07.
La Buissière: +33 (0)4 75 63 02 51.
La Maison de Marinette: +33 (0)6 15 76 24 55.
Margot: +33 (0)4 75 63 08 05.
Le Matignier: +33 (0)6 09 45 12 52.
La Petite Véronne: +33 (0)4 75 63 15 53.
Gîtes and vacation rentals
Further information: +33 (0)4 75 63 10 88
https://valleedeladrome-tourisme.com
Campsites
La Poche**: +33 (0)4 75 63 02 88.

🍴 Eating Out
Annie's en Provence: +33 (0)6 72 23 61 45.
Atelier Café Patine: +33 (0)4 75 41 21 82.

Café Bert, local bistro, pizzeria: +33 (0)4 75 56 18 51.
♥ La Capitelle: +33 (0)4 75 63 02 72.
Chez Margot: +33 (0)4 75 63 08 05.
Crêperie La Dinette: +33 (0)4 75 41 06 76.

🧺 Local Specialties
Food and Drink
Seasonal fruit juice, fruit, and vegetables • Drôme *vins de pays*.
Art and Crafts
Jewelry designer • Painters • Potters • Silkscreen printer • Sculptors • Glassmaker • Gifts • Antiques • Dressmaker • Art galleries.

🔢 Events
March: Nature trail.
April–September: Concerts and exhibitions at the Église Sainte-Foy.
October: Plant and garden fair.
December: Torchlight walks; village Nativity scenes.

🐕 Outdoor Activities
Husky dogs and walking with dogs (summer) • Walking • Mountain-biking.

🌾 Further Afield
• Cliousclat, pottery village (1 mile/2 km).
• Crest (11 miles/18 km).
• Montélimar (11 miles/18 km).
• Dieulefit (19 miles/31 km).
• Forêt de Saoû (20 miles/32 km).
• *Le Poët-Laval (21 miles/34 km), see p. 122.
• Gervanne valley (22 miles/35 km).
• Grignan (25 miles/40 km).
• *La Garde-Adhémar (26 miles/42 km), see p. 98.

Montbrun-les-Bains

Thermal treatments at the gateway to Provence

Drôme (26) • Population: 430 • Altitude: 1,969 ft. (600 m)

At Montbrun, sandwiched between the Lure and Ventoux mountains, the region of Drôme takes on Provençal features: it is adorned with lavender, *garrigue* scrubland, and vines. Tiered on the steep sides of a hill, the high façades of Montbrun are pierced with windows like arrow slits. They stand as the last line of defense protecting the imposing remains of an historic medieval castle. Rebuilt during the Renaissance, the castle was looted during the French Revolution. From the Place de l'Horloge and its belfry as far as the Sainte-Marie gate, narrow cobblestone alleyways lead from fountain to fountain, right to the 12th-century church. This houses a splendid Baroque altar and several paintings, including *Coronation of the Virgin* by Pierre Parrocel. At the foot of the village, thermal baths in a modern building benefit from a spring that the Romans used: the waters help respiratory and rheumatic ailments, and improve fitness.

By road: Expressway A7, exit 19–Bollène (46 miles/74 km); expressway A51, exit 22–Vallée du Jabron (32 miles/52 km). **By train:** Carpentras station (33 miles/53 km); Orange TGV station (44 miles/71 km). **By air:** Avignon-Caumont airport (52 miles/84 km).

ⓘ Tourist information:
+33 (0)4 75 28 82 49
www.montbrunlesbainsofficedutourisme.fr

👁 Highlights
• **Church** (12th century): Baroque building, painting by Pierre Parrocel (key at town hall).
• **Village:** Further information:
+33 (0)4 75 28 82 49.

🗝 Accommodation
Hotels
Hôtel des Voyageurs*: +33 (0)4 75 28 81 10.
Aparthotels
Le Château des Gipières***:
+33 (0)4 75 28 87 33 or +33 (0)4 85 88 02 37.
Le Hameau des Sources:
+33 (0)4 75 26 96 88.
Guesthouses
L'Abbaye**: +33 (0)4 75 28 83 12.
Le Bellevue: +33 (0)4 75 28 84 92 .
Le Deffend de Redon: +33 (0)4 75 28 68 19.
La Ferme du Vallon: +33 (0)4 75 27 43 29.
La Maison de Marguerite:
+33 (0)4 75 28 41 23.
Gîtes, walkers' lodges, and vacation rentals
Further information: +33 (0)4 75 28 82 49.
Vacation villages
Léo Lagrange: +33 (0)4 75 28 89 00.
VVF: +33 (0)4 75 28 82 35.
Campsites
Le Pré des Arbres: +33 (0)4 75 28 85 41.

🍴 Eating Out
L'Ô Berge de l'Anary: +33 (0)4 75 28 88 14.
L'Ô des Sources: +33 (0)4 75 27 11 09.
La Tentation, pizzeria:
+33 (0)4 75 28 87 26.
Les Voyageurs: +33 (0)4 75 28 81 10.

🧺 Local Specialties
Food and Drink
Goat cheese • Honey, herbs, and spices • Einkorn wheat • Organic produce.
Art and Crafts
Potter • Perfumes and herbs.

📅 Events
Market: Saturday mornings, Place de la Mairie.
April: Cheese and craft market (1st Sunday).
September: Journée Bien-être au Naturel (plant and wellbeing fair); local saint's day and fireworks, Saturday evening (2nd weekend).

🍃 Outdoor Activities
Canyoning and climbing • Via Ferrata • Horse-riding • Walking: Route GR 9 and 10 marked trails • Thermal baths and convalescence (mid-March–end November).

🌿 Further Afield
• Sault (7½ miles/12 km).
• Buis-les-Baronnies (16 miles/26 km).
• Nyons (19 miles/31 km).
• Toulourenc valley; Vaison-la-Romaine (20 miles/32 km).
• Mont Ventoux (24 miles/39 km).

Montclus

Clothed in vineyards and lavender

Gard (30) • Population: 159 • Altitude: 295 ft. (90 m)

Sitting at a bend in the Cèze river, Monclus exudes all the charm of a Languedoc village.

Inhabited since prehistoric times, the site attracted fishing tribes to settle before it became Castrum Montecluso in the Middle Ages, earning its name from its hilltop position at the foot of a mountain. In the 13th century both the abbey of Mons Serratus and an imposing fortified castle were built here. A few ruins of the old troglodyte Benedictine monastery remain, used as a chapel by the Knights Templar, as well as a vast room hewn out of the rock, while the massive square tower of the castle still casts its long shadow over the pink-tiled roofs. From the Place de l'Église, narrow alleys, steps, and covered passageways punctuate the village. As you wander, you catch occasional glimpses, beyond the bright stone façades of lovingly restored residences, of lush green gardens tumbling down to the Cèze.

By road: Expressway A7, exit 19–Bollène (21 miles/34 km); expressway A9, exit 23–Remoulins (32 miles/51 km); N86 (14 miles/23 km). **By train:** Bollène-La Croisière station (18 miles/29 km); Avignon TGV station (37 miles/60 km). **By air:** Avignon-Caumont airport (40 miles/64 km); Nîmes-Arles-Camargues airport (55 miles/89 km).

ⓘ Tourist information—Gard Rhodanien: +33 (0)4 66 82 30 02 www.village-montclus.fr

👁 Highlights
• **Church** (Tuesday mornings in July and August).
• **Castle** (Tuesday mornings in July and August): Main hall, spiral staircase. Guided tours by appointment only. Further information: Association des Amis du Château: +33 (0)6 14 49 48 20.
• **Village:** Guided tours in summer. Further information: +33 (0)4 66 82 30 02.

🛠 Accommodation
Hotels
La Magnanerie de Bernas***: +33 (0)4 66 82 37 36.
Guesthouses
La Micocoule: +33 (0)4 66 82 76 09.
Le Moulin: +33 (0)9 65 38 78 07.
Nid d'Abeilles: +33 (0)6 82 86 83 00 or +33 (0)6 33 09 03 84.
Aparthotels
L'Entremont: +33 (0)6 84 90 39 05.
Campsites, farm campsites, gîtes, and vacation rentals
Further information: +33 (0)4 66 82 30 02.

🍴 Eating Out
Le Mûrier: +33 (0)4 66 82 59 98.

🧺 Local Specialties
Food and Drink
Honey • Olive oil • Lavender essence.
Art and Crafts
Painter • Joiner • Ironworker.

🗓 Events
Market: Provençal market Tuesday mornings (July–August).
July and August: Cultural activities and shows.
August: Local saint's day (1st weekend).

🦋 Outdoor Activities
Swimming • Canoeing • Walking • Horse-riding • Mountain-biking.

🌿 Further Afield
• Aven d'Orgnac, sinkhole (5½ miles/9 km).
• Cornillon; Goudargues (6 miles/9.5 km).
• *Aiguèze (9½ miles/15.5 km), see pp. 84–85.
• *La Roque-sur-Cèze (9½ miles/15.5 km), see pp. 124–25.
• Valbonne: monastery (11 miles/18 km).
• Bagnols-sur-Cèze: market (15 miles/24 km).
• Pont-Saint-Esprit (15 miles/24 km).
• *Lussan (15½ miles/25 km), see p. 111.
• Gorges of the Ardèche (21 miles/34 km).

Montpeyroux
A labyrinth of sandstone

Puy-de-Dôme (63) • Population: 355 • Altitude: 1,499 ft. (457 m)

Perched on a mound to the south of Clermont-Ferrand and winding around its castle keep, the medieval village offers a panoramic view of the Auvergne volcanos.

Sitting on the ancient Régordane Way linking the Auvergne with Languedoc, Montpeyroux brings a flavor of southern France. Over the centuries, its inhabitants have lived off the proceeds of its vineyards and its arkose quarry. Arkose is a sandstone rich in crystalline feldspar; the stone lights up Montpeyroux's houses with golden glints, and was used to build the major Romanesque churches in the Auvergne—Saint-Austremoine at Issoire and Notre-Dame-du-Port at Clermond. The vineyards of Montpeyroux disappeared at the end of the 19th century during the outbreak of phylloxera, and the quarry closed in 1935, heralding the village's decline. However, restoration began in the 1960s, and Montpeyroux has recovered its vigor through growing vines again and encouraging artists and craftspeople to come. With its massive, gold-flecked winegrowers' houses and its roofs of round tiles, Montpeyroux is one of the jewels of the Allier valley.

By road: Expressway A75, exit 7–Montpeyroux (1 mile/1.5 km).
By train: Clermont-Ferrand station (19 miles/31 km).
By air: Clermont-Ferrand Auvergne airport (15 miles/24 km).

(i) Tourist information—Pays d'Issoire:
+33 (0)4 73 89 15 90
www.issoire-tourisme.com
www.montpeyroux63.com

👁 Highlights
• Ferme Pédagogique de la Moulerette: Discover farm animals:
+33 (0)4 73 96 62 68.
• Montpeyroux tower (13th century): Exhibition and audiovisual presentation:
+33 (0)4 73 96 62 68.
• Village: Guided tours for groups by appointment only: +33 (0)4 73 89 15 90. Special tours for the visually impaired (tactile models of the tower, the 12th-century gate, and the village) by appointment: +33 (0)4 73 96 62 68.

🗝 Accommodation
Guesthouses
Les Pradets****: +33 (0)4 73 96 63 40.
Le Cantou***: +33 (0)4 73 96 92 26.
L'Écharpes d'Iris***: +33 (0)6 77 19 19 77.
Le Petit Volcan***: +33 (0)4 73 89 11 41 or +33 (0)6 78 84 86 64.
Chez Helen: +33 (0)6 81 13 28 23.

🍴 Eating Out
Déco Thé, tea room:
+33 (0)4 73 96 69 67.
Le Donjon, bar/crêperie:
+33 (0)4 73 96 69 25.
L'Hortus: +33 (0)4 73 71 11 23 or +33 (0)6 64 63 27 06.
Mon Bistrot Zen—CZ:
+33 (0)4 73 96 63 46.

🛒 Local Specialties
Local produce
AOC Côtes d'Auvergne wines.
Art and Crafts
Jewelry • Ceramic artists • Art galleries • Painters • Visual artists.

📅 Events
May: Potters' sale (8th).
September: Art'n Rock, art and craft fair.

🐾 Outdoor Activities
Fishing • Walking: 1 marked trail, "L'Arkose" (5½ or 7½ miles/9 or 12 km) • Mountain-biking.

🌿 Further Afield
• Issoire (9½ miles/15.5 km).
• Clermont-Ferrand (12 miles/19 km).
• Saint-Nectaire; Besse-en-Chandesse; Massif de Sancy (12–25 miles/19–40 km).
• *Usson (15 miles/24 km), see p. 146.
• La Chaîne des Puys, series of volcanic domes; Vulcania, theme park (31 miles/50 km).

📖 Did you know?
As an 80th birthday present for her husband, Pablo, Jacqueline Picasso bought a house in Montpeyroux. Restored, then later sold, this house still stands in the village.

Moustiers-Sainte-Marie

The star of Verdon

Alpes-de-Haute-Provence (04) • Population: 740 • Altitude: 2,100 ft. (640 m)

Moustiers sits at the entrance to the Grand Canyon du Verdon, protected by a golden star suspended on a chain high above the village between two rocky cliffs.

Moustiers owes its existence to a body of water, and its fame to an Italian monk. The water is the Adou river: it made medieval Moustiers a village of stationers, potters, and drapers. In the 17th century, a monk from Faenza brought the secret of enameling (tin-glazed earthenware) here, and Moustiers became the capital of "the most beautiful and the finest faience in the kingdom." Although the faience industry disappeared in the 19th century, it has been revitalized in recent years, and now over a dozen studios marry tradition with innovation. The Adou river tumbles through the village and is spanned by little stone bridges. On both sides, the golden houses topped with Romanesque tiles huddle round small courtyards and line alleys linked by steps and vaulted passageways. At the heart of the village, the church has been altered several times and contains a pre-Roman vault, a nave dating to the 14th and 16th centuries, and a square Lombard tower. A flight of 262 steps links the village with the chapel of Notre-Dame-de-Beauvoir, which blends charming Gothic and Romanesque architecture.

By road: Expressway A51, exit 18–Manosque (34 miles/55 km); expressway A8, exit 36–Draguignan (47 miles/76 km). **By coach:** LER No. 27 from Aix-en-Provence bus station (58 miles/93 km; Monday and Saturday April 1–June 30, and daily July–August). **By train:** Digne-les-Bains station (34 miles/55 km); Manosque station (35 miles/56 km). **By air:** Marseille-Provence airport (71 miles/114 km).

ⓘ Tourist information:
+33 (0)4 92 74 67 84
www.moustiers.eu

👁 Highlights

• Chapelle Notre-Dame-de-Beauvoir (12th and 16th centuries).
• **Parish church** (12th and 14th centuries).
• **Musée de la Faïence:** History of faience ceramics, 17th century to today, a collection of over 400 pieces; temporary exhibitions: +33 (0)4 92 74 61 64.
• **Village:** Guided tours for individuals, Tuesdays 10 a.m. and Thursdays 5 p.m. July–August; groups all year by appointment: +33 (0)4 92 74 67 84.

🔑 Accommodation

Hotels
La Bastide de Moustiers****:
+33 (0)4 92 70 47 47.
La Bastide du Paradou***:
+33 (0)4 88 04 72 01.
♥ Le Colombier***: +33 (0)4 92 74 66 02.
La Ferme Rose***: +33 (0)4 92 75 75 75.
Les Restanques***: +33 (0)4 92 74 93 93.
La Bonne Auberge**: +33 (0)4 92 74 66 18.
Le Clos des Iris**: +33 (0)4 92 74 63 46.
Le Relais**: +33 (0)4 92 74 66 10.
Le Belvédère: +33 (0)4 92 74 66 04.

Guesthouses
Angouire Bn'B***: +33 (0)6 08 48 71 87.
Ferme du Petit Segries***:
+33 (0)4 92 74 68 83.
Le Mas du Loup***: +33 (0)4 92 74 65 61.
Maison de Melen: +33 (0)4 92 74 44 93.
Other guesthouses, gîtes, walkers' lodges, vacation rentals, and campsites
Further information: +33 (0)4 92 74 67 84
www.moustiers.eu

🍴 Eating Out

Au Coin Gourmand: +33 (0)6 81 25 66 66.
La Bastide de Moustiers:
+33 (0)4 92 70 47 47.
Le Belvédère: +33 (0)4 92 74 66 04.
La Bonne Auberge: +33 (0)4 92 74 60 40.
La Bouscatière: +33 (0)4 92 74 67 67.
La Cantine: +33 (0)4 92 77 46 64.
La Cascade: +33 (0)4 92 74 66 06.
Chez Benoit, brasserie: +33 (0)4 92 77 45 07.
Clérissy, crêperie/pizzeria:
+33 (0)4 92 77 29 30.
Côté Jardin: +33 (0)4 92 74 68 91.
Le Da Vinci: +33 (0)4 92 77 24 69.
L'Étoile de Mer: +33 (0)4 92 74 62 24.
Ferme Sainte-Cécile: +33 (0)4 92 74 64 18.
La Grignotière: +33 (0)4 92 74 69 12.
Jadis, pizzeria: +33 (0)4 92 74 63 01.
Les Magnans, brasserie:
+33 (0)4 92 74 61 20.
Le Relais: +33 (0)4 92 74 66 10.
Les Santons: +33 (0)4 92 74 66 48.
Les Tables de Cloître: +33 (0)6 31 61 72 40.
La Treille Muscate: +33 (0)4 92 74 64 31.

🧺 Local Specialties

Food and Drink
Cookies • Artisan preserves, salted produce • Olive oil • Lavender honey.
Art and Crafts
Faience workshops • Painters.

📅 Events

Markets: Fridays 8 a.m.–1 p.m, Place de l'École; Wednesdays 6–11 p.m. July–August, Place de la Mairie.
August–September: "Fête de la Diane," festival (August 31–September 8).

🦋 Outdoor Activities

Walking: Route GR 4 and 12 marked trails • White-water sports: canyoning, kayaking, pedalo • Climbing, paragliding • Mountain-biking.

🌿 Further Afield

• Lac de Sainte-Croix, lake (3 miles/5 km).
• Le Grand Canyon du Verdon; Castellane (6–28 miles/9.5–45 km).
• Riez; Valensole; Gréoux-les-Bains: spa; Manosque (9½–31 miles/15.5–50 km).

ℹ Did you know?

According to the account by Frédéric Mistral (1830–1914), the star was hung between the two cliffs over Moustiers as an expression of thanks to the Virgin Mary. It was put there on the wishes of Blacas, a crusader knight imprisoned by the Saracens; he had promised that if he returned safely to his village, he would hang a star and his chain in that spot.

Oingt
A golden nugget at the heart of vineyards

Rhône (69) • Population: 614 • Altitude: 1,804 ft. (550 m)

Overlooking the Beaujolais vineyards, Oingt is a jewel amid the *pierres dorées* (golden stones), rich in iron oxide, found in this region.

Built on a ridge overlooking the Roman roads between Saône and Loire, this former Roman *castrum* saw its heyday in the Middle Ages. It was around the year 1000 CE that the Guichard d'Oingt lords, powerful *viguiers* (judges) for the count of Le Forez, built a motte-and-bailey castle and its chapel here, and in the 12th century a keep was added. Today, the fortified Nizy Gate at the entrance to the village provides the first sign of its medieval past. Houses with yellow-ocher walls, where the play of light and shadow constantly changes, line the road leading to the old chapel, which became a parish church in 1660. Next to it are the remains of the castle's residential buildings and keep, which have now been made into a museum. From the terrace, there is an exceptional view of the Beaujolais vineyards, the Azergues valley, and the Lyonnais mountains.

By road: Expressway A6, exit 31.2–Roanne (10 miles/16 km); expressway A89, exit Saint-Romain-de-Popey (8½ miles/14 km); N7 (8½ miles/13.5 km).
By train: Villefranche-sur-Saône station (9½ miles/15.5 km); Lyon-Part-Dieu TGV station (24 miles/39 km).
By air: Lyon-Saint-Exupéry airport (41 miles/66 km).

ⓘ Tourist information—Pays des Pierres Dorées: +33 (0)4 74 60 26 16
www.tourismepierresdorees.com
www.oingt.com

👁 Highlights
• **Musée de la Tour** (12th century): Museum of the village's history, panoramic terrace with viewpoint indicator: +33 (0)6 68 39 32 43.
• **Église Saint-Matthieu** (10th century): 12th-century polychrome sculptures, Stations of the Cross, Pietà, pulpit; liturgical museum.
• **Musée de la Musique mécanique et de l'Orgue de Barbarie:** Display of old objects (collection of 60 European instruments) plus music demonstrations.
• **Musée Automobile, Viticole, et Agricole:** Vintage cars from 1927 to 1967: +33 (0)4 74 71 20 52 or +33 (0)6 07 45 75 75.
• **Maison Commune** (16th century): Exhibition of the works of regional artists (painters, sculptors, ceramicists), April–October: +33 (0)4 74 71 21 24.
• **Village:** Guided tour, booking essential: +33 (0)6 68 39 32 43.

🔑 Accommodation
Guesthouses
M. and Mme Bourbon***:
+33 (0)4 74 71 24 41 or
+33 (0)6 80 50 27 93.
Gîtes
Mme Marie-Pierre Guillard***:
+33 (0)4 74 71 20 52.
M. and Mme Lucien Guillard*:
+33 (0)4 74 71 20 49 or
+33 (0)6 87 25 62 39.
Mme Banes: +33 (0)4 78 43 03 32.

🍴 Eating Out
Chez Marguerite: +33 (0)4 74 71 20 13.
Chez Marlies: +33 (0)4 74 71 66 18.
La Clef de Voûte: +33 (0)4 74 71 29 91.
La Table du Donjon: +33 (0)4 74 21 20 24.
La Vieille Auberge: +33 (0)4 74 71 21 14.

🏛 Local Specialties
Food and Drink
Honeyberries • AOC Beaujolais wines.
Art and Crafts
Calligrapher • Ceramicist • Textile designer • Interior designer • Mosaic artist • Potter • Sculptor • Stained-glass artist • Art galleries.

📅 Events
Market: Thursday, Place de Presberg, 3 p.m.–7 p.m.
February: "Fête de l'Amour," Oingt craftsmen celebrate Valentine's Day.
July: "Rosé Nuit d'Eté," aperitif and concert (1st week).
September: Festival International d'Orgue de Barbarie et de Musique Mécanique, organ festival (1st weekend).
November: Beaujolais Nouveau festival (3rd Thursday).
December–January: Oingt en Crèches, Oingt nativity scenes (last 3 weeks of December and 1st week of January).

🦋 Outdoor Activities
Walking • Mountain-biking (marked trails).

🌿 Further Afield
• Pays des Pierres Dorées, region: golden stone villages (2½–12 miles/4–19 km).
• Villefranche-sur-Saône (8½ miles/13.5 km).
• Lyon (23 miles/37 km).

Pérouges
The cobblestones of Ain

Ain (01) • Population: 1,250 • Altitude: 919 ft. (280 m)

At the top of a hill, the medieval village of Pérouges forms a circle around its square, which is shaded by a 200-year-old lime tree.

Long coveted for its prosperity, created by its weaving industry, and for its strategic position overlooking the plain of the Ain river, the town was ruled by the province of Dauphiné, and then the region of Savoy, before becoming French at the dawn of the 17th century. Despite being besieged several times, Pérouges was saved from ruin in the early 19th century and has retained an exceptional heritage inside its ramparts, with no fewer than eighty-three listed buildings. The fortified church, with its ramparts, arrow-slits, and keystones bearing the Savoyard coat of arms, is one of its principal treasures. Surrounded by corbeled and half-timbered mansions built in the 13th century, the Place du Tilleul, shaded by its "tree of freedom," planted in 1792, reflects several centuries of history in the narrow cobblestone streets that lead off the square, with their central gutter to channel away dirty water.

By road: Expressway A42, exit 7–Pérouges (3½ miles/5.5 km). By train: Villars-les-Dombes station (13 miles/21 km); Lyon-Saint-Exupéry TGV station (21 miles/34 km). By air: Lyon-Saint-Exupéry airport (20 miles/32 km).

ⓘ Tourist information:
+33 (0)4 74 46 70 84
www.perouges.org

👁 Highlights
• **Fortified church** (15th century): Altarpiece, wooden statues.
• **Maisons des Princes:** Musée d'Art et d'Histoire du Vieux Pérouges et Hortulus, watchtower, medieval garden.
• **Village:** Guided tours for individuals and groups; dramatized evening tours in July and August; accessible tours for the visually impaired (sensory tour, large print and Braille guidebooks, audioguides). Further information: +33 (0)4 74 46 70 84.

🗝 Accommodation
Hotels
Hostellerie du Vieux Pérouges*** and ****: +33 (0)4 74 61 00 88.
La Bérangère**: +33 (0)4 74 34 77 77.
Guesthouses
Casa la Signora di Perugia***: +33 (0)4 74 61 47 03.
Chez Françoise: +33 (0)6 99 31 98 69.
Com' à la Maison: +33 (0)7 77 76 89 11.
La Ferme de Rapan: +33 (0)4 74 37 01 26.
Le Grenier à Sel: +33 (0)6 98 87 62 16.
The Resid for Calixte: +33 (0)6 72 14 95 18.

🍷 Eating Out
L'Auberge du Coq: +33 (0)4 74 61 05 47.
Hostellerie du Vieux Pérouges: +33 (0)4 74 61 00 88.

Le Ménestrel: +33 (0)4 74 61 11 43.
Le Relais de la Tour: +33 (0)4 74 61 01 03.
Les Terrasses de Pérouges: +33 (0)4 74 61 38 68.
Le Veneur Noir: +33 (0)4 74 61 07 06.

🍴 Local Specialties
Food and Drink
Chocolates • Galettes de Pérouges • Bugey wine.
Art and Crafts
Antique dealers • Ceramicist • Costumer • Papermaker.

2 Events
April–November: Exhibitions and creative workshops.
May 1: Crafts market.
May–June: Printemps Musical de Pérouges, spring music festival; plants fair.
June: Medieval festival (1st fortnight).
July: "Pérouges de Cape et d'Épée," "cape and sword" historical weekend.
August: Mechanical music festival.
October: Automnales Oenologiques (autumn wine fair).
December: Christmas market.

🦋 Outdoor Activities
Étang de l'Aubépin (lake) • Étangs des Dombes (lakes) • Walking: 4 marked trails.

🌿 Further Afield
• Villars-les-Dombes: bird sanctuary (11 miles/18 km).
• Ambérieu-en-Bugey: Château des Allymes (11 miles/18 km).
• Ambronay: abbey (13 miles/21 km).
• Lyon (22 miles/35 km).

Piana

On Corsica—the Isle of Beauty

Corse-du-Sud (2A) • Population: 439 • Altitude: 1,437 ft. (438 m)

At the entrance to the magnificent Calanque de Piana ("Calanche" in Corsican), which is listed as a UNESCO World Heritage Site, stands Piana, looking down over the Gulf of Porto.

The site was inhabited intermittently from the late Middle Ages until the early 16th century, but the founding of the current village dates back to the 1690s. Twenty years later, the village had thirty-two households, and the Chapelle Saint-Pierre-et-Saint-Paul was built on the ruins of a medieval oratory. It was decided that another, larger church should be built. Completed in 1792, it was dedicated to Sainte-Marie. Its bell tower, which was finished in the early 19th century, is a replica of the one at Portofino, on the Ligurian coast. It was on the sandy beach at Arone, near Piana, on February 6, 1943, that the first landing of arms and munitions for the Corsican Maquis (Resistance fighters) took place, delivered by the submarine *Casabianca* from Algeria.

By road: D81 and D84.
By train: Ajaccio station (42 miles/68 km).
By sea: Ajaccio harbor (42 miles/68 km).
By air: Ajaccio-Campo Dell'Oro airport (44 miles/70 km); Calvi-Sainte-Catherine airport (49 miles/79 km).

(i) Tourist information:
+33 (0)9 66 92 84 42
www.otpiana.com

🍴 Eating Out
Auberge U' Spuntinu: +33 (0)4 95 27 80 02.
Campanile: +33 (0)4 95 27 81 71.
Capo Rosso: +33 (0)4 95 27 82 40.
Casabianca, Arone: +33 (0)4 95 20 70 40.
Casa Corsa: +33 (0)4 95 24 57 93.
Le Casanova, pizzeria: +33 (0)4 95 27 84 20.
Chez Jeannette: +33 (0)4 95 27 81 73.
L'Onda, Arone: +33 (0)4 95 73 58 86.
La Plage, Arone: +33 (0)4 95 20 17 27.
Les Roches Rouges: +33 (0)4 95 27 81 81.
La Voûte: +33 (0)4 95 27 80 46.

📅 Events
Good Friday: La Granitola procession.
July: Rencontres Interconfréries, Mass and procession (last Sunday).
July and August: Exhibitions.
August 15: Festival and procession.
All year round: Exhibition of photographs by André Kertész (town hall).

👁 Highlights
• **Church** (Baroque style): Polychrome wooden door, frescoes, miniature portraits by Paul-Mathieu Novellini: +33 (0)9 66 92 84 42.
• **Chapelle Sainte-Lucie** (hamlet of Vistale): Byzantine-style frescoes, view of the Gulf of Porto. Open July and August.
• **E Calanche di Piana:** UNESCO World Heritage Site: +33 (0)9 66 92 84 42.

🔑 Accommodation
Hotels
Capo Rosso****: +33 (0)4 95 27 82 40.
Mare e Monti***: +33 (0)4 95 28 82 14.
Les Roches Rouges***: +33 (0)4 95 27 81 81.
Le Scandola***: +33 (0)4 95 27 80 07.
La Calanche: +33 (0)4 95 27 82 08.
Guesthouses
Giargalo: +33 (0)9 84 58 40 18.
San Pedru: +33 (0)9 53 75 72 94.
Gîtes and vacation rentals
Marina d'Arone: +33 (0)6 18 97 93 37.
Résidence U Casinu: +33 (0)4 95 10 78 66.
Campsites
Plage d'Arone***: +33 (0)4 95 20 64 54.

🦋 Outdoor Activities
Swimming • Walking • Mountain-biking.

🌿 Further Afield
• Calanche (2 miles/3 km).
• Scandola: nature reserve (6 miles/9.5 km, access by sea from Porto).
• Porto (7½ miles/12 km).
• Cargèse (12 miles/19 km).
• Gorges de la Spelunca: rocky trail (12 miles/19 km).
• Forêt d'Aïtone, forest (19 miles/31 km).

Le Poët-Laval

On the roads to Jerusalem

Drôme (26) • Population: 957 • Altitude: 1,007 ft. (307 m)

Surrounded by lavender and aromatic plants, this village was once a commandery.

Le Poët-Laval, bathed in Mediterranean light, emerged from a fortified commandery of the order of the Knights Hospitaller, soldier-monks watching over the roads to Jerusalem. At the summit of the village, on a steep slope of the Jabron valley, stands the massive keep of the castle, built in the 12th century. Rebuilt twice, in the 13th and 15th centuries, and topped with a dovecote, it has now been restored and hosts permanent and temporary exhibitions. Of the Romanesque Saint-Jean-des-Commandeurs chapel, situated below the castle, there remains part of the nave and the chancel, topped by a bell gable, against which the fortifications surrounding the village were built. At the southwestern corner of the ramparts, the Renaissance façade of the Salon des Commandeurs harks back to the order's heyday in the 15th century, before the village rallied to Protestantism, as witnessed by the former Protestant church, now a museum, near the Grand Portail.

By road: Expressway A7, exit 17–Montélimar (22 miles/35 km). **By train:** Montélimar station (16 miles/26 km). **By air:** Valence-Chabeuil airport (45 miles/72 km); Marseille-Provence airport (106 miles/171 km).

ⓘ Tourist information—Pays de Dieulefit-Bourdeaux: +33 (0)4 75 46 42 49
www.paysdedieulefit.eu
www.lepoetlaval.org

👁 Highlights

• **Castle** (12th, 13th, and 15th centuries): Permanent exhibition on the reconstruction of the village and temporary exhibitions open April–October: +33 (0)4 75 46 44 12.
• **Centre d'Art Yvon Morin:** Exhibitions, concerts: +33 (0)4 75 46 49 38.
• **Musée du Protestantisme Dauphinois:** Old 15th-century residence that became a church in the 17th century; history of Protestantism in Dauphiné, from the Reformation to the present day; collections of contemporary mosaics: +33 (0)4 75 46 46 33.
• **Village:** Free guided tour Wednesday mornings in July and August: +33 (0)4 75 46 42 49.

🗝 Accommodation

Hotels
Les Hospitaliers***: +33 (0)4 75 46 22 32.
Guesthouses
Le Mas des Alibeaux***:
+33 (0)4 75 46 35 59.
Ferme Saint-Hubert: +33 (0)4 75 46 48 71.
Le Mas des Vignaux: +33 (0)4 75 46 55 47.
Les Terrasses du Château:
+33 (0)4 75 50 20 30.
Gîtes, walkers' lodges, and vacation rentals
Further information: +33 (0)4 75 46 42 49
www.paysdedieulefit.eu
Campsites
Lorette**, May–September:
+33 (0)4 75 91 00 62.

🍴 Eating Out

Les Hospitaliers: +33 (0)4 75 46 22 32.
La Rose des Vents, tea room, April–October: +33 (0)4 75 00 43 28.
Tous les Matins du Monde, in Gougne: +33 (0)4 75 46 46 00.

🧺 Local Specialties

Art and Crafts
Jewelry and clothing • Artists/galleries • Potters.

② Events

July: "Jazz à Poët" festival; three-day local saint's festival in Gougne (last weekend).
August: Les Musicales de Poët-Laval, chamber music (early August).

🦋 Outdoor Activities

Walking: Route GRP "Tour du Pays de Dieulefit," route GR 965: departure point of the Sentier International des Huguenots and 2 short marked trails • Horse-riding • Mountain-biking.

🦋 Further Afield

• Dieulefit: Maison de la Céramique (2½ miles/4 km).
• La Bégude-de-Mazenc: (4½ miles/7 km).
• Comps: 12th-century church; "Ruches du Monde" (beehives of the world) exhibition (6 miles/9.5 km).
• Rochefort-en-Valdaine: 10th-century castle; 14th-century chapel (9½ miles/15.5 km).
• Marsanne (13 miles/21 km).
• Grignan; Nyons (17–22 miles/27–35 km).
• *Mirmande (21 miles/34 km), see p. 113.
• Crest (23 miles/37 km).
• *La Garde-Adhémar (24 miles/39 km), see p. 98.

Pradelles
Taking the Stevenson Trail

Haute-Loire (43) • Population: 651 • Altitude: 3,796 ft. (1157 m)

Protecting pilgrims and mule-drivers on the Régordane Way, Pradelles was—in the 11th century—the "stronghold of the high pastures."

Overlooking the Haut Allier valley, with the Margeride mountains to the west, Mont Lozère to the south, and the Tanargue range to the east, Pradelles was for a long time a stronghold surrounded by ramparts. A stopping place on the Régordane Way linking the Auvergne to the Languedoc, the village was also a crossroads for pilgrims traveling to Le Puy-en-Velay or Saint-Gilles-du-Gard; for merchants bringing in salt, oil, and wines from the south by mule; and for armies and free companies (of mercenaries) transporting weapons and ammunition. Throughout the ages, Pradelles' high façades have thus seen generations of travelers as diverse as Saint Jean-François Régis who, in the 17th century, preached the Catholic faith in lands bordering the Cévennes, which had been won over by Protestantism; the 18th-century highwayman and popular hero Louis Mandrin; and, more recently, Robert Louis Stevenson, who, with his donkey, traveled the route that now bears his name.

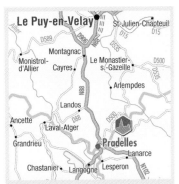

By road: Expressway A75, exit 20– Le Puy-en-Velay (60 miles/97 km), then N102-N88. **By train:** Langogne station (4½ miles/7 km); Puy-en-Velay station (21 miles/34 km). **By air:** Clermont-Ferrand-Auvergne airport (95 miles/153 km).

ⓘ Tourist information:
+33 (0)4 71 00 82 65 / www.gorges-allier.com
www.pradelles-43.com

👁 Highlights
• Musée du Cheval de Trait (draft-horse museum; in summer): Miniature village, 19th-century horse-drawn carts and carriages, multimedia show recounting the travels of Robert Louis Stevenson, stables: +33 (0)4 71 00 87 87.
• Village: Guided tour by appointment only: +33 (0)4 71 00 82 65.

🗝 Accommodation
Hotels
L'Arche**: +33 (0)4 71 00 85 20.
Gîtes, communal gîtes, walkers' lodges, and vacation rentals
Further information: +33 (0)4 71 00 82 65 or +33 (0)4 71 00 85 74.
Campsites
Le Rocher du Grelet*: +33 (0)4 71 00 85 74.
Holiday villages
La Valette: +33 (0)4 71 00 85 74.

🍴 Eating Out
L'Arche: +33 (0)4 71 00 82 98.
L'Auvergnat Gourmand: +33 (0)4 71 07 60 62.
Aux Légendes: +33 (0)4 71 00 88 00.
Brasserie du Musée: +33 (0)4 71 00 87 88.
La Ferme de Livarat: +33 (0)4 71 02 91 69.
Le Panorama: +33 (0)4 71 00 25 32.
Le Renaissance: +33 (0)4 71 02 47 03.

🧺 Local Specialties
Food and Drink
Salted meats and fish.

2️ Events
August: Procession of floral floats to celebrate local saint's day (15th).

🦋 Outdoor Activities
Hunting • Fishing • Swimming pool • Horse-riding • Donkey hire • Walking: Routes GR 70 (Stevenson Trail), GR 470 (Sources et Gorges de l'Allier), and GR 700 (Régordane Way); marked trails • Vélorail (pedal-powered railcars) • Mountain-biking.

🌿 Further Afield
• Langogne: Lac de Naussac, watersports base (4½ miles/7 km).
• Lanarce: L'Auberge Rouge, (Red Inn) (5 miles/8 km).
• Lac de Coucouron, lake (7½ miles/12 km).
• *Arlempdes (11 miles/18 km), see p. 88.
• Lac du Bouchet, lake; Devès, volcanic field (12–22 miles/19–35 km).
• Lac d'Issarlès, lake; Mont Gerbier-de-Jonc; Mont Mézenc, (16–28 miles/26–45 km).
• Cascade de la Beaume, waterfall (16 miles/26 km).
• Le Puy-en-Velay (22 miles/35 km).

La Roque-sur-Cèze

Stone, vines, and water

Gard (30) • Population: 178 • Altitude: 295 ft. (90 m)

Surrounded by *garrigue* scrubland, La Roque-sur-Cèze has established itself on a rocky slope overlooking the Cèze river and surrounding vineyards.

Past the Pont Charles-Martel with its twelve arches, along steep, winding, cobbled streets, lies an endless jumble of buildings, rooftops, and covered terraces, whose sun-weathered stone walls and Genoese tiles give them a Tuscan feel. When you reach the top of the village, after a certain amount of physical exertion, the ruins of the 12th-century castle and its Romanesque chapel are reminders of the strategic position that the site enjoyed in the Middle Ages on the Roman road leading from Nîmes to Alba. Presenting a sharp contrast with the serenity and aridity of the village are the dramatic waterfalls, rapids, and crevices of the Cascades du Sautadet, including the magnificent "giants' cauldrons"—cylindrical cavities, some of them huge, cut into the Cèze; they require great caution but offer a refreshing place to relax in the wilderness.

By road: Expressway A7, exit 19–Bollène (17 miles/28 km); expressway A9, exit 22–Roquemaure (19 miles/31 km); N86 (6 miles/9.5 km). **By train:** Bollène-La Croisière station (15 miles/24 km); Avignon TGV station (29 miles/47 km). **By air:** Avignon-Caumont airport (32 miles/51 km); Nîmes-Alès-Camargue-Cévennes airport (50 miles/80 km).

ⓘ Tourist information—
Gard Rhodanien: +33 (0)4 66 82 30 02
tourisme.gardrhodanien.media
www.laroquesurceze.fr

Le Mas du Bélier: +33 (0)4 66 82 21 39.
Pizzeria Camping Les Cascades:
+33 (0)4 66 82 08 42.
Wine and Food: +33 (0)4 66 79 08 89.

🧺 Local Specialties

Food and Drink
AOC Côtes du Rhône wines.

📅 Events

May: "En mai fais ce qu'il te plait," month-long festival of food, wine, and nature.
Mid-August: Jam fair.
Throughout the summer: Concerts and entertainment as part of "Les Arts de la Voix" festival.

🦋 Outdoor Activities

Walking and mountain-biking •
Swimming • Canoeing • Fishing.

🌿 Further Afield

- Chartreuse de Valbonne, monastery (3½ miles/5.5 km).
- Cornillon; Goudargues (5 miles/8 km).
- Pont-Saint-Esprit (6 miles/9.5 km).
- Bagnols-sur-Cèze: market (7½ miles/12 km).
- Gorges of the Cèze (9½ miles/15.5 km).
- *Montclus (9½ miles/15.5 km), see p. 115.
- *Aiguèze (11 miles/18 km), see pp. 84–85.
- *Lussan (12½ miles/20 km), see p. 111.
- Méjannes-le-Clap: Grotte de la Salamandre (14 miles/23 km).
- Barjac: market (15 miles/24 km).
- Gorges of the Ardèche; Aven d'Orgnac, sinkhole; Vallon-Pont-d'Arc (19–25 miles/31–40 km).
- Uzès (19 miles/31 km).
- Orange (22 miles/35 km).
- Pont du Gard, Roman aqueduct (25 miles/40 km).
- Avignon (27 miles/43 km).

👁 Highlights

- **Village:** Guided tour by arrangement: +33 (0)4 66 82 30 02.
- **Church (10th century):** restored in 2013, contemporary stained-glass windows.
- **Chapelle du Presbytères:** exhibitions.

🗝 Accommodation

Guesthouses
Mme Welland**: +33 (0)4 66 79 27 76.
M. and Mme Dupart: +33 (0)6 23 09 17 09.
Gîtes and vacation rentals
Further information: +33 (0)4 66 82 30 02
www.tourisme-gard-rhodanien.com
Campsites
Les Cascades****: +33 (0)4 66 82 72 97.
La Vallée Verte****: +33 (0)4 66 79 08 89.

🍽 Eating Out

L'Auberge des Cascades:
+33 (0)4 66 50 80 98.
Le Bistrot de la Roque: +33 (0)4 66 82 78 60.
Cèze Grand Rue: +33 (0)4 66 82 08 42.
Chez Piou, open-air café/restaurant (summer only): +33 (0)4 66 82 77 72.
Enfin Voilà l'Été (summer only):
+33 (0)6 68 02 89 26.

Roussillon

The flame of the Luberon

Vaucluse (84) • Population: 1348 • Altitude: 1,066 ft. (325 m)

Sparkling with colors in its verdant setting, Roussillon, north of Marseille, is a jewel in its ocher surroundings.

In Roman times, the ocher of Mont Rouge was transported to the port of Marseille, and from there it was shipped to the East. Taking over from silk farming, which was responsible for the village's rise in fortunes from the 14th century, the ocher industry developed in the late 18th century thanks to a local man, Jean-Étienne Astier, who devised the idea of extracting the pigment from the sands. Since then, Roussillon has built its reputation on this brightly colored mineral. Today, ocher presents visitors with an almost infinite palette in every narrow street and on house fronts, and can be seen, too, in its natural setting, on the ocher trail, with its spectacular sites sculpted by water, wind, and humankind. On the Place de la Mairie, a lively meeting place for both locals and visitors, the Hôtel de Ville and the houses facing it date from the 17th century.

By road: Expressway A7, exit 24–Avignon sud (23 miles/37 km); expressway A51, exit 18–Valensole (34 miles/55 km), D900 (16 miles/26 km). **By train:** Cavaillon station (19 miles/31 km); Avignon TGV station (32 miles/51 km). **By air:** Avignon-Caumont airport (25 miles/40 km); Marseille-Provence airport (54 miles/87 km).

ⓘ Tourist information:
+33 (0)4 90 05 60 25
www.luberon-apt.fr
www.roussillon-provence.fr

• **Sentier des Ocres** (ocher trail): July and August, 9 a.m.–7.30 p.m.; off-season: +33 (0)4 90 05 60 16.

🔑 Accommodation

Hotels
La Clé des Champs***:
+33 (0)4 90 05 63 22.
Le Clos de la Glycine***:
+33 (0)4 90 05 60 13.
♥ Hôtel des Ambres***:
+33 (0)4 90 05 65 46.
Les Sables d'Ocre***: +33 (0)4 90 05 55 55.
La Maison des Ocres**:
+33 (0)4 90 05 60 50.

Guesthouses
Le Clos des Cigales: +33 (0)4 90 05 73 72.
La Lavandine: +33 (0)4 90 05 63 24.
La Mauderle: +33 (0)4 90 05 61 14.
Les Passiflores: +33 (0)4 90 71 43 08.
Poterie de Pierroux: +33 (0)4 90 05 68 81.
La Villa des Roses: +33 (0)4 90 04 98 20.

Gîtes and vacation rentals
Further information: +33 (0)4 90 05 60 25
www.luberon-apt.fr

Campsites
Arc-en-Ciel***: +33 (0)4 90 05 73 96.

🍴 Eating Out

Le Bistrot: +33 (0)4 90 05 74 45.
Le Café des Couleurs:
+33 (0)4 90 05 62 11.
Le Castrum, crêperie:
+33 (0)4 90 05 62 23.
Chez Nino: +33 (0)4 90 74 29 17.
Le Comptoir des Arts: +33 (0)4 90 74 11 92.
David: +33 (0)4 90 05 60 13.
La Grappe de Raisin: +33 (0)4 90 71 38 06.

👁 Highlights

• **Conservatoire des Ocres:** Guided tour on the manufacture, geology, and heritage of ocher; workshops and courses. +33 (0)4 90 05 66 69.

L'Ocrier: +33 (0)4 90 05 79 53.
Le Piquebaure: +33 (0)4 90 05 79 65.
Le P'tit Gourmand: +33 (0)4 90 71 82 58.
La Sirmonde: +33 (0)4 90 75 70 41.
La Treille: +33 (0)4 90 05 64 47.

🧺 Local Specialties

Food and Drink
Olive oil • Fruit juices • AOC Côtes du Luberon and Côtes du Ventoux wines.

Art and Crafts
Candles • Ceramicists • Ocher-based crafts • Interior designers • Fossils and minerals • Art galleries • Artists • Sculptors.

2 Events

Market: Thursday mornings, Place du Pasquier.
June: Saint-Jean des Couleurs, Les Vieux Tracteurs (old tractors; exhibition and country fair).
July: Beckett festival (late July).
August: String quartet festival.
July and August: Outdoor film festival.
September: Le Livre en Fête, book fair.
November: Salon du Livre et de l'Illustration Jeunesse (books and illustrations for children fair, late November).

🦋 Outdoor Activities

Walking: Routes GR 6 and 97, and 4 marked trails • Hot-air balloon flights.

🌿 Further Afield

• Apt (6 miles/9.5 km)
• *Gordes (6 miles/9.5 km), see pp. 102–3.
• Luberon, region (6–12 miles/9.5–19 km).
• *Ménerbes (11 miles/18 km), see p. 112.
• *Lourmarin (14 miles/23 km), see pp. 109–10.
• *Venasque (15 miles/24 km), see pp. 147–48.
• L'Isle-sur-la-Sorgue (17 miles/27 km).
• Cavaillon (19 miles/31 km).
• *Ansouis (21 miles/34 km), see pp. 86–87.

🗡 Did you know?

Raymond d'Avignon, lord of Roussillon, having neglected his wife, Sermonde, to go off hunting, discovered she was enjoying the company of the troubadour Guillaume de Cabestan. In a jealous rage, Raymond killed his wife's lover, tore out his heart, and fed it to Sermonde, before revealing to her the nature of the dish. In despair, the lady threw herself from the cliff top. And this is why, it is said, the cliffs of Roussillon have been blood red ever since.

Saint-Antoine-l'Abbaye

Miracles in medieval Dauphiné

Isère (38) • Population: 1,039 • Altitude: 1,247 ft. (380 m)

Deep in a verdant valley surrounded by the Vercors massif, the Abbaye Saint-Antoine watches over the village that bears its name.

The history of Saint-Antoine-l'Abbaye began in the 11th century, when Geilin, a local lord, brought back from his pilgrimage to the Holy Land the relics of Saint Anthony of Egypt, who was believed to have performed many miracles. In around 1280, building started on the abbey that was to house these famous relics, which were said to have the power to cure "Saint Anthony's Fire," a poisoning of the blood that was treated by the Hospitallers (who had settled in the village after chasing out the Benedictines) in their institutions. The Wars of Religion brought this prosperous period of pilgrimages to an end. Reconstruction work undertaken in the 17th century has enabled visitors to admire the abbey—considered to be one of the most remarkable Gothic buildings in the Dauphiné region—and its rich interior. At the foot of this mighty building, the village bears living witness to the medieval and Renaissance eras: noblemen's houses built in the 15th–18th centuries from *molasse* stone and featuring mullioned windows link—via *goulets* (half-covered narrow streets)—with old shops with half-timbered façades and the medieval covered market.

By road: Expressway A49, exit 9–Saint-Marcellin (8 miles/13 km); expressway A48, exit 9–La Côte-Saint-André (26 miles/42 km).
By train: Saint-Marcellin station (8 miles/13 km); Romans station (15 miles/24 km).
By air: Grenoble-Saint-Geoirs airport (19 miles/31 km); Lyon-Saint-Exupéry airport (63 miles/101 km).

ⓘ Tourist information:
+33 (0)4 76 38 53 85
www.tourisme.pays-saint-marcellin.fr
www.saint-antoine-labbaye.fr

👁 Highlights

• **Abbey church** (12th–15th centuries): Murals, Aubusson tapestries, wood paneling, 17th-century organ: +33 (0)4 76 38 53 85.
• **Abbey treasury:** Liturgical vestments, surgical instruments, antiphonaries, 17th-century ivory Christ, one of the largest reliquaries in France: +33 (0)4 76 38 53 85.
• **Musée de Saint-Antoine-l'Abbaye** (museum of the Isère *département*): Housed in 17th- and 18th-century convent buildings; exhibitions on the Hospitallers of Saint-Antoine, therapeutic perfumes, and the history of the gardens; temporary exhibitions: +33 (0)4 76 36 40 68. www.musee-saint-antoine.fr
• **Jardin Médiéval de l'Abbaye** (medieval garden): In the Cour des Grandes Écuries, four symmetrical gardens filled with luxuriant plants, herbs, flowers, and fruit trees, together with a fountain and pools: +33 (0)4 76 36 40 68. www.musee-saint-antoine.fr

• **Stonemason's workshop:** Housed in the abbey's old infirmary; a presentation of building construction techniques in the Middle Ages, with demonstrations: +33 (0)4 76 36 44 12.
• **Village:** Self-guided discovery trail, "Le Sentier du Flâneur" (leaflet available from tourist information center); guided tours all year round for groups and April–October for individuals: +33 (0)4 76 38 53 85.

⚒ Accommodation

Hotels
Chez Camille: +33 (0)4 76 36 86 98.
Guesthouses
L'Antonin***: +33 (0)4 76 36 41 53.
Mme Philibert***: +33 (0)4 76 36 41 65.
La Grange du Haut: +33 (0)4 76 64 30 74.
Philibert Patricia: +33 (0)6 11 96 74 26.
La Vourelyne: +33 (0)4 76 36 05 91.
Treehouses
Les Cabanes de Fontfroide: +33 (0)4 76 36 46 84.

Gîtes and vacation rentals
Les Genets*** and **: +33 (0)4 76 36 43 81.
Mme Nivon**: +33 (0)4 76 40 79 40.
Le Dictambule: +33 (0)6 64 02 68 00.
La Grange du Haut: +33 (0)4 76 64 30 74.
Jean-Marc Renevier: +33 (0)4 76 64 91 65.
Les Reynauds: +33 (0)6 72 22 18 19.
Community accommodation
Communauté de l'Arche: +33 (0)4 76 36 45 97.

🍴 Eating Out
L'Auberge de l'Abbaye: +33 (0)4 76 36 42 83.
L'Auberge du Chapeau Rouge: +33 (0)4 76 36 45 29.
Le Belier Rouge: +33 (0)4 76 64 54 82.
Chez Camille: +33 (0)4 76 36 86 98.
Goûts du Safran, La Calèche: +33 (0)4 76 64 12 77.
Hostellerie du Vieux Saint-Antoine: +33 (0)4 76 36 40 51.
Mon Manège à Moi, pizzeria: +33 (0)4 76 36 40 53.
Les Tentations d'Antoine: +33 (0)4 76 36 71 77.

🛍 Local Specialties

Food and Drink
Honey, mead, hippocras, *pain d'épice* (spice cake) • Fruit wines • Teas.

Art and Crafts
Jewelry designer • Ready-to-wear clothing designer • Cabinetmaker • Potter • Bookbinder • Stonemason and sculptor in stone • Milliner • Painter and mixed-media artist • Antique-furniture restorer • Local artists' galleries and studios.

🗓 Events

Market: Local produce and crafts market, May–October, Friday 4–7 p.m., Place de la Halle.
January: Fête de la Truffe and Marché des Tentations, truffle festival (Sunday after 17th).
May: Rare flower and plant fair (3rd Sunday).
June: "Pig'halle," concerts.
Late June–late September: Sacred music festival (organ recitals Sundays at 5 p.m. in the abbey church).

July: "Textes en l'Air" festival, contemporary theater (last week); "Les Nuits Antonines" music festival (2nd week).
August: Saint-Antoine en Moyen Âge (medieval festival, early August); antiques, secondhand goods, and collectors' fair (3rd Sunday).
October: Foire à l'Ancienne et aux Potirons, local produce and pumpkin fair (4th Sunday).
December: "Noël des Tentations": Christmas fair with local produce and crafts (2nd weekend).

🦋 Outdoor Activities

Miripili, l'Île aux Pirates theme park, Étang de Chapaize • Walking and mountain-biking.

🌿 Further Afield

• La Sône: Jardin des Fontaines Pétrifiantes (exotic plants, rocks, and water; closed from mid-October to May 1); Royans-Vercors paddle steamer (7½ miles/12 km).
• Saint-Marcellin (8 miles/13 km).
• Pont-en-Royans: Musée de l'Eau, water museum; "suspended" houses (14 miles/23 km).
• Romans: Musée de la Chaussure, shoe museum; collegiate church of Saint-Barnard (14 miles/23 km).
• Parc Naturel Régional du Vercors, nature park (14 miles/23 km).
• Grotte de Choranche, cave (16 miles/26 km).
• Hauterives: Postman Cheval's Palais Idéal, naive architecture (19 miles/31 km).

Saint-Guilhem-le-Désert

Romanesque architecture and wilderness

Hérault (34) • Population: 250 • Altitude: 292 ft. (89 m)

At the bottom of a wild gorge, Saint-Guilhem surrounds its abbey, one of the finest examples of Romanesque architecture in the Languedoc.

A stopping place on the Saint James's Way, Saint-Guilhem was, in the Middles Ages, a center of Christianity, where believers, Crusaders, and pilgrims came to pray and to venerate a piece of the True Cross. Although little remains of the original abbey, founded by Saint Guilhem in the 9th century, the present church is a gem of Romanesque architecture, listed as a UNESCO World Heritage Site. The heart of the village is the delightful Place de la Liberté. There is an impressive plane tree, more than 150 years old; fountains dating from 1907; and an old 18th-century covered market with arches, making the square a magical place where people like to gather to enjoy the cool evenings on café terraces. Huddled together along the main streets, sturdy houses, with their sun-weathered façades and traditional pink barrel-tiled roofs, are adorned with double Romanesque windows, Gothic lintels, and Renaissance mullions.

By road: Expressway A75, exit 58–Gignac-Font d'Encauvi (8 miles/13 km).
By train: Montélimar TGV station (27 miles/43 km). **By air:** Montpellier-Méditerranée airport (37 miles/60 km).

ⓘ Tourist information:
+33 (0)4 67 56 41 97 or
+33 (0)4 67 57 58 83
www.saintguilhem-valleeherault.fr
www.saint-guilhem-le-desert.com

👁 Highlights

• **Abbaye de Gellone:** Abbey church of the 11th, 12th, and 15th centuries; treasury: +33 (0)4 67 57 58 83.
• **Musée Lapidaire de l'Abbaye:** Collection of Romanesque and Gothic sculpture, remains of the cloister (restored); film on the history of the abbey and its rebuilding (April–October), by appointment for groups: +33 (0)6 98 04 74 72.
• **Musée d'Antan:** History of the village and its traditional trades: +33 (0)4 67 57 77 07.
• **Village:** Daily tours for groups and by appointment: +33 (0)4 67 57 00 03.

🗝 Accommodation

Hotels
Le Guilhaume d'Orange: +33 (0)4 67 57 24 53.
La Taverne de l'Escuelle: +33 (0)4 67 57 72 05.
Gîtes and vacation rentals
Alain Duverge**: +33 (0)4 67 57 40 22.
Le Lieu Plaisant: +33 (0)4 67 58 07 61.
Lou Cap del Mund: +33 (0)4 67 71 76 67.
Lucette Diez: +33 (0)4 67 22 42 70.
La Maison des Légendes: +33 (0)6 85 39 73 70.

Walkers' lodges, group accommodation
CAF: +33 (0)6 89 77 17 59.
Gîte Saint-Elie: +33 (0)4 67 57 75 80.
Further information: +33 (0)4 67 57 70 17
www.saint-guilhem-le-desert.com

🍴 Eating Out

L'Oustal Fonzes: +33 (0)4 67 57 39 85.
Le Petit Jardin: +33 (0)4 67 57 35 18.
La Source: +33 (0)6 59 29 56 34.
Sur le Chemin: +33 (0)4 99 63 93 71.
La Table d'Aurore: +33 (0)4 67 57 24 53.
La Taverne de l'Escuelle: +33 (0)4 67 57 72 05.
Le Val de Gellone, pizzeria: +33 (0)4 67 57 33 99.
Vent de Soleil, light meals: +33 (0)4 67 57 78 85.
La Voûte Gourmande, light meals: +33 (0)4 67 57 33 65.

Crêperies and tea rooms
La Belliloise, crêperie: +33 (0)4 67 58 89 20.
Isa and Luc, tea room: +33 (0)4 67 58 83 31.
Le Logis des Pénitents, crêperie:
+33 (0)4 67 57 48 63.
Le Musée d'Antan, tea room:
+33 (0)4 67 57 77 07.

🛒 Local Specialties

Food and Drink
Olive oil and grapes • Trout and crawfish •
Wine and truffles.

Art and Crafts
Craftsmen • Painters • Potters • Sculptors.

🗓 Events

July–September: Music season and
heures d'orgues (organ recitals), theater,
exhibitions, secondhand book fair.
December: Christmas concert (abbey
church).

🦋 Outdoor Activities

Swimming • Fishing • Canoeing • Walks
for all levels • Caving.

🕊 Further Afield

• Pont du Diable, bridge; Grotte de
Clamouse, cave (2 miles/3 km).
• Saint-Jean-de-Fos: Argileum, pottery
workshop (2½ miles/4 km).
• Clermont-l'Hérault; Lac de Salagou,
lake (16 miles/26 km).

Saint-Véran

"Where hens peck at the stars"

Hautes-Alpes (05) • Population: 235 • Altitude: 6,699 ft. (2,042 m)

The highest inhabited village in Europe—hence its motto, "where hens peck at the stars"—Saint-Véran lies at the heart of the Queyras regional nature park.

As Saint-Véran has been accessible by road for little more than a century, the inhabitants had plenty of time to learn to pull together in this extreme environment (altitude of 6,699 ft./2,042 m). They battled floods, avalanches, and fires; and worked shale and larch in the Queyras to build the *fustes* and *casets* (traditional dwellings that shelter animal fodder and livestock under protruding roofs). They also smelted copper, carved wood, tapped the water from the hillsides for their fountains, and harnessed the sun's rays for their brightly colored sundials. Moreover, they devised both winter and summer tourism, which capitalizes on the great outdoors while respecting their traditions. The mission crosses, erected in tribute to missionaries who came to convert this Queyras backwater, symbolize the area's fervent religious belief and practice, and form part of its heritage.

By road: Expressway A32, exit 12–Oulx Circonvalazzione (50 miles/80 km); N94 (35 miles/56 km). **By train:** Montdauphin-Guillestre station (24 miles/39 km); Briançon station (30 miles/48 km). **By air:** Marseille-Provence airport (162 miles/261 km).

ⓘ Tourist information—Queyras: +33 (0)4 92 45 82 21 www.saint-veran-queyras.com **Les Amis de Saint-Véran** www.saintveran.com

👁 Highlights

• **Church** (17th century): Stone lions, font.
• **Old copper mine exhibition:** In the communal oven at Les Forannes.
• **Maison Traditionnelle:** Traditional house, inhabited and shared with animals until 1976; preserved (furniture, everyday objects, clothes): +33 (0)4 92 45 82 39.
• **Musée Le Soum:** The oldest house in the village (1641); discover village life and traditions in bygone days: +33 (0)4 92 45 86 42.
• **Observatory** (alt. 9,633 ft./2,936 m): Tour of the dome and its equipment; further information, Saint-Véran Culture Développement: +33 (0)6 60 31 23 33.
• **Maison du Soleil:** Complex dedicated to solar observation, interactive experience, themed visits, educational workshops, and seasonal activities; further information, Saint-Véran Culture Développement: +33 (0)4 92 45 83 91.
• **Village:** Guided tour for groups only, by reservation. Further information: +33 (0)4 92 45 82 21.

🗝 Accommodation

Hotels
L'Alta Peyra****: +33 (0)4 92 22 24 00.
Les Chalets du Villard***: +33 (0)4 92 45 82 08.
Le Grand Tétras**: +33 (0)4 92 45 82 42.
Auberge Coste Belle: +33 (0)4 92 45 82 17.
Auberge L'Estoilies: +33(0)4 92 45 82 65.
La Baïta du Loup, gîte-hotel: +33 (0)4 92 54 00 12.

Guesthouses
Cascavelier: +33 (0)4 92 45 88 31.
La Chevrette: +33 (0)4 92 45 81 42.
Jacqueline and Eric Turina: +33 (0)4 92 45 81 77.

Gîtes and vacation rentals
Further information: +33 (0)4 92 45 82 21 or +33 (0)4 92 51 04 23/ www.saintveran.com

Family vacation centers, accommodation for groups
Les Perce-Neige: +33 (0)4 92 45 82 23.

Vacation villages
Centre de montagne OVL Saint-Ouen: +33 (0)4 92 45 82 28.

Walkers' lodges
Le Chalet des Routiers: +33 (0)4 75 02 01 12.
Le Chant de l'Alpe: +33 (0)4 92 54 22 41.
Les Gabelous: +33 (0)4 92 45 81 39.
Les Perce-Neige: +33 (0)4 92 45 82 23.

Mountain refuges
Refuge de la Blanche (alt. 8,202 ft./2,500 m): +33 (0)4 92 45 80 24.

RV parks (June–September): +33 (0)4 92 45 83 91

🍴 Eating Out

Auberge L'Estoilies: +33 (0)4 92 45 82 65.
La Baïta du Loup: +33 (0)4 92 54 00 12.
Coste Belle: +33 (0)4 92 45 82 17.
Le Bouticari: +33 (0)4 92 45 89 20.
Les Chalets du Villard—La Gratinée: +33 (0)4 92 45 82 08.
Le Dardaya : +33 (0)4 92 22 24 00.
La Fougagno: +33 (0)4 92 45 86 39.
Le Grand Tétras: +33 (0)4 92 45 82 42.
La Maison d'Élisa: +33 (0)4 92 45 82 48.
La Marmotte: +33 (0)4 92 45 84 77.
Refuge de la Blanche: +33 (0)4 92 45 80 24.
Le Roc Alto: +33 (0)4 92 22 24 00.

🧺 Local Specialties

Food and Drink
Queyras honey.
Art and Crafts
Craft courses (plant collecting, lace-making, weaving, knitting) • Cutler-blacksmith • Wood-carvers.

🎬 Events

January: Cross-country skiing in the Queyras (last Sunday).
February–early March: Tasting workshops, snowshoe outings, torchlit descents.

July: Franco-Italian pilgrimage to Clausis chapel (16th); Saint Anne's day at Raux (Sunday nearest 26th).

July–August: Sale of bread baked at the communal oven; "Astro-Raquette" (snowshoeing and star-gazing); guided tours in the steps of the miners.

August: "Fête des Traditions" festival.

🦋 Outdoor Activities

Climbing • Forest adventure course • Fishing • Walking • Pack-donkey or packhorse rides • Skiing: Alpine, cross-country, ski touring, snowshoeing • Mountain-biking.

🌿 Further Afield

• Château-Queyras (8½ miles/13.5 km).
• Aiguilles; Abriès (10–13miles/16–21 km).
• Col d'Agnel and the Italian border (12 miles/19 km).
• Guillestre; Mont-Dauphin (24 miles/ 39 km).
• Col de l'Izoard (30 miles/48 km).
• Briançon (30 miles/48 km).

⚑ Did you know?

In the old days, using wood as a fuel for heating caused many fires. To prevent blazes from ripping through the village, the inhabitants carved up their settlement into five distinct areas, each separated from the others by open spaces in which building was prohibited. This created small neighborhoods that still exist today. Each neighborhood had its own bread oven and fountain—made up of a circular part, used as an animal drinking trough, and a rectangular part acting as a laundry area. Each neighborhood also worshiped separately in its own chapel and with its own mission cross.

Sainte-Agnès

A balcony over the Mediterranean

Alpes-Maritimes (06) • Population: 1,191 • Altitude: 2,559 ft. (780 m)

Perched nearly 2,600 ft. (800 m) in the air, the highest coastal village in Europe has an amazing panorama over the Mediterranean from Cap-Martin to the Italian Riviera.

Sainte-Agnès is a strategic site that has been fought over for centuries. It was initially a fortified Roman camp, then the site of a defensive castle built in the 12th century by the House of Savoie, and in 1932–38 its fort was dug out of the rock to become the most southerly post on the Maginot Line, built to defend the Franco-Italian border. Today the village is valued for its unique location away from the crowds and concrete of the coast. The village has an authentic feel, with its crisscrossing alleyways (some of which recall the tales of Saracen inhabitants), old cobblestones, secret vaults, and higgledy-piggledy houses. The lofty ruins of the fortified castle now contain a medieval garden designed on the theme of courtly love. From its highest point, a 360-degree panorama gives the viewer a superb contrast between the blue Mediterranean and, in winter, the snowy peaks of the Mercantour National Park.

By road: Expressway A8, exit 59– Menton (6 miles/9.5 km). **By train:** Menton station (6 miles/9.5 km). **By air:** Nice-Côte-d'Azur airport (26 miles/42 km).

(i) Town hall: +33 (0)4 93 35 84 58
www.sainteagnes.fr

👁 Highlights

• **Espace Culture et Traditions:** Local heritage museum, archeology, painting, and sculpture: +33 (0)4 93 28 35 31.
• **Maginot Line fort:** 6,500 sq. ft. (2,000 sq. m) of galleries, multimedia exhibition: +33 (0)6 88 75 70 89.
• **Église Notre-Dame-des-Neiges** (16th century): Gilded wooden altar, 16th-century stone font, 17th-century statue of Saint Agnes, 16th- and 18th-century paintings, chandeliers from Monaco Cathedral.
• **Castle site:** Tour of the ruins and medieval garden.
• **Village:** Guided tour by Menton tourist information center, Tuesday afternoons; audioguides.

🔑 Accommodation

Hotels
Le Saint-Yves: +33 (0)4 93 35 91 45.
Private gîtes
+33 (0)4 93 35 84 58 / www.sainteagnes.fr

🍴 Eating Out

Le Logis Sarrasin: +33 (0)4 93 35 86 89.
Le Righi: +33 (0)4 92 10 90 88.
Le Saint-Yves: +33 (0)4 93 35 91 45.

🧺 Local Specialties

Art and Crafts
Leather and cloth crafts • Painter • Master glassblower.

2️⃣ Events

January 21: Mass and procession for Saint Agnes's day.
May 1: Walking rally.
July: Fête de la Lavande et du Temps Passé, lavender and history festival (2nd fortnight).
October: Fête des Champignons et de l'Automne, mushroom and autumn produce festival (mid-October); "Cinéma sous les Étoiles" festival, outdoor cinema.

🌾 Outdoor Activities

Treasure hunt • Mountain-biking • Horse-riding • Walking.

🌿 Further Afield

• Hilltop villages of Castellar, Gorbio, Peille (3–12 miles/5–19 km).
• Menton (7 miles/11.5 km).
• Monaco (12 miles/19 km).
• *Coaraze (24 miles/39 km), see p. 97.
• Nice (27 miles/43 km).

❗ Did you know?

A princess named Agnès was once caught in a torrential storm. She prayed to her namesake, Saint Agnes, who showed her a grotto in which to shelter. In gratitude, she decided to build a sanctuary dedicated to the saint near this grotto, around which the present village grew up. There is now a military outwork on the site of this chapel, and an oratory next to the fort. Saint Agnes's day is celebrated on January 21.

Sainte-Croix-en-Jarez

A charterhouse reborn as a village

Loire (42) • Population: 450 • Altitude: 1,378 ft. (420 m)

Sainte-Croix-en-Jarez has taken root in a former Carthusian monastery, with the Pilat regional nature reserve as a backdrop. A school, town hall, and dwellings occupy the former monks' cells, which were abandoned during the French Revolution. The monastic church, with decorative paneling and Gothic stalls, contains a reproduction of Andrea Mantegna's famous *Martyrdom of Saint Sebastian* and polychrome wood statues. In the choir of the medieval church are early 14th-century wall paintings. The charterhouse kitchen still has its enormous fireplace. A restored and furnished cell, the iron grille forged in 1692; the clock tower, its fortified façade altered in the 17th century; the cloisters; and the grand staircase all similarly remain intact from the old monastery. In the hamlet of Jurieu, the village also boasts a 12th-century chapel and the megalithic site of Roches de Marlin.

By road: Expressway A47, exit 11– Rive-de-Gier (7½ miles/12 km). **By train:** Rive-de-Gier station (5 miles/8 km); Saint-Etienne station (19 miles/31 km). **By air:** Saint-Étienne-Bouthéon airport (29 miles/47 km); Lyon-Saint-Exupéry airport (39 miles/63 km).

(i) Tourist Information: +33 (0)4 77 20 20 81
www.chartreuse-saintecroixenjarez.com

👁 Highlights
• **Former charterhouse** (13th century): Bakery, Brothers' court, cloisters, medieval church with 14th-century wall paintings, parish church, Fathers' court, kitchen, cells; hanging garden, covered paths. Standard and themed guided visits for groups and individuals. Further information: +33 (0)4 77 20 20 81

⚔ Accommodation
Hotels
Le Prieuré: +33 (0)4 77 20 20 09.
Guesthouses
Le Clos de Jeanne***: +33 (0)4 77 54 82 28.
La Rose des Vents: +33 (0)4 77 20 29 72 or +33 (0)4 77 20 22 58.
Gîtes
Le Chant du Ruisseau***:
+33 (0)4 77 20 20 86.
L'Elixir***: +33 (0)4 77 20 20 81.

🍴 Eating Out
Le Cartusien: +33 (0)4 77 20 29 72.
Le Prieuré: +33 (0)4 77 20 20 09.

🛍 Local Specialties
Food and Drink
Charcuterie • Cheese • Honey.
Art and Crafts
Basketry • Local crafts (shop and information point).

📅 Events
March–November: Art exhibitions.
Pentecost: Traditional fair.
June: "Festin Musical," music festival.
July–September: Medieval supper and tour by lamplight.
September: "Les Musicales," classical music festival.
September–March: Family activities (giant Cluedo, "Festinmoyenajeux", treasure hunts, tours in costume); .
December: Provençal crib and Christmas activities.

🐦 Outdoor Activities
Fishing • Walking: 3 marked trails • Mountain-biking.

🌿 Further Afield
• Monts du Pilat (14 miles/23 km).
• Saint-Étienne (19 miles/31 km).
• Lyon (29 miles/47 km).

Sainte-Énimie
Amid the wonders of the Tarn Gorges

Lozère (48) • Population: 548 • Altitude: 1,591 ft. (485 m)

The Merovingian princess Énimie gave her name to the village: legend has it that she was cured of leprosy in spring waters here.

The village is encircled by the cliffs of the limestone plateaus of Sauveterre and Méjean, through which the Tarn has gouged its gorges. Sainte-Énimie retains its distinctive steep alleyways, massive limestone residences that evoke its prosperous past, and half-timbered workshops and houses. The Romanesque church of Notre-Dame-du-Gourg contains some splendid statues from the 12th and 15th centuries. At the top of the village, the chapel of Sainte-Madeleine and a chapter house are all that remain of a Benedictine monastery. At its feet flows the Burle river, which is supposed to have healing properties, and several paths lead to the cell to which Saint Énimie retreated. From here, there is a superb view of the village and the spectacular scenery of the Tarn, Jonte, and Causses gorges, all listed as UNESCO World Heritage Sites.

By road: Expressway A75, exit 40–La Canourgue (17 miles/28 km); N88 (12 miles/19 km); N106 (2½ miles/4 km).
By train: Mende station (17 miles/27 km).
By air: Rodez-Marcillac airport (65 miles/105 km); Nîmes-Arles-Camargue airport (94 miles/151 km).

ⓘ Tourist information—Cévennes-Gorges du Tarn: +33 (0)4 66 45 01 14
www.cevennes-gorges-du-tarn.com

👁 Highlights
• **Église Notre-Dame-du-Gourg** (13th–14th centuries): Statues, notable artifacts.
• **Refectory known as the "salle capitulaire"** (12th century).
• **Chapelle Sainte-Madeleine** (13th century).
• **Hermit's hut:** Semi-troglodyte hut over the natural grotto (45 minutes' walk from the village); viewpoint.
• **Village:** Self-guided tour, heritage discovery trail available from tourist information center; guided evening tour at 9:30 p.m., Mondays and Wednesdays in July–August; tour with forge demonstration Thursdays in July–August: +33 (0)4 66 45 01 14.

🗝 Accommodation
Hotels
Auberge du Moulin***: +33 (0)4 66 48 53 08.
Auberge de la Cascade**: +33 (0)4 66 48 52 82.
Le Chante-Perdrix**: +33 (0)4 66 48 55 00.
Bleu Nuit: +33 (0)4 66 48 50 01.
Burlatis: +33 (0)4 66 48 52 30.
Guesthouses, gîtes, walkers' lodges, and vacation rentals
Further information: +33 (0)4 66 45 01 14
www.gorgesdutarn.net

Campsites
Couderc***: +33 (0)4 66 48 50 53.
Les Fayards***: +33 (0)4 66 48 57 36.
Les Gorges du Tarn*: +33 (0)4 66 48 59 38.
Le Site: +33 (0)4 66 48 58 08.

🍽 Eating Out
Auberge de la Cascade:
+33 (0)4 66 48 52 82.
Auberge du Moulin: +33 (0)4 66 48 53 08.
Au Vieux Moulin, pizzeria:
+33 (0)4 66 48 58 04.
Le Bel Été: +33 (0)4 66 48 18 24.
La Calabrèse, pizzeria: +33 (0)4 66 31 67 90.
La Cardabelle: +33 (0)4 66 48 50 49.
Les Deux Sources, pizzeria:
+33 (0)4 66 48 53 87.
L'Eden: +33 (0)4 66 45 66 71.
Les Gorges du Tarn: +33 (0)4 66 48 50 10.
La Halle au Blé: +33 (0)4 66 48 59 34.
Le Pêcheur de Lune, crêperie:
+33 (0)4 66 48 58 12.
Restaurant du Nord: +33 (0)4 66 48 53 46.
La Tendelle: +33 (0)4 66 47 48 87.

🧺 Local Specialties
Food and Drink
Lozère and local wines • Cheese •
Charcuterie.
Art and Crafts
Jeweler • Potter.

② Events
June: cartoon and book festival; music
festival.
July: Pottery market; fireworks (14th).
July–August: Concerts, theater,
exhibitions; evening market (Thursdays);
medieval shows (Tuesdays).
October: Village fête and pilgrimage
(1st Sunday).

🦋 Outdoor Activities
Canoeing, canyoning • Caving • Fishing •
Swimming • Climbing • Adventure park •
Via Ferrata and Via Cordata • Horse-
riding • Walking • Mountain-biking.

🌿 Further Afield
• Causse de Sauveterre, plateau: Utopix;
Boissets farm (5 miles/8 km).
• Causse Méjean: Dargilan caves and Aven
Armand cave (4½–11 miles/7–18 km).
• Parc National des Cévennes, national
park (6 miles/9.5 km).

🕯 Did you know?
Énimie was the daughter of Chlothar II
(584–629) and the sister of Dagobert I
(603–639), both Frankish kings. She was the
founder of the monastery whose remains
can still be seen at the top of the village.

Sant'Antonino

In the skies over the Balagne

Haute-Corse (2B) • Population: 113 • Altitude: 1,624 ft. (495 m)

From its eagle's nest high above the Balagne, Sant'Antonino surveys the Mediterranean and Corsica's mountains.

Although the Chapelle de la Trinité outside the village was built in the 12th century, families began to settle here only in the 15th century. They fused their homes together in the rock so that they became a protective wall to withstand invaders. The houses are so tightly packed that there was not enough space to build churches. Only the Chapelle Sainte-Anne is in the village itself; all the others, including the Chapelle de la Trinité and the parish church of L'Annonciade, were built in a meadow outside the village. Sant'Antonino is one of Corsica's oldest villages, with origins reputedly dating back to the 9th century. Stone reigns supreme here: in the tall façades of houses gripping the granite; in cobblestones mingling with rock in narrow, winding alleyways; in vaulted passageways leading to the old castle ruins. From here you can see right across the plain and the olive-planted hills of the Balagne, all the way to the shining sea. In a secluded spot on the former threshing ground at the foot of the village, the Baroque church of L'Annonciade houses an organ by the Italian artist Giovanni Battista Pomposi, dating from 1744.

By road: N197 (6 miles/9.5 km).
By boat: L'Île Rousse port (7½ miles/ 12 km).
By air: Calvi-Sainte-Catherine airport (12 miles/19 km).

ⓘ Town hall: +33 (0)4 95 61 78 38
www.santantonino.fr

② Events

June: Corsican shepherd songs.
July: Religious festival at Notre-Dame-des-Grâces.
August: Fête de Saint Roch.

ꙮ Outdoor Activities

Donkey rides • Walking: 3 marked trails • Mountain-biking.

ꙮ Further Afield

• Cateri (2½ miles/4 km).
• Lavatoggio (3 miles/5 km).
• Lumio (7 miles/11 km).
• Aregno; Corbara; L'Île-Rousse (10 miles/ 16 km).
• Calvi (11 miles/18 km).

ꙮ Did you know?

Sant'Antonino was founded in the early 9th century by Guido Savelli, the lieutenant of Ugo Colonna (a significant figure in Corsican history who conquered the Moors to take the island). The Savellis were a warrior family who won fame for their independent spirit through the centuries: during the Genoese occupation they invited the occupiers to a banquet just so that they could massacre them. Similarly, during the siege of Calvi, Savelli refused to surrender the village, even after seeing his son killed before his own eyes.

◉ Highlights

• Église de l'Annonciade (17th century): 18th-century organ, historic paintings.
• Chapelle de la Trinité (12th century).

ꙮ Accommodation

Gîtes and vacation rentals
Further information: +33 (0)4 95 65 16 67
www.calvi-tourisme.com

ꙮ Eating Out

A Casa Corsa: +33 (0)4 95 47 34 20.
A Stalla: +33 (0)4 95 61 33 74.
Le Bellevue: +33 (0)4 95 61 73 91.
U Lazzu, light meals: +33 (0)6 43 11 72 08.
I Scalini: +33 (0)4 95 47 12 92.
U Spuntinu, light meals:
+33 (0)6 12 96 94 43.
La Taverne Corse: +33 (0)4 95 61 70 15.
La Voûte, pizzeria: +33 (0)4 95 61 74 71.

ꙮ Local Specialties

Food and Drink
Almonds • Citrus fruits • Jams • Wines, muscats • Olive oil • Corsican charcuterie and cheeses.
Art and Crafts
Jeweler • Potter.

Séguret
The vineyards of Montmirail

Vaucluse (84) • Population: 945 • Altitude: 886 ft. (270 m)

With a front-row seat, Séguret overlooks the Rhône valley from the foot of the Dentelles de Montmirail mountain chain.

On a hillside dominated by its medieval castle tower, Séguret rises above a landscape of vineyards. Inhabited since prehistoric times and improved in the Gallo-Roman era, the village proper was built in the 10th–12th centuries. Until the French Revolution it was a papal state, then rejoined France in 1792. Its heritage is considerable: winding streets, cobblestones, the Reynier Gate, the 15th-century belfry, the Romanesque Saint-Denis church (12th–13th centuries), the chapel of Notre-Dame-des-Grâces (17th century), and the Mascarons fountain (17th century). The Place des Arceaux and the Place de l'Église command marvelous views over the Comtat plain, as far as the Rhône and the Cévennes rivers. The village has great respect for its traditions, and every Christmas celebrates the Bergié, a mystery play that has been handed down orally from generation to generation since the Middle Ages.

By road: Expressway A7, exit 22–Orange Sud (14 miles/23 km). By train: Orange TGV station (12 miles/19 km); Avignon TGV station (29 miles/47 km). By air: Avignon-Caumont airport (33 miles/53 km); Marseille-Provence airport (71 miles/114 km).

ⓘ Tourist information—Pays de Vaison Ventoux en Provence:
+33 (0)4 90 36 02 11 or +33 (0)4 90 67 32 64
www.vaison-ventoux-tourisme.com
www.seguret.fr

👁 Highlights
• Chapelle Notre-Dame-des-Grâces (17th century): By appointment only: +33 (0)4 90 46 91 08.
• Chapelle Sainte-Thècle (18th century): Exhibition of paintings and *santons* (crib figures). Further information: +33 (0)4 90 36 02 11.
• Église Saint-Denis (12th–13th century): By appointment only: +33 (0)4 90 46 91 08.
• Village: Signposted walk.

🗝 Accommodation
Hotels
Domaine de Cabasse***: +33 (0)4 90 46 91 12.
La Bastide Bleue: +33 (0)4 90 46 83 43.
Guesthouses
Amour Provence: +33 (0)4 90 46 89 39.
Bouquet de Séguret: +33 (0)4 90 28 13 83.
Maison Sadina: +33 (0)6 09 84 89 13.
Patios des Vignes: +33 (0)4 90 65 47 96.
Le Vieux Figuier: +33 (0)4 90 46 84 38.
Gîtes and vacation rentals
Further information: +33 (0)4 90 36 02 11
www.vaison-ventoux-tourisme.com

🍽 Eating Out
La Bastide Bleue: +33 (0)4 90 46 83 43.
Côté Terrasse: +33 (0)4 90 28 03 48.
L'Églantine, tea room: +33 (0)4 90 46 81 41.
♥ La Table de Cabasse: +33 (0)4 90 46 91 12.
Le Mesclun: +33 (0)4 90 46 93 43.

🧺 Local Specialties
Food and Drink
AOC Côtes du Rhône and local wines.
Art and Crafts
Postcard publisher • Pottery • *Santons* (crib figures) • Art gallery • Sculptor • Jeweler • Painter.

🗓 Events
July: Local saint's day (3rd Sunday).
July–August: "Musiques à Séguret," music festival (July–August); book fair (August 15); "Fête d'Hue Vin," wine-tasting and traditional activities (end August); harvest festival (end August).
December: "Bergié de Séguret," mystery play (24th); Journée des Traditions, heritage fair (3rd Sunday).
December–January: *Santons* (crib figures) exhibition.

🦋 Outdoor Activities
Hunting • Fishing • Cycle routes • Climbing in the Dentelles de Montmirail • Walking: Route GR 4.

🌿 Further Afield
• Dentelles de Montmirail, chain of mountains (3 miles/5 km).
• Vaison-la-Romaine (5 miles/8 km).
• Orange (14 miles/23 km).
• Carpentras (14 miles/23 km).
• *Venasque (21 miles/34 km), see pp. 147–48.
• Avignon (25 miles/40 km).
• Mont Ventoux (25 miles/40 km).
• *La Garde-Adhémar (25 miles/40 km), see p. 98.

Seillans

Tradition and innovation in a Provençal village

Var (83) • Population: 2,561 • Altitude: 1,201 ft. (366 m)

From below, Seillans looks like a huge staircase, its tall façades scaling the slope in steps.

Gathered at the top, as if on a throne, are the Sarrasine Gate, a medieval castle, a former priory of monks from Saint-Victor Abbey in Marseille, and the 11th-century church of Saint-Léger. Inside its three consecutive walls, Seillans is a patchwork of light and shade, an enticing maze of paved streets still echoing to the sound of horse hooves, steeply sloping cobbled alleys, vaulted passageways, and shady corners in which fountains tinkle musically. On the square at the entrance to the village stands the statue "Génie de la Bastille" by Max Ernst (1891–1976), a permanent reminder that he fell so in love with Seillans that he moved here with his wife, Dorothea Tanning, and used to enjoy playing *pétanque* with the locals on this very spot. In the valley below, where pines, olive trees, and vineyards jostle for space, the chapel of Notre-Dame-de-l'Ormeau protects an altarpiece unique in Provence. The village welcomes artists and craftspeople to its silk farm and old cork factory, emblems of its past economic life, and also spotlights events that celebrate artistic expertise and innovation.

By road: Expressway A8, exit 39–Les Adrets-de-l'Estérel (13 miles/21 km). **By train:** Arcs-Draguignan TGV station (19 miles/31 km); Saint-Raphaël-Valescure TGV station (22 miles/35 km). **By bus:** 3601 from Saint-Raphaël bus station (25 miles/40 km) and 3001 from Grasse bus station (20 miles/32 km). **By air:** Nice-Côte-d'Azur airport (40 miles/64 km).

ⓘ Tourist information:
+33 (0)4 94 76 85 91
www.paysdefayence.com / www.seillans.fr

👁 Highlights
• **Chapelle Notre-Dame-de-l'Ormeau**
(12th century): Provençal Cistercian
building; 16th-century polychrome wood-
carved altarpiece, unique in Provence.
Tours all year round by appointment
for groups 5+, Thursdays 11.15 a.m.:
+33 (0)4 94 76 85 91.
• **Max Ernst, Dorothea Tanning, and
Stan Appenzeller Collections:** In the
Maison Waldberg (mid-13th-century
mansion), a collection of lithographs by
surrealist artists Max Ernst and Dorothea
Tanning, made while the couple lived in
Seillans; a collection of works by artist
Stanislas Appenzeller (1901–1980). Guided
tours all year round for groups of 5+ by
appointment: +33 (0)4 94 76 85 91.
• **Village:** Guided tours, Thursdays,
10 a.m. all year round, for groups of 5+,
by reservation: +33 (0)4 94 76 85 91.

🗝 Accommodation
Hotels
Les Deux Rocs***: +33 (0)4 94 76 87 32.
Guesthouses
La Magnanerie de Seillans: +33 (0)4 94 50
83 56 or +33 (0)6 20 13 73 67.
La Maison de Jenny: +33 (0)4 83 11 61 10
or +33 (0)6 11 11 78 86.
Le Mas de Combelongues:
+33 (0)9 82 12 15 04 or +33 (0)6 24 77 20 23.
**Gîtes, vacation rentals, and vacation
centers**
Further information: +33 (0)4 94 76 85 91
www.paysdefayence.com
Rural campsite
Le Rouquier: +33 (0)4 94 76 86 71 or
+33 (0)6 88 18 00 05.
RV park
Further information: +33 (0)4 94 76 85 91.

🍴 Eating Out
Bar Charlot, light meals:
+33 (0)4 94 76 40 82.
Chez Hugo: +33 (0)4 94 85 54 70.
Les Deux Rocs: +33 (0)4 94 76 87 32.
La Gloire de Mon Père: +33 (0)4 94 76 98 68.
Pepperoni and Co, pizzeria, snack bar:
+33 (0)4 94 68 15 85.
Tilleul Citron, tea room:
+33 (0)4 94 50 47 64.

🧺 Local Specialties
Food and Drink
Honey • AOC Côtes de Provence wine •
Olive oil • Farm produce • Goat cheese •
Institut Gastronomique (cookery courses).
Art and Crafts
Art galleries and studios • Ceramicist •
Wrought ironwork • Figurine maker and

history painter • Engraver • Model-maker •
Leather craftsman • Painters • Beadmaker •
Soap-maker • Silk screening • Sculptor.

📅 Events
Market: Wednesday mornings, 8 a.m.–
12.30 p.m.
February: Cycle tour, Haut Var (last
weekend).
March: Marché Gourmand, gourmet
market (1st Sunday).
May: "Salon de Mai," art exhibition;
art and crafts, and local produce market.
May–June: "Les Rencontres de la
Photographie et de l'Image," photography
exhibition.
July: Feast day of Saint Cyr and Saint Léger
(last weekend).
August: "Aïoli des Selves" (1st weekend);
"Musique Cordiale," music festival (1st
fortnight); pottery market (15th); art and
crafts market.
September: Art and crafts market.
September–October: Provençal
heritage and history exhibition
(mid-September–mid-October).
October: "Musique en Pays de Fayence,"
music festival (last week).
November: Fête de l'Olive, olive festival
(last weekend); Christmas market (last
Sunday).
December: Christmas exhibition, craft
fair, and "13 Desserts" (Provençal dessert
tasting), animated Nativity scene.

🦋 Outdoor Activities
Sports park with multisports area •
Pétanque • Horse-riding • Swimming pool
(July–August) • Walking: 15 marked trails.

🌿 Further Afield
• Pays de Fayence, region: hilltop villages
(3–12 miles/5–19 km).
• Gorges of the Siagnole (9½–12 miles/
15.5–19 km).
• Lac de Saint-Cassien, lake (12 miles/
19 km).
• Grottes de Saint-Cézaire, caves
(19 miles/31 km).
• *Bargème (21 miles/34 km), see p. 90.
• Draguignan (22 miles/35 km).
• Grasse (22 miles/35 km).
• La Corniche d'Or, coastal drive;
Saint-Raphaël; Fréjus (24 miles/39 km).
• *Tourtour (27 miles/43 km),
see pp. 144–45.
• Les Gorges du Verdon, gorges
(31 miles/50 km).

Semur-en-Brionnais

Cluny history in Burgundy

Saône-et-Loire (71) • Population: 649 • Altitude: 1,299 ft. (396 m)

Birthplace of Saint Hugh, one of the great abbots at the powerful monastery of Cluny, Semur is the historic capital of the Brionnais region, in the depths of Burgundy.

Founded on a rocky spur, in the 10th century Semur-en-Brionnais became a defensive site ruled by the counts of Chalon. The Château Saint-Hugues is considered one of the oldest fortresses in Burgundy, and its keep is intact. Inside, a collection of posters evokes the French Revolution, during which time the guards' rooms functioned as a prison. The Romanesque church dedicated to Saint Hilaire was erected by Geoffroy V in the 12th and 13th centuries. Its gate shows the saint defending the Catholic orthodoxy against Arians at the Council of Seleucia. Inside, the triple elevation of the nave and the corbeled gallery are directly inspired by Cluny. The chapter house, founded in 1274 by Jean de Châteauvillain, provides information about the Romanesque style in the Brionnais. The main square contains the 18th-century law courts (now the town hall), 16th-century men-at-arms' houses, and the salt store, whose ceiling is decorated with allegorical paintings. The rampart walk still exists, as does the postern gate. Nestled in the valley, the 11th-century church of Saint-Martin-la-Vallée is decorated with 14th-century wall paintings.

By road: Expressway A6, exit 33–Balbigny (36 miles/58 km); N79 (12 miles/19 km); expressway A89, exit 5.1–Balbigny (40 miles/64 km), then N82-N7 (18 miles/29 km). **By train:** Paray-le-Monial station (17 miles/27 km); Le Creusot-Montceau TGV station (49 miles/79 km). **By air:** Lyon-Saint-Exupéry airport (79 miles/127 km).

ⓘ Tourist information:
+33 (0)3 85 25 13 57
www.semur-en-brionnais.fr

👁 Highlights

• ♥ **Château Saint-Hugues** (10th century): Keep, towers, medieval warfare room; French Revolution poster collection; family tree of Hugh of Semur, abbot of Cluny: +33 (0)3 85 25 13 57.
• **Collegiate church of Saint-Hilaire** (12th–13th centuries): Pre-eminent Romanesque church in the region; polychrome wood statues.
• **Église Saint-Martin-la-Vallée** (11–12th centuries): 15–16th-century wall paintings.
• **Maison du Chapitre:** Hall with ceiling and fireplace painted late 16th century; exhibition about Romanesque art in the region.
• **Salt store:** Building where salt tax was paid; ceiling decorated with allegorical paintings from end of 16th century.
• **Former law courts** (now the town hall) (18th century): Louis XVI-style building.
• **Saint-Hugues priory:** Chapel, reception hall (exhibition).
• **Village:** Various guided tours for groups, May–November. Further information: "Les Vieilles Pierres" association: +33 (0)3 85 25 13 57.

🔑 Accommodation

Guesthouses
Maison Guillon Kopf: +33 (0)3 85 81 55 59.
Gîtes
Belle Vue***, farm accommodation:
+33 (0)6 42 70 03 89.
M. Lorton: +33 (0)3 85 25 36 63.

🍴 Eating Out

L'Entrecôte Brionnaise:
+33 (0)3 85 25 10 21.

🧺 Local Specialties

Food and Drink
Brionnais wines.
Art and Crafts
Monastic crafts.

📅 Events

May–October: Exhibitions in the salt store.
July: La Madeleine, patron saint's day
(1st weekend after 14th).
August: Art market (1st Sunday).

🦋 Outdoor Activities

Walking • Mountain-biking.

🌿 Further Afield

• Marcigny: museums and exhibitions
(3 miles/5 km).
• Voie Verte, picturesque greenway
(3 miles/5 km).
• Saint-Christophe-en-Brionnais:
cattle market (5 miles/8 km).
• Romanesque churches in Brionnais
region: Anzy-le-Duc, Iguerande,
Montceaux-l'Étoile, Saint-Julien-de-Jonzy
(6–9½ miles/9.5–15.5 km).
• Charlieu: abbey (12 miles/19 km).
• Paray-le-Monial (16 miles/26 km).
• Château de Drée (16 miles/26 km).
• Roanne (20 miles/32 km).

❗ Did you know?

In 1024 Hugh was born at Semur castle;
he later became the sixth chief abbot
of the Cluniac order. For 60 years, until
his death, he led the order of more than
10,000 monks across the Christian world.
He also built the great abbey church, sadly
destroyed after the French Revolution,
which was the largest church in all
Christendom before the construction
of Saint Peter's in Rome.

Tourtour

In the skies above Provence

Var (83) • Population: 593 • Altitude: 2,133 ft. (650 m)

Perched on a plateau soaring above Provence, with vineyards to the south and lavender to the north, Tourtour exudes the perfume of thyme and olive trees.

Tourtour was fortified in the early Middle Ages to protect itself from frequent Saracen attacks. From this long-distant and precarious past, it still has some fortifications and its street plan, in which streets encircle the old castle. The narrow alleyways of the medieval village boast buildings of old stone and curved tiles, and they accommodate a traditional oil mill and a fascinating fossil museum. Alleyways, steps, and vaulted passageways are dotted with fountains, refreshing passersby exhausted by the sun. Intertwined streets surround the two castles—a medieval one with two towers, and a 17th-century one with four towers. The church stands high above both village and landscape; built in the 11th century and restored in the 19th, it provides an exceptional view of inland Provence, from Sainte-Baume and Mont Sainte-Victoire as far as the Maures massif and the Mediterranean.

By road: Expressway A8, exit 36–Draguignan (20 miles/32 km), N555 (11 miles/18 km); expressway A51, exit 18–Valensole (41 miles/66 km). **By train:** Draguignan station (13 miles/21 km). **By air:** Toulon-Hyères airport (58 miles/93 km); Nice-Côte d'Azur airport (66 miles/106 km).

ⓘ Tourist information:
+33 (0)4 94 70 59 47
www.tourtour.org

👁 Highlights

• **Église Saint-Denis** (11th century): Summer concerts.
• **Traditional olive mill:** In operation November–February; art exhibitions mid-May–mid-September.
• **Musée des Fossiles:** Collection of ammonites and local fossils (especially dinosaur eggs).
• **Town hall:** Sculptures by Bernard Buffet (1928–1999) of giant insects and permanent exhibition of drawings by Ronald Searle (1920–2011) at the town gallery.
• **Village:** Guided tours of the village, mill, and museum for groups all year round by appointment: +33 (0)4 94 70 59 47.

🗝 Accommodation

Hotels
La Bastide de Tourtour****:
+33 (0)4 98 10 54 20.
Auberge St-Pierre***:
+33 (0)4 94 50 00 50.
Le Mas des Collines: +33 (0)4 94 70 59 30.
La Petite Auberge: +33 (0)4 98 10 26 16.
Guesthouses
Chanteciel: +33 (0)6 95 92 59 69.
Le Colombier: +33 (0)4 94 70 53 93.
Maison de la Treille: +33 (0)6 15 17 37 64.
Villa Pharima: +33 (0)6 23 74 41 67.

Gîtes
Further information: +33 (0)4 94 70 59 47
www.tourtour.org

🍴 Eating Out

L'Aléchou, crêperie: +33 (0)4 94 70 54 76.
Auberge St-Pierre: +33 (0)4 94 50 00 50.
La Bastide de Tourtour:
+33 (0)4 98 10 54 20.
La Farigoulette: +33 (0)4 94 70 57 37.
Le Mas des Collines: +33 (0)4 94 70 59 30.
La Mimounia, Moroccan cuisine:
+33 (0)4 94 47 67 89.
Les Ormeaux, bar: +33 (0)4 94 70 57 07.
La Petite Auberge: +33 (0)4 98 10 26 16.
Les Pins Tranquilles: +33 (0)4 94 50 40 39.
La Place: +33 (0)4 94 84 32 13.
Le Relais de Saint-Denis:
+33 (0)4 94 70 54 06.
La Table, gourmet restaurant:
+33 (0)4 94 70 55 95.

🏛 Local Specialties

Food and Drink
Organic produce (fruit, vegetables, fruit juice) • Olive oil.
Art and Crafts
Gifts • Art galleries and artists' studios • Fashion.

② Events
Market: Small Provençal market, Wednesday and Saturday mornings.
February: "Roustide," olive oil festival.
Easter: "Fête de l'Œuf," Easter festival (Sunday and Monday).
June–September: Exhibitions at the oil mill.
July: "Courts, Courts," short-film festival (last weekend); Journées des Galeries, art fair.
August: Village fair, ball (1st Sunday).
July–August: "Piano dans le Ciel," music festival.
October: Saint Denis's feast day.
December: Christmas market.
December–January: "La Pastorale," Nativity play.

🦋 Outdoor Activities
Boules area • Walking and mountain-biking • Horse-riding.

🌿 Further Afield
• Villecroze: park, caves, and waterfalls (4½ miles/7 km).
• Salernes; Sillans-la-Cascade; Cotignac; Bargemon; Draguignan; Châteaudouble: gorges (7–18 miles/11.5–29 km).
• Lac de Sainte-Croix, lake (18 miles/ 29 km).
• Le Thoronet Abbey, Sainte-Roseline chapel (19 miles/31 km).
• *Seillans (27 miles/43 km), see pp. 140–41.
• *Bargème (29 miles/47 km), see p. 90.
• Le Grand Canyon du Verdon (31 miles/ 51 km).

Usson

A gilded cage for Queen Margot

Puy-de-Dôme (63) • Population: 263 • Altitude: 1,772 ft. (540 m)

On the fringes of the regional nature park of Livradois-Forez, Usson perches on a volcanic mound and surveys the vast panorama of the mountains of Puy de Dôme, Mont Dore, and Cézallier. The village, overshadowed by a statue of the Virgin, used to be overlooked by an impressive castle. After improvements by Jean de Berry and restoration work by Louis XI in the late 15th century, the castle of Usson housed the exiled Queen Margaret (1553–1615), known as Margot—sister of Charles IX and foolish young wife of the future Henri IV. She eloped with her lover, the equerry Jean d'Aubiac, but they were discovered at Ybois; her lover was executed and Margaret was held at Usson. She remained there for nineteen years, leading both a courtly and religious life. In July 1605, aged 52, she returned to Paris, having managed to get Usson exempted from taxation and offering a grant in perpetuity for the local poor. Behind the village's basalt façades remain parts of its triple surrounding walls flanked by towers, which were destroyed under Cardinal Richelieu (1585–1642). The Église Saint-Maurice, Romanesque in origin, was extended in the 16th century with the addition of the Queen's Chapel, under whose starry vault Margaret prayed. The tabernacle shutters, made in 1622, show her in old age personified as Saint Radegonde and wearing a gown and crown decorated with fleurs-de-lys, beside her husband, Henri IV. South of this building, a path leads to the village's impressive basalt columns and to a summit that towers above the village.

By road: Expressway A75, exit 13–Sauxillanges (6 miles/9.5 km). **By train:** Issoire station (7½ miles/12 km); Clermont-Ferrand station (26 miles/42 km). **By air:** Clermont-Ferrand-Auvergne airport (29 miles/47 km).

ⓘ Tourist information—Pays d'Issoire: +33 (0)4 73 89 15 90
www.issoire-tourisme.com

👁 Highlights
• Église Saint-Maurice (12th–16th centuries): 17th-century tabernacle, statues, paintings +33 (0)4 73 71 05 90.
• Basalt columns: Above the village.
• Old forge: Restored with all its tools (e.g. hearth, bellows, anvil).
• Village: Guided tour of the village and church for groups by reservation: +33 (0)4 73 89 15 90.
• Exhibition on the history and culture of Usson (at the Usson tourist office): +33 (0)4 73 71 05 90

🗝 Accommodation
Hotels
Auberge de Margot: +33 (0)4 73 71 97 92.
Gîtes
Gérard Serre: +33 (0)4 73 96 84 88.
Jean-Claude Millot: +33 (0)7 62 89 15 04.
Jean-Claude Roux: +33 (0)4 73 96 80 69.

🍴 Eating Out
Auberge de Margot: +33 (0)4 73 71 97 92.

🧺 Local Specialties
Art and Crafts
Workers in glass, wood, and stone.

📅 Events
May: Pilgrimage to Notre-Dame-d'Usson (Ascension).
July: Flea market (last Sunday).

🦋 Outdoor Activities
Fishing • Walking: 2 marked trails.

🌾 Further Afield
• Château de Parentignat (5 miles/8 km).
• Issoire (7 miles/11.5 km).
• Hilltop villages: Nonette, Auzon (9½–16 miles/15.5–26 km).
• *Montpeyroux (15 miles/24 km), see p. 116.
• Billom (20 miles/32 km).
• Clermont-Ferrand (28 miles/45 km).
• Massif du Livardois; Ambert (32 miles/51 km).

Venasque
The taste of Provence

Vaucluse (84) • Population: 1,180 • Altitude: 1,050 ft. (320 m)

Giving its name to the Comtat Venaissin region, Venasque is a crow's nest towering above a sea of *garrigue* scrubland, vineyards, and cherry orchards.

At the foot of Mont Ventoux, Venasque has molded itself to the shape of a rocky spur at the northwestern tip of the Vaucluse plateau, high above the Carpentras plain, where the Gorges of the Nesque open out. Occupied in Neolithic times, then during the Roman era, this naturally defensive site is reinforced by a rampart and three towers. The Église Notre-Dame was rebuilt in the 13th century, on the site of a 6th-century church probably built by Saint Siffredus, and contains a Crucifixion from 1498 attributed to a primitive painter of the Avignon school. Below, a stunning baptistery in the form of a Greek cross contains marble columns from Roman buildings. Dotted along the steep alleyways are houses with golden façades, built in the 14th–17th centuries, which echo the old hospice in Rue de l'Hôpital, very close to a delightful 18th-century Provençal fountain. The village is proud of its local heritage, and is the capital of cherry growing, a fruit celebrated each June.

By road: Expressway A7, exit 22–Orange-Sud (21 miles/34 km). **By train:** Avignon station (20 miles/32 km); Orange station (23 miles/37 km); Avignon TGV station (27 miles/43 km). **By air:** Avignon-Caumont airport (28 miles/45 km).

ⓘ Tourist information:
+33 (0)4 90 66 11 66
www.tourisme-venasque.com

Venasque Vaucluse

◉ Highlights
• **Baptistery** (6th century, much altered): Decorated blind arches and various decorated capitals. Further information: +33 (0)4 90 66 62 01.
• **Église Notre-Dame** (13th century): Avignon school Crucifixion, and 1498 processional cross.
• **Village:** Information boards; guided tours Thursday, 5 p.m. in summer, book at tourist information center; accessible tours for the visually impaired; "Visites en Scènes," musical and theatrical history show, presented by TRAC in July–August: +33 (0)4 90 66 11 66.

✗ Accommodation
Hotels
La Garrigue**: +33 (0)4 90 66 03 40.
Les Remparts: +33 (0)4 90 66 02 79.
Guesthouses
Mme Lubiato***: +33 (0)4 90 66 60 71.
Mme Maret***: +33 (0)4 90 66 03 04.
M. and Mme Ruel***: +33 (0)4 90 66 02 84.
M. Velay***: +33 (0)4 90 66 63 98.
Mme Charles**: +33 (0)4 90 66 14 20.
Mme C. Ruel**: +33 (0)4 90 66 02 84.
Mme Dulière: +33 (0)4 90 66 04 69.
Mme Laroche: +33 (0)4 90 34 84 11.
Mme Leroy: +33 (0)4 90 60 64 05.
Le Mas du Kaïros: +33 (0)4 90 30 99 18.
M. Tourrette: +33 (0)4 90 66 03 71.
Gîtes, vacation rentals, and houses
Further information:
+33 (0)4 90 66 11 66
www.tourisme-venasque.com

⑪ Eating Out
Côté Fontaine: +33 (0)4 90 66 64 85.
Maison de Charme La Fontaine, tea room and wine bar: +33 (0)4 90 60 64 05.
Le Petit Chose, snack bar:
+33 (0)4 90 66 02 79.
Les Remparts: +33 (0)4 90 66 02 79.

🧺 Local Specialties
Food and Drink
Cherries and dessert grapes.
Art and Crafts
Ceramicists • Weaver • Painters • Potters • Sculptor.

② Events
Market: Fridays, 5–8 p.m., mid-June–mid-September.
April: Venasque rally-driving.
June: Festival de la Cerise, cherry festival (outdoor tasting sessions, and discovery and sale of produce).
July: July 14 festival.
June-August: Art exhibitions in the vaulted gallery behind the church.
July–August: Art exhibitions at Salle Romane.
August: Local saint's day (around 15th); Journée Arts et Artisans dans les rues, street art fair (15th).
December: Christmas market.

🦋 Outdoor Activities
Climbing • Horse-riding • Walking • Golf • Cycle touring.

🌿 Further Afield
• Hilltop villages: Beaucet, La Roque-sur-Pernes (3–6 miles/5–9.5 km).
• Pernes-les-Fontaines (4½ miles/7 km).
• Carpentras (7 miles/11.5 km).
• Gorges of the Nesque (9½ miles/15.5 km).
• *Gordes (9½ miles/15.5 km), see pp. 102–3.
• *Ménerbes (15 miles/24 km), see p. 112.
• *Roussillon (15 miles/24 km), see pp. 126–27.
• Avignon (19 miles/31 km).
• *Séguret (21 miles/34 km), see p. 139.
• Mont Ventoux (22 miles/35 km).
• Vaison-la-Romaine (24 miles/39 km).
• Pays de la Lavande, region; Sault (25 miles/40 km).

Vogüé

A castle in the south of France

Ardèche (07) • Population: 1,020 • Altitude: 486 ft. (148 m)

Nestled in an amphitheater at the foot of a cliff, Vogüé dips its toes in the almost Mediterranean-like waters of the Ardèche river.

The riverside roads dotted with arched passageways lead to the castle that dwarfs the village. This ancestral home of the Vogüés, one of the most illustrious families in the region, was rebuilt in the 16th and 17th centuries. It has a tower at each corner, and façades decorated with mullioned windows. It is now managed by Vivante Ardèche and houses an exhibition on the region's history and architecture, the works of Ardèche engraver Jean Chièze (1898–1975), and contemporary art. In the old village streets, medieval houses roofed with curved tiles are interspersed with arcades. Their stepped terraces overflow with flowers, and in the Midi sunshine everything radiates a Mediterranean air.

By road: Expressway A7, exit 17–Montélimar (30 miles/48 km); N102 (4½ miles/7 km). **By train:** Montélimar station (23 miles/37 km). **By air:** Lyon-Saint-Exupéry airport (123 miles/198 km).

ⓘ Tourist information—Pont-d'Arc Ardèche: +33 (0)4 28 91 24 10
pontdarc-ardeche.fr

👁 Highlights
• **Castle** (16th and 17th centuries): 12th-century state room, keep, and kitchen, Jean Chièze room, Vogüé room, chapel, hanging garden; temporary art and craft exhibitions:
+33 (0)4 75 37 01 95.
• **Wine cellar:** +33 (0)4 75 37 71 14.
• **Village:** Guided tours by reservation in summer: +33 (0)4 28 91 24 10.

🗝 Accommodation
Hotels
Les Falaises: +33 (0)4 75 37 72 59.
Guesthouses
Le Mas des Molines****:
+33 (0)6 61 72 83 78.
Les Carriers: +33 (0)6 84 43 35 73.
Gîtes
Further information: +33 (0)4 28 91 24 10
http://pontdarc-ardeche.fr
Aparthotels
Domaine Lou Capitelle:
+33 (0)4 75 37 71 32.
Campsites
L'Oasis des Garrigues***:
+33 (0)4 75 37 03 27.
Les Chênes Verts**: +33 (0)4 75 37 71 54.
Les Roches*: +33 (0)4 75 37 70 45.
Residential leisure parks
Les Roulottes de Saint-Cerice:
+33 (0)6 11 49 75 33.

🍴 Eating Out
L'Ardèche: +33 (0)4 75 37 03 71.
Au Cabanon: +33 (0)6 61 19 67 81.
Chez Papytof: +33 (0)4 75 37 01 62.
L'Esparat: +33 (0)4 75 38 86 21.
La Falaise: +33 (0)4 75 37 72 59.
La Rôtisserie: +33 (0)4 75 88 40 78.
Le Temps'Danse: +33 (0)4 75 37 72 52.
La Voguette, crêperie:
+33 (0)4 75 37 01 61.

🛍 Local Specialties
Food and Drink
Honey • Coteaux de l'Ardèche wines.

② Events
Market: Monday mornings, July–August.
July–August: Musical theater shows; art exhibitions.
August: Flea market (1st Sunday).
Easter–All Saints' Day: Contemporary art exhibitions at the castle.

🦋 Outdoor Activities
Canoeing • Climbing • Walking: *Topoguide*, book of walks, available at tourist information center • Mountain-biking.

🌿 Further Afield
• Sauveplantade: church; Rochecolombe (1–2½ miles/1.5–4 km).
• *Balazuc (4½ miles/7 km), see p. 89.
• Aubenas (6 miles/9.5 km).
• Le Pradel: estate of Olivier de Serre; Coiron plateau (8–12 miles/13–19 km).
• Ruoms: winegrowers' boutique (9½ miles/15.5 km).
• Gorges of the Ardèche; Vallon-Pont-d'Arc; Grotte du Pont-d'Arc, cave (12 miles/19 km).

Yvoire

Medieval reflections in the waters of Lake Geneva

Haute-Savoie (74) • Population: 911 • Altitude: 1,181 ft. (360 m)

Yvoire combines the pleasures of a lakeside village with the strength of its medieval heritage as a sentry overlooking an important waterway. Its strategic position between the Petit Lac and the Grand Lac inspired the count of Savoy, Amadeus V the Great, to begin important fortification works here in 1306, at the height of the Delphino-Savoyard war. He built the castle on the site of a former stronghold and surrounded it with a fortified village. Castle, ramparts, gates, ditches, and medieval houses have miraculously survived an extremely stormy past. The whole village is overflowing with flowers in all colors of the rainbow, which makes for a wonderful sight against the stone squares and façades. The flower display changes with the seasons, so that there is always something new to discover. The dazzling setting—with its dramatic backdrop of mountains and lake, and the bustle of fishing boats, yachts, and steamers on the water—make it easy to see why Yvoire is known as the "pearl of Lake Geneva."

By road: Expressway A40, exit 14– Annemasse (18 miles/29 km); expressway A41-A40, exit 15–Vallée Verte (18 miles/ 29 km). **By train:** Thonon-les-Bains station (10 miles/16 km); Geneva station (16 miles/26 km). **By air:** Geneva airport (19 miles/31 km).

ⓘ Tourist information:
+33 (0)4 50 72 80 21
www.yvoiretourism.com

👁 Highlights

• **Le Jardin des Cinq Sens** (classified as "remarkable" by the Ministry of Culture): Plant maze on the theme of the five senses in the castle's old vegetable garden, recreating the style and symbolism of medieval gardens: +33 (0)4 50 72 88 80.

• **La Maison de l'Histoire:** Permanent exhibition, "Un Patrimoine Écrit Exceptionnel": documents from Yvoire's heritage: +33 (0)4 50 72 80 21.
• **Le Domaine de Rovorée-La Châtaignière:** Nature reserve of 59 acres (24 ha); walking trails: +33 (0)4 50 72 80 21.

• **La Châtaignière** (mansion, 20th-century architecture typical of the lakeside): "Domaine Départemental d'Art et de Culture" (exhibitions), June–September: +33 (0)4 50 72 26 67.
• **La Grange à la Marie:** Restored small 19th-century farm: +33 (0)4 50 72 80 21.
• **Village:** Guided tours with tour guides from "Patrimoine des Pays de Savoie"; for individuals June–September, for groups all year round by appointment: +33 (0)4 50 72 80 21.

🗝 Accommodation
Hotels
Le Jules Verne****: +33 (0)4 50 72 80 08.
Le Port****: +33 (0)4 50 72 80 17.
Villa Cécile****: +33 (0)4 50 72 27 40.
Le Pré de la Cure***: +33 (0)4 50 72 83 58.
Le Vieux Logis: +33 (0)4 50 72 80 24.
Gîtes
La Falescale**: +33 (0)4 50 72 92 95.
La Pointe d'Yvoire: +33 (0)6 09 17 85 26.
Campsites
Léman I**: +33 (0)4 50 72 84 31.

🍽 Eating Out
Le Bacouni: +33 (0)4 50 72 85 67.
Le Bar des Pêcheurs: +33 (0)4 50 72 80 26.
Le Bateau Ivre: +33 (0)4 50 72 81 84.

Le Café de la Marine: +33 (0)4 50 72 87 82.
Le Chardon, brasserie: +33 (0)4 50 72 81 71.
La Crêperie d'Yvoire: +33 (0)4 50 72 80 78.
Les Cygnes, brasserie: +33 (0)4 50 72 82 88.
La Dîme, pizzeria: +33 (0)4 50 72 89 87.
Les Galets, crêperie: +33 (0)4 50 72 69 73.
♥ Les Jardins du Léman:
+33 (0)4 50 72 80 32.
Le Jules Verne: +33 (0)4 50 72 80 08.
La Perche: +33 (0)4 50 72 89 30.
Petit Cabri: +33 (0)4 50 72 88 55.
Le Pirate: +33 (0)4 50 72 83 61.
Le Port: +33 (0)4 50 72 80 17.
Le Pré de la Cure: +33 (0)4 50 72 83 58.
La Traboule: +33 (0)4 50 72 83 73.
La Vieille Porte: +33 (0)4 50 72 80 14.
Le Vieux Logis: +33 (0)4 50 72 80 24.
Villa Cécile: +33 (0)4 50 72 27 40.

🏛 Local Specialties
Food and Drink
Lake Geneva perch • Artisan ice creams •
Artisan cookies • Savoy produce.
Art and Crafts
Wood crafts • Crystal artist • Lacemaker •
Art galleries • Potter • Rocks and minerals
specialist • Basketmaker • Glassblowers •
Contemporary artists.

📅 Events
Seasonal market: "Rencontres
Gourmandes" (local produce): monthly
events in June, July, and August
April: "Fête de la Cuisine," food fair.
May: Parade Vénitienne, Venetian
parade.
July–August: Yvoire Jazz Festival; "Fête
du Sauvetage," festival organized by the
Yvoire Lifesavers association; "Ginguettes
des Mouettes," music festival; local fairs,
concerts.
September: Journée du Patrimoine,
heritage festival.
October: Fête des Ânes, donkey fair;
Marché Bio, organic market.

🦋 Outdoor Activities
Boat trips on Lake Geneva • Walking.

🌿 Further Afield
• Nernier (1 mile/1.5 km).
• Château d'Allinges (9½ miles/15.5 km).
• Thonon-les-Bains; Ripaille: castle;
Évian-les-Bains (10–16 miles/16–26 km).
• Geneva (17 miles/27 km).
• Nyon (20 minutes by boat).

❗ Did you know?
At dusk on September 29, 1844, the
traveler and writer Alfred de Bougy arrived
at Yvoire. In a chapter titled "Chez les
sauvages du Léman" ("Among the savages
of Lake Geneva"), he wrote this damning
description of Yvoire as, "A jumble of ugly
huts, hovels that resemble pig-sties." He
added that he "would never have imagined
such a sordid collection of uncivilized men
at the heart of Europe." He spoke of "the
most detestable village," and finished by
saying that "when the magnificent steam
boats tour the lake, they pass in sight of
Yvoire, they round its protruding headland,
but they take care not to put into port
there." It's fair to say that Yvoire has had its
revenge on both fate and history.

Southwest

Scale 1: 2,600,000

0   50 km
0   40 miles

Atlantic Ocean

Les Sables-
d'Olonne
Pointe de l'Aiguille

Vouva

Île de Ré   p. 196
Ars-en-Ré   La Flotte   Niort
p. 155

La Rochelle
Île d'Oléron   Rochefort   Surgères
St-Jean-d'Ang
Brouage   Mornac-
p. 172   s.-Seudre   Sain
p. 218
Royan

Talmont-
s.-Gironde
p. 259

Blaye

Bordeaux
Arcachon
Cap Ferret

**Mont-de-
Marsan**

Dax   Aire-s.-l'Adou

Santander

Bayonne
Anglet   La Bastide-   Orthez
Biarritz   Clairence   Navarrenx
Sare   p. 162   Pa
Bilbao   San Sebastián   p. 252   Ainhoa
p. 154   Oloron-
Ste-Marie   Pa

St-Jean-
Pied-de-Port
p. 246

Vitoria-
Gasteiz

Pamplona

Logroño

Burgos

SPAIN

©éditerra

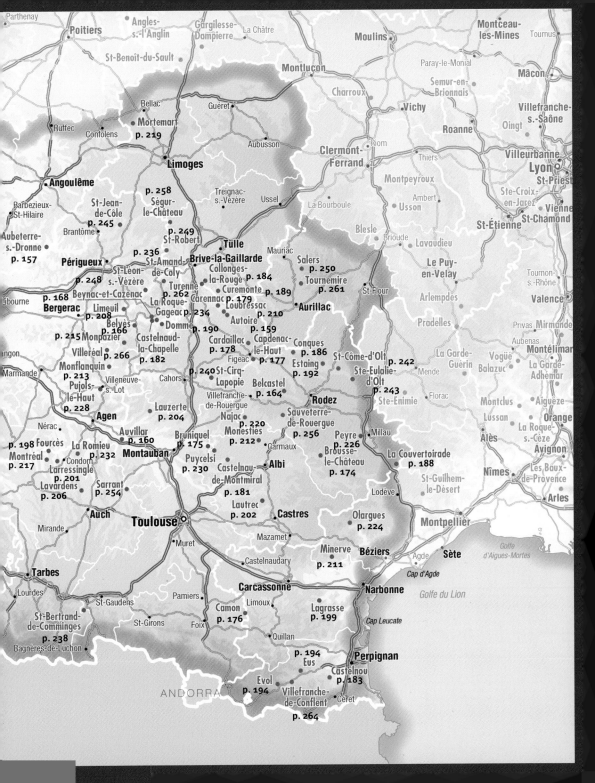

Ainhoa

All the colors of the Basque Country

Pyrénées-Atlantiques (64) • Population: 680 • Altitude: 394 ft. (120 m)

Marrying its green hillsides with the red-and-white façades of its Labourdin and Navarrese houses, Ainhoa displays the colors of the Basque Country along its single street. In the 13th century, the Roman Catholic religious order known as the Premonstratensians set up a vicariate at Ainhoa to provide assistance to pilgrims traveling to Santiago, and a *bastide* (fortified town) emerged from the plain to provide for their welcome. Rebuilt in the 17th century, its finest façades face east. The rings for tying up mules on the *lorios* (doors) of some houses bear witness to their former role as merchant inns on the road to Pamplona. Further back, gardens extend at the rear of the houses. The immaculate house fronts, some of which have balconies, are full of character, with typically Basque red and green shutters and timbering. Next to the *fronton* (Basque pelota court), which still hosts a few games in summer, the 13th-century church has been rebuilt, but the cut stones of its lower parts date back to the founding of the *bastide*. Higher up, the Notre-Dame-d'Arantzazu chapel (*arantza* means "hawthorn" in Basque; it is also known as Notre-Dame-de-l'Aubépine in French) stands on the Atsulai mountainside.

By road: Expressway A63, exit 5–Bayonne Sud (16 miles/26 km). **By train:** Cambo-les-Bains station (8 miles/13 km); Biarritz station (15 miles/24 km). **By air:** Biarritz-Bayonne-Anglet airport (16 miles/26 km).

ⓘ Tourist information:
+33 (0)5 59 29 93 99
www.ainhoa-tourisme.com

👁 Highlights
• Église Notre-Dame-de-l'Assomption: Spanish-style gilded wooden altarpiece.
• Maison du Patrimoine: Exhibition, film on the history of the village and the border area: +33 (0)5 59 29 93 99.
• Village: *Bastide, fronton*, church, and open-air washhouse. Guided tour from June to September; groups of 7+ all year by appointment: +33 (0)5 59 29 93 99.

🗝 Accommodation
Hotels
Argi-Eder**** : +33 (0)5 59 93 72 00.
Ithurria**** : +33 (0)5 59 29 92 11.
Oppoca*** : +33 (0)5 59 29 90 72.
Ur-Hegian** : +33 (0)5 59 29 91 16.
Etchartenea* : +33 (0)5 59 29 90 26.
Guesthouses
Ohantzea*** : +33 (0)5 59 29 57 17.
Maison Goxoki: +33 (0)6 21 20 92 34.
Maison Xaharenea: +33 (0)6 21 37 40 71.
Gîtes, vacation rentals, and campsites
For information: +33 (0)5 59 29 93 99
www.ainhoa-tourisme.com

🍴 Eating Out
Argi-Eder: +33 (0)5 59 93 72 00.
Auberge Alzate: +33 (0)5 59 29 77 15.
Ithurria: +33 (0)5 59 29 92 11.
Ohantzea, tea room:
+33 (0)5 59 29 90 50.
Oppoca: +33 (0)5 59 29 90 72.
Pain d'Épice d'Ainhoa, tea room:
+33 (0)5 59 29 34 17.
Ur-Hegian: +33 (0)5 59 29 91 16.

🏛 Local Specialties
Food and Drink
Pain d'épice (spice cake) • Salted meats and fish • Basque specialties.
Art and Crafts
Artisan perfumer • Jeweler, artist-creator.

🗓 Events
April: Mountain-biking tour.
Pentecost: Pilgrimage to Notre-Dame-de-l'Aubépine (Monday).
May: Journée de la Nature et du Terroir, desmonstrations relating to farm animals and plants by local producers and breeders.
June–September: Basque pelota games, Basque songs in the church.
July: "Xareta Oinez" hiking trail (3rd Sunday).
August: *Romeria* (open-air meal) and *xahakoa* (wineskin) drinking championship; festivals (15th).
October: Fête de la Palombe, pigeon festival, including cooking demonstrations, Basque songs, local produce and craft fair.

🏐 Outdoor Activities
Basque pelota • Walking: Routes GR 8 and 10, and 5 marked trails • Mountain-biking: 1 marked trail.

🦋 Further Afield
• Urdax and Zugarramurdi caves (3–5 miles/5–8 km).
• Espelette (4 miles/6.5 km).
• *Sare (5 miles/8 km), see pp. 252–53.
• Cambo-les-Bains (7 miles/11.5 km).
• Saint-Pée-sur-Nivelle (7½ miles/12 km).
• Saint-Jean-de-Luz; Bayonne; Biarritz (14–17 miles/23–27 km).
• *La Bastide-Clairence (19 miles/31 km), see pp. 162–63.
• *Saint-Jean-Pied-de-Port (27 miles/43 km), see pp. 246–47.

Ars-en-Ré

Between port and marshes

Charente-Maritime (17) • Population: 1,315 • Altitude: 10 ft. (3 m)

At the far west of the island, the village's bell tower keeps vigil over the ocean and the Fiers d'Ars marshes. Born from the salt marshes created in the 11th century and still exploited by more than sixty salt merchants, Ars is one of the Île de Ré's oldest parishes. The church retains its 12th-century door and its 15th-century bell tower, whose 130 ft. (40 m) black-and-white spire used to serve as a day-mark for seafarers. In the Rue des Tourettes, the two corner towers of the Maison du Sénéchal, built in the 16th century, are a reminder that the village was once under the jurisdiction of a seneschal. Abandoned by ships coming from Northern Europe to load salt, the port now provides shelter for pleasure craft. Pleasant to explore on foot or bike, the narrow streets, dotted with hollyhocks, are lined with white houses with green or light blue shutters, typical of the traditional architecture of this region.

By road: Expressway A10, exit 33–La Rochelle (58 miles/93 km), N11-N237 (17 miles/27 km).
By train: La Rochelle station (22 miles/35 km).
By air: La Rochelle-Laleu airport (19 miles/31 km).

(i) **Tourist information:** +33 (0)5 46 29 46 09
www.iledere-arsenre.com

👁 Highlights
• Église Saint-Étienne (12th, 15th, and 17th centuries): Romanesque style; arched door, rich furnishings.
• **Tours of the bell tower and salt marshes:** April to September.
• **Huîtrière de Ré, oyster farm:** Guided tours April to September, Wednesday evening with tasting and Thursday evening: +33 (0)5 46 29 44 24.

🗝 Accommodation
Hotels
Le Clocher***: +33 (0)5 46 29 41 20.
Le Martray***: +33 (0)5 46 29 40 04.
Le Sénéchal***: +33 (0)5 46 29 40 42.
Le Parasol**: +33 (0)5 46 29 46 17.
Thalassotherapy resorts
Côté Thalasso Ile de Ré***:
+33 (0)5 46 29 10 00.
Vacation rentals and guesthouses
Further information: +33 (0)5 46 29 46 09
www.iledere-arsenre.com
Holiday villages
La Salicorne, VVF: +33 (0)5 46 29 45 13.

Campsites
Le Cormoran*****: +33 (0)5 46 29 68 27.
Les Dunes****: +33 (0)5 46 29 41 41.
ESSI***: +33 (0)5 46 29 44 73.
Le Soleil***: +33 (0)5 46 29 40 62.
La Combe à l'Eau*: +33 (0)5 46 29 46 42.

🍽 Eating Out
Le 20 [vingt], wine bar, world cuisine:
+33 (0)5 46 29 69 52.
L'Annexe: +33 (0)5 46 34 06 71.
Au Goûter Breton: +33 (0)5 46 29 41 36.
Aux Frères de la Côte, brasserie:
+33 (0)5 46 29 04 54.
Le Bistrot du Martray:
+33 (0)5 46 29 40 04.
La Cabane du Fier: +33 (0)5 46 29 64 84.
Le Café du Commerce, brasserie/crêperie:
+33 (0)5 46 29 41 57.
Chez Rémi: +33 (0)5 46 29 40 26.
Le Clocher: +33 (0)5 46 29 41 20.
Le Grenier à Sel: +33 (0)5 46 29 08 62.
Le K'Ré d'Ars: +33 (0)5 46 29 94 94.
L'Océane: +33 (0)5 46 29 24 70.
Ô de Mer: +33 (0)5 46 29 23 33.

Le Parasol: +33 (0)5 46 29 46 17.
La Pointe de Grignon: +33 (0)5 46 29 10 00.
Sans Foie ni Loix, beer and tapas bar:
+33 (0)9 50 44 37 97.
Le Soleil d'Ars: +33 (0)5 46 43 09 27.
La Tour du Sénéchal, light meals, seafood: +33 (0)5 46 29 41 12.
Le "V": +33 (0)5 46 29 45 56.

🧺 Local Specialties
Food and Drink
Strawberries • Shrimp • Oysters • AOP early potatoes • Salt and *fleur de sel* sea salt • Wine and Pineau.
Art and Crafts
Antique dealers • Artists.

📅 Events
Markets: Daily 8 a.m.–1 p.m., Place du Marché-d'Été (April–September) or Tuesdays and Fridays 8 a.m.–1 p.m., Place Carnot (Winter).
July and August: Concerts, "Embrasement du Clocher," firework display and dance, regattas.

🦋 Outdoor Activities
Bathing: La Grange beach • Cycling: Cycle paths across the marshes to the nature reserve at Fiers d'Ars • Walking: 3 marked trails • Sailing • Riding • Thalassotherapy.

🌿 Further Afield
• Saint-Clément-des-Baleines: Lighthouse and Parc des Incas (3 miles/5 km).
• Les Portes-en-Ré: Maison du Fier et de la Nature (6 miles/9.5 km).
• Loix-en-Ré: Écomusée du Marais Salant, local heritage museum (7½ miles/12 km).
• Saint-Martin-de-Ré: fortifications (7½ miles/12 km).
• *La Flotte (11 miles/18 km), see pp. 196–97.
• La Rochelle (21 miles/34 km).

🗡 Did you know?
Producing more than 2,000 tons of salt every year, the salt marshes lie behind the development of Ars. The huge *salorge*, where the salt was stored, now houses the covered market, and some fine merchant houses are still visible on the Rue du Havre.

Aubeterre-sur-Dronne

Monolithic grandeur amid the white rocks

Charente (16) • Population: 422 • Altitude: 295 ft. (90 m)

Nestled against a chalky limestone cliff, Aubeterre overlooks the verdant valley of the Dronne river and boasts an extraordinary cultural heritage. Around its central square, a labyrinth of roofs and house fronts bedecked with wooden galleries and balconies stretches out. Facing the castle of this old fortress town, which was destroyed by the English and then by the Huguenots, and whose imposing gate still overlooks the Dronne, stands the Église Saint-Jacques, with its fine Romanesque façade. At the turn of every street and steep alleyway, the visitor is reminded of Aubeterre's religious past: pilgrims on their way to Santiago de Compostela would stop at the church and three former convents, and the village also features the monolithic Église Saint-Jean, which was carved into the rock near a primitive worship site in the 12th century. For an unforgettable experience, explore the underground building and necropolis beneath its high vaults of light and shade.

By road: Expressway A89, exit 11–Coutras (27 miles/43 km). **By train:** Chalais station (7½ miles/12 km). **By air:** Bergerac-Roumanière airport (43 miles/69 km).

ⓘ **Tourist information:**
+33 (0)5 45 98 57 18
www.sudcharentetourisme.fr
www.aubeterresurdronne.com

👁 Highlights

• **Église Saint-Jacques:** Originally built in the 12th century but rebuilt in the 17th century; Romanesque façade with finely carved vaulted archways and Moorish ornamentation.
• **Monolithic underground Église Saint-Jean:** Hewn into the cliff face in the 12th century. A unique construction housing a reliquary, a central relic pit, and a necropolis containing more than 160 stone sarcophagi.
• **Musée-espace Ludovic-Trarieux:** An exhibition focusing on human rights and on Ludovic Trarieux, the founder of the French Human Rights League.
• **Village:** Guided tours all year round by appointment only for groups; in the summer, possibility of individual visits: +33 (0)5 45 98 57 18 or +33 (0)6 79 85 81 26.

🗝 Accommodation

Hotels
Hostellerie du Périgord**:
+33 (0)5 45 98 50 46.
Guesthouses
Aubeterre-sur-Dronne:
+33 (0)5 45 98 04 08.
Gaillardon: +33 (0)6 22 13 39 40.
♥ Les Logis de la Tour:
+33 (0)6 43 61 40 77.
Gîtes
Further information: +33 (0)5 45 98 57 18
www.sudcharentetourisme.fr
Campsites
Bord de Dronne***: +33 (0)6 87 29 18 36.

🍽 Eating Out

Au Cochon Prieur: +33 (0)5 45 78 87 43.
Le Comptoir d'Alba Terra:
+33 (0)5 45 78 38 45.
Crêperie de la Source, in summer:
+33 (0)5 45 98 61 78.
Cupcakes, tea room: +33 (0)5 45 78 32 68.
Le Garage, light meals:
+33 (0)5 45 98 18 19.
Hostellerie du Périgord:
+33 (0)5 45 98 50 46.
Hôtel de France: +33 (0)5 45 98 50 43.
Restaurant de la Plage, in summer:
+33 (0)5 45 78 22 91.
La Ruchette, tea room:
+33 (0)9 66 98 40 15.
Sel et Sucre, crêperie, in summer:
+33 (0)5 45 98 60 91.
La Tapazzeria: +33 (0)5 45 98 37 11.
La Taverne de Pierre Véry:
+33 (0)5 45 98 15 53.

🧺 Local Specialties

Food and Drink
Foie gras and duck confit • Pineau • Cognac.
Art and Crafts
Antique dealer • Cabinetmaker • Potters • Wood turners • Metalworker • Ceramicist • Dressmaker • Leatherwork.

🗓 Events

May: Fête de l'Ascension; artists' festival.
July: Fête de la Saint-Jacques (last weekend).
July and August: Evening musical events in the monolithic church.

🦋 Outdoor Activities

Swimming • Canoeing • Fishing • Walking.

🌿 Further Afield

• Romanesque churches at Pillac, Rouffiac, and Saint-Aulaye (5 miles/8 km).
• Chalais: medieval town (7 miles/11.5 km).
• Villebois-Lavalette: castle; covered market (12 miles/19 km).
• Cognac and Bordeaux vineyards (28 miles/45 km).
• Angoulême (30 miles/48 km).
• Périgueux (34 miles/55 km).

⚑ Did you know?

Hewn into the hillside on which the castle stands, Aubeterre-sur-Dronne's subterranean church is one of the largest in Europe. The vault carved into the limestone is 56 ft. (17 m) high. A stairway cut into the rock provides access to the upper gallery, which surrounds the church on three sides. In the sanctuary there is a hexagonal reliquary, 20 ft. (6 m) high and 10 ft. (3 m) in diameter, which was carved from a single block of stone during the Romanesque period.

Autoire

Medieval stone and red tiles amid vines and tree-covered hills

Lot (46) • Population: 345 • Altitude: 738 ft. (225 m)

The village takes its name from the Autoire, the mountain stream that rushes down from the Causse de Gramat limestone plateau in a series of waterfalls before reaching the first ocher manor houses.

At the center of a cirque—a deep, high-walled basin—square dovecotes and the corbeled façades of rustic dwellings stand next to the turrets of manor houses. The Laroque-Delprat manor and the Château de Limargue are located downhill from the village. Higher up, the Château de Busqueille, built in the late 16th century, rises above the brown-tiled roofs. In the 14th century Autoire was besieged by the English, who had already been victorious in the region of Haut Quercy. One of the village's castles (the Château des Anglais) served as a hideout for traveling mercenaries during the Hundred Years War. Autoire was laid waste by the Calvinists in 1562 and did not see peace again until 1588. The only remains of the village's fortified ensemble is the Église Saint-Pierre, which dates back to the 11th and 12th centuries. The square bell tower is covered with flat stone *lauzes* (schist tiles) rather than the tiles used on other roofs in the village.

By road: Expressway A20, exit 54–Gramat (24 miles/39 km). **By train:** Biars-sur-Cèren station (9½ miles/15.5 km). **By air:** Brive-Vallée de la Dordogne airport (30 miles/48 km).

ⓘ Tourist information—Vallée de la Dordogne: +33 (0)5 65 33 22 00 www.vallee-dordogne.com

👁 Highlights
• Église Saint-Pierre (11th–12th centuries).
• **Village:** Guided tours in July and August: +33 (0)5 65 33 81 36.

🗝 Accommodation
Hotels
Auberge de la Fontaine: +33 (0)5 65 10 85 40.
Guesthouses
M. Sebregts: +33 (0)6 71 71 07 89.
Gîtes and vacation rentals
M. Blankoff: +33 (0)1 43 80 69 76.
Mlle Chovanec: +33 (0)5 65 38 15 61.
M. Fouilhac: +33 (0)5 65 38 12 02.
M. Frauciel: +33 (0)5 65 10 98 86.
M. Lacam: +33 (0)9 70 91 23 20.
M. Lemonnier: +33 (0)2 33 95 13 16.
M. Magnac: +33 (0)6 10 02 53 25.
M. Marchandet: +33 (0)5 65 38 13 50.
M. Santolaria: +33 (0)2 33 94 22 54.
M. Sebregts: +33 (0)6 71 71 07 89.
Mme Trassy: +33 (0)5 65 38 21 74.

🍽 Eating Out
Auberge de la Fontaine: +33 (0)5 65 10 85 40.
La Cascade, crêperie: +33 (0)6 07 86 90 62 or (0)5 65 38 20 02.

🧺 Local Specialties
Food and Drink
Cabécou cheese • Mushrooms • Honey • Wine.

Art and Crafts
Weaving workshop.

📅 Events
July: Flea market (14th); local saint's day with firework display (last weekend).
August: Gourmet market.

🦋 Outdoor Activities
Rock climbing • Fishing • Mountain-biking • Walking: Route GR 480 and 8 marked trails.

🌿 Further Afield
• Cascade d'Autoire, waterfall (½ mile/1 km).
• *Loubressac (3 miles/5 km), see p. 210.
• Saint-Céré (3 miles/5 km).
• Grotte de Presque, caves (4½ miles/7 km).
• Montal and Castelnau castles (4½ miles/7 km).
• Gouffre de Padirac, chasm (6 miles/9.5 km).
• *Carennac (8 miles/13 km), see pp. 179–80.
• Rocamadour (12 miles/19 km).
• *Curemonte (16 miles/26 km), see p. 189.
• *Collonges-la-Rouge (22 miles/35 km), see p. 184–85.
• *Turenne (22 miles/35 km), see pp. 262–63.
• *Capdenac-le-Haut (29 miles/47 km), see p. 177.

Auvillar

A port on the Garonne river

Tarn-et-Garonne (82) • Population: 999 • Altitude: 377 ft. (115 m)

A stopping place on one of the pilgrimage routes to Santiago de Compostela, the former fiefdom of the kings of Navarre still watches over the Garonne river.

Located on the Via Podiensis linking Le Puy-en-Velay to the Chemin de Saint-Jacques-de-Compostelle (Saint James's Way), on the banks of the Garonne, Auvillar bears traces of its dual religious and trading role. Unique in the southwest, the covered market, built in 1824 during the city's heyday, is composed of an outer circular building—embellished with Tuscan columns—and a central structure. Inside, you can still see stone and metal grain measures, recalling the importance of the market for locally produced cereals. Serving as its setting, the magical triangular plaza, which dates from the Middle Ages, has 15th- and 17th-century half-timbered red-brick mansions. This former stronghold stands on a rocky spur and has retained traces of its fortifications, including a door crowned with a brick-and-stone clock tower dating from the late 17th century. Outside of the upper town, the former Benedictine priory attached to the Abbaye de Moissac has become the Église Saint-Pierre (12th and 14th centuries), and is considered one of the finest in the diocese of Montauban. For a long time an inland shipping center, the port has retained its chapel dedicated to Saint Catherine, the patron saint of mariners.

By road: Expressway A62, exit 8–Valence-d'Agen (3 miles/5 km). **By train:** Valence-d'Agen station (3½ miles/5.5 km); Moissac station (12 miles/19 km). **By air:** Agen-La Garenne airport (21 miles/34 km); Toulouse-Blagnac airport (56 miles/90 km).

ⓘ **Tourist information:**
+33 (0)5 63 39 89 82
www.auvillar.eu

👁 Highlights
• **Chapelle Sainte-Catherine** (in summer): Murals: +33 (0)5 63 39 89 82.
• **Église Saint-Pierre:** Contains a remarkable Baroque altarpiece.
• **Musée de la Faïence:** Museum of popular art and traditions with a collection of 18th- and 19th-century Auvillar earthenware: +33 (0)5 63 39 89 82.
• **Musée de la Batellerie:** Located in the clock tower, the museum presents the history of navigation on the Garonne river in past centuries. Further information: +33 (0)5 63 39 89 82.
• **Village:** Guided tour for groups of 10+. Further information and bookings: +33 (0)5 63 39 89 82.

🗝 Accommodation
Hotels
L'Horloge: +33 (0)5 63 39 91 61.
Guesthouses
Allison Feeley****: +33 (0)5 81 11 51 26.
L'Arbudet***: +33 (0)6 64 62 07 52.
Claude Dassonville***: +33 (0)5 63 29 07 43.
Jacques Sarraut***: +33 (0)5 63 39 62 45.
Nicole Lamer**: +33 (0)5 63 39 70 02.
Further information and other guest rooms:
+33 (0)5 63 39 89 82 / www.auvillar.eu

Gîtes
Gisèle Chambaron***:
+33 (0)5 63 29 04 31.
Gîte communal d'Étape et de Séjour***
Patrice Cagnati***: +33 (0)6 89 29 58 08.
Marie-Thérèse Desprez***:
+33 (0)5 63 39 01 08.
Further information: +33 (0)5 63 39 89 82
www.auvillar.eu

🍽 Eating Out
Al Dente, pizzeria: +33 (0)5 63 32 20 55.
Alta Villa: +33 (0)5 63 29 20 09.
Le Bacchus: +33 (0)5 63 29 12 20.
Le Baladin, crêperie/steak house (summer only): +33 (0)5 63 39 73 61.
L'Horloge: +33 (0)5 63 39 91 61.
Le Petit Palais: +33 (0)5 63 29 13 17.

🧺 Local Specialties

Food and Drink
Fruit juice, fruit produce • Brulhois wines • Jams and honey.

Art and Crafts
Calligrapher • Potter • Ceramicist • Art galleries • Artists • Soap.

2 Events

Market: Sunday mornings, farmers' market.
Palm Sunday: Dressmakers' market.
May–August: Music events.
Pentecost: Saint-Noé, Fête des Vignerons et des Félibres, winemakers' and Provençal poets' festival (1st weekend after Pentecost).
July: Antiques fair (July 13–14); Craftsmen's event (last weekend); dramatized evening walks.

August: Dog show (2nd weekend), port festival (15th).
October: Pottery market (2nd weekend).
December: Christmas evening market (2nd Saturday).
All year round: Art and crafts exhibitions.

🦋 Outdoor Activities

Hunting • Fishing • Walking: Route GR 65 and various trails.

🦋 Further Afield

• Voie Verte, picturesque greenway (3 miles/5 km).
• Golfech: nuclear site, "fish elevator" linking two canals (3½ miles/5.5 km).
• Donzac : Musée de la Ruralité (5 miles/8 km).
• Fortified towns of Dune, Castelsagrat, and Monjoi (8–17 miles/13–27 km).

• Moissac (12 miles/19 km).
• Agen (21 miles/34 km).
• *Lauzerte (21 miles/34 km), see pp. 204–5.

🛈 Did you know?

Auvillar potters have used clay and marl from the deposits found in the Garonne plains since Gallo-Roman times. Earthenware manufacture was very important here in the 18th and 19th centuries. Auvillar earthenware is distinguished by its colored—combed or sponged—edges, and predominant colors of blue and red. The Musée du Vieil Auvillar has an interesting collection of it on display.

La Bastide-Clairence

A bastide for the arts in Basque Country

Pyrénées-Atlantiques (64) • Population: 1,016 • Altitude: 164 ft. (50 m)

La Bastide-Clairence has a Basque face and a Gascon accent, with its white façades and its attractive half-timbering painted in red or green.

Bastida de Clarenza was founded in 1312 to secure a river port on the Joyeuse, and thus provide the kingdom of Navarre with a new maritime outlet. The founding charter signed by the king of Navarre, the future Louis X the Headstrong, granted land and tax benefits to the city, which developed throughout the Middle Ages and was home to the states of Navarre from 1627 to 1706. The town planning of the *bastides* of Aquitaine has been retained here; a grid pattern is observed with, in the center of the village, the Place des Arceaux. Characteristic spaces separate not only the houses but also the *cazalots*. These small gardens at the rear of the houses, built originally on identical plots known as *plaza*, were allocated to the first settlers, Basques, Gascons, and "Francos"—Compostela pilgrims who stayed on here. In one of the streets leading from the square, the world's oldest *trinquet* or *jeu de paume* court, dating from 1512, is still in use. The church of Notre-Dame-de-l'Assomption, built in 1315, is remarkable for its porch, the only remains of the original 14th-century building, and its lateral cloisters paved with tombstones. Next to the Christian cemetery, the Hebrew inscriptions in the Jewish cemetery, like the Hebrew names of some of the houses, are a reminder that in the 17th and 18th centuries La Bastide-Clairence welcomed an important Sephardic community fleeing the Spanish and Portuguese inquisitions. Motivated by its artisanal past, the village is currently home to more than a dozen artists and craftspeople, who combine tradition with innovation.

By road: Expressway A64, exit 4–Urt (3½ miles/5.5 km). **By train:** Cambo-les-Bains station (11 miles/18 km); Biarritz station (22 miles/35 km). **By air:** Biarritz-Bayonne-Anglet airport (23 miles/37 km).

ⓘ **Tourist information:**
+33 (0)5 59 29 65 05.
www.labastideclairence.com

👁 **Highlights**
• **Village:** Guided tours for groups all year round by appointment only:
+33 (0)5 59 29 65 05.
• **Discovery trail, "Les murs vous racontent"** ("the walls tell a story"; available in French only): +33 (0)5 59 29 65 05.
• **MP3 audioguide:** The history of the *bastide* told around the streets, with stories from locals (available in French only).
• *Trinquet:* The oldest *jeu de paume* court still in use (1512).

🔑 **Accommodation**
Guesthouses
Maxana****: +33 (0)5 59 70 10 10.
Argizagita***: +33 (0)5 59 70 15 54.
Le Clos Gaxen***: +33 (0)5 59 29 16 44.
La Maison Marchand***:
+33 (0)5 59 29 18 27.
Gîtes and vacation rentals
Further information: +33 (0)5 59 29 65 05
www.labastideclairence.com
Aparthotels
♥ Les Collines Iduki****:
+33 (0)5 59 70 20 81.
Holiday villages
Les Chalets de Pierretoun:
+33 (0)5 59 29 68 88.

🍴 **Eating Out**
Les Arceaux: +33 (0)5 59 29 66 70.
Iduki Ostatua: +33 (0)5 59 56 43 04.

La Table Gourmande de Ghislaine
Potentier: +33 (0)5 59 70 22 78.

🧺 Local Specialties
Food and Drink
Beef and farm produce • Basque
country cider • Foie gras and duck
confit • Sheep cheese • Macarons •
Gâteau basque.

Art and Crafts
Jeweler • Luthier • Picture framer •
Perfumer • Wood-carvers • Sculptor
in stone • Lacemaker • Multimedia
designer • Upholsterer-decorator •
Glassblower • Potters • Cosmetics
made from asses' milk • Textile designer •
Leather craftsman • Artist • Floral art •
Medieval art • Galleries.

2️⃣ Events
Market: July and August, farmers' market,
every Friday evening 7–10 p.m.
Easter: Show by the group Esperantza.
May: Book fair.
July and August: *Sardinade*, La Bastide-
Clairence festival, neighborhood festivities
(La Chapelle, Pont de Port, Pessarou,
La Côte).
September: Pottery market
(2nd weekend).

🦋 Outdoor Activities
Basque pelota • Fishing • Walking:
2 marked trails.

🦋 Further Afield
- Hasparren (5 miles/8 km).
- Isturitz and Oxocelhaya prehistoric
caves (8 miles/13 km).
- Cambo-les-Bains (9½ miles/15.5 km).
- Arbéroue valley (12 miles/19 km).
- Bayonne (16 miles/26 km).
- *Ainhoa (19 miles/31 km), see p. 154.
- *Sare (24 miles/39 km), see pp. 252–53.
- *Saint-Jean-Pied-de-Port (27 miles/
43 km), see pp. 246–47.

Belcastel

A medieval gem on the banks of the Aveyron

Aveyron (12) • Population: 219 • Altitude 1,335 ft. (407 m)

Clinging to vertiginous wooded slopes, Belcastel village is dominated by its spectacular fortified castle and dips its toes in the Aveyron river at its base.

In the 13th century, the fortress belonged to the lords of Belcastel, whose influence extended along both sides of the Aveyron, before entering into the hands of the Saunhac family at the end of the 14th century. Abandoned during the 18th century, the fortress gradually fell into disrepair. It was in 1973 that the renowned architect Fernand Pouillon discovered the ruins: he bought the site and began eight years of renovation work on it, encouraging the inhabitants of Belcastel to restore their village streets and homes too. The château-fortress now looks fondly down on the renovated village with its cobbled streets, its oven, metalworking trades, and old fountain. The 15th-century church houses the tomb of its founder, Alzias de Saunhac, who built the stone bridge with its unique altar, where passersby paid for their crossing with prayers and offerings. A stone's throw from the village, the fortified site of the Roc d'Anglars dates from the 5th century.

By road: Expressway A75, exit 42–Rodez (44 miles/70 km); D994 (15 miles/24 km).
By train: Rodez station (15 miles/24 km).
By air: Rodez-Marcillac airport (14 miles/23 km); Toulouse-Blagnac airport (103 miles/166 km).

(i) Tourist information—
Pays Rignaçois/Belcastel:
+33 (0)5 65 64 46 11
www.tourisme-pays-rignacois.fr

👁 Highlights
• **Castle:** 11th-century fortress; 16th-century arms and armour collection; contemporary art galleries inspired by the Animazing Gallery in Soho, New York: +33 (0)5 65 64 42 16.
• **Church** (15th century): Way of the Cross by Casimir Ferrer, recumbent statue on the tomb of Alzias de Saunhac, 15th-century statues: +33 (0)5 65 64 46 11.
• **Maison de la Forge et des Anciens Métiers** (smithy and traditional crafts): Tours of the village's old smithy and exhibition of tools; permanent exhibition of "sylvistructure" wood sculptures by the artist Pierre Leron-Lesur. Further information: +33 (0)5 65 64 46 11.
• **Village:** Guided tour and audioguide: +33 (0)5 65 64 46 11.

🗝 Accommodation
Hotels
Le Vieux Pont***: +33 (0)5 65 64 52 29.
Guesthouses
Le Château: +33 (0)5 65 64 42 16.
M. Rouquette: +33 (0)5 65 64 40 61.
Gîtes
www.mairie-belcastel.fr
Campsites
Camping de Belcastel**: +33 (0)5 65 63 95 61 or +33 (0)6 47 11 24 76.

ⅲ Eating Out

Le 1909 [mille neuf cent neuf]:
+33 (0)5 65 64 52 26.
Auberge Rouquette, farmhouse inn:
+33 (0)5 65 64 40 61.
Chez Anna, light meals:
+33 (0)5 65 63 95 61 or
+33 (0)6 47 11 24 76.
Le Vieux Pont: +33 (0)5 65 64 52 29.

🗓 Events

Market: July–August, sampling and purchase of local products every Friday evening.
Throughout the summer: Art exhibition of paintings, photography, and sculpture.
June: "Feu de la Saint-Jean," Saint John's Eve bonfire (last Saturday).
July: Local saint's day with village supper, fireworks, multimedia show (penultimate weekend).
September: Fête Nationale des Villages (national celebration of villages) and flea market.

🦋 Outdoor Activities

Fishing • Walking: Route GR 62B and 7 marked trails.

🌿 Further Afield

• Château de Bournazel (9½ miles/15.5 km).
• Rodez (16 miles/26 km).
• *Sauveterre-de-Rouergue (17 miles/27 km), see pp. 256–57.
• Peyrusse-le-Roc (20 miles/32 km).
• Villefranche-de-Rouergue (23 miles/37 km).
• *Capdenac-le-Haut (24 miles/39 km), see p. 177.
• *Conques (24 miles/39 km), see pp. 186–87.

ⓘ Did you know?

The village's most unusual feature, which affords a good view of the village and its valley, is the rock of Roquecante, which has seven seats cut into it. According to legend, these "lords' seats," which probably date to the 16th century, were used when the local lords were dispensing justice.

Belvès

The village of seven bell towers

Dordogne (24) • Population: 1,482 • Altitude: 591 ft. (180 m)

Dominating the verdant valley of the Nauze river from its hilltop position, Belvès provides a sweeping panorama across the landscape of Périgord Noir.

Owing to its strategic position, the village has had a turbulent past, despite the protection it received from both its rampart walls and from Pope Clement V, who granted Belvès the status of papal town when he was archbishop of Bordeaux (1297–1305). The town was besieged and invaded seven times by English forces during the Hundred Years War, and was later under siege again from Protestant forces during the Wars of Religion. It is miraculous that many legacies of Belvès' tumultuous past have survived: troglodyte cave dwellings, apparently occupied since prehistoric times; towers and bell towers from the Middle Ages; and residences and mansions in which Gothic flamboyance blends with Renaissance artistry. In the heart of the village, a historic covered market comes to life once a week, and here you can sample the many tasty products of Périgord, which change with the seasons. Beyond the gates of the town, the marked trails of the vast Bessède forest welcome walkers, horse-riders, and mountain-bikers all year round for both competition and leisure.

By road: Expressway A89, exit 17–Saint-Yrieix-la-Perche (33 miles/53 km); expressway A20, exit 55 (39 miles/63 km).
By train: Belvès station.
By air: Bergerac-Roumanière airport (30 miles/48 km); Brive-Vallée de la Dordogne airport (50 miles/80 km).

ⓘ Tourist information—
Vallée Dordogne Forêt Bessède:
+33 (0)5 53 29 10 20
www.perigordnoir-valleedordogne.com

👁 Highlights

• **Troglodyte dwellings:** Discover how peasants lived in these caves in the 13th to 18th centuries; games book for children aged 6-13. Further information and bookings: +33 (0)5 53 29 10 20.
• **Castrum:** Guided tours in summer, self-guided visits and audioguides all year round. Further information: +33 (0)5 53 29 10 20.
• **Église de Notre-Dame-de-l'Assomption:** Renaissance painting; guided tours in summer, self-guided visits all year round. Further information: +33 (0)5 53 29 10 20.
• **Castle and wall paintings** (14th–16th centuries): Visit the principal furnished rooms; only wall paintings in Aquitaine representing the Nine Valiant Knights of legend, as well as a historical scene of Belvès in 1470. Further information: +33 (0)5 53 29 10 20.
• **La Filature** (spinning mill) **de Belvès:** Spinning mill and impressive machine room, testament to the village's industrial past. Self-guided visits and activities for children. Further information: +33 (0)5 53 31 83 05.
• **La Dédale:** Contemporary art trail through the heart of the medieval town.

• **Village:** Guided tours for groups by arrangement: +33 (0)5 53 29 10 20; self-guided family trail with educational booklet for children, free audio-guided route available to download: +33 (0)5 53 29 10 93.

🔑 Accommodation

Hotels
♥ Le Clément V***: +33 (0)5 53 28 68 80.
Le Home*: +33 (0)5 53 29 01 65.
Guesthouses
Le Manoir de la Moissie:
+33 (0)5 53 29 93 49 or +33 (0)6 85 08 80 26.
Le Petit Bonheur: +33 (0)5 53 59 67 88.
Gîtes, walkers' lodges, and vacation rentals
Le Madelon: +33 (0)5 53 31 15 70.
Further information: +33 (0)5 53 29 10 20
www.perigordnoir-valleedordogne.com
Holiday villages
Domaine de la Bessède: +33 (0)5 53 31 94 60.
L'Échappée Verte: +33 (0)5 53 29 15 51.
Les Hauts de Lastours: +33 (0)5 53 29 00 42.

Campsites
Le Moulin de la Pique****:
+33 (0)5 53 29 01 15.
Les Nauves***: +33 (0)5 53 29 12 64
or +33 (0)6 85 15 32 73.

🍴 Eating Out
La Brasserie de la Halle:
+33 (0)5 47 96 93 68.
Le Café de Paris, brasserie:
+33 (0)5 53 59 62 40.
Le Calascio, pizzeria: +33 (0)6 23 82 39 84.
L'Échappée: +33 (0)6 07 18 73 51.
Le Madelon, brasserie:
+33 (0)5 53 31 15 70.
Le Médiéval Café, brasserie:
+33 (0)5 53 30 29 83.
Le Parfum des Mets:
+33 (0)5 53 59 60 34.
Le Pourquoi Pas, tea room:
+33 (0)5 53 29 46 18.
Les Terrasses de Belvès:
+33 (0)5 53 28 25 48.

🧺 Local Specialties
Food and Drink
Foie gras • Honey • Farm produce •
Truffles • Farmers' market.
Art and Crafts
Antique dealer • Cutler • Cabinetmaker •
Metalworker • Painters • Wool spinner •
Sculptor • Stained-glass artist • Mosaic
artist.

📅 Events
Market: Saturday mornings, Place
de la Halle.
April: "Les 100 km du Périgord Noir,"
ultra-marathon (last Saturday).
July: Flea market (1st Sunday),
Republican supper (14th).
July–August: Bach festival; gourmet
market (Wednesday evenings).
August: Medieval festival (1st Sunday),
air display (15th), open-air rummage sale.
September: Pilgrimage to Notre-Dame-
de-Capelou (start of the month).

🦋 Outdoor Activities
Swimming • Horse-riding • Fishing • Walking:
75 miles (121 km) of marked trails, Route
GR 36 and other routes in the Dordogne
valley along the Saint James's Way to
Santiago de Compostela • Aerial sports.

🌿 Further Afield
• Abbaye de Cadouin (8½ miles/14 km).
• Dordogne valley: *Castelnaud-la-Chapelle
(11 miles/18 km), see p. 182; *Limeuil
(12 miles/19 km), see pp. 208–9; *Beynac-et-
Cazenac (14 miles/23 km), see pp. 168–69;
*La Roque-Gageac (14 miles/23 km), see
pp. 234–35; *Domme (15 miles/24 km),
see pp. 190–91.
• Pays des Bastides (9–19 miles/14.5–31 km):
*Monpazier (10 miles/16 km), see
pp. 215–16.
• Sarlat (22 miles/35 km).
• Vézère valley (16–31 miles/26–50 km):
*Saint-Léon-sur-Vézère (24 miles/39 km),
see p. 248.

Beynac-et-Cazenac
Two villages, one castle, and a river

Dordogne (24) • Population: 511 • Altitude: 427 ft. (130 m)

Curled at the foot of an imposing castle that surveys the Dordogne, Beynac-et-Cazenac is a beautiful spot enhanced by both the sublime river and the food of the region.

Occupied since the Bronze Age (c. 2000 BCE) in a settlement that has been reconstructed in the current archeological park, the naturally defensive site of Beynac became the seat of one of the four baronies of Périgord during the Middle Ages. Besieged by Richard the Lionheart in 1197, then demolished by Simon de Montfort, the castle was rebuilt before being captured and recaptured during the Hundred Years War (1337–1453) by the armies of both the English and French kings. It was then abandoned during the French Revolution. Its owner began restoration work in 1961 and opened it to the public. The impressive castle towers over the village's *lauze* (schist-tiled) rooftops and golden façades. Nestling between river and cliff, and protected by a wall in which only the Veuve gateway remains, for many years Beynac made its living from the passing trade on the Dordogne. The *gabares* (sailing barges) have abandoned the old port, which is now a park, and are today used for river trips, sharing the water with other boats and canoes. On the plateau dominating the valley, the chapel at Cazenac, a village joined to Beynac in 1827, is moving in its simplicity.

By road: Expressway A89, exit 18–Terrasson-la-Villedieu (39 miles/63 km); expressway A20, exit 55 (27 miles/43 km).
By train: Sarlat-la-Canéda station (7 miles/11.5 km).
By air: Brive-Vallée de la Dordogne airport (35 miles/56 km); Bergerac-Roumanière airport (40 miles/64 km).

ⓘ Tourist information—
Sarlat-Périgord Noir: +33 (0)5 53 31 45 45
www.sarlat-tourisme.com

👁 **Highlights**
• **Château de Beynac:** Range of 12th–17th century buildings, restored in 20th century: +33 (0)5 53 29 50 40.
• **Archeological park:** How our ancestors lived from the Neolithic period to the Iron Age; guided tours. Educational workshops for children: +33 (0)5 53 29 51 28.
• **Village:** Regular guided tours June–September, by appointment the rest of the year: +33 (0)5 53 31 45 42. Special event August 15: guided tour.
• ♥ **Gabarres de Beynac:** Boat trips along the Dordogne river: +33 (0)5 53 28 51 15.

⚔ **Accommodation**
Hotels
Hostellerie Maleville–Hôtel Pontet**: +33 (0)5 53 29 50 06.
Hôtel du Château**: +33 (0)5 53 29 19 20.
Café de la Rivière: +33 (0)5 53 28 35 49.
Guesthouses
Guy Gauthier: +33 (0)5 53 29 51 45.
Résidence Versailles: +33 (0)5 53 29 35 06.
Vacation rentals and gîtes
Further information: +33 (0)5 53 29 43 08 in season or +33 (0)5 53 31 45 45 off-season
www.sarlat-tourisme.com

Campsites
Le Capeyrou***: + 33 (0)5 53 29 54 95.

🍴 Eating Out
Auberge Lembert: +33 (0)5 53 29 50 45.
Café de la Rivière: +33 (0)5 53 28 35 49.
Hostellerie Maleville–Hôtel Pontet:
+33 (0)5 53 29 50 06.
La Petite Tonnelle: +33 (0)5 53 29 95 18.
Restaurant du Château: +33 (0)5 53 29 19 20.
La Taverne des Remparts:
+33 (0)5 53 29 57 76.

🧺 Local Specialties
Food and Drink
Duck, goose • Traditional preserves.
Art and Crafts
Painter • Painter-enamelists • Potters •
Metal artist.

📅 Events
Mid-June to mid-September: Farmers'
market every Monday morning,
La Balme car park.
August: Fireworks (15th).

🦋 Outdoor Activities
Canoeing on the Dordogne • Fishing •
Walking: 2 marked trails • Balloon flights •
Mountain-biking: 5 marked trails.

🌿 Further Afield
• Dordogne valley: Château de Marqueyssac:
park and hanging gardens (1 mile/1.5 km);
Château de Castelnaud; Château des
Milandes; *Castelnaud-la-Chapelle:
Ecomusée de la Noix, walnut museum
(2½ miles/4 km), see p. 182; *La Roque-
Gageac (3 miles/5 km), see pp. 234–35;
*Domme (7 miles/11.5 km)o, see pp. 190–91;
*Belvès (14 miles/23 km), see pp. 166–67;
*Limeuil (18 miles/29 km), see pp. 208–9.
• Sarlat (7 miles/11.5 km).
• Les Eyzies; Vézère valley (16–31 miles/
26–50 km).
• *Saint-Léon-sur-Vézère (21 miles/34 km),
see p. 248.
• *Saint-Amand-de-Coly (22 miles/35 km),
see pp. 236–37.
• *Monpazier (24 miles/39 km), see pp. 215–16.

ℹ Did you know?
The *gabares* sailing barges evolved from
a different kind of barge that plied the
waters of the Dordogne. They carried
locally made wines to the port of
Bordeaux. Many *gabares* used to dock
at the old port of Beynac right up until
the 19th century.

Blesle

Benedictine memories at the gateway to the Haute-Loire

Haute-Loire (43) • Population: 653 • Altitude: 1,706 ft. (520 m)

At the end of a narrow, isolated valley that invites meditation, the echoes of Benedictine monks' prayers have for centuries blended with the murmurs of the rivers that bring life to the village of Blesle.

At the end of the 9th century, Ermengarde, countess of Auvergne, founded an abbey dedicated to Saint Peter here; then, two centuries later, the barons de Mercoeur built an impressive fortress. The village grew up under the protection of these two powers: one spiritual and the other temporal. It became one of the thirteen *bonnes villes* (which received privileges and protection from the king in exchange for providing a contingent of armed men) of Auvergne, and welcomed lawyers and merchants; they rubbed shoulders with tanners, weavers, and wine producers. Sheltered within its medieval surrounding wall, Blesle invites visitors to discover more than ten centuries of heritage. Several towers that were part of the old wall can still be seen on Boulevard du Vallat, itself built on the site of earlier ditches. Only the keep and a watchtower remain of the fortress, but the Église de Saint-Pierre and nearly fifty houses, many of which are half-timbered, preserve the memory of the Benedictine founders and the many trades that brought prosperity to the village.

By road: Expressway A75, exit 22–Blesle (5 miles/8 km). **By train:** Brioude station (14 miles/23 km). **By air:** Clermont-Ferrand Auvergne airport (46 miles/74 km).

ⓘ **Tourist information:**
+33 (0)4 71 74 97 49
www.tourismeblesle.fr

👁 Highlights

• Abbey church of Saint-Pierre: 12th–13th centuries.
• Église de Saint-Pierre: Liturgical vestments, silver plate, statues from the abbey; visits by appointment only: +33 (0)4 71 74 97 49.
• Musée de la Coiffe: Headdresses, bonnets, ribbons, hats from the region (late 18th century–early 20th century): +33 (0)4 71 74 97 49.
• Village: Guided tours in summer by appointment for individuals, all year for groups; accessible tours for visually impaired (large-print and Braille guidebooks): +33 (0)4 71 74 97 49.

🗝 Accommodation

Hotels
La Bougnate***: +33 (0)4 71 76 29 30.
Le Scorpion: +33 (0)4 71 76 28 98.
Guesthouses
Chez Margaridou***: +33 (0)4 71 76 22 29.
Aux Amis de Bacchus, M. and Mme Doremus: +33 (0)4 71 76 21 38 or +33 (0)6 84 50 97 12.
Le Bailli de Chazelon: +33 (0)4 71 76 21 98.
Gîtes, vacation rentals, and walkers' lodges
Further information: +33 (0)4 71 74 97 49.
Campsites
Camping municipal de la Bessière**: +33 (0)4 71 76 25 82 or +33 (0)4 71 76 20 75 off-season.

🍴 Eating Out

La Barrière: +33 (0)4 71 74 64 22.
♥ La Bougnate: +33 (0)4 71 76 29 30.
Le Scorpion: +33 (0)4 71 76 28 98.
La Tour: +33 (0)4 71 76 22 97.

🧺 Local Specialties

Food and Drink
Charcuterie, salted meats, and fish •
Local cheeses • Local beers • Auvergne
liqueurs and wines.
Art and Crafts
Antiques dealer • Potter.

📅 Events

July: Painting and sketching competition
in the village streets (2nd Saturday); flea
market and open-air rummage sale (last
Sunday).
July–August: Local market (preserves,
foie gras), Fridays from 5 p.m., Place
du Vallat.
August: Festival of Les Apéros Musique
(weekend of 15th); Fête d'Été summer fair
(weekend before 15th); flea market.
November: Saint-Martin Fair (11th).

🦋 Outdoor Activities

Fishing • Walking: 17 trails, 2 mountain-
biking trails.

🌿 Further Afield

• Gorges of the Alagnon: Chateaux
of Montgon, Torsiac, and Léotoing
(3–6 miles/5–9.5 km).
• Cézallier (4½–12 miles/7–19 km).
• Château de Lespinasse (6 miles/9.5 km).
• Gorges of the Sianne (6 miles/9.5 km).
• Brioude (14 miles/23 km).
• Ardes-sur-Couze: safari park (16 miles/26 km).
• *Lavaudieu (19 miles/31 km), see p. 108.
• Issoire (22 miles/35 km).
• Saint-Flour (24 miles/39 km).

ℹ️ Did you know?

Blesle has had many famous residents:
Gaspard de Chavagnac, friend of the
prince of Condé (Protestant leader during
the Wars of Religion); Laurent Bas, who
arrested Charlotte Corday after she killed
Marat in the French Revolution; the abbé
de Pradt, Napoléon's chaplain; the author
Maurice Barrès; the 19th-century artist
Édouard Onslow; and even the holy
martyr Natalène, who was beheaded by
her father and then buried in a spot that
became the spring that bears her name.

Brouage (commune of Hiers-Brouage)

Fortified town in the marshes

Charente-Maritime (17) * Population: 650 * Altitude: 10 ft. (3 m)

Between the Île d'Oléron and Rochefort, the fortified town of Brouage looks down over the gulf of Saintonge and its marshland. This singular landscape, a veritable paradise for hundreds of species of birds, was shaped by man, who in the Middle Ages made it the salt cellar for the whole of Northern Europe. The 12th-century fortifications were built by order of Cardinal Richelieu, then governor of Brouage, in order to provide military resistance to the Protestants of La Rochelle. The town was created by Samuel de Champlain, founder of the city of Quebec and father of New France, and still bears witness to its rich history in its food market, foundries, underground ports, gunpowder magazine, and church. If, beyond the ramparts, the manufacture of salt has given way to oyster farming, mussel farming, and animal husbandry, inside the village shops and artists' workshops have taken the place of market stalls and bring the simple, bright façades typical of Charentes architecture to life.

By road: Expressway A89-A10, exit 35– Île d'Oléron–Saintes. **By train:** Stations at Rochefort (12 miles/20 km), Saintes (28 miles/45 km), La Rochelle (31 miles/ 50 km). **By air:** Rochefort-Charente-Maritime airport (6 miles/ 10 km) Rochelle-Île-de-Ré (37 miles/60 km).

(i) Tourist information:
+33 (0)5 46 85 19 16
www.hiers-brouage-tourisme.fr

👁 Highlights

• **Église Saint-Pierre** (17th century): Memorial to the religious origins of New France, tombs of rich salt merchants (17th century), soldiers, and governors; stained-glass windows celebrating friendship between France and Quebec.
• **Halle aux Vivres** (17th–20th centuries): Permanent exhibition on the history of Brouage and the salt trade; information center on military architecture: +33 (0)5 46 85 19 16.
• **Ramparts:** 1 mile (2 km) long and 26 ft. (8 m) high, reinforced with 7 bastions and 19 watchtowers; panoramic views over the marshland from the rampart walk.
• ♥ **Village:** Self-guided visit, treasure hunt on the theme of Champlain; guided or dramatized tours: +33 (0)5 46 85 19 16.

🗝 Accommodation

Hotels
Hôtel Le Brouage: +33 (0)5 46 85 03 06.
Guesthouses
La Marouette: +33 (0)5 46 76 14 01.
Mme Rabette: +33 (0)6 09 73 42 75.
Gîtes
Mme Mylène Bernard: +33 (0)5 46 85 32 21 or +33 (0)5 46 36 37 07.
M. Pierre Bugeon: +33 (0)5 46 75 12 05.

M. Jean-Luc Chassat: +33 (0)5 46 85 11 16.
Mme Huguette Gaillard:
+33 (0)5 46 95 62 98.
Mme Marie-Claire Lefebvre:
+33 (0)6 37 34 91 05.
M. Vincent Meriglier: +33 (0)5 46 36 88 27.
Mme Natacha Renoux: +33 (0)5 46 36 42 87
or +33 (0)6 17 50 43 65.
M. André Sauve: +33 (0)7 50 87 86 82.
Le Temps d'une Pause (M. and Mme Duc):
+33 (0)5 46 85 11 35 or +33 (0)6 28 27 12 83.

🍽 Eating Out
L'Auberge Saint-Denis: +33 (0)5 46 75 45 46.
La Belle Epoque: +33 (0)5 46 47 95 98.
Le Brouage: +33 (0)5 46 85 03 06.
Le Champlain: +33 (0)5 46 76 72 68.
La Citadelle: +33 (0)5 46 85 30 65.
L'Escale du Roy: +33 (0)6 78 22 28 56.
Le P'tit Biniou: +33 (0)5 46 85 13 89.

🏛 Local Specialties
Food and Drink
Salt • Oysters • Artisan candy • Local and
Quebec products.
Art and Crafts
Potter • Artisan jewelry • Painter on canvas •
Leatherwork artisan • Lace-maker •
Glassblower.

📅 Events
April to September: Art exhibitions in
military buildings (forges, cooperage,
La Brèche gunpowder magazine).
May: Flower fair in village streets (8th).
May–September: Cycling museum open
every afternoon.
June: Costumed historical fête (end
of June).
July and August: Nuits Buissonnières
(tales by torchlight), "Jeudis de Brouage"
(free family activities on Thursdays),
designers' markets.
November: Flea market in village streets
(1st).

🦋 Outdoor Activities
Walking.

🌿 Further Afield
• Marennes (4 miles/7 km).
• St-Just-Luzac and le Moulin des Loges
(6 miles/10 km).
• Bourcefranc-le-Chapus and le Fort
Louvois (7 miles/11 km).
• Île d'Oléron (9 miles/15 km).
• Rochefort-sur-Mer (11 miles/18 km).
• Saint-Sornin and la Tour de Broue
(11 miles/18 km).

• *Mornac-sur-Seudre (19 miles/30 km),
see p. 218.
• Pays Royannais (22 miles/35 km).
• Saintes (26 miles/42 km).
• *Talmont-sur-Gironde (31 miles/50 km),
see pp. 259–60.

❗ Did you know?
In the 17th century, Brouage was the
setting for an impossible love affair
between the French King Louis XIV and
Marie Mancini, niece of Cardinal de
Mazarin. The cardinal was fiercely opposed
to the union and exiled his niece to the
palace of the governor of Brouage, which
is no longer standing. The staircase that
the young Sun King climbed to reach the
ramparts in order to weep for his lost love
can still be seen flanking the Royal Forge.

Brousse-le-Château

Medieval stopover at the confluence of the Tarn and the Alrance

Aveyron (12) • Population: 171 • Altitude: 787 ft. (240 m)

Brousse stands on the banks of the Alrance river, overlooked by the imposing silhouette of its medieval castle that gives the village its name. In 935, when the Château de Brousse was first mentioned in historical records, it was just a modest fort above the Tarn. Between the 10th and 17th centuries, the fort grew steadily until it filled the whole rock. Dominating the village, it also strengthened the position of the counts du Rouergue and then, from 1204 onward, the d'Arpajon family, one of whom became a duke and French dignitary in the 17th century. Restoration work started in 1963, funded by the Vallée de l'Amitié charity, and the castle opened to the public. Between the Middle Ages and the Renaissance, Brousse was a typical fortress: its keep, towers, ramparts, arrow-slits, crenellations, and machicolations indicate its military function, while the lord's apartments and the gardens reveal the level of comfort that was to be found there. Ancient winding lanes lead to the 15th-century fortified church, which sits between a graveyard and a small chapel. Crossing the 14th-century stone bridge over the Alrance brings you to the road at the bottom of the village. Stepped terraces, cut into the sloping banks of the Alrance and the Tarn, show that vines used to grow here; these, along with chestnut groves, used to be the main source of income for Brousse-le-Château.

By road: Expressway A75, exit 46–Saint-Rome-de-Cernon (32 miles/51 km).
By train: Albi station (32 miles/51 km); Millau or Rodez stations (37 miles/60 km). **By air:** Rodez-Marcillac airport (42 miles/68 km); Toulouse-Blagnac airport (93 miles/150 km).

(i) Tourist information—Raspes du Tarn: +33 (0)5 65 99 45 40 / www.tourisme-muse-raspes.com / www.brousselechateau.net

⚲ Highlights

• **Castle:** Typical of the medieval Rouergue military style. Interior includes lord's apartments, well and water tank, bread oven: +33 (0)5 65 99 45 40.
• **Church** (15th century): Dedicated to Saint James the Greater: +33 (0)5 65 99 41 14.
• **Illuminations** of château, church, and chapel.

⚷ Accommodation

Hotels
Le Relays du Chasteau**:
+33 (0)5 65 99 40 15.
Gîtes
M. Miron***: +33 (0)5 65 35 48 04.
M. and Mme Rolland**:
+33 (0)5 65 99 47 18.
M. Tuffery**: +33 (0)4 90 75 62 79.
M. Daures*: +33 (0)5 65 99 41 45.
M. and Mme Platet: +33 (0)6 22 99 52 67.
M. and Mme Rugen: +33 (0)5 65 55 18 11.
M. and Mme Sénégas: +33 (0)5 65 99 40 15.

ⓜ Eating Out

♥ Le Relays du Chasteau:
+33 (0)5 65 99 40 15.

⛶ Local Specialties

Art and Crafts: Potter.

② Events

July: Bonfire and fireworks at the castle (13th); flea market.
July–August: Activities, music, exhibitions.
August: Local saint's day for Saint Martin de Brousse with traditional stuffed chicken (3rd weekend).

⚜ Outdoor Activities

Swimming • Fishing • Canoeing • Rowing • Walks • Mountain-biking.

⚘ Further Afield

• Châteaux de Coupiac, de Saint-Izaire, and de Montaigut (9–12 miles/14.5–19 km).
• Peyrebrune tower, Saint-Louis dolmen, Ayssènes, Saint-Victor, and Melvieu (12 miles/19 km).
• Valley of Dourdou and Saint-Affrique (21 miles/34 km).
• Pays de la Muse, region; Raspes du Tarn, gorges; Lévezou lakes (22 miles/35 km).

Bruniquel
Defying the enemy from the cliff top

Tarn-et-Garonne (82) • Population: 583 • Altitude: 541 ft. (165 m)

Bruniquel and its two medieval castles sit atop a high rocky promontory, dominating the village and surveying the confluence of the Aveyron and Vère rivers. Bruniquel certainly shows its defensive side to approaching visitors: the high, massive façades of its 600-year-old castles perched on the escarpment are truly impressive. But the village feels completely different as you explore its flower-filled paths, pass through historic gateways opening onto the ramparts, or hear the clock in the belfry. Everything is picturesque—the sculptured figures, a pair of trefoil or mullioned windows, an arched doorway. And the byword here is stone, both gray and golden. Everything about the architecture and the heritage of the village reveals Bruniquel's past lives. It was a stronghold of the counts of Toulouse and then of Louis XIII. Later it became a center of the wine, hemp, and saffron trades; this brought it an international reputation that can still be discerned today in the Maison Payrol, built in the 12th century by monks, which became home to the governors of the town in the 15th century. After that it was an industrial town, with ores from its mines feeding forges and sawmills, right up until the middle of the 20th century. Today it is a village brought to life by its craftsmen.

By road: Expressway A20, exit 59–Saint-Antonin-Noble-Val (13 miles/21 km).
By train: Montauban station (18 miles/ 29 km). **By air:** Toulouse-Blagnac airport (51 miles/82 km).

(i) **Tourist information:**
+33 (0)5 63 67 29 84
www.bruniquel.fr

👁 Highlights
• **Chateaux:** Vaulted chambers, chapel, and Renaissance gallery; museum of prehistory: +33 (0)5 63 67 27 67.
• **Village:** All-year-round audioguide tours for individuals: +33 (0)5 63 67 29 84.

⚔ Accommodation
Guesthouses
Mme Waleryszak***: +33 (0)5 63 67 25 00.
Mme Artusi*: +33 (0)5 63 24 15 26.
M. and Mme Bouvet: +33 (0)5 63 67 75 68.
M. Caulliez: +33 (0)5 63 24 17 31.
Mme Estanove: +33 (0)5 63 67 23 09.

Le Moulin de Mirande: +33 (0)5 63 24 50 50.
M. Rouquet: +33 (0)6 78 30 78 47.
Gîtes, vacation rentals, and campsites
Further information: + 33 (0)5 63 67 29 84
www.bruniquel.fr

🍴 Eating Out
Les Bastides: +33 (0)5 63 67 21 87.
Le Café Elia: +33 (0)5 63 24 19 87.
Le Délice des Papilles: +33 (0)5 63 20 30 26.
Les Gorges de l'Aveyron:
+33 (0)5 63 24 50 50.
La Taverne du Temps:
+33 (0)5 63 65 35 96.

🛒 Local Specialties
Art and Crafts
Jewelry maker • Ceramic artist • Leather engraver • Artists • Art photographer • Potter • Glassblower • Weaver.

🗓 Events
May: "Vert-Tige" plant market
(1st Sunday).
End July–early August: Offenbach Festival.
September: Les Nuits Frappées de Bruniquel, drumming festival
(1st Saturday).
December: À la Rencontre des Créateurs de Bruniquel, craft festival (1st weekend).

🦋 Outdoor Activities
Walking: Route GR 46 and 5 marked trails.
Trail with pack mules: L'Abri-Niquel:
+33 (0)5 63 24 15 26.

🌿 Further Afield
• Montricoux; Bioule; Montauban
(3–19 miles/5–31 km).
• Gorges of the Aveyron and Caylus
(4½–22 miles/7–35 km).
• *Puycelsi (8 miles/13 km), see pp. 230–31.
• *Castelnau-de-Montmiral
(14 miles/23 km), see p. 181.

Camon

The village of 100 roses

Ariège (09) • Population: 147 • Altitude: 1,148 ft. (350 m)

Nestling at the bottom of a valley in Ariège, Camon has a historic fortress-abbey within the ring of its ramparts.

The village is situated on a bend in the Hers river, on the boundary between Ariège and Aude, and grew out of an abbey that had been founded in the 10th century by Benedictine monks. The monastery became a priory belonging to the abbey at Lagrasse in 1068, but it was destroyed on June 18, 1279, by a catastrophic flood, caused when the natural barrier holding back the waters of the Lac de Puivert broke. Restored during the 14th century, the priory was again devastated in 1494 by bands of rovers and was abandoned. In the early 16th century, Philippe de Lévis, the new bishop of Mirepoix, rebuilt and fortified it, at the same time as reconstructing the church shared by the monks and local inhabitants. He guaranteed them protection by enclosing the town within a second defensive wall. At the end of the 16th century, Cardinal George d'Armagnac, then prior of Camon, strengthened the fortifications and gave the village and the priory their current appearance. Typical of the fortified villages of the Ariège *département*, whose houses made from local materials hunch together cheek by jowl and are covered in curved tiles, Camon is also dubbed "the village of 100 roses" and celebrates this delicate flower every May.

By road: Expressway A66, exit 6–Mirepoix (21 miles/34 km); expressway A61, exit 22–Foix (25 miles/40 km). **By train:** Foix station (29 miles/47 km). **By air:** Carcassonne-Salvaza airport (35 miles/56 km); Toulouse-Blagnac airport (70 miles/113 km).

ⓘ **Tourist information:**
+33 (0)5 61 68 83 76
www.camon09.org

👁 Highlights
• **Village** (abbey, church, ramparts): Guided tours. Further information: +33 (0)5 61 68 88 26.
• *Cabanes* (stone huts) **of Camon:** Themed path around the historic dry-stone winegrowers' huts; wild orchids in springtime; guided tours: +33 (0)5 61 68 88 26.
• **Roseraie:** Fragrant rose garden (free entry).

🗝 Accommodation
Guesthouses
L'Abbaye–Château de Camon: +33 (0)5 61 60 31 23.
Gîtes
Gîtes de Daurat, Mme Vercauteren: +33 (0)5 61 68 24 92.
Campsites
La Pibola***: +33 (0)5 61 68 12 14.
La Besse**, farm campsite: +33 (0)5 61 68 84 63.

🍽 Eating Out
L'Abbaye–Château de Camon (evenings; booking essential): +33 (0)5 61 60 31 23.
La Bergerie: +33 (0)6 95 40 28 85.
La Besse, light meals and seasonal farm produce: +33 (0)5 61 68 84 63.
La Camonette, light meals using local, seasonal ingredients (summer only): +33 (0)6 86 72 80 21.

🧺 Local Specialties
Food and Drink
Charcuterie • Croustades (flaky fruit pastries) • Grapes and grape juice.
Art and Crafts
Ceramics (sale and workshops).

★ Events
May: Fête des Roses (3rd Sunday).

🐾 Outdoor Activities
Canoeing • Fishing (accessible fishing facilities) • Walking • Voie Verte, picturesque greenway (disused railway line, Lavelanet–Mirepoix): suitable for walking, mountain-biking, and horse-riding.

🍃 Further Afield
• Chalabre, fortified town; Lac de Montbel, lake; Puivert: castle, museum; Nébias: natural maze (6–12 miles/ 9.5–19 km).
• Mirepoix; Vals (7½–16 miles/12–26 km).
• Lavelanet; Château de Montségur (10–22 miles/16–35 km).
• Carcassonne (31 miles/50 km).

Capdenac-le-Haut
The figurehead on the ship's prow

Lot (46) • Population: 1,111 • Altitude: 853 ft. (260 m)

Perched on a protruding rock, more than 360 ft. (110 m) above a meander in the Lot river, Capdenac "on high" suffered attacks by Julius Caesar and Simon de Montfort.

Shaped like the figurehead at the prow of a ship, Capdenac allegedly got its Occitan name from the configuration of the site. It was coveted for its strategic position, and what we know today as the medieval fortress was conquered in the 13th century by the count of Toulouse. However, well before that, this was the location of one of the most important Roman towns in Quercy: Uxellodunum, the site of Roman Emperor Julius Caesar's last battle against the Gauls. The Gaulish spring and Caesar's spring, fed by magnificent underground cisterns, are reminders of these ancient times. The monumental gates to the citadel, the keep, and several handsome 18th-century residences show Capdenac's second face—a place that navigated the trials and tribulations of the Middle Ages, and in which lived Maximilien de Béthune, duke of Sully (1560–1641), Henri IV's loyal minister.

By road: Expressway A20, exit 56–Rodez (32 miles/51 km). **By train:** Capdenac-Gare station (2 miles/3 km); Figeac station (3½ miles/5.5 km). **By air:** Rodez-Marcillac airport (31 miles/50 km).

ⓘ Tourist information—
Pays de Figeac: +33 (0)5 65 38 32 26
or +33 (0)5 65 34 06 25
www.capdenac-lot.fr

👁 Highlights
• **Keep** (13th and 14th centuries): Exhibition on the prehistoric, Gallo-Roman, and medieval periods: +33 (0)5 65 38 32 26.
• **Fontaine des Anglais:** Troglodyte spring with two underground pools: +33 (0)5 65 38 32 26.
• **Jardin des 1001 Pattes:** Ecological garden featuring an enormous "insect hotel".
• **Jardin Médiéval Cinq Sens:** Plants arranged according to the five senses—smell, sight, touch, taste, and a fountain to stimulate hearing; medicinal plants: +33 (0)5 65 38 32 26.
• **Village:** Torchlit visits in July and August: +33 (0)5 65 38 32 26.

⚔ Accommodation
Hotels
Le Relais de la Tour***: +33 (0)5 65 11 06 99.
Gîtes and vacation rentals
La Maison Eclusière***: +33 (0)7 80 51 18 40
or +33 (0)7 79 50 96 14.
M. Couderc**: +33 (0)5 65 34 19 50.
M. Tayrac**: +33 (0)5 65 34 03 81.
M. Vibe: +33 (0)6 03 94 00 99.

🍽 Eating Out
L'Oltis, crêperie: +33 (0)5 65 34 05 85.
Le Relais de la Tour: +33 (0)5 65 11 06 99.

🧺 Local Specialties
Food and Drink
Goat cheese • *Fouaces* (brioche/cake).
Art and Crafts
Organic soap-maker • Mosaic artist.

📅 Events
Summer market: Wednesday mornings in July and August, Place de la Mairie.
April: Foire aux Chevaux, horse fair (3rd Saturday).
May–September: Exhibitions in the keep.
July–August: Evening markets, concerts, art exhibitions, open-air cinema, guided visits.
September: Local saint's day (3rd weekend).

🦋 Outdoor Activities
Walking: 1 marked trail:
+33 (0)5 65 38 32 26.

🌿 Further Afield
• Figeac: Musée Champollion (3½ miles/5.5 km).
• *Cardaillac (10 miles/16 km), see p. 178.
• Peyrusse-le-Roc (11 miles/18 km).
• Decazeville (14 miles/23 km).
• Villefranche-de-Rouergue (21 miles/34 km).
• *Belcastel (24 miles/39 km), see pp. 164–65.
• *Conques (26 miles/42 km), see pp. 186–87.
• *Autoire (29 miles/47 km), see p. 159.

Cardaillac

The powerhouse of Quercy

Lot (46) • Population: 614 • Altitude: 1,175 ft. (358 m)

The powerful feudal Cardaillac family founded this village on the fringes of Quercy and Ségala, and gave it its name.

When Pépin the Younger (714–768) granted Cardaillac lands to his knight Bertrand and descendants, he guaranteed a bright future for the village. The fort, completed in the 12th century, sits on a triangular spur, two cliffs providing natural fortifications. Three towers are all that survive of the ramparts: the round tower, the clock tower (which served as the prison), and the tower of Sagnes, which affords a panoramic view of the village. Cardaillac was attacked during both the Hundred Years War and the Wars of Religion; these events drove the local people to become the most fervent Protestant community in Haut Quercy, and they participated in the destruction of Saint Julian's Church. The church was restored to Catholicism by the Edict of Nantes, then rebuilt in the 17th century, when the fort passed into the hands of Protestant reformers. At the Revocation of the Edict of Nantes, the ramparts and towers were razed to the ground.

By road: Expressway A20, exit 56–Rodez (27 miles/43 km).
By train: Figeac station (7½ miles/12 km).
By air: Rodez-Marcillac airport (41 miles/66 km).

ⓘ **Tourist information—**
Pays de Figeac: +33 (0)5 65 34 06 25
www.tourisme-figeac.com

👁 Highlights

• **Fort:** Ruins of 11th-century medieval fort (Sagnes and clock towers); guided visits in summer. Further information: +33 (0)5 65 34 06 25.
• **Medieval kitchen garden:** Medicinal plants and plants used in dyeing; self-guided visit with information boards.
• **Musée Éclaté:** Multisite museum; visit several sites that tell the story of the village and its people since the Middle Ages. Visit La Maison du Semalier (13th century), containing the workshop of Émile Cros—poet, inventor, and last master craftsman of the *comporte* baskets used for brining in the grape harvest; La Maison de l'Oustal, house of the Cardaillac-Thémines (fortified medieval house), collection of farming equipment and craftsman's tools; *l'étuve à pruneaux* (plum steam-room) and the bread oven, the *saboterie* (clogmaker), and the *moulin à huile de noix* (walnut mill): +33 (0)5 65 40 10 63 or +33 (0)5 65 40 15 65.
• **Village:** Signposted route with information boards; guided tours by appointment only: +33 (0)5 65 34 06 25.

⚷ Accommodation

Guesthouses
Le Pressoir***: +33 (0)5 65 34 68 75.
Le Relais de Conques: +33 (0)5 65 40 17 22.
Gîtes and vacation rentals
Isabelle de la Rosa***: +33 (0)5 65 34 18 95.
Le Chalet du Ségala: +33 (0)5 65 34 56 88.
Raymond Davet: +33 (0)5 65 40 16 39.

🍽 Eating Out

Auberge du Mercadiol: +33 (0)5 65 33 19 97.
Le Bar du Fort: +33 (0)5 65 11 08 86.

📅 Events

Market: Sunday mornings, 8.30 a.m.–1 p.m., Place du Boulodrome.
May: Foire du Renouveau, flea market, crafts, local produce.
June: National gardens day.
July–August: Ciné-village, film sceening preceded by a meal at the village hall; exhibitions; local saint's day; Fête de la Peinture, painting festival.
November: Saint Martin's Fair, flea market, trees and flowers, local produce.

🦋 Outdoor Activities

Children's playground • Picnic area • *Boules* court • Hunting • Fishing (lake; Murat 1st category permit) • Mountain-biking • Walking: Route GR 6 and marked trails.

🍃 Further Afield

• Figeac (6 miles/9.5 km).
• *Capdenac-le-Haut (11 miles/18 km), see p. 177.
• Lacapelle-Marival (9½ miles/15.5 km).
• Célé valley (16 miles/26 km).
• Rocamadour (22 miles/35 km).
• Saint-Céré (22 miles/35 km).
• *Autoire (24 miles/39 km), see p. 159.
• Gouffre de Padirac, chasm (25 miles/40 km).

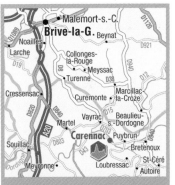

Carennac
Renaissance elegance and Quercy charm

Lot (46) • Population: 386 • Altitude: 387 ft. (118 m)

Carennac sits on the banks of the Dordogne, facing the Île de Calypso, where it shelters Renaissance houses adorned with sculptured windows.

In the days when it was called Carendenacus, the village huddled around a church that was dedicated to Saint Sernin and annexed to Beaulieu Abbey. On the orders of Cluny Abbey, the parish became a priory, and in the 11th century it built the existing Romanesque Église de Saint-Pierre, whose door is decorated with a magnificent 12th-century tympanum. The Flamboyant part-Romanesque, part-Gothic cloisters stretch out on either side of a hexagonal tower and contain a chapter house with a 16th-century sculpture of the Entombment, 15th-century bas-reliefs of Christ's life and passion, and various statues by different craftsmen. In the Château des Doyens, the heritage center hosts an exhibition staged by the Pays d'Art et d'Histoire association, of which Carennac is a member. The village houses, nestling up to this exquisite building, live up to the beauty of the church. Built in stone, some boast ornate mullioned windows, while others have watchtowers or exterior staircases, and they are covered in a patchwork of steeply sloping brown-tiled roofs, typical of this area.

By road: Expressway A20, exit 56–Rodez (27 miles/43 km). **By train:** Rocamadour station (14 miles/23 km); Gramat station (19 miles/31 km); Brive-la-Gaillarde station (30 miles/48 km). **By air:** Brive-Vallée de la Dordogne airport (21 miles/34 km).

ⓘ Tourist information—Vallée de la Dordogne-Rocamadour-Padirac: +33 (0)5 65 33 22 00 www.vallee-dordogne.com

Highlights

• Église de Saint-Pierre and its cloister
(11th–12th centuries).
• **Espace Patrimoine, heritage center**
(16th-century building): Permanent
exhibition on the area's natural,
architectural, and patrimonial wealth:
+33 (0)5 65 33 81 36.
• **Priory and village:** Guided tours
by appointment only. Further
information: +33 (0)5 65 33 81 36 or
+33 (0)5 65 33 22 00.

 Accommodation

Hotels
Hostellerie Fénelon**: +33 (0)5 65 10 96 46.
Guesthouses
La Farga: +33 (0)5 65 33 18 97 or +33
(0)6 73 73 56 79.
La Petite Vigne: +33 (0)5 65 50 25 84.
Vacation rentals
Further information: +33 (0)5 65 33 22 00
www.vallee-dordogne.com
Campsites
L'Eau Vive**: +33 (0)5 65 10 97 39.

Eating Out

La Bodega: +33 (0)5 65 39 77 77.
L'Epicure: +33 (0)5 65 40 34 52.
Le Fénelon: +33 (0)5 65 10 96 46.
Le Prieuré: +33 (0)5 65 39 76 74.

Local Specialties

Art and Crafts
Ceramic artist • Marquetry • Sculptor
(summer).

Events

Market: July–August, local products
on Tuesdays, 5–8 p.m.
July–September: Painting and sculpture
exhibitions.
August: Journée de la Prune Dorée de
Carennac, plum festival and market
(1st Monday).
November: Mois de la Pierre, "month
of the stone" exhibition.
December: Christmas market.

Outdoor Activities

Canoeing • Fishing • Walking: Route GR 52 •
Mountain-biking.

Further Afield

• *Loubressac (6 miles/9.5 km), see p. 210.
• Castelnau and Montal castles, Saint-Céré
(6–10 miles/9.5–16 km).
• Gouffre de Padirac, chasm; Rocamadour
(6–12 miles/9.5–19 km).
• *Autoire (8 miles/13 km), see p. 159.
• *Curemonte (9½ miles/15.5 km),
see p. 189.
• Dordogne valley (11–22 miles/18–35 km).
• Martel (11 miles/18 km).
• *Collonges-la-Rouge (14 miles/23 km),
see pp. 184–85.
• *Turenne (15 miles/24 km),
see pp. 262–63.

Did you know?

After the Wars of Religion, the 17th
century saw the return of prosperity to
Carennac, thanks to the peace established
by Henri IV (1553–1610). The priory of
Carennac became part of the fiefdom of
the Salignac family of La Mothe-Fénelon,
whose most famous member was François
Fénelon, prior of the abbey from 1681
to 1685 and later bishop of Cambrai.
He chose this "happy corner of the globe"
in which to write his instructional novel
The Adventures of Telemachus.

Castelnau-de-Montmiral

The treasure of the counts of Armagnac

Tarn (81) • Population: 1,000 • Altitude: 951 ft. (290 m)

The *bastide* of Castelnau-de-Montmiral boasts a rich heritage bequeathed by the counts of Toulouse and Armagnac.

Proudly perched on its rocky outcrop, the village is ideally situated as a lookout and, in the Middle Ages, saw remarkable growth and the building of a seignorial castle coupled with an impregnable fortress. The castle was destroyed in the 19th century, but part of the fortifications have been preserved, along with the Porte des Garrics, dating from the 13th century. At the center of the *bastide*, founded in 1222 by the Count of Toulouse Raymond VII, 16th- and 17th-century houses surround the covered square and old well. The Église Notre-Dame-de-l'Assomption contains a superb Baroque altarpiece, a Pietà, and a Pensive Christ from the 15th century, as well as the reliquary cross of the consuls from the late 14th century: a masterpiece of southern religious goldsmithery, which was originally decorated with 354 precious stones.

By road: Expressway A68, exit 9–Gaillac (12 miles/19 km); expressway A20, exit 59–Saint-Antonin-Noble-Val (26 miles/42 km). **By train:** Gaillac station (7 miles/11.5 km). **By air:** Toulouse-Blagnac airport (50 miles/80 km).

ⓘ **Tourist information:**
+33 (0)8 05 40 08 28
www.tourisme-vignoble-bastides.com

👁 Highlights
• Église Notre-Dame-de-l'Assomption (15th–16th centuries): 14th-century reliquary cross, altarpiece, Pensive Christ, Pietà, frescoes.
• Permanent exhibition: "Castelnau, Pages d'Histoire" at the tourist information center.
• Château de Mayragues (12th–17th centuries): Open for visits on Thursdays in July and August. Further information: +33 (0)8 05 40 08 28.
• Village: Guided tour for groups by appointment only; in summer also for individuals: +33 (0)8 05 40 08 28..

Accommodation
Hotels
Les Consuls***: +33 (0)5 63 33 17 44.
Guesthouses
M. Burd***: +33 (0)5 63 40 47 93.
M. Coquillat***: +33 (0)5 63 40 17 25.
Mme Geddes***: +33 (0)5 63 33 94 08.
Mme Tuffal***: +33 (0)5 63 33 50 41 or +33 (0)6 19 02 26 65.
Mme Camalet: +33 (0)5 63 33 12 02.
Mme Robert-Vautier: +33 (0)6 76 57 20 59.
M. and Mme Van Nimmen: +33 (0)5 63 33 40 67.
Gîtes and walkers' lodges
Further information: +33 (0)8 05 40 08 28
www.tourisme-vignoble-bastides.com

Campsites
Domaine du Chêne Vert***: +33 (0)5 63 33 16 10.

🍽 Eating Out
Les Arcades: +33 (0)5 63 33 20 88.
Au Baladin de la Grésigne, light meals: +33 (0)5 63 42 78 99.
Marina Pizza: +33 (0)5 63 34 47 43.
Le Ménagier: +33 (0)5 63 42 08 35.

🧺 Local Specialties
Food and Drink
Foie gras, duck confit, duck breast (*magret*) • AOC Gaillac wines.
Art and Crafts
Perfumer • Artists • Art gallery.

🗓 Events
Market: All year round, Tuesday mornings, Place des Arcades.

Pentecost: Village festival (weekend).
July and August: "Les Musicales," rock, blues, and pop festival (mid-July); "Architecture et Musique," festival of music in fine settings (late July–early August).
August 15: Honey and local produce fair, village festival.

🦋 Outdoor Activities
Base de Vère-Grésigne: Swimming, fishing, paddleboat, mountain-bike trail departure point • Walking: Routes GR 36 and 46 and 3 marked trails.

🦋 Further Afield
• Gaillac (7½ miles/12 km).
• *Puycelsi (8 miles/13 km), see pp. 230–31.
• *Bruniquel (14 miles/23 km), see p. 175.
• Cordes-sur-Ciel (14 miles/23 km).
• Albi (20 miles/32 km).
• *Monestiés (20 miles/32 km), see p. 212.

Castelnaud-la-Chapelle

A tale of two châteaux

Dordogne (24) • Population: 461 • Altitude: 459 ft. (140 m)

Clinging to the cliffside overlooking the confluence of the Dordogne and Céou rivers, the Château de Castelnaud and its houses, which are typical of the Périgord region, are arranged in tiers along the steep, narrow streets. Built in the 12th century on a strategic site for controlling the region's main river and land transportation routes, the Château de Castelnaud was much coveted during the many wars that marked the Middle Ages. Abandoned during the French Revolution, it was even used as a stone quarry in the 19th century, until, in 1966, it was listed as a historic monument and was thus prevented from falling into total ruin. Today, after extensive restoration, it once again casts its shadow over the valley, offering an exceptional view over the neighboring villages. It houses the Musée de la Guerre au Moyen Âge (medieval warfare museum). In the village, the characteristic houses, with their pale façades and brown sloping roofs, contrast with the green vegetation of the area. Not far from the river, the Château des Milandes preserves the memory of the French jazz entertainer Josephine Baker, who owned the property from 1947 to 1968.

By road: Expressway A20, exit 55–Sarlat (23 miles/37 km). **By train:** Sarlat-la-Canéda station (7½ miles/12 km). **By air:** Brive-Vallée de la Dordogne airport (35 miles/56 km); Bergerac-Roumanière airport (42 miles/68 km).

ⓘ Tourist information—Vallée et Coteaux du Céou:
+33 (0)5 53 29 88 84
www.tourisme-ceou.com

👁 Highlights
• Château de Castelnaud (12th century, restored): Musée de la Guerre au Moyen Âge in the halls of the seigneurial home, a collection of 200 items of weapons and armor, collection of furniture, scenography: +33 (0)5 53 31 30 00.
• Château des Milandes (15th century): Permanent exhibition on the life of Josephine Baker; garden: +33 (0)5 53 59 31 21.
• Écomusée de la Noix du Périgord: History and culture of the walnut in Périgord in an old restored farmhouse surrounded by a walnut grove. Museum, discovery tour, oil press: +33 (0)5 53 59 69 63.
• Gardens of the Château de Lacoste: Boxwood and rose garden, vegetable garden, park: +33 (0)5 53 29 89 37.

🗝 Accommodation
Guesthouses
Le Petit Bois: +33 (0)5 53 28 29 32.
La Tour de Cause: +33 (0)5 53 30 30 51.
Gîtes and vacation rentals
Carpignac: +33 (0)5 58 74 33 81.
La Chambre à Four: +33 (0)5 53 31 45 40.
L'Escale: +33 (0)5 53 31 45 40.
Fondaumier: +33 (0)5 53 31 45 40.
La Grange au Puits: +33 (0)5 53 29 55 50.

Campsites and holiday villages
Camping Maisonneuve***:
+33 (0)5 53 29 51 29.
Camping-village de Vacances Lou Castel***: +33 (0)5 53 29 89 24.

🍽 Eating Out
Bar du Château: +33 (0)5 53 29 51 16.
La Cour de Récré: +33 (0)5 53 31 89 85.
Les Machicoulis, crêperie:
+33 (0)5 53 28 23 15.
La Plage, pizzeria/snack bar:
+33 (0)5 53 29 40 87.
La Taverne du Château:
+33 (0)5 53 31 30 00.
Les Tilleuls, brasserie: +33 (0)5 53 29 58 54.
Le Tornoli: +33 (0)5 53 29 31 21.
Le Tournepique: +33 (0)5 53 29 51 07.

🏺 Local Specialties
Art and Crafts: Miniature models.

📅 Events
July: Fête de la Plage (beach festival, weekend after the 14th).

🦋 Outdoor Activities
Municipal canoeing center:
+33 (0)5 53 29 40 07 • Walking: Route GR 64 and marked trails • Mountain-biking • Horse-riding.

🍂 Further Afield
• Dordogne Valley: *La Roque-Gageac (2 miles/3 km), see pp. 234–35; *Beynac-et-Cazenac (2½ miles/4 km), see pp. 168–69; *Domme (6 miles/9.5 km), see pp. 190–91; *Belvès (11 miles/18 km), see pp. 166–67; *Limeuil (21 miles/34 km), see pp. 208–09.
• Sarlat (8 miles/13 km).
• Les Eyzies (15 miles/24 km).
• *Monpazier (21 miles/34 km), see pp. 215–16.
• *Saint-Amand-de-Coly (22 miles/35 km), see pp. 236–37.
• Vézère valley: *Saint-Léon-sur-Vézère (23 miles/37 km), see p. 248.

Castelnou

In the foothills of the Pyrenees

Pyrénées-Orientales (66) • Population: 365 • Altitude: 804 ft. (245 m)

Nestled in the Aspres, foothills accentuated by the magnificent Canigou mountain, Castelnou is a village that typifies Catalan rural architecture. Surrounded by two limestone plateaus—the Causse de Thuir and the Roc de Majorque—the village, founded in the 10th century, seems to have been forgotten by time after having been the capital of the viscountcy of Vallespir for more than three centuries. The castle follows the natural shape of the rock and forms a pentagon. The steepness of the rock, the castle's 10-ft. (3-m) thick walls, and the 14th-century fortified walls surrounding the village, of which eight towers remain, assured its defense. To the northeast of the village, a tower erected on a hill allowed for the sending of smoke signals between France and the kingdom of Spain. The harshness of this steep, tiered, stone-built site contrasts with the intimacy of the narrow flower-filled streets lined with warm-hued houses with round-tiled roofs. To the north of the village, the Église Santa Maria del Mercadal (Saint Mary of the marketplace) is in the Catalan Romanesque style.

By road: Expressway A9, exit 42–Perpignan Sud (10 miles/16 km). **By train:** Perpignan station (12 miles/19 km). **By air:** Perpignan-Rivesaltes airport (17 miles/27 km).

ⓘ Tourist information— Aspres-Thuir: +33 (0)4 68 28 32 38 or +33 (0)4 68 53 45 86 www.aspres-thuir.com

👁 Highlights
• Église Santa Maria del Mercadal (12th century).
• **Village:** Guided tour by appointment only.

🏃 Accommodation
Guesthouses
La Figuera***: +33 (0)4 68 53 18 42.
Les Coricos: +33 (0)6 76 96 47 00.
La Planquette: +33 (0)4 68 53 48 13.
Gîtes
Further information: +33 (0)4 68 53 45 72 www.aspres-thuir.com

🍽 Eating Out
Restaurants
D'Ici et d'Ailleurs: +33 (0)4 68 53 23 30.
L'Hostal: +33 (0)4 68 53 45 42.
Light meals
Au Pré de Carlos: +33 (0)4 34 54 18 29 or +33 (0)6 34 49 40 01.
Le Coin Catalan: +33 (0)4 68 53 26 88.
La Font: +33 (0)4 68 53 66 25 or +33 (0)6 87 12 73 72.

🧺 Local Specialties
Food and Drink
Foie gras, preserves • Farm produce • Honey • Castelnou wine.
Art and Crafts
Artists' and craftsmen's studios and galleries • Cutler • Wirework workshop • Artist-mosaicist • Potters • Wood turner • Artworks made from eggshells • Sculptural ceramicist • Lampshades • Objects created from recycled paper • Jewelry design • Crafts using natural materials.

📅 Events
Market: Mid-June–mid-September, Tuesday 9 a.m.–7 p.m., at the foot of the church.
April–October: Temporary exhibitions, Carré d'Art Gili.
June: Les Lucioles de Castelnou, 11-mile/18-km night race; "Feu de la Saint-Jean," Saint John's Eve bonfire (end of June).
October: Farmers' market (2nd weekend).

🦋 Outdoor Activities
Walking • Mountain-biking.

🌿 Further Afield
• Camélas; Fontcouverte; Monastir-del-Camp; Sainte-Colombe; Serrabonne (2½–9½ miles/4–15.5 km).
• Thuir (Byrrh wine cellars), Perpignan (13 miles/21 km).
• Céret; Tech valley (18 miles/29 km).
• *Eus (18 miles/29 km), see p. 194.
• Elne; Collioure (19 miles/31 km).
• *Villefranche-de-Conflent (23 miles/37 km), see pp. 264–65.

Collonges-la-Rouge
Russet-colored Corrèze

Corrèze (19) • Population: 455 • Altitude: 755 ft. (230 m)

On the border between Limousin and Quercy, the red sandstone of Collonges harmonizes with the green of the vines rambling on its façades. Built up around a Benedictine priory founded in the 8th century, the village came under the lordship of the powerful neighboring viscount of Turenne in the 13th century and was the place of residence of his judicial officers. Collonges then acquired the Renaissance castles of Maussac, Vassinhac, Benge, and Beauvirie. With its imposing proportions, *lauze* (schist stone) roofs, towers, turrets, and watchtowers, both rural and bourgeois, robust and refined, Collonges-la-Rouge displays a rare homogeneity and has been remarkably well preserved. Every building, every monument declares the village's rich history. The Église Saint-Pierre, built in the 11th and 12th centuries, bears witness to the time when Collonges was one of the stopping places on the Saint James's Way pilgrim route via Rocamadour. The Priory gate, which is vaulted and ogival shaped, and the Flat gate (it has no tower) are the only remains of the village's former ramparts. At the center of the village, the former grain and wine market dating from the 16th century recalls the village's commercial activity and prosperous history, and still houses the communal bread oven. The Chapelle des Pénitents, which can be admired today thanks to restoration work by the Friends of Collonges, was, from 1765 to the end of the 19th century, home to the Brotherhood of Black Penitents, whose charitable missions included burying the dead free of charge.

By road: Expressway A20, exit 52–Collonges-la-Rouge (9½ miles/15.5 km). **By train:** Brive-la-Gaillarde station (12 miles/19 km). **By air:** Brive-Vallée de la Dordogne airport (14 miles/23 km).

(i) Tourist information—Vallée de la Dordogne: +33 (0)5 65 33 22 00
www.vallee-dordogne.com

👁 Highlights

• **Chapelle des Pénitents (15th century):**
Restored in 1927 by the Friends of
Collonges.
• **Église Saint-Pierre (11th–12th centuries):**
Carved tympanum.
• **Maison de la Sirène (16th century):**
A typical Collonges house with furniture
and everyday objects from the past,
explaining the history of the village.

🗝 Accommodation

Hotels
Le Relais Saint-Jacques**:
+33 (0)5 55 25 41 02.
Guesthouses
Domaine de Peyrelimouse***:
+33 (0)5 55 84 07 17 or
+33 (0)6 73 57 08 99.
La Douce France***: +33 (0)5 55 84 39 59
or +33 (0)6 88 65 69 95.
La Vigne Grande**: +33 (0)5 55 25 39 20.
Le Jardin de la Raze: +33 (0)5 55 25 48 16
or +33 (0)6 04 18 89 91.
Holiday villages
Les Vignottes: +33 (0)5 55 25 30 91.
Campsites
Moulin de la Valane***:
+33 (0)5 55 25 41 59 or
+33 (0)6 84 40 36 23.

🍴 Eating Out

L'Auberge de Benges: +33 (0)5 55 85 76 68.
Lou Brasier, pizzeria: +33 (0)6 16 59 69 49.
Le Cantou: +33 (0)5 55 84 25 15.
Le Collongeois: +33 (0)5 55 84 59 16.
La Ferme de Berle, farmhouse inn,
booking essential: +33 (0)5 55 25 48 06.
Le Pause & Vous: +33 (0)5 55 22 67 03.
Le Pèlerin: +33 (0)6 77 71 80 16.
Le Pèlerin et la Sorcière, crêperie:
+33 (0)5 55 74 23 49.
Les Pierres Rouges: +33 (0)5 55 74 19 46.
♥ Le Relais Saint-Jacques:
+33 (0)5 55 25 41 02.

🧺 Local Specialties

Food and Drink
Duck • Purple mustard • Walnuts.
Art and Crafts
Leatherworkers • Hats • Cutlery •
Decoration • Art galleries • Linen •
Artists • Pottery • Glass • Artisan perfumes.

📅 Events

May: Local saint's day (3rd weekend).
Mid-July–mid-August: Theater on
Tuesday evenings.
August: Fête du Pain, bread festival
(1st weekend); painting and visual arts
festival (15th).

🦋 Outdoor Activities

Walking: Route GR 480 and several
marked trails.

🦋 Further Afield

• Ligneyrac, Noailhac, and Saillac: churches
(2 miles/3 km).
• *Turenne (6 miles/9.5 km), see pp. 262–63.
• Dordogne valley (6 miles/10 km).
• *Curemonte (7½ miles/12 km), see p. 189.
• Brive-la-Gaillarde: market
(12 miles/19 km).

Varetz: Jardins de Colette, gardens
(12½ miles/20 km).
• *Carennac (15 miles/24 km), see pp. 179–80.
• *Loubressac (21 miles/34 km), see p. 210.
• Souillac (21 miles/34 km).
• *Autoire (22 miles/35 km), see p. 159.

🎗 Did you know?

The incomparable color of this stone is due
to a geological phenomenon dating back
millions of years. The "Meyssac Fault,"
which passes through Collonges-la-Rouge,
was formed by the sliding of the red
sandstone of the Massif Central beneath
Aquitaine's limestone plate. The oxidized
iron of the sandstone of Corrèze gives the
stone its dark red color, which is
characteristic of the Meyssac Fault.

Conques
Muse of Romanesque artists

Aveyron (12) • Population: 283 • Altitude: 820 ft. (250 m)

A hotspot for Romanesque art, Conques contains treasures inspired by the faith of artists in the Middle Ages.

Conques was established on the slope of a valley shaped like a shell (*concha* in Latin, hence its name), at the heart of a rich forested massif situated at the confluence of two rivers: the Ouche and the Dourdou. Its heyday, in the 11th and 12th centuries, coincided with the building of the abbey church, a true masterpiece of Romanesque architecture. Beneath its vaults, 250 capitals are enhanced by contemporary stained-glass windows designed by Pierre Soulages (b. 1919), and on the tympanum of its western portal 124 figures in stone illustrate the Last Judgment. Depicted in all her splendor, Saint Foy keeps watch, with an enigmatic expression, over a unique collection of reliquaries covered in gold, silver, enamelwork, and precious stones. The Barry and Vinzelle gates, remains of the ramparts built during the same period, flank a village where stone reigns. Lining the narrow cobbled streets, the village houses, the oldest of which date from the late Middle Ages, display façades that combine half-timbering, yellow limestone, and red sandstone, and are topped with splendid silver shale roofs.

By road: Expressway A75, exit 42–Rodez, N88-Rodez, D 901 (24 miles/39 km).
By train: Saint-Christophe-Vallon station (21 miles/34 km); Rodez station (28 miles/45 km). **By air:** Rodez-Aveyron airport (21 miles/34 km).

(i) **Tourist information:**
+33 (0)5 65 72 85 00
www.tourisme-conques.fr

👁 Highlights
• **Abbatiale Sainte-Foy:** Guided tour of the tympanum, the lower level of the church, and the tribunes to discover the Roman column heads and Soulages stained-glass; for information on days and times: +33 (0)5 65 72 85 00. Evening tours of the tribunes with organ and lights daily at 9 p.m. from May to September. Guided tour for groups all year round, booking essential: +33 (0)5 65 72 85 00.
• **Trésor de Sainte-Foy:** Abbey treasury: daily, for times: +33 (0)5 65 72 85 00; guided tour for groups all year round, booking essential: +33 (0)5 65 72 85 00.
• **Tour of the village:** July and August: +33 (0)5 65 72 85 00; accessible tours for visually impaired (tatcile models, reliefs,

guidebooks in Braille and large print). Further information: +33 (0)5 65 72 85 00.

⚔ Accommodation
Hotels
Hervé Busset—Domaine de Cambelong****: +33 (0)5 65 72 84 77.
Auberge Saint-Jacques**:
+33 (0)5 65 72 86 36.
Sainte-Foy: +33 (0)5 65 69 84 03.
Guesthouses
Au Nid d'Angèle***: +33 (0)6 60 87 28 61.
La Maison des Sources***:
+33 (0)5 65 47 04 54 or
+33 (0)6 19 49 23 92.
Les Chambres de Marie Scépé**:
+33 (0)5 65 72 83 87 or +33 (0)7 78 24 34 45.
Les Chambres de Montignac**:
+33 (0)5 65 69 84 29.

Chez Alice et Charles**:
+33 (0)5 65 72 82 10 or +33 (0)6 87 19 17 59.
Le Castellou: +33 (0)5 65 78 27 09 or
+33 (0)6 48 15 66 91.
Les Grangettes de Calvignac:
+33 (0)6 75 50 59 19.
Gîtes and vacation rentals
Further information: 05 65 72 85 00
www.tourisme-conques.fr
Bunkhouses and walkers' lodges
Maison Familiale de Vacances Relais Cap France: +33 (0)5 65 69 86 18.
Centre d'Accueil de l'Abbaye Sainte-Foy:
+33 (0)5 65 69 89 43.
Communal walkers' lodge:
+33 (0)5 65 72 82 98.
Campsites
Le Beau Rivage*** (mobile home rentals), Le Faubourg: +33 (0)5 65 69 82 23.

🍴 Eating Out
Auberge Saint-Jacques: +33 (0)5 65 72 86 36.
Au Parvis, crêperie/brasserie:
+33 (0)5 65 72 82 81.
Le Charlemagne, crêperie/ice cream parlor: +33 (0)5 65 69 81 50.
Chez Dany Lo Romiu, pizzeria/snack bar:
+33 (0)5 65 46 95 01.
Le Conqu'errant: +33 (0)7 81 87 52 42.
Hervé Busset—Domaine de Cambelong:
+33 (0)5 65 72 84 77.

Sainte-Foy: +33 (0)5 65 69 84 03.
Sur le Chemin du Thé, tea room/organic
food: +33 (0)9 60 02 81 95.

🏛 Local Specialties
Food and Drink
Conquaises (walnut shortbread) •
Conques wine.
Art and Crafts
Antique dealer • Beadmaker • Art gallery •
Etcher • Engraver • Leather craftsmen •
Artist • Sadler • Wood-carvers • Sculptor-
stonemason • Low-warp tapestry • Art
foundry • Ceramicists • Bookbinding •
Felt-worker.

📅 Events
July and August: Music festival.
October: Procession de la Sainte-Foy
(the 6th or the 1st Sunday after the 6th).
All year round: Lectures, concerts, shows,
workshops, etc.

🦋 Outdoor Activities
Fishing • Walking: Routes GR 62, 65,
and 465, and 7 marked trails.

🌿 Further Afield
• Dourdou valley and gorge: viewpoint
at Le Bancarel (1 mile/1.5 km).
• Lot valley (4½ miles/7 km).
• La Vinzelle (7½ miles/12 km).
• Vallon de Marcillac, AOP vineyards and wine
route (11 miles/18 km).
• Salles-la-Source, waterfall (16 miles/26 km).
• *Belcastel (24 miles/39 km), see pp. 164–65.
• *Estaing (24 miles/39 km), see pp. 192–93.
• Rodez: cathedral and Musée Soulages
(24 miles/39 km).

La Couvertoirade

In the footsteps of the Templars

Aveyron (12) • Population: 188 • Altitude: 2,546 ft. (776 m)

At the heart of the wide-open spaces of the Causse du Larzac, La Couvertoirade is the work of the Templars and Hospitallers. Built in the 12th century, the Château de La Couvertoirade formed part of the command network developed by the Templars throughout the West and in the Holy Land. After they were declared heretics in the early 14th century by Philippe le Bel, the Templars were replaced by the Hospitallers, who inherited all their assets. The latter, too, were soldier-monks and encircled the city with ramparts in the 15th century to protect it from attack and from epidemics. From the top of the ramparts, the view stretches over Larzac and the whole of the village: at the foot of the 12th-century church, a labyrinth of narrow streets lined with "Caussenard"-style houses (built of thick stone to protect the men and livestock inside) and 16th- and 17th-century mansions provides an enticing place to stroll.

By road: Expressway A75, exit 49–Le Caylar (4½ miles/7 km). **By train:** Millau station (30 miles/48 km). **By air:** Montpellier-Méditerranée airport (58 miles/93 km).

ⓘ Tourist information—
La Couvertoirade: +33 (0)5 65 58 55 59
www.lacouvertoirade.com
Tourist information—Larzac et Vallées:
+33 (0)5 65 62 23 64
www.tourisme-larzac.com

◉ Highlights

• Village: 15th-century ramparts, 17th-century castle, Hospitallers' church, 14th-century oven. Self-guided visit (audioguide) or guided tour, evening tours in summer. Further information: +33 (0)5 65 58 55 59.

⚷ Accommodation

Guesthouses
M. et Mme Augustin, La Salvetat: +33 (0)5 65 62 13 15.
Gîte de la Cité: +33 (0)6 01 81 94 18.
Les Mourguettes: +33 (0)6 11 08 35 30 or +33 (0)6 14 57 12 31.
Gîtes, walkers' lodges, and vacation rentals
Further information: 05 65 62 23 64
www.tourisme-larzac.com
Rural campsites
Les Canoles, La Blaquèrerie: +33 (0)5 65 62 15 12.

ⓜ Eating Out

L'Auberge du Chat Perché: +33 (0)5 65 42 14 61.
Au 20 [vingt], light meals/wine bar: +33 (0)5 65 62 19 64.
Café Montes, crêperie: +33 (0)5 65 58 10 71.
Café des Remparts: +33 (0)5 65 62 11 11.
Les Fées des Causses, tea room: +33 (0)5 65 58 14 23.
Les Gourmandises de l'Aveyron, light meals: +33 (0)6 83 03 61 31.
L'Hospitalier, tea room: +33 (0)6 38 51 88 31.
Le Médiéval: +33 (0)5 65 62 27 01.
Tour Valette: +33 (0)5 65 62 09 69.

🛍 Local Specialties

Food and Drink
Sheep cheese • Duck produce.
Art and Crafts
Art gallery • Workshops in summer (potters, weavers, soap-makers, sculptors).

▣ Events

July and August: "Les Mascarades," medieval village festival; country market (Thursday evenings); children's days; lectures, concerts, etc.

🦋 Outdoor Activities

Geo-caching: Treasure-hunting with GPS • Pony rides • Trail through the rocks • Walking: Routes GR 71 C and GR 71 D and circular walks around the village • Mountain-biking.

🌿 Further Afield

• Saint-Jean-du-Bruel: Noria, Maison de l'Eau (11 miles/18 km).
• Larzac Templar and Hospitaller sites: La Cavalerie; Sainte-Eulalie-de-Cernon (reptilarium, rail bike; Viala-du-Pas-de-Jaux; Saint-Jean-d'Alcas (12–19 miles/19–31 km).
• Lodève (15 miles/24 km).
• Gorges of the Dourbie; Nant: Romanesque churches (16 miles/26 km).
• Cirque de Navacelles (21 miles/34 km).
• Millau Viaduct (22 miles/35 km).
• Caves de Roquefort (29 miles/47 km).

Curemonte

A village of lords and winegrowers

Corrèze (19) • Population: 216 • Altitude: 689 ft. (210 m)

Punctuated by the towers of its three castles, the profile of Curemonte stands out above the Sourdoire and Maumont valleys.

The village is built on a long sandstone spur. Seen from the top of the village, its medieval architecture is astonishing. Standing near the three castles (the square-towered Saint-Hilaire, the round-towered Plas, and La Johannie), the Romanesque Église Saint-Barthélemy contains an altarpiece from 1672, and altars of Saint John the Baptist and the Virgin Mary from the 17th and 18th centuries. The late 18th-century covered market houses a Gothic cross shaft. In an enduringly simple and rural atmosphere, Renaissance mansions stand side by side with old winegrowers' houses in a harmony of pale sandstone and brown roof tiles. Outside the village, the Romanesque Église Saint-Genest, decorated with 15th-century paintings, houses a museum of religious artifacts, while the recently restored Église de La Combe is a masterpiece of 11th-century architecture and one of the oldest churches in Corrèze.

By road: Expressway A20, exit 52–Noailles (11 miles/18 km). **By train:** Brive-la-Gaillarde station (19 miles/31 km). **By air:** Brive-Vallée de la Dordogne airport (17 miles/27 km).

(i) Tourist information—Vallée de la Dordogne:
+33 (0)5 65 33 22 00 or +33 (0)5 55 25 47 57
www.vallee-dordogne.com

👁 Highlights
• **Église Saint-Barthélemy** (12th century): 17th-century wooden altarpiece.
• **Église de La Combe** (11th century): Exhibitions in summer.
• **Église Saint-Genest:** Museum of religious artifacts.

Accommodation
Guesthouses
Mme Raynal***: +33 (0)5 55 25 35 01.
Gîtes and vacation rentals
Gîte de la Barbacane***:
+33 (0)5 55 87 49 26.
La Maison de la Halle***:
+33 (0)5 55 85 20 92.
La Maison Lale***: +33 (0)5 55 84 00 09.

Gîte de la Mairie**:
+33 (0)5 55 27 38 38.
Lou Pé Dé Gril: +33 (0)5 55 25 45 53.
La Maison de Marguerite:
+33 (0)4 42 01 77 13.
Le Roc Blanc: +33 (0)5 55 25 48 02.

🍽 Eating Out
Auberge de la Grotte, farmhouse inn:
+33 (0)5 55 25 35 01.
La Barbacane: +33 (0)5 55 25 43 29.

🛒 Local Specialties
Food and Drink
Garlic and shallots • Aperitifs and jams made from dandelion flowers • Strawberries and jams • Artisanal beer.

2 Events
July and August: Festive market, sale of regional produce followed by a barbecue (Wednesdays at 4 p.m.).

🦋 Outdoor Activities
Hunting • Fishing • Walking: Route GR 480 and the "Boucle Verte" linking Curemonte with Collonges-la-Rouge.

🌿 Further Afield
• La Chapelle-aux-Saints: prehistoric site; museum (2 miles/3 km).
• Dordogne valley: Beaulieu; Argentat (6–22 miles/9.5–35 km).
• *Collonges-la-Rouge (7½ miles/12 km), see pp. 184–85.
• *Carennac (8½ miles/13.5 km), see pp. 179–80.
• *Turenne (11 miles/18 km), see pp. 262–63.
• *Loubressac (14 miles/23 km), see p. 210.
• *Autoire (16 miles/26 km), see p. 159.
• Brive-la-Gaillarde: Jardins de Colette, gardens; market (25 miles/40 km).

🍴 Did you know?
In 1940, the French novelist Colette came here to seek refuge with her daughter, Colette de Jouvenel, owner of the Châteaux de Saint-Hilaire et de Plas. In the tranquility of the village, the writer wrote part of her novel *Looking Backwards*.

Domme

A panoramic viewpoint over the Dordogne

Dordogne (24) • Population: 1,019 • Altitude: 689 ft. (210 m)

On the edge of a breathtakingly high cliff, Domme offers a remarkable view over the Dordogne valley.

Towering 492 ft. (150 m) over the meandering river, Domme's exceptional site accounts for it being one of the most beautiful *bastides* in the southwest of France, as well as a coveted place marked by a long and turbulent history. Its ramparts, fortified gates, and towers, which served as prisons first for the Templars in the early 14th century, then for French and English soldiers during the Hundred Years War, stand as imposing witnesses of its past. From the Place de la Rode, randomly dotted along flower-decked streets, are fine houses with golden façades and irregular roofs covered with brown tiles, such as the Maison du Batteur de Monnaie, embellished with a triple mullioned window, and the former courthouse of the seneschal, both built in the 13th century. Continuing on from the Place de la Halle, Domme offers a panoramic view of the Dordogne valley, rural landscapes, cultivated land, and a few local heritage sites, such as the Château de Monfort, the village of La Roque-Gageac, and the Jardins de Marqueyssac.

By road: Expressway A20, exit 55–Sarlat (22 miles/35 km). **By train:** Sarlat-la-Canéda station (7½ miles/12 km). **By air:** Brive-Vallée de la Dordogne airport (33 miles/53 km).

ⓘ Tourist information—
Périgord Noir:
+33 (0)5 53 33 71 00
www.perigordnoir-valleedordogne.com

👁 Highlights
• **Église Notre-Dame-de-l'Assomption:** Open daily.
• **Templar graffiti:** Seven pictures linked to religious iconography engraved by the Templars on the walls of the Porte des Tours. Guided tours: +33 (0)5 53 33 71 00.
• ♥ **Cave with stalactites:** The largest accessible cave in the Périgord Noir. More than a quarter of a mile (450 m) of tunnels beneath the *bastide*; ascent by panoramic elevator with a view of the Dordogne valley. Further information: +33 (0)5 53 33 71 00.
• **L'Oustal du Périgord** (popular arts and traditions museum): Collection of 19th- and 20th-century farming objects. Further information: +33 (0)5 53 33 71 00.
• **Village:** Guided tours in July and August and by appointment only off-season +33 (0)5 53 33 71 00; tour of the village by tourist train.

✎ Accommodation
Hotels
L'Esplanade***: +33 (0)5 53 28 31 41.
Nouvel Hôtel**: +33 (0)6 38 32 91 23.
Guesthouses
Le Manoir du Rocher***:
+33 (0)6 15 25 91 75.
1 Logis à Domme: +33 (0)9 75 44 51 68.

Vacation rentals and campsites
Further information: +33 (0)5 53 31 71 00
www.perigordnoir-valleedordogne.com
Holiday villages
La Combe: +33 (0)5 53 29 77 42.
Les Ventoulines: +33 (0)5 53 28 36 29.
Village du Paillé: +33 (0)6 73 38 32 94.

🍴 Eating Out
Auberge de la Rode: +33 (0)5 53 28 36 97.
Aux'Bar: +33 (0)5 53 28 53 47.
Le Belvédère: +33 (0)5 53 31 12 01.
La Borie Blanche, farmhouse inn:
+33 (0)5 53 28 11 24.
Cabanoix et Châtaignes: +33 (0)5 53 31 07 11.
Le Carreyrou: +33 (0)6 82 01 08 36.
Le Chalet: +33 (0)5 53 29 32 73.
L'Esplanade: +33 (0)5 53 28 31 41.
Le Jacquou Gourmand: +33 (0)5 53 28 36 81.
Le Médiéval: +33 (0)5 53 28 24 57.
La Pizzeria des Templiers: +33 (0)6 06 45 15 09.
La Poivrière: +33 (0)5 53 28 32 52.

🏛 Local Specialties
Food and Drink: Geese • Walnuts.
Art and Crafts: Jeweler • Artist.

② Events

Market: Thursday morning, Place de la Halle.
June: Fête de la Saint-Clair (1st weekend); "Feux de la Saint-Jean," Saint John's Eve bonfire; music festival; amateur dramatics festival.
July 14: Torchlight procession, fireworks.
July and August: Crafts market (Thursdays); "Domme Contemporaine Pas à Pas," art exhibition.

🦋 Outdoor Activities

Canoeing • Tennis • Mountain-biking • Walking: Route GR 64 and marked trails • Air sports: Light aircraft and microlights.

🦋 Further Afield

• Sarlat (7½ miles/12 km).
• Dordogne valley: *La Roque-Gageac (3 miles/5 km), see pp. 234–35; *Castelnaud-la-Chapelle (6 miles/9.5 km), see p. 182; *Beynac-et-Cazenac (6 miles/9.5 km), see pp.168–69; *Belvès (16 miles/26 km), see pp. 166–67.
• *Gourdon (17 miles/27 km), see pp. 104–5.
• Les Eyzies (21 miles/34 km).
• *Saint-Amand-de-Coly (23 miles/37 km), see pp. 236–37.
• *Limeuil (24 miles/39 km), see pp. 208–9.
• Vézère valley: *Saint-Léon-sur-Vézère (24 miles/39 km), see p. 248.
• *Monpazier (27 miles/43 km), see pp. 215–16.

🗡 Did you know?

At the beginning of the 14th century, Philippe Le Bel, king of France from 1285 to his death in 1314, suppressed the Christian military organization the Knights Templar. Some knights of neighboring commanderies were confined in the *bastide* of Domme. Their prison, the Porte des Tours, commemorates those years of captivity. Engraved in the stone, messages bear witness to both their distress and their faith.

Estaing

One family, one castle

Aveyron (12) • Population: 610 • Altitude: 1,050 ft. (320 m)

A short distance from the Gorges of the Lot, set against a backdrop of greenery, Estaing is distinguished by an imposing castle that overlooks the *lauze* (schist stone) roofs of the shale houses.

The illustrious Estaing family left its mark on the history of Rouergue, but also on that of France. The Château des Comtes d'Estaing (11th century to present) mixes Romanesque, Gothic, Flamboyant, and Renaissance styles. On the Place François Annat, named after Louis XIV's confessor, the 15th-century church, which has some remarkable altarpieces and stained-glass windows, houses the relics of Saint Fleuret. The fine Renaissance houses at the heart of the village continue to draw tourists. Providing a magnificent entrance point from the Saint James's Way, the 16th-century Gothic gateway is on the UNESCO World Heritage list and boasts unique views over the castle, the village's crowning feature.

By road: Expressway A75, exit 42–Rodez (34 miles/55 km). **By train:** Rodez station (24 miles/39 km). **By air:** Rodez-Marcillac airport (30 miles/48 km).

ⓘ Tourist information—
Espalion-Estaing: +33 (0)5 65 33 03 22
www.tourisme-espalion.fr

👁 Highlights
• **Castle** (11th century to present): Birthplace of the Estaing family. Open to the public in season: self-guided visit of the restored rooms; guided tour by appointment only: +33 (0)5 65 44 72 24.
• **Église Saint-Fleuret** (15th century): Gilded wooden altarpieces (17th and 18th centuries), relics of Saint Fleuret; contemporary stained-glass windows by Claude Baillon.
• **Chapelle de l'Ouradou** (16th century).
• **Village:** Guided tour for groups by appointment only: +33 (0)5 65 44 03 22.

🗝 Accommodation
Hotels
Auberge Saint-Fleuret**: +33 (0)5 65 44 01 44.
Aux Armes d'Estaing**: +33 (0)5 65 44 70 02.
B and B Manoir de la Fabrègues: +33 (0)5 65 66 37 78.
Guesthouses
Lou Bellut: +33 (0)6 80 66 77 79.
M. Disols: +33 (0)5 65 44 71 51.

La Marelle***: +33 (0)5 65 44 66 78.
L'Oustal de Cervel***: +33 (0)5 65 44 09 89.
Gîtes, vacation rentals, and campsites
Further information: +33 (0)5 65 44 03 22
www.tourisme-espalion.fr

🍴 Eating Out
Auberge Saint-Fleuret +33 (0)5 65 44 01 44.
Aux Armes d'Estaing: +33 (0)5 65 44 70 02.
Brasserie du Château: +33 (0)5 65 44 12 89.
Chez Mon Père, pizzeria: +33 (0)5 65 44 02 70.
Le Chrislou, light meals: +33 (0)5 65 44 35 56.
Le Ch'ti Estagnol: +33 (0)7 68 31 15 51.
Le Plaisir du Goût, crêperie/salad bar: +33 (0)5 65 48 27 43.

🧺 Local Specialties
Food and Drink
AOC and IGP Aveyron wines.
Art and Crafts
Bags and accessories designer • Jewelers • Cutlery maker • Artist • Illuminator • Unique handcrafted objects.

📅 Events
Market: July and August, gourmet market, Place du Foirail, Fridays from 7 p.m.
June 15–September 15: "Son et Lumière d'Estaing, 1500 ans d'histoire," sound and light show (Wednesday evenings).
July: Fête de la Saint-Fleuret, traditional parade (1st Sunday).
August: Nuit Lumière, illumination of the village by candlelight, sound and light show, fireworks (15th).
September: Les Médiévales d'Estaing, Estaing celebrates its medieval past (2nd weekend).

🦋 Outdoor Activities
Trout-fishing • Walking: Routes GR 65 and 6; topographic guide (23 circular walks), and walking tour of the village.

🌿 Further Afield
• Maison de la Vigne, du Vin, et des Paysages d'Estaing (all things wine-related) (3 miles/5 km).
• Espalion: Château de Calmont (8 miles/ 13 km).
• *Saint-Côme-d'Olt (8½ miles/13.5 km), see p. 242.
• Villecomtal (9½ miles/15.5 km).
• Gorges of the Truyère (16 miles/26 km).
• Laguiole; l'Aubrac (16 miles/26 km).
• *Sainte-Eulalie-d'Olt (21 miles/34 km), see p. 243–44.
• Rodez (22 miles/35 km).
• *Conques (24 miles/39 km), see pp. 186–87.

Eus

A feel of the South

Pyrénées-Orientales (66) • Population: 435 • Altitude: 1,270 ft. (387 m)

Eus is filled with the fragrance of orchards, old olive groves, and the *garrigue*. Built on terraces sheltered from the wind, the village takes its name from the surrounding *yeuses* (holm oaks). Designed for defense, Eus repelled the French in 1598 and, in 1793, the Spanish army, which at that time dominated the region. The 18th-century Église Saint-Vincent stands on the site of the Roman camp that kept watch over the road from Terrenera to Cerdagne, and of the former castle chapel, Notre-Dame-de-la-Volta, built in the 13th century. At the entrance to Eus, a Romanesque chapel is dedicated to the patron saint of winegrowers and to Saint Gaudérique. It opens onto a 13th-century porch made from pink marble from Villefranche-de-Conflent. Clinging to the steep, cobblestone streets, the old restored shale-stone houses give the village a harmonized feel.

By road: Expressway A9, exit 42–Perpignan Sud (25 miles/40 km).
By train: Prades-Molitg-les-Bains station (3½ miles/5.5 km). **By air:** Perpignan-Rivesaltes airport (29 miles/47 km).

ⓘ Tourist information—
Prades-Conflent: +33 (0)4 68 05 41 02
www.prades-tourisme.fr / www.eus.fr

👁 Highlights

• **Romanesque chapel** (11th–13th centuries): Listed as a historical monument.
• **Église Saint-Vincent** (18th century): Altarpieces and statues.
• **Musée La Solana:** Popular traditions.
• **Village:** Guided tour by arrangement: +33 (0)4 68 96 22 69.
• **Pépinières d'Agrumes Bachès** (citrus fruit nursery): Guided tours for groups by appointment only October–February: +33 (0)4 68 96 42 91.

🗝 Accommodation

Guesthouses
Casa Ilicia: +33 (0)6 95 34 15 32.
Gîtes and vacation rentals
Les Calendulas***: +33 (0)6 84 35 06 11.
Destination Méditerranée***:
+33 (0)4 68 68 42 88.
Julia Marie**: +33 (0)4 68 96 41 00.
Alexine*: +33 (0)4 34 56 00 26.
Amelia*: +33 (0)4 34 56 00 26.
Other gîtes and vacation rentals
Further information: +33 (0)4 68 68 42 88
or +33 (0)4 68 05 41 02
www.prades-tourisme.fr

🍴 Eating Out

Des Goûts et des Couleurs, tea room:
+33 (0)6 09 53 32 47.
El Lluert, bar & tapas: +33 (0)4 68 05 37 28.
Le Vieux Chêne d'Eus: +33 (0)4 68 96 35 29.

🧺 Local Specialties

Food and Drink
Regional fruit and vegetables • Fruit juice • Honey.

Art and Crafts
Murano glass jewelry • Ceramics • Wrought ironwork • Cutlery • Paintings • Photographs • Sculptures • Stained-glass windows • Herbs, oils, and perfumes.

🗓 Events

January: Feast of Saint Vincent (22nd).
Easter Monday: "Goig Dels Ous," Catalan Easter songs presented by the Cant'Eus choir.
June: Croisée d'Arts, contemporary art festival.
August: Festa Major festival; "Nits d'Eus," cultural festival; Course des Lézards, lizard-racing (last Sunday).

🦋 Outdoor Activities

Walking: 5 marked trails • Adventure park (10 trails): tubing, paintball, dével'mountain (downhill course on a scooter).

🦅 Further Afield

• Prades; Abbaye Saint-Michel-de-Cuxa (3½ miles/5.5 km).
• Marcevol: priory (5 miles/8 km)
• *Villefranche-de-Conflent (7½ miles/12 km), see pp. 264–65.
• Vernet-les-Bains; Abbaye Saint-Martin-du-Canigou (11 miles/18 km).
• Serrabone: priory (14 miles/23 km).
• *Évol (15 miles/24 km), see p. 195.
• *Castelnou (17 miles/27 km), see p. 183.
• Têt valley; Perpignan (27 miles/43 km).
• Rivesaltes; Salses fort (30 miles/48 km).

Évol

"A piece of sky on the mountain"

Pyrénées-Orientales (66) • Population: 40 • Altitude: 2,625 ft. (800 m)

In the foothills of the Massif du Madrès, on the side of a valley, the hamlet of Évol emerged from the mountain.

According to Catalan bard Ludovic Massé, who was born here in 1900, Évol, "far from everything," was "a piece of the sky on the mountain whose only shade is from cloud." Invisible from the road that leads from the plain to Cerdagne, the village emerges like a jewel in its verdant setting. Overlooked by the old fortress of the viscounts of So and the bell tower of its Romanesque church, Évol remains in perfect communion with the mountain, which provides a livelihood for its shepherds and is present in the shale of its walls and the blue *lauze* (schist tiles) of its roofs, the cutting of which was one of the occupations undertaken by locals in winter. Along the winding, flower-filled streets, bread ovens, a fig-drying kiln, barns, and interior courtyards bear witness to the daily life of a bygone era.

By road: Expressway A9, exit 42–Perpignan Sud (39 miles/63 km).
By train: Prades-Molitg-les-Bains station (12 miles/19 km). **By air:** Perpignan-Rivesaltes airport (42 miles/68 km).

(i) Tourist information:
+33 (0)4 68 05 39 09 or
+33 (0)6 07 23 31 24
www.evol66.fr

👁 Highlights
• **Église Saint-André** (11th century): Conjuratory (small religious building), John the Baptist altarpiece (15th century), and Romanesque statue of the Virgin (13th century).
• **Viscounts' castle** (13th century).
• **Chapelle Saint-Étienne** (13th century).
• **Cabinet Littéraire Ludovic-Massé:** Literary room devoted to the Catalan writer, storyteller, and bard, born in Évol in 1900.
• **Musée des Arts et Traditions Populaires:** Museum of popular arts and traditions housed in a former local school, featuring old tools; "Si Évol m'était conté," exhibition. Guided tour by appointment only, Évol la Médiévale association:
+33 (0)4 68 97 09 72 or
+33 (0)6 13 04 19 86.
• **Église Saint-André at Olette** (11th–13th centuries).

🔑 Accommodation
Guesthouses
La Fontaine, Olette: +33 (0)4 68 97 03 67.
Gîtes and vacation rentals
Gîtes de France: +33 (0)4 68 68 42 88.
Communal gîtes
Further information: +33 (0)4 68 97 02 86.

🍴 Eating Out
La Casa del Sol, Catalan bistro:
+33 (0)4 68 97 10 45.
L'Houstalet: +33 (0)4 68 97 03 90.

📅 Events
Market: Traditional market at Olette, Thursdays 8 a.m.–1 p.m, Place du Village.
May: Transhumance des Mérens, moving the horse herd.
June: Fête de la Transhumance (1st weekend).
August: Open-air rummage sale.
October: Sheep, cattle, and local produce fair (3rd or 4th weekend).

🐎 Outdoor Activities
Trout fishing (Évol river) • La Bastide lakes • Walking • Mountain-biking: "Madres-Coronat" biking area.

🌿 Further Afield
• Train Jaune: Olette station (1 mile/1.5 km).
• Saint-Thomas-les-Bains (6 miles/9.5 km).
• *Villefranche-de-Conflent (8 miles/13 km), see pp. 264–65.
• Prades (11 miles/18 km).
• Vernet-les-Bains: Abbaye Saint-Martin-du-Canigou (12 miles/19 km).
• Mont-Louis (14 miles/23 km).
• *Eus (15 miles/24 km), see p. 194.

La Flotte Charente-Maritime

La Flotte
Port on the Île de Ré

Charente-Maritime (17) • Population: 2,893 • Altitude: 56 ft. (17 m)

Facing the Pertuis Breton tidal estuary and the mainland, the pretty houses of La Flotte-en-Ré circle the harbor and reflect the ocean's light.

Now effectively a peninsula, located as it is at the end of a long bridge, Ré still retains its magical light, which changes with the tides; its gentle landscapes, which combine coastal flowers, vines, and salt marshes with oyster beds and fields of fruit and vegetables; and the dazzling white of its green-shuttered houses. To this "sandy, windswept island," as Richelieu called it, in a natural environment that has been very well preserved, La Flotte adds the soulful remains of the Abbaye des Châteliers, built by Cistercian monks in the 12th century; the imposing Fort de La Prée, built in the 17th century in the face of English invasions and the Protestant La Rochelle; a maze of restored and flower-decked alleyways around the Église Sainte-Catherine, and the old round-tile-covered market; and a picturesque harbor that is enlivened year round with fishing boats and pleasure craft. The other side of its double pier, the ocean still separates the "white island" from the mainland.

By road: N11-N237 (7 miles/11.5 km).
By train: La Rochelle station (14 miles/23 km).
By air: La Rochelle-Laleu airport (8 miles/13 km).

(i) **Tourist information:** +33 (0)5 46 09 60 38
www.laflotte-iledere.fr

👁 Highlights

• **Fort de La Prée** (17th century): A Vauban construction; guided tour by appointment only: +33 (0)5 46 09 61 39.
• **La Maison du Platin:** Museum dedicated to life on the Île de Ré, with collections on the island's traditional occupations, its relations with the mainland, housing, and costumes; temporary exhibitions: +33 46 09 61 39.
• **Ruins of the Cistercian Abbaye des Châteliers** (12th century): Self-guided visit or guided tour.
• **Village:** Guided tour by arrangement: +33 (0)5 46 09 61 39.

🔑 Accommodation

Hotels
Le Richelieu***** : +33 (0)5 46 09 60 70.
Le Français** : +33 (0)5 46 09 60 06.
♥ La Galiote** : +33 (0)5 46 09 50 95.
L'Hippocampe** +33 (0)5 46 09 60 68.
Aparthotels
Les Hauts de Cocraud** Odalys:
+33 (0)5 46 68 29 21 or
+33 (0)8 25 56 25 62.
Guesthouses
Stéphanie Gaschet: +33 (0)5 46 09 05 78.
M. Rocklin: +33 (0)5 46 09 51 28.
Mme Vanoost: +33 (0)5 46 09 12 89.
Mme Wyart: +33 (0)5 46 09 63 93.
Gîtes, vacation rentals, and campsites
Further information: +33 (0)5 46 09 60 38
www.laflotte-iledere.fr

🍽 Eating Out
À la Plancha: +33 (0)5 46 68 10 34.
Chez Nous Comme Chez Vous, bistro/
wine bar: +33 (0)5 46 09 49 85.
La Croisette: +33 (0)5 46 09 06 06.
L'Écailler, gourmet: +33 (0)5 46 09 56 40.
L'Endroit du Goinfre: +33 (0)5 46 09 50 01.
L'Escale, brasserie: +33 (0)5 46 05 63 37.
La Fiancée du Pirate, crêperie/pizzeria:
+33 (0)5 46 09 52 46.
Le Français: +33 (0)5 46 09 60 06.
Il Gabbiano, Italian specialties:
+33 (0)5 46 09 60 08.
Le Nautic: +33 (0)9 67 37 31 73.
Les Pieds dans l'Eau, crêperie:
+33 (0)5 46 09 45 68.
Le Pinocchio, pizzeria: +33 (0)5 46 09 13 13.
La Poissonnerie du Port, except January
and February: +33 (0)5 46 09 04 14.
Le Richelieu, gourmet:
+33 (0)5 46 09 60 70.
Le Saint-Georges: +33 (0)5 46 09 60 18.

🧺 Local Specialties
Food and Drink
Ré oysters • Spring vegetables • Pineau,
wines • *Sel de Ré* (salt).
Art and Crafts
Decoration • Earthenware • Art galleries •
Artists • Painter-decorator.

📅 Events
Market: Medieval market daily, 8 a.m.–
1 p.m., Rue du Marché.
June: Firework display; flea markets.
July: Journée des Peintres, artists' day.
July–August: Regattas, musical events at
the harbor (every evening); evening crafts
market.
July 1–September 15: Concerts in
the Église Sainte-Catherine and tours;
classical concerts at the harbor.
August: Gathering of traditional sailing
vessels (1st fortnight); music and firework
display (mid-August).

🦋 Outdoor Activities
Swimming (lifeguard) in July and August
(Plage de l'Arnérault) • Riding • Pleasure
boating • Shellfish gathering • Bike rides
(rental) • Watersports: swimming, sailing,
windsurfing • Thalassotherapy.

🌿 Further Afield
• La Rochelle (9½ miles/15.5 km).
• *Ars-en-Ré (11 miles/18 km),
see pp. 155–56.
• Islands of Aix, Madame, and Oléron
(19–28 miles/31–45 km).
• Marais Poitevin, region (25 miles/40 km).
• Rochefort (25 miles/40 km).

Fourcès

A medieval circle in Gascony

Gers (32) • Population: 295 • Altitude: 213 ft. (65 m)

In a loop of the Auzoue river, at the end of a bridge, Fourcès forms a circle around a central square shaded by plane trees.

Set on the banks of the Auzoue, and facing the Église Saint-Laurent on the other side of the river, Fourcès has a circular shape that is unique in Gascony. The village developed in the 11th century under the protection of a castle, which occupied the main square, and ramparts, of which the Porte de l'Horloge remains. In 1279, Fourcès fell into the hands of Edward I of England who, ten years later, made it a *bastide* by granting it a charter of customs. Every year, in a theatrical setting of arches and half-timbered façades, the square hosts an exceptional flower market. The late 15th-century Château des Fourcès escaped ruin by becoming a hotel-restaurant; since 2010 it has been a guesthouse.

By road: Expressway A62, exit 6–Nérac (28 miles/45 km).
By train: Agen station (32 miles/51 km).
By air: Agen-La Garenne airport (30 miles/48 km).

ⓘ Tourist information—Ténarèze:
+33 (0)5 62 28 00 80
www.tourisme-condom.com

👁 Highlights
• Arboretum: Free entry.
• Église Saint-Laurent and Église Sainte-Quitterie.
• Village.

🗝 Accommodation
Guesthouses
♥ Le Château de Fourcès****:
+33 (0)5 62 29 49 53.
Du Côté de Chez Jeanne****:
+33 (0)9 53 06 04 06.
Solange and Pierre Mondin, Bajolle**:
+33 (0)5 62 29 42 65.
Gîtes and vacation rentals
Further information: +33 (0)5 62 28 00 80
www.tourisme-condom.com
RV parks
Further information: +33 (0)5 62 29 40 13.

🍴 Eating Out
L'Auberge: +33 (0)5 62 29 40 10.
Le Carroussel Gourmand, tea room:
+33 (0)9 53 06 04 06.

🧺 Local Specialties
Food and Drink
Armagnac • Foie gras, duck fillet and confit • AOC Côtes de Gascogne wines.
Art and Crafts
Antique dealers • Jewelry and accessories designer • Cardboard crafts • Embroidery.

📅 Events
April: Flower market (last weekend).
May–November: Flea market (2nd Sunday of each month).
June: Artists in the street.
July: Antiquarian book fair (3rd Sunday); aperitif and concert.
August: "Marciac in Fourcès," jazz concert (mid-August); village fair (3rd weekend).
December: Christmas market.

🦋 Outdoor Activities
Hunting • Fishing • Theme park, adventure playground for children • Walking • *Pétanque.*

🕊 Further Afield
• *Montréal (3½ miles/5.5 km), see p. 217.
• Poudenas (5 miles/8 km).
• Mézin, fortified town (5½ miles/9 km).
• *Larressingle (6 miles/9.5 km), see p. 201.
• Condom (8 miles/13 km).
• Château de Cassaigne (9½ miles/15.5 km).
• Abbaye de Flaran (11 miles/18 km).
• Trésor d'Eauze, archeological museum (13 miles/21 km).
• Nérac (15 miles/24 km).
• *Lavardens (25 miles/40 km), see pp. 206–7.

Lagrasse

An abbey amid the vineyards

Aude (11) • Population: 615 • Altitude: 433 ft. (132 m)

At the heart of the Corbière mountains, where vines mingle with perfumed Mediterranean *garrigue* scrubland, Lagrasse is a rare bloom in Cathar country.

The Benedictine abbey of Lagrasse, founded in 800 CE in the valley on the left bank of the Orbieu river, is considered to have been one of the oldest and richest in France, and is still today the biggest abbey in the Aude. Its material, political, and spiritual influence extended beyond the Pyrenees. During the French Revolution, the abbey became state property, and it was split into two sections—as can be seen by the two entrance gates—before being sold. Mainly medieval, the oldest part can be visited and hosts concerts, exhibitions, and other cultural events all year round. Lagrasse is linked to this architectural jewel by a medieval bridge straddling the Orbieu. It is delightful to wander along its picturesque lanes, to share the wonderful atmosphere on its terraces or in its lively market hall, as people have been doing since the 14th century, and to appreciate the skills of its many craftspeople.

By road: Expressway A61, exit 25–Lézignan-Corbières (10 miles/16 km). **By train:** Lézignan-Corbières station (12 miles/19 km). **By air:** Carcassonne-Salvaza airport (35 miles/56 km).

ⓘ Tourist information:
+33 (0)4 68 43 11 56
https://vivonslagrasse.org/fr

👁 Highlights

• **Abbaye Saint-Marie d'Orbieu** (9th–18th centuries): Guided tour available: +33 (0)4 68 43 15 99.
• **Église Saint-Michel** (14th century): Gothic style, paintings by the studio of Giuseppe Crespi (1665–1747) and by Jacques Gamelin (1738–1803), 13th-century) wood sculpture of the Virgin.
• **Maison du Patrimoine, heritage center:** Former presbytery, 15th-century painted ceilings; permanent exhibition on the painted ceilings of Languedoc-Roussillon; restored works from three Renaissance painted ceilings in Lagrasse, and a rare medieval painted ceiling from a mansion in Montpellier: +33 (0)4 68 43 11 56.
• **"Le 1900":** Over 3,000 sq. ft. (300 sq. m) exhibition with audioguide about life and traditional skills in 1900; rare-object collections; 4D show about the disused tramway: +33 (0)4 68 32 18 87.
• **Village:** Guided visit for groups by appointment only: +33 (0)6 81 42 79 63.

🗝 Accommodation

Hotels
Hostellerie des Corbières**: +33 (0)4 68 43 15 22.
Guesthouses
Les Glycines***: +33 (0)4 68 43 14 54.
Château Villemagne*: +33 (0)4 68 24 06 97.
Further information: +33 (0)4 68 43 11 56
https://vivonslagrace.org/fr
Gîtes
♥ Le Studio Blanc: +33 (0)6 78 96 64 72.
Further information: +33 (0)4 68 43 11 56
https://vivonslagrace.org/fr
Campsites
Camping Boucocers: +33 (0)4 68 43 15 18 or +33 (0)4 68 43 10 05.

🍴 Eating Out

L'Affenage: +33 (0)4 68 43 16 59.
Au Coupa Talen, pizzeria: +33 (0)4 68 43 19 36.
Café de la Promenade: +33 (0)4 68 43 15 89.
La Cocotte Fêlée: +33 (0)4 68 75 90 54.
Hostellerie des Corbières: +33 (0)4 68 43 15 22.
La Petite Maison, tea room: +33 (0)4 68 91 34 09.
Le Recantou, ice-cream parlor, tapas: +33 (0)4 68 49 94 73.
Le Temps des Courges: +33 (0)4 68 43 10 18.
Les Trois Grâces: +33 (0)4 68 43 18 17.

🧺 Local Specialties

Food and Drink
Olive oil • Vinegar • Honey • AOC Corbières wines.
Art and Crafts
Antiques • Leather craftsman • Jewelry maker • Furniture designer • Wrought ironworker • Painters • Ceramic artist • Sculptor and caster • Fashion and hat designer • Upholsterer • Stained-glass artist.

📅 Events

Market: Saturday mornings, Place de la Halle.
May–September: Flea markets.
July: Piano festival (early July); village fête (13th); "Les Abracadagrasses," music festival (3rd weekend).
August: Summer banquet, literature, and philosophy festival (1st fortnight); potters' market; "Les P'tibals," folk festival (end of August).
September: "Les Loges Musicales," chamber music festival (1st fortnight).

🦋 Outdoor Activities

Fishing • Saint-Jean Lake • Walking: Route GR 36 and themed family trails.

🌿 Further Afield

• Termes and Villerouge-Termenès castles (12 miles/19 km).
• Abbaye de Fontfroide (17 miles/27 km).
• Carcassonne (22 miles/35 km).
• Narbonne (27 miles/43 km).

Larressingle
A mini-Carcassonne in the Midi-Pyrenees

Gers (32) • Population: 217 • Altitude: 469 ft. (143 m)

Towering above the vines, the fortress-village of Larressingle cultivates the Gascon way of life.

The village lies beyond a fortified gateway, just past a bridge straddling a green moat. It backs onto a crown of ramparts encircling the castle keep (for many years the residence of the bishops of Condom) and a high church with two naves. Larressingle was saved from ruin by the enthusiastic duke of Trévise, who created a rescue committee financed by generous Americans. Today the village is a delightful collection of heritage buildings from the area's rich medieval past, including the castle, dating from the 13th, 14th, and 16th centuries, which has three floors and a pentagonal tower, a fortified gateway, and the remains of its surrounding walls; the Romanesque church of Saint-Sigismond; and the charming and finely built residences, decorated with mullioned windows and roofed with ocher tiles. Rooted to the land, Larressingle is a showcase for local Gers produce, particularly Armagnac, foie gras, and apple croustade.

By road: Expressway A62, exit 7–Périgueux (25 miles/40 km).
By train: Auch station (29 miles/47 km); Agen station (29 miles/47 km).
By air: Agen-La Garenne airport (25 miles/40 km); Toulouse-Blagnac airport (68 miles/109 km).

ⓘ **Tourist information—Ténarèze:**
+33 (0)5 62 68 22 49 or +33 (0)5 62 28 00 80
www.tourisme-condom.com

👁 Highlights
• **Medieval siege camp:** Camp with siege engines for attack and defense, firing demonstrations of war machines: +33 (0)5 62 68 33 88.
• **Église Saint-Sigismond** (12th-century): Modern Madonna and Child stained-glass windows inspired by Marc Chagall paintings.
• **Musée de la Halte du Pèlerin** (pilgrim's rest): Representation of medieval life; 75 life-size wax characters: +33 (0)5 62 28 11 58 or +33 (0)5 62 28 08 08.
• **Orchard:** Series of vineyards around the village ramparts. 7-acre (3-hectare) agro-ecological site comprised of a vineyard of dessert grapes (23 varieties) and an orchard (65 varieties); historic and local collection: +33 (0)6 89 12 92 33.
• **Village:** Self-guided visit; guided tour (admission fee) by appointment only in summer for individuals: +33 (0)5 62 28 00 80.

⚔ Accommodation
Hotels
Auberge de Larressingle**: +33 (0)5 62 28 29 67.
Guesthouses
Maider Papelorey***: +33 (0)5 62 28 26 89.
Martine Valeri: +33 (0)5 62 77 29 72.
Gîtes
M. Teoran, "Couchet": +33 (0)5 62 28 17 50.
Walkers' lodges
Further information: +33 (0)5 62 68 82 49 or +33 (0)5 62 28 00 80.

Campsites
Mme Danto, la Ferme de Laillon, farm campsite: +33 (0)5 62 28 19 71 or +33 (0)6 07 69 14 19.

🍽 Eating Out
Auberge de Larressingle: +33 (0)5 62 28 29 67.
Aux Délices de Flor, tea room: +33 (0)5 62 68 10 23.
Crêperie du Château: +33 (0)5 62 68 48 93.
L'Estanquet, pizzeria: +33 (0)9 83 95 20 23.
Glacier Art: +33 (0)6 80 10 90 66.

🛍 Local Specialties
Food and Drink
Armagnac • Floc de Gascogne aperitif • Free-range duck preserves (confit, foie gras), and free-range pork • Organic wines.
Art and Crafts
Antiques • Painter • Glassblower.

☑ Events
July: Medieval fair.
July–August: Theater productions; night visit to the fortified village with falconry demonstration; night markets.

🦋 Outdoor Activities
Walking: Route GR 65 and short marked trails.

🌿 Further Afield
• Pont de l'Artigues (½ mile/1 km).
• Condom (3 miles/5 km).
• Mouchan Priory belonging to Cluny (3½ miles/5.5 km).
• Château de Cassaigne (4½ miles/7 km).
• Abbaye de Flaran (6 miles/9.5 km).
• *Fourcès (6 miles/9.5 km), see p. 192.
• *Montréal (6 miles/9.5 km), see p. 217.
• *La Romieu: collegiate church (10 miles/16 km), see pp. 232–33.
• Trésor d'Eauze, archeological museum (15 miles/24 km).
• Lectoure (16 miles/26 km).
• *Lavardens (20 miles/32 km), see pp. 206–7.
• Auch (28 miles/45 km).

Lautrec

Pays de Cocagne—the land of milk and honey

Tarn (81) • Population: 1,750 • Altitude: 1,033 ft. (315 m)

This medieval town in the heart of Tarn's Pays de Cocagne is the birthplace of painter Toulouse-Lautrec's family. From the top of La Salette hill there are far-reaching views over the whole Casters plain and the Montagne Noire. A castle stood here; now there is a Calvary cross and a botanical trail. For many years the village was the only fortified place between Albi and Carcassonne, and some of its ramparts remain. Its shady plane-tree promenade runs alongside them, and each year Lautrec, the center of pink garlic farming, holds garlic markets. The gateway of La Caussade leads straight from the rampart walk to the central square. The Rue de Mercadial also leads there, passing an old Benedictine convent, which became the town hall after the French Revolution. The square still holds a traditional Friday morning market under the beams of its covered hall. With its well and its lovely half-timbered and corbeled residences, it remains a delightful part of Lautrec. The Rue de l'Église leads to the collegiate church of Saint-Rémy, built in the 14th century then extended. The pastel blue walls celebrate a color that brought riches to Lautrec, earning the Pays de Cocagne its name—from the *coques* or *cocagnes* (balls of dried woad) that were ground down to produce dye—as well as its reputation as an earthly paradise.

By road: Expressway A68, exit 9–Gaillac (18 miles/29 km). By train: Castres station (10 miles/16 km). By air: Castres-Mazamet airport (15 miles/24 km); Toulouse-Blagnac airport (47 miles/76 km).

ⓘ Tourist information—Lautrécois-Pays d'Agout: +33 (0)5 63 97 94 41
www.lautrectourisme.com
www.lautrec.fr

👁 Highlights

• Clogmaker's workshop: Recreated workshop that existed until the 1960s, with vintage machines and tools: +33 (0)7 86 91 98 77.
• Église Collégiale Saint-Rémy (14th–16th centuries): Marble altarpiece by Caunes-Minervois, sculpted lectern (17th century).
• La Salette windmill: For opening hours: +33 (0)5 63 97 94 41. By appointment off-season.
• La Salette botanical trail: Self-guided walk to learn about the plants of the Lautrec region, plus panoramic view of the area with viewpoint indicator.
• Village: Daily guided tours for groups of 10+ people, by reservation: +33 (0)5 63 97 94 41.

🗝 Accommodation

Guesthouses
Cadalen****: +33 (0)7 86 02 88 48.
Château de Montcuquet***: +33 (0)5 63 75 90 07.
La Fontaine de Lautrec***: +33 (0)5 63 50 15 72.
Temps de Pause***: +33 (0)6 62 89 66 03.
Les Amis de Mes Amis: +33 (0)9 60 19 59 66.

Les Chambres de la Caussade: +33 (0)5 63 75 33 21.
Château de Brametourte: +33 (0)5 63 75 01 25.
Gîtes and vacation rentals, bunkhouses
16 gîtes (1–4*) and bunkhouse. Further information: +33 (0)5 63 97 94 41
www.lautrectourisme.com
Campsites and RV parks
Aire Naturelle de Brametourte: +33 (0)5 63 75 30 31.
RV park with facilities: further information at tourist information center.

🍴 Eating Out

Auberge Le Garde-Pile, booking essential: +33 (0)5 63 75 34 58.
Au Pied du Moulin: +33 (0)6 52 72 22 29.
Café Plüm: +33 (0)5 63 70 83 30.
Le Clos d'Adèle: +33 (0)5 81 43 61 91.
L'Embuscade, pizzeria: +33 (0)9 54 63 15 94.
La Ferme dans l'Assiette: +33 (0)5 63 74 23 29.
Relais Loisirs de Brametourte, booking essential: +33 (0)5 63 75 30 31.
Les Terrasses, brasserie: +33 (0)5 63 75 37 10.

🛍 Local Specialties

Food and Drink

Lautrec pink garlic, garlic specialties (bread, vinegar, pâté) • *Croquants aux amandes* (almond cookies) • Duck foie gras • *Gelée de plantes* (herb and aromatic plant jellies).

Art and Crafts

Ceramic artist • Cabinetmaker • Leather craftsman • Pastel dyeing • Art galleries • Jewelry • Household linen • Clothing.

2 Events

Market: Fridays 8–12 a.m., Place Centrale.
Pink garlic market: Mid-July to mid-February, Fridays 8–10 a.m., on the promenade.
May: Fêtes de Lautrec (last weekend).
June: Fête des Moulins, windmill festival and open-air rummage sale (3rd Sunday).
July: Fête du Livre, festival of books and book craftsmanship (1st fortnight, odd-numbered years); Fête du Sabot et des Anciens Métiers, festival of clogs and traditional skills (3rd Sunday).
August: Fête de l'Ail rose, pink garlic festival (1st Friday and Saturday); Fête du Pain–Fête du Goût, tasting fair (15th); "Festivaoût," 3 days of concerts (around the 15th).
September: Festival of the Arts in Pays de Cocagne (1st weekend).
October: "Outilautrec," traditional tool and machine festival (1st weekend).

🦋 Outdoor Activities

Aquaval watersports (open mid-June–end August): swimming, beach volleyball, *boules* area, minigolf, model-making, fishing, field volleyball, family games • *Boules* area: Place du Mercadial (*pétanque* competition on Friday evenings in summer) • Horse-riding: marked trails • Cycling and walking: marked trails.

🌿 Further Afield

• Lombers: Écomusée du Pigeon, pigeon museum (5½ miles/9 km).
• Réalmont, royal walled town (7 miles/11 km).
• Castres (Musée Goya) and Le Sidobre (9½–14 miles/15.5–23 km).
• Saint-Paul-Cap-de-Joux: Musée du Pastel and Château de Magrin (12 miles/19 km).
• Albi, UNESCO World Heritage Site: Musée Toulouse-Lautrec, museum (19 miles/31 km).
• Cascade d'Arifat, waterfall (19 miles/31 km).

❗ Did you know?

Pink garlic appeared in Lautrec during the Middle Ages. An itinerant merchant stopped at the place known as L'Oustallarié at Lautrec, wanting a feast. Since he had no money, he settled his bill with pretty pink garlic cloves. The hotelier planted the cloves and pink garlic began to grow in the region.

Lauzerte
A walled town in Quercy Blanc

Tarn-et-Garonne (82) • Population: 1,535 • Altitude: 722 ft. (220 m)

Lauzerte dominates the surrounding valleys and hills from its lofty position atop a spur of land. In the late 12th century, the count of Toulouse began construction of this fortified town. Granted an official charter in 1241, Lauzerte was simultaneously a trading town, a stronghold, and a staging post along the ancient Via Podiensis, or Saint James's Way, the pilgrims' route to Santiago de Compostela. Many buildings tell the prestigious history of this successful and wealthy town: the old fortifications, the 13th-century church of Saint-Barthélémy (restored on several occasions), houses that once belonged to local notables, and the Place des Cornières, the town's commercial and artistic center. Today Lauzerte hosts numerous festivals, cultural events, and markets. It makes *cocagne* dyes, and its fertile farmlands and temperate climate also produce the Chasselas grape, Quercy melons, plums, peaches, pears, and nectarines, as well as poultry, foie gras, and confits.

By road: Expressway A62, exit 8–Cahors (22 miles/35 km) or exit 9–Castelsarrasin (21 miles/34 km); expressway A20, exit 58–Cahors Sud (20 miles/32 km).
By train: Moissac station (15 miles/24 km).
By air: Toulouse-Blagnac airport (62 miles/100 km).

ⓘ **Town hall:** +33 (0)5 63 94 65 14
www.lauzerte.fr

👁 Highlights
• **Église Saint-Barthélemy** (13th–18th centuries): Stalls, paintings, Baroque altarpiece, painted paneling attributed to Joseph Ingres (1755–1814) and his pupils.
• **Jardin du Pèlerin** (pilgrim's garden): Designed as a game of giant snakes and ladders on the theme of the pilgrimage to Santiago; history, life as a medieval pilgrim, European cultural and linguistic heritage are explored through play.
• **Village:** Guided visits; evening tour by torchlight. Further information: +33 (0)6 19 13 66 53.

🗝 Accommodation
Hotels
Le Belvédère***: +33 (0)5 63 95 51 10.
Le Luzerta*: +33 (0)5 63 94 64 43.
Le Quercy*: +33 (0)5 63 94 66 36.
Guesthouses
Bounetis Bas: +33 (0)5 63 39 56 61.
Camp Biche: +33 (0)5 63 29 23 86.
Castelmac: +33 (0)5 63 94 55 51.
Chez Françoise: +33 (0)6 99 62 79 12.
Domaine Saint Fort: +33 (0)9 67 02 04 28.
Les Figuiers: +33 (0)5 63 94 61 29.
L'Horizon: +33 (0)5 63 32 55 04.
Le Jardin Secret: +33 (0)5 63 94 80 01.
Lavande en Quercy: +33 (0)5 63 94 66 19.
Millial: +33 (0)6 09 63 81 41.
Mme Turti: +33 (0)5 63 94 66 19.
Moulin de Tauran: +33 (0)5 63 94 60 68.
Sainte Claire: +33 (0)5 63 39 08 62.
Saint-Fort: +33 (0)6 89 03 09 49.
La Stinoise: +33 (0)5 63 95 21 90.
Villa Lucerna: +33 (0)6 33 98 03 97.
Wallon-nous dormir?: +33 (0)5 63 04 56 44.
Gîtes, walkers' lodges, and vacation rentals
Further information: +33 (0)5 63 94 61 94.
Campsites
Le Beau Village***: +33 (0)5 63 29 13 68.

🍽 Eating Out
L'Auberge d'Auléry: +33 (0)5 63 04 79 13.
Auberge des Carmes, brasserie: +33 (0)5 63 94 64 49.
Aux Sarrazines du Faubourg, crêperie: +33 (0)5 65 20 10 12.
Le Belvédère: +33 (0)5 63 95 51 10.
L'Etna, pizzeria: +33 (0)5 63 94 18 60.
Le Local: +33 (0)5 63 32 24 84.
Le Luzerta: +33 (0)5 63 94 64 43.
Le Puits de Jour, music café and light meals: +33 (0)5 63 94 70 59.
Le Quercy: +33 (0)5 63 94 66 36.
La Table des 3 Chevaliers: +33 (0)5 63 95 32 69.

🏛 Local Specialties
Food and Drink
Foie gras and other duck products • Fruit, Chasselas grapes AOP de Moissac • Macarons.
Art and Crafts
Ceramic artists • Illuminator • Metalworker • Leather and wood engravers • Sculptors • Photographers • Leather crafts • Jeweler.

2️⃣ Events
Markets: Wednesday mornings, Foirail; Saturday mornings, Cornières.
April: "Place aux fleurs," flower market (3rd Sunday).
April–November: "Espace Points de Vue," exhibitions.
June: "Fête de la Musique," music festival.
July: Ball and fireworks (14th); "Métalik' Art," metallic sculpture symposium (2nd weekend); Pottery market (3rd weekend).
July–August: Guided visit (Mondays); open-air cinema (Tuesdays); "Place aux artistes," art market (Wednesdays); food and music festival (Thursdays).
August: Afro-Latino music and dance festival (1st weekend); professional flea market (15th).

September: "Place aux Nouvelles," book festival (2nd weekend).
November: "Journée de L'Arbre et du Bois," tree and wood festival (penultimate Sunday).
December: "Place à Noël," poetry and drinks (2nd Wednesday).

🦋 Outdoor Activities
Horse-riding • Fishing • Walking: Route GR 65 on the Saint James's Way, and shorter walks.

🌿 Further Afield
• Saint-Sernin-du-Bosc: Romanesque chapel (2½ miles/4 km).
• Montcuq (6 miles/9.5 km).
• Moissac (16 miles/26 km).
• *Auvillar (21 miles/34 km), see pp. 160–61.

Lavardens

A stone nave in the Gascon countryside

Gers (32) • Population: 407 • Altitude: 646 ft. (197 m)

Like a ship moored on a rocky outcrop, the imposing Château de Lavardens dominates the green crests and troughs of central Gascony.

Once the military capital of the counts of Armagnac, the medieval fortress of Lavardens was besieged and destroyed in 1496 on the order of Charles VII. The castle passed into the hands of the d'Albret and later the de Navarre families, and was granted by Henri IV to his friend Antoine de Roquelaure in 1585. De Roquelaure began rebuilding the castle out of love for his young wife, Suzanne de Bassabat. This work was interrupted several years later when he died in a plague outbreak, and was completed by the Association de Sauvegarde du Château de Lavardens (which restores and manages the castle) only in the 1970s. Its work respects all the individuality of this unique architectural site: the space, the ocher tiles and original bricks of the rooms, the exterior galleries, and the squinch towers—a unique architectural feature. At the foot of this white-stone sentinel, the charming 18th-century village houses line the cobbled streets, which are bordered with hollyhocks.

By road: Expressway A62, exit 7–Auch (36 miles/58 km); N21 (14 miles/23 km).
By train: Auch station (14 miles/23 km).
By air: Agen-La Garenne airport (40 miles/ 64 km); Toulouse-Blagnac airport (54 miles/87 km).

ⓘ **Tourist information—Grand Auch:**
+33 (0)5 62 05 22 89
www.auch-tourisme.com

👁 Highlights

• **Castle** (12th–17th centuries): Including guardroom, ballroom, games room, chapel; exhibitions: +33 (0)5 62 58 10 61.
• **Church** (13th century): Pulpit, stalls.
• **Chapelle Sainte-Marie des Consolations:** Medieval chapel with views over the village.
• **Petit Musée du Téléphone:** Telephone museum. By appointment only: +33 (0)5 62 64 56 61.
• **Village:** Guided visits in summer, and for groups all year round by appointment: +33 (0)5 62 05 22 89; "Passengus" guided visit by appointment: www.passe-en-gus.fr.

🗝 Accommodation

Guesthouses
M. and Mme Chaput, Lo Campestre****: +33 (0)5 62 58 24 30.
M. and Mme Delhaye, Domaine de Mascara***: +33 (0)5 62 64 52 17.
Mme Ulry, at Nabat*: +33 (0)5 62 64 51 21.
Gîtes and vacation rentals
M. Lloyd**: +33 (0)6 62 64 57 66.
M. Monello: +33 (0)5 62 64 56 92.

🍽 Eating Out

Le Malthus, brasserie: +33 (0)5 62 64 57 18.
Le Restaurant du Château: +33 (0)5 62 66 20 83.

🧺 Local Specialties

Food and Drink
Gers green lentils.
Art and Crafts
Stonecutters.

📅 Events

March–June: Art exhibition at the castle.
July–August: Evening markets.
August: "Rétromotion," exhibition of antique and exceptional cars.
September: Village fête (3rd weekend).
October–January: *Santon* (crib figures) exhibition at the castle.
December: Christmas market.

🦋 Outdoor Activities

Walking.

🌿 Further Afield

• Jégun, fortified town (3½ miles/5.5 km).
• Castéra-Verduzan: spa, sports, recreation park, racetrack (6 miles/9.5 km).
• Biran: castle, church (10 miles/16 km).
• Saint-Jean-Poutge: castles; canoeing on the Baïse river (10 miles/16 km).
• Valence-sur-Baïse: Abbaye de Flaran (14 miles/23 km).
• Auch: cathedral (14 miles/23 km).
• *Larressingle (20 miles/32 km), see p. 201.
• *Montréal (24 miles/39 km), see p. 217.
• *Fourcès (25 miles/40 km), see p. 198.
• *Sarrant (27 miles/43 km), see pp. 254–55.

Limeuil

Barges and boatmen—
a bustling trading center

Dordogne (24) • Population: 354 • Altitude: 295 ft. (90 m)

Where the Dordogne and Vézère rivers meet, the once-flourishing port of Limeuil is now a welcoming and shady bank. The village knew dark days defending itself against the Vikings and then, during the Hundred Years War, the English. Three fortified gateways remain from this time, which visitors pass through to reach the village, built on a steep slope. The houses wind along its lanes, showing their façades of golden stone decorated with coats of arms. Halfway up, at the Place des Fossés, the castle comes into view, medieval in origin but renovated in the Moorish style. Down below, an arched double bridge straddles both rivers, and the Place du Port is a reminder that Limeuil was an important commercial center in the 19th century. In the valley not far from the village stands the 12th-century chapel of Saint-Martin, considered one of the most beautiful Romanesque chapels in Périgord.

By road: Expressway A89, exit 16–Périgueux Est (25 miles/40 km). N221 (24 miles/38 km).
By train: Buisson-de-Cadouin station (3½ miles/5.5 km); Bergerac station (29 miles/47 km). **By air:** Bergerac-Roumanière airport (28 miles/45 km).

ⓘ **Tourist information:**
+33 (0)5 53 63 38 90
www.limeuil-en-perigord.com

👁 **Highlights**
• Chapelle Saint-Martin (12th century): Frescoes: +33 (0)5 53 63 33 66.
• **Panoramic gardens** (castle park): Gardens on the themes of colors, sorcerers, water, arboretum, landscaped garden; discovery trails on the themes of trees, landscape, river transport, and seamanship; craft workshops: +33 (0)5 53 57 52 64.
• **Village and park:** Self-guided visit (information panels). Further information: +33 (0)5 53 63 38 90.

🗝 **Accommodation**
Hotels
Les Terrasses de Beauregard**:
+33 (0)5 53 63 30 85.
Guesthouses
Au Bon Accueil: +33 (0)5 53 63 30 97.
Le Béquie: +33 (0)5 53 63 01 59.
La Rolandie Haute: +33 (0)5 53 73 16 12.
Gîtes and vacation rentals
Further information: +33 (0)5 53 63 38 90
www.limeuil-en-perigord.com
Aparthotels
Domaine de la Vitrolle**:
+33 (0)5 53 61 58 58.
Campsites
La Ferme de Perdigat***:
+33 (0)5 53 63 31 54.
La Ferme des Poutiroux***:
+33 (0)5 53 63 31 62.

🍽 **Eating Out**
À l'Ancre de Salut, bar/brasserie:
+33 (0)5 53 63 39 29.
Au Bon Accueil: +33 (0)5 53 63 30 97.
Le Chai, crêperie/pizzeria:
+33 (0)5 53 63 39 36.
Garden Party: +33 (0)5 53 73 36 65.
Les Terrasses de Beauregard:
+33 (0)5 53 63 30 85.

🧺 **Local Specialties**
Food and Drink
Local beer • Périgord apples and vin de pays • Organic produce.

Art and Crafts

Jewelry • Art gallery • Silver/goldsmith • Painters • Potters • Glassblowers • Beadmaker • Straw-weaver.

2 Events

Market: Sunday mornings, local produce, Place du Port (1st weekend in July through last weekend in August).

July: Flea market, local saint's day (weekend closest to 14th); pottery market (last weekend).

July–August: Evening markets (every Sunday); exhibitions.

🐦 Outdoor Activities

Swimming (no lifeguard) • Canoeing • Fishing • Walking, horse-riding, or mountain-biking: Route GR 6, Boucle de Limeuil (8 miles/13 km) and Route de Périgueux (3 miles/5 km).

🍃 Further Afield

• Vézère valley (3–25 miles/5–40 km): Le Bugue; Les Eyzies; *Saint-Léon-sur-Vézère (19 miles/31 km), see. p 248; Lascaux; *Saint-Amand-de-Coly (29 miles/ 47 km), see pp. 236–37.

• Cingle de Trémolat, meander; Bergerac (6–26 miles/9.5–42 km).

• Walled towns and medieval villages (6–25 miles/9.5–40 km): Cadouin; *Belvès (12 miles/19 km), see pp. 166–67; *Monpazier (17 miles/27 km), see pp. 215–16; Issigeac.

• Dordogne valley: *Beynac-et-Cazenac (18 miles/29 km), see pp. 168–69; *Castelnaud-la-Chapelle (21 miles/34 km), see p. 182; *La Roque-Gageac (21 miles/ 34 km), see pp. 234–35.

• Sarlat (22 miles/35 km).

Loubressac
Pointed roofs in the Dordogne valley

Lot (46) • Population: 536 • Altitude: 1,115 ft. (340 m)

From its cliff top, Loubressac commands a panoramic view of the valley of the Dordogne. Loubressac was ruined during the Hundred Years War but came back to life when the people of the Auvergne and Limousin moved back in, and it owes its current appearance to their efforts. Today, the flower-decked village lanes meet at a shady village square, where the church of Saint-Jean-Baptiste, dating from the 12th and 15th centuries, stands tall. The limestone medieval houses topped with antique tiles turn golden in the warm rays of the sun. Dominated by its castle perched on a natural promontory, the village offers far-reaching views of the Dordogne and Bave valleys. Numerous walking trails, which start in Loubressac, crisscross the area, linking the surrounding villages. Taking one of these snaking paths leads the visitor past springs or prehistoric dolmens to emerge on the limestone Causse plateau nearby.

By road: Expressway A20, exit 54–Gramat (27 miles/43 km); expressway A89, exit 21–Aurillac (40 miles/64 km).
By train: Gramat station (10 miles/16 km).
By air: Brive-Vallée de la Dordogne airport (34 miles/55 km).

ⓘ Tourist information—Vallée de la Dordogne: +33 (0)5 65 33 22 00
www.vallee-dordogne.com
www.loubressac.fr

👁 Highlights
• La Ferme de Siran: Angora goat farm and movie on how mohair is produced: +33 (0)5 65 38 74 40.
• Village: Guided tour organized by local culture group Le Pays d'Art et d'Histoire de La Vallée de la Dordogne Lotoise: +33 (0)5 65 33 81 36.

⚷ Accommodation
Hotels
Le Relais de Castelnau***: +33 (0)5 65 10 80 90.
Lou Cantou**: +33 (0)5 65 38 20 58.
Gîtes and vacation rentals
Further information:
www.vallee-dordogne.com

Campsites
La Garrigue: +33 (0)5 65 38 34 88.

🍴 Eating Out
Lou Cantou: +33 (0)5 65 38 20 58.
Le Relais du Castelnau: +33 (0)5 65 10 80 90.
Le Vieux Pigeonnier, crêperie in Py hamlet: +33 (0)5 65 38 52 09.

🧺 Local Specialties
Food and Drink
Cabécou goat cheese • Walnut oil • Flour.
Art and Crafts
Handicrafts • Painters • Artist-potters • Mohair clothing.

📅 Events
May: Spring festival, art and crafts, flowers, local produce (1st Sunday).
July: Local saint's day, book festival (2nd Sunday).
August: Marché de Producteurs, farmers' market, and food-lovers' picnic (2nd Thursday); flea market (4th Sunday).

🦋 Outdoor Activities
Walking • Mountain-biking.

🌿 Further Afield
• *Autoire (3 miles/5 km), see p. 159.
• Château de Castelnau (3½ miles/5.5 km).
• Gouffre de Padirac, chasm (3½ miles/5.5 km).
• *Carennac (5½ miles/9 km), see pp. 179–80.
• Château de Montal; Saint-Céré (5½ miles/9 km).
• Rocamadour (12 miles/19 km).
• *Curemonte (14 miles/23 km), see p. 189.
• *Collonges-la-Rouge (19 miles/31 km), see pp. 184–85.
• *Turenne (19 miles/31 km), see pp. 262–63.

Minerve

Vines and stone

Hérault (34) • Population: 122 • Altitude: 745 ft. (227 m)

Commanding a dominant position in the Languedoc landscape, Minerve is a stone ship beached in the *garrigue* scrubland.

Below this wine-producing village, the Brian and Cesse rivers meet and carve out deep gorges. A viscounty in the Middle Ages, Minerve erected a Romanesque church to Saint-Étienne in the 11th century and built a ring of ramparts up against a castle. This system of defense allowed the inhabitants of the village, who had converted to the heretic Cathar religion, to resist Simon de Montfort's crusading army for seven weeks. The Rue des Martyrs and a monument near the church keep alive the memory of 180 Cathars burned at the stake after the town fell on July 22, 1210. The castle was destroyed in the 17th century; only one octagonal tower remains. A path at the bottom of the village leads from the southern postern to the Cesse river, following the course of the river underground for some 900 feet (300 meters) through impressive limestone caves.

By road: Expressway A9, exit 36–Castres (29 miles/47 km); expressway A61, exit 24–Carcassonne Est (24 miles/39 km).
By train: Lézignan-Corbières station (14 miles/23 km); Narbonne station (22 miles/35 km). **By air:** Carcassonne-Salvaza airport (30 miles/48 km); Béziers-Vias airport (40 miles/64 km); Montpellier-Méditerranée airport (75 miles/121 km).

ⓘ **Tourist information—Minervois:**
+33 (0)4 68 91 81 43
www.minervois-tourisme.fr

👁 Highlights
• Musée Archéologique et Paléontologique (Archeology and Paleonthology Museum): "3,000 Years of History" exhibition: +33 (0)4 68 91 22 92.
• Musée Hurepel: History of the Cathars and the Crusades: +33 (0)4 68 91 12 26.

• **Village:** Guided tour for groups only and by appointment only: +33 (0)4 68 91 81 43; videoguides for hire at Musée Archéologique.

🗝 Accommodation
Hotels
Relais Chantovent: +33 (0)4 68 91 14 18.
Guesthouses
La Barbacane: +33 (0)4 68 49 10 21.
L'Étape Minervoise: +33 (0)4 68 75 50 54.
Gîtes
Further information: +33 (0)4 68 91 81 43
www.minervois-tourisme.fr
Campsites
Le Maquis: +33 (0)4 67 23 94 77.

🍴 Eating Out
Le 1210 [mille deux cent dix], pizzeria/salad bar: +33 (0)4 68 75 50 68.
M. and Mme Poumayrac, farmhouse inn: +33 (0)4 67 97 05 92.
Relais Chantovent: +33 (0)4 68 91 14 18.
La Table des Troubadours, steak house: +33 (0)4 68 91 27 61.
La Terrasse: +33 (0)4 68 65 11 58.

🛍 Local Specialties
Food and Drink
Goat cheese • AOC Minèrve wines.
Art and Crafts
Local crafts • Gifts • Bookshop • Paintings and sculptures.

🗓 Events
July: Activities and commemorative concert "1210" (around 22nd).

🦋 Outdoor Activities
Swimming • Walking: Route GR 77 and 2 marked trails.

🌿 Further Afield
• Caunes-Minervois; Lastours; Carcassonne (16–28 miles/26–45 km).
• Montagne Noire (19 miles/31 km).
• Narbonne (20 miles/32 km).
• Oppidum d'Ensérune, archeological site; Béziers (28 miles/45 km).
• *Olargues (29 miles/47 km), see pp. 224–25.

❗ Did you know?
The name Minerve is an adaptation of "Menerba" in the Romance language, Occitan. In turn, this probably derives from the Celtic words *men* (stone or rock) and *herbec* (refuge, sanctuary).

Monestiés

Hispanic influences in France's southwest

Tarn (81) • Population: 1,430 • Altitude: 689 ft. (210 m)

Coiled in a loop of the Cérou river, Monestiés lies in a valley that has been occupied since the Iron Age.

The once-fortified medieval village grew up around the Église Saint-Pierre, a seat of religious and political power from the 10th century. Monestiés has retained its historic maze of streets and lanes lined with old residences. Throughout the village, half-timbered houses, doors with carved lintels, a fountain, and corbeled arcades and houses all reflect the warm colors and simple style typical of villages in southwest France. One of these buildings today houses the Bajèn-Vega museum of painting, dedicated to two artists who were political refugees from Spain. While the Chapelle Saint-Jacques, at the gates to the village, no longer welcomes the pilgrims from Santiago who used to seek refuge in the hospital, it still contains an exceptional 15th-century altarpiece. It is composed of twenty life-size polychrome stone statues, which depict the last three Stations of the Cross: the Crucifixion, the Pièta, and the Entombment.

By road: Expressway A68-N88 (5 miles/8 km); expressway A20, exit 58–Villefranche-de-Rouergue (53 miles/86 km). **By train:** Carmaux station (4½ miles/7 km). **By air:** Rodez-Marcillac airport (48 miles/77 km); Toulouse-Blagnac airport (68 miles/109 km).

ⓘ **Tourist information:**
+33 (0)5 63 76 19 17
www.tourisme-monesties.fr

👁 Highlights
• **Chapelle Saint-Jacques** (16th century): Monumental 15th-century group in polychrome limestone representing the three last Stations of the Cross: +33 (0)5 63 76 19 17.
• **Musée Bajèn-Vega:** Collection of works by Francisco Bajèn and Martine Vega, important members of the 20th-century Tarnaise art movement: +33 (0)5 63 76 19 17.
• **"Discovery Pass":** Single ticket for visits to the Chapelle Saint-Jacques and the Musée Bajèn-Véga. Further information: +33 (0)5 63 76 19 17.

• **Église Saint-Pierre** (10th and 16th centuries): Monumental 17th-century altarpiece and 18th-century painting (*Swooning Virgin Supported by Saint John*).
• **Village:** Guided tour for groups of 15+ by appointment all year round: +33 (0)5 63 76 19 17.

⚒ Accommodation
Guesthouses, gîtes, bunkhouses, and vacation rentals
Further information: +33 (0)5 63 43 46 44 www.tourisme-monesties.fr
Campsites
Camping municipal Les Prunettes*, mid-June–mid-September: +33 (0)5 63 76 19 17.

🍴 Eating Out
Further information: +33 (0)5 63 76 19 17 or +33 (0)5 63 43 46 44.

🛒 Local Specialties
Food and Drink
Green lentils • Vegetable oils • Honey • Herbs and medicinal plants • AOC Gaillac wine.
Art and Crafts
Luthier and bow-maker.

📅 Events
May: Flea market (beginning of the month).
June: Dressmakers' flea market; Fête de l'Âne, donkey festival.
July–August: Art exhibitions, village fêtes; eco-friendly market (every Thursday, 5.30 p.m.).
September: Journées du Patrimoine, heritage festival.
November: Flea market (beginning of the month).
December: Christmas market.

🦋 Outdoor Activities
Horse-riding • Fishing • Tennis • Walking and mountain-biking: Marked trails • "Les Secrets de la Rivière" (botanical river trail) • Watersports: La Roucarié lakeside park.

🌿 Further Afield
• Cagnac-les-Mine: Musée de la Mine, mining museum (5 miles/8 km).
• Carmaux: Musée du Verre, glasswork museum (5 miles/8 km).
• Le Garric: Cap'Déecouverte, outdoor activities center (5 miles/8 km).
• Cordes-sur-Ciel (9½ miles/15.5 km).
• Albi; Gaillac (12–17 miles/19–27 km).
• *Najac (19 miles/31 km), see pp. 220–21.
• *Castelnau-de-Montmiral (22 miles/35 km), see p. 181.
• *Sauveterre-de-Rouergue (23 miles/37 km), see pp. 256–57.
• *Bruniquel (30 miles/48 km), see p. 175.

Monflanquin
A Tuscan air

Lot-et-Garonne (47) • Population: 2,398 • Altitude: 594 ft. (181 m)

French writer Stendhal (1783–1842) called the landscape around Monflanquin in the southwest of France "a little Tuscany."

Founded in 1256 by Alphonse de Poitiers, brother of Louis IX (Saint Louis), Monflanquin is one of about 300 fortified towns or villages that were typically built by the kings of France and England or the counts of Toulouse, who were fighting for control of the southwest of France. At the end of the 14th century, the village became the center of a bailiwick and was enclosed within ramparts punctuated by fortified gates and topped with towers. The ramparts were destroyed in 1622 by royal proclamation after the clashes of the Wars of Religion. Monflanquin has nevertheless retained its characteristic checkerboard street plan. At the heart of the village, the Place des Arcades features a broad colonnade supported by stone pillars; it contains stunning residences, including the House of the Black Prince. From the Cap del Pech there is a spectacular view over the Lède valley.

By road: Expressway A62, exit 7–Périgueux (34 miles/55 km); expressway A89, exit 15–Agen (58 miles/93 km), N21 (8½ miles/13.5 km). **By train:** Monsempron-Libos station (11 miles/18 km); Agen station (30 miles/48 km). **By air:** Bergerac-Roumanière airport (31 miles/50 km); Agen-La Garenne airport (35 miles/56 km).

ⓘ Tourist information:
+33 (0)5 53 36 40 19
www.monflanquin-tourisme.com

213

👁 Highlights

• **Musée des Bastides:** Exhibition about fortified towns, the new towns of the Middle Ages; interactive family guide, escape game, calligraphy studio, and children's games: +33 (0)5 53 36 40 19.
• **Village:** For thrilling tales and amazing sights, take a discovery walk through the lanes of the fortified town with your jester guide Janouille la Fripouille, a medieval troubadour. Tour for individuals in July–August, by day or evening, and special events; throughout the year only for booked groups: +33 (0)5 53 36 40 19.
• **"Pollen," contemporary art hub and artists' residence:** Exhibitions, education, and talks: +33 (0)5 53 36 54 37.

🗡 Accommodation

Hotels
Monform**: +33 (0)5 53 49 85 85.
La Bastide des Oliviers: +33 (0)5 53 36 40 01.

Guesthouses
Le Nid à Nane***: +33 (0)6 82 41 26 95.
La Cambra dé Monflanquin: +33 (0)5 53 71 61 17.
Château Ladausse: +33 (0)5 53 36 71 63.
Les Fleurs des Îles: +33 (0)5 53 40 22 38.
Vignes de la Justice: +33 (0)5 53 36 32 54.

Gîtes
Les Augustins: +33 (0)2 51 61 65 02.
Le Bossu: +33 (0)5 53 36 40 61.
Les Bourdeaux: +33 (0)6 89 78 16 93.
Bruguet: +33 (0)5 53 01 67 10.
Chez Max: +33 (0)6 81 19 14 79.
Les Figuiers: +33 (0)6 74 57 14 53.
Le Mayne de Boulède: +33 (0)6 75 35 38 00.
Moulin de Calviac: +33(0)5 53 70 20 72.
Nicou: +33 (0)6 79 72 08 96.
Les Noisetiers: +33 (0)6 85 40 73 67.
Le Vignal: +33 (0)6 95 08 40 18.

Aparthotels
Résidence du Lac***, Pierre et Vacances: +33 (0)5 53 49 72 00.
Résidence du Lac Mondésir: +33 (0)5 53 49 03 27.

🍽 Eating Out

Aldayaa: +33 (0)9 64 06 15 55.
La Baldoria, pizzeria: +33 (0)5 53 49 09 35.
La Bastide, crêperie: +33 (0)5 53 36 77 05.
La Bastide des Oliviers: +33 (0)5 53 36 40 01.
Le Bistrot du Prince Noir: +33 (0)5 53 36 63 00.
La Grappe de Raisin: +33 (0)5 53 36 31 52.
Le Jardin: +33 (0)5 53 36 54 15.
Le Restaurant du Lac: +33 (0)5 53 49 85 86.
La Terrasse des Arts'cades, brasserie: +33 (0)5 53 36 32 18.

🏛 Local Specialties

Food and Drink
Foie gras • Cheese • Organic produce • Hazelnuts • Prunes • Wine.

Art and Crafts
Flea market and antiques • Contemporary art • Ceramic artist • Cartoonist • Wooden toys • Painters • Soap • Clothes and jewelry • African, Lebanese, and Moroccan crafts • Art galleries.

📷 Events

Markets: Traditional market, Thursday mornings, Place des Arcades.
Little market, Sunday mornings, entrance to the fortified town, July–August.
Throughout the year: exhibitions, concerts, and theater.
February: Photography festival.
April: Spring fair, book fair, and horse-racing.
June: "Nuit de la Saint-Jean," Saint John's Eve ball with traditional music.
July: Antiques fair (mid-July); "Les Soirées Baroques de Monflanquin,"Baroque music (2nd fortnight); village concerts: world music.
July–August: Local farmers' market (Thursday evenings).
August: "Soirée des Étoiles," stargazing (early August); "Les Arts'Franchis," jazz, symphony orchestra, musical theater (early August); medieval fair (mid-August).
December: Saint André's day (1st Monday in December and preceding weekend).

🦋 Outdoor Activities

Boules area • Horse-riding • Fishing: Lac de Coulon (1st and 2nd categories) • Walking and mountain-biking.

🌿 Further Afield

• Montagnac-sur-Lède: mill (5 miles/8 km).
• Castle at Gavaudun (7 miles/11.5 km).
• Fortified towns of Villeréal, Villeneuve-sur-Lot, Castillonnès, and Beaumont-du-Périgord (7½–18 miles/12–29 km).
• Medieval towns of Cancon, Penne-d'Agenais, and Issigeac (7½–18 miles/ 12–29 km).
• Saint-Avit: Musée Bernard-Palissy, museum (7½ miles/12 km).
• Château de Biron (11 miles/18 km).
• *Monpazier (14 miles/23 km), see pp. 215–16.
• Château de Bonaguil (14 miles/23 km).
• *Pujols-le-Haut (16 miles/26 km), see pp. 228–29.
• *Belvès (24 miles/39 km), see pp. 166–67.
• Bergerac (28 miles/45 km).
• Agen (31 miles/50 km).

🗡 Did you know?

The Black Prince was Edward of Woodstock, Prince of Wales (1330–1376), eldest son of the English king Edward III. His dark nickname perhaps has its origins in an act of revenge perpetrated by him during the sack of Limoges in 1370, where one chronicler claimed he killed more than 3,000 citizens, though other sources suggest this was much exaggerated.

Monpazier
An iconic fortified town

Dordogne (24) • Population: 534 • Altitude: 650 ft. (198 m)

Eight hundred years after its foundation, Monpazier retains its original street plan and remains an excellent example of a medieval fortified town. It was founded in 1284 by Edward I, king of England. Given that the Hundred Years War, famine, and epidemics all hit Monpazier hard during the Middle Ages, the town is remarkably well preserved. Amid the three hundred fortified towns of the southwest, Monpazier's singularity and exemplarity as a masterpiece of architecture and urban planning earned it a certain reputation: both 19th-century architect Viollet le Duc and Le Corbusier considered it to be a model for all fortified towns. Crisscrossed by *carreyras* (streets) and *carreyrous* (alleys), the village is laid out around the delightful Place des Cornières. Perfectly square, this is lined with 18th-century buildings and surrounded by 14th- and 18th-century arcades. Among the superb medieval structures are the 13th-century central market, which still has its grain measures; the Église Saint-Dominique (13th and 15th centuries); the square tower; the oldest (1292) and tallest chapter house in Monpazier; Dîmes barn, and also the three fortified gates. Nearby is the historic Récollets convent and the Bastideum, which houses the Centre d'Interprétation de l'Architecture et du Patrimoine (architecture and heritage center).

By road: Expressway A89, exits 16– Angoulême (41 miles/66 km) and 13– Bergerac (43 miles/69 km); N21 (17 miles/ 27 km). **By train:** Belvès station (10 miles/ 16 km); Bergerac station (27 miles/43 km). **By air:** Bergerac-Roumanière airport (29 miles/47 km).

(i) Tourist information:
+33 (0)5 53 22 68 59
www.pays-bergerac-tourisme.com
www.monpazier.fr

👁 Highlights

• **Bastideum:** Centre d'Interprétation de l'Architecture et du Patrimoine. Archive documents, oral testimonies, 3D reconstruction of the fortified town, several ancient games, medieval garden: +33 (0)5 53 57 12 12.
• **Église Saint-Dominique** (13th and 15th centuries): Stalls.
• **Village:** Guided tour in French, Tuesdays at 11 a.m. in July–August for individuals, throughout the year for groups by appointment only. Tours by torchlight, Mondays at 9.30 p.m. in July–August; accessible tours for the visually impaired (tactile models, guidebooks in Braille and large print). Further information: +33 (0)5 53 22 68 59.

🗝 Accommodation

Hotels
♥ Hôtel Edward Ier***: +33 (0)5 53 22 44 00.
Guesthouses
Les Hortensias***: +33 (0)5 53 58 18 04.
Anatôle: +33 (0)6 79 34 47 68.
Chez Janou: +33 (0)6 73 70 09 13.
Les Fleurs: +33 (0)5 53 27 97 12.
Gîtes and vacation rentals
Further information: +33 (0)5 53 22 68 59
www.pays-bergerac-tourisme.com

🍴 Eating Out

Eleonore, gourmet restaurant:
+33 (0)5 53 22 44 00
La Bastide: +33 (0)5 53 22 60 59.

Le Bistrot 2 [deux]: +33 (0)5 53 22 60 64.
Le Bonheur est dans le Pot, crêperie:
+33 (0)6 18 51 29 69.
Le Chêne Vert, pizzeria and light meals:
+33 (0)5 53 74 17 82.
Chez Minou, pizzeria: +33 (0)5 53 22 46 59.
Le Croquant: +33 (0)5 53 22 62 63.
Galerie M: +33 (0)9 61 67 97 14.
Le Privilège du Périgord:
+33 (0)5 53 22 43 98.

🧺 Local Specialties

Food and Drink
Local Périgord specialties (foie gras etc.) • Wine.

Art and Crafts

Jewels • Turned wood • Ceramics • Dress design • Bookbinding • Gilding on wood • Framing • Clock-maker • Leather goods • Marquetry • Painting • Glass painting • Glassblowing • Wall coverings • Soft furnishings • Ladies' fashion.

📅 Events

Markets: Market on Thursday mornings;. Marché aux Cèpes, mushroom market (according to yield), every afternoon in autumn.
Marché aux Truffes, truffle market, December–February.
April: Theater; "Printemps de Minou," concerts (2nd Saturday).
May: "Printemps des Bastides," intercultural events; Fête des Fleurs, flower festival; horse races (end of May).
June: "Rendez-vous aux Jardins," open gardens (1st weekend); flea market (2nd weekend); Journée Nationale de l'Archéologie, archeology festival.
July: Horse-racing (2nd Sunday); cycling after dark (last Thursday); Fête du Livre, book festival (last Sunday).
August: "Eté Musical en Bergerac," music festival (beginning of August); horse-racing (1st Sunday); flea market (2nd weekend); "Adoreed," endurance horse competition (last weekend).
July–August: Open-air cinema; farmers' market.
September: "Pour l'amour de l'art," art and crafts fair.
October: Flea market (2nd weekend).

🦋 Outdoor Activities

Boules area • Sports playing field • Walking.

🌿 Further Afield

• Château de Biron (5 miles/8 km).
• Abbaye de Cadouin (10 miles/16 km).
• *Belvès (10 miles/16 km), see pp. 166–67.
• *Monflanquin (14 miles/23 km), see pp. 213–14.
• Dordogne valley: *Limeuil (17 miles/27 km), see pp. 208–9; * Castelnaud-la-Chapelle (21 miles/34 km), see p. 182; *Beynac-et-Cazenac (24 miles/39 km), see pp. 168–69; *La Roque-Gageac (24 miles/39 km), see pp. 234–35; *Domme (25 miles/40 km), see pp. 190–91.
• Château de Bonaguil (19 miles/31 km).
• Issigeac (19 miles/31 km).
• Monbazillac (27 miles/43 km).
• Bergerac (28 miles/45 km).

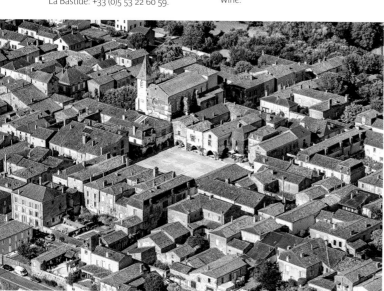

Montréal
Ancient and medieval Gascony

Gers (32) • Population: 1,266 • Altitude: 427 ft. (130 m)

The fortified town of Montréal is surrounded by vineyards and stands proudly at the heart of Gascony in the southwest of France.

In 1255, Alphonse de Poitiers, brother of Louis IX (Saint Louis), built the first Gascon *bastide* (fortified town) on a rocky spur around which twists the Auzoue river. Following the classic grid pattern, roads and cobbled streets lead to the central square, which has arcades on three sides. The 13th-century Gothic church of Saint-Philippe-et-Saint-Jacques is built into the fortifications, and its flat, square tower looks down on half-timbered houses. An ogee gate survives from the fortifications. To the north, the pre-Romanesque church of Saint-Pierre-de-Genens (11th century) has a reused Roman colonnade and a Chi-Rho (symbol for Christ) carved into the antique marble. With its Flamboyant Gothic plan and vaulting, the chapel of Luzanet represents an architectural style that is rare in southwest France. Just over a mile (2 km) from Montréal, the 4th-century Séviac Roman villa is an enormous palace boasting sumptuous mosaics and vast thermal baths. This luxurious wine-growing estate dominated the territory of Elusa (Eauze), capital city of the Roman province of Novempopulania.

By road: Expressway A62, exit 6–Nérac (34 miles/55 km); N124 (29 miles/47 km). **By train:** Auch station (33 miles/53 km); Agen station (34 miles/55 km). **By air:** Agen-La Garenne airport (31 miles/50 km); Toulouse-Blagnac airport (78 miles/126 km).

ⓘ **Tourist information—Ténarèze:**
+33 (0)5 62 29 42 85 or +33 (0)5 62 28 00 80
www.tourisme-condom.com

👁 Highlights
- Collegiate church of Saint-Philippe-et-Saint-Jacques (13th century).
- Église Saint-Pierre-de-Genens (11th century): Carved portal, white marble tympanum.
- Séviac Gallo-Roman villa: Vast multicolored mosaic floor, thermal baths. Further information: +33 (0)5 62 29 48 57 www.elusa.fr.
- Winemaking discovery center: +33 (0)5 62 29 42 85.
- Village: Guided tour of the fortified town on request: +33 (0)5 62 29 42 85.

⚷ Accommodation
Guesthouses
Carpe Diem***: +33 (0)5 62 28 37 32.
Le Couloumé***: +33 (0)5 62 29 47 05.
Lou Prat de la Ressego***:
+33 (0)5 62 29 49 55.
Château de Malliac:
www.vie-de-chateau.com
La Pôse de Mont Royal: +33 (0)6 74 80 07 48.
Aparthotels
Résidence Hotesia***: +33 (0)5 62 68 38 93.
Gîtes, walkers' lodges, and vacation rentals
La Métairie du Clos Saint-Louis:
+33 (0)6 09 99 43 72.
Victorian Lodge Belès: +33 (0)5 62 29 42 35.
Further information: +33 (0)5 62 29 42 85.
www.tourisme-condom.com

Campsites
M. Lussagnet, farm campsite:
+33 (0)5 62 29 44 78.

🍴 Eating Out
Chai Juan: +33 (0)5 62 28 24 06.
L'Escale: +33 (0)5 62 29 59 05.
Mura & Co, tea room:
+33 (0)5 62 29 45 91.
La Petite Escale: +33 (0)5 62 28 82 05.

🧺 Local Specialties
Food and Drink
Preserves (foie gras, duck confit, etc.) • Cheese • Honey • Wine, Floc de Gascogne, and Armagnac.
Art and Crafts
Ceramic artist • Paintings on cardboard • Painters • Statues in reconstituted marble.

🔲 Events
Market: Fridays 8 a.m.–1 p.m.
July: Hamlet of Arquizan's weekend festival (last weekend); "À Brass Ouverts," brass band festival.
July–August: Evening medieval fair; evening walk (every Thursday).
August: "Courses Landaises," bullfighting, and Montréal festival (1st fortnight).
November: "Flamme de l'Armagnac," Armagnac festival (3rd weekend).

🦋 Outdoor Activities
Recreation area • Fishing • Walking: PR and GR routes.

🌿 Further Afield
- Auzoue valley: *Fourcès (3½ miles/5.5 km), see p. 200; Nérac (21 miles/34 km).
- *Larressingle (6 miles/9.5 km), see p. 201.
- Condom (9½ miles/15.5 km).
- *Lavardens (26 miles/42 km), see pp. 206–7.

Mornac-sur-Seudre

A pearl in the marshes

Charente-Maritime (17) • Population: 840 • Altitude: 16 ft. (5 m)

Typical of Charente-Maritime, the house façades in the little port of Mornac, trimmed with hollyhocks, are bleached by the sun.

During Gallo-Roman times, the attractions of the Seudre river turned the budding village of Mornac into a small fishing town on a hill near the present castle. As commerce developed, attractive low houses began to replace modest huts. Today, Mornac-sur-Seudre is a center of oyster farming and salt production, which you can see by visiting the marshes. Brimming with medieval charm, the old town is crisscrossed by alleys leading to the port. The Romanesque church, built in the 11th century over a Merovingian shrine, is topped by a fortified square tower and has a magnificent chevet.

By road: Expressway A10, exit 35–Saintes (24 miles/39 km); N150, exit D14–Saujon/ La Tremblade (5½ miles/9 km).
By train: Royan station (7½ miles/12 km).
By air: La Rochelle-Laleu airport (45 miles/72 km); Bordeaux-Mérignac airport (100 miles/161 km).

ⓘ Tourist information:
+33 (0)5 46 22 92 46
www.tourisme-mornac-sur-seudre.fr

👁 Highlights
• Église Saint-Pierre (11th century): Medieval frescoes, reliquary treasure.
• Seudre marshes: Guided biodiversity walk: +33 (0)5 46 22 92 46.
• Musée Ferroviaire (railroad museum): In Mornac-sur-Seudre's 150-year-old disused railway station: +33 (0)7 51 66 92 36.
• Village: Guided tours: +33 (0)5 46 22 92 46.
• Salt-marsh tour: Meet salt producer Sébastien Rossignol: +33 (0)6 71 09 03 03.

🗝 Accommodation
Guesthouses
Côté Chenal: +33 (0)5 46 02 14 57.
Marjorie: +33 (0)5 46 22 60 87.
Le Mornac: +33 (0)5 46 22 63 20.
Gîtes, vacation rentals, and campsites
M. Cougot: +33 (0)5 46 50 63 63.
Michel Vinay, farm campsite:
+33 (0)5 46 22 72 25.
Further information: +33 (0)5 46 22 92 46
www.tourisme-mornac-sur-seudre.fr

🍴 Eating Out
Le Bar'Ouf: +33 (0)5 46 22 75 24.
Les Basses Amarres: +33 (0)5 46 22 63 31.
Le Café des Arts, crêperie:
+33 (0)5 46 06 40 43.
La Cambuse: +33 (0)9 83 27 62 24.
Les Ecluses Vertes: +33 (0)6 11 77 09 53.
La Gourmandine : +33 (0)5 46 23 38 47.
L'Insolite: +33 (0)5 46 22 76 53.

Le Marais: +33 (0)5 46 23 16 78.
Le Moulin, crêperie: +33 (0)5 46 05 59 36.
Ô Saline: +33 (0)5 46 06 49 53.
Le Parc des Graves: +33 (0)5 46 22 75 14.

🍽 Local Specialties
Food and Drink
Candy • Oysters • Shrimps • Seafood preserves • Salt.
Art and Crafts
Leather crafts • Jewelry • Bag, fashion, and accessories designer • Crafts from natural materials • Salt dough • Painters and sculptors • Potters • Torch glass artist.

📅 Events
Market: Wednesdays and Sundays, 9 a.m.–12.30 p.m.
April: Romanesque fair.
May: Storytelling festival.
July–August: "Jeudis Musicaux et Nocturne des Artisans," evening music and craft fairs (every Thursday); exhibitions at the port; evening tours of the village.
August (depending on tide): "Voiles de Mornac," annual gathering of traditional sailboats.
September: Pottery market.
December: Christmas market.

🦋 Outdoor Activities
Seudre river cruises • Horse-riding • Canoeing • Fishing • Walking: 3 marked trails • Cycling: 1 marked trail • Microlights.

🌿 Further Afield
• Saujon: Le Train des Mouettes, tourist steam train (6 miles/9.5 km).
• Royan (7½ miles/12 km).
• La Palmyre: zoo (9½ miles/15.5 km).
• Saint-Georges-de-Didonne: Parc de l'Estuaire, nature reserve (9½ miles/15.5 km).
• *Talmont-sur-Gironde (18 miles/29 km), see pp. 259–60.
• Marennes; Isle of Oléron (19 miles/31 km).
• *Brouage (20 miles/32 km), see pp. 172–73.

Mortemart

The great and the good in Limousin

Haute-Vienne (87) • Population: 118 • Altitude: 984 ft. (300 m)

A flower-bedecked Limousin town with a glorious past, Mortemart resonates with ten centuries of history. Established on a marshy plain that gave the village its name (*Morte mortuum*; "dead sea"), Mortemart did not remain primitive for long. In 995, as a reward for his victorious defense of the neighboring town of Bellac against Count Guillaume de Poitiers, Abon Drut, lord of Mortemart, was authorized to build the Château des Ducs. This became the birthplace of the Rochechouart-Mortemart family; Madame de Montespan, born into the family in 1640, was a favorite of Louis XIV's. In the 10th-century castle, while the fortifications have disappeared, the keep, courtroom, and guards' room are a reminder of the perils that threatened medieval towns, as are the drawbridge, pond, and dried-up moat. The Carmelite and Augustinian convents, designed to a square grid, were begun in 1330 but were not completed until the 18th century. The Augustinian chapel, which became the parish church, contains 15th-century carved wooden stalls: their misericords, which allowed monks to rest, recall the long church services of times gone by. The historic market and the superb houses of prominent townsfolk evoke a thriving 17th-century commercial town.

By road: Expressway A20, exit 23–Bellac (27 miles/43 km); N145 (9½ miles/15.5 km); N141, exit Bellac (11 miles/18 km). **By train:** Bellac station (8 miles/13 km); Limoges-Bénédictins station (28 miles/45 km). **By air:** Limoges-Bellegarde airport (24 miles/39 km).

ⓘ **Tourist information:**
+33 (0)5 55 68 12 79
www.mortemarttourismelimousin.com

👁 Highlights
• Château des Ducs (10th century): Keep, courtroom, guards' room (July–August).
• Carmelite convent (14th–17th centuries): Monumental staircase; art and craft gallery.
• Church: 15th-century stalls, 17th-century altarpiece.
• Village: Guided visits for groups by appointment only: +33 (0)5 55 68 12 79.

🗝 Accommodation
Guesthouses
Thomas Raymond***:
+33 (0)5 55 60 20 23.
Gisèle Ribette: +33 (0)5 55 68 35 99.

🍴 Eating Out
Le Café du Marché: +33 (0)5 55 68 98 61.

🧺 Local Specialties
Art and Crafts
Poetry publisher • Artists and craftspeople at Carmelite convent.

🎫 Events
Market: Sunday mornings, local produce, at La Halle covered market (July–August).
April: Plant fair (3rd weekend, alternate years); natural wine fair.
June: Concert by the Josquin des Prés vocal ensemble.
July–August: Concerts; painting and sculpture exhibitions; Haut Limousin music and heritage festival; "Peintres dans la Rue," street painting competition.
September: Open-air rummage sale.
November: Local fruit festival (3rd weekend); local trail discovery day, on dog sleds.

🦋 Outdoor Activities
Walking: 3 marked trails • Mountain-biking • Golf Club Villars (9 holes) • Electric bike rental • Horse-drawn carriage rides.

🌿 Further Afield
• Monts de Blond, uplands (1–9½ miles/1.5–15.5 km).
• Bellac; Le Dorat (8–16 miles/13–26 km).
• Oradour-sur-Glane: Centre de la Mémoire, center for remembrance (9½ miles/15.5 km).
• Confolens: folklore festival (19 miles/31 km).
• Saint-Junien, Vienne valley (22 miles/35 km).
• Limoges; Site Corot, porcelain factory (25 miles/40 km).

Najac

Tumbling rooftops in the Aveyron

Aveyron (12) • Population: 754 • Altitude: 1,115 ft. (340 m)

Set on a steep hill, the fortress of Najac dominates the village and wild gorges of this southern French region.

A simple square tower in the 12th century, the Château de Najac became a fortress a century later by order of Louis IX (Saint Louis). Its strategic position made it the linchpin of the valley and earned it a turbulent history. Kings of France and England, counts of Toulouse, Protestants, and locals have all desired this "key to the whole land." From round towers, the view plunges to the valley of the Aveyron and over the village's *lauze* (schist tile) rooftops. The inhabitants converted to the "Cathar heresy" in the 1200s, and were sentenced by the Inquisition to build the Église Saint-Jean at their own expense. Its southern-French style of pointed arch makes it one of the first Gothic churches in the area. The village extends over the rocky crest at the foot of the castle. At its center, the Place du Barry evokes the village's role as a commercial center: its stone or half-timbered houses from the 15th and 16th centuries feature arcades to shelter merchandise.

By road: Expressway A20, exit 59–Rodez (31 miles/50 km); expressway A75, exit 42–Rodez (75 miles/120 km), N88 (33 miles/53 km); expressway A68, exit 9–Gaillac (36 miles/58 km). **By train:** Najac station; Villefranche-de-Rouergue station (14 miles/22 km). **By air:** Rodez-Marcillac airport (50 miles/81 km); Toulouse-Blagnac airport (77 miles/124 km).

ⓘ **Tourist information:**
+33 (0)5 65 29 72 05
www.tourisme-najac.com

👁 Highlights

• **Royal fortress** (12th and 13th centuries): Keep, Saint-Julien's Chapel (frescoes), governor's chamber (panoramic view from the terrace): +33 (0)5 65 29 71 65.
• **Église Saint-Jean** (13th and 14th centuries).
• **Village:** Guided tours Tuesdays 10 a.m., June 15–September 15; for groups off-season by appointment; torchlit tours July–August; "Le Maître des Secrets de Najac," treasure hunt for children (age 6–12): +33 (0)5 65 29 72 05.

🗝 Accommodation

Hotels
Le Belle Rive***: +33 (0)5 65 29 73 90.
L'Oustal del Barry**:
+33 (0)5 65 29 74 32.
Guesthouses
Marie Delerue**, La Prade Haute:
+33 (0)5 65 29 74 30.
J.-P. Verdier**, La Prade Basse:
+33 (0)5 65 29 71 51.
La Bastide: +33 (0)5 65 45 08 07 or
+33 (0)6 81 92 54 93.
El Camino de Najac: +33 (0)5 65 81 29 19.
Sylvie Frazier, La Contie:
+33 (0)5 65 29 70 79.

Gîtes, walkers' lodges, vacation rentals
Further information: +33 (0)5 65 29 72 05
www.tourisme-najac.com
Vacation villages
Les Hauts de Najac, VVF Villages:
+ 33 (0)8 25 39 49 59; site reception:
+33 (0)5 65 29 74 31.
Campsites
Le Païsserou***, information and booking:
+33 (0)5 65 29 73 96.
Camping des Étoiles*:
+33 (0)5 65 29 77 05.
La Prade Basse, farm campsite:
+33 (0)5 65 29 71 51.
RV parks
Further information: +33 (0)5 65 29 71 34.

🍴 Eating Out
La Belle Rive: +33 (0)5 65 29 73 90.
La Cantine Pirate: +33 (0)5 65 81 59 27.
Il Cappello, pizzeria: +33 (0)5 65 29 70 26.
Les Hauts de Najac: +33 (0)5 65 29 74 31.
♥ L'Oustal del Barry: +33 (0)5 65 29 74 32.
La Salamandre: +33 (0)5 65 29 74 09.
Tartines et Compagnie: +33 (0)5 65 29 57 47.

🧺 Local Specialties
Food and Drink
Ostrich and duck (confits, foie gras) •
Fouace de Najac • Cheese • *Gâteau à la
broche* (fire-baked cake) • *Astet najacois*
(roast stuffed pork).
Art and Crafts
Jewelry designer • Cutler • Potter.

2️⃣ Events
Market: Sunday 8 a.m.–1 p.m, June–
September.
April: "Salon du Goût," tasting fair
(1st weekend).
June: "Nuit des Chiens Bleus,"
music festival; medieval festival; hot-air
balloon day (every other year).
July: Open-air cinema.
July–August: Contemporary art
exhibitions, "Ateliers du Patrimoine" and
"L'Été des 6–12 ans"; flea market (Sundays
mid-July–mid-August); evening market
(Wednesdays).
August: "Festival en Bastides," theater
and street performances (1st week),
village fête (3rd weekend); book fair;
"Les Musicales du Rouergue," music
festival.
September: Jazz festival.
October: "Lame à Najac," cutlery fair.

🦋 Outdoor Activities
Canoeing • Orienteering • Climbing •
Horse-riding • Fishing • Via Ferrata •
Mountain-biking (cross-country mountain-
biking area) • Walking: Route GR 36 and
8 marked trails.

🌿 Further Afield
• Abbaye de Beaulieu; Caylus
(9½–12 miles/15.5–19 km).
• Fortified towns of Villefranche-de-
Rouergue and Villeneuve (14–22 miles/
23–35 km).
• Château de Saint-Projet (16 miles/26 km).
• Cordes-sur-Ciel (16 miles/26 km).
• Gorges of the Aveyron; Saint-Antonin-
Noble-Val (17 miles/27 km).
• *Monestiés (19 miles/31 km), see p. 212.
• *Sauveterre-de-Rouergue (27 miles/
43 km), see pp. 256–57.
• Albi (31 miles/50 km).

ℹ️ Did you know?
A local specialty, the *fouace de Najac* was
originally cooked in the ashes of a fire (the
word comes from the Latin *focus*, meaning
hearth). Nowadays the bread is made of
flour, yeast, eggs, milk, sugar, orange-
blossom water, and salt, and is presented
in the shape of a crown.

Navarrenx
The first fortified town in France

Pyrénées-Atlantiques (64) • Population: 1,131 • Altitude: 394 ft. (120 m)

Situated at the place where the Gave d'Oloron river and the Saint James's Way meet, Navarrenx is one of the oldest towns in the old independent state of Béarn.

Navarrenx has its origins in the 1st century CE, but it was in the Middle Ages that the town had its glory days. Built as a *bastide* (walled town) in 1316, Navarrenx enjoyed a number of privileges that helped it to expand. From 1538 onward Henri II d'Albret, king of Navarre, made important alterations to it in an attempt to protect this vital commercial center and crossroads from the Spanish. The designer was Italian architect Fabricio Siciliano; his work is still visible today in the historic stronghold, and his style was copied a century later by Vauban (commissioner for fortifications in the 17th century). The impressive ramparts 33 ft. (10 m) high, from which you can see the Pyrenees, provide a magnificent view over the Gave d'Oloron, as well as over several bastions and military structures. Navarrenx, once an important stopover on the path to Santiago de Compostela, now gives a nod to the village's defensive past by welcoming pilgrims in search of peace to the historic 17th-century arsenal, partly converted into gîtes. The Gave d'Oloron, the longest salmon river in France, has also given Navarrenx its reputation as a "salmon capital," and freshwater fishermen still enjoy its bounties.

By road: Expressway A64, exit Salies-de-Béarn (17 miles/27 km) and exit 9–Mourenx (14 miles/23 km), N117 (13 miles/21 km). **By train:** Orthez station (14 miles/23 km); Pau station (25 miles/40 km). **By air:** Pau-Pyrénées airport (25 miles/40 km); Biarritz-Anglet-Bayonne airport (50 miles/80 km).

ⓘ Tourist information—Béarn des Gaves: +33 (0)5 59 38 32 85
www.tourisme-navarrenx.com

👁 Highlights
• **Centre d'Interprétation, visitor center:** Museum inside the former arsenal, dedicated to the history of Navarrenx, e.g. models, plans: +33 (0)5 59 66 10 22.
• **"La Poudrière":** Permanent exhibition on gunpowder: +33 (0)5 59 38 32 85.
• **La Porte Saint-Antoine:** Musée des Vieux Outils, museum of old tools: +33 (0)5 59 38 32 85.
• **La Maison du Cigare:** Production site of the luxury cigar "Le Navarre," combining French and Cuban expertise; see the different stages of production of premium cigars and a cigar-rolling demonstration. Open throughout the year, Monday–Friday: +33 (0)5 59 66 51 96.
• **Village:** Self-guided tour using leaflet (available from tourist information center); themed tour for individuals led by tour guide from "Pays d'Art et d'Histoire"; guided group tour throughout the year by appointment; guided view of model of the fortified town at tourist information center.

🔑 Accommodation
Hotels
Hôtel du Commerce** : +33 (0)5 59 66 50 16.
Guesthouses
Le Cri de la Girafe: +33 (0)5 59 66 24 22.
Lalanne: +33 (0)6 89 46 80 76.
Monique and Jean-Pierre Lasarroques: +33 (0)5 59 66 27 36 or +33 (0)6 75 59 36 56.
Le Relais du Jacquet: +33 (0)5 59 66 57 25 or +33 (0)6 75 72 89 33.
Gîtes and vacation rentals
Le Relais du Jacquet** : +33 (0)5 59 66 57 25 or +33 (0) 06 75 72 89 33.
Peter French: +33 (0)5 59 66 01 18.
Madeleine Laberthe: +33 (0)5 59 66 51 69.
Bernadette Nargassans: +33 (0)5 59 66 08 39.
Christiane Palas: +33 (0)5 59 66 50 35).
Walkers' lodges
Further information: + 33 (0)5 59 38 32 85
www.tourisme-navarrenx.com

Campsites
Camping Beau Rivage***:
+33 (0)5 59 66 10 00.

🍴 Eating Out
Auberge du Bois:
+33 (0)5 59 66 10 40.
Bar des Sports: +33 (0)5 59 66 50 63.
Le Commerce: +33 (0)5 59 66 50 16.
La Taverne de Saint-Jacques:
+33 (0)5 59 66 25 25.

🛒 Local Specialties
Food and Drink
Salted products • Jam • Artisan beers •
Gave river salmon and trout.
Art and Crafts
Artist and interior designer • Jewelry
designer • Photographer • Potter •
Stylist and designer.

📅 Events
Markets: Wednesday mornings,
Place Darralde; summer market,
Sunday mornings, at the town hall
(June–September).
January: Large agricultural and second-
hand equipment fair; book fair.
Easter weekend: Craft fair.
June: "Feu de la Saint-Jean," Saint John's
(Midsummer's) Eve bonfire.
July–August: "Festival des Pierres Lyriques,"
tapas evening, and "Alto" concerts in Béarn.
August: Patron saint's feast (beginning
of August); medieval fête (end of August).
December: Christmas markets and
activities (first three Sundays).

🦋 Outdoor Activities
Walking: several marked trails • Mountain-
biking: Navarrenx mountain-biking base—
140 miles (225 km) of marked trails •
Salmon and trout fishing (1st category) •
Rafting, mini-rafts, canoeing, stand-up
paddle-boarding • Le Domaine Nitot leisure
complex • Golf: 18-hole course • "Piste
du Brané": national motocross track.

🦋 Further Afield
• Gurs former internment camp (3½ miles/
5.5 km).
• Laàs castle and gardens (6 miles/9.5 km).
• Église de l'Hôpital-Saint-Blaise, UNESCO
World Heritage Site (9½ miles/15.5 km).
• Église Saint-Girons-de-Monein (11 miles/
18 km).
• Sauveterre-de-Béarn, medieval town
(12 miles/19 km).
• Orthez, former medieval capital (14 miles/
23 km).
• Salies-de-Béarn, salt city (19 miles/31 km).

Olargues
The natural charm of the Languedoc

Hérault (34) • Population: 600 • Altitude: 600 ft. (183 m)

Situated in a bend in the Jaur river, Olargues provides walks flavored with history at the heart of the Haut-Languedoc regional nature park. At the foot of Mont Caroux, the "mountain of light," Olargues combines the coolness of Massif Central rivers with the sunshine of the South, and its landscapes of chestnut and cherry trees with vineyards and olive groves. Although this exceptional site has been occupied since prehistoric times, it was in the 12th century that lords in the region built a castle and fortified village here. From the old bridge over the Jaur, *calades* (decorative cobblestones) invite visitors to discover stone houses, now covered with barrel tiles rather than the traditional *lauzes* (schist rooftiles); the remains of the ramparts; the covered stairway of the commandery, and the Église Saint-Laurent, built in the 17th century with stones from the original Romanesque church, whose bell tower was formerly a castle keep.

By road: Expressway A75, exit 57– Clermont-l'Hérault (34 miles/55 km); expressway A9, exit 36–Valras Plage (42 miles/68 km). **By train:** Bédarieux station (14 miles/23 km); Béziers station (40 miles/64 km). **By air:** Béziers-Cap-d'Agdes-en-Languedoc airport (40 miles/ 64 km); Montpellier-Méditerranée airport (73 miles/117 km); Toulouse-Blagnac airport (93 miles/150 km).

ⓘ Tourist information—Caroux:
+33 (0)4 67 23 02 21
www.ot-caroux.fr

👁 Highlights
• **Centre Cebenna:** An ecosystems study and research center. Multimedia library, 3D projection, giant kaleidoscope; exhibitions, activities, and nature tours: +33 (0)4 67 97 88 00.
• **Musée des Arts et Traditions Populaires** (May–September): Museum of village history, old tools, the geology of the region, famous people, models of life in the past, life-size reproduction of a forge, medieval hall: +33 (0)4 67 23 02 21.
• **Forge:** restored tool-making forge. Tours by appointment: +33 (0)4 67 23 02 21
• **Village:** Self-guided visit and guided tours every Monday at 6 p.m. in July and August; by appointment only off-season for 10+ people: +33 (0)4 67 23 02 21.

⚔ Accommodation
Hotels
Laissac-Speiser: +33 (0)4 67 97 70 89.
Guesthouses
Les Quatr' Farceurs**: +33 (0)4 67 97 81 33.
Fleurs d'Olargues: +33 (0)4 67 97 27 04 or +33 (0)6 80 51 96 55.

Gîtes, walkers' lodges, and vacation rentals
Further information: +33 (0)4 67 23 02 21
www.ot-caroux.fr
Campsites
Further information: +33 (0)4 67 23 02 21.

Eating Out
Brasserie L' École: +33 (0)6 30 42 76 13.
Fleurs d'Olargues: +33 (0)4 67 97 27 04.
Le Funambule: +33 (0)4 67 97 72 06.
Laissac-Speiser: +33 (0)4 67 97 70 89.
La Lampisterie, pizzeria:
+33 (0)6 23 87 32 51.

Local Specialties
Food and Drink
Olargues chestnut-based specialties •
Wild plants and fruits.
Art and Crafts
Artists • Luthiers • Artisan potter.

Events
Market: Sunday mornings, Place
de la Mairie.
May: Fête de la Brouette, wheelbarrow
festival (mid-May).
August: "Festibaloche," contemporary
music festival; "Estival de la Bio," organic
produce festival; "Autour du Quatuor,"
classical music festival.
September: Fête Médiévale d'Olargues,
medieval fête (3rd weekend in September).
November: Fête du Marron et du Vin
Nouveau, chestnuts and wine (1st weekend
after All Saints).
December: Christmas market.

Outdoor Activities
Swimming • *Boules* area • Canoeing,
canyoning, caving • Rock climbing •
Walking • Mountain-biking and hybrid
biking • "Passa Païs": Haut Languedoc
greenway for walkers and cyclists from
Mazamet to Bédarieux (47 miles/76 km).

Further Afield
• Le Caroux, massif; Gorges of the Héric
(3½ miles/5.5 km).
• Gorges of the Orb; Vieussan (5 miles/
8 km).
• Monts de l'Espinouse (7½ miles/12 km).
• Saint-Pons-de-Thomières (11 miles/18 km).
• Roquebrun (12 miles/19 km).

Peyre
(commune of Comprégnac)
A vertiginous viaduct

Aveyron (12) • Population: 251 • Altitude: 1,214 ft. (370 m)

Clinging to a sheer cliff where the original church was built, Peyre overlooks the Tarn downstream of Millau.

Beneath the plateau of the Causse Rouge, dotted with *caselles* (drystone shelters) whose *lauze* (schist-tiled) roofs protected shepherds and winegrowers, the lower village, crisscrossed with narrow, cobbled, stepped streets, descends steeply toward the river. The top of Peyre stretches out at the foot of a high tufa cliff, whose corbeled overhang towers above the village. Like the houses that surround it, the Église Saint-Christophe backs onto this cliff face. Fortified in the 17th century to serve as a refuge for residents of the parish, it has retained brattices and murder holes that bear witness to its defensive history. Recently restored as a venue for concerts and exhibitions, the church, which is bathed in changing light diffused by its glass and crystal stained-glass windows, now faces another symbol of modernity: the P2 pier, which, soaring upward from the Tarn, makes the Millau Viaduct the tallest bridge in the world.

By road: Expressway A75, exit 45–Millau (7½ miles/12 km). **By train:** Millau station (5 miles/8 km). **By air:** Rodez-Marcillac airport (62 miles/100 km); Montpellier-Méditerranée airport (84 miles/135 km).

ⓘ Tourist information—Millau:
+33 (0)5 65 60 02 42
www.millau-viaduc-tourisme.fr
www.compregnac12.fr

👁 Highlights
• **Église Saint-Christophe:** Partially dug into the rock face, this church holds contemporary art exhibitions from June to September.
• **Village:** Guided tour from July 1 to National Heritage Days in September, by appointment only: +33 (0)5 65 60 02 42.
• **Colombier du Capelier,** Comprégnac (14th century): Self-guided visit.
• **Maison de la Truffe,** Comprégnac: Presentation of truffle cultivation, and typical architecture from the Causses.

🔑 Accommodation
Guesthouses
M. Espinasse: +33 (0)5 65 58 15 52 or +33 (0)6 84 90 32 07.
Les Terrasses de Pérouges:
+33 (0)6 21 79 61 82.
Gîtes
M. Espinasse: +33 (0)5 65 58 15 52 or +33 (0)6 84 90 32 07.
Campsites
Le Katalpa, Comprégnac:
+33 (0)5 65 62 30 05.

🍴 Eating Out
L'Estival, July and August:
+33 (0)5 65 62 39 37.

🧺 Local Specialties
Food and Drink
Truffles and truffle-based produce.
Art and Crafts
Gifts, tableware • Potter • Atelier Terralhas, Comprégnac.

📅 Events
June: Chœurs de Peyre, choirs and concerts.
July: Fête de la Saint-Christophe, festival (last weekend).
Mid-July–mid-August: Festival de la Vallée et des Gorges du Tarn.
Late July–early August: Fête du Pain au Four Communal, bread festival.

December: Truffle festival at Comprégnac and local produce market (weekend before Christmas).

🦋 Outdoor Activities

Aire de Loisirs des Pyramides, on the banks of the Tarn: children's games, picnic area • Walking: *caselles* (drystone shelters) discovery trails, circular walks of 3 miles (5 km, 1½ hrs) or 4½ miles (7 km, 3 hrs) leaving from Peyre or Comprégnac, and (short) "Randocroquis" drawing trails around the village.

🦋 Further Afield

- Millau (5 miles/8 km)
- Millau Viaduct discovery area (9½ miles/15.5 km).
- Castelnau-Pégayrolles (12 miles/19 km).
- Gorges of the Dourbie (13–24 miles/21–39 km).
- Saint-Léon: Micropolis, insect museum and birthplace of the entomologist Henri Fabre (16 miles/26 km).
- Chaos de Montpellier-le-Vieux (17 miles/27 km).
- Larzac Templars and Hospitallers sites (17–32 miles/27–51 km).
- Gorges of the Jonte (17–30 miles/27–48 km).
- Gorges of the Tarn (17–39 miles/27–63 km).
- *La Couvertoirade (30 miles/48 km), see p. 188.

see p. 188.

🛈 Did you know?

Periodically, following prolonged heavy rain, rumblings that warn of an inflow of underground water wake up some locals, and water pours down the rock overhanging the village. The water forms an impressive cascade, hurtling down the slope toward the Tarn. This phenomenon, which can last for several days, attracts a lot of local attention.

Pujols-le-Haut
A former stronghold in the Albi region

Lot-et-Garonne (47) • Population: 3,844 (Pujols commune) • Altitude: 614 ft. (187 m)

A fiefdom of the heretics, Pujols was destroyed during the Albigensian Crusade then rebuilt; it has preserved its medieval character. The former stronghold of the barony of Pujols has lived through many troubled times in the course of its history, from the Hundred Years War to the French Revolution, yet most of its 13th-century architectural heritage has been preserved. In addition to part of the outer wall and the castle, there remain two fortified gates, one of which serves as the bell tower to the old seigniorial chapel of Saint-Nicolas. The Église Sainte-Foy has retained its 16th-century frescoes. On the square, the covered market, built in 1850 with materials recovered from the Église Saint-Jean-des-Rouets, faces some fine late 13th-century half-timbered houses. The stone walls of the ground floor are topped with black oak beams interspersed with flat bricks.

By road: Expressway A62, exit 6–Aiguillon (25 miles/40 km)/exit 7–Agen (21 miles/ 34 km), N21 (15 miles/24 km). By train: Agen station (18 miles/29 km). By air: Agen-Lagarenne airport (22 miles/ 35 km); Bordeaux-Mérignac airport (93 miles/150 km).

ⓘ Tourist information—Villeneuvois: +33 (0)5 53 36 78 69
www.tourisme-villeneuvois.fr
www.pujols47.fr

👁 Highlights
• Collégiale Saint-Nicolas (16th century): Old castle chapel, collegial church since 1547; fine Flamboyant Gothic architecture.
• Église Sainte-Foy (15th century): 16th-century frescoes.
• Village: Guided tours for individuals by appointment: +33 (0)5 53 36 78 69; guided tours for groups by arrangement, and workshops for young people: +33(0)9 64 41 87 73.

🗝 Accommodation
Hotels
Campanile**: +33 (0)5 53 40 27 47.
Bel Air: +33 (0)5 53 36 89 43.
Guesthouses
Pech des Renards: +33 (0)5 53 36 04 93.
Gîtes and vacation rentals
Les Chênes***: +33 (0)5 53 47 80 87.
Gîte des Copains et du Pigeonnier***: +33 (0)5 53 01 22 93.
Gîte Plaine de Fourtou***: +33 (0)6 08 24 72 42.
Le Gîte Salabert***: +33 (0)5 53 66 11 82.
La Petite Maison**: +33 (0)5 53 70 78 14.
Les Moulinières: +33 (0)5 53 71 11 14.
La Parenthèse: +33 (0)6 81 72 80 94.
Further information: +33 (0)5 53 36 78 69
www.tourisme-villeneuvois.fr

Campsites
Camping Lot & Bastides***:
+33 (0)5 53 36 86 79.

🍽 Eating Out
Aux Délices du Puits, pizzeria:
+33 (0)5 53 71 61 66.
Campanile: +33 (0)5 53 40 27 47.
Le Fournil de Pujols: +33 (0)5 53 70 15 55.
Le Pianothé, crêperie: +33 (0)5 53 71 90 91.
La Toque Blanche: +33 (0)5 53 49 00 30.
Villa Smeralda: +33 (0)5 53 36 72 12.

🛍 Local Specialties
Food and Drink
Walnut, hazelnut, and prune-kernel oils •
Walnuts, chocolate-covered walnuts •
Macarons and shortbread cookies • Prunes.
Art and Crafts
Artists • Potters • Toys • Artists' association.

📅 Events
Market: Sunday mornings, Place Saint-
Nicolas (all year round).
April–October: Painting and sculpture
exhibitions at the Église Sainte-Foy and
at the Salle Culturelle.

May: "Mai de la Photo" photo exhibition.
July and August: Gourmet market
(Wednesday evenings); "Couleurs du
Monde" festival (1st week of August).
August: Book sale (1st Sunday); potters'
market (3rd Sunday).
September: Fête des Associations,
societies' fair (2nd Saturday).
December: Christmas market and activities.

🦌 Outdoor Activities
Hunting • Horse-riding • Fishing • Walking
and mountain-biking: Route GR 652 and
3 marked trails.

🌿 Further Afield
• Villeneuve-sur-Lot (2 miles/3 km).
• Grottes de Lastournelle, caves
(3 miles/5 km).
• Penne-d'Agenais (9½ miles/15.5 km).
• Le Temple-sur-Lot (11 miles/18 km).
• *Monflanquin (14 miles/23 km),
see pp. 213–14.
• Agen (18 miles/29 km).
• Bonaguil: castle (22 miles/35 km).
• *Monpazier (29 miles/47 km),
see pp. 215–16.

Puycelsi
Forest fortress

Tarn (81) • Population: 484 • Altitude: 981 ft. (299 m)

At the edge of the Grésigne forest, Puycelsi watches over the Vère valley.

Occupied since prehistoric times, then besieged by the Celts and later by the Romans, Puycelsi passed, in the late 12th century, into the ownership of the counts of Toulouse, who made it one of their favorite fortified residences. Because of its strategic position and its walls, the village was able to resist many sieges: those of Simon de Montfort from 1211 to 1213 during the Albigensian Crusade; the Shepherds' Crusade in 1320; Duras's English troops in 1386; and the Huguenots during the Wars of Religion. Confined within its medieval walls, of which there remain more than 875 yards (800 meters) of ramparts and the Irissou double gate, Puycelsi offers splendid views over the Grésigne forest, the Vère valley, and the Causses du Quercy from its wall walks. At the heart of the village, the Église Saint-Corneille, with its listed altarpiece, is bordered by a medicinal-herb garden and surrounded by mostly 14th- and 15th-century houses, which combine stone with wood and brick beneath fine hollow-tile roofs. On the horizon, the Grésigne forest can be seen, on the outskirts of which the village's master glassworkers located their workshops, in order to be close to a wood source.

By road: Expressway A20, exit 59–Saint-Antonin-Noble-Val (20 miles/32 km); expressway A68, exit 9–Gaillac (17 miles/27 km). **By train:** Gaillac (15 miles/24 km) station; Caussade (19 miles/31 km) station; Montauban-Ville Bourbon station (27 miles/43 km). **By air:** Toulouse-Blagnac airport (59 miles/95 km).

ⓘ Tourist information—
Bastides and Vignoble du Gaillac:
+33 (0)8 05 40 08 28
www.tourisme-vignoble-bastides.com
www.puycelsi.fr

👁 Highlights

• Église Saint-Corneille (15th and 17th centuries): Statuary, altarpiece, 18th-century bell tower.
• Institut International du Darwinisme: Further information: +33 (0)5 63 33 86 59.
• Heritage walk: Free entry.
• Research and conservation orchard: For old species of fruit trees (cherry, peach, pear, apple) and vines; option of guided tours: +33 (0)5 63 33 19 41.
• Village: Guided tour, booking essential; map of the historic village available from tourist information center.

🔑 Accommodation

Hotels
L'Ancienne Auberge★★★:
+33 (0)5 63 33 65 90.
Guesthouses
La Bâtisse Belhomme:
+33 (0)9 53 17 53 51.
Chez Delphine: +33 (0)5 63 33 13 65.
La Première Vigne: +33 (0)9 75 30 06 13.
Gîtes, vacation rentals, and campsites
Further information: +33 (0)8 05 40 08 28
www.tourisme-vignoble-bastides.com

🍽 Eating Out

Au Cabanon de Puycelsi, local bistro:
+33 (0)5 63 33 11 33.
Le Jardin des Lys, local bistro:
+33 (0)5 63 33 15 69.
Le Puycelsi Roc Café, snack bar:
+33 (0)5 63 33 13 67.

🧺 Local Specialties

Food and Drink
Cookies and crackers • Fruits, fruit purées, juices, and sorbets • Honey • AOC Gaillac wines.
Art and Crafts
Artists and craftsmen (Artistes Créateurs à Puycelsi) • Ceramicist • Painter-sculptor • Potters • Painting and model-making workshop.

📅 Events

July: "Le Festival de Puycelsi Grésigne," choral festival (2nd fortnight).
August: "Fêtes de Puycelsi," village festival (end of August).

🦋 Outdoor Activities

Walking: Route GR 46, heritage walks, Grésigne forest.

🍃 Further Afield

• *Bruniquel (8 miles/13 km), see p. 175.
• *Castelnau-de-Montmiral (8 miles/13 km), see p. 181.
• Gorges of the Aveyron: from Bruniquel to Saint-Antonin-Noble-Val (9½–22 miles/15.5–35 km).
• Gaillac (13 miles/21 km).
• Caussade (16 miles/26 km).
• Montauban (24 miles/39 km).
• *Monestiés (27 miles/43 km), see p. 212.
• Albi (28 miles/45 km).

ℹ Did you know?

In 1386, having been unable to take the fortress, English troops decided to reduce the villagers' resistance by besieging them. With no supplies left, the villagers walked their last squealing pig several times around the ramparts in order to make the enemy believe they still had resources despite the siege. The English eventually left. It is for this reason that a little pig can be seen carved into the stone on the church door.

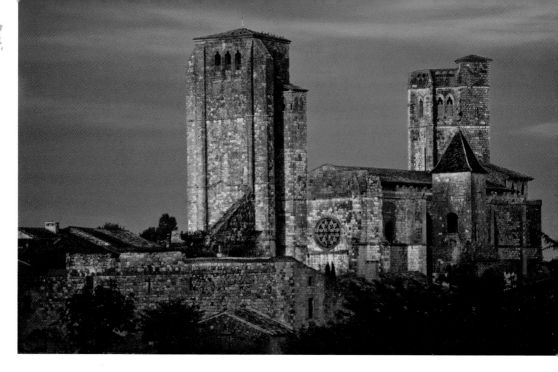

La Romieu

At the crossing of the ways

Gers (32) * Population: 573 * Altitude: 614 ft. (187 m)

Amid the simplicity and charm of the Gascon countryside, La Romieu and its collegiate church are a stopping place at the intersection of paths leading from Puy and Rocamadour to Santiago de Compostela. Taking its name from the Gascon word *roumiou*, meaning "pilgrimage," the village was founded at the end of the 11th century by Albert, a German monk returning from a pilgrimage to Rome. The area gained greater importance in the 15th century when the powerful Cardinal Arnaud d'Aux, cousin of Pope Clement V and a native of the village, established the collegiate church of Saint-Pierre here. This building, which has been on the UNESCO World Heritage list since 1998, survived the agonies of the Wars of Religion and the French Revolution, and today provides visitors with a remarkable example of Southern Gothic architecture. The solemn beauty of its cloisters, its high, octagonal bell tower, and the recently restored frescoes in the sacristy are among the building's riches. At its feet, the village blends in seamlessly. While the ancient *sauveté*—a refuge for pilgrims—retains only some of its fortifications, the arcaded square and the houses with their bright stone façades typical of the region create a unified and graceful ensemble around the religious site. Like everywhere in the Gers, La Romieu is a destination prized for its local specialties—in particular its fruit, vegetables, and poultry—carefully produced by outlying farms.

By road: Expressway A62, exit 7–Agen (17 miles/27 km).
By train: Agen station (21 miles/33 km); Auch station miles (48 km).
By air: Agen-La Garenne airport (17 miles/30 km); Toulouse-Blagnac airport (68 miles/110 km).

(i) Tourist information—Gascogne-Lomagne: +33 (0)5 62 64 00 00
www.gascogne-lomagne.com
www.la-romieu.fr

👁 Highlights
• **Collégiale Saint-Pierre** (14th century): Church, cloisters, octagonal tower, sacristy with polychrome frescoes, bell, Cardinal's Palace (remains). Self-guided and guided tours throughout the year; combined ticket with Les Jardins de Coursiana: +33 (0)5 62 28 86 33.
• **Les Jardins de Coursiana**: 15-acre (6-hectare) vegetable garden, English landscape garden, medicinal plant garden, aromatic and scented garden, arboretum, kitchen garden, and orchard (April–October): +33 (0)5 62 68 22 80 or +33 (0)6 61 95 01 89.

🗝 Accommodation
Guesthouses
Clairière des Sept Hountas: +33 (0)5 62 28 81 37 or +33 (0)6 88 73 95 02.
L'Étape d'Angeline: +33 (0)5 62 28 10 29 or +33 (0)6 69 63 88 99.
Maison d'Artiste: +33 (0)5 62 28 23 22 or +33 (0)6 73 16 63 61.
♥ La Maison d'Aux: +33 (0)5 62 28 14 89 or +33 (0)6 82 76 66 59.
Le Perrouet: +33 (0)5 81 68 13 11.
Gîtes and vacation rentals
L'Étable****: +33 (0)5 62 28 10 93.
Beausoleil**: +33 (0)5 62 68 48 22 or +33 (0)6 71 58 50 21.
Boulevard Quintilla 3: +33 (0)5 62 61 79 00.
Gratuzous: +33 (0)5 62 28 03 17.
Lepine: +33 (0)6 80 17 85 42.
Pellecahus: +33 (0)5 62 28 03 89 or +33 (0)6 76 29 73 73.

Walkers' lodges
Le Couvent de La Romieu: +33 (0)5 62 28 73 59.
Le Refuge du Pèlerin: +33 (0)6 80 05 09 31.
Campsite
Le Camp de Florence****: +33 (0)5 62 28 15 58.

🍴 Eating Out
Le Cardinal: +33 (0)5 62 68 42 75.
L'Étape d'Angéline: +33 (0)5 62 28 10 29.
Restaurant du Camping: +33 (0)5 62 28 15 58.

🧺 Local Specialties
Food and Drink
Honey • Prunes • Apples • Strawberries • Melons • Garlic • Asparagus • Côtes de Gascogne wines.
Art and Crafts
Art galleries and artists' studios.

📅 Events
May: Rose market.
June: "L'Art au mieux" art festival.
July: "Musique en Chemin" music festival.
September: Marché de Potiers, potters' market.

🦋 Outdoor Activities
Walking: Route GR 65 Chemin du Puy and GR 652 Voie de Rocamadour • Mountain-biking (marked trails) • Caving (karst trail).

🌿 Further Afield
• Condom: cathedral (7 miles/11 km).
• Lectoure: cathedral (9 miles/15 km).
• *Larressingle (11 miles/17 km), see p. 201.
• Cassaigne: castle (12 miles/20 km).
• Valence-sur-Baïse: Flaran Cistercian abbey (12 miles/20 km).
• *Fourcès (16 miles/25 km), see p. 198.
• *Montréal (16 miles/26 km), see p. 217.
• Séviac: Gallo-Roman villa (17 miles/28 km).
• Agen: fine art museum (19 miles/31 km).
• *Lavardens: castle (19 miles/31 km), see pp. 206–7.
• Auch: cathedral (31 miles/50 km).

ℹ Did you know?
In the Middle Ages, during a terrible famine, the inhabitants of La Romieu had to eat their own cats in order to survive. But without its cats the village was rapidly invaded by rats, which destroyed the harvests. A young local girl, Angéline, who had hidden her two felines, managed to get rid of these rodents thanks to her cats' numerous descendants. To keep this legend alive, about twenty cat sculptures by Maurice Serreau decorate façades on Place Bouet and Rue Surmain. To this day La Romieu is known as the "village of cats."

La Roque-Gageac
Sheltered by a cliff

Dordogne (24) • Population: 430 • Altitude: 430 ft. (131 m)

Protected from the coldest weather by the cliff behind, La Roque-Gageac's golden buildings catch the sun's rays and are reflected in the Dordogne river.

An important stronghold in the Middle Ages, the village gained its fine mansions, including that of humanist Jean Tarde (1561–1636), during the Renaissance. In the 19th century, it saw heavy traffic of *gabares* (flat-bottomed boats) on the Dordogne river that transported wines from Domme to Bordeaux. Sheltered by the south-facing cliffs, and overlooked by the 16th-century church, Mediterranean and tropical plants flourish along the village's streets and in its gardens. The yellow-stone façades and pitched roofs covered with brown tiles contrast with their green setting. The beauty and character of the houses of La Roque-Gageac can also be admired from a boat on the Dordogne.

By road: Expressway A20, exit 55–Sarlat (22 miles/35 km). **By train:** Sarlat-la-Canéda station (8 miles/13 km). **By air:** Brive-Vallée de la Dordogne airport (32 miles/51 km); Bergerac-Roumanière airport (42 miles/68 km).

ⓘ Tourist information—
Sarlat-Périgord Noir:
+33 (0)5 53 31 45 45
www.sarlat-tourisme.com

◉ Highlights
• **Jardin Exotique:** Mediterranean and tropical plants. Free self-guided visit: +33 (0)5 53 29 40 29.
• **Bambouseraie:** Self-guided tour to discover different varieties of bamboo. Open 10 a.m.–7 p.m.: +33 (0)7 81 69 00 56.
• **Jardin de la Ferme Fleurie:** Terraced gardens (romantic garden, grandmother's garden, wild garden, medicinal-herb garden): +33 (0)5 53 28 33 39.
• **Village:** Guided tour June–September. Further information: +33 (0)5 53 31 45 45.

✎ Accommodation
Hotels
La Belle Étoile***: +33 (0)5 53 29 51 44.
Auberge des Platanes**: +33 (0)5 53 29 51 58.
Le Périgord**: +33 (0)5 53 28 36 55.
Guesthouses
La Ferme Fleurie**: +33 (0)5 53 28 33 39.
Mme Alla: +33 (0)5 53 28 33 01.
Le Clos Gaillardou: +33 (0)5 53 59 53 97.
Les Hauts de Gageac: +33 (0)5 47 27 51 30.
La Maison d'Anne Fouquet: +33 (0)6 37 76 83 81.
M. and Mme Menu: +33 (0)5 53 59 65 63.
Le Pigeonnier de Labrot: +33 (0)5 53 28 37 00.
Gîtes, walkers' lodges, and vacation rentals
Further information: +33 (0)5 53 31 45 45
www.sarlat-tourisme.com

Campsites
Beau Rivage***: +33 (0)5 53 28 32 05.
La Butte**: +33 (0)5 53 28 30 28.
Verte Rive*: +33 (0)5 53 28 30 04.

🍴 Eating Out
L'Ancre d'Or: +33 (0)5 53 31 27 66.
Auberge des Platanes: +33 (0)5 53 29 51 58.
La Belle Étoile: +33 (0)5 53 29 51 44.
"Chez Tom," pizzeria: +33 (0)5 53 29 71 97.
Le Colombier, farmhouse inn: +33 (0)5 53 28 33 97.
La Ferme Fleurie, Périgord Noir country inn: +33 (0)5 53 28 33 39.
Ô Plaisir des Sens: +33 (0)5 53 29 58 53.
Le Palmier: +33 (0)5 53 29 42 61.
Le Patio: +33 (0)5 53 30 22 13.
Le Périgord: +33 (0)5 53 28 36 55.
Les Prés Gaillardou: +33 (0)5 53 59 67 89.

🧺 Local Specialties
Food and Drink
Foie gras • Périgord specialties.

234

Art and Crafts
Enameler • Metalworker • Painter-decorator.

② Events
Market: Friday mornings (May–September).
August: Village festival; gourmet food market.

🦋 Outdoor Activities
Swimming (no lifeguard) in the Dordogne • *Gabare* (traditional flat-bottomed boat) • Canoeing • Fishing • *Boules* area • Périgord hot-air balloons • Walking • Mountain-biking • Cycling.

🌿 Further Afield
• Dordogne valley: *Castelnaud-la-Chapelle (2 miles/3 km), see p. 182; *Beynac-et-Cazenac (3 miles/5 km), see pp. 168–69; *Domme (3½ miles/5.5 km), see pp. 190–91; *Belvès (14 miles/23 km), see pp. 166–67; *Limeuil (21 miles/34 km), see pp. 208–09.
• Marqueyssac: park and gardens (2½ miles/4 km).
• Sarlat (8 miles/13 km).
• Vézère valley: Les Eyzies (16 miles/26 km), *Saint-Amand-de-Coly (21 miles/34 km), see pp. 238–39; *Saint-Léon-sur-Vézère (22 miles/35 km), see p. 248.
• *Monpazier (24 miles/39 km), see pp. 215–16.

ℹ Did you know?
The village, which faces south, enjoys an amazing microclimate and, thanks to a resident of the village, Mr. Dorin, who founded it, a Mediterranean and tropical plant garden has grown up along the narrow streets. Palms, banana trees, date palms, albizias, yuccas, bamboos, and oleanders flourish beneath the Périgord sun.

Saint-Amand-de-Coly

An abbey in Périgord

Dordogne (24) • Population: 405 • Altitude: 568 ft. (173 m)

Nestled at the intersection of three wooded valleys, the abbey at Saint-Amand-de-Coly watches over houses that are typical of the Périgord Noir region. The village owes both its name and its religious heritage to the monk Amand, who came to evangelize the Coly valley in the 6th century. The abbey was founded in the 12th century and ensured Saint-Amand's prosperity for two centuries. Before the Hundred Years War and the development of defense systems, the abbey church was considered the most beautiful fortified church in Périgord. The splendid 100-ft. (30-m) tall bell-tower porch, its huge Gothic arch, and its triple-arched door have a simple strength about them that is sustained inside the building. Indeed, the nave is a fine expression of the subtle balance between the sobriety of Romanesque architecture and the soaring verticality of the Gothic period. Around the church, which continues to make the village famous and which is the venue for excellent classical concerts throughout the year, are houses built in a typically Périgord style. In a harmonious contrast of ocher and gray tones, Sarlat stones and *lauze* (schist tile) roofs dress both grand and humble elements of the village's heritage: the abbey, houses, dovecotes, and old tobacco-drying barns.

By road: Expressway A89, exit 17 (10 miles/16 km). **By train:** Condat-le-Lardin station (6 miles/9.5 km); Sarlat-la-Canéda station (15 miles/24 km); Brive-la-Gaillarde station (22 miles/35 km). **By air:** Brive-Vallée de la Dordogne airport (34 miles/55 km).

ⓘ **Tourist information—Lascaux-Dordogne Vallée Vézère:**
+33 (0)5 53 51 04 56
www.lascaux-dordogne.com
www.saint-amand-de-coly.org
Maison du Patrimoine (July and August):
+33 (0)9 64 01 46 39

👁 Highlights
• **Guided tour of the abbey-church** (12th century): In July and August: +33 (0)9 64 01 46 39; off-season by appointment only: +33 (0)5 53 51 47 85.
• **Maison du Patrimoine:** +33 (0)9 64 01 46 39.
• **La Ferme du Peuch:** Walnut groves, harvesting, drying, and cracking of walnuts; tour of the oil press: +33 (0)5 53 51 27 87.
• **Signposted walk:** Historical trail and recreational nature trail.

🗝 Accommodation
Hotels
Hôtel de l'Abbaye**: +33 (0)5 53 51 68 50.
Guesthouses
M. and Mme Delbos: +33 (0)5 53 51 60 48 or +33 (0)6 84 57 11 08.
La Ferme du Peuch, rooms and evening meal: +33 (0)5 53 51 27 87.
M. Lajoinie: +33 (0)5 53 51 68 76.
Gîtes
Further information: +33 (0)9 64 01 46 39 or +33 (0)5 53 51 47 85
www.lascaux-dordogne.com

Campsites
Lascaux Vacances**: +33 (0)5 53 50 81 57.
Hamelin Périgord Vacances: +33 (0)5 53 51 60 64.

🍴 Eating Out
Restaurant de l'Abbaye: +33 (0)5 53 51 68 50.

🧺 Local Specialties
Food and Drink
Walnut, walnut oil, Périgord *choconoiseries* (chocolate-covered walnuts), walnut preserves.
Art and Crafts
Copperwork.

🗓 Events
July: "Saint-Amand Fait Son Intéressant," concerts and shows in the street (around the 14th); "Les Fabulesques," theatre festival (end of July).
July and August: Périgord Noir classical music festival (late July–early August); local farmers' market (Tuesday, 6 p.m.–10 p.m.).
August: Village festival (Saint-Hubert Mass, drawing competition) (15th).
October: Marché aux Saveurs de l'Automne, fall produce market (last weekend).
All year round: Concerts, lectures.

🦋 Outdoor Activities
Walking, horse-riding, and mountain-biking (70 marked trails): Périgord Noir mountain-biking center.

🌿 Further Afield
• Montignac (5½ miles/9 km).
• Prehistoric sites at Lascaux (7½ miles/ 12 km) and Eyzies (19 miles/31 km).
• *Saint-Léon-sur-Vézère (12 miles/19 km), see p. 248.
• Sarlat (14 miles/23 km).
• Dordogne valley: *La Roque-Gageac (20 miles/32 km), see pp. 234–36; *Beynac-et-Cazenac (21 miles/34 km), see pp. 168–69; *Castelnaud-la-Chapelle (21 miles/34 km), see p. 182; *Domme (22 miles/35 km), see pp. 190–91; *Limeuil (29 miles/47 km), see pp. 208–9.

ⓘ Did you know?
Here's how people greet one another in Saint-Amand-de-Coly: "Adieu soit, brave monde (homme), si vous l'êtes, et à se revoir," or, in Occitan, "Adiussatz brave monde, si sou setz, e a nous tourna veire." ("Farewell good men/man, if such you be, and until we meet again.")

Saint-Bertrand-de-Comminges

Ancient guardian of the Pyrenees

Haute-Garonne (31) * Population: 259 * Altitude: 1,700 ft. (518 m)

Saint-Bertrand-de-Comminges owes its name to the bishop who built its cathedral. Located at the foot of the Pyrenees, the village still contains the ruins of a Roman forum, established in 72 BCE by Pompey on his return from Spain. Considered to be King Herod's place of exile, the town grew up around a basilica in the 4th century before it was destroyed by the Vandals and then the Burgundians. Bertrand, bishop of Comminges, rebuilt the village from its ruins and installed an episcopal court here. Military in appearance, the Cathédrale Sainte-Marie, which was remodeled in the 14th century by the future pope Clement V, retains its 12th-century bell tower, its cloisters giving onto the Pyrenees, and its portal representing the Adoration of the Magi, the Virgin and Child, and Saint Bertrand. A rood screen stands in front of the choir and its sixty-six carved oak stalls and 16th-century episcopal throne. Fine dwellings from the 16th–18th centuries huddle around the cathedral. Forming a girdle around the old town, the ramparts are punctuated by the Majou, Cabirole, and l'Hyrisson gateways.

By road: Expressway A64, exit 17–Luchon (4 miles/6 km).
By train: Montréjeau station (4½ miles/7 km).
By air: Tarbes, Ossun, Lourdes airport (45 miles/72 km); Toulouse-Blagnac airport (72 miles/116 km).

ⓘ Tourist information:
Saint-Gaudinois: +33 (0)5 61 94 77 61
www.tourisme-stgaudens.com

👁 Highlights
• **Cathédrale Sainte-Marie** (11th–14th centuries): Tympanum showing the Adoration of the Magi, the Virgin and Child, and Saint Bertrand; ensemble of 66 stalls carved from wood; 16th-century corner organ. Self-guided or guided tours, audioguides: +33 (0)5 61 89 04 91.
• **Early Christian basilica:** Remains of a basilica (date unknown, but 4th-century coins were found inside date) whose foundations incorporate 28 sarcophagi in marble from the Pyrenees.
• **Chapelle Saint-Julien:** 19th-century reconstruction of an ancient chapel.
• **Les Olivetains Cultural and Tourist Center:** Archaeological museum, bookstore, contemporary art exhibitions: +33 (0)5 61 95 44 44.
• **Musée du Blason et des Ordres de Chevalerie** (heraldry museum): Renaissance mansion housing a collection of over 2,000 coats of arms, coins, illuminated manuscripts, and medieval weapons; retells legends concerning the orders of chivalry: +33 (0)6 22 35 30 10.
• **Village:** Guided tour for groups, only by prior arrangement: +33 (0)5 61 95 44 44.

🔑 Accommodation
Hotels
L'Oppidum**: +33 (0)5 61 88 33 50.
Les Comminges*: +33 (0)5 61 88 31 43.
Guesthouses
La Randonnée de Saint-Jacques:
+33 (0)6 76 15 32 13.
Gites, walkers' lodges, and vacation rentals
Further information: +33 (0)5 61 95 44 44.
Campsite
Es Pibous**: +33 (0)5 61 94 98 20.

🍴 Eating Out
Restaurants
Le Bistrot Gourmand – Chez Martine:
+33 (0)6 27 29 08 63.
Chez Simone: +33 (0)5 61 94 91 05.
La Vieille Auberge: +33 (0)5 61 88 36 60.

🧺 Local Specialties

Food and Drink
Cassoulet • Foie gras • *Porc noir de Bigorre* (rare-breed pork) • Croustade (flaky fruit pastry) • Tome des Pyrénées cheese

Art and Crafts
Jewelry, fossils, and minerals • Leatherwork, saddlery • Umbrella-maker • Blacksmith • Clogs.

📅 Events
July: Local fête.
July and August: Gourmet food markets; "Nocturnes de Saint-Bertrand," themed strolls, cathedral meditation (each Thursday except 1st week July).
July–September: "Festival du Comminge," classical music festival.

🦋 Outdoor Activities
Walks: GR 656 and 2 trails.

🌿 Further Afield
• Valcabrère: basilica (1 mile/2 km).
• Barbazan (3 miles/5 km).
• La Barousse valley (4½ miles/7 km).
• Gargas: caves (5 miles/8 km).
• Montréjeau and Saint-Gaudens (5½–11 miles/9–17 km).
• Bagnères-de-Luchon (20 miles/32 km).

Saint-Cirq-Lapopie
A panoramic viewpoint

Lot (46) • Population: 223 • Altitude: 722 ft. (220 m)

Perched on an escarpment whose ridge is silhouetted against a background of high cliffs, Saint-Cirq-Lapopie overlooks a bend in the Lot river.

Controlling the Lot valley, which for a long time saw a flourishing trade in the transportation of goods by barge, the site of Saint-Cirq has been occupied since Gallo-Roman times. In the Middle Ages it became a powerful fortified complex that included the castles of the four dynasties that shared power here (Cardaillac, Castelnau, Gourdon, and Lapopie). Owing to its coveted strategic position, Saint-Cirq was constantly besieged. Although Richard the Lionheart failed to capture the fortress in the 12th century, it passed alternately under English and French rule during the Hundred Years War. In the late 16th century, the Huguenots twice seized it, before Henri IV—following the example set by Louis XI and Charles VIII—totally demolished it. Its castles thus vanished, and only the Rocamadour Gate still stands, but Saint-Cirq remains a place of rare harmony between the village, its architecture, and its landscapes. Of the numerous artists and writers who succumbed to the magic of this place in the 19th century, it is probably André Breton who paid it its finest tribute. Discovering the village one evening in 1950, like "an impossible rose in the night," he made the old Auberge des Mariniers his summer residence and ceased "wishing to be elsewhere."

By road: Expressway A20, exit 57 (from Paris) or 58 (from Toulouse)–Cahors Centre (19 miles/31 km).
By train: Cahors station (16 miles/26 km).
By air: Rodez-Marcillac airport (52 miles/84 km); Brive-Vallée de la Dordogne airport (62 miles/100 km); Toulouse-Blagnac airport (84 miles/135 km).

ⓘ Tourist information—Saint-Cirq-Lapopie: +33 (0)5 65 31 31 31
www.saint-cirqlapopie.com

👁 Highlights

• **Musée Départemental Rignault:**
Permanent collections of furniture and
works of art assembled by the collector
Émile Joseph-Rignault; temporary
exhibitions; gardens with an exceptional
view of the Lot: +33 (0)5 65 31 23 22.
• **Village:** Guided tours all year round:
+33 (0)5 65 31 31 31; by appointment
for groups: +33 (0)5 65 24 13 95.

🗝 Accommodation

Hotels
Auberge du Sombral**:
+33 (0)5 65 31 26 08.
Hôtel du Causse: +33 (0)5 65 21 76 61.
Guesthouses
À la Source: +33 (0)5 65 23 56 98.
M. Balmes, farmhouse guest rooms:
+33 (0)5 65 31 26 02.
Chambres de Cantagrel:
+33 (0)5 65 23 81 45.
Gîtes, vacation rentals, and walkers' lodges
Further information:
+33 (0)5 65 31 31 31
www.saint-cirqlapopie.com
Campsites
La Plage****: +33 (0)5 65 30 29 51.
La Truffière***: +33 (0)5 65 30 20 22.

🍴 Eating Out

Auberge du Sombral: +33 (0)5 65 31 26 08.
Brasserie Lou Faouré:
+33 (0)5 65 30 20 36.
Le Cantou: +33 (0)5 65 35 59 03.
Le Gourmet Quercynois:
+33 (0)5 65 31 21 20.
Hôtel du Causse: +33 (0)5 65 21 76 61.
Le Lapopie: +33 (0)5 65 30 27 44.
Lou Bolat: +33 (0)5 65 30 29 04.
L'Oustal: +33 (0)5 65 31 20 17.
La Plage, pizzeria: +33 (0)5 65 30 29 51.
La Table du Producteur:
+33 (0)5 65 22 18 37.
La Tonnelle, brasserie:
+33 (0)5 65 31 21 20.

🧺 Local Specialties

Food and Drink
Duck foie gras • Walnuts • Truffles •
Saffron • Cahors wine.
Art and Crafts
Leather crafts • Jewelry • Hats • Ceramics •
Gifts, tableware • Wooden toys • Paintings •
Engraving • Sculpture • Wood turning •
Clothing.

📅 Events

Market: Farmers' market, Wednesdays
4–8 p.m., Place du Sombral
(July and August).
June–September: Cinema; dance;
theater; concerts.
July: Village festival (3rd weekend).
All year round: Exhibitions, workshops,
concerts, cultural events at the
Maison de la Fourdonne,
www.maisondelafourdonne.com.

🦋 Outdoor Activities

Canoeing • Walking: Route GR 36 and
1 marked trail.

🌿 Further Afield

• Château de Cénevières (5½ miles/9 km).
• Célé valley: Cabrerets, Pech Merle caves,
Marcilhac (6–16 miles/9.5–26 km).
• Causse de Limogne, Villefranche-de-
Rouergue (9½–24 miles/15.5–39 km).
• Cajarc; Figeac (12–28 miles/19–45 km).
• Cahors (16 miles/26 km).

Saint-Côme-d'Olt

A pilgrims' stopping place on the Lot river

Aveyron (12) • Population: 1,364 • Altitude: 1,234 ft. (376 m)

Located on the Saint James's Way in the fertile Lot valley, Saint-Côme-d'Olt is distinguished by its twisted spire and its delightful houses.

Bordered on the south side by the green hills that overlook the basaltic mass of Roquelaure, and to the north by terraces of old vineyards, the village has built up over time inside the circular ditches of the old medieval town, of which three fortified gates remain. The 16th-century church, whose twisted spire dominates the village, is of Flamboyant Gothic style. Its heavy carved-oak doors are reinforced with 365 wrought-iron nails. The 11th-century Chapelle des Pénitents, with its *ajouré* (pierced) bell tower, is topped with a hull roof. The Château des Sires de Calmont, built in the 12th century and rebuilt in the 15th, presents a Renaissance façade and has two 14th-century towers. The narrow streets retain old medieval shops and houses from the 10th and 16th centuries, such as the Consul of Rodelle's house, which has mullioned windows and is embellished with sculptures. The Ouradou, a building with an octagonal roof, was erected in memory of the victims of the 1586 plague.

By road: Expressway A75, exit 28–Espalion (54 miles/87 km) or exit 42–Rodez (27 miles/43 km), N88 (12 miles/19 km). **By train:** Rodez station (21 miles/34 km). **By air:** Rodez-Marcillac airport (27 miles/43 km).

ⓘ Tourist information—Espalion: +33 (0)5 65 44 10 63 or +33 (0)5 65 48 24 46 www.tourisme-espalion.fr

👁 Highlights

• Chapelle des Pénitents (11th century): Exhibition on Romanesque architecture and the White Penitents.
• Église Saint-Côme-et-Saint-Damien (16th century): Twisted spire, 16th-century wooden Christ, 18th-century altarpiece, listed 16th-century oak doors.
• Village: Guided tours all year round by arrangement; themed visits, discovery tour June–August: +33 (0)5 65 48 24 46.

🗝 Accommodation

Hôtel
Espace Rencontre Angèle Mérici 2**: +33 (0)5 65 51 03 20.
Guesthouses
M. Burguière*: +33 (0)5 65 44 10 61.
Les Jardins d'Éliane: +33 (0)5 65 48 28 06.
Le Plateau: +33 (0)5 65 48 07 04.
Walkers' lodges
Gîte de Combes***: +33 (0)5 65 48 21 58.
Gîte Compagnon de Route: +33 (0)5 65 48 18 16.
Gîte Del Roumiou: +33 (0)5 65 48 28 06.
Gîte La Halte d'Olt: +33 (0)5 65 44 12 58.
Campsites
Camping Bellerive**: +33 (0)5 65 44 05 85.

🍴 Eating Out

Brasserie du Théron: +33 (0)5 65 48 01 10.
La Fontaine: +33 (0)5 65 44 05 82.
Le Passage: +33 (0)5 65 44 39 68.

🧺 Local Specialties

Art and Crafts
Jewelry • Potter.

🎟 Events

Market: Sunday mornings.
May: "La Transhumance Aubrac," moving cattle to new pastures (Sunday nearest 25th).
July: Evening market (Wednesday following 15th August).
August: Folk festival (2nd Saturday); evening market (Wednesday nearest 15th); local saint's day festivities (4th Sunday).

🦋 Outdoor Activities

Boules area • Bowling • Canoeing • Fishing • Walking: Route GR 65, Chemin de Compostelle (Saint James's Way) and 10 marked trails • Mountain-biking.

🌿 Further Afield

• Flaujac, fortified hamlet (1 mile/1.5 km).
• Roquelaure: castle, lava flow (2–3 miles/3–5 km).
• Espalion: Musée du Scaphandre, Calmont d'Olt medieval castle, 11th-century Romanesque chapel of Perse and Pont-Vieux, Chapelle des Pénitents (2½ miles/4 km).
• Abbaye de Bonneval, Laguiole, and L'Aubrac (6–19 miles/9.5–31 km).
• *Estaing (8 miles/13 km), see pp. 192–93.
• Trou de Bozouls, horseshoe gorge (9½ miles/15.5 km).
• *Sainte-Eulalie-d'Olt (12 miles/19 km), see p. 243.

Sainte-Eulalie-d'Olt

Creativity and artistry in the Lot valley

Aveyron (12) • Population: 377 • Altitude: 1,345 ft. (410 m)

Deep in the Lot valley, numerous artists and craftspeople are breathing life into the old stones of Sainte-Eulalie-d'Olt.

This typically medieval village is laid out in a series of alleyways and small squares around the Place de l'Église. Wealthy residences from the 15th and 16th centuries are reminders of the village's prosperous past, and houses built in Lot shingle up to the 18th century are architectural jewels. The large wheel of the restored flour mill rumbles away once again. The church, cited in records in 909, has a Romanesque choir surrounded by impressive cylindrical columns, while the nave and the chapel are Gothic in style. Three apsidal chapels open off the ambulatory, and a reliquary chest contains two thorns supposedly from Christ's crown. Also worth seeing in the village are the Château des Curières de Castelnau, dating from the 15th century, and a corbeled Renaissance residence, whose façade is punctuated with fourteen windows. This rich heritage, and the views that Sainte-Eulalie-d'Olt commands over the Lot valley, have encouraged numerous artists to make this village their home and inspiration.

By road: Expressway A75, exit 41–Campagnac (16 miles/26 km). **By train:** Campagnac-Saint-Geniez station (12 miles/19 km). **By air:** Rodez-Marcillac airport (33 miles/53 km).

ⓘ Tourist information:
+33 (0)5 65 47 82 68
www.sainteeulaliedolt.fr

👁 Highlights
• Romanesque and Gothic church (11th, 12th, and 16th centuries): Relics.
• "Eulalie d'Art" and various artists' studios: Art and craft studios, demonstrations, exhibitions, workshops: +33 (0)5 65 47 82 68.
• Musée-Galerie Marcel Boudou: Temporary exhibitions, July–August: +33 (0)5 65 47 82 68.
• Village: Self-guided visit (information boards and map available at tourist information center); guided tour for individuals, Mondays and Fridays 5 p.m., July–August; for groups by appointment all year round, except January 1 and May 1: +33 (0)5 65 47 82 68.

🪛 Accommodation
Hotels
Au Moulin d'Alexandre**: +33 (0)5 65 47 45 85.
Guesthouses
Chambres d'Olt: +33 (0)6 70 46 57 93.
La Draye: +33 (0)5 65 70 46 45.
Gîtes and vacation rentals
Further information: +33 (0)5 65 47 82 68.
Aparthotels
La Cascade***: +33 (0)6 88 84 52 65.
Campsites and RV parks
La Grave**, municipal campsite, May 15–September 15: +33 (0)5 65 47 44 59.
Brise du Lac, rural campsite: +33 (0)5 65 47 55 55.
RV park (open all year): +33 (0)5 65 47 44 59.

🍴 Eating Out
Au Moulin d'Alexandre: +33 (0)5 65 47 45 85.
Café de la Place, brasserie and ice-cream parlor: +33 (0)5 65 70 45 60.
Caravan Kitchen, light meals using local ingredients (in summer): +33 (0)6 78 74 12 89.

🧺 Local Specialties
Food and Drink
Traveling home distiller (November 1–end April) • Wood-baked *pain au levain* bread • Organic chicken • Fruit farm.
Art and Crafts
Potter • Enamel engraver • Glassblower • Wooden caravan builder • Jewelry designer • Artist • Sculptor • Dressmaker • Leaf-painter.

🔢 Events
Market: Monday mornings, Place de l'Église (July–August).
May: "Marché des Senteurs et Saveurs," local produce market (1st Sunday); fishing competition (Thursday of Ascension).
June: "Feu de la Saint-Jean," Saint John's (Midsummer's) Eve bonfire with fireworks.
July: Historic procession of the Holy Thorn (2nd Sunday) and local saint's day; Vallée d'Olt classical music festival; book fair; concerts.
July–September: "Les Rencontres Photographiques," photography festival.
August: Fishing competition; writers' events; concerts.

September: "Trophée Cabanac," European carp fishing competition (end of September).
November 1: "Poule Un," charity auction to redeem souls in Purgatory.

🐟 Outdoor Activities
Canoeing • Stand-up paddle-boarding • Motorboats • Fishing • Walking and mountain-biking • Electric bikes • Swimming • Solar-powered boat.

🌿 Further Afield
• Hamlets of Cabanac, Lous, Malescombes (2–4½ miles/3–7 km).
• Saint-Geniez-d'Olt (2 miles/3 km).
• Parc Naturel Régional des Grands Causses, nature park (3½ miles/5.5 km).
• Pierrefiche; Galinières: keep (3½–6 miles/5.5–9.5 km).
• L'Aubrac (6 miles/9.5 km).
• *Saint-Côme-d'Olt (12 miles/19 km), see p. 242.
• *Estaing (19 miles/31 km), see pp. 192–93.
• Gorges of the Tarn (25 miles/40 km).

ℹ Did you know?
Legend has it that the nickname "Encaulats"—cabbage eaters—was given in jest to the local inhabitants because cabbages grew in every garden. Every winter since 2000, the inhabitants of Sainte-Eulalie have gathered together for a huge annual cabbage dinner.

Saint-Jean-de-Côle
Architectural symphony in Périgord Vert

Dordogne (24) • Population: 359 • Altitude: 489 ft. (149 m)

Nestling in the hills, Saint-Jean-de-Côle is an inviting place to dream and meditate in an exceptional architectural setting. Overlooking the village square, the Château de la Marthonie has replaced the original fortress that was built here in the 11th century to defend the Périgord and Limousin borders. Burned during the Hundred Years War, the latter made way for a 15th- and 16th-century building that combines Renaissance elegance and classical precision in its two wings, which share a magnificent straight-flight staircase. Adjoining a priory with cloisters and ambulatory, the Romanesque–Byzantine-style church was built in the 12th century. It contains some beautiful paintings and a polychrome stone Madonna from the 17th century. At the edge of the village, near the old mill, a medieval bridge with cutwaters spans the Côle river. This prestigious architectural ensemble is completed by the village's unusual little streets and old houses, some of which are half-timbered.

By road: Expressway A89, exit 15–Agen (31 miles/50 km); N21 (5 miles/8 km).
By train: Thiviers station (5 miles/8 km).
By air: Périgueux-Bassillac airport (24 miles/39 km); Limoges-Bellegarde airport (42 miles/68 km).

ⓘ **Tourist information:**
+33 (0)5 53 62 14 15
www.perigordgourmand.com
www.saintjeandecole.fr

👁 Highlights
• **Château de la Marthonie** (12th, 15th, 16th, and 17th centuries): Castle exterior only.
• **Église Saint-Jean-Baptiste** (11th and 12th centuries): Wood paneling, paintings; interior sound and light show.

• **Priory** (12th century): Braille guide available from tourist information center. +33 (0)5 53 62 14 15.
• **Village:** Audioguide tour; treasure hunt for children. Further information: +33 (0)5 53 62 14 15.

🗝 Accommodation
Guesthouses
Le Moulin du Pirrou:
+33 (0)5 53 52 35 38.
Le Relais de Montgeoffroy:
+33 (0)6 37 20 85 81 or
+33 (0)6 13 46 29 29.
M. Wolff: +33 (0)5 53 52 53 09.
Gîtes and vacation rentals
Further information:
+33 (0)5 53 62 14 15
www.perigordgourmand.com

🍴 Eating Out
Chez Robert: +33 (0)5 53 52 53 09.
Le Moulin du Pirrou:
+33 (0)5 53 52 35 38.
La Perla Café, in summer:
+33 (0)5 53 52 38 11.
Le Saint-Jean: +33 (0)5 53 52 23 20.
Le Temps des Mets: +33 (0)9 67 78 25 72.

🧺 Local Specialties
Art and Crafts
Ceramicist • Art gallery • Painter.

2 Events
May: Flower show (weekend nearest May 8).
June: "Musicôle," combining the "Fête de la Musique" music festival and the bonfires of Saint John.
July and August: Classical music concerts; street theater (Énigme du Peiregord).

🦋 Outdoor Activities
Fishing • Voie Verte (11 miles/18 km): greenway for walkers, riders, and mountain-bikers; marked trails and railway-themed signposted walk.

🌿 Further Afield
• Thiviers: Maison du Foie Gras (4½ miles/7 km).
• Villars: Château de Puyguilhem; caves; Abbaye de Boschaud ruins (5–7 miles/8–11.5 km).
• Limousin-Périgord regional nature park (6 miles/9.5 km).
• Corgnac-sur-l'Isle: Château de Laxion (8½ miles/13.5 km).
• Sorges: Écomusée de la Truffe, truffle trail (9½ miles/15.5 km).
• Brantôme (12 miles/19 km).
• Jumilhac: castle and gold museum (15½ miles/25 km).
• Périgueux (22 miles/35 km).
• *Ségur-le-Château (28 miles/45 km), see p. 258.

Saint-Jean-Pied-de-Port

Fortified town in the Pays Basque

Pyrénées-Atlantiques (64) • Population: 1,801 • Altitude: 525 ft. (160 m)

Situated on the banks of the Nive river, between the Basque coast and the Spanish border, this historically defensive site now watches over pilgrims on their way to Santiago de Compostela.

At the end of the 12th century, the king of Navarre ordered a fortress to be built on a hill overlooking the Nive river, in the foothills of the mountains around Cize, in a bid to secure control of the main passage through the Pyrenees via Roncevalles. Shortly afterward, a new town was constructed around the fortress. The strategic position of this "key town" in the kingdom of Navarre meant that it was not only a military linchpin but also a thriving commercial center. The town assumed an enduring religious importance when it was made an indispensable stop on the pilgrimage to Santiago de Compostela. This three-pronged identity can still be seen in the village's architecture: from the citadel—founded on the site of the former castle of the kings of Navarre in the 17th century and reworked by Vauban—to the 13th-century ramparts of the upper town, and from the Rue d'Espagne, lined with artisans' and traders' houses that are typical of the region's traditional architecture, to the Porte Saint-Jacques, and the Église Notre-Dame-du-Bout-du-Pont (13th–14th centuries), built in pink sandstone from nearby Arradoy. With a backdrop spanning the verdant valleys of the Cize countryside, the vineyards of Irouleguy, and the Pyrenees, Saint-Jean-Pied-de-Port encapsulates all the colors and flavors of Basque culture.

By road: Expressway A63, exit 5–Bayonne Sud (30 miles/48 km); expressway A64, exit 7–Salies-de-Béarn (36 miles/58 km).
By train: Saint-Jean-Pied-de-Port station; Bayonne station (35 miles/56 km).
By air: Pau-Pyrénées airport (72 miles/116 km); Biarritz-Bayonne-Anglet airport (35 miles/56 km).

ⓘ Tourist information—Saint-Jean-Pied-de-Port–Saint-Etienne de Baïgorry: +33 (0)5 59 37 03 57
www.saintjeanpieddeport-paysbasque-tourisme.com

👁 Highlights
• **Citadel** (17th century): Bastioned fortification overhauled by Vauban. Guided visits on Monday and Wednesday in July and August: +33 (0)5 59 37 03 57.
• **Prison des Évêques** (14th century): Medieval building used as a warehouse, then as a prison. Permanent exhibition on the pilgrimage to Santiago de Compostela. Open from Easter until All Saints' Day: +33 (0)5 59 37 00 92.
• **Église Notre-Dame-du-Bout-du-Pont** (13th–14th centuries): One of the most important Gothic church buildings in the French Basque Country. Open every day.
• **Village:** Guided tour for groups all year round by appointment only and guided tour for individuals by a "Raconteur de Pays" (specialist) from July to August: +33 (0)5 59 37 03 57; audioguide tour (route can be downloaded from tourist information website); tourist train from April to October: +33 (0)5 59 37 00 92.

⚷ Accommodation
Hotels
Hôtel Les Pyrénées****: +33 (0)5 59 37 01 01.
Hôtel Itzalpea**: +33 (0)5 59 37 03 66.
Hôtel Les Remparts **: +33 (0)5 59 37 13 79.
Hôtel Ramuntcho**: +33 (0)5 59 37 03 91.
Hôtel Central: +33 (0)5 59 37 00 22.
Guesthouses
Maison Harria***: +33 (0)5 59 37 09 74.
Maison Garicoitz: +33 (0)6 80 00 49 51.
Maison Gure Lana: +33 (0)5 24 34 14 97.
Mme Paris: +33 (0)5 59 37 22 32.
Casas Rurales Portaleburu:
+33 (0)5 59 49 10 74.
Further information: +33 (0)5 59 37 03 57
www.pyrenees-basques.com
Gîtes and vacation rentals
Appartement Sejournant***:
+33 (0)6 64 43 88 96.
M. and Mme Iribarne***:
+33 (0)5 59 37 28 37.
Appartement Aguergaray**:
+33 (0)5 59 37 10 61.
M. and Mme Elizalde**: +33 (0)5 59 37 37 81.
Mme Larre**: +33 (0)5 59 37 30 18.
Further information: +33 (0)5 59 37 03 57
www.pyrenees-basques.com
Stopover gîtes and bunkhouses
Further information: +33 (0)5 59 37 03 57
www.saintjeanpieddeport-paysbasque-
tourisme.com
Holiday villages
VVF Villages Garazi: +33 (0)5 59 37 06 90.
Campsites and RV parks
Camping municipal Plaza Berri**:
+33 (0)5 59 37 11 19.
RV park: +33 (0)5 59 37 00 92.

🍽 Eating Out
Café de la Paix, brasserie/pizzeria:
+33 (0)5 59 37 00 99.
Café Ttipia, wine bistro:
+33 (0)5 59 37 11 96.
Le Central: +33 (0)5 59 37 00 22.
Le Chaudron: +33 (0)5 59 37 20 15.
Cidrerie Hurrup Eta Klik:
+33 (0)5 59 37 09 18.
Crêperie Kuka: +33 (0)5 59 49 08 86.
Oillarburu: +33 (0)5 59 37 06 44.
Les Pyrénées, gourmet restaurant:
+33 (0)5 59 37 01 01.
Ramuntcho: +33 (0)5 59 37 03 91.
Le Relais de la Nive: +33 (0)5 59 37 04 22.
Txitxipapa, world cuisine:
+33 (0)5 59 37 36 74.
La Vieille Auberge – Chez Dédé:
+33 (0)5 24 34 11 49.

🍴 Local Specialties
• **Food and Drink**
AOP Ossau-Iraty cheese • AOC Irouleguy wine • AOC Kintoa Basque pork • Distilled spirits • *Gâteau basque* • Macarons • Banka trout.
• **Art and Crafts**
Artisan sandal-maker • Potter • Gallery of local arts.

📅 Events
Markets: Monday, all day, Place Charles de Gaulle; Monday until 1 p.m. at covered market; farmers' market on Thursdays in season.

April–October: Exhibitions at the townhall and Prison des Évêques.
June–September: Exhibitions of local arts and crafts.
Mid-August: Patron saint's day (around the 15th); theater festival (late August).
September: Irouleguy vineyards festival; village festivals.

🦋 Outdoor Activities
• Walking: Routes GR 10 and GR 65; several marked trails • Mountain-biking: "Grande Traversée du Pays Basque" • Fly fishing.

🌾 Further Afield
• Saint-Jean-le-Vieux: archeological museum (3 miles/5 km).
• Spanish border (4½ miles/7 km).
• Irouleguy (5 miles/8 km).
• Esterençuby: Grottes d'Harpea, caves (5½ miles/9 km).
• Saint-Etienne de Baïgorry (7 miles/11 km).
• Vallée des Aldudes, valley (7 miles/11 km).
• Bidarray, frontier village (12½ miles/20 km).
• Forêt d'Iraty, forest (19 miles/30 km).
• Cambo-les-Bains (21 miles/34 km).
• Espelette (22 miles/36 km).
• Mauléon-Licharre (25 miles/40 km).
• *Ainhoa and *La Bastide-Clairence (27 miles/43 km), see pp. 154 and 162–63.
• *Sare (31 miles/50 km), see p.252–53.

Saint-Léon-sur-Vézère
Treasure of the Vézère valley

Dordogne (24) • Population: 429 • Altitude: 230 ft. (70 m)

Tucked away in a bend in the Vézère river, halfway between Lascaux and Les Eyzies, Saint-Léon is at the heart of this cradle of civilization. Occupied since prehistoric times, as evidenced in the remains of dwellings at Conquil, Saint-Léon is named after one of the first bishops of Périgueux. Located near a Roman road, the village was, until the arrival of the railway, a thriving port on the Vézère river, earning itself the name Port-Léon during the French Revolution. From the cemetery's expiatory chapel at the entrance to the village, the road leads past the Château de Clérans and the Manoir de La Salle, to a 12th-century Romanesque church with a *lauze* (schist-tiled) roof, which is one of the venues for the popular Périgord Noir music festival. Its plan resembles that of Byzantine churches. Near the Côte de Jor, the Château de Chabans dates from the Middle Ages to the 17th century.

By road: Expressway A89, exit 17 (14 miles/23 km). **By train:** Condat-le-Lardin station (12 miles/19 km); Sarlat-la-Canéda station (23 miles/37 km). **By air:** Brive-Vallée de la Dordogne airport (40 miles/64 km); Périgueux-Bassillac airport (43 miles/69 km).

ⓘ **Tourist information:**
+33 (0)5 53 51 08 42
www.lascaux-dordogne.com
www.saint-leon-sur-vezere.fr

👁 Highlights
• **Buddhist study and meditation center:** The main European center for the preservation of the Kagyupa Buddhist tradition; meditation, Buddhist philosophy courses: +33 (0)5 53 50 70 75.
• **Romanesque church** (12th century): Frescoes.
• **Le Conquil prehistoric theme park:** Cave site, dinosaur park.

🗝 Accommodation
Hotels
Le Relais de la Côte de Jor**:
+33 (0)5 53 50 74 47.
Guesthouses
Le Clos des Songes: +33 (0)5 53 42 25 72.
Esprit Nature: +33 (0)5 53 51 35 71.
Gîtes and vacation rentals
Argiler: +33 (0)7 85 53 79 98.
♥ Le Bel Orme: +33 (0)7 87 14 81 08.
La Chênaie du Roc, eco-gîte:
+33 (0)6 79 60 31 77.
La Fouillousse: +33 (0)5 53 50 70 64.
Les Landes-La Bugadie: +33 (0)5 53 50 70 64.
Lou Camillou: +33 (0)6 58 53 92 57.
Maison Rouge: +33 (0)5 53 50 70 64.
Le Pigeonnier: +33 (0)5 53 50 70 64.
Villa Butzelaar: +33 (0)7 85 53 79 98.
Campsites and RV parks
Le Paradis*****: +33 (0)5 53 50 72 64.
Municipal campsite: +33 (0)5 53 51 08 42.
RV park: +33 (0)5 53 51 08 42.

🍴 Eating Out
L'Auberge du Pont: +33 (0)5 53 50 73 07.
Le Déjeuner sur l'Herbe, local light meals:
+33 (0)5 53 50 69 17.
Lou Camillou: +33 (0)6 58 53 92 57.
Le Martin Pêcheur: +33 (0)5 33 02 12 58.
Le Restaurant de la Poste:
+33 (0)5 53 50 73 08.

🏺 Local Specialties
Art and Crafts
Artists • Jewelry designers • Wood-carver • Ivory sculptor • Workers in felt and glass.

② Events
Market: Gourmet and crafts market, Thursdays in July and August from 6 p.m.
July: Flea market (1st or 2nd Sunday).
August: Périgord Noir music festival: concerts in the Romanesque church (mid-August); village festival (2nd weekend).

🦋 Outdoor Activities
Canoeing • Fishing • Forest adventure park • Horse-riding • Walking: Route GR 36 (3 marked trails) • Hang gliding • Mountain-biking • *Boules*.

🌿 Further Afield
• Côte de Jor: viewpoint (2 miles/3 km).
• Vallée de l'Homme, prehistoric sites:
Lascaux, Les Eyzies (2–9½ miles/3–15.5 km).
• Montignac-sur-Vézère (6 miles/9.5 km).

• Grotte de Rouffignac, cave (11 miles/18 km).
• *Saint-Amand-de-Coly (11 miles/18 km),
see pp. 236–37.
• Dordogne valley: *Limeuil (19 miles/31 km),
see pp. 208–9; *Beynac-et-Cazenac (21 miles/34 km), see pp. 168–69; *La Roque-Gageac (22 miles/35 km), see pp. 234–35; *Castelnaud-la-Chapelle (23 miles/37 km), see p. 182; * Belvès (24 miles/39 km), see pp. 166–67; *Domme (24 miles/39 km), see pp. 190–91.
• Sarlat (22 miles/35 km).

Saint-Robert
The hill of the Benedictines

Corrèze (19) • Population: 350 • Altitude: 1,148 ft. (350 m)

Built around a monastery founded by Saint Robert's disciples, the village was named after the founder of La Chaise-Dieu Benedictine abbey in the Auvergne.

The village stands on a hill, in landscape typical of Corrèze, on the site of an old Merovingian city. On the Saint-Robert plateau, the ruins of a curtain wall encircle the Benedictine monastery and its Romanesque abbey church. The prosperous-looking cut-stone buildings, small castles, and houses with towers were, in their time, home to noblemen. The fortified church has preserved its 12th-century structure almost intact. The ambulatory once displayed saints' relics to pilgrims on their way to Santiago; scenes charged with biblical symbolism are engraved on the capitals, and a 13th-century, life-size Christ, carved in wood, testifies to the religious intensity of the Middle Ages. Saint-Robert, a city-state on the borders of Périgord, was itself the scene of violent religious clashes.

By road: Expressway A20, exit 50–Objat (14 miles/23 km); expressway A89, exit 17–Thenon (16 miles/26 km).
By train: Objat station (8 miles/13 km); Brive-la-Gaillarde station (17 miles/27 km).
By air: Brive-Vallée de la Dordogne airport (24 miles/39 km).

ⓘ Tourist information—Brive et Son Pays: +33 (0)5 55 24 08 80
www.brive-tourisme.com

👁 Highlights
• Église Notre-Dame (12th century).
• **Village:** Guided tour on Tuesdays at 11 a.m. and Thursdays at 4.30 p.m. in July and August; by appointment only the rest of the year: +33 (0)5 55 25 21 01.

🗝 Accommodation
Guesthouses
Le Saint-Robert: +33 (0)5 55 25 58 09.
Gîtes and vacation rentals
Further information: +33 (0)5 55 24 08 80
www.brive-tourisme.com

🧺 Local Specialties
Food and Drink
Foie gras and confit • Bread baked in a wood-fired oven.
Art and Crafts
Local crafts.

📅 Events
Spring: Milk-fed veal prize-giving fair.
July and August: Festive markets, classical music festival.
August: Local saint's day (15th).
October: Fête du Vin Nouveau, wine festival (2nd Sunday).

November: Milk-fed veal prize-giving fair (2nd Monday).

🦋 Outdoor Activities
Walking: 2 marked trails.

🌿 Further Afield
• Église de Saint-Bonnet-la-Rivière and Yssandon site (7½ miles/12 km).
• Château de Hautefort (10 miles/16 km).
• Pompadour (14 miles/23 km).
• Vézère valley; Terrasson (14 miles/23 km).
• Brive (16 miles/26 km).
• *Ségur-le-Château (17 miles/27 km), see p. 258.

🕯 Did you know?
Filming of the French TV mini-series adapted from the novel *Firelight and Woodsmoke* by local author Claude Michelet remains etched on the memory of villagers. The story reflected the history of their village in its depiction of the Vialhe family living through the momentous changes of the 20th century.

Salers

Volcanic majesty and gastronomic delights

Cantal (15) • Population: 353 • Altitude: 3,117 ft. (950 m)

In the majestic scenery of the Monts du Cantal, Salers prides itself on its geological beauty and its unique regional taste sensations.

Salers stands right at the edge of an ancient lava flow, surveying the Maronne valley from a height of 3,117 ft. (950 m). The village was the seat of a baronetcy whose lords distinguished themselves in the First Crusade, and in 1428 it was granted a license by Charles VII to build ramparts, from which the Beffroi and La Martille gates survive. Here, in 1550, Henri II established the royal bailiwick of the Hautes-Montagnes d'Auvergne. On Place Tyssandier-d'Escous, the former bailiwick is surrounded by magistrates' residences, including Hôtel de Ronade, Maison de Flogeac, and Maison de Bargues. The house of commander de Mossier, Knight of Malta, has been turned into a museum celebrating the history and folklore of Salers. The Église de Saint-Mathieu boasts a Romanesque portal, five 17th-century Aubusson tapestries, and a 15th-century Entombment sculpture. At the village's eastern end, the Barrouze Esplanade overlooks the Puy Violent peak and the Monts du Cantal. Acclaimed equally for meat and cheese, from Salers's own breed of cows, the village represents the high point of gastronomy in the Auvergne.

By road: Expressway A89, exit 22–Egletons (41 miles/66 km).
By train: Mauriac station (12 miles/19 km); Aurillac station (26 miles/42 km).
By air: Aurillac-Tronquières airport (27 miles/43 km); Brive-Vallée de la Dordogne airport (81 miles/130 km); Clermont-Ferrand-Auvergne airport (89½ miles/144 km).

ⓘ Tourist information—Pays de Salers:
+33 (0)4 71 40 58 08
www.salers-tourisme.fr
www.salers.fr

👁 Highlights

• **Maison du Commandeur:** Known as the Templars' House. Museum of the history of Salers and its folk traditions; Renaissance residence and historic pharmacy; temporary exhibitions; open April–November 1st: +33 (0)4 71 40 75 97.

• **Cellar of Salers:** Cheese-ageing cellar specializing in AOP Salers cheese. Tours, exhibitions, and tastings; open all year round: +33 (0)4 71 69 10 48.
• **Village:** Guided tour by tourist information center, June–September; by appointment only: +33 (0)4 71 40 58 08.

🗝 Accommodation

Hotels
Le Bailliage***: +33: (0)4 71 40 71 95.
Le Gerfaut***: +33 (0)4 71 40 75 75.
Les Remparts***: +33 (0)4 71 40 70 33.
Le Beffroi: +33 (0)4 71 40 70 11.
Saluces: +33 (0)4 71 40 70 82.

Guesthouses
L'Asphodele***: +33 (0)4 71 40 70 82.
Le Jardin du Haut Mouriol***:
+33 (0)4 71 40 74 02.
La Maison de Barrouze***:
+33 (0)4 71 40 78 08.
Les Sagranières: +33 (0)4 71 40 70 50.

Gîtes and vacation rentals
Au Petit Nid Douillet***:
+33 (0)4 71 68 79 10.
Le Gîte de Barrouze***:
+33 (0)4 71 40 76 42.
Le Gîte Chareyrade***:
+33 (0)4 71 40 70 67.
Le Gîte de la Jourdanie***:
+33 (0)4 71 40 29 80.
Le Gîte du Foirai**: +33 (0)4 71 40 70 13.
La Petite Maison Sagranière**:
+33 (0)4 71 67 34 75.
Gîte d'Étape Équestre La Grange:
+33 (0)4 71 40 70 67.

Campsites
Camping Municipal Le Mouriol***:
+33 (0)4 71 40 73 09.

🍴 Eating Out
Le Bailliage: +33 (0)4 71 40 71 95.
Le Beffroi: +33 (0)4 71 40 70 11.
La Diligence: +33 (0)4 71 40 75 39.
Le Drac, crêperie: +33 (0)4 71 40 72 12.
L'Evasion: +33 (0)4 71 40 74 56.
La Poterne: +33 (0)4 71 40 75 11.
La Préfète, brasserie:
+33 (0)4 71 40 70 55.
Les Remparts: +33 (0)4 71 40 70 33.
Le Rétro, crêperie: +33 (0)4 71 40 72 00.
Les Templiers: +33 (0)4 71 40 71 35.

🛍 Local Specialties
Food and Drink
Carré de Salers (cookie) • Salers gentian
aperitif • Salers meat • Salers cheese.
Art and Crafts
Jewelry • Wooden toys • Lithographs and
watercolors • Pottery • Wood carvings •
Glassworking • Cutlery • Foundry • Horn
sculpture • Fashion • Art photography.

🎫 Events
Market: Wednesday mornings.
May: "Salon des Sites Remarquables du
Goût," food fair (1st); "La Pastourelle,"
walking, running, and mountain-biking
races.
June: Fête de la Montagne, mountain
festival.
July: Fête Chasse et Nature, hunting and
nature festival.
July–August: Concerts.
August: Journée de la Vache et du
Fromage, cow and cheese festival; Folklore
gala (15th); pottery market.

🦋 Outdoor Activities
Auvergne Volcanoes regional natural
reserve • Walking, bike tours, and bridle
paths • La Peyrade: rock-climbing.

🌿 Further Afield
• Route du Puy May, scenic drive:
Les Burons de Salers, shepherds' huts
(2½ miles/4 km); Récusset and Falgoux,
volcanic landscape (7½ miles/12 km);
Puy Mary, volcano (12½ miles/20 km).
• Route de Mauriac, scenic drive: Maison
de la Salers (3 miles/5 km); Château
de la Trémolière (7 miles/11 km);
Estuves pathways (10½ miles/17 km).
• Route de Saint-Paul-de-Salers, scenic
drive: monolithic Fontanges chapel
(3½ miles/6 km); Puy Violent, summit
(7 miles/11 km); Château de Saint-
Chamant (11 miles/18 km); *Tournemire
and Château d'Anjony (17½ miles/28 km),
see p. 261; Jordanne gorges (19 miles/
31 km)
• Route des Crêtes, scenic drive: Aurillac
(28 miles/ 45 km).

Sare
Frontier traditions

Pyrénées-Atlantiques (64) • Population: 2,411 • Altitude: 230 ft. (70 m)

The Rhune and the Axuria, legendary mountains of the Basque Country, tower over this village, famous for both its tradition of hospitality and its festivals.

Ringed by mountains separating it from the Bay of Biscay and from Spanish Navarra, Sare honors vibrant Basque Country traditions. In particular, the tradition of the "Etxe," the Basque house, finds full expression here. Among the eleven scattered parts of this former shepherds' village, the Ihalar neighborhood is one of the oldest, and here houses date from the 16th and 17th centuries. Ortillopitz is an authentic residence from 1660, restored by a local family keen to keep their history and the significance of the Basque home alive for future generations; the house allows visitors to experience "L'Etxe où bat le cœur des hommes" ("The house where human hearts beat"). Numerous chapels and shrines contain votive offerings of thanks for survival in storms at sea—reminders that Sare inhabitants were also seafarers. A tradition of smuggling, made famous by Pierre Loti's classic novel *Ramuntcho* (1897), is also revisited each summer in a walking trail.

By road: Expressway A63, exit 4–Saint-Jean-de-Luz (10 miles/16 km); expressway A64, exit 5–Bayonne-Sud (15 miles/24 km). **By train:** Saint-Jean-de-Luz station (8½ miles/13.5 km). **By air:** Biarritz-Bayonne-Anglet station (18 miles/29 km).

ⓘ **Tourist information:**
+33 (0)5 59 54 20 14
www.sare.fr

👁 Highlights
• **Grottes de Sare, prehistoric caves:** New multimedia show tour about the geology of the site, and the origins and mythology of the Basque people: +33 (0)5 59 54 21 88.
• **La Maison Basque du Sare, Ortillopitz, traditional Basque house** (1660): Explore the Labourd architecture of the "Etxe," its authentic furniture, and Basque family life, on a substantial estate: +33 (0)5 59 85 91 92.
• **Musée du Gâteau Basque** (Maison Haranea): Explore the history, flavor, and appeal of the *gâteau basque* (filled cake), and learn how it was traditionally made: +33 (0)5 59 54 22 09.
• **Etxola animal park:** Many different types of domestic animal from France and abroad: +33 (0)6 15 06 89 51.
• **Village:** Church, Basque pelota court, medieval way, oratoires, evocation of Basque traditions and customs. Guided tours June–September; all year for groups by appointment: +33 (0)5 59 54 20 14.
• **Bell tower:** Guided tours of the bell tower and the most ornate bell in France; tower with oak floor and beams. Guided tours June–September for individuals; all year for groups by appointment: +33 (0)5 59 54 20 14.

• **La Rhune tourist train** (alt. 2,969 ft./905 m): 35-minute climb to the top of La Rhune: +33 (0) 59 54 20 26.
• **Suhalmendi, Basque pork discovery trail:** See Basque pigs in their natural habitat on a family walk up to the peak of Suhalmendi. Further information: +33 (0)5 59 54 20 14.

🔑 Accommodation
Hotels
Arraya***: +33 (0)5 59 54 20 46.
Lastiry***: +33 (0)5 59 54 20 07.
Baratxartea**: +33 (0)5 59 54 20 48.
Pikassaria**: +33 (0)5 59 54 21 51.
Guesthouses
Further information: Gîtes de France: +33 (0)5 59 46 37 00.
Locals' guest rooms, gîtes, walkers' lodges, and vacation rentals
Further information: +33 (0)5 59 54 20 14 www.sare.fr
Vacation villages
VVF Villages Ormodia: +33 (0)5 59 54 20 95.
Campsites
La Petite Rhune***, chalets for rent: +33 (0)5 59 54 23 97.
Tellechea*: +33 (0)5 59 54 26 01.
Goyenetche (including rural campsite): +33 (0)5 59 54 28 34.

🍽 Eating Out
Arraya: +33 (0)5 59 54 20 46.
Baketu: +33 (0)6 37 38 01 22.
Baratxartea: +33 (0)5 59 54 20 48.
Berrouet: +33 (0)5 59 54 21 96.
Halty: +33 (0)5 59 54 24 84.
Lastiry: +33 (0)5 59 54 20 07.
Olhabidea: +33 (0)5 59 54 21 85.
Pikassaria: +33 (0)5 59 54 21 51.
Pleka: +33 (0)5 59 54 22 06.
Le Pullman: +33 (0)5 59 54 20 11.
Les Trois Fontaines: +33 (0)5 59 54 20 80.
Urtxola: +33 (0)5 59 54 21 31.

🏛 Local Specialties

Food and Drink
Gâteau basque • Farm produce • Cheese • Honey • Cider.

Art and Crafts
Bentas (border shops) • Fabric and Basque designs.

📅 Events

Markets: Farmers' market and craft market, Fridays 4.30 p.m.–8.30 p.m. (April–September).
Farmers' market, Saturdays 9 a.m.–1 p.m. (November–March).
Summer fair (craft market), Mondays 8 a.m.–1 p.m. (September–October).
February or March: Carnival.
Easter Monday: "Biltzar," Basque Country writers' fair.
June: Sare mountain-biking excursion (last Sunday).
July–August: Basque singing and dancing, trials of strength, *boules* games.
July: National Pottok horse competition (3rd Saturday).
August: "Cross des Contrebandiers," cross-country race (Sunday after 18th).
September: Sare festival (2nd week, Saturday–Wednesday).
October: "Les Charbonnières," traditional charcoal fires (demonstrations, workshops, etc.); "La Palombe," wood pigeon hunt.
November: Santa Katalina's day (3rd Sunday).
December: La Rhune, ascent by train, descent on foot (1st Saturday).

🦋 Outdoor Activities

Hunting wood pigeons (October–November) • Wild-salmon river fishing (tuition and guide) • Horse-riding • Basque pelota • Walking: Routes GR 8 and GR 10, and 8 marked trails; hiking across the Spanish border • Mountain-biking: 3 trails.

🌿 Further Afield

• Old farms in Ihalar, Istilart, Lehenbiskaï, and Xarbo Erreka (1 mile/1.5 km).
• Église Saint-Martin (17th century) (1 mile/ 1.5 km).
• Xareta: *Ainhoa, see p. 154; Urdax; Zugarramurdi (5–6 miles/8–9.5 km).
• Ascain, Ahetze, Arbonne, Biriatou, Ciboure, Guéthary, Hendaye, Saint-Jean-de-Luz, Saint-Pée-sur-Nivelle, Urrugne (8½–10 miles/13.5–16 km).
• Espelette (9½ miles/15.5 km).
• Cambo-les-Bains: poet and dramatist Edmond Rostand's house (12 miles/19 km).
• Biarritz, Bayonne (12–15 miles/19–24 km).
• Bidassoa valley (14–28 miles/23–45 km).
• *La Bastide-Clairence (24 miles/39 km), see pp. 162–63.
• Saint-Jean-Pied-de-Port (31 miles/50 km), p. 246.

🛈 Did you know?

Sare has a frontier 18 miles (29 km) long, which gives it the longest shared boundary with Spanish Navarra in the whole province. Smuggling began as an act of solidarity, as a means of providing basic essentials, but was equally an expression of the common values and identity the Basques shared. Among the many stories linked to this tradition, a popular one tells of a movie filmed at Sare in 1937, based on Pierre Loti's novel *Ramuntcho*, about a Basque smuggler. The orchestra of 120 singers and musicians was a little unusual as it included a number of smugglers—as well as the popular Basque singer Luis Mariano, who was making his debut.

Sarrant

A circular stronghold

Gers (32) • Population: 400 • Altitude: 410 ft. (125 m)

Sitting on the ancient Roman road between Toulouse and Lectoure, at the edges of the Lomagne, Sarrant wraps itself around the church of Saint-Vincent.

Sarrant's ancient origins are known because Roman maps include "Sarrali" along one of the five main routes out of Toulouse. The village started to expand in 1307, thanks to the "charter of customs" and the privileges it was accorded by Philippe Le Bel. Sarrant is separated from the simple chapel of Notre-Dame-de-la-Pitié and its cemetery by a wide boulevard shaded by plane trees, and its main entrance is a 14th-century vaulted gate cut into a massive square tower, a vestige of Sarrant's protective walls. While the ramparts, blocked off by the houses embedded in them, have in part disappeared, and the ditches been filled in, the village itself has kept its circular street plan. Inside the historic center, the main street is lined with tall, stone houses whose upper stories are frequently corbeled and are made from cob and half-timbering. The parish church stands in the middle of the circle; it was rebuilt and enlarged after the Wars of Religion, before being topped in the 19th century by a fine octagonal flèche that soars above the beautiful rooftops of Sarrant.

By road: Expressway A20, exit 65–Agen (31 miles/50 km); expressway A624–N124, exit L'Isle-Jourdain (15 miles/24 km).
By train: L'Isle-Jourdain station (14 miles/23 km); Auch station (24 miles/39 km).
By air: Toulouse-Blagnac airport (35 miles/56 km).

ⓘ Tourist information:
+33 (0)5 62 65 00 32 / www.sarrant.com

👁 Highlights
• **Église Saint-Vincent and medieval village:** Guided tours by appointment: +33 (0)5 62 06 79 70; program of children's activities exploring the Middle Ages, www.quenouille-tambourin.com.
• **Tour of the town gate:** Exhibitions.
• **Medieval garden:** Free entry.
• **Jardin des Sources:** Learn about herbs, medicinal plants, and plants used in dyeing: +33 (0)5 62 59 39 83.
• **Roman fountain.**

🔑 Accommodation
Guesthouses
Domaine Mahourat★★★★: +33 (0)6 70 28 26 43.
En Louison: +33 (0)7 85 10 34 56.
Gîtes
Au Terrascle★★★: +33 (0)5 62 65 00 33.
Les Clarettes★★★: +33 (0)5 62 65 02 89.
Le Clos de Sarrali★★★: +33 (0)6 76 38 59 20.
En Gardian★★★: +33 (0)5 62 61 79 00.
Les Gruets★★: +33 (0)5 62 07 49 32.
Lefèvre★★: +33 (0)5 62 65 19 40.
Lo Riberot★★: +33 (0)6 61 21 49 04.
La Clé des Champs, gypsy caravan: +33 (0)5 62 65 01 40.
Ferradou: +33 (0)5 62 65 01 87.
Plaisance: +33 (0)6 77 82 20 41.

RV parks
Route de Solomiac: +33 (0)5 62 65 00 34.

🍴 Eating Out
Des Livres et Vous, bookshop and restaurant; 11 a.m.–6 p.m.; evening booking recommended: +33 (0)5 62 65 09 51.

🛍 Local Specialties
Food and Drink
Aperitifs and homemade jams • Foie gras.
Art and Crafts
Wood turner and -carver.

📅 Events
May: "Tatoulu," young people's literature prize: +33 (0)5 62 65 09 51.
July: "Les Estivales de l'Illustration," art and illustration festival (Thursday–Sunday, after 14th).

July–August: Exhibitions at the chapel.
August: Local festival (last weekend).
December: Christmas market
(1st weekend).

🦋 Outdoor Activities

Donkey rides and carriage rides • Walking and mountain-biking: 3 marked trails.

🦋 Further Afield

- Brignemont: mill (3 miles/5 km).
- Cologne, fortified village (4½ miles/7 km).
- Mauvezin, fortified village (5 miles/8 km).
- Château de Laréole (7 miles/11.5 km).
- Beaumont-de-Lomagne, fortified village (9½ miles/15.5 km).
- L'Isle-Jourdain (14 miles/23 km).
- Fleurance (17 miles/27 km).
- Auch: cathedral (25 miles/40 km).
- *Lavardens (27 miles/43 km),
see pp. 206–7.

⚡ Did you know?

During the French Revolution, Sarrant became an enclave of such fierce resistance to Republican abuses of power that it was dubbed "New Vendée," after the Vendée area of France that rebelled violently against the French Republic. On Palm Sunday 1793, young revolutionaries capitalized on a rainy night to cut down the tree of liberty, a symbol of the Republic, which had been planted the previous year in front of the town gate. Such a crime could only bring trouble on those who committed it: they were imprisoned at Auch, in Armagnac Tower, whence none of them came out alive.

Sauveterre-de-Rouergue

Royal fortified village rich in arts and crafts

Aveyron (12) • Population: 803 • Altitude: 1,575 ft. (480 m)

The royal *bastide* of Sauveterre-de-Rouergue, halfway between Albi and Rodez, is brought alive by the passion and expertise of its crafts-people.

From its medieval past the village has kept its original 1281 street plan, the Saint-Christophe and Saint-Vital fortified gates, the rectilinear streets, and the central square complete with forty-seven arcades. The history of this centuries-old, lively site is told through its superbly corbeled stone and half-timbered houses, its 14th-century collegiate church of Saint-Christophe and its contents, and its coats of arms and stone carvings sprinkled across the façades. Proud of its illustrious past as an important center for artisanal skills, the village had new life breathed into it a few decades ago by pioneering modern artists. Widely acknowledged as a center for arts and crafts, Sauveterre continues to showcase its cultural heritage, passion for beauty, and commitment to excellence.

By road: Expressway A75, exit 42–Rodez (55 miles/89 km), N88, exit Baraqueville (8 miles/13 km); expressway A68, then N88, exit Naucelle (5½ miles/9 km). **By train:** Naucelle station (5½ miles/9 km). **By air:** Rodez-Marcillac airport (31 miles/50 km); Toulouse-Blagnac airport (86 miles/138 km).

(i) **Tourist information:**
+33 (0)5 65 72 02 52
www.sauveterre-de-rouergue.fr

Les Quatre Saisons (in summer), light meals: +33 (0)5 65 78 49 32.
Le Sénéchal: +33 (0)5 65 71 29 00.
La Terrasse du Sénéchal: +33 (0)5 65 71 29 00.

🧺 Local Specialties
Food and Drink
Duck and foie gras • *Tripous* (sheep's tripe) and charcuterie • *Échaudés* (Aveyron cakes) • Goat cheese.
Art and Crafts
Painters • Jeweler • Ceramicist-engraver • Cutlers • Glassblowers • Cabinetmaker • Leather crafts • Painted furniture • Illustrator • Sculptor • Landscape watercolorist • Photographer • Luthiers.

🗓 Events
Market: Sundays 8 a.m.–1 p.m.; evening market, Fridays (July–August).
May: "Soft'R," contemporary music festival.
August: Fête de la Lumière, festival of lights (2nd Saturday).
September: "Fête du Melon et de l'Accordéon," festival of rock music and melon-eating (1st Sunday).
October: "Root'sergue," reggae and world music festival (last Saturday); Fête de la Châtaigne et du Cidre Doux, chestnut and cider festival (last Sunday).

🏞 Outdoor Activities
La Gazonne recreation areas: swimming pool, disc golf: 18 baskets, fitness circuit • *Boules* area • Walking and moutain-biking: 4 marked trails.

🌿 Further Afield
• Pradinas: wildlife park (6 miles/9.5 km).
• Château du Bosc (9½ miles/15.5 km).
• Viaur Viaduct (11 miles/18 km).
• *Belcastel (17 miles/27 km), see pp. 164–65.
• Rodez (22 miles/35 km).
• *Monestiés (23 miles/37 km), see p. 212.

👁 Highlights
• **Collegiate Church of Saint-Christophe** (14th century): Southern Gothic style; 17th-century altarpiece.
• **Village:** Guided tours by appointment, from tourist information center.
• **"La Bastide au 16e Siècle":** Multimedia exhibition of life in the fortified town in the 16th century, based on the travel diary of a Swiss student who visited here.
• **Espace Lapérouse:** Permanent and temporary craft exhibitions; tour of art and craft studios by arrangement with tourist information center.

🗝 Accommodation
Hotels
Auberge du Sénéchal***: +33 (0)5 65 71 29 00.
La Grappe d'Or: +33 (0)5 65 72 00 62.
Guesthouses
Lou Cambrou***: +33 (0)7 86 68 41 87.
Les Lilas: +33 (0)6 19 90 06 92.
Villa Elia: +33 (0)6 63 98 36 60.
Gîtes
Further information: +33 (0)5 65 72 02 52
www.sauveterre-de-rouergue.fr
Chalets
Les Chalets de la Gazonne: +33 (0)5 65 72 02 46.
Campsites
Le Sardou, rural campsite: +33 (0)5 65 72 02 52.

🍽 Eating Out
Le Bar des Amis, pizzeria: +33 (0)5 65 72 02 12.
La Grappe d'Or: +33 (0)5 65 72 00 62.

❗ Did you know?
The family of naval officer and explorer Jean-François de Galaup owned properties in and around Albi, and in Sauveterre, from where his mother and grandmother came. The family house in the village was for a long time the presbytery, but it has recently been restored, and now artists and craftspeople work and exhibit there. It is called the Espace Lapérouse and is part of the fortified village's artistic center.

Ségur-le-Château

A safe haven in the depths of Limousin and Périgord

Corrèze (19) • Population: 240 • Altitude: 984 ft. (300 m)

Birthplace of the viscounts of Limoges, Ségur is lit up brightly at night, and the reflections of its fortress shimmer in the waters of the Auvezère.

Ségur comes from the French *lieu sûr*, meaning "place of safety," and it is exactly that: situated on a rocky outcrop, surrounded by forbidding hills, and encircled by a network of outpost castles. All these factors helped a village to develop here, huddling against the protective fortress walls. Then craft and commercial activities expanded. The village's reputation spread during the 15th to 18th centuries, owing to the presence of a court of appeal, responsible for dispensing justice to 361 seignorial estates between Limousin and Périgord. From this prosperous period, there remain noble houses with turrets or half-timbering, towers with spiral staircases, huge fireplaces, and carved granite mullioned windows. Among the village's other noteworthy buildings are a 15th-century granite residence topped with a tower and turrets, the watchtower, the tower of Saint Laurent, and Maison Henri-IV.

By road: Expressway A20, exit 44–Saint-Ybard (16 miles/26 km); expressway A89, exit 17–Thenon (29 miles/47 km); N21 (24 miles/39 km). **By train:** Saint-Yrieix-la-Perche station (9½ miles/15.5 km). **By air:** Limoges-Bellegarde airport (42 miles/68 km); Brive-Vallée de la Dordogne airport (47 miles/76 km).

ⓘ Tourist information—
Pays de Saint-Yrieix:
+33 (0)5 55 73 39 92
www.tourisme-saint-yrieix.com

👁 Highlights
• Église Saint-Léger (19th century): Stained-glass window by contemporary artist Vincent Corpet, symbolizing Saint-Léger's torture.
• **Village:** Guided tours Mondays and Fridays, 10.30 a.m., July–August; by appointment out of season for groups of 10 or more. Further information: +33 (0)5 55 73 39 92.

🗝 Accommodation
Gîtes
Village gîte: +33 (0)5 55 73 53 21.

🍽 Eating Out
L'Auberge Henri-IV, brasserie: +33 (0)5 55 73 38 50.
La Part des Anges: +33 (0)5 55 73 35 27.
Le Vert Galant, brasserie: +33 (0)5 55 73 18 02.

🛏 Local Specialties
Food and Drink
Trout • *Cul noir* (black-bottomed) farm pigs.
Art and Crafts
Terra-cotta sculptures and models • Donkey-milk beauty products • Porcelain painter.

2️⃣ Events
July: Exhibitions.
July–August: Farmers' market (Mondays, 4 p.m.); exhibitions.
August: "Fête des Culs Noirs," pig festival (1st Sunday); flea market/outdoor rummage sale (2nd Sunday); street-painters' fair (close to 15th).

🦋 Outdoor Activities
Fishing • Walking: 4 marked trails.

🦋 Further Afield
• Château de Coussac-Bonneval (6 miles/9.5 km).
• Château de Pompadour; stud farm (6 miles/9.5 km).
• Vaux: ecomuseum of local heritage; paper-maker (6 miles/9.5 km).
• Saint-Yrieix-la-Perche (9½ miles/15.5 km).
• Uzerche (16 miles/26 km).
• *Saint-Robert (17 miles/27 km), see p. 249.
• Hautefort (25 miles/40 km).
• Brive (28 miles/45 km).
• *Saint-Jean-de-Côle (28 miles/45 km), see p. 245.

Talmont-sur-Gironde

Fortified village on an estuary

Charente-Maritime (17) • Population: 78 • Altitude: 16 ft. (5 m)

The Talmont promontory, girded by ramparts and crowned by its Romanesque church, seems to rise above the waves, in defiance of the waters of the Gironde.

This walled town was built in 1284 on the orders of Edward I of England, who also ruled Aquitaine. On a promontory encircled by the Gironde estuary, Talmont has kept its original medieval street plan. The streets and alleyways are punctuated by flowers, dotted with monolithic wells and sundials, and enlivened by craftspeople and traders. Streets lead to the tip of the promontory, where the 12th-century church of Saint Radegonde watches over the largest estuary in Europe. From the Romanesque church, a stop on one of the routes to Santiago de Compostela, the rampart walk follows the cliff to the port, still used by traditional skiffs. Unmissable features of Talmont's landscape and heritage are the stunning panorama over the bay, the port, the village, the estuary, and the fishermen's huts.

By road: Expressway A10, exit 36–Jonzac (17 miles/27 km). **By train:** Royan station (13 miles/21 km). **By air:** Angoulême-Brie-Champniers airport (70 miles/113 km); Bordeaux-Mérignac airport (81 miles/130 km).

ⓘ Tourist information:
+33 (0)5 46 90 16 25
www.talmont-sur-gironde.fr

259

Talmont-sur-Gironde Charente-Maritime

👁 Highlights
• Église Sainte-Radegonde (6th–7th centuries).
• **Musées Historique et de la Pêche:** Local history museum on the site's geology; the church; the construction of the fortified town by Edward I, king of England; the American port built in 1917; and fishing in the lower Gironde estuary. Further information: +33 (0)5 46 90 16 25.
• **Naval cemetery:** Unique on the Atlantic coast; many memorials overflowing with hollyhocks.
• **Village:** Guided tour by appointment: +33 (0)5 46 90 16 25.

🗝 Accommodation
Hotels
L'Estuaire**: +33 (0)5 46 90 43 85.
Guesthouses
Le Portail du Bas**: +33 (0)5 46 90 44 74.
La Maison de l'Armateur: +33 (0)5 46 93 68 01.
La Talamo: +33 (0)5 46 91 16 66.
La Vieille Maison de la Douane: +33 (0)6 79 87 44 18.
Gîtes and vacation rentals
Chantevent: +33 (0)5 46 02 50 97.
L'Escale: +33 (0)6 02 24 03 98.
Gîte du Puits: +33 (0)6 48 47 24 08.
Jarriault: +33 (0)6 82 40 95 70.
Mille Fleurs: +33 (0)5 46 86 03 06.
L'Oubliance: +33 (0)6 48 47 24 08.
Pigeonnier: +33 (0)6 88 34 81 04.
Portail du Bas: +33 (0)5 46 90 44 74.
La Presqu'île: +33 (0)5 46 95 58 02.
Rose Trémière: +33 (0)6 34 52 34 51.
Talum Mundi: +33 (0)5 46 98 10 56.

🍴 Eating Out
L'Âne Culotté: +33 (0)5 46 90 41 58.
La Brise, pizzeria: +33 (0)5 46 90 40 10.
Les Délices de l'Estuaire, tea room: +33 (0)5 46 96 31 44.
L'Estuaire: +33 (0)5 46 90 43 85.
La Petite Cour, crêperie: +33 (0)5 46 90 16 25.
Le Promontoire: +33 (0)5 46 90 40 66.
Les Saveurs de Talmont, tea room: +33 (0)6 48 47 24 08.
La Talmontaise: +33 (0)5 46 93 28 24.

🧺 Local Specialties
Food and Drink
Charente produce • Talmont wines.
Art and Crafts
Jewelry and clothes • Handmade gifts • Rocks, fossils, gems • Artists • Pottery • Moroccan crafts • Soap • Leather goods • Lace.

📅 Events
Market: Farmers' market, Sundays 9 a.m.–5 p.m (April 1–October 31).
April–October: Art exhibitions, Salle du Presbytère.
May: "Fête du Vent," kite festival.
July–August: Wander the village by candlelight, shops remain open, Tuesdays from 9 p.m.; multimedia show.
August: Talmont grand fair (2nd Sunday).

🦋 Outdoor Activities
Fishing • Mountain-biking and hybrid biking • Walking: Route GR 36 and walk to Caillaud cliff • Scooter trips (in summer).

🌿 Further Afield
• Le Caillaud: vineyard activity trail (½ mile/1 km).
• Barzan: Fâ, Gallo-Roman site (1 mile/1.5 km).
• Arces-sur-Gironde: 12th-century church of Saint-Martin (2½ miles/4 km).

• Meschers-sur-Gironde: cave dwellings; beaches; estuary walks (3 miles/5 km).
• Cozes: church; covered market (5 miles/8 km).
• Saint-Georges-de-Didonne (6 miles/9.5 km).
• Royan (11 miles/18 km).
• *Mornac-sur-Seudre (18 miles/29 km), see p. 218.
• Saintes (22 miles/35 km).
• La Palmyre: zoo (25 miles/40 km).
• *Brouage (31 miles/50 km), see pp. 172–73.

❗ Did you know?
Around 1917, during the Russian Revolution, a Romanov princess was exiled to this area. When visiting Talmont-sur-Gironde, she was horrified to see sturgeon eggs being thrown to the hens and ducks. She brought in an expert, who taught the fishermen the real value of caviar; since then the little port has become an important center for its production.

Tournemire

A battle for supremacy

Cantal (15) • Population: 142 • Altitude: 2,625 ft. (800 m)

Set in the Volcans d'Auvergne regional nature park, Tournemire dominates the Doire river valley. In medieval times, two families fought for control of this village of tufa stone, which stretches down as far as the Château d'Anjony. In the Middle Ages the Tournemire family built a fortress on the tip of the Cantal massif, but a rivalry with the Anjony family, whose own castle, built in 1435, was close to the keep at Tournemire, signaled destruction for this fortress—nothing but ruins remain today. However, the Château d'Anjony, with its square body and four corner towers, remains intact, as does the low wing added in the 18th century. Inside, the building still has its vaulted lower hall at basement level. The chapel and knights' hall are decorated by 16th-century murals. Flanked by 14th- and 15th-century houses, the 12th-century village church is characteristic of the Auvergne Romanesque style. It contains wood carvings and the Holy Thorn, brought back from the Crusades by Rigaud de Tournemire.

By road: Expressway A75, exit 23–Aurillac (52 miles/84 km); N122 (18 miles/29 km); expressway A89, exit 22–Egletons (54 miles/87 km). **By train:** Aurillac station (14 miles/23 km). **By air:** Aurillac-Tronquières airport (16 miles/26 km).

ⓘ Tourist information—Pays de Salers: +33 (0)4 71 40 58 08
www.salers-tourisme.fr

👁 Highlights

• **Château d'Anjony** (15th century): Guided tours, concerts: +33 (0)4 71 47 61 67.
• **Church** (12th century): Sculptures, reliquary.

⚓ Accommodation

Hotels
Auberge de Tournemire:
+33 (0)4 71 47 61 28.

Gîtes
Gîte***: +33 (0)4 71 40 70 68 or +33 (0)4 71 48 64 20.

🍴 Eating Out

Auberge de Tournemire:
+33 (0)4 71 47 61 28.
La Petite Boutique, picnic bags, every day in summer
La Pizza des Volcans, street food, Tuesdays (July–August).

🛒 Local Specialties

Food and Drink
Traditional Auvergne produce.
Art and Crafts
Painter • Strip-cartoon illustrator.

📅 Events

Market: Country market, Wednesdays 6 p.m. (July–August).
April: Journées Européennes des Métiers d'Art, European crafts festival (1st weekend).
August: Local saint's day.
September: Journées du Patrimoine, heritage festival.
December: Christmas market.

🦋 Outdoor Activities

Walking.

🌿 Further Afield

• Col de Legal (7½ miles/12 km).
• Aurillac (16 miles/26 km).
• *Salers (17 miles/27 km), see pp. 250–51.
• Puy Griou and Puy Mary, volcanoes (22 miles/35 km).

Turenne

A powerful ruling family in southwest France

Corrèze (19) • Population: 811 • Altitude: 886 ft. (270 m)

Located at the foot of an old citadel bearing still-impressive remains, Turenne was for ten centuries the seat of an important viscountcy.

The Caesar and Trésor towers, on top of a limestone mound (an outlier of the Causse de Martel), mark the site of the earlier fortress of the viscounts of Turenne, who ruled the Limousin, Périgord, and Quercy regions until 1738. Along its narrow streets and on its outskirts, the village has kept a remarkably homogeneous architectural heritage from this period of history. There are mansions from the 15th to 17th centuries, sporting turrets and watchtowers, and simple houses-cum-workshops too, all topped by *ardoise* (slate) tiles and presenting spotlessly white façades to the hot sun in this southern part of Limousin. They rub shoulders with the collegiate church of Saint-Pantaléon, consecrated in 1661, and the 17th-century Chapel of the Capuchins.

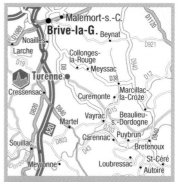

By road: Expressway A20, exit 52–Noailles (5½ miles/9 km). **By train:** Brive-la-Gaillarde station (9½ miles/15.5 km). **By air:** Brive-Vallée de la Dordogne airport (5 miles/8 km).

ⓘ **Tourist information—Brive et Son Pays:** + 33 (0)5 55 24 08 80
www.brive-tourisme.com
www.turenne.fr

La Vicomté: +33 (0)5 55 85 91 32.
Le Vieux Séchoir: +33 (0)5 55 85 90 46.

🧺 Local Specialties
Food and Drink
Walnut oil • Honey • Farmhouse bread.
Art and Crafts
Wood turner.

📅 Events
March or April (Maunday Thursday):
"Foire aux Bœufs," cattle show.
July: Local saint's day (1st weekend);
torchlit tour (3rd weekend); "Festival
de la Vézère," music festival.
August: Outdoor rummage sale
(3rd weekend).

🦋 Outdoor Activities
Fishing • Walking: Routes GR 46 and
GR 480, and 6 marked trails.

🌿 Further Afield
• Gouffre de la Fage, cave (4½ miles/7 km).
• *Collonges-la-Rouge (6 miles/9.5 km),
see pp. 184–85.
• Brive-la-Gaillarde (11 miles/18 km).
• Lac du Causse, lake (11 miles/18 km).
• *Curemonte (11 miles/18 km), see p. 189.
• *Carennac (15 miles/24 km),
see pp. 179–80.
• Abbaye d'Aubazine (16 miles/26 km).
• Dordogne valley (16 miles/26 km).
• *Loubressac (19 miles/31 km), see p. 210.
• *Autoire (22 miles/35 km), see p. 159.
• Padirac; Rocamadour (22 miles/35 km).
• *Saint-Robert (25 miles/40 km), see p. 249.

ℹ Did you know?
The viscount gained substantial benefits
from his geographical location. These
privileges were granted by the kings of
England and France. The viscount raised an
army, minted coins, ennobled his faithful
servants, and answered only to the king.
His subjects did not pay the king's taxes,
did not accommodate his soldiers, and
assembled each year to vote their
viscount's grant. Until the estate was
purchased by Louis XV in 1738, the
viscountcy was what we would today call
a tax haven, practically autonomous from
the authority of the kings of France, with
the right even to summon the Estates
(nobles, clergy, and commoners). These
freedoms aroused the envy of its neighbors
and the bitterness of royal functionaries.
No wonder the French have the adage
"as proud as a Viscount"!

👁 Highlights
• **Castle:** César and Trésor towers,
and garden: +33 (0)5 55 85 90 66.
• **Village:** Historical tours, interactive
costumed tours, and evening visits
in summer; group tours available:
+33 (0)5 55 85 59 97.

🗝 Accommodation
Hotels
La Maison des Chanoines***:
+33 (0)5 55 85 93 43.
Guesthouses
Au Bon Temps***: +33 (0)5 55 85 97 72.

Le Clos Marnis***: +33 (0)5 55 22 05 28.
Château de Coutinard:
+33 (0)5 55 85 91 88.
La Rocaille: +33 (0)5 55 22 05 73.
Gîtes and vacation rentals
Further information: +33 (0)5 55 24 08 80
www.brive-tourisme.com
Vacation villages
La Gironie: +33 (0)5 55 85 91 45.

🍴 Eating Out
Au Temps Gourmand: +33 (0)9 84 34 93 06.
La Maison des Chanoines:
+33 (0)5 55 85 93 43.

Villefranche-de-Conflent

A trading center and defensive site

Pyrénées-Orientales (66) • Population: 225 • Altitude: 1,417 ft. (432 m)

Villefranche-de-Conflent owes its reputation as a commercial center to its founder, Guillaume Raymond, count of Cerdagne, and its fortifications to the works of Vauban (1633–1707), a marshal of France.

Lying in a deep valley where the Cady and Têt rivers meet, the village occupied a strategic site since its foundation at the end of the 11th century; it later became the capital of the Conflent region. The belfry tower of La Viguerie was the administrative center, and the many shops are reminders that Villefranche was a commercial center. In the 17th century, the military engineer Vauban strengthened its role as military capital of this border region by adding his fortifications to the medieval ramparts, today listed as a UNESCO World Heritage Site. The Liberia Fort, linked to the village by the Mille Marches steps built up the mountainside, is an ingenious network of galleries equipped with twenty-five cannon ports. Inside the fortifications, the buildings and the finest residences have stunning pink marble façades, and the Romanesque church of Saint-Jacques, filled with remarkable artifacts, is a reminder that Villefranche was on one of the key routes into Spain and on to Santiago.

By road: Expressway A9, exit 42–Perpignan-Sud (31 miles/50 km), N116.
By train: Villefranche-Vernet-les-Bains-Fuilla station (1 mile/1.5 km); Prades-Molitg-les-Bains station (5½ miles/9 km).
By air: Perpignan-Rivesaltes airport (34 miles/55 km).

ⓘ Tourist information—Conflent-Canigou: +33 (0)4 68 96 22 96.

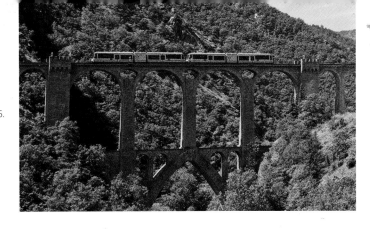

👁 Highlights
• Église Saint-Jacques (11th–14th centuries): 12th-century Romanesque carved portal, Baroque furniture (altarpiece by Joseph Sunyer, 1715). Further information: +33 (0)4 68 96 22 96.
• Ramparts. Further information: +33 (0)4 68 05 87 05.
• Fort Liberia (17th century): Tours of Vauban's site: +33 (0)4 68 96 34 01.
• Petites and Grandes Canalettes grottoes, stalactites, and stalagmites: Stunning geological display and multimedia show: +33 (0)4 68 05 20 20.
• Cova Bastéra (prehistoric grotto): Cave fortified by Vauban.
• Village: Village, ramparts, etc; guided tour (sensory tour, audioguides, Braille, and large-print guidebooks available). Further information: +33 (0)4 68 05 87 05.

🗝 Accommodation
Aparthotels
Le Vauban** : +33 (0)4 68 96 18 03.
Guesthouses
♥ L'Ancienne Poste**** : +33 (0)4 68 05 76 78.
Gîtes and vacation rentals
Further information: +33 (0)4 68 05 87 05
villefranchedeconflent-tourisme.blogspot.fr

🍴 Eating Out
L'Alchimiste, snack bar: +33 (0)6 70 91 40 94.
Ar'Bilig, crêperie: +33 (0)6 47 73 68 57.
Auberge Saint-Paul: +33 (0)4 68 96 30 95.
La Barak' a' M'semen, Moroccan cuisine: +33 (0)4 68 05 30 99.

La Bonafogassa, light meals: +33 (0)4 68 96 33 52.
Le Canigou, country bistro: +33 (0)4 68 05 25 87.
L'Échauguette: +33 (0)4 68 96 21 58.
La Forge d'Auguste, crêperie: +33 (0)4 68 05 08 65.
Forza Real, pizzeria: +33 (0)6 17 06 74 48.
Le Patio: +33 (0)4 68 05 01 92.
La Pizzeria des Remparts: +33 (0)6 09 45 10 29.
Le Relais: +33 (0)4 68 96 31 63.
Le Saint-Jean: +33 (0)4 68 05 70 81.
La Senyera: +33 (0)4 68 96 17 65.
Le Vauban, light meals: +33 (0)4 68 96 18 03.

🧺 Local Specialties
Food and Drink
Artisanal apple juice • Farmhouse goat cheese • *Tourteaux à l'anis* (aniseed cake).
Art and Crafts
Jeweler • Leather crafts • Ceramicist • Cabinetmaker • Wrought ironworker •

Lapidary studio • Wax painting • Potters • Witch doll manufacturer • Soap and candles.

📅 Events
Easter Sunday: "Fêtes des Géants," Easter festival.
Easter Monday: "Aplec," pilgrimage to Notre-Dame-de-Vie.
June: Saint-Jean's and Saint-Pierre's feast days.
July: Saint-Jacques's feast day.

🦋 Outdoor Activities
Adventure park • Canyoning, caving • Walking.

🌿 Further Afield
• Saint-Martin-du-Canigou (5 miles/ 8 km).
• Saint-Michel-de-Cuxa (5 miles/8 km).
• *Eus (7½ miles/12 km), see p. 194.
• *Évol (8 miles/13 km), see p. 195.
• Cerdagne valley (19 miles/31 km).
• *Castelnou (23 miles/37 km), see p. 183.

🛈 Did you know?
Each Easter, Villefranche-de-Conflent hosts the "Fête des Géants"—the festival of giants. In this traditional Catalan festival, two enormous papier-maché figures—nearly 10 ft. (3 m) high—dressed in medieval costumes and with a person inside, represent the founders of the village, Guillaume Raymond de Cerdagne and his wife, Sancia de Barcelona. They wander the streets accompanied by musicians playing traditional instruments, as well as "giants" invited from other villages or towns in France and southern Catalonia.

Villeréal

Royal bastide and artistic center

Lot-et-Garonne (47) * Population: 1,260 * Altitude: 338 ft. (103 m)

Overhanging the Dropt valley, on the borders of Lot-et-Garonne and the Dordogne, the royal *bastide* of Villeréal combines a vibrant history with a gentle pace of life and an artistic vocation. Founded in 1267 by Alphonse de Poitiers, the *bastide* of Villeréal tells the tale, as do a number of its neighbours, of how Aquitaine was fought over at this time by England and France. The village has the classic arrangement of streets at right angles lined with half-timbered houses, but is also unique in having two squares. As is typically the case, the Place aux Cornières has a remarkable early 16th-century market hall in its center, whose upper storey is supported by impressive oak pillars; since 1269 it has teemed with life during the weekly market. Not far away, the 13th-century church overlooks the second square. Its massive silhouette, crenellated rampart walk, and two towers with pointed roofs linked by a gallery are reminders that this religious building also had a defensive role. Today, it is satisfying to see that the village has retained one of its original purposes as an active commercial center. In addition to the various markets that showcase local products (foie gras and confits, cheese, organic meat and vegetables, prunes) throughout the year, more than 130 traders and artisans provide for the inhabitants' daily needs. For a decade or so, a theater festival presenting plays created by the village's artists in residence has reinforced the cultural fiber of Villeréal. Indeed, from its horse festival to its jazz festival, not forgetting the "Feria de la Grande Bodega," this village is dedicated to bringing art into the heart of the community.

By road: Expressway A62, exit 7–Agen (22 miles/35 km); expressway A89, exit 13–Mussidan (35 miles/56 km); expressway A20, exit 15–Périgueux (30 miles/48 m).
By train: Bergerac station (22 miles/35 km); Agen station (37 miles/60 km); TGV Bordeau-Saint-Jean (93 miles/150 km).
By air: Bergerac-Dordogne-Périgord airport (19 miles/30 km); Agen–La Garenne airport (40 miles/64 km); Bordeaux-Mérignac airport (91 miles/147 km).

ⓘ Tourist information:
Coeur de Bastides: +33 (0)5 53 36 09 65
www.coeursdebastides.com/mairie-villereal.fr

👁 Highlights
• Église Notre-Dame de Villeréal (13th century): Fortified church with crenellated rampart walk: +33 (0)5 53 36 43 84.
• Guided tour of the *bastide*: Further information: +33 (0)5 53 36 00 37.

⚔ Accommodation
Hôtel
Hôtel de l'Europe: +33 (0)5 53 36 00 35.
Guesthouses
La Maison Bleue***: +33 (0)5 53 70 34 20.
Lys de Vergne**: +33 (0)5 53 36 61 54.
Chambre Sainte Colombe:
+33 (0)5 53 71 29 11.
Lune et Croissant: +33 (0)9 54 70 00 58.
M. Noyelle: +33 (0)9 63 21 46 05.

Gîtes and vacation rentals
La Colombière: +33 (0)5 53 36 02 41.
Gîte de Jeancel***: +33 (0)5 53 36 06 15.
Gîte de Laplagne**: +33 (0)5 56 84 94 11.
Gîte de Rouilles: +33 (0)5 53 36 04 49.
Gîte de Rouquet: +33 (0)5 53 36 06 97.
Le Jeanquet de Villeréal:
+33 (0)5 53 36 09 33.
Maison Sirgue: +33 (0)6 33 57 22 99.
Moulin de Barbot: +33 (0)5 53 36 62 82.
Le Moulin de la Haute Fage:
+33 (0)5 53 36 02 55.
Mme and M. Pichet: +33 (0)5 53 71 79 35.
Une Maison Rue Saint Michel:
+33 (0)6 40 64 58 64.

🍴 Eating Out
Restaurants
Le Boudoir: +33 (0)7 67 83 46 90.
La Dolce Vita: +33 (0)5 53 71 64 02.
Fromages et Plus, wine bar and regional light meals: +33 (0)5 53 49 25 39.
Le Gourmet: +33 (0)5 47 99 05 36.
Les Marronniers: +33 (0)5 53 36 03 33.
Le Moderne: +33 (0)5 53 40 78 39.
La Roma: +33 (0)5 53 71 27 52.
Tea rooms
Le Boudoir: +33 (0)7 67 86 46 90.
Pâtisserie Blanchard: +33 (0)5 53 36 00 61.

🏛 Local Specialties
Food and Drink
Products from southwest France • Flour.
Art and Crafts
Potter • Upholsterer and interior designer.

🗓 Events
Market: Saturdays at the market hall; July to mid-September, farmers' market every Monday evening
May: Antiques market (1st).
June–September: Concerts beneath the market hall (every Sunday).

July: Villeréal Festival (theater); "Feria la Grande Bodega," music festival (last Sunday).
July–August: Horse racing at the racetrack.
August: Rummage sale (3rd Sunday).
September: Horse festival (last Sunday).
All year round: Flea market (2nd Sunday of every month); live opera broadcasts from the Metropolitan Opera House, New York, and performances from the Comédie Française.

🦋 Outdoor Activities
Walking (2 circuits from Villeréal) • Tour of the *bastide* by bike.

🌿 Further Afield
• Château de Biron (7 miles/12 km).
• Monflanquin (7 miles/12 km), see pp. 213–14.

• Monpazier: Musée des Bastides (9 miles/15 km), see pp. 215–16.
• Beaumont-du-Périgord (11 miles/17 km).
• Château de Gavaudun (11 miles/17 km).
• Château de Monbazillac (17 miles/28 km).
• Cloître de Cadouin (18 miles/29 km).
• Belvès (19 miles/31 km), see pp. 216–17.
• Château de Bonaguil (19 miles/31 km).
• Pujols-le-Haut (21 miles/33 km), see pp. 228–29.

ℹ Did you know?
The *bastide* of Villeréal was founded through a *paréage*—a collaborative agreement in feudal law—made between Gaston III de Gontaut, who was lord of Biron, the abbots of Aurillac, and Alphonse de Poitiers, who was the brother of Louis IX. The new royal town (*ville royale*) thus obtained its name from its prestigious connections.

Hell-Bourg
(commune of Salazie)

Creole heritage at the heart of the "intense island"

La Réunion (97) • Population: 2,000 • Altitude: 886 ft. (270 m)

By road: N2 (16 miles/26 km), D48.
By air: Saint-Denis airport (31 miles/50 km).

ⓘ Tourist information—
Intercommunal de l'Est:
+33 (0)2 62 47 89 89
est.reunion.fr / www.ville-salazie.fr

On the southern side of the Cirque de Salazie amphitheater, the natural entrance to the "peaks, cirques, and ramparts" designated as a UNESCO World Heritage Site, Hell-Bourg devotes itself to Creole tradition, lifestyle, and hospitality.

The Cirque de Salazie (a volcanic caldera) sets the scene for Hell-Bourg: ravines plunge into the Rivière du Mât, and waterfalls gush down the rock face, its lush vegetation maintained by the humidity of the trade winds blowing in from the Indian Ocean. For a long time the refuge of slaves fleeing from plantations on the coast, the Hell-Bourg area was colonized from 1830. With the discovery, the following year, of therapeutic springs, Hell-Bourg became a fashionable spa that was frequented by the island's well-to-do families every summer. Thatched huts gave way to villas adorned with pediments and mantling and surrounded by verandas opening onto gardens with bubbling freshwater fountains. Since the thermal springs dried up as the result of a cyclone in 1948, Hell-Bourg has maintained and perpetuated the architectural heritage of this lavish period, and has sought to return to the roots of its Creole heritage.

👁 Highlights

• **La Case Tonton:** Creole home, beliefs, and traditions. Guided tour daily from 8.30 a.m. Further information: Freddy Lafable, +33 (0)6 92 15 32 32, or Guid'A Nou, +33 (0)6 92 86 32 88.
• **Tour of Creole huts.** Guided tour by Freddy Lafable, +33 (0)6 92 15 32 32, or Guid'A Nou, +33 (0)6 92 86 32 88; self-guided tour with audioguide, rental from tourist information center.
• **Villa Folio and its garden:** 19th-century Creole house, visitor interpretive center, park, garden. Guided tours for individuals and groups: +33 (0)2 62 47 80 98.
• **Old thermal spa:** Explore the history of the former spa. Guided tour or self-guided tour. Further information: +33 (0)2 62 47 89 89.
• **Mare à Poule d'Eau:** Explore the tropical flora and fauna of one of La Réunion's most beautiful stretches of water. Guided tour with Guid'A Nou: +33 (0)6 92 86 32 88.
• Landscaped cemetery.
• **Museum of Musical Instruments:** +33 (0)2 62 46 72 23.

🗝 Accommodation

Hotels
Les Jardins d'Héva**: +33 (0)2 62 47 87 87.
Relais des Cimes**: +33 (0)2 62 47 81 58.
Guesthouses
Le Relais des Gouverneurs***: +33 (0)2 62 47 76 21.
L'Orchidée Rose: +33 (0)2 62 47 87 22.
Gîtes and vacation rentals
Further information: +33 (0)2 62 47 89 89.
Campsites
Le Relax, farm campsite: +33 (0)2 62 47 83 06.

🍽 Eating Out

Chez Alice: +33 (0)2 62 47 86 24.
Chez Maxime's, fast-food restaurant: +33 (0)6 93 13 07 71.
La Cuisine d'Héva: +33 (0)2 62 47 87 87.
Le Gouléo, fast-food restaurant: +33 (0)6 92 62 36 24.
L'Orchidée Rose: +33 (0)2 62 47 87 22.
P'tit Koin Kréol, fast-food restaurant: +33 (0)6 92 32 61 16.
Relais des Cimes: +33 (0)2 62 47 81 58.
Ti Chouchou: +33 (0)2 62 47 80 93.
Villa Marthe: +33 (0)6 92 08 64 37.

🧺 Local Specialties

Food and Drink
Creole produce.
Art and Crafts
Local creations: basketry, pottery, paintings • Chayote straw-braiding.

📅 Events

May: Transrun by Decathlon, race.
June: Fête du Chouchou, festival devoted to the chayote fruit, the emblem of the Cirque de Salazie (tasting sessions, demonstrations, concerts, visits, etc.).
July: Memwar Nout Terroir, festival; Trail de La Réunion Hell-Bourg Ste-Marie, mountain race.
August: "La Cimasalazienne" mountain race; CiMaSa race.
September: Trail des Masters, race.
October: Trail de Bourbon, race.
December 20: Abolition of slavery festival.

🦋 Outdoor Activities

Walking (60 miles/100 km of trails) • Rock climbing • Canyoning • Trail bike station dedicated to nature sports.

🌿 Further Afield

• Natural and heritage sites of Salazie: Bé-Maho viewpoint, Mare à Poule d'Eau, Voile de la Mariée (2–10 miles/ 3–16 km).
• Bras-Panon: vanilla cooperative (16 miles/26 km).
• Grand-Îlet: Église Saint-Martin, church (19 miles/31 km).
• Saint-André: Tamil temples, Parc du Colosse, Bois-Rouge sugar refinery, and Savanna rum distillery (25 miles/ 40 km).
• Plaines des Palmistes plains, national park headquarters (31 miles/50 km).
• Saint-Denis (31 miles/50 km).
• Sainte-Rose: lava tunnels of the Piton de la Fournaise volcano (31 miles/50 km).

Index of Villages

Photographic Credits

With the exception of pages 8, 49, 50, 53, 65, 97, 111, 174, 179, 208–209, and 217, all of the photographs featured in this book are published courtesy of the Hemis photographic agency:

4–9: Philippe Body; 15t: Philippe Blanchot; 15b: Hervé Levain; 16: Jean-Daniel Sudres; 17g: John Frumm; 17d: Christophe Boisvieux; 18–19: Franck Guiziou; 20: Francis Cormon; 21t: Jean-Daniel Sudres; 21b: René Mattes; 22: Francis Leroy; 23: Philippe Body; 24: Francis Leroy; 25: Hervé Lenain; 26: Franck Guiziou; 27–28: Hervé Lenain; 29 and 30b: Bertrand Rieger; 30t: Emmanuel Berthier; 31–32t: Francis Cormon; 32b: Franck Guiziou; 33–34: Emmanuel Berthier; 35: Hervé Lenain; 36: Philippe Body; 37: Arnaud Chicurel; 38t: Hervé Hughes; 38b: Philippe Body; 39: René Mattes; 40: Philippe Roy; 41–42: Francis Cormon; 43: Philippe Body; 45: Hervé Lenain; 46–47: Philippe Body; 48: Jean-Daniel Sudres; 51: Bertrand Rieger; 52: Francis Leroy; 56–57: Hervé Lenain; 58: Franck Guiziou; 59: Arnaud Chicurel; 60: Sylvain Sonnet; 61t: René Mattes; 61b: Denis Caviglia; 62:Bertrand Gardel; 63t: Denis Caviglia; 64: Sylvain Cordier; 66: Denis Caviglia; 67t: Denis Bringard; 67m and b: Denis Caviglia; 68: Hervé Lenain; 69: René Mattes; 70: Denis Bringard; 71: Denis Caviglia; 72: Philippe Moulu; 73: Franck Guiziou; 74: Andrea Pistolesi ; 75–76: René Mattes; 77: Denis Bringard; 78: Denis Caviglia; 79: Arnaud Chicurel; 80: Christian Guy; 81t: Christophe Boisvieux; 81b: Hervé Lenain; 84–85: Franck Guiziou; 86: Michel Cavalier; 87t: Camille Moirenc; 87b: Michel Renaudeau; 88: Guy Christian; 89: Sylvain Sonnet; 90: Jean-Pierre Degas; 91–92: Franck Guiziou; 93: Pierre Jacques; 94: René Mattes; 95: Hervé Lenain; 96: Denis Caviglia; 98: Matthieu Colin; 99: Franck Guiziou; 100: Michel Cavalier; 101: Franck Chapus; 102–103: Jean-Pierre Degas; 103: Camille Moirenc; 104–105: Pierre Jacques; 105: Denis Caviglia; 106: Lionel Montico; 107: Franck Guiziou; 108: Hervé Lenain; 109: Franck Guiziou; 110: Michel Cavalier; 112: Franck Guiziou; 113: Lionel Montico; 114: Franck Guiziou; 115: Pierre Jacques; 116: Denis Caviglia; 117: Lionel Montico; 118: Camille Moirenc; 119: Lionel Montico; 120: Franck Guiziou; 121: René Mattes; 122: Jean-Daniel Sudres; 123: Denis Caviglia; 124–125: Pierre Jacques; 126: Franck Guiziou; 127: Michel Gotin; 129: Franck Guiziou; 131t: Pierre Jacques; 131b: Franck Guiziou; 133t: Lionel Montico; 133b: Laurent Giraudou; 134: Denis Caviglia; 136: Franck Guiziou; 137t: Westend 61; 137b: Pierre Jacques; 138: Denis Caviglia; 139: Franck Guiziou; 140–141: Michel Cavalier; 142: Christian Guy; 143: Denis Caviglia; 144: Denis Caviglia; 145t: Jean-Pierre Degas; 145b: Sylvain Sonnet;

146: Denis Caviglia; 147: Christian Guy; 148: José Nicolas; 149: Franck Guiziou; 150–151: Pierre Jacques; 154: Pierre Jacques; 155: Philippe Body; 156: Didier Zylberyng; 157–158: Hervé Lenain; 159: Jean-Paul Azam; 160: Hervé Lenain; 161: Jean-Paul Azam; 162–163b: Denis Caviglia; 163t: Jean-Daniel Sudres; 164–165: Pierre Jacques; 167: Bertrand Gardel; 168–169: Francis Cormon; 170–171b: Denis Caviglia; 171h–172: Hervé Lenain; 173: Francis Leroy; 175: Francis Leroy; 176: Franck Guiziou; 177: Philippe Body; 178: Francis Leroy; 180–181: Jean-Paul Azam; 182: Arnaud Chicurel; 183: Franck Guiziou; 184: Bertrand Gardel; 185: Jean-Paul Azam; 186: Stéphane Lemaire; 187: Jean-Paul Azam; 188: Pierre Jacques; 189: Jean-Paul Azam; 191t: Philippe Body; 191b: Robert Harding; 192–193: Jean-Pierre Degas; 193: Jean-Paul Azam; 194: Francis Leroy; 195: Franck Guiziou; 196: Francis Leroy; 197: Franck Guiziou; 198: Jean-Daniel Sudres; 199–200: Franck Guiziou; 201: Jean-Paul Azam; 202: Didier Zylberyng; 203–205: Jean-Paul Azam; 206: Jean-Marc Barrere; 207: Jean-Paul Azam; 210: Arnaud Chicurel; 211: Franck Guiziou; 212: Jean-Paul Azam; 213: Jean-Marc Barrère; 214: Denis Caviglia; 217: Patrick Escudero; 216t: Denis Caviglia; 216b: Francis Leroy; 218: Philippe Body; 219: Francis Leroy; 220: Jean-Paul Azam; 221: Jean-Pierre Degas; 223: Jean-Marc Barrere; 224–225: Franck Guiziou; 227: Pierre Jacques; 228: Hervé Lenain; 229t: Denis Caviglia; 229b: Jean-Marc Barrere; 230–231: Jean-Paul Azam; 232–233: Jean-Daniel Sudres; 234–235: Patrick Escudero; 235b–236: Denis Caviglia; 237: Patrick Escudero; 239t: Hervé Tardy; 239b: Jean-Paul Azam; 240: Jean-Marc Barrere; 241: Jean-Paul Azam; 242–244: Hervé Lenain; 245: Jean-Daniel Sudres; 246: Philippe Roy; 247: Christian Guy; 248: Gregory Gerault; 249: Jean-Paul Azam; 250: Jean-Daniel Sudres; 251: Hervé Tardy; 252–253: Jean-Paul Azam; 255t: Francis Leroy; 255b: Jean-Paul Azam; 256: Christian Guy; 259: Francis Leroy; 260: Hervé Lenain; 261: Jean-Pierre Degas; 262–263: Christian Guy; 264: Jean-Paul Azam; 265t: Franck Guiziou; 265b: Jean-Daniel Sudres; 266: Francis Leroy; 267: Romain Cintract; 268: imageBROKER; 269: Gil Giuglio.

8: Marielsa Niels/PBVF; 49: P. Bernard/PBVF; 50: Association Veul'Images; 53: Dlebigot/PBVF; 65: Kazutoshi Yoshimura; 97: P. Bernard/PBVF; 111: Max Labeille/PBVF; 174: Kazutoshi Yoshimura; 179: Kazutoshi Yoshimura ; 208–209: Y. Lemaître/PBVF ; 217: M. Laffargue/PBVF.

All maps featured in this book were produced by Éditerra.

Flammarion would like to thank the Plus Beaux Villages de France association (Anne Gouvernel, Cécile Vaillon, and Pascal Bernard) and Éditerra (Sophie Lalouette).